W9-AVR-566

DEVIL'S BRIDE

A RAKE'S VOW

The Bar Cynster Family Tree

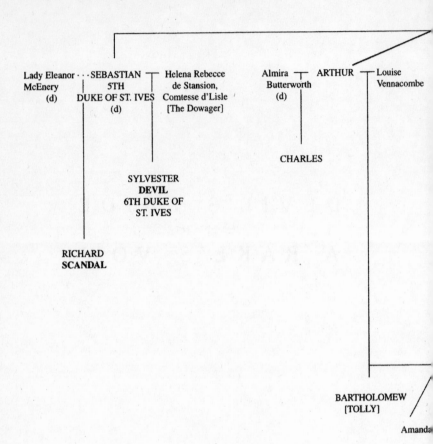

Lady Eleanor··· SEBASTIAN ─┬─ Helena Rebecce
McEnery   5TH   de Stansion,
(d)   DUKE OF ST. IVES Comtesse d'Lisle
                (d)   [The Dowager]

Almira ─┬─ ARTHUR ─┬─ Louise
Butterworth   Vennacombe
(d)

SYLVESTER
DEVIL
6TH DUKE OF
ST. IVES

CHARLES

RICHARD
SCANDAL

BARTHOLOMEW
[TOLLY]

Amanda

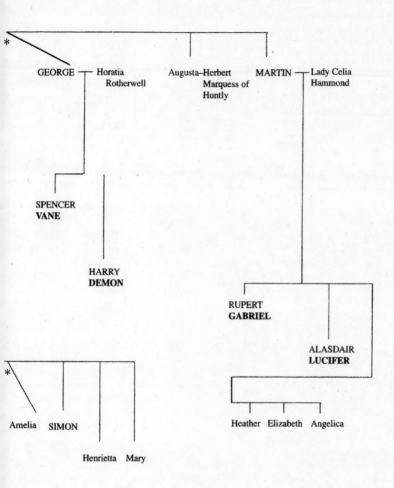

*

GEORGE — Horatia Rotherwell

Augusta–Herbert Marquess of Huntly

MARTIN — Lady Celia Hammond

SPENCER VANE

HARRY DEMON

RUPERT GABRIEL

ALASDAIR LUCIFER

*

Amelia   SIMON

Henrietta   Mary

Heather   Elizabeth   Angelica

Stephanie Laurens

DEVIL'S BRIDE

A RAKE'S VOW

Rhapsody
Garden City, New York

This edition was especially created in 2004 for Rhapsody by arrangement with Avon Books, an imprint of HarperCollins Publishers.

Published by Rhapsody, 401 Franklin Avenue, Garden City, New York 11530

ISBN: 1-58288-107-3

Book design by Christos Peterson

Printed in the United States of America

Contents

DEVIL'S BRIDE

Chapter 1

Somersham, Cambridgeshire
August 1818

"THE DUCHESS IS SO very . . . very . . . well, really, most *charming*. So . . ." With an angelic smile, Mr. Postlethwaite, the vicar of Somersham, gestured airily. "*Continental*, if you take my meaning."

Standing by the vicarage gate while she waited for the gig to be brought around, Honoria Wetherby only wished she could. Wringing information from the local vicar was always one of her first actions on taking up a new position; unfortunately, while her need for information was more acute than usual, Mr. Postlethwaite's comments were unhelpfully vague. She nodded encouragingly—and pounced on the one point which might conceivably mean something. "Is the duchess foreign-born?"

"*Dowager* Duchess." Mr. Postlethwaite beamed. "She likes to be called that now. But foreign?" Head to one side, he considered the point. "I suppose some might call her so—she *was* French-born and -bred. But she's been amongst us so long, she seems a part of our landscape. Indeed"—his eyes brightened—"she's something of a *feature* on our limited horizon."

That much, Honoria had gleaned. It was one reason she needed to know more. "Does the Dowager join the congregation here? I didn't see any ducal arms about." Glancing at the neat stone church beyond the vicarage, she recalled numerous commemorative inscriptions honoring the deceased from various

3

lordly houses, including some scions of the Claypoles, the family whose household she joined last Sunday. But no ducal plaques, helpfully inscribed with name and title, had she discovered anywhere.

"On occasion," Mr. Postlethwaite replied. "But there's a private church at the Place, quite *beautifully* appointed. Mr. Merryweather is chaplain there. The duchess is always reliable in her devotions." He shook his head sadly. "Not, I'm afraid, a general characteristic of that family."

Honoria resisted a strong urge to grind her teeth. *Which family?* She'd been chasing that information for the past three days. Given that her new employer, Lady Claypole, seemed convinced that her daughter Melissa, now Honoria's charge, was destined to be the next duchess, it seemed the course of wisdom to learn what she could of the duke and his family. The family name would help.

By choice, she had spent little time amongst the *haut ton* but, thanks to her brother Michael's long letters, she was reliably informed of the current status of the families who made up that gilded circle—the circle into which she'd been born. If she learned the name, or even the major title, she would know a great deal more.

However, despite spending an hour on Sunday explaining in excruciating detail just why Melissa was destined to be a duchess, Lady Claypole had not used the lucky duke's title. Assuming she would learn it easily enough, Honoria had not specifically questioned her ladyship. She'd only just met the woman; advertising her ignorance had seemed unnecessary. After taking stock of Melissa and her younger sister Annabel, she'd vetoed any idea of asking them; showing ignorance to such was inviting trouble. The same reason had kept her from inquiring of the Claypole Hall staff. Sure that she would learn all she wished while being welcomed to the local Ladies Auxiliary, she'd arranged for her afternoon off to coincide with that most useful of village gatherings.

She'd forgotten that, within the local area, the duke and Dowager Duchess would always be referred to in purely generic terms. Their neighbors all knew to whom they referred—she still did not. Unfortunately, the patent scorn with which the other ladies viewed Lady Claypole's ducal aspirations had made asking a simple question altogether too awkward. Undaunted, Honoria had endured a lengthy meeting over raising sufficient funds to replace the church's ancient roof, then scoured the church, reading every plaque she could find. All to no avail.

Drawing a deep breath, she prepared to admit to ignorance. "To which—"

"There you are, Ralph!" Mrs. Postlethwaite came bustling down the path. "I'm so sorry to interrupt, my dear." She smiled at Honoria, then looked at her spouse. "There's a boy come from old Mrs. Mickleham—she's asking for you urgently."

"Here you are, miss."

Honoria whirled—and saw the vicar's gardener leading the bad-tempered grey the Claypole Hall groom had harnessed to the gig. Shutting her lips, she nodded graciously to Mrs. Postlethwaite, then sailed through the gate the vicar held wide. Taking the reins with a tight smile, she allowed the gardener to assist her to the seat.

Mr. Postlethwaite beamed. "I'll look to see you on Sunday, Miss Wetherby."

Honoria nodded regally. "Nothing, Mr. Postlethwaite, could keep me away." *And*, she thought, as she set the grey in motion, *if I haven't found out by then who this blessed duke is, I won't let go of you until I have!*

Brooding darkly, she drove through the village; only as the last of the cottages fell behind did she become aware of the heaviness in the air. Glancing up, she saw thunderclouds sweeping in from the west.

Tension gripped her, locking her breath in her chest. Abruptly looking forward, Honoria focused on the intersection immediately ahead. The road to Chatteris led straight on, then curved north, into the path of the storm; the long lane to Claypole Hall gave off it three miles on.

A gust of wind plucked at her, whistling mockingly. Honoria started; the grey jibbed. Forcing the horse to a halt, Honoria berated herself for remaining out so long. A ducal name was hardly of earth-shattering importance. The approaching storm was.

Her gaze fell on the lane joining the road at the signpost. It wended away through stubbled fields, then entered a dense wood covering a low rise. She'd been told the lane was a shortcut, ultimately joining the Claypole Hall lane mere yards from the Hall gates. It seemed her only chance of reaching the Hall before the storm broke.

One glance at the roiling clouds growing like a celestial tidal wave to her right made up her mind. Stiffening her spine, Honoria clicked the reins and directed the grey left. The beast stepped out eagerly, carrying her past the golden fields, darkening as the clouds thickened.

A dull *crack!* cut through the heavy stillness. Honoria looked ahead, scanning the trees swiftly drawing nearer. Poachers? Would they be out in such weather when the game was in deep cover, sheltering from a storm? She was still puzzling over the odd sound when the wood rose before her. The grey trotted on; the trees engulfed them.

Determined to ignore the storm, and the unease it raised within her, Honoria turned to contemplation of her latest employers, and the niggle of doubt she felt over their worth as recipients of her talents. Beggars couldn't be choosers, which was what any *other* governess would say. Fortunately, she wasn't just any governess. She was wealthy enough to live idly; it was by her own eccentric will that she eschewed a life of quiet ease for one which allowed her to use her skills. Which meant she *could* choose her employers, and usually did so most reliably. This time, however, fate had intervened and sent her to the Claypoles. The Claypoles had failed to impress.

The wind rose in a bansheelike screech, then died to a sobbing moan. Branches shifted and swayed; boughs rubbed and groaned.

Honoria wriggled her shoulders. And refocused her thoughts on the Claypoles—on Melissa, their eldest daughter, the prospective duchess. Honoria grimaced. Melissa was slight and somewhat underdeveloped, fair, not to say faded. In terms of animation, she had taken the "to be seen and not heard" maxim to heart—she never had two words to say for herself. Two intelligent words, anyway. The only grace Honoria had yet discovered in her was her carriage, which was unconsciously elegant—on all the rest she'd have to work hard to bring Melissa up to scratch. To a duke's scratch at that.

Taking comfort from her irritation—it distracted her from the thought of what she could not see through the thick canopy overhead—Honoria set aside the vexing question of the duke's identity to reflect on the qualities Lady Claypole had ascribed to the phantom.

He was thoughtful, an excellent landowner, mature but not old, ready, so her ladyship assured her, to settle down and begin filling his nursery. This paragon had no faults to which any might take exception. The picture her ladyship had painted was of a sober, serious, retiring individual, almost a recluse. That last was Honoria's addition; she couldn't imagine any duke other than a reclusive one being willing, as Lady Claypole had declared this one was, to apply for Melissa's hand.

The grey tugged. Honoria kept the ribbons taut. They'd passed the entrance to two bridle paths, both winding away into trees so dense it was impossible to glimpse anything beyond a few yards. Ahead, the lane swung left, around a virtually blind curve. Tossing his head, the grey paced on.

Honoria checked for the curve, noting that their upward climb had ended. As the weight of his load lessened, the grey surged. Honoria's grip slipped—the reins slithered through her fingers. Cursing, she grabbed wildly and caught the ribbons firmly; leaning back, she wrestled with the beast.

The grey shied. Honoria shrieked and yanked hard, for once uncaring of the horse's mouth. Her heart racing, she forced the grey to a halt. Abruptly, the horse stood stock-still, quivering, coat aflicker. Honoria frowned. There'd been no thunderclaps yet. She glanced along the lane. And saw the body slumped beside the verge.

Time stood still—even the wind froze.

Honoria stared. *"Dear God."*

At her whisper, the leaves sighed; the metallic taint of fresh blood wafted along the lane. The grey sidled; Honoria steadied him, using the moment to swallow the knot of shock in her throat. She didn't need to look again to see the dark, glistening pool growing beside the body. The man had been shot recently— he might still be alive.

Honoria eased from the gig. The grey stood quietly, head drooping; edging to the verge, Honoria looped the reins about a branch and pulled the knot tight. Stripping off her gloves, she stuffed them in her pocket. Then she turned and, taking a deep breath, walked down the lane.

7

The man was still alive—she knew that the instant she knelt on the grass beside him; his breathing was rattly and harsh. He was lying on his side, slumped forward; grasping his right shoulder, she rolled him onto his back. His breathing eased—Honoria barely noticed, her gaze transfixed by the jagged hole marring the left side of his coat. With every ragged breath the man drew, blood welled from the wound.

She had to staunch the flow. Honoria looked down; her handkerchief was already in her hand. Another glance at the wound confirmed its inadequacy. Hurrying, she stripped off the topaz-silk scarf she wore over her dun-colored gown and wadded it into a pad. Lifting the sodden coat, she left the man's ruined shirt undisturbed and pressed her improvised dressing over the gaping hole. Only then did she glance at his face.

He was young—surely too young to die? His face was pale; his features were regular, handsome, still holding traces of youthful softness. Thick brown hair lay disheveled across a wide brow; brown brows arched over his closed eyes.

Sticky dampness rose beneath Honoria's fingers, her kerchief and scarf no match for the relentless flow. Her gaze fell on the youth's cravat. Unhooking the pin securing the linen folds, she unwound the cravat, folded it, then positioned the thick wad and carefully pressed down. She was bent over her patient when the thunder struck.

A deep resounding *boom*, it rent the air. The grey screamed, then shot down the lane, a sharp crack accompanying the thud of hooves. Heart pounding, Honoria watched in helpless dismay as the gig rushed past, the branch with the reins still wrapped about it bumping wildly in its wake.

Then lightning cracked. The flash was hidden by the canopy yet still lit the lane in garish white. Honoria shut her eyes tight, blocking her memories by sheer force of will.

A low moan reached her. Opening her eyes, she looked down, but her charge remained unconscious.

"Wonderful." She glanced around; the truth was impossible to avoid. She was alone in a wood, under trees, miles from shelter, without means of transport, in a countryside she'd first seen four days ago, with a storm lashing the leaves from the trees—and beside her lay a badly wounded man. How on earth could she help him?

Her mind was a comfortless blank. Into the void came the sound of hoofbeats. At first, she thought she was dreaming, but the sound grew steadily louder, nearer. Giddy with relief, Honoria rose. She stood in the lane, fingertips on the pad, listening as the hoofbeats drew rapidly nearer. At the last minute, she stood upright, turning and stepping boldly to the center of the lane.

The ground shook; thunder engulfed her. Looking up, she beheld Death.

A massive black stallion screamed and reared over her, iron-tipped hooves flailing within inches of her head. On the beast's back sat a man to match the horse, black-clad shoulders blocking out the twilight, dark mane wild, features harsh—satanic.

The stallion's hooves thudded to the ground, missing her by a bare foot. Furious, snorting, eyes showing white, the beast hauled at the reins. It tried to swing its huge head toward her; denied, it attempted to rear again.

Muscles bunched in the rider's arms, in the long thighs pressed to the stallion's flanks. For one eternal minute, man and beast did battle. Then all went still, the stallion acknowledging defeat in a long, shuddering, horsy sigh.

Her heart in her throat, Honoria lifted her gaze to the rider's face—and met his eyes. Even in the dimness, she was sure of their color. Pale, lucent green, they seemed ancient, all-seeing. Large, set deep under strongly arched black brows, they were the dominant feature in an impressively strong face. Their glance was penetrating, mesmerizing—unearthly. In that instant, Honoria was sure that the devil had come to claim one of his own. And her, too.

Then the air about her turned blue.

Chapter 2

❧

"*WHAT IN THE* **devil's own name are you about, woman?**"
Ending a string of decidedly inventive curses, that question, delivered with enough force to hold back the storm itself, jerked Honoria's wits into place. She focused on the commanding figure atop the restless stallion, then, with haughty dignity, stepped back, gesturing to the body on the verge. "I came upon him a few minutes ago—he's been shot, and I can't stop the bleeding."

The rider's eyes came to rest on the still figure. Satisfied, Honoria turned and headed back to the injured man, then realized the rider hadn't moved. She looked back, and saw the broad chest beneath what she now recognized as a dark hacking jacket expand—and expand—as the rider drew in an impossibly deep breath.

His gaze switched to her. "Press down on that pad—hard."

Without waiting to see if she obeyed, he swung down from his horse, the movement so eloquent of harnessed power, Honoria felt giddy again. She hurriedly returned to her patient. "That's precisely what I *was* doing," she muttered, dropping to her knees and placing both hands on the pad.

The rider, busy tying the stallion's reins about a tree, glanced her way. "Lean over him—use all your weight."

Honoria frowned but shuffled closer and did as he said.

There was a note in the deep voice that suggested he expected to be obeyed. Given that she was counting on him to help her deal with the wounded man, now, she decided, was not the time to take umbrage. She heard him approach, footsteps firm on the packed earth. Then the footfalls slowed, became hesitant, then stopped altogether. She was about to glance up when he started forward again.

He came to the other side of the wounded man, avoiding the large pool of blood. Hunkering down, he gazed at the youth.

From beneath her lashes, Honoria gazed at him.

At closer range, the effect of his face diminished not one whit—if anything, the impact of strong, angular planes, decidedly patrician nose, and lips that were long, thin, and provocatively mobile was even more pronounced. His hair was indeed midnight black, thick and wavy enough to form large locks; his eyes, fixed on their common charge, were hooded. As for the rest of him, Honoria decided it was wiser not to notice—she needed all her wits for helping the wounded man.

"Let me see the wound."

Was that a quaver she heard running through that dark voice, so deep it half resonated through her? Honoria glanced swiftly at her rescuer. His expression was impassive, showing no hint of any emotion—no, she'd imagined the quaver.

She lifted the sodden wad; he bent closer, angling his shoulders to let light reach the wound. He grunted, then nodded, rocking back on his heels as she replaced the pad.

Looking up, Honoria saw him frown. Then his heavy lids lifted and he met her gaze. Again she was struck by his curious eyes, transfixed by their omniscient quality.

Thunder rolled; the echoes were still reverberating when lightning lit up the world.

Honoria flinched, struggling to control her breathing. She refocused on her rescuer; his gaze hadn't left her. Raindrops pattered on the leaves and spattered the dust of the lane. He looked up. "We'll have to get him—and ourselves—under cover. The storm's nearly here."

He rose, smoothly straightening his long legs. Still kneeling, Honoria was forced to let her eyes travel upward, over top boots and long, powerfully muscled thighs, past lean hips and a narrow waist, all the way over the wide acreage of his chest to find

11

his face. He was tall, large, lean, loose-limbed yet well muscled—
a supremely powerful figure.

Finding her mouth suddenly dry, she felt her temper stir. "To
where, precisely? We're miles from anywhere." Her rescuer
looked down, his disturbing gaze fixing on her face. Honoria's
confidence faltered. "Aren't we?"

He looked into the trees. "There's a woodsman's cottage
nearby. A track leads off a little way along the lane."

So he was a local; Honoria was relieved. "How will we move
him?"

"I'll carry him." He didn't add the "of course," but she
heard it. Then he grimaced. "But we should pack the wound
better before shifting him."

With that, he shrugged off his jacket, tossed it over a nearby
branch, and proceeded to strip off his shirt. Abruptly, Honoria
transferred her gaze to the wounded man. Seconds later, a fine
linen shirt dangled before her face, suspended from long, tanned
fingers.

"Fold the body of the shirt and use the arms to tie it about
him."

Honoria frowned at the shirt. Lifting one hand, she took it,
then looked up, directly into his face, studiously ignoring the
tanned expanse of his bare chest and the crisply curling black
hair that adorned it. "If you can take over here and keep your
eyes on the wound, I'll donate my petticoat. We'll need more
fabric to bind against the hole."

His black brows flew up, then he nodded and hunkered
down, placing long strong fingers on the pad. Honoria withdrew
her hand and stood.

Briskly, trying not to think about what she was doing, she
crossed to the other side of the lane. Facing the trees, she lifted
the front of her skirt and tugged at the drawstring securing her
lawn petticoat.

"I don't suppose you've a penchant for underdrawers?"

Stifling a gasp, Honoria glanced over her shoulder, but her
devilish rescuer was still facing in the opposite direction. When
she didn't immediately answer, he went on: "It would give us
even more bulk."

Honoria's petticoat slithered down her bare legs. "Unfortunately not," she replied repressively. Stepping free, she swiped up her offering and stalked back across the lane.

He shrugged. "Ah, well—I can't say I'm a fan of them myself."

The vision his words conjured up was ridiculous. Then Honoria's wits clicked into place. The look she cast him as she dropped to her knees should have blistered him; it was wasted—his gaze was trained on the wounded man's face. Inwardly humphing, Honoria ascribed the salacious comment to ingrained habit.

Folding the petticoat, she combined it with the shirt; he removed his hand, and she applied the thick pad over her earlier insignificant one.

"Leave the sleeves hanging. I'll lift him—then you can reach under and tie them tight."

Honoria, wondered how even he would cope with the long, heavy weight of their unconscious charge. Amazingly well was the answer; he hefted the body and straightened in one fluid movement. She scrambled to her feet. He held the youth against his chest; with one sleeve in her hand she ducked and felt about for the other. Her searching fingertips brushed warm skin; muscles rippled in response. She pretended not to notice. Locating the wayward sleeve, she pulled it taut, tying the ends in a flat knot.

Her rescuer expelled a long breath through his teeth. For one instant, his strange eyes glittered. "Let's go. You'll have to lead Sulieman." With his head, he indicated the black monster cropping grass beside the lane.

Honoria stared at the stallion. "Sulieman was a treacherous Turk."

"Indeed."

She transferred her gaze back to the man. "You're serious, aren't you?"

"We can't leave him here. If he gets loose, panicked by the storm, he could damage something. Or someone."

Unconvinced, Honoria retrieved his jacket from the branch. She studied the stallion. "Are you sure he won't bite?" When no answer came, she turned to stare, openmouthed, at her rescuer. "You expect me to—?"

"Just take the reins—he'll behave himself."

His tone held enough irritated masculine impatience to have her crossing the lane, albeit with no good grace. She glared at the stallion; he stared levelly back. Refusing to be intimidated—by a horse—Honoria crammed the jacket under the saddle, then tugged the reins free. Holding them firmly, she started along the lane. And came to an abrupt halt when the stallion didn't budge.

"Sulieman—walk."

At the command, the huge horse started forward. Honoria scurried ahead, trying to keep beyond the range of the monster's teeth. Her rescuer, after one comprehensive glance, turned and strode on.

They were deep within the densest part of the wood, thickly leaved canopies interwoven overhead. As if flexing its muscles, the wind gusted, riffling the leaves and flinging a shower of raindrops upon them.

Honoria watched as her rescuer angled his awkward burden through a tight curve. As he straightened, the muscles in his back shifted, smoothly rippling under taut skin. A single raindrop fell to tremble, glistening, on one tanned shoulder, then slowly slid down his back. Honoria tracked it all the way; when it disappeared beneath his waistband, she swallowed.

Why the sight affected her so, she couldn't understand—men's bare torsos, viewed from childhood in the fields and forge, had never before made it difficult to breathe. Then again, she couldn't recall seeing a chest quite like her rescuer's before.

He glanced back. "How did you come to be in the lane alone?" He paused, shifted the youth in his arms, then strode on.

"I wasn't exactly alone," Honoria explained to his back. "I was returning from the village in the gig. I saw the storm coming and thought to take a shortcut."

"The gig?"

"When I saw the body I went to investigate. At the first thunderclap, the horse bolted."

"Ah."

Honoria narrowed her eyes. She hadn't seen him glance heavenward, but she knew he had. "It wasn't my knot that came undone. The branch I tied the reins to broke."

He glanced her way; while his face was expressionless, his lips were no longer perfectly straight. "I see."

The most noncommittal two words she had ever heard. Honoria scowled at his infuriating back, and trudged on in awful silence. Despite his burden, he was forging ahead; in her kid half boots, not designed for rough walking, she slipped and slid trying to keep up. Unfortunately, with the storm building by the second, she couldn't hold the pace he was setting against him.

The disgruntled thought brought her mentally up short. From the instant of encountering her rescuer, she'd been conscious of irritation, a ruffling of her sensibilities. He'd been abrupt, distinctly arrogant—quite impossible in some ill-defined way. Yet he was doing what needed to be done, quickly and efficiently. She ought to be grateful.

Negotiating a tangle of exposed tree roots, she decided it was his assumption of command that most irked—she had not before met anyone with his degree of authority, as if it was his unquestionable right to lead, to order, *and* to be obeyed. Naturally, being who she was, used to being obeyed herself, such an attitude did not sit well.

Finding her eyes once more glued to his back, entranced by the fluid flexing of his muscles, Honoria caught herself up. Irritation flared—she clung to its safety. He was impossible—in *every* way.

He glanced back and caught her black frown before she had a chance to wipe it from her face. His brows quirked; his eyes met hers, then he faced forward. "Nearly there."

Honoria released the breath that had stuck in her throat. And indulged in a furious scowl. Who the devil *was* he?

A gentleman certainly—horse, clothes, and manner attested to that. Beyond that, who could tell? She checked her impressions, then checked again, but could find no hint of underlying unease; she was perfectly certain she was safe with this man. Six years as a governess had honed her instincts well—she did not doubt them. Once they gained shelter, introductions would follow. As a well-bred lady, it wasn't her place to demand his name, it was his duty to make himself known to her.

Ahead, the dimness beneath the trees lightened; ten more steps brought them into a large clearing. Directly in front, backing onto the wood, stood a timber cottage, its thatch in good repair. Honoria noted the opening of two bridle paths, one to the right, one to the left. His stride lengthening, her rescuer headed for the cottage door.

"There's a stable of sorts to the side. Tie Sulieman in there." He flicked a glance her way. "To something unbreakable."

The glare she sent him bounced off his broad back. She quickened her pace, egged on by the rising whine of the wind. Leaves whirled like dervishes, clutching at her skirts; the black monster trotted at her heels. The stable was little more than a rude shack, built against the cottage wall.

Honoria scanned the exposed timbers for a hitching post. "I don't suppose it's what you're accustomed to," she informed her charge, "but you'll have to make do." She spied an iron ring bolted to the cottage wall. "Ah-hah!"

Looping the reins through, she hung on the ends to tighten the knot. She grabbed the jacket and was about to turn away when the huge black head swung toward her, one large eye wide, its expression strangely vulnerable. Briskly, she patted the black nose. "Stay calm."

With that sage advice, she picked up her skirts and fled for the cottage door. The storm chose that precise moment to rend the sky—thunder rolled, lightning crackled, the wind shrieked— so did Honoria.

She flew through the open door, whirled, and slammed it shut, then slumped back against it, eyes closed, hands clutching the soft jacket to her breast. Rain drummed on the roof and pelted the panels at her back. The wind shook the shutters and set the rafters creaking. Honoria's heart pounded; on the inside of her eyelids she saw the white light she knew brought death.

Catching her breath on a hiccup, she forced her eyes open. And saw her rescuer, the youth in his arms, standing beside a pallet raised on a crude frame. The cottage was dark, lit only by dim remnants of light leaking through the slatted shutters.

"Light the candle, then come and set the covers."

The simple command prodded Honoria into action. She crossed to the table that dominated the single-roomed abode. A candle stood in a simple candlestick, tinder beside it. Laying the jacket aside, she struck a spark and coaxed the candle into flame. A soft glow spread through the room. Satisfied, she headed for the pallet. An odd assortment of furniture crowded the small cottage—an old wing chair sat beside the stone hearth, a huge carved chair with faded tapestry cushions facing it. Chairs, bed, and table took up much of the available space; a chest and two rough dressers hugged the walls. The bed stood out into the room, its head against one wall; Honoria reached for the neatly folded blankets left on its end. "Who lives here?"

"A woodsman. But it's August so he'll be in the woods by Earith. These are his winter quarters." He leaned forward, lowering his burden, as Honoria flipped the blanket out along the bed.

"Wait! He'll be more comfortable if we remove his coat."

Those unearthly eyes held hers, then he looked down at the body in his arms. "See if you can ease the sleeve off."

She'd been careful not to catch the coat when she'd secured their improvised bandage. Honoria gently tugged; the sleeve shifted inch by inch.

Her rescuer snorted. "Silly clunch probably took an hour to get into it."

Honoria looked up—this time she was sure. His voice had shaken on the "clunch." She stared at him, a dreadful premonition seeping through her. "Pull harder—he can't feel anything at the moment."

She did; between them, by yanking and tugging, they managed to free one arm. With a sigh of relief, he laid the body down, drawing the coat off as he eased his hands free. They stood and stared at the deathly pale face, framed by the faded blanket.

Lightning cracked; Honoria shifted and glanced at her rescuer. "Shouldn't we fetch a doctor?"

Thunder rolled, echoing and booming. Her rescuer turned his head; the heavy lids lifted, and his strange eyes met hers. In the clear green—timeless, ageless, filled with desolate bleakness—Honoria read his answer. "He's not going to recover, is he?"

The compelling gaze left her; his black mane shook in a definite negative.

"Are you sure?" She asked even though she suspected he was right.

His long lips twisted. "Death and I are well acquainted." The statement hung in the suddenly chill air. Honoria was grateful when he elaborated: "I was at Waterloo. A great victory we were later told. Hell on earth for those who lived through it. In one day I saw more men die than any sane man sees in a lifetime. I'm quite certain—" Thunder crashed, nearly drowning out his words. "He won't see out the night."

His words fell into sudden silence. Honoria believed him; the bleakness that hung about him left no room for doubt.

"You saw the wound—how the blood kept pulsing? The ball nicked the heart—either that, or one of the big vessels close by. That's why we can't stop the bleeding." He gestured to where blood was staining the thick pad. "Every time his heart beats, he dies a little more."

Glancing at the youth's innocent face, Honoria drew in a slow breath. Then she looked at her rescuer. She wasn't sure she believed the impassive face he wore. His very stoicism fed her suspicion; compassion stirred.

Then he frowned, black brows slashing down as he held up the youth's coat. Honoria watched as he examined the button opposite the bloody hole. "What is it?"

"The button deflected the ball. See?" He held the button to the light so she could see the dent in its rim, the scorching beside it. Eyes measuring the coat against the youth, he added: "If it hadn't been for the button, it would have been a clean shot through the heart."

Honoria grimaced. "A pity perhaps." When he glanced her way, green eyes strangely empty, she gestured helplessly. "In the circumstances, I mean—a slow death, rather than a fast one."

He said nothing but continued to frown at the button. Honoria pressed her lips together, trying to deny the impulse, and failed. "But?"

"But . . ." He hesitated, then went on: "A clean shot through the heart with a long-barreled pistol—small bore, so it wasn't a shotgun or even horse pistol—at reasonable range—closer would have left more of a burn—is no mean feat. Pulling off such a shot takes remarkable skill."

"And remarkable cold-bloodedness, I imagine."

"That, too."

Rain beat against the walls, the shutters. Honoria straightened. "If you light the fire, I'll heat some water and wash away the worst of the blood." The suggestion earned her a surprised look; she met it with implacable calm. "If he has to die, then at least he can die clean."

For an instant, she thought she'd shocked him—his gaze appeared truly arrested. Then he nodded, his permission so clearly implied she could not doubt that he considered the injured youth in his care.

She headed for the hearth; he followed, soft-footed for such a large man. Pausing before the fire, Honoria glanced over her shoulder—and nearly swallowed her heart when she found him directly beside her.

He was big—bigger than she'd realized. She was often referred to as a "Long Meg"; this man towered over her by a full head, cutting her off from the candlelight, his dramatic face in deep shadow, his black hair a dark corona about his head. He was the Prince of Darkness personified; for the first time in her life, she felt small, fragile, intensely vulnerable.

"There's a pump near the stable." He reached past her; candlelight glimmered on the curved contours of his arm as he lifted the kettle from its hook. "I'd better check Sulieman, too, but I'll get the fire going first."

Honoria quickly shifted to the side. Only when he had crouched before the hearth, laying logs from the woodbox in the grate, did she manage to breathe again. At close range, his voice reverberated through her, a decidedly unnerving sensation.

By the time he had a blaze established, she had her attention firmly fixed on the dressers, discovering clean cloths and a canister of tea. She heard him move past; reaching high, he lifted a bucket from a hook. The latch clicked; Honoria glanced around—he stood in the doorway, bare to the waist, silhouetted by a searing flash of light—an elemental figure in an elemental world. The wind funneled in, then was abruptly cut off; the door shut and he was gone.

She counted seven rolls of thunder before he returned. As the door closed behind him, the tension gripping her eased. Then she noticed he was dripping wet. "Here." She held out the largest of the cloths she'd found and reached for the kettle. She busied herself by the fire, setting the kettle to boil, quite sure she didn't need to watch him drying that remarkable chest. The kettle hissed; she reached for the bowl she'd set ready.

He was waiting by the bed; she considered ordering him to dry himself by the fire, then decided to save her breath. His gaze was fixed on the youth's face.

Setting the bowl on the chest by the bed, she squeezed out a cloth, then gently sponged the youth's face, removing the grit and dust of the lane. Cleanliness emphasized his innocence, and highlighted the obscenity of his death. Pressing her lips together, Honoria bent to her task. Until she came to the badly stained shirt.

"Let me."

She shifted back. Two well-judged rips, and the left side of the shirt was free.

"Give me a cloth."

She squeezed one out and handed it over. They worked side by side in the flickering light; she was amazed by how gentle such large hands could be, was moved by how reverently one so powerfully alive dealt with the dying.

Then they were done. Settling another blanket over their silent charge, she gathered the soiled cloths and loaded them into the bowl. He preceded her to the fire; she set the bowl on the table and straightened her back.

"Devil?"

The call was so faint she only just heard it. Honoria whirled and flew back to the bed. The youth's lids fluttered. "Devil. Need . . . Devil."

"It's all right," she murmured, laying her hand on his brow. "There's no devil here—we won't let him get you."

The youth frowned; he shook his head against her hand. "No! Need to *see* . . ."

Hard hands closed about Honoria's shoulders; she gasped as she was lifted bodily aside. Freed of her touch, the youth opened glazed eyes and struggled to rise.

"Lie back, Tolly. I'm here."

Honoria stared as her rescuer took her place, pressing the youth back to the bed. His voice, his touch, calmed the dying man—he lay back, visibly relaxing, focusing on the older man's face. "Good," he breathed, his voice thin. "Found you." A weak smile flickered across his pale face. Then he sobered. "Have to tell you—"

His urgent words were cut off by a cough, which turned into a debilitating paroxysm. Her rescuer braced the youth between his hands, as if willing strength into the wilting frame. As the coughing subsided, Honoria grabbed up a clean cloth and offered it. Laying the youth down, her rescuer wiped the blood from the boy's lips. "Tolly?"

No answer came—their charge was unconscious again.

"You're related." Honoria made it a statement; the revelation had come the instant the youth opened his eyes. The resemblance lay not only in the wide forehead but in the arch of the brows and the set of the eyes.

"Cousins." Animation leached from her rescuer's harsh face. "First cousins. He's one of the younger crew—barely twenty."

His tone made Honoria wonder how old *he* was—in his thirties certainly, but from his face it was impossible to judge. His demeanor conveyed the impression of wordly wisdom, wisdom earned, as if experience had tempered his steel.

As she watched, he put out one hand and gently brushed back a lock of hair from his cousin's pallid face.

The low moan of the wind turned into a dirge.

Chapter 3

⬥

SHE WAS STRANDED in a cottage with a dying man and a man known to his intimates as Devil. Ensconced in the wing chair by the fire, Honoria sipped tea from a mug and considered her position. It was now night; the storm showed no sign of abating. She could not leave the cottage, even had that been her most ardent desire.

Glancing at her rescuer, still seated on the pallet, she grimaced; she did not wish to leave. She'd yet to learn his name, but he'd commanded her respect, and her sympathy.

Half an hour had passed since the youth had spoken; Devil—she had no other name for him—had not left his dying cousin's side. His face remained impassive, showing no hint of emotion, yet emotion was there, behind the facade, shadowing the green of his eyes. Honoria knew of the shock and grief occasioned by sudden death, knew of the silent waiting and the vigils for the dead. Returning her gaze to the flames, she slowly sipped her tea.

Sometime later, she heard the bed creak; soft footfalls slowly neared. She sensed rather than saw him ease into the huge carved chair, smelled the dust that rose from the faded tapestry as he settled. The kettle softly hissed. Shifting forward, she poured boiling water into the mug she'd left ready; when the steam subsided, she picked up the mug and held it out.

He took it, long fingers brushing hers briefly, green eyes lifting to touch her face. "Thank you."

He sipped in silence, eyes on the flames; Honoria did the same.

Minutes ticked by, then he straightened his long legs, crossing his booted ankles. Honoria felt his gaze on her face.

"What brings you to Somersham, Miss . . . ?"

It was the opening she'd been waiting for. "Wetherby," she supplied.

Instead of responding with his name—Mr. Something, Lord Someone—he narrowed his eyes. "Your *full* name?"

Honoria held back a frown. "Honoria Prudence Wetherby," she recited, somewhat tartly.

One black brow rose; the disturbing green gaze did not waver. "Not Honoria Prudence *Anstruther*-Wetherby?"

Honoria stared. "How did you know?"

His lips quirked. "I'm acquainted with your grandfather."

A disbelieving look was her reply. "I suppose you're going to tell me I look like him?"

A short laugh, soft and deep, feathered across her senses. "Now you mention it, I believe there is a faint resemblance— about the chin, perhaps?"

Honoria glared.

"Now that," her tormentor remarked, "is very like old Magnus."

She frowned. "What is?"

He took a slow sip, his eyes holding hers. "Magnus Anstruther-Wetherby is an irascible old gentleman, atrociously high in the instep and as stubborn as bedamned."

"You know him well?"

"Only to nod to—my father knew him better."

Uncertain, Honoria watched him sip; her full name was no state secret—she simply didn't care to use it, to claim relationship with that irascible, stubborn old gentleman in London.

"There was a second son, wasn't there?" Her rescuer studied her musingly. "He defied Magnus over . . . I remember—he married against Magnus's wishes. One of the Montgomery girls. You're their daughter?"

Stiffly, Honoria inclined her head.

"Which brings us back to my question, Miss Anstruther-

Wetherby. What the deuce are you doing here, gracing our quiet backwater?"

Honoria hesitated; there was a restlessness in the long limbs, a ripple of awareness—not of her, but of the body on the pallet behind them—that suggested conversation was his need. She lifted her chin. "I'm a finishing governess."

"A *finishing* governess?"

She nodded. "I prepare girls for their come-out—I only remain with the families for the year before."

He eyed her with fascinated incredulity. "What in all the heavens does old Magnus think of that?"

"I've no idea. I've never sought his opinion."

He laughed briefly—that same throaty, sensuous sound; Honoria suppressed an urge to wriggle her shoulders. Then he sobered. "What happened to your family?"

Inwardly, Honoria shrugged. It couldn't hurt to tell her tale, and if it distracted him, well and good. "My parents died in an accident when I was sixteen. My brother was nineteen. We lived in Hampshire, but after the accident, I went to stay with my mother's sister in Leicestershire."

He frowned. "I'm surprised Magnus didn't intervene."

"Michael informed him of the deaths, but he didn't come down for the funeral." Honoria shrugged. "We hadn't expected him. After the falling-out between him and Papa, there'd been no contact." Her lips lifted fleetingly. "Papa swore he'd never ask for quarter."

"Stubbornness is clearly a family trait."

Honoria ignored the comment. "After a year in Leicestershire, I decided to try my hand at governessing." She looked up, into far-too-perceptive green eyes.

"Your aunt wasn't exactly welcoming?"

Honoria sighed. "No—she was *very* welcoming. She married beneath her—not the mild *mesalliance* the Anstruther-Wetherbys got so heated over but truly out of her class." She paused, seeing again the rambling house filled with dogs and children. "But she was happy and her household was welcoming *but* . . ." She grimaced and glanced at the dark face watching her. "Not for me."

"Fish out of water?"

"Precisely. Once I came out of mourning, I considered my

options. Funds, of course, were never a problem. Michael wanted me to buy a small house in some safe country village and live quietly *but . . ."*

"Again, not for you?"

Honoria tilted her chin. "I couldn't conceive of a life so tame. I think it unfair that women are forced to such mild existences and only gentlemen get to lead exciting lives."

Both black brows rose. "Personally, I've always found it pays to share the excitement."

Honoria opened her mouth to approve—then caught his eye. She blinked and looked again, but the salacious glint had disappeared. "In my case, I decided to take control of my life and work toward a more exciting existence."

"As a governess?" His steady green gaze remained ingenuously interested.

"No. That's only an intermediary stage. I decided eighteen was too young to go adventuring in Africa. I've decided to follow in Lady Stanhope's footsteps."

"*Good God!*"

Honoria ignored his tone. "I have it all planned—my burning ambition is to ride a camel in the shadow of the Great Sphinx. One would be ill-advised to undertake such an expedition too young; governessing in a manner that requires spending only a year with each family seemed the ideal way to fill in the years. As I need provide nothing beyond my clothes, my capital grows while I visit various counties, staying in select households. That last, of course, eases Michael's mind."

"Ah, yes—your brother. What's he doing while you fill in your years?"

Honoria eyed her inquisitor measuringly. "Michael is secretary to Lord Carlisle. Do you know him?"

"Carlisle? Yes. His secretary, no. I take it your brother has political ambitions?"

"Lord Carlisle was a friend of Papa's—he's agreed to stand as Michael's sponsor."

His brows rose fleetingly, then he drained his mug. "What made you decide on governessing as your temporary occupation?"

Honoria shrugged. "What else was there? I'd been well educated, prepared for presentation. Papa was adamant that I be

25

presented to the *ton*, puffed off with all the trimmings—paraded beneath my grandfather's nose. He hoped I'd make a wonderful match, just to show Grandfather no one else shared his antiquated notions."

"But your parents were killed before you were brought out?"

Honoria nodded. "Lady Harwell, an old friend of Mama's, had a daughter two years younger than I. After putting off black gloves, I broached my idea to her—I thought with my background, my preparation, I could teach other girls how to go on. Lady Harwell agreed to a trial. After I finished coaching Miranda, she landed an earl. After that, of course, I never wanted for positions."

"The matchmaking mama's delight." An undercurrent of cynicism had crept into the deep voice. "And who are you coaching around Somersham?"

The question returned Honoria to reality with a thump. "Melissa Claypole."

Her rescuer frowned. "Is she the dark one or the fair one?"

"The fair one." Propping her chin in her hand, Honoria gazed into the flames. "An insipid miss with no conversation— God knows how I'm supposed to render her attractive. I was booked to go to Lady Oxley but her six-year old caught chicken pox, and then old Lady Oxley died. I'd declined all my other offers by then, but the Claypoles' letter arrived late, and I hadn't yet replied. So I accepted without doing my usual checks."

"Checks?"

"I don't work for just anyone." Stifling a yawn, Honoria settled more comfortably. "I make sure the family is good *ton*, well connected enough to get the right invitations and sufficiently beforehand not to make a fuss over the milliner's bills."

"Not to mention those from the modistes."

"Precisely. Well"—she gestured briefly—"no girl is going to snare a duke if she dresses like a dowd."

"Indubitably. Am I to understand the Claypoles fail to meet your stringent requirements?"

Honoria frowned. "I've only been with them since Sunday, but I've a nasty suspicion . . ." She let her words trail away, then shrugged. "Luckily, it appears Melissa is all but spoken for—by a duke, no less."

A pause followed, then her rescuer prompted: "A duke?"

"So it seems. If you live about here you must know of him—sober, reserved, rather reclusive, I think. Already tangled in Lady Claypole's web, if her ladyship speaks true." Recollecting her burning question, Honoria twisted around. "Do you know him?"

Clear green eyes blinked back at her; slowly, her rescuer shook his head. "I can't say I've had the pleasure."

"Humph!" Honoria sank back in her chair. "I'm beginning to think he's a hermit. Are you sure—"

But he was no longer listening to her. Then she heard what had caught his attention—the rattly breathing of the wounded youth. The next instant, he was striding back to the bed. He sat on the edge, taking one of the youth's hands in his. From the chair, Honoria listened as the youth's breathing grew more ragged, more rasping.

Fifteen painful minutes later, the dry rattle ceased.

An unearthly silence filled the cottage; even the storm was still. Honoria closed her eyes and silently uttered a prayer. Then the wind rose, mournfully keening, nature's chant for the dead.

Opening her eyes, Honoria watched as Devil laid his cousin's hands across his chest. Then he sat on the pallet's edge, eyes fixed on the pale features that would not move again. He was seeing his cousin alive and well, laughing, talking. Honoria knew how the mind dealt with death. Her heart twisted, but there was nothing she could do. Sinking back in the chair, she left him to his memories.

She must have dozed off. When next she opened her eyes, he was crouched before the hearth. The candle had guttered; the only light in the room was that thrown by the flames. Half-asleep, she watched as he laid logs on the blaze, banking it for the night.

During their earlier conversation, she'd kept her eyes on his face or the flames; now, with the firelight sculpting his arms and shoulders, she looked her fill. Something about all that tanned male skin had her battling a fierce urge to press her fingers to it, to spread her hands across the warm expanse, to curve her palms about hard muscle.

Arms crossed, hands safely clutching her elbows, she shivered.

In one fluid motion he rose and turned. And frowned.

"Here." Reaching past her, he lifted his soft jacket from the table and held it out.

Honoria stared at it, valiantly denying the almost overwhelming urge to focus, not on the jacket, but on the chest a yard behind it. She swallowed, shook her head, then dragged her gaze straight up to his face. "No—you keep it. It was just that I woke up—I'm not really cold." That last was true enough; the fire was throwing steady heat into the room.

One black brow very slowly rose; the pale green eyes did not leave her face. Then the second brow joined the first, and he shrugged. "As you wish." He resumed his seat in the old carved chair, glancing about the cottage, his gaze lingering on the blanket-shrouded figure on the bed. Then, settling back, he looked at her. "I suggest we get what sleep we can. The storm should have passed by morning."

Honoria nodded, immensely relieved when he spread his jacket over his disturbing chest. He laid his head against the chairback, and closed his eyes. His lashes formed black crescents above his high cheekbones; light flickered over the austere planes of his face. A strong face, hard yet not insensitive. The sensuous line of his lips belied his rugged jaw; the fluid arch of his brows offset his wide forehead. Wild locks of midnight black framed the whole—Honoria smiled and closed her eyes. He should have been a pirate.

With sleep clouding her mind, her body soothed by the fire's warmth, it wasn't hard to drift back into her dreams.

Sylvester Sebastian Cynster, sixth Duke of St. Ives, known as That Devil Cynster to a select handful of retainers, as Devil Cynster to the *ton* at large and simply as Devil to his closest friends, watched his wife-to-be from beneath his long lashes. What, he wondered, would his mother, the Dowager Duchess, make of Honoria Prudence Anstruther-Wetherby?

The thought almost made him smile, but the dark pall that hung over his mind wouldn't let his lips curve. For Tolly's death there was only one answer; justice would be served, but vengeance would wield the sword. Nothing else would appease him or the other males of his clan. Despite their reckless propensities, Cynsters died in their beds.

But avenging Tolly's death would merely be laying the past

to rest. Today he had rounded the next bend in his own road; his companion for the next stretch shifted restlessly in the old wing chair opposite.

Devil watched her settle, and wondered what was disturbing her dreams. Him, he hoped. She was certainly disturbing him—and he was wide-awake.

He hadn't realized when he'd left the Place that morning that he was searching for a wife; fate had known better. It had placed Honoria Prudence in his path in a manner that ensured he couldn't pass her by. The restless dissatisfaction that had gripped him of late seemed all of a piece, part of fate's scheme. Jaded by the importunities of his latest conquest, he'd come to the Place, sending word to Vane to meet him for a few days' shooting. Vane had been due to join him that evening; with a whole day to kill, he'd thrown a saddle on Sulieman and ridden out to his fields.

The wide lands that were his never failed to soothe him, to refocus his mind on who he was, what he was. Then the storm had risen; he'd cut through the wood, heading for the back entrance to the Place. That had put him on track to find Tolly—and Honoria Prudence. Fate had all but waved a red flag; no one had ever suggested he was slow to see the light. Seizing opportunity was how he'd made his name—he'd already decided to seize Honoria Prudence.

She would do very well as his wife.

For a start, she was tall, with a well-rounded figure, neither svelte nor fleshy but very definitely feminine. Hair of chestnut brown glowed richly, tendrils escaping from the knot on the top of her head. Her face, heart-shaped, was particularly arresting, fine-boned and classical, with a small straight nose, delicately arched brown brows, and a wide forehead. Her lips were full, a soft blush pink; her eyes, her finest feature, large, wide-set and long-lashed, were a misty grey. He'd told true about her chin—it was the only feature that reminded him of her grandsire, not in shape but in the determination it managed to convey.

Physically, she was a particularly engaging proposition—she'd certainly engaged his notoriously fickle interest.

Equally important, she was uncommonly level-headed, not given to flaps or starts. That had been clear from the first, when she'd stood straight and tall, uncowering beneath the weight of the epithets he'd so freely heaped on her head. Then she'd favored him with a look his mother could not have bettered and directed him to the matter at hand.

He'd been impressed by her courage. Instead of indulging in a fit of hysterics—surely prescribed practice for a gentlewoman finding a man bleeding to death in her path?—she'd been resourceful and practical. Her struggle to subdue her fear of the storm hadn't escaped him. He'd done what he could to distract her; her instantaneous response to his commands—he'd almost seen her hackles rising—had made distracting her easy enough. Taking his shirt off hadn't hurt, either.

His lips twitched; ruthlessly he straightened them. That, of course, was yet another good reason he should follow fate's advice.

For the past seventeen years, despite all the distractions the *ton*'s ladies had lined up to provide, his baser instincts had remained subject to his will, entirely and absolutely. Honoria Prudence, however, seemed to have established a direct link to that part of his mind which, as was the case with any male Cynster, was constantly on the lookout for likely prospects. It was the hunter in him; the activity did not usually distract him from whatever else he had in hand. Only when he was ready to attend to such matters, did he permit that side of his nature to show.

Today, he had stumbled—more than once—over his lustful appetites.

His question over underdrawers was one example, and while taking off his shirt had certainly distracted her, that fact, in turn, had also distracted him. He could feel her gaze—another sensitivity he hadn't been prey to for a very long time. At thirty-two, he'd thought himself immune, hardened, too experienced to fall victim to his own desires.

Hopefully, once he'd had Honoria Prudence a few times—perhaps a few dozen times—the affliction would pass. The fact that she was Magnus Anstruther-Wetherby's granddaughter, rebellious granddaughter at that, would be the icing on his wedding cake. Devil savored the thought.

He hadn't, of course, told her his name. If he had, she wouldn't have fallen asleep, restlessly or otherwise. He'd realized almost immediately that she didn't know who he was. There was no reason she should recognize *him*. She would, however, recognize his name.

Her peculiar profession would make keeping up with *ton* gossip imperative; he had not a doubt that, had he favored her with his name, she would have made the connection and reacted accordingly. Which would have been trying for them both.

Convincing her that she had no reason to fret would have taken a great deal of effort, which he did not, at the moment, have to spare. He still had Tolly's murder to contend with—he needed her calm and composed. He found her directness, her unfussy, almost wifely matter-of-factness, refreshing and strangely supportive.

The fire glowed, gilding her face. Devil studied the delicate curve of her cheek, noted the vulnerable softness of her lips. He would confess his identity in the morning—he wondered what she would say. The possibilities were, he judged, wide-ranging. He was mulling over the most likely when she whimpered and stiffened in her chair.

Devil opened his eyes fully. And simultaneously became aware of the renewed ferocity of the storm. Thunder rolled, rumbling ever nearer. The wind rose on a sudden shriek; a sharp crack echoed through the wood.

Honoria gasped and came to her feet. Eyes closed, hands reaching, she stepped forward.

Devil surged from his chair. Grabbing her about the waist, he lifted her away from the fire.

With a wrenching sob, she turned and flung herself against him. Her arms slipped about him; she clung tightly, pressing her cheek to his chest. Reflexively, Devil closed his arms about her and felt the sobs that racked her. Off-balance, he took a step back; the old chair caught him behind his knee.

He sat down; Honoria did not slacken her hold. She followed him down, drawing up her legs; she ended curled in his lap. Sobbing silently.

Tilting his head, Devil peered at her face. Her eyes were closed but not tightly. Tears coursed down her face. She was, in fact, still asleep.

Trapped in her nightmare, she shuddered. She gulped down a sob, only to have another rise in its place.

Watching her, Devil felt a sharp ache twist through his chest.

The tears welled from beneath her lids, gathered, then rolled slowly, steadily, down her cheeks.

His gut clenched. Hard. Gently, he tipped up her face. She didn't wake; the tears continued to fall.

He couldn't stand it. Devil bent his head and set his lips to hers.

Engulfed in sorrow so black, so dense, not even lightning could pierce it, Honoria became aware of lips warm and firm pressed against her own. The unexpected sensation distracted her, breaking the hold of her dream. Blackness receded; she pulled back and caught her breath.

Strong fingers curved about her jaw; the distracting lips returned. Warmth seeped into her bones, her skin, driving out death's chill. The lips held to hers, reassuringly alive, a link from one dream to the next. She made the transition from nightmare to a sense of peace, of rightness, reassured by the strength surrounding her and the steady beat of a heart not her own.

She was no longer alone in misery. Someone was here, keeping her warm, holding the memories at bay. The ice in her veins melted. Her lips softened; tentatively, she returned the kiss.

Devil caught his baser instincts an instant before they bolted. She was still asleep—the last thing he intended was to scare her awake. The battle to resist his demons, clamoring for him to deepen the caress into something far from innocent, was furious, as ferocious as the storm. He won—but the effort left him shaking.

She drew back. Lifting his head, he heard her sigh softly. Then, lips curving in a distinctly feminine smile, she shifted, settling herself in his lap.

Devil caught his breath; he bit his lip.

Pressing her cheek once more to his chest, she slid into peaceful slumber.

At least he'd stopped her tears. Jaw clenched, Devil reminded himself that that—and only that—had been his aim. Thanks to fate, he'd have time and more to claim recompense for the pain she was causing him, to claim a suitable reward for his remarkable rectitude. His halo, for once, ought to be glowing.

It took half an hour of thinking of something else before he could risk relaxing. By then she was deeply asleep. Shifting carefully, he settled more comfortably, then noticed the fire was dying. Reaching down, he snagged his jacket, then draped it carefully over his wife-to-be.

Lips curving, he rested his head against the chairback and closed his eyes.

He woke with his cheek pillowed on her curls.

Devil blinked. Sunlight slanted through the shutters. Honoria was still asleep, snuggled against him, legs curled across his thighs. Then he heard the clop of hooves approaching. Vane, no doubt, come to seek him out.

Straightening, Devil winced as cramped muscles protested. His wife-to-be did not stir. Gathering her in his arms, he stood; Honoria mumbled, resettling her head against his shoulder. Devil gently deposited her in the wing chair, tucking his jacket about her. A frown fleetingly puckered her brows as her cheek touched the cold chintz, then her features eased and she slid deeper into sleep.

Devil stretched. Then, running his fingers across his chest, he headed for the door. Yawning, he opened it.

His breath hissed in through his teeth. "Hell and the devil!" Taking stock of the arrivals, he cursed beneath his breath. He'd been right about Vane—his cousin, mounted on a black hunter, had just pulled up. Another horseman halted alongside. Devil's features blanked as he nodded to his only older cousin, Charles—Tolly's half brother.

That, however, was not the worst. From the other bridle path, a party of four trotted forward—Lord Claypole, Lady Claypole, and two grooms.

"Your *Grace*! How surprising to come upon you here." A sharp-featured woman with crimped hair, Lady Claypole barely glanced at Vane and Charles before returning her gaze to Devil, her protruberant blue eyes widening.

"I was stranded by the storm." Bracing one forearm against the doorframe, Devil blocked the doorway.

"Indeed? Beastly night." Lord Claypole, a short, rotund gentleman, wrestled his bay to a halt. "Might I inquire, Your Grace, if you've seen anything of our governess? Took the gig out to Somersham yesterday—gig came home without her—haven't seen hide nor hair of her since."

Devil looked blank. "The storm was quite wild."

"Quite, quite." His lordship nodded briskly. "Daresay the horse got loose and bolted home. Testy brute. Sure to find Miss Wetherby safe and sound at the vicarage, what?" His lordship looked at his wife, still absorbed with the view. "Don't you think so, m'dear?"

Her ladyship shrugged. "Oh, I'm sure she'll be all right. So terribly inconsiderate of her to put us to all this fuss." Directing a weary smile at Devil, Lady Claypole gestured to the grooms. "We felt we should mount a search, but I daresay you're right, my lord, and she'll be sitting snug at the vicarage. Miss Wetherby," her ladyship informed Devil archly, "comes with the *highest* recommendations."

Devil's brows rose. "Does she indeed?"

"I had it from Mrs. Acheson-Smythe. Of the *highest* calibre—*quite* exclusive. Naturally, when she learned of my Melissa, she set aside all other offers and—" Lady Claypole broke off, protruberant eyes starting. Her mouth slowly opened as she stared past Devil's bare shoulder.

Heaving an inward sigh, Devil lowered his arm, half-turning to watch Honoria's entrance. She came up beside him, blinking sleepily, one hand pressed to her back; with the other, she brushed errant curls from her face. Her eyes were heavy-lidded, her topknot loose, releasing wispy tendrils of gold-shot brown to wreathe auralike about her head. She looked deliciously tumbled, her cheeks lightly flushed, as if they had indeed been entertaining each other in the manner the Claypoles were imagining.

Honoria looked past him—momentarily, she froze. Then she straightened, cool grace dropping like a cloak about her. Not a glimmer of consternation showed in her face. Devil's lips quirked—in approval, in appreciation.

"*Well*, miss!"

Lady Claypole's strident tones overflowed with indignant outrage. Devil fixed her with a clear, very direct glance that any sane person would have read as a warning.

Her ladyship was not so acute. "A *fine* broiling, indeed! Well, Miss Wetherby—if *this* is what you get up to when you *say* you're visiting the vicar, you need not think to cross the Claypole Hall threshold again!"

"Ahem!" More observant than his lady, Lord Claypole plucked at her sleeve. "My dear—"

"To *think* that I've been so misled! Mrs. Acheson-Smythe will hear about—"

"*No*! Really, Margery—" One eye on Devil's face, Lord Claypole fought to restrain his wife from committing social suicide. "No need for any of that."

"No *need*?" Lady Claypole stared at him as if he'd taken leave of his senses. Shaking off his hand, she drew herself up and haughtily declaimed: "If you will send word of your direction, we'll send your boxes on."

"How kind." Devil's purring murmur held sufficient steel to succeed where Lord Claypole had failed. "You may send Miss Anstruther-Wetherby's boxes to the Place."

A long silence greeted his edict.

Lady Claypole leaned forward. "*Anstruther*-Wetherby?"

"The Place?" The soft echo came from Charles Cynster; his horse shifted and stamped.

Abruptly, Lady Claypole switched her gaze to Honoria. "Is this true, miss? Or is it merely a piece of flummery you've succeeded in coaxing His Grace to swallow?"

His *Grace*? For one discrete instant, Honoria's brain reeled. She glanced sideways at the devil beside her—his eyes, cool green, fleetingly met hers. In that moment, she would have given all she possessed to rid herself of everyone else and take to him as he deserved. Instead, she lifted her chin and calmly regarded Lady Claypole. "As His Grace," she invested the title with subtle emphasis, "has seen fit to inform you, I am, indeed, one of the Anstruther-Wetherbys. I choose to make little of the connection, to avoid unwarranted, ill-bred interest."

The comment failed to rout her ladyship. "I really don't know *how* I'm going to explain this to my daughters."

"I suggest, madam,"—his gaze on Lady Claypole's face, Devil caught Honoria's hand, squeezing her fingers warningly as he raised them to his lips—"that you inform your daughters that they've had the honor of being instructed, albeit for so short a time, by my duchess."

"Your *duchess*!" The exclamation burst from three throats— of the gentry, only Vane Cynster remained silent.

Honoria's brain reeled again; the grip on her fingers tightened. Her expression serene, her lips gently curved, she glanced affectionately at her supposed fiancé's face; only he could see the fell promise in her eyes.

"*Really*, Your Grace! You *can't* have considered." Lady Claypole had paled. "This matter hardly warrants such a sacrifice—I'm sure Miss Wetherby will be only too happy to reach some agreement . . ."

Her voice trailed away, finally silenced by the expression on Devil's face. For one, long minute, he held her paralyzed, then switched his chill gaze to Lord Claypole. "I had expected, my lord, that I could count on you and your lady to welcome my duchess." The deep flat tones held a definite menace.

Lord Claypole swallowed. "Yes indeed! No doubt of it— none whatever. Er . . ." Gathering his reins, he reached for his wife's. "Felicitations and all that—daresay we should get on. If you'll excuse us, Your Grace? Come, m'dear." With a yank, his lordship turned both his and his wife's horses; with remarkable speed, his party quit the clearing.

Relieved, Honoria studied the remaining horsemen. One glance was enough to identify the one nearest as a relative of . . . the duke called Devil. Her mind tripped on the thought, but she couldn't catch the connection. The horseman in question turned his head; hands negligently crossed on the pommel, he was strikingly handsome. His coloring—brown hair, brown brows—was less dramatic than Devil's, but he seemed of similar height and nearly as large as the man beside her. They shared one, definitive characteristic—the simple act of turning his head had been invested with the same fluid elegance that characterized all Devil's movements, a masculine grace that titillated the senses.

The horseman's gaze traveled rapidly over her—one comprehensive glance—then, lips curving in a subtle smile, he looked at Devil. "I take it you don't need rescuing?"

Voice and manner confirmed their relationship beyond question.

"Not rescuing—there's been an accident. Come inside."

The horseman's gaze sharpened; Honoria could have sworn some unspoken communication passed between him and Devil. Without another word, the horseman swung down from his saddle.

Revealing his companion, still atop his horse. An older man with pale thinning hair, he was heavily built, his face round, his features more fleshy than the aquiline planes of the other two men. He, too, met Devil's eye, then he hauled in a breath and dismounted. "Who are they?" Honoria whispered, as the first man, having secured his horse, started toward them.

"Two other cousins. The one approaching is Vane. At least, that's what we call him. The other is Charles. Tolly's brother."

"Brother?" Honoria juggled the image of the heavyset man against that of the dead youth.

"Half brother," Devil amended. Grasping her elbow, he stepped out of the cottage, drawing her with him.

It had been some time since anyone had physically compelled Honoria to do anything—it was certainly the first time any man had dared. His sheer presumption left her speechless; his sheer power rendered noncompliance impossible. Her heart, having finally slowed after the jolt he'd given it by kissing her fingers, started racing again.

Five paces from the door, he halted and, releasing her, faced her. "Wait over there—you can sit on that log. This might take a while."

For one pregnant instant, Honoria hovered on the brink of open rebellion. There was something implacable behind the crystal green, something that issued commands in the absolute certainty of being obeyed. She ached to challenge it, to challenge him, to take exception to his peremptory dictates. But she knew what he faced in the cottage.

Lips compressed, she inclined her head. "Very well."

She turned, skirts swirling; Devil watched as she started toward the log, set on stumps to one side of the clearing. Then she paused; without looking back, she inclined her head again. "Your Grace."

His gaze fixed on her swaying hips, Devil watched as she continued on her way. His interest in her had just dramatically increased; no woman before had so much as thought of throwing his commands—he knew perfectly well they were autocratic—back in his teeth. She'd not only thought of it—she'd nearly done it. If it hadn't been for Tolly's body in the cottage, she would have.

She reached the log. Satisfied, Devil turned; Vane was waiting at the cottage door.

"What?"

Devil's face hardened. "Tolly's dead. Shot."

Vane stilled, his eyes fixed on Devil's. "Who by?"

"That," Devil said softly, glancing at Charles as he neared, "I don't yet know. Come inside."

They stopped in a semicircle at the foot of the rude pallet, looking down on Tolly's body. Vane had been Devil's lieutenant at Waterloo; Charles had served as an adjutant. They'd seen death many times; familiarity didn't soften the blow. In a voice devoid of emotion, Devil recounted all he knew. He related Tolly's last words; Charles, his expression blank, hung on every syllable. Then came a long silence; in the bright light spilling through the open door, Tolly's corpse looked even more obscenely wrong than it had the night before.

"My *God. Tolly*!" Charles's words were broken. His features crumpled. Covering his face with one hand, he sank to the edge of the pallet.

Devil clenched his jaw, his fists. Death no longer possessed the power to shock him. Grief remained, but that he would handle privately. He was the head of his family—his first duty was to lead. They'd expect it of him—he expected it of himself. And he had Honoria Prudence to protect.

The thought anchored him, helping him pull free of the vortex of grief that dragged at his mind. He hauled in a deep breath, then quietly stepped back, retreating to the clear space before the hearth.

A few minutes later, Vane joined him; he glanced through the open door. "She found him?"

Devil nodded. "Thankfully, she's not the hysterical sort." They spoke quietly, their tones subdued. Glancing at the bed, Devil frowned. "What's Charles doing here?"

"He was at the Place when I arrived. Says he chased Tolly up here over some business matter. He called at Tolly's rooms— Old Mick told him Tolly had left for here."

Devil grimaced. "I suppose it's as well that he's here."

Vane was studying his bare chest. "Where's your shirt?"

"It's the bandage." After a moment, Devil sighed and

straightened. "I'll take Miss Anstruther-Wetherby to the Place and send a cart."

"And I'll stay and watch over the body." A fleeting smile touched Vane's lips. "You always get the best roles."

Devil's answering smile was equally brief. "This one comes with a ball and chain."

Vane's eyes locked on his. "You're serious?"

"Never more so." Devil glanced at the pallet. "Keep an eye on Charles."

Vane nodded.

The sunshine outside nearly blinded him. Devil blinked and squinted at the log. It was empty. He cursed and looked again—a terrible thought occurred. What if she'd tried to take Sulieman?

His reaction was instantaneous—the rush of blood, the sudden pounding of his heart. His muscles had already tensed to send him racing to the stable when a flicker of movement caught his eye.

She hadn't gone to the stable. Eyes adjusting to the glare, Devil watched her pace back and forth, a few steps to the side of the log. Her dun-colored gown had blended with the boles of the trees, momentarily camouflaging her. His panic subsiding, he focused his gaze.

Honoria felt it—she looked up and saw him, bare-chested still, the very image of a buccaneer, watching her, unmoving, irritation in every line. Their gazes locked—a second later, she broke the contact. Nose in the air, she stepped gracefully to her right—and sat primly on the log.

He waited, sharp green gaze steady, then, apparently satisfied that she'd remain where she'd been put, he headed for the stable.

Honoria ground her teeth, and told herself that he didn't matter. He was an expert in manipulation—and in intimidation—but why should that bother her? She would go to this Place of his, wait for her boxes, and then be on her way. She could spend the time meeting the Dowager Duchess.

At least she'd solved one part of the mystery plaguing her—she'd met her elusive duke. The image she'd carried for the past three days—the image Lady Claypole had painted—of a mild, unassuming, reclusive peer, rose in her mind. The image didn't fit the reality—the duke called Devil was not mild or unassuming. He was a first-class tyrant. And as for Lady Claypole's claim that he was caught in her coils, her ladyship was dreaming.

But at least she'd met her duke, even if she had yet to learn his name. She was, however, having increasing difficulty believing that the notion of introducing himself had not, at some point in the past fifteen hours, passed through his mind. Which was a thought to ponder.

Honoria wriggled, ruing the loss of her petticoat. The log was rough and wrinkly; it was making painful indentations in her flesh. She could see the stable entrance; from the shifting shadows, she surmised Devil was saddling his demon horse. Presumably he would ride to the Place and send conveyances for her and his cousin's body.

With the end of her unexpected adventure in sight, she allowed herself a moment's reflection. Somewhat to her surprise, it was filled with thoughts of Devil. He was overbearing, arrogant, domineering—the list went on. And on. But he was also strikingly handsome, could be charming when he wished and, she suspected, possessed a suitably devilish sense of humor. She'd seen enough of the duke to accord him her respect and enough of the man to feel an empathetic tug. Nevertheless, she had no desire to spend overmuch time in the company of a tyrant called Devil. Gentlemen such as he were all very well—as long as they weren't related to you and kept a respectful distance.

She'd reached that firm conclusion when he reappeared, leading Sulieman. The stallion was skittish, the man somber. Honoria stood as he neared.

Stopping in front of her, he halted Sulieman beside him; with the log immediately behind her, Honoria couldn't step back. Before she could execute a sideways sidle, Devil looped the reins about one fist—and reached for her.

By the time she realized his intention, she was perched precariously sidesaddle on Sulieman's back. She gasped, and locked her hands about the pommel. "What on *earth* . . . ?"

Unlooping the reins, Devil threw her an impatient frown. "I'm taking you home."

Honoria blinked—he had a way with words she wasn't sure she appreciated. "You're taking me to *your* home—the Place?"

"Somersham Place." The reins free, Devil reached for the

pommel. With Honoria riding before him, he wasn't intending to use the stirrups.

Honoria's eyes widened. "*Wait!*"

The look Devil cast her could only be achieved by an impatient man. "What?"

"You've forgotten your jacket—it's in the cottage." Honoria fought to contain her panic, occasioned by the thought of his chest—bare—pressed against her back. Even within a foot of her back. Within a foot of any of her.

"Vane'll bring it."

"*No!* Well—whoever heard of a duke riding about the countryside bare-chested? You might catch cold—I mean . . ." Aghast, Honoria realized she was looking into pale green eyes that saw far more than she'd thought.

Devil held her gaze steadily. "Get used to it," he advised. Then he vaulted into the saddle behind her.

Chapter 4

HE ONLY BENEFIT Honoria could discover in her position on Sulieman's back was that her tormentor, behind her, could not see her face. Unfortunately, he could see the blush staining not only her cheeks but her neck. He could also feel the rigidity that had gripped her—hardly surprising—the instant he'd landed in the saddle behind her, he'd wrapped a muscled arm about her and pulled her against him.

She'd shut her eyes the instant he'd touched her; panic had cut off her shriek. For the first time in her life she thought she might actually faint. The steely strength surrounding her was overwhelming; by the time she subdued her flaring reactions and could function rationally again, they were turning from the bridle path into the lane.

Glancing about, she looked down—and clutched at the arm about her waist. It tightened.

"Sit still—you won't fall."

Honoria's eyes widened. She could *feel* every word he said. She could also feel a pervasive heat emanating from his chest, his arms, his thighs; wherever they touched, her skin burned. "Ah . . ." They were retracing the journey she'd taken in the gig; the curve into the straight lay just ahead. "Is Somersham Place your principal residence?"

"It's home. My mother remains there most of the year."

There was no duke of Somersham. As they rounded the curve, Honoria decided she had had enough. Her hips, her bottom, were wedged firmly between his rock-hard thighs. They were exceedingly close, yet she didn't even know his name. "What *is* your title?"

"Titles." The stallion tried to veer to the side of the lane but was ruthlessly held on course. "Duke of St. Ives, Marquess of Earith, Earl of Strathfield, Viscount Wellsborough, Viscount Moreland, . . ."

The recital continued; Honoria leaned back against his arm so she could see his face. By the time names ceased to fall from his lips, they'd passed the place of yesterday's tragedy and rounded the next bend. He looked down; she narrowed her eyes at him. "Are you quite finished?"

"Actually, no. That's the litany they drummed into me when I was in shortcoats. There are more recent additions, but I've never learned where they fit."

He glanced down again—Honoria stared blankly back at him. She'd finally caught the elusive connection.

Cynsters hold St. Ives. That was a line of the rhyme her mother had taught her, listing the oldest families in the *ton*. And if Cynsters still held St. Ives, that meant . . . Abruptly, she focused on the chiseled features of the man holding her so easily before him. "You're *Devil Cynster?*"

His eyes met hers; when she continued to stare in dumbfounded accusation, one black brow arrogantly rose. "You want proof?"

Proof? What more proof could she need? One glance into those ageless, omniscient eyes, at that face displaying steely strength perfectly melded with rampant sensuality, was enough to settle all doubts. Abruptly, Honoria faced forward; her mind had reeled before—now it positively whirled.

Cynsters—the *ton* wouldn't be the same without them. They were a breed apart—wild, hedonistic, unpredictable. In company with her own forebears, they'd crossed the Channel with the Conqueror; while her ancestors sought power through politics and finance, the Cynsters pursued the same aim through more direct means. They were and always had been warriors supreme—strong, courageous, intelligent—men born to lead. Through the centuries, they'd thrown themselves into any likely-

43

looking fray with a reckless passion that made any sane opponent think twice. Consequently, every king since William had seen the wisdom of placating the powerful lords of St. Ives. Luckily, by some strange quirk of nature, Cynsters were as passionate about land as they were over battle.

Added to that, whether by fate or sheer luck, their heroism under arms was matched by an uncanny ability to survive. In the aftermath of Waterloo, when so many noble families were counting the cost, a saying had gone the rounds, born of grudging awe. The Cynsters, so it went, were invincible; seven had taken the field and all seven returned, hale and whole, with barely a scratch.

They were also invincibly arrogant, a characteristic fueled by the fact that they were, by and large, as talented as they thought themselves, a situation which engendered in less-favored mortals a certain reluctant respect.

Not that Cynsters demanded respect—they simply took it as their due.

If even half the tales told were true, the current generation were as wild, hedonistic, and unpredictable as any Cynsters ever were. And the current head of the clan was the wildest, most hedonistic, and unpredictable of them all. The present duke of St. Ives—he who had tossed her up to his saddle and declared he was taking her home. The same man who'd told her to get used to his bare chest. The piratical autocrat who had, without a blink, decreed she was to be his duchess.

It suddenly occurred to Honoria that she might be assuming too much. Matters might not be proceeding quite as she'd thought. Not that it mattered—she knew where life was taking her. Africa. She cleared her throat. "When next you meet them, the Claypole girls might prove trying—they are, I'm sorry to say, their mother's daughters."

She felt him shrug. "I'll leave you to deal with them."

"I won't be here." She made the statement firmly.

"We'll be here often enough—we'll spend some of the year in London and on my other estates, but the Place will always be home. But you needn't worry over me—I'm not fool enough to face the disappointed local aspirants without availing myself of your skirts."

"I beg your pardon?" Turning, Honoria stared at him.

He met her gaze briefly; his lips quirked. "To hide behind."

The temptation was too great—Honoria lifted an arrogant brow. "I thought Cynsters were invincible."

His smile flashed. "The trick is not to expose oneself unnecessarily to the enemy's fire."

Struck by the force of that fleeting smile, Honoria blinked—and abruptly faced forward. There was, after all, no reason she should face *him* unnecessarily either. Then she realized she'd been distracted. "I hate to destroy your defense, but I'll be gone in a few days."

"I hesitate to contradict you," came in a purring murmur just above her left ear, "but we're getting married. You are, therefore, not going anywhere."

Honoria gritted her teeth against the shivery tingles that coursed down her spine. Turning her head, she looked directly into his mesmerizing eyes. "You only said that to spike Lady Claypole's guns." When he didn't respond, just met her gaze levelly, she looked forward, shrugging haughtily. "You're no gentleman to tease me so."

The silence that followed was precisely gauged to stretch her nerves taut. She knew that when he spoke, his voice deep, low, velvet dark. "I never tease—at least not verbally. And I'm not a gentleman, I'm a nobleman, a distinction I suspect you understand very well."

Honoria knew what she was meant to understand—her insides were quaking in a thoroughly distracting way—but she was not about to surrender. "I am not marrying you."

"If you think that, my dear Miss Anstruther-Wetherby, I fear you've overlooked a number of pertinent points."

"Such as?"

"Such as the past night, which we spent under the same roof, in the same room, unchaperoned."

"Except by a dead man, your cousin, who everyone must know you were fond of. With his body laid out upon the bed, no one will imagine anything untoward occurred." Convinced she'd played a winning card, Honoria wasn't surprised by the silence which followed.

They emerged from the trees into the brightness of a late-summer morning. It was early; the crisp chill of the night had yet to fade. The track followed a water-filled ditch. Ahead, a line of gnarled trees lay across their path.

"I had intended to ask you not to mention how we found Tolly. Except, of course, to the family and the magistrate."

Honoria frowned. "What do you mean?"

"I'd rather it was thought that we found him this morning, already dead."

Honoria pursed her lips, and saw her defense evaporate. But she could hardly deny the request, particularly as it really mattered not at all. "Very well. But why?"

"The sensationalism will be bad enough when it becomes known he was killed by a highwayman. I'd rather spare my aunt, and you, as much of the consequent questioning as possible. If it's known he lived afterward and we found him before he died, you'll be subjected to an inquisition every time you appear in public."

She could hardly deny it—the *ton* thrived on speculation. "Why can't we say he was already dead when we found him yesterday?"

"Because if we do, it's rather difficult to explain why I didn't simply leave you with the body and ride home, relieving you of my dangerous presence."

"Given you appear impervious to the elements, why didn't you leave after he died?"

"It was too late by then."

Because the damage to her reputation had already been done? Honoria swallowed an impatient humph. Between the trees, she could see a stone wall, presumably enclosing the park. Beyond, she glimpsed a large house, the roof and the highest windows visible above tall hedges. "Anyway," she stated, "on one point Lady Claypole was entirely correct—there's no need for any great fuss."

"Oh?"

"It's a simple matter—as Lady Claypole will not give me a recommendation, perhaps your mother could do so?"

"I think that's unlikely."

"Why?" Honoria twisted around. "She'll know who I am just as you did."

Pale green eyes met hers. "That's why."

She wished narrowing her eyes at him had some effect—she

tried it anyway. "In the circumstances, I would have thought your mother would do all she can to help me."

"I'm sure she will—which is precisely why she won't lift a finger to help you to another position as governess."

Stifling a snort, Honoria turned forward. "She can't be that stuffy."

"I can't recall her ever being described as such."

"I rather think somewhere to the north might be wise—the Lake District perhaps?"

He sighed—Honoria felt it all the way to her toes. "My dear Miss Anstruther-Wetherby, let me clarify a few details. Firstly, the tale of us spending the night alone in my woodsman's cottage will out—nothing is more certain. Regardless of all injunctions delivered by her put-upon spouse, Lady Claypole will not be able to resist telling her dearest friends the latest scandal involving the duke of St. Ives. All in absolute confidence, of course, which will ensure the story circulates to every corner of the *ton*. After that, your reputation will be worth rather less than a farthing. Regardless of what they say to your face, not a single soul will believe in your innocence. Your chances of gaining a position in a household of sufficient standing to set your brother's mind at rest are currently nil."

Honoria scowled at the trees, drawing ever nearer. "I take leave to inform you, Your Grace, that I'm hardly a green girl. I'm a mature woman of reasonable experience—no easy mark."

"Unfortunately, my dear, you have your cause and effect confused. If you had, indeed, been a fresh-faced chit just out of the schoolroom, few would imagine I'd done anything other than sleep last night. As it is . . ." He paused, slowing Sulieman as they neared the trees. "It's well-known I prefer more challenging game."

Disgusted, Honoria humphed. "It's ridiculous—there wasn't even a bed."

The chest behind her quaked, then was still. "Trust me—there's no requirement for a bed."

Honoria pressed her lips shut and glared at the trees. The path wended through the stand; beyond stood the stone wall, two feet thick and eight feet high. An archway gave onto an avenue lined with poplars. Through the shifting leaves, she sighted the house, still some way to the left. It was huge—a long central block with perpendicular wings at each end, like an E without the middle stroke. Directly ahead lay a sprawling stable complex.

The proximity of the stables prompted her to speech. "I suggest, Your Grace, that we agree to disagree over the likely outcome of last night. I acknowledge your concern but see no reason to tie myself up in matrimony to avoid a few months' whispers. Given your reputation, you can hardly argue." That, she felt, was a nicely telling touch.

"My dear Miss Anstruther-Wetherby." His gentle, perfectly lethal purr sounded in her left ear; tingles streaked down her spine. "Let me make one point perfectly clear. I don't intend to argue. You, an Anstruther-Wetherby, have been compromised, however innocently, by me, a Cynster. There is, therefore, no question over the outcome; hence, there can be no argument."

Honoria gritted her teeth so tightly her jaw ached. The struggle to suppress the shudder that purring murmur of his evoked distracted her all the way to the stable arch. They rode beneath it, Sulieman's hooves clattering on the cobbles. Two grooms came running but pulled up short of where Devil reined in his black steed.

"Where's Melton?"

"Not yet about, Y'r Grace."

Honoria heard her rescuer—or was that captor?—curse beneath his breath. Entirely without warning, he dismounted—by bringing his leg over the pommel, taking her to the ground with him. She didn't have time to shriek.

Catching her breath, she realized her feet had yet to reach earth—he was holding her still, firmly caught against him; another shudder threatened. She drew breath to protest—on the instant, he gently set her down.

Lips compressed, Honoria haughtily brushed down her skirts. Straightening, she turned toward him—he caught her hand, grabbed the reins, and headed for the stable block, towing her and his black demon behind him.

Honoria swallowed her protest; she'd rather go with him than cool her heels in the stable yard, a prey to his grooms' curiosity. Gloom, filled with the familiar smells of hay and horses, engulfed her. "Why can't your grooms brush him down?"

"They're too frightened of him—only old Melton can handle him."

Honoria looked at Sulieman—the horse looked steadily back.

His master stopped before a large stall. Released, Honoria leaned against the stall door. Arms crossed, she pondered her predicament while watching her captor—she was increasingly certain that was a more accurate description of him—rub down his fearsome steed.

Muscles bunched and relaxed; the sight was positively mesmerizing. He'd told her to get used to it; she doubted she ever could. He bent, then fluidly straightened and shifted to the horse's other side; his chest came into view. Honoria drew in a slow breath—then he caught her eye.

For one instant, their gazes held—then Honoria looked away, first at the tack hanging along the stable wall, then up at the rafters, inwardly berating herself for her reaction, simultaneously wishing she had a fan to hand.

It was never wise to tangle with autocrats, but, given she had no choice, she needed to remember that it was positively fatal to acknowledge he had any power over her.

Determined to hold her own, she ordered her mind to business. If he believed honor demanded he marry her, she'd need to try a different tack. She frowned. "I do not see that it's fair that, purely because I was stranded by a storm and took shelter in the same cottage as you, I should have to redirect my life. I am not a passive spectator waiting for the next occurrence to happen—I have plans!"

Devil glanced up. "Riding in the shadow of the Great Sphinx?" He could just imagine her on a camel—along with a hovering horde of Berber chieftains who looked remarkably like him and thought like him, too.

"Precisely. And I plan to explore the Ivory Coast as well—another exciting place so I've heard."

Barbary pirates and slave traders. Devil tossed aside the currying brush and dusted his hands on his breeches. "You'll just have to make do with becoming a Cynster—no one's ever suggested it's a mundane existence."

"I am not going to marry you."

Her flashing eyes and the set of her chin declared her

Anstruther-Wetherby mind was made up; Devil knew he was going to seriously enjoy every minute it took to make her change it. He walked toward her.

Predictably, she backed not an inch, although he saw her muscles lock against the impulse. Without breaking stride, he closed his hands about her waist and lifted her, setting her down with her back against the stall wall. With commendable restraint, he removed his hands, locking one on the top of the half-closed door, bracing the other, palm flat, on the wall by her shoulder.

Caged, she glared at him; he tried not to notice how her breasts rose as she drew in a deep breath. He spoke before she could. "What have you got against the proposition?"

Honoria kept her eyes locked on his—standing as he was, her entire field of vision was filled with bare male. Once her heart had ceased to thud quite so loudly, she raised her brows haughtily. "I have no desire whatever to marry purely because of some antiquated social stricture."

"That's the sum of your objections?"

"Well, there's Africa, of course."

"Forget Africa. Is there any reason other than my motives in offering for you that in your opinion constitutes an impediment to our marriage?"

His arrogance, his high-handedness, his unrelenting authority—his chest. Honoria was tempted to start at the top of her list and work her way down. But not one of her caveats posed any serious impediment to their marriage. She searched his eyes for some clue as to her best answer, fascinated anew by their remarkable clarity. They were like crystal clear pools of pale green water, emotions, thoughts, flashing like quicksilver fish in their depths. "No."

"Good."

She glimpsed some emotion—was it relief?—flash through his eyes before his heavy lids hid them from view. Straightening, he caught her hand and headed for the stable door. Stifling a curse, she grabbed up her skirts and lengthened her stride. He made for the main archway; beyond lay his house, peaceful in the morning sunshine.

"You may set your mind at rest, Miss Anstruther-Wetherby." He glanced down, the planes of his face granite-hard. "I'm not marrying you because of any social stricture. That, if you consider it, is a nonsensical idea. Cynsters, as you well know, do not give a damn about social strictures. Society, as far as we're concerned, can think what it pleases—*it* does not rule *us*."

"But . . . if that's the case—and given your reputation I can readily believe it is—why insist on marrying me?"

"Because I want to."

The words were delivered as the most patently obvious answer to a simple question. Honoria held on to her temper. "Because you *want* to?"

He nodded.

"That's it? Just because you want to?"

The look he sent her was calculated to quell. "For a Cynster, that's a perfectly adequate reason. In fact, for a Cynster, there *is* no better reason."

He looked ahead again; Honoria glared at his profile. "*This* is ridiculous. You only set eyes on me yesterday, and now you want to marry me?"

Again he nodded.

"*Why?*"

The glance he shot her was too brief for her to read. "It so happens I need a wife, and you're the perfect candidate." With that, he altered their direction and lengthened his stride even more.

"I am *not* a racehorse."

His lips thinned, but he slowed—just enough so she didn't have to run. They'd gained the graveled walk that circled the house. It took her a moment to replay his words, another to see their weakness. "That's still ridiculous. You must have half the female population of the *ton* waiting to catch your handkerchief every time you blow your nose."

He didn't even glance her way. "At least half."

"So why *me*?"

Devil considered telling her—in graphic detail. Instead, he gritted his teeth and growled: "Because you're unique."

"*Unique?*"

Unique in that she was arguing. He halted, raised his eyes to the heavens in an appeal for sufficient strength to deal with an Anstruther-Wetherby, then looked down and trapped her gaze. "Let me put it this way—*you* are an attractive Anstruther-Wetherby female with whom I've spent an entire night in private—and I've yet to bed you." He smiled. "I assume you would prefer we married before I do?"

The stunned shock in her eyes was balm to his soul. The grey orbs, locked on his, widened—then widened even more. He knew what she was seeing—the sheer lust that blazed through him had to be lighting his eyes.

He fully expected her to dissolve into incoherent, ineffectual, disjointed gibberings—instead, she suddenly snapped free of his visual hold, blinked, drew a quick breath—and narrowed her eyes at him.

"I am *not* marrying you just so I can go to bed with you. I mean—" She caught herself up and breathlessly amended, "So that you can go to bed with me."

Devil watched the telltale color rise in her cheeks. Grimly, he nodded. "Fine." Tightening his grip on her hand, he turned and stalked on.

All the way from the cottage, she'd shifted and wriggled against him; by the time they'd reached the stable, he'd been agonizingly aroused. How he'd managed not to throw her down in the straw and ease his pain, he had no idea. But he now had a roaring headache, and if he didn't keep moving—keep her moving—temptation might yet get the upper hand. "*You*," he stated, as they rounded the corner of the house, "can marry me for a host of sensible, socially acceptable reasons. *I'll* marry you to get you into my bed."

He felt her dagger glance. "That is—*Good God!*"

Honoria stopped; stock-still, she stared. Somersham Place lay spread before her, basking in the morning sunshine. Immense, built of honey-colored stone at least a century before, it sprawled elegantly before her, a mature and gracious residence overlooking a wide lawn. She was dimly aware of the lake at the bottom of the lawn, of the oaks flanking the curving drive, of the stone wall over which a white rose cascaded, dew sparkling on the perfumed blooms. The clack of ducks drifted up from the lake; the air was fresh with the tang of clipped grass. But it was the house that held her. Durable, inviting, there was grandeur in every line, yet the sharp edges were muted, softened by the years. Sunbeams glinted on row upon row of lead-paned windows; huge double oak doors were framed by a portico of classic design. Like a lovely woman mellowed by experience, his home beckoned, enticed.

He was proposing to make her mistress of all this.

The thought flitted through her mind; even though she knew he was watching, she allowed herself a moment to imagine, to dwell on what might be. For this had she been born, reared, trained. What should have been her destiny lay before her. But becoming his duchess would mean risking . . .

No! She'd promised herself—never again.

Mentally shutting her eyes to the house, the temptation, she drew a steadying breath, and saw the crest blazoned in stone on the portico's facade, a shield sporting a stag rampant on a ground of fleur-de-lis. Beneath the shield ran a wide stone ribbon bearing a carved inscription. The words were Latin—it took her a moment to translate. "To have . . . and to hold?"

Hard fingers closed about hers. "The Cynster family motto."

Honoria raised her eyes heavenward. An irresistible force, he drew her toward the steps. "Where are you taking me?" A vision of silk cushions and gauze curtains—a pirate's private lair—flashed into her mind.

"To my mother. Incidentally, she prefers to be addressed as the Dowager."

Honoria frowned. "But you're not married."

"Yet. It's her subtle way of reminding me of my duty."

Subtle. Honoria wondered what the Dowager—his mother, after all—would do if she wished to make a point forcefully. Whatever, it was time and past to make a stand. It would be unwise to cross his threshold—beyond which, she had not the slightest doubt, he ruled like a king—without coming to some agreement as to their future relationship, or lack thereof.

They reached the porch; he halted before the doors and released her. Facing him, Honoria straightened. "Your Grace, we must—"

The doors swung inward, held majestically wide by a butler, one of the more imposing of the species. Cheated of her moment, Honoria only just managed not to glare.

The butler's eyes had gone to his master; his smile was genuinely fond. "Good morning, Your Grace."

His master nodded. "Webster."

Honoria stood her ground. She was not going to cross his threshold until he acknowledged her right to ignore—as he did whenever it suited him—society's dictates.

He shifted to stand beside her, gesturing for her to precede him. Simultaneously, Honoria felt his hand at the back of her waist. Without her petticoat, only a single layer of fabric separated her skin from his hard palm. He didn't exert any great pressure; instead, seductively questing, his hand traveled slowly, very slowly, down. When it reached the curve of her bottom, Honoria sucked in a quick breath—and stepped quickly over the threshold.

He followed. "This is Miss Anstruther-Wetherby, Webster." He looked her way; Honoria glimpsed triumph in his eyes. "She'll be staying—her boxes should arrive this morning."

Webster bowed low. "I'll have your things taken to your room, miss."

Stiffly, Honoria inclined her head—her heart was still fluttering in her throat; her skin felt hot and cold in the strangest places. She couldn't fault the butler's demeanor; he seemed unsurprised by his master's lack of attire. Was she the only one who found his bare chest at all remarkable? Stifling an urge to sniff disbelievingly, she elevated her nose another inch and looked about the hall.

The impression created by the exterior extended within doors. A sense of graciousness pervaded the high-ceilinged hall, lit by sunlight pouring through the fanlight and the windows flanking the front doors. The walls were papered—blue fleur-de-lis on an ivory ground; the paneling, all light oak, glowed softly. Together with the blue-and-white tiles, the decor imparted an airy, uncluttered atmosphere. Stairs of polished oak, their baluster ornately carved, led upward in a long, straight sweep, then divided into two, both arms leading to the gallery above.

Webster had been informing his master of the presence of his cousins. Devil nodded curtly. "Where's the Dowager?"

"In the morning room, Your Grace."

"I'll take Miss Anstruther-Wetherby to her. Wait for me."

Webster bowed.

The devil glanced down at her. With a languid grace that set her nerves on end, he gestured for her to accompany him.

She was still quivering inside—she told herself it was due to indignation. Head high, she swept down the hall.

His instruction to his butler to wait had recalled what their sparring had driven from her mind. As they neared the morning-room door, it occurred to Honoria that she might have been arguing for no real reason. Devil reached for the doorknob, his fingers closing about hers—she tugged. He looked up, incipient impatience in his eyes.

She smiled understandingly. "I'm sorry—I'd forgotten. You must be quite distracted by your cousin's death." She spoke softly, soothingly. "We can discuss all this later, but there's really no reason for us to wed. I daresay, once the trauma has passed, you'll see things as I do."

He held her gaze, his eyes as blank as his expression. Then his features hardened. "Don't count on it." With that, he set the door wide and handed her through. He followed, closing the door behind him.

A petite woman, black hair streaked with grey, was seated in a chair before the hearth, a hoop filled with embroidery on her lap. She looked up, then smiled—the most gloriously welcoming smile Honoria had ever seen—and held out her hand. "There you are, Sylvester. I'd wondered where you'd got to. And who is this?"

His mother's French background rang clearly in her accent; it also showed in her coloring, in the hair that had once been as black as her son's combined with an alabaster complexion, in the quick, graceful movements of her hands, her animated features and the candid, appraising glance that swept Honoria.

Inwardly ruing her hideously creased skirts, Honoria kept her head high as she was towed across the room. The Dowager hadn't so much as blinked at her son's bare chest.

"*Maman.*" To her surprise, her devilish captor bent and kissed his mother's cheek. She accepted the tribute as her due; as he straightened, she fixed him with a questioning glance every bit as imperious as he was arrogant. He met it blandly. "You told me to bring you your successor the instant I found her. Allow me to present Miss Honoria Prudence Anstruther-Wetherby." Briefly, he glanced at Honoria. "The Dowager Duchess of St. Ives." Turning back to his mother, he added:

55

"Miss Anstruther-Wetherby was residing with the Claypoles—
her boxes will arrive shortly. I'll leave you to get acquainted."

With the briefest of nods, he proceeded to do just that, closing the door firmly behind him. Stunned, Honoria glanced at the
Dowager, and was pleased to see she wasn't the only one left
staring.

Then the Dowager looked up and smiled—warmly, welcomingly, much as she had smiled at her son. Honoria felt the glow
touch her heart. The Dowager's expression was understanding,
encouraging. "Come, my dear. Sit down." The Dowager waved
to the *chaise* beside her chair. "If you have been dealing with
Sylvester, you will need the rest. He is often very trying."

Resisting the temptation to agree emphatically, Honoria
sank onto the chintz.

"You must excuse my son. He is somewhat . . ." The Dowager paused, clearly searching for the right word. She grimaced.
"*Detressé.*"

"I believe he has a number of matters on his mind."

The Dowager's fine brows rose. "His mind?" Then she
smiled, eyes twinkling as they rested once more on Honoria's
face. "But now, my dear, as my so-*detressé* son has decreed, we
will get acquainted. And as you are to be my daughter-in-law, I
will call you Honoria." Again, her brows rose. "Is that not
right?"

Her name became " 'Onoria"—the Dowager couldn't manage the "H." Honoria returned her smile, and sidestepped the
leading question. "If you wish it, ma'am."

The Dowager's smile grew radiant. "My dear, I wish it with
all my heart."

Chapter 5

*A*FTER AN HOUR of subtle interrogation, Honoria escaped the Dowager, pleased that, while she'd parted with her life history, she'd successfully avoided all mention of Tolly's death. Shown to an elegant suite, she washed and changed; her self-confidence renewed, she descended—into mayhem.

The magistrate had arrived; while Devil dealt with him, Vane had broken the news to the Dowager. When Honoria entered the drawing room, the Dowager was in full histrionic spate. While grief was certainly present, it had been overtaken by indignant fury.

Instantly, the Dowager appealed to her for details. "You need not apologize for not telling me before. I know just how it was—that oh-so-male son of mine sought to keep the matter from me, Cynster that he is."

Waved to a chair, Honoria dutifully complied. She'd barely finished her tale when the scrunch of wheels on gravel heralded Devil's reappearance.

"What's the verdict?" Vane asked.

Devil met his gaze levelly. "Death through shooting by some person unknown. Possibly a highwayman."

"A highwayman?" Honoria stared at him.

Devil shrugged. "Either that or a poacher." He turned to the Dowager. "I've sent for Arthur and Louise."

Lord Arthur Cynster and his wife Louise proved to be Tolly's parents.

There followed a detailed discussion of who to notify, the appropriate arrangements, and how to accommodate the expected crowd, which encompassed a goodly proportion of the *ton*. While Devil undertook the first two aspects, organizing rooms and sustenance fell to the Dowager.

Despite her firm intention to remain aloof from Devil's family, Honoria simply could not stand by and allow such a weight to descend on the Dowager's fragile shoulders. Especially not when she was more than well qualified to lighten the load. As, however reluctantly, an Anstruther-Wetherby who had been present when Tolly had died, she would be expected to attend the funeral; she would need to remain at the Place at least until after that. That being so, there was no reason not to offer her aid. Besides which, to sit idly in her room while about her the household ran frantic, would be entirely beyond her.

Within minutes, she was immersed in lists—initial lists, then derived lists and eventually lists for cross-checking. The afternoon and evening passed in intense activity; Webster and the housekeeper, a matronly woman known as Mrs. Hull, coordinated the execution of the Dowager's directives. An army of maids and footmen labored to open up rooms. Helpers from the nearby farms tramped in to assist in the kitchens and stables. Yet all the bustle was subdued, somber; not a laugh was heard nor a smile seen.

Night fell, restless, disturbed; Honoria awoke to a dull day. A funereal pall had settled over the Place—it deepened with the arrival of the first carriage.

The Dowager met it, taking her grieving sister-in-law under her wing. Honoria slipped away, intending to seek refuge in the summerhouse by the side of the front lawn. She was halfway across the lawn when she caught sight of Devil, heading her way through the trees. He had gone with the chaplain, Mr. Merryweather, and a party of men to mark out the grave. Devil had seen her; Honoria halted.

He came striding out of the shade, long legs encased in buckskin breeches and shiny top boots. His fine white shirt with billowing sleeves, opened at the throat, was topped by a leather waistcoat. Despite his less-than-conventional attire, with his dramatic coloring, he still looked impressive—and every inch a pirate.

His gaze traveled swiftly over her, taking in her gown of soft lavender-grey, a color suitable for half-mourning. His expression was set, impassive, yet she sensed his approval.

"Your aunt and uncle have arrived." She made the statement while he was still some yards away.

One black brow quirked; Devil didn't pause. "Good morning, Honoria Prudence." Smoothly collecting her hand, he placed it on his arm and deftly turned her back toward the house. "I trust you slept well?"

"Perfectly, thank you." With no choice offering, Honoria strolled briskly beside him. She suppressed an urge to glare. "I haven't made you free of my name."

Devil looked toward the drive. "An oversight on your part, but I'm not one to stand on ceremony. I take it *Maman* has my aunt in hand?"

Her eyes on his, Honoria nodded.

"In that case," Devil said, looking ahead, "I'll need your help." Another crepe-draped carriage came into view, rolling slowly toward the steps. "That will be Tolly's younger brother and sisters."

He glanced at Honoria; she exhaled and inclined her head. Lengthening their strides, they reached the drive as the carriage rocked to a halt.

The door burst open; a boy jumped down. Eyes wide, he looked dazedly toward the house. Then he heard their footsteps and swung their way. Slender, quivering with tension, he faced them, his face leached of all color, his lips pinched. Recognition flared in his tortured eyes. Honoria saw him tense to fly to Devil, but he conquered the impulse and straightened, swallowing manfully.

Devil strode to the boy, dropping a hand on his shoulder and squeezing reassuringly. "Good lad."

He looked into the carriage, then beckoned to the occupants. "Come."

He lifted first one silently sobbing girl, then another, down. Both possessed a wealth of chestnut ringlets and delicate complexions, presently blotchy. Four huge blue eyes swam in pools of tears; their slender figures shook with their sobs. They were,

Honoria judged, about sixteen—and twins. Without any show of consciousness or fear, they clung to Devil, arms locking about his waist.

One arm about each, Devil turned them to face her. "This is Honoria Prudence—Miss Anstruther-Wetherby to you. She'll look after you both." He met Honoria's gaze. "She knows how it feels to lose someone you love."

Both girls and the boy were too distressed to render the prescribed greeting. Honoria didn't wait for it but smoothly took her cue. Devil deftly detached himself from the girls' clinging arms; gliding forward, she took his place. Slipping a comforting arm around each girl, she turned them toward the house. "Come—I'll show you to your room. Your parents are already inside."

They allowed her to shepherd them up the steps. Honoria was aware of their curious glances.

On the porch, both girls paused, gulping back their tears. Honoria cast a swift glance behind and saw Devil, his back to them, one arm draped across the boy's slight shoulders, head bent as he spoke to the lad. Turning back, she gathered her now shivering charges and urged them on.

Both balked.

"Will we have to . . . I mean—" One glanced up at her.

"Will we have to look at him?" the other forced out. "Is his face badly damaged?"

Honoria's heart lurched; sympathy—long-buried empathy—welled. "You won't have to see him if you don't want to." She spoke softly, reassuringly. "But he looks wonderfully peaceful—just like I imagine he always did. Handsome and quietly happy."

Both girls stared at her, hope in their eyes.

"I was there when he died," Honoria felt compelled to add.

"You were?" There was surprise and a touch of youthful skepticism in their tones.

"Your cousin was there as well."

"Oh." They glanced back at Devil, then both nodded.

"And now we'd better get you settled." Honoria glanced back; a maid had hopped down from the carriage; footmen had materialized and were unstrapping boxes from the boot and the roof. "You'll want to wash your faces and change before the rest of the family arrives."

With sniffs and watery smiles for Webster, encountered in the hall, they allowed her to usher them upstairs.

The chamber allotted to the girls was near the end of one wing; promising to fetch them later, Honoria left them in their maid's care and returned downstairs.

Just in time to greet the next arrivals.

The rest of the day flew. Carriages rolled up in a steady stream, disgorging matrons and stiff-necked gentlemen and a goodly sprinkling of bucks. Devil and Vane were everywhere, greeting guests, fielding questions. Charles was there, too, his expression wooden, his manner stilted.

Stationed by the stairs, Honoria helped the Dowager greet and dispose of family and those friends close enough to claim room within the great house. Anchored to her hostess's side, the keeper of the lists, she found herself introduced by the Dowager, with a gently vague air.

"And this is Miss Anstruther-Wetherby, who is keeping me company."

The Cynster cousin to whom this was addressed, presently exchanging nods with Honoria, immediately looked intrigued. Speculation gleamed in the matronly woman's eyes. "Indeed?" She smiled, graciously coy. "I'm very pleased to make your acquaintance, my dear."

Honoria replied with a polite, noncommittal murmur. She'd failed to foresee her present predicament when she'd offered her aid; now she could hardly desert her post. Fixing a smile on her lips, she resolved to ignore her hostess's blatant manipulation. The Dowager, she'd already realized, was even more stubborn than her son.

The family viewing of the body was held late that afternoon; remembering her promise, Honoria went to fetch Tolly's sisters from the distant wing.

They were waiting, pale but composed, intensely vulnerable in black muslin. Honoria ran an experienced eye over them, then nodded. "You'll do." They came forward hesitantly, clearly dreading what was to come. Honoria smiled encouragingly. "Your cousin omitted to mention your names."

"I'm Amelia, Miss Anstruther-Wetherby." The closest bobbed a curtsy.

Her sister did the same, equally gracefully. "I'm Amanda."

Honoria raised her brows. "I presume calling 'Amy' will bring you both?"

The simple sally drew two faint smiles. "Usually," Amelia admitted.

Amanda had already sobered. "Is it true—what Devil said? About you knowing about losing one you love?"

Honoria met her ingenuous gaze levelly. "Yes—I lost both my parents in a carriage accident when I was sixteen."

"Both?" Amelia looked shocked. "That must have been terrible—even worse than losing a brother."

Honoria stilled, then, somewhat stiffly, inclined her head. "Losing any family member is hard—but when they leave us, we still have to go on. We owe it to them—to their memory— as much as to ourselves."

The philosophical comment left both girls puzzling. Honoria seized the moment to get them headed downstairs, to the private chapel off the gallery.

Halting in the doorway, the twins nervously surveyed the black-clad ranks of their aunts and uncles and older male cousins, all silent, most with heads bowed.

Both girls reacted as Honoria had hoped: their spines stiffened—they drew deep breaths, straightened their shoulders, then paced slowly down the quiet room. Hand in hand, they approached the coffin, set on trestles before the altar.

From the shadows by the door, Honoria watched what was, in essence, a scene from her past. The somber peace of the chapel held her; she was about to slip into the back pew when Devil caught her eye. Commandingly formal in black coat and black trousers, white shirt and black cravat, he looked precisely what he was—a devilishly handsome rake—and the head of his family. From his position beyond the coffin, he raised one brow, his expression a subtle melding of invitation and challenge.

Tolly was no relative of hers, but she'd been present when he died. Honoria hesitated, then followed Tolly's sisters down the aisle.

Clinging to each other, the twins moved on, slipping into the pew behind their weeping mother. Honoria paused, looking down on an innocence not even death could erase. As she had said, Tolly's face was peaceful, serene; no hint of the wound in his chest showed. Only the grey pallor of his skin bore witness that he would not again awake.

She'd seen death before, but not like this. Those before had been taken by God; they had only needed to be mourned. Tolly had been taken by man—a vastly different response was required. She frowned.

"What is it?" Devil's voice came from beside her, pitched very low.

Honoria looked up. Frowning, she searched his eyes. He *knew*—how could he not? Why, then . . . ? A chill touched her soul—she shivered and looked away.

"Come." Devil took her arm; Honoria let him hand her to a pew. He sat beside her; she felt his gaze on her face but did not look his way.

Then Tolly's mother rose. Supported by her husband, she placed a white rose in the coffin; the viewing was at an end. No one spoke as they slowly filed out, following the Dowager and Tolly's parents to the drawing room.

In the front hall, Devil drew Honoria aside, into the shadows of the stairs. As the last stragglers passed, he said, his voice low: "I'm sorry—I shouldn't have insisted. I didn't realize it would remind you of your parents."

Honoria looked up, directly into his eyes. They were not, she realized, particularly useful for *hiding* emotions—the clear depths were too transparent. Right now, they looked contrite.

"It wasn't that. I was simply struck—" She paused, again searching his eyes. "By how *wrong* his death was." Impulsively, she asked: "Are you satisfied with the magistrate's verdict?"

His face hardened into a warrior's mask. His lids lowered, screening those too-revealing eyes, his lashes a distracting veil. "Perfectly." Languidly, he gestured toward the drawing room. "I suggest we join the others."

His abrupt dismissal was not quite a slap in the face, but it certainly gave Honoria pause. Cloaked in her customary poise, she allowed him to lead her into the drawing room, then inwardly cursed when so many eyes swung their way. Their entrance together, separate from the earlier crowd, supported the image Devil and the Dowager were intent on projecting—the image of her as Devil's bride. Such subtle nuances were life and breath to the *ton*, Honoria knew it—she was usually adept at using such signals to her own advantage, but, in the present case, she was clearly fencing with a master.

Make that two masters, simultaneously—the Dowager was no newcomer to the game.

The drawing room was full, crowded with family, connections and close acquaintances. Despite the subdued tones, the noise was substantial. The Dowager was seated on the *chaise* beside Tolly's mother. Devil steered Honoria to where Amelia and Amanda were nervously conversing with a very old lady.

"If you need help with names or connections, ask the twins. It'll make them feel useful."

Honoria inclined her head and coolly returned: "Much as I'd like to distract them, there's really no need. It is, after all, unlikely I'll meet any of your family again." Regally aloof, she raised her head—and met the dark, frowning glance Devil sent her with implacable calm.

Amanda and Amelia turned as they came up, an identical look of pleading in their eyes.

"Ah—Sylvester." The old lady put out a crabbed hand and gripped Devil's sleeve. "A shame it has to be such a sad occasion on which I see you again."

"Indeed, Cousin Clara." Fluidly, Devil drew Honoria into their circle, trapping her hand on his sleeve the instant before she removed it. "I believe," he drawled, "that you've already met . . ." An untrustworthy gleam lit his eyes; inwardly aghast, her gaze locked with his, Honoria held her breath—and saw his lips curve as he looked down at Cousin Clara. "Miss Anstruther-Wetherby?"

Honoria almost sighed with relief. Her serene smile somewhat strained, she trained it on Clara.

"Oh, yes! Dear me, yes." The old lady visibly brightened. "Such a *great* pleasure to meet you, dear. I've been looking forward to—" Catching herself up, Clara glanced impishly at Devil, then smiled sweetly at Honoria. "Well—you know." Reaching out, she patted Honoria's hand. "Suffice to say we're all *perfectly delighted*, my dear."

Honoria knew one person who was less than perfectly delighted, but, with Amanda and Amelia looking on, she was forced to allow Clara's transparent supposition to pass with nothing more than a gracious smile. Looking up, she fleetingly met Devil's gaze—she could have sworn she detected a satisfied gleam in his eyes.

He immediately broke the contact. Releasing her, he covered Clara's hand with his, stooping so she did not have to look up so far. "Have you spoken to Arthur?"

"Not yet." Clara glanced about. "I couldn't find him in this crush."

"He's by the window. Come—I'll take you to him."

Clara beamed. "So kind—but you always were a good boy." With brief nods to the twins, and a gracious one for Honoria, the old lady allowed Devil to lead her away.

Honoria watched them go, Devil so large and powerful, so arrogantly commanding, making not the smallest fuss over the creases Clara's sparrowlike claws were leaving in his sleeve. A good boy? She inwardly humphed.

"Thank goodness you came." Amanda swallowed. "She wanted to talk about Tolly. And I—we—didn't know how to . . ."

"Stop her?" Honoria smiled reassuringly. "Don't worry—it's only the very old who'll ask such questions. Now—" She glanced around—"tell me who the younger ones are—Devil told me their names, but I've forgotten."

That was untrue, but the exercise served to distract the twins. Aside from themselves, Simon, and their two younger sisters, Henrietta and Mary, ten and three, they had three younger cousins.

"Heather's fourteen. Elizabeth—we call her Eliza—is thirteen, and Angelica's ten, the same as Henrietta."

"They're Uncle Martin's and Aunt Celia's daughters. Gabriel and Lucifer are their older brothers."

Gabriel and Lucifer? Honoria opened her mouth to request clarification—simultaneously, the Dowager caught her eye.

The Dowager's expression was an outright appeal for help. Her sister-in-law's hands still gripped hers tightly. With her eyes, the Dowager signaled to Webster, standing unobtrusively before the door. The tension in his stately figure conveyed very clearly that something was amiss.

Honoria looked back at the Dowager—she understood what was being asked of her, and that a positive response would be interpreted as confirmation of another understanding—a matrimonial understanding between Devil and herself. But the appeal in the Dowager's eyes was very real, and of all the ladies present, she was unquestionably in the best state to deal with whatever disaster had befallen.

Torn, Honoria hesitated, then inwardly grimaced and nodded. She stepped toward the door, then remembered the twins. She glanced over her shoulder. "Come with me."

She swept regally across the room. Webster opened the door and stood back; Honoria sailed through. After waiting for her two escorts to pass, Webster followed, closing the door behind him.

In the hall, Honoria found Mrs. Hull waiting. "What's happened?"

Mrs. Hull's gaze flicked to Webster's face, then returned to Honoria's. The significance of that glance was not lost on Honoria; Webster had confirmed that she'd been deputed by the Dowager.

"It's the cakes, miss. What with all we've had to do, we sent out for them to the village. Mrs. Hobbs is excellent with cakes. We've often used her in such circumstances."

"But this time she hasn't lived up to expectations?"

Mrs. Hull's face tightened. "It's not that, miss. I sent two grooms with the gig, like I always do. Hobbs had the cakes ready—the boys loaded them in their trays. They were most of the way back"—Mrs. Hull paused to draw in a portentous breath—"when that *demon* horse of the master's came racing up, rearing and screaming, and spooked the old mare in the gig. The cakes went flying"—Mrs. Hull's eyes narrowed to flinty shards—"and that *devil* horse ate most of them!"

Pressing her fingers to her lips, Honoria looked down. Then she glanced at Webster. His face was expressionless.

"His Grace did not have time to ride the horse today, miss, so the head stableman turned him out for a run. The track from the village runs through the stable paddock."

"I see." Honoria's jaw ached. Despite all—the solemnity of the occasion and the impending crisis—the vision of Sulieman chomping on delicate petit fours was simply too much.

"So, you see, miss, I don't know what we're to do, with all these visitors and not even enough biscuits to go around." Mrs. Hull's expression remained severe.

"Indeed." Honoria straightened, considering possibilities. "Scones," she decided.

"Scones, miss?" Mrs. Hull looked surprised, then her expression turned calculating.

Honoria glanced at the clock on the wall. "It's just four—they won't be expecting tea for at least half an hour. If we arrange some distraction . . ." She looked at Webster. "What time were you intending to serve dinner?"

"Seven, miss."

Honoria nodded. "Put dinner back to eight—notify the valets and ladies' maids. Mrs. Hull, you've an hour to produce scones in quantity. Take whatever helpers you need. We'll have plain scones with jam—do you have any blackberry jam? That would be a nice touch."

"Indeed, miss." Mrs. Hull was transformed. "We have our own blackberry jam—there's no other like it."

"Very good—we'll have cream for those that wish it, and we'll have cheese scones and spiced scones as well."

"I'll get onto it immediately, miss." With a quick bob, Mrs. Hull sped back to her kitchen.

"You spoke of a distraction, miss—to gain half an hour for Mrs. Hull?"

Honoria met Webster's eye. "Not an easy task, given the cause of this gathering."

"Indeed not, miss."

"Can we help?"

Both Honoria and Webster turned to view the twins.

Amanda colored. "With the distraction, I mean."

Slowly, Honoria's brows rose. "I wonder . . . ?" She looked along the hall. "Come with me."

With Webster following, they entered the music room, next to the drawing room. Honoria waved at the instruments ranged along one wall. "What do you play?"

Amelia blinked. "I play the pianoforte."

"And I play the harp," Amanda supplied.

Excellent examples of both instruments stood before them; Webster hurried to maneuver the required pieces into place. Honoria turned to the girls. "You play together?" They nodded. "Good. What pieces can you play? Think of slow, mournful pieces—requiems or sections thereof."

To her relief, the twins were true to their class, well taught and with decent repertoires. Five minutes later, she'd also discovered they possessed considerable skill.

"Excellent." Honoria exchanged a relieved glance with Webster. "Don't let anyone distract you—we need you to play for at least forty minutes. Start at the beginning of your list and start repeating once you've finished. You can stop when the tea trolley arrives."

The girls nodded, and commenced a liturgical excerpt.

"Shall I open the doors, miss?" Webster whispered.

"Yes—the ones to the terrace as well." Both the music room and the drawing room gave onto the long terrace. Webster set the two doors flanking the fireplace wide, joining the two rooms. Heads turned as the haunting chords flowed over the conversations.

Gradually, tempted by the music, both ladies and gentlemen strolled in. The twins, used to performing before their elders, did not falter. There were chairs aplenty; gentlemen obligingly set them out, the ladies subsiding in groups, the gentlemen standing beside them.

From her position by the open terrace door, Honoria watched her distraction take hold. Suddenly, she felt a familiar presence behind her.

"*This* was inspired."

Glancing back, she met Devil's green eyes; they scanned her face.

"What was wrong?"

Honoria wondered if there was anyone in the entire assembly who had missed her assumption of the Dowager's authority. She'd been prepared to swear Devil had been deep in conversation at the far side of the room at the time. "Your devil-horse ate the tea cakes. Mrs. Hull is not impressed. I believe she has visions of turning your steed into cat's meat."

He was close, his shoulder propped against the doorframe behind her; she felt his chest quake with suppressed laughter. "Hully wouldn't do that."

"Just mention your horse and watch her reach for her cleaver."

He was silent, looking out over the room. "Don't tell me you don't play?"

Honoria caught herself just in time—and reframed her answer. "I play the harpsichord, but I'm not Tolly's sister. Incidentally," she continued, in the same mild tone, "I give you fair warning that regardless of whatever imbroglio you and your mother concoct, I will *not* be marrying you."

She felt his gaze on her face; when he spoke, the words feathered her spine. "Would you care to wager on that?"

Honoria lifted her chin. "With a reprobate like you?" She waved dismissively. "You're a gamester."

"One who rarely loses."

The deep words reverberated through her; Honoria abandoned speech and opted for a haughty shrug.

Devil didn't move. His gaze swept her face, but he said nothing more.

To Honoria's relief, her strategem worked. The tea, when it arrived, was perfect, the scones fresh from the oven, the jam sweet. The twins retired to subdued but sincere applause; one glance at their faces showed just how much their contribution had meant to them.

"We'll get them to play again tomorrow," Devil murmured in her ear.

"Tomorrow?" Honoria fought to quell an unhelpful shiver.

"At the wake." Devil met her eyes. "They'll feel better to be doing something useful again."

He left her musing—and returned with a cup of tea for her. She took it, only then realizing how much in need of refreshment she was. Other than understanding her too well, Devil behaved himself, smoothly introducing her to family friends. Honoria didn't need to exercise her imagination over how the company viewed her—their deference was marked. The events of the afternoon, orchestrated by Devil and the Dowager, aided and abetted by Devil's demon horse, had conveyed a clear message—that she was to be Devil's bride.

The evening passed swiftly; dinner, attended by everyone, was a somber meal. No one was inclined to entertainment; most retired early. A brooding, melancholy silence descended over the house, as if it mourned, too.

In her chamber, cocooned in down, Honoria thumped her pillow and ordered herself to fall asleep. Five minutes of restless rustling later, she turned onto her back, and glared at the canopy.

It was all Devil's fault, his and his mother's. She'd *tried* to avoid acting as his duchess-to-be, unfortunately unsuccessfully. Worse, as Devil had stated, on a superficial level, she was perfect for the position, a fact apparently obvious to any who considered the matter. She was starting to feel like she was fighting fate.

Honoria shuffled onto her side. She, Honoria Prudence *Anstruther*-Wetherby, was not going to be pressured into anything. It was patently obvious both Devil and the Dowager would do everything possible to tempt her, to convince her to accept his proposal—the proposal he hadn't made. That last was not a fact she was likely to forget—he'd simply taken it for granted that she would marry him.

She'd known from the first he was impossible, even when she'd thought him a mere country squire; as a duke, he was doubly—triply—so. Aside from anything else—his chest, for example—he was a first-class tyrant. Sane women did not marry tyrants.

She clung to that eminently sound declaration, drawing strength from its unarguable logic. Keeping Devil's image in mind helped enormously—one glance at his face, at the rest of him, was all it took to reinforce her conclusion.

Unfortunately, that image, while helpful on the one hand, brought the source of her deeper unease into stronger focus. No matter how she tried, she couldn't escape the conclusion that for all his vaunted strength of character, for all his apparent family feeling, even despite his Cousin Clara's belief, Devil was turning his back on his dead cousin. Sweeping his death under the proverbial rug, presumably so it wouldn't interfere with his hedonistic pursuit of pleasure.

She didn't want to believe it, but she'd heard him herself. He'd stated that Tolly had been killed by a highwayman or a poacher. Everyone believed him, the magistrate included. He was the head of the family, one step removed from a despot; to them and the *ton*, what Devil Cynster, duke of St. Ives, stated, was.

The only one inclined to question him was herself. Tolly hadn't been shot by a highwayman, nor a poacher.

Why would a highwayman kill an unarmed young man? Highwaymen ordered their victims to stand and deliver; Tolly had carried a heavy purse—she'd felt it in his pocket. Had Tolly been armed and, with the impetuosity of youth, attempted to defend himself? She'd seen no gun; it seemed unlikely he could have flung it far from him while falling from the saddle. A highwayman did not seem at all likely.

As for a poacher, her devilish host had narrowed the field there. Not a shotgun, he had said, but a pistol. Poachers did not use pistols.

Tolly had been murdered.

She wasn't sure when she had reached that conclusion; it was now as inescapable as the dawn.

Honoria sat up and thumped her pillow, then fell back and stared into the night. Why was she so incensed by it—why did she feel so involved? She felt as if a responsibility had been laid upon her—upon her soul—to see justice done.

But that wasn't the cause of her sleeplessness.

She'd heard Tolly's voice in the cottage, heard the relief he'd felt when he'd realized he'd reached Devil. He'd thought he'd reached safety—someone who would protect him. In the cottage, she would have sworn Devil cared—cared deeply. But his behavior in ignoring the evidence of Tolly's murder said otherwise.

If he truly cared, wouldn't he be searching for the murderer, doing all he could to catch him? Or was his "caring" merely an attitude, only skin-deep? Beneath that facade of strength, was he truly weak and shallow?

She couldn't believe it. She didn't want to believe it.

Honoria closed her eyes. And tried to sleep.

Chapter 6

❧❖❧

I T WAS AN illusion—all an illusion—a typically arrogant sleight of hand. The scales fell from Honoria's eyes late the next morning, right in the middle of Tolly's funeral.

The crowd attending was considerable. A short service had been held in the church in the grounds, a stone building ringed by ancient trees shading monuments to Cynsters long gone.

Then the pallbearers—Devil and his cousins—had carried the coffin to the grave, set in a small clearing beyond the first circle of trees. Contrary to her intention to merge with the crowd, Honoria had been partnered first by Vane, who had given her his arm, thus including her in the family procession to the church, then later claimed by Amanda and Amelia, who had steered her to the grave, admitting they were acting on Devil's orders. A funeral was no place to make a stand. Resigned, Honoria had capitulated, accepting a position behind the twins at the graveside.

It was then the truth struck her.

The males of the family lined the other side of the grave. Directly opposite stood Tolly's brothers, Charles, with Simon beside him. Devil stood next to Simon; as Honoria watched, he placed a hand on Simon's shoulder. The boy looked up; Honoria witnessed their shared glance, that silent communication at which Devil excelled.

Vane stood next to Devil; behind and around them stood a solid phalanx of male Cynsters. There was no doubt of their connection—their faces, seen all together, held the same unyielding planes, their features the same autocratic cast. They numbered six, not counting Simon and Charles, both set apart, one by age, the other by character. Between the six, hair color varied, from Devil's black to light chestnut; eye color, too, differed. Nothing else did.

There was enormous strength in the group facing her—powerful, masculine, it emanated from them. Devil was their leader yet they were a group of individuals, each contributing to the whole. Elsewhere about the grave, grief was amorphous. The grief of Tolly's male cousins held purpose, melding into a cohesive force, directed, focused.

Focused on Tolly's grave.

Honoria narrowed her eyes. People were still shifting, finding places in the crowd; both Amelia and Amanda were tense. Honoria leaned forward and whispered: "Tell me the names of your older male cousins."

The twins glanced at her, then across the grave. Amelia spoke first. "Vane's next to Devil, but you know him."

"That can't be his real name."

"His real name's *Spencer*," Amanda whispered. "But don't *ever* call him that."

"The one behind Devil is Richard—he's called Scandal. He's Devil's brother."

"And the one behind Vane is his younger brother, Harry. They call him Demon."

"Demon Harry?"

"That's right." Amanda nodded. "The one next to Vane is Gabriel."

"His real name's Rupert—he's Uncle Martin's eldest son."

"And I suppose the one behind Gabriel is Lucifer?" Honoria asked. "His brother?"

"That's right—he's really Alasdair."

Straightening, Honoria spent one minute wondering how they'd come by their pseudonyms—one question she was not about to ask the twins. She looked across the grave at those six male faces, and saw them clearly. No force on earth would stop them bringing Tolly's murderer to justice.

Being Cynsters, they could be counted on to avenge Tolly's death. Also being Cynsters, they would ensure their womenfolk, their elders and juniors—all those they considered in their care—were not disturbed or touched by such violence. Death and vengeance was their province, the home fires for the rest.

Which was all very well, *but* . . .

The last prayer was said; earth struck the coffin. Tolly's mother sagged in her sisters-in-law's arms; her husband hurried to her side. Amelia and Amanda tugged at Honoria's hands. Reluctantly, she turned from the grave—from the tableau on its opposite side.

Charles and the older Cynsters had left, but Simon, Devil, and the five others remained, their gazes still locked on the coffin. Just before she turned, Honoria saw Simon look up, into Devil's face, a question in his wide eyes. She saw Devil's response, the tightening of his hand on Simon's shoulder, the quiet promise he bent his head to give.

She had no doubt of the substance of that promise.

In company with the twins, Honoria crossed the lawns, musing on her situation. She would send for her brother Michael tomorrow, but he would take some days to reach her. Those days could be useful.

She needed to see justice done; she had a duty to avenge innocence—that was doubtless why Tolly's face haunted her. Impossible to send adult Cynster males to avenge innocence; their vengeance would be fueled by their warriors' reasons—the defending of their family, their clan. *She* would be the defender of innocence—she had a role to play, too.

She'd been looking for excitement, for adventure and intrigue—fate had landed her here. Far be it from her to argue.

The wake was a crush. Many of the bucks and bloods who had come up from London stayed for the final scene. In half an hour, Honoria had been introduced to more dangerous blades than she'd thought to meet in a lifetime. Luckily, her inclusion within the family group had sent a clear message; she was not troubled by any of the visitors.

The twins again took to their instruments; the crowd filled the music room and the drawing room and overflowed onto the terrace.

While chatting with Cynster relatives and *ton*nish family acquaintances, Honoria kept a careful eye on Devil and his five accomplices. A pattern was soon apparent. Devil stood in the drawing room, his back to the open terrace doors; the others roamed the crowd, every now and then either stopping by Devil's side quietly to impart some information or catching his eye.

She could do nothing to intercept that silent communication; as for the other, however, . . . Honoria focused on Lady Sheffield, her present interrogator.

"Of course," her ladyship intoned, "this distressing business will delay matters somewhat."

Deliberately vague, Honoria raised her brows. "Indeed?"

Lady Sheffield eyed her consideringly. "Three months of mourning—that makes it December."

"Winter," Honoria helpfully observed. She smiled at Lady Sheffield, and gave her something for her pains. "Pray excuse me, ma'am—I must speak with Webster."

With a smile, she glided to the door, quite certain how her words would be interpreted. In the hall, she wove through the knots of guests. Plates piled with tiny sandwiches sat waiting on a sideboard; picking one up, she proceeded through the music room and onto the terrace.

Reaching the spot immediately behind Devil's back, she took up her position, her back to the drawing room. The sandwiches on her plate instantly attracted suitable cover.

"Lady Harrington," an older lady introduced herself. "Know your grandfather well, miss. Haven't seen him for a while. Daresay he's keeping well?"

"I daresay," Honoria replied, keeping her voice low.

"Hurst knows nothing, nor does Gilford."

Without turning around and risking one of Devil's cousins noticing her, Honoria couldn't tell which one was reporting. But she knew Devil's voice. "Vane's checked with Blackwell. Try Gelling."

"Nice sandwiches, these." Lady Harrington took another. "There's Lady Smallworts—she knows your grandfather, too. Here—Dulcie!"

Lady Harrington waved at another bedizened lady; behind Honoria, another report was coming in. "Nothing from Dashwood and yes, I leaned heavily. He's not holding anything back. Not his style, this sort of caper."

There was silence, then Devil asked: "Anyone else here from that part of town?"

"I'll try Giles Edgeworth."

Some older gentleman approached Devil, and he was forced to converse; Honoria grasped the opportunity to give her attention to Lady Smallworts.

"Dear me, yes!" Lady Smallworts was examining her face through lorgnettes. "There's a definite likeness there, don't you think, Arethusa? About the chin."

Making a mental note to examine her chin when next she glanced in her mirror, Honoria plastered a smile on her lips and set herself to getting the two old dames chatting. Then she tuned her ears to the activity behind her.

"No luck with Farnsworth, nor Girton either."

Devil sighed. "There has to be something, somewhere."

"Must be—we'll just have to keep looking until we find it." After a pause, whichever cousin it was said: "I'll try a touch on Caffrey."

"Careful—I don't want this all over town by morning."

"Trust me."

Honoria could almost see the Cynster smile that went with the words.

Again Devil's attention was claimed by others; Honoria put her tuppence worth into the discussion over whether sprigged muslin would still be all the rage next Season.

It was some time before another of his cousins came to Devil's side. Guests were starting to depart when Vane reported; Honoria recognized his voice. "Forget Hillsworth or, I suspect, any of that ilk. If the problem's in that line, we'll need to get Harry to dig deeper."

"Speak of the Demon . . ."

"No go with any of my lot."

"Here come the others," Vane said.

"Not a whisper—not so much as a twitch."

"No luck."

"Not so much as a hint of a suspicion."

"Which means," Devil said, "that we'll have to go hunting."

"But in which direction?"

"In all directions." Devil paused. "Demon, you take the tracks and all connected enterprises. Vane, the guards and the taverns. Gabriel, the dens and finance in general. Scandal—you can do what you do best—chat up the ladies. Which leaves the catteries to Lucifer."

"And you?" Vane asked.

"I'll take the local angle."

"Right—I'm for London tonight."

"So am I."

"And me—I'll give you a lift if you like. I've got a prime 'un between the shafts."

Their deep voices faded, blending with the murmurs of the crowd. Lady Smallworts and Lady Harrington had moved onto the mysteries of the latest poke bonnets. It was time for Honoria to retreat—she'd heard all she needed. "If you'll excuse me, ladies?"

"Actually, my dear." Lady Harrington grasped Honoria's wrist. "I had meant to ask whether it's true."

"True?"

On the word, Honoria heard from behind her: "Dear me, coz—what trouble you do get into when you don't have me covering your back."

It was Vane's drawl; Honoria knew the instant Devil turned and saw her—she felt his gaze on her neck, her shoulders. She stiffened. She longed to swing about, but her ladyship clung tight.

"Why, yes." Lady Harrington smiled. "About you and—" She broke off, gaze lifting to a point beyond Honoria's left shoulder, eyes widening with delight. "Ah—good afternoon, St. Ives."

"Lady Harrington."

It wasn't his voice, and the subtle menace beneath it, that sent shock waves coursing through Honoria—it was the large hand that curved possessively about her waist.

Devil captured the hand Lady Harrington freed. Honoria watched her fingers, trapped in his, rise inexorably toward his long lips. She steeled herself to feel his lips on her fingers.

He reversed her hand and pressed his lips to her wrist.

If she'd been a weaker woman, she'd have fainted.

Smoothly, Devil turned to Lady Harrington. "You were saying, ma'am?"

Lady Harrington beamed. "Nothing of any importance—think you've given me all the answer I need." She all but winked at Honoria, then jabbed Lady Smallworts in the arm. "Come along, Dulcie—I saw Harriet on the lawn. If we hurry, we might catch her before she leaves. Your Grace." Her ladyship nodded to Honoria. "We'll see you in town, my dear. Give my regards to your grandfather."

"Yes, of course," Honoria half gasped. Her lungs had seized, courtesy of the long fingers spread over her ribs. If he kissed her wrist again, she *would* faint.

"Wave to their ladyships," her tormentor instructed.

"With what," she hissed back. "The plate?"

"I really don't think you need the plate anymore—Thomas will take it."

A footman appeared and relieved her of the plate. There were few people left on the terrace. Honoria waited, but the grip on her waist did not ease. Instead, Devil wrapped his other arm about her waist, too, her hand still held in his. She could feel him, his chest, his thighs, steely-hard behind her, his arms an unbreakable cage about her.

"Did you learn much, out here on the terrace?" The words, soft, deep and low, tickled her ear.

"Reams about sprigged muslin. And did you know that the latest poke bonnets have a ruched rim?"

"Indeed? What next?"

"Precisely what Lady Smallworts wanted to know."

"And what do you want to know, Honoria Prudence?"

He had a distinctly lethal way of saying her name—he rolled the "r"s, just slightly, so the perfectly prim English words transformed into something more sensuous. Honoria fought down a shiver. "I want to know what you're about."

She felt him sigh. "What am I to do with you, you meddlesome woman?" He rocked her, slightly, to and fro.

The sensation of losing touch with the earth made Honoria gasp. He hadn't even shifted his grip. "You can put me *down* for a start!"

She was saved by the Dowager. "Sylvester! What on earth are you doing? Put Honoria down *at once!*"

He obeyed—reluctantly; the second Honoria's feet touched earth, the Dowager took her arm. "Come, my dear—there's someone I want you to meet."

Without a backward glance, Honoria escaped with the Dowager.

She took care to play least-in-sight for the rest of the day. While most guests left directly after the wake, many of the family lingered. Honoria had no intention of finding herself unexpectedly alone with Devil in his present mood. The summerhouse, a white-timber hexagon wreathed by a yellow rambler, became her refuge.

Her embroidery in her lap, she watched the carriages roll down the drive—watched Devil play the host and wave them on their way. Afternoon was fading to evening when Charles Cynster descended the front steps and started across the lawn, heading straight for the summerhouse.

Inclining his head gravely, he entered. "Good evening, my dear. I wanted to speak with you before I left—Sylvester told me where to find you."

So much for her refuge. Honoria studied Tolly's older brother critically. He was certainly older than Devil, which made him the oldest of the Cynster cousins. He cut an impressive figure, six feet tall and solidly built, but lacked the lean Cynster lines. His face was rounder, with heavy jowls. His eyes, resting on her, were plain brown; given his recent loss, Honoria was surprised by how intent his expression was.

The summerhouse boasted a long wickerwork settee with chintz cushions, and nothing else. With a wave, she invited Charles to sit; somewhat to her relief, he declined the settee to settle on a windowsill. Facing her. Honoria raised a polite brow. Presumably, Devil had sent Charles to persuade her to leave Tolly's death to the Cynsters.

"I wanted to thank you for aiding Tolly. Sylvester mentioned you'd helped." Charles's lips twisted in a fleeting smile. "To use his phrase, 'above and beyond what might reasonably be expected of a lady of your station.' "

Graciously, Honoria inclined her head. "Despite your cousin's beliefs, I did nothing more than any lady of practical sensibilities."

"Be that as it may . . ." Charles's words trailed away; Honoria glanced up and met his gaze. "My dear Miss Anstruther-Wetherby, I hope you will excuse me if I speak plainly?"

"I would prefer you did so." Setting aside her embroidery, Honoria folded her hands and gave him her full attention.

"It appears to me that, rather than being rewarded for your help, you have been placed in an invidious position." Charles glanced at her. "Forgive me—this is a delicate subject. But I understand that, by virtue of rendering assistance to Tolly and thus being stranded by the storm, you were forced to spend the night in company with Sylvester, and thus now find yourself compromised and, not to put too fine a point on it, forced to accept his offer."

Honoria opened her lips—Charles raised his hand. "No, if you please—allow me to finish. I realize that many ladies would be *aux anges* over becoming the duchess of St. Ives, whatever the circumstances. I can see, however, that you are not of that giddy ilk. You're an Anstruther-Wetherby, daughter of an old and ancient line—quite as proud as we Cynsters. You are a woman of sound sense, independence, and—as you acknowledged—of a practical bent.

"You have, I believe, chosen to live life quietly—it hardly seems fair that in return for your good offices, you should be forced to become Sylvester's wife, a role that will not only be demanding but also very likely less than rewarding." He paused, then added: "For a lady of sensitivity." He hesitated, weighing his words, then continued: "Sylvester bears a very specific reputation, as do most of the Cynsters. It seems unlikely that a leopard so devoted to hunting will readily change his spots."

He looked at Honoria; she raised her brows haughtily. "There is little in your assessment with which I would argue, Mr. Cynster."

Charles's brief smile did not light his eyes. "Indeed, my dear, I believe we are two who would understand each other well, which is why I hope you will understand my motives in proposing an alternative solution to your undeserved predicament."

"An alternative?" Honoria was conscious of increasing unease. She had not expected Charles to undermine Devil; she was truly surprised that he had.

"A more acceptable alternative to a lady of your sensibility."

Honoria looked her question.

"Marrying Sylvester would not be in your best interests—anyone with understanding can see that. You stand, however, in need of an offer, in restitution if nothing else. As Tolly was my brother, in order to retrieve your standing, I would be happy to offer you my hand. My estate, of course, is nothing compared to Sylvester's; it is, however, not inconsiderable."

Honoria was stunned; only years of training kept the fact from her face. She did not have to think to frame her reply—the words came spontaneously to her lips. "I thank you for your offer, sir, but I am not of a mind to marry—not for this nor, indeed, any other foreseeable reason."

Charles's face blanked. After a moment, he asked, "You don't intend to accept Sylvester's offer?"

Lips compressed, Honoria shook her head. "I have no intention of marrying at all." With that firm declaration, she reached for her embroidery.

"You will be pressured to accept Sylvester's offer—both by the Cynsters and your own family."

Honoria's eyes flashed; she raised her brows haughtily. "My dear sir, I am not at all amenable to unwarranted interference in my life."

Silence ensued, then Charles slowly stood. "I apologize, Miss Anstruther-Wetherby, should I have given offense." He paused, then added: "However, I urge you to remember that, should a time come when you feel it necessary to marry to escape the situation arising from Tolly's death, you have an alternative to marrying Sylvester."

Engrossed in jabbing her needle into her canvas, Honoria did not look up.

"Your humble servant, Miss Anstruther-Wetherby."

Barely glancing at Charles's bow, Honoria stiffly inclined her head. Charles turned on his heel and descended the steps; Honoria watched, narrow-eyed, as he returned to the house. When he disappeared, she frowned and wriggled her shoulders.

If she ever had to marry a Cynster, she'd rather try taming the tyrant.

The tyrant came knocking on her door late that evening.

Devil's uncles, aunts, and younger cousins had stayed for

dinner, then all except Tolly's family had departed, letting the staff catch their collective breath. A cloak of calm had settled over the Place, a restful silence only found in those houses that had seen birth and death many times.

Leaving the Dowager and Tolly's parents swapping bitter-sweet memories, Honoria had retired to her chamber. She had intended to compose her letter to Michael. Instead, the peace outside drew her to the window; she sank onto the window seat, her mind sliding into the night.

The knock that interrupted her undirected reverie was so peremptory she had no doubt who was there. She hesitated, then, stiffening her spine, rose and crossed to the door.

Devil was standing in the corridor, looking back toward the stairs. As she set the door wide, he turned and met her gaze. "Come for a walk."

He held out his hand; Honoria held his gaze steadily—and slowly raised one brow. His lips twitched, then he fluidly sketched a bow. "My dear Honoria Prudence, will you do me the honor of strolling with me in the moonlight?"

She preferred his order to his request; the effortless charm lurking beneath his words, uttered in that soft, deep voice, was enough to turn any lady's head. But it needed no more than the blink of an eye to decide why he was here. "I'll get my shawl."

The swath of fine Norwich silk lay on a chair; draping it about her shoulders, Honoria pinned the ends, then headed for the door. She intended making it plain that she was not about to pull back from her interest in Tolly's murder.

Devil took her hand and drew her over the threshold and shut the door, then settled her hand on his sleeve. "There's another stairway that gives onto the side lawn."

In silence, they left the house to stroll beneath the huge trees dotting the lawn, passing from shadow to moonlight and back again.

The silence was soothing; the pervasive tang of leaves, green grass, and rich earth, scents Devil always associated with his home, was tonight spiced with a subtle fragrance, an elusive scent he had no difficulty placing.

It was her—the fragrance of her hair, of her skin, of her perfume—lily of the valley with a hint of rose—an expensive, alluring mix. Beneath all wafted the heady scent of woman, warm and sensual, promising all manner of earthly delights. The evocative scent teased his hunter's senses and heightened the tension gripping him.

Tonight, he was prey to two driving desires—at the moment, he could pursue neither goal. There was nothing he could do to avenge Tolly's death—and he could not take Honoria Prudence to his bed. Not yet. There was, however, one point he could address—he could do something about her chin.

He had no intention of letting her involve herself with Tolly's murder, but his action on the terrace had been ill-advised. Intimidation would not work with this particular lady. Luckily, an alternative strategy lay to hand, one much more to his liking. Using it would kill two birds with one stone. Cloaked in shadow, Devil smiled—and turned their steps toward the summerhouse.

She lost patience before they reached it. "What steps are you taking to apprehend your cousin's killer?"

"The matter will be dealt with—rest assured of that."

He felt her glare. "That's not what I asked."

"That is, however, all the answer you need."

She stiffened, then sweetly inquired: "Has anyone informed you, Your Grace, that you are without doubt the most arrogant man in Christendom?"

"Not in those precise words."

The comment robbed her of speech long enough for him to lead her up the summerhouse steps. He halted in the pavillion's center, releasing her. Shafts of moonlight streaked the floor, patterned with the shadows of the leaves. Through the dimness, he saw her breasts swell.

"*Be* that as it may—"

Honoria's words ended on a half squeak; one instant, her tormentor was standing, loose-limbed and relaxed, before her—the next, long fingers had firmed about her chin. And he was suddenly much closer. "What are you *doing*?" Her eyes had flown wide; she was breathless. She didn't try to free her chin; his grip felt unbreakable.

His lids lifted; his eyes, even paler in the weak light, met hers. "Distracting you."

His deep murmur was certainly distracting; Honoria felt it in her bones. Other than on her chin, he wasn't touching her, yet she felt herself sliding into his hold. He drew her upward and she stretched, her head tilting further; her heart tripped, then started to race. His eyes held hers, mesmerizing in the moonlight, ageless, seductive, all-knowing. His head slowly lowered—her lips softened, parted.

She could not have pulled back had the heavens fallen.

The first touch of his lips sent an aching shudder through her; his arms immediately closed about her, drawing her against him. Hardness surrounded her; muscles with less give than steel caged her. His head angled; the pressure of his lips increased.

They were hard, like the rest of him—commanding, demanding; a heartbeat later they were warm, enticing, seductively persuasive. Honoria stilled, quivering, on some invisible threshold—then he tugged and she plunged forward, into the unknown.

It was not the first time she'd been kissed, yet it was. Never before had there been magic in the air, never before had she been taken by the hand and introduced to a world of sensation. Pleasure rose, warm and enthralling, then whirled through her, a kaleidoscope of delight, leaving her giddy. Pleasurably giddy.

What little breath she managed to catch, he took, weaving his web until she was caught beyond recall. The tip of his tongue traced her lips, a beguilingly artful caress. She knew she'd be wise to ignore it; he was leading her into realms beyond her knowledge, where he would be her guide. A most unwise situation—a dangerous situation.

His lips firmed; heat welled, melting all resistance. On a sigh, she parted her lips farther, yielding to his arrogant demand.

He took what he wanted—the intimate caress sent sensation streaking through her, a bolt of lightning striking to her core. Shocked, Honoria drew back on a gasp.

He let her retreat—just so far. Stunned, her wits reeling, she searched his face. One black brow slowly arched; his arms tightened.

"No." Honoria braced against his hold—or tried to; her muscles had the consistency of jelly.

"There's no need to panic—I'm only going to kiss you."

Only? Honoria blinked wildly. "That's bad enough. I mean—" She hauled in a breath and tried to focus her wayward wits. "You're dangerous."

He actually chuckled; the sound shredded her hard-won control—she shivered.

"I'm not dangerous to you." His hands stroked soothingly, seductively, down her back. "I'm going to marry you. That puts the shoe on the other foot."

Had her wits been completely addled? Honoria frowned. "What shoe—and which foot?"

His teeth gleamed. "According to all precepts, Cynster wives are the only beings on earth of whom Cynster men need be wary."

"Really?" He was pulling her leg. Honoria tried to whip up her indignation, an impossible task given he had bent his head and was gently nibbling her lips.

"Just kiss me." He whispered the words against her lips as he drew her hard against him. The contact set her nerves quivering again; his lips, lightly teasing, left her mind in no state to quibble.

Devil kissed her again, waiting with the patience of one who knew, until she yielded completely. Her melting surrender was all the more sweet, knowing as he did that she would prefer it was otherwise. Too wise, too experienced, he did not push her too far, keeping a tight rein on his passions. She lay softly supple in his arms, her lips his to enjoy, the sweet cavern of her mouth his to taste, to plunder, to claim; for tonight, that would have to be enough.

He would much rather have claimed her—taken her to his bed and filled her, celebrated life in that most fundamental of ways—a natural response to death's presence. But she was innocent—her skittering reactions, her quiescence, spoke to him clearly. She would be his and his alone—but not yet.

The reality of his need impinged fully on his mind; Devil mentally cursed. Her softness, pressed from breast to thigh against him, was a potent invocation, feeding his demons, calling them, inciting them. He drew back; chest swelling, he studied her face, wondering . . . even while he shackled his desires. Her eyes glinted beneath her lashes.

Her mind still adrift, Honoria let her gaze roam his face. There was no softness in his features, no hint of gentleness, only strength and passion and an ironclad will. "I am not going to marry you." The words went directly from her brain to her lips—an instinctive reaction.

He merely raised a brow, irritatingly supercilious.

"I'm going to send for my brother tomorrow to come and escort me home."

His eyes, silver in the night, narrowed fractionally. "Home—as in Hampshire?"

Honoria nodded. She felt unreal, out of touch with the world.

"Write a note for your brother—I'll frank it tomorrow."

She smiled. "And I'll put it in the post myself."

He smiled back—she had a premonition he was laughing at her though his chest, so close, was not quaking. "By all means. We'll see what he thinks of your decision."

Honoria's smile turned smug; she felt quite lightheaded. He, Cynster that he was, thought Michael would support his cause. Michael, of course, would agree with her—he would see, as instantly as she had, that for her, marrying Devil Cynster was not a good idea.

"And now, if we've settled your immediate future to your satisfaction . . ." His lips brushed hers; instinctively, Honoria tracked them.

A twig cracked.

Devil raised his head, every muscle tensing. He and Honoria looked out into the night; the sight that met their incredulous eyes had him straightening. "What the . . . ?"

"*Sssh!*" Honoria pressed her hand to his lips.

He frowned and caught her hand, but remained silent as the small procession drew nearer, then passed the summerhouse. Through moonlight and shadow, Amelia, Amanda and Simon led the little band. Henrietta, Eliza, Angelica and Heather with Mary in tow followed. Each child carried a white rose. Devil's frown deepened as the dense shadow of the trees swallowed them; of their destination there could be little doubt. "Wait here."

Honoria stared at him. "You must be joking." She picked up her skirts and hurried down the steps.

He was on her heels as they slipped from shadow to shadow, trailing the small band. The children halted before Tolly's freshly filled grave. Honoria stopped in the deep shadows beneath an oak; Devil stopped behind her. Then his hands gripped her waist; he lifted her to put her aside.

She twisted in his hold and flung herself against him. "*No!*" Her furious whisper made him blink. Her hands gripping his shoulders, she whispered: "You mustn't!"

He frowned at her, then lowered his head so he could whisper in her ear: "Why the hell not? They're not frightened of me."

"It's not that!" Honoria frowned back. "You're an adult—not one of them."

"So?"

"So this is their moment—their time to say good-bye. Don't spoil it for them."

He searched her face, then his lips thinned. Lifting his head, he looked at the contingent lined up at the foot of the grave but made no further move to join them.

Honoria wriggled and he let her go; she turned to watch. The chill beneath the trees penetrated her thin gown—she shivered. The next instant, Devil's arms came around her, drawing her back against him. Honoria stiffened, then gave up and relaxed, too grateful for his warmth to quibble.

A conference had taken place at the graveside; now Amelia stepped forward and threw her rose on the mound. "Sleep well, Tolly."

Amanda stepped up. "Rest in peace," she intoned, and flung her rose to join her twin's.

Next came Simon. "Good-bye, Tolly." Another rose landed on the grave.

One by one, the children added their roses to the small pile, each bidding Tolly farewell. When they were done, they looked at each other, then re-formed their procession and hurried back to the house.

Honoria held Devil back until the children passed by. He sent her an unreadable, distinctly Cynster look when she finally let him loose, then took her hand; together, they trailed the children back to the lawn.

There was dew on the grass; it was heavy going, particularly for little Mary. Devil grunted and lengthened his stride—Honoria flung herself at him again. "No!" She glared furiously and pressed him back under the trees.

Devil glared back. "They'll get wet feet—I can carry two of them."

He gripped her waist: Honoria clung to his shoulders. "They'll guess you know where they've been—they'll guess you watched. It'll spoil it for them. A little water won't hurt them— not if they're true Cynsters."

A gleam marked Devil's reluctant smile. He waited, grudgingly, until the children disappeared through the side door, then, her hand locked in his, strode for the house. The children were still negotiating the stairs when they reached the foot. Devil went straight on, treading close by the wall. When they reached the upper landing, the children were only partway up the next flight—Devil yanked Honoria into an alcove.

She gasped as she landed against his chest. One arm locked about her; hard fingers lifted her face. His lips were on hers before she drew breath; she tried to hold firm, but beneath the pleasure he lavished upon her, her resistance wilted, then melted away.

To be replaced by something so insidious, so soul-stealingly compulsive, so innately enthralling, she couldn't pull back. He was hungry—she sensed it in the leashed passion that hardened his lips, that, when she opened to him, set him plundering more rapaciously than before. The tension investing his every muscle spoke of rigid control; the turbulence behind it frightened and fascinated. His tongue tangled with hers, intimately enticing, then settled to a slow, repetitive, probing rhythm. Her mouth was his; his possession set her senses whirling—no man had touched her like this. A warm flush rushed through her, a sweet fever unlike anything she'd known. Beyond that and the shocking intimacy of his caress, she knew only one thing. He was ravenously hungry—for her. The sudden, almost overwhelming impulse to give herself to him, to assuage that rampant need, shook her to the core—and still she could not pull back.

How long they stood locked together in the dark she had no idea; when he lifted his head, she'd lost touch with the world.

He hesitated, then brushed her lips with his. "Do I frighten you?"

"Yes." In a way he did. Wide-eyed, her pulse tripping, Honoria searched his shadowed eyes. "But it's not you I'm frightened of." He was making her feel, making her yearn. "I—" Frowning, she stopped, for once lost for words.

In the dark, Devil smiled crookedly. "Don't worry." He took her mouth in one last, searching kiss before putting her from him. "Go. Now." It was a warning—he wasn't sure she understood.

She blinked up at him through the dimness, then nodded. "Good night." She slipped out of the alcove. "Sleep well."

Devil nearly laughed. He wouldn't have a good night—he wouldn't sleep well. He could feel another headache coming on.

Chapter 7

~≈≈≈≈≈~

$\mathcal{N}$EXT MORNING, HONORIA attended Sunday service in the church in the grounds, then strolled back with Louise Cynster. Tolly's mother thanked her for helping her son; Honoria politely disclaimed. With little encouragement, Louise spoke of Tolly and his relationship with Devil. Hero worship seemed the most apt description.

The object of Tolly's reverence had not seen fit to attend church. When the ladies reached the breakfast table, it was apparent he'd been there before them. Honoria made quick work of tea and toast, then headed upstairs.

Devil, she felt sure, would have gone riding. It was a perfect day—he would be out surveying his fields astride his cake-eating demon. Which should leave nearer precincts clear.

It was the work of three minutes to don her stylish topaz riding habit. Her clothes were the one item she'd always insisted lived up to her Anstruther-Wetherby background. She flicked the feather on her matching toque so that it draped rakishly over one temple, then headed for the door.

There was no one in the stable yard. Unperturbed, she entered the main stable. The stall walls were high; she couldn't see over them. The tack room was at the end—she stepped purposefully down the aisle.

A large hand reached out and hauled her into a stall.

"*What . . . ?*" Warm steel encircled her. Honoria focused—and realized her danger. "Don't you *dare* kiss me—I'll scream if you do!"

"And who do you imagine will rescue you?"

Honoria blinked—and tried to think of the right answer.

"Anyway, you won't be able to scream while I'm kissing you."

She parted her lips and hauled in a deep breath.

By the time she realized that was not a wise move, it was too late—he'd taken full advantage. A vague notion of struggling wafted into her mind—then out, as heat, warmth and insidious pleasure burgeoned within her. His lips moved on hers, arrogantly confident; his tongue slid between in a deliciously languid caress, an unhurried caress that went on and on, until she was heated through. Honoria felt the fever rise—she tried to tell herself this was wrong—scandalously wrong—while every sense she possessed purred in appreciation.

She couldn't think or hear when he kissed her. She made that discovery when Devil finally raised his head; up until the instant his lips left hers, her mind had been thought-free, blissful in its vacancy. The sounds of the stable rushed in on her, compounding her breathlessness. Her bones had liquefied, yet she was still upright—then she realized it was due to him that she was so. He was holding her against himself; her toes only just touched the floor.

"Great heavens!" Blinking wildly, she lowered her heels to earth. Had she labeled him dangerous? He was lethal.

"Good morning, Honoria Prudence." His deep purr sent a shiver down her spine. "And where are you headed?"

"Ah . . ." Gazing, wide-eyed, into his too-knowing green eyes, Honoria marshaled her wits. "I was looking for a horse. Presumably you have more than one?"

"I believe there's a hoity, wilful mare that should suit. But where were you thinking of riding?"

"Oh—just out about the lanes." He was holding her too securely for her to pull away; she tried to ease back—his hold gave not an inch.

"You don't know this country—you'll get lost. You'll be safer riding with me."

Dispensing with all subtlety, Honoria reached behind her

and tried to pry his arms loose. He chuckled and let her tug—all to no avail. Then he bent his head and feathered delicate kisses about her left ear.

Breathless, quite ridiculously flustered, Honoria glared. "Whoever called you Devil had the right of it!"

"Hully?"

Honoria blinked, directly into his eyes. "Mrs. *Hull* gave you your nickname?"

He grinned—devilishly. "She used to be my nursemaid. I was three when she christened me 'That Devil Cynster.' "

"You must have been a tyrant even then."

"I was."

A furious clearing of a throat spared Honoria the necessity of replying. Devil looked around, then released her, turning so he hid her from view. "What is it, Martin?"

"Sorry t'interrupt, Y'r Grace, but one of the flanges on the North Number One's split—Mister Kirby was a-wondering if you'd swing past that way. He was hoping you'd check the lay before he reset the blade."

The message made no sense to Honoria; she peered around Devil's shoulder. A workman, his cap in his hands, stood waiting in the aisle. She glanced up—and discovered his master's green gaze on her.

"Tell Kirby I'll be there within the half-hour."

"Yes, Y'r Grace." Martin hurried out.

Honoria straightened. "What was that about?"

"One of the windmills is out of action."

"Mills?" Honoria recalled numerous windmills dotting the fields. "There seem to be a lot about."

Devil's lips twitched. He reached for her hand. "This is fen country, Honoria Prudence—the mills drive pumps which drain the land."

"Oh." Honoria found herself being towed down the aisle. "Where are you taking me?"

He raised both brows at her. "To find a horse. Wasn't that what you wanted?"

Ten minutes later, atop a frisky chestnut mare, Honoria clattered out of the stable yard—in Devil's wake. The notion of a surreptitious detour occurred only to be dismissed; he'd overtake her in an instant.

They left the park by a different route from that which led through the woods; beyond the park walls, the clack of windmills became noticeable, steadily increasing as they headed north. The mill in question was a large one; Devil dismounted in its shadow to confer with his foreman.

For Honoria, their discussion held little interest. As they cantered back to the Place, she took the devil by the horns. "Have you any idea who the 'highwayman' might be?" It seemed a clear enough question.

His response was a dissertation on the mechanics of fen drainage. By the time they reached the stable yard, Honoria had heard enough to verify the adage about Cynsters being as passionate about their land as they were in their other pursuits. She'd also gained a very firm idea of what her host thought of her interest in his cousin's murder.

The next morning, she watched from her window until she *saw* her nemesis ride out. Then she headed for the stables. The grooms saw nothing odd in her request that the mare be saddled again. When she passed under the arch leading out of the park, Honoria whooped with delight. Smiling inanely, she headed for the wood.

She ended going the long way around via the village. It was an hour and more before she finally reached the straight where Tolly had been shot. The mare seemed to sense the fatal spot; Honoria drew rein and slid from the saddle, tethering the horse some yards down the lane.

Brisk and full of purpose, she crossed the lane—the rumble of hoofbeats reached her. Halting, she listened; the unknown horseman was heading her way. "Damn!" She whisked about and hurried back to the mare.

She couldn't remount. In disbelief, Honoria looked right and left. The hoofbeats drew steadily nearer. In that moment, she would have traded her entire wardrobe for a suitable log; none was to be found.

The unknown presence was likely some local no more threatening than Mr. Postlethwaite. Honoria stepped to the mare's head and assumed a haughty, nonchalant expression. If she wished to stand beside her horse in the lane, who had the right to gainsay her?

The oncoming horse rounded the curve and burst into view. The rider wasn't Mr. Postlethwaite.

The black demon halted beside her; Devil looked down at her. "What are you doing here?"

Honoria opened her eyes wide—even wider than they already were. "I stopped to stretch my legs."

He didn't blink. "And admire the view?"

They were hemmed in on all sides by the wood. Honoria narrowed her eyes at him. "What are *you* doing here?"

Devil met her look, his expression implacable, then swung down from the saddle. Jaw set, he knotted the reins about a tree; without a word, he turned and strode to the spot where Tolly had fallen.

Honoria marched determinedly in his wake. "You don't believe it was a highwayman any more than I do—and it certainly wasn't a poacher."

Devil snorted. "I'm not daft." He shot her a piercing glance, then looked away, flexing his shoulders as if throwing off some restraint.

Honoria watched him study the ground. "Well? Who do you think did it?"

"I don't know, but we'll find out."

"*We'll?*" Honoria was perfectly certain he didn't mean *her* and him. "You're all searching, aren't you—you and your cousins?"

The look he cast her brimmed with masculine long suffering; his short sigh underscored it. "As you've so accurately deduced, it wasn't a highwayman; nor was it a poacher—Tolly was murdered. Behind such a murder there must be a reason—we're looking for the reason. The reason will lead us to the man."

"From what I heard, you haven't any clue as to what the reason might be." His glance, razor-sharp, touched her face; Honoria tried not to look conscious.

"Tolly lived a full life. While I'm going over the ground here, the others are quartering London—the balls, the hells—anywhere a Cynster might have been."

Recalling the assignments he'd delegated to his cousins, Honoria frowned. "Was Tolly particularly partial to cats?"

Devil stared at her, his expression utterly blank.

"The catteries?"

He blinked, slowly, then his gaze, devoid of expression, met hers. "The salons. Of the *demimonde*."

Honoria managed to keep the shock from her eyes. "He was *only* twenty."

"So?" The word dripped arrogance. "Cynsters start young."

He was the archetype—presumably he knew. Honoria decided to leave that subject—Devil had stepped into the undergrowth. "What are you looking for? A gun?"

"Tolly didn't carry a gun."

"So?" Her version dripped impatience.

His lips thinned. "I'm looking for anything that shouldn't be here." He stopped and looked around. "The wind could have blown things either side of the lane."

It was a daunting task. While Devil tramped back the undergrowth close by where Tolly had fallen, Honoria peered and poked at the verges farther along the lane. A strong stick in one hand, she followed in his wake, prodded likely-looking clumps of grass and lifted leaf mold. Devil glanced around and grunted, then continued more swiftly, scanning the area as he went, leaving the finer details to her.

When they'd covered an area going back a yard from the lane, Honoria straightened and pushed back the feather trying to poke her in the eye. "Why do you think Tolly was in the lane?"

Devil answered without looking up. "I assume he was coming to the Place."

"Your aunt thought it likely he was coming to seek your advice."

He looked up at that. "You asked Aunt Louise?"

His tone had Honoria straightening to attention. "We were just chatting—she doesn't suspect anything." His censorious expression didn't alter; gesturing airily, she shrugged. "You said it was a highwayman, so it was a highwayman. Everyone believes it—even your mother."

"Thank God for that." With a last, saber-edged glance, Devil returned to his search. "The last thing I need is females interfering."

"Indeed?" Wielding her stick, she scattered a pile of leaves. "I suppose it never occurred to you that we females might contribute something?"

"If you saw the contribution my mother thought of making you wouldn't ask. She penned a note to the magistrate that would have made his hair stand on end—if he could have deciphered it."

Honoria flicked over a clod. "If we weren't left feeling so frustratingly helpless—set to one side and told to knit mittens—perhaps we wouldn't react quite so wildly." Swinging about, she waved her stick at him. "Just think how frustrated *you* would feel if you knew you, personally, could never achieve *anything*."

He looked at her—steadily—for what seemed a long time. Then his features hardened; he gestured at the ground. "Just keep searching."

Though they searched both sides of the lane, they found precisely nothing. Remounting, they cantered through the fields, then through the gate into the park, both absorbed with thoughts of Tolly's death.

As they rode between the ranks of golden poplars, Honoria glanced at Devil. "Your aunt intends to give you the silver hip flask you gave Tolly for his birthday as a keepsake—he had it on him when he was shot." When he merely nodded, his gaze fixed ahead, she added somewhat tartly: "It seems the 'highwayman' forgot it."

That got her a glance—a warning one.

"Your aunt also mentioned," she plowed on, "that if he was in trouble, Tolly would turn to you first, as head of the family, rather than to his father or Charles. Do you think that the reason he was killed could be the same as his reason for seeking you?"

Devil's gaze sharpened; in that instant, Honoria knew triumph. She'd beaten him to that conclusion, and he thought she was right. He said nothing, however, until they reached the stable yard. Lifting her down, he held her before him. "Don't say anything to *Maman* or Aunt Louise—there's no need to start hares."

Honoria met his gaze with one of bland hauteur.

"And if you should hear or discover anything, tell me."

She opened her eyes innocently wide. "And you'll tell me whatever you discover?"

His expression turned grim. "Don't press your luck, Honoria Prudence."

Chapter 8

~≈❖≈~

TWO MORNINGS LATER, Devil descended the main stairs, tugging on his driving gloves. As he started down the last flight, Webster appeared, heading for the front door.

"Your curricle should be waiting, Your Grace."

"Thank you." Reaching the front door, Devil looked back.

Hand on the latch, Webster paused. "Is anything amiss, Your Grace?"

Devil turned as Webster opened the door—revealing his curricle drawn up before the steps, along with a figure in pale lilac. Devil smiled. "No, Webster—everything's as I expected."

Strolling out, Devil paused in the shadows of the porch to relish the picture Honoria presented. His bride-to-be had a certain style, an innate elegance. Her hair was piled high in a fashionable knot, fine errant curls wreathing her face. A frilled parasol protected her complexion; her hands and feet were encased in tan leather. Her lilac carriage dress had been cut with skill, neatly fitting her slender waist, emphasizing the ripe swell of her hips and the generous curves of her breasts. It took conscious effort to wipe the wolfish smile from his face.

Adopting a bland, impassive expression, he strolled down the steps.

Twirling her parasol, Honoria watched him approach. "I gather you intend driving to St. Ives, Your Grace. I wonder if I might accompany you? I have a keen interest in old chapels—I believe the bridge-chapel at St. Ives is a particularly fine example of its kind."

"Good morning, Honoria Prudence." Halting before her, Devil claimed her right hand; smoothly raising it, he pressed his lips to her inner wrist, left bare by her glove.

Honoria nearly dropped her parasol. She shot him a glare and tried to calm her racing heart. "Good morning, Your Grace."

Without another word—without the argument she had primed herself to win—he led her to the curricle's side and lifted her to the seat. Effortlessly. She had to calm her wayward heart all over again. Shifting along, she clung to the rail as the seat tipped as he climbed up. Once it resettled, she rearranged her skirts, then fussed with her parasol.

Devil took the reins, dismissed his groom, then they were bowling down the drive. Honoria drew a deep breath; the cool air beneath the oaks revived her wits—and brought the last minutes into sharper focus. Abruptly narrowing her eyes, she turned them on Devil. "You *knew*!"

He glanced her way, his expression mildly indulgent. "I'm generally considered a fast learner."

An unnerving suspicion leapt to mind. "Where are you taking me?"

This time his expression was innocence incarnate. "To St. Ives—to see the bridge-chapel."

Honoria looked into his eyes—they were crystal-clear. Twisting about, she looked behind—and saw a horse on a leading rein following the curricle. She turned back. "You're going to St. Ives to return the horse Tolly was riding the afternoon he was shot."

Devil's gaze turned sharp, his expression irritated. "I don't suppose I can persuade you to leave the matter in my hands?"

Honoria frowned. "Is it Tolly's horse—or could it be the murderer's?"

Devil's jaw firmed. "It must be the horse Tolly was riding—it was found fully saddled in a field near the wood the day after the storm. It's from the stables Tolly usually used. And the murderer presumably left the scene on horseback." A straight stretch lay before them; he slowed his matched bays and looked at Honoria. "Honoria Prudence, you might have come upon Tolly a few minutes before I did, but there's no reason you should take an active role in tracking down his killer."

Honoria put her nose in the air. "I take leave to disagree, Your Grace."

Devil scowled. "For God's sake, stop 'Your Gracing' me—call me Devil. We are, after all, going to be man and wife."

"That," Honoria declared, her chin rising another notch, "is unlikely."

Devil eyed the tip of her chin, and debated the wisdom of arguing. Instead, he said, his tone edged but even: "Honoria, I'm the head of this family—my shoulders are broader than yours and my back is a good deal stronger. Finding Tolly's murderer is *my* responsibility—rest assured I'll fulfill it."

She looked at him. "You do realize you've just contradicted yourself? One minute, you declare I'm to be your bride—the next you forbid me to act as either your wife or your bride should."

"As far as I'm concerned my wife, prospective or actual, which is to say *you*, should refrain from all dangerous activities." Forced to look to his horses, Devil heard his own growl; his frown deepened. "Murder is violent; tracking a murderer is dangerous. *You* should not be involved."

"Entrenched opinion states that a wife should give her husband aid and succor in all his enterprises."

"Forget the aid—I'll settle for the succor."

"I'm afraid you cannot separate the two—they come as a package. Besides," Honoria added, her eyes widening, "if I'm to stay away from all danger, however could we wed?"

He glanced at her, his expression arrested; he searched her face, then narrowed his eyes. "You know you stand in no danger from me. You wouldn't be here if you did."

That, Honoria inwardly admitted, was true; he was far too potent a force to challenge without cast-iron assurances. But her position was unassailable—given he viewed her as his bride, he would uphold her honor, even against himself. She could have no more formidable protector. Secure in that knowledge, she smiled serenely. "Have your cousins learned anything yet?"

He muttered something and looked ahead—she didn't try too hard to catch his words. His jaw was set—granite would have been softer. He took the next turn at speed, then whipped up his horses. Unperturbed, she sat back, idly scanning the flat fields past which they flew.

Devil barely checked his team for Somersham,

Honoria glimpsed Mr. Postlethwaite by the vicarage. She waved; he blinked, then smiled and waved back. Had it really been only a week since she'd taken the lane through the wood?

Tolly's family had left the previous day, having spent the days since the funeral coming to terms with their grief. She had taken the twins in hand, encouraging them to turn their thoughts to the futures that lay before them. She had also broken one of her golden rules and taken the younger girls, Henrietta and little Mary, under her wing; there'd been no one else suited to the task. Supporting Tolly's sisters had only strengthened her resolution to ensure that his killer was brought to justice.

The roofs of St. Ives lay ahead before Devil finally spoke. "Vane sent a messenger yesterday—no one has unearthed the smallest clue or heard the slightest whisper. Nothing to suggest what sent Tolly this way or why he might have been killed."

Honoria studied his profile. "You were expecting more, weren't you?"

"I put off returning the horse, hoping to have a description of the man we're seeking. He must have got to the wood somehow. If he followed Tolly or came earlier from London, he may have hired a horse in St. Ives."

"Perhaps he drove?"

Devil shook his head. "If he had, he would have had to drive out of the wood *away* from Somersham. Otherwise, he would have encountered you. There was a group of my laborers in the fields below the wood—any carriage going that way would have passed them. None did."

"What about a horseman?"

"No, but the wood's riddled with bridle paths. There are any number a horseman could have taken."

"Is it possible to ride up from London?"

"Possible but not likely." Devil checked his pair; the first houses of St. Ives were before them. "A horse ridden that far at any reasonable speed could not have participated in any subsequent flight."

They'd reached the main street; Devil slowed the bays to a walk.

"So," Honoria concluded, "we're looking for a man, identity and description unknown, who hired a horse on the day of the shooting."

She felt Devil's gaze on her face—and heard the short, irritated, aggravated sigh he gave before saying: "*We're* looking for precisely that."

Five minutes later, sitting in the curricle, listening as he questioned the stablemaster, Honoria was still struggling with her triumph. She knew better than to let it show—the last thing she wanted was to bruise his masculine sensibilities and have him rescind his decision. Yet victory was so sweet it was hard to keep the smile from her lips—every time she was sure he couldn't see it, she gave in to the urge and smiled.

The curricle rocked as Devil climbed up. "You heard?"

"No horseman except Tolly. Are there other stables in town?"

There were two, but the answers there were the same as at the first. No man had hired a horse on that day—no one had noticed any horseman riding through. "What now?" Honoria asked as Devil headed his team back up the main street.

"I'll send men to check at Huntingdon, Godmanchester, and Ely. Chatteris as well, though that's even less likely."

"What about Cambridge?'

"That," Devil stated, "is the main chance. It's closer to town, and the coaches are more frequent on that route."

Honoria nodded. "So when are we going there?"

Devil flicked her a glance. "*We* aren't—any more than we're going to the other towns."

Honoria narrowed her eyes at him—only to see his lips twitch.

"I'm too well known to ask questions without inviting comment. St. Ives is different—it's the family town and has few other major families living close. And *you* can't ask either. But my grooms can chat up the ostlers over a pint or two and learn all we need without anyone being the wiser."

"Hmm." Honoria eyed him suspiciously.

"I'll send Melton to Cambridge."

"Your head stableman?"

"So to speak."

Honoria had yet to sight the man. "He doesn't seem to be much about."

"Melton is *never* around when I need him. It's a point of honor with him."

Honoria stared. "Why do you put up with him?"

Devil shrugged. "He's old."

"That's it? Because he's old?"

"No."

Intrigued, Honoria watched the hard face soften, not a great deal, but enough to show.

"Melton put me on my first pony—you could say he taught me to ride. He's been at the Place all his life, and no one knows more about horses—not even Demon. I couldn't turn him out to grass, not after a lifetime in the position. Luckily, his son-in-law, Hersey, is a sensible man—he's my understableman and actually does all the work. Other than on special occasions—and with handling Sulieman—Melton's position is purely titular."

"But he never turns up when you bring Sulieman in."

"Or when I take him out. As I said, it's a point of honor with him." Devil glanced at Honoria, his lips twisting wryly. "To make sure I don't forget all he's taught me. According to him, just because I'm a duke doesn't excuse me from currying my horse."

Honoria choked, then gave up and laughed unrestrainedly.

Devil cast her a disgusted glance—and drove on.

She was wiping her eyes, still racked by the occasional giggle, when he checked his team. They were a mile or so short of Somersham; Honoria sobered when Devil turned the horses off the road, eased them along a narrow lane, then swung onto a wide grassy patch and reined in.

"Behold—north Cambridgeshire."

She could hardly miss it—the county lay spread before her, a tapestry of greens and golds, edged with the darker hues of woods and hedgerows.

"This is the closest we come to a lookout in these parts."

Honoria studied the landscape—while her wariness escalated in leaps and bounds. They were on a grassy plateau, a stand of trees screening them from the road. Essentially private.

"Over there," Devil pointed to the right, "you can see the roofs of Chatteris. The first dark green line beyond is the Forty-Foot Drain, the second is the Old Nene."

Honoria nodded; she recalled the names from his earlier lecture on the fens.

"And now . . ." Devil secured the reins. "It's time for lunch."

"Lunch?" Honoria swung around, but he'd already leapt down from the curricle. An instant later, she heard him rummaging in the boot. He reappeared, a rug in one hand, a picnic basket in the other.

"Here." He tossed the rug at her. Reflexively, she caught it—then caught her breath as his free arm snaked about her waist and he swung her to the ground. He smiled down at her, pure wolf in his eyes. "Why don't you chose a suitable place to spread the rug?"

Honoria glared—she couldn't speak; her heart was blocking her throat, her breathing had seized. She barely had enough strength to whisk herself free of his encircling arm. Marching across the grass as determinedly as her suddenly shaky limbs allowed, all too aware he prowled close behind, she spread the rug over the first reasonable patch, then, remembering her parasol, returned to the safety of the curricle to retrieve it.

The move gave her time to calm her senses, to take a firm grip on her wayward wits—to remind herself of how safe she really was. As long as she didn't allow him to kiss her again, all would be well.

She could hardly be held responsible for the previous kisses he'd stolen—like the buccaneer he reminded her of, he'd surprised her, captured her and taken what he wished. This time, however, while she might unwittingly have walked into his trap, she did know it was a trap. He hadn't sprung it yet—as a virtuous lady it was clearly her duty to ensure his planning came to nought.

His kisses, and the desire behind them, were far from innocent; she could not, in all conscience, indulge in such scandalous dalliance.

Which made her role very clear—circumspection, caution, and unassailable virtue. She headed back to the rug, repeating that litany. The sight of the repast he'd unpacked—the two wineglasses, the champagne, cool in a white linen shroud, the delicacies designed to tempt a lady's palate—all bore testimony to his intent. She narrowed her eyes at him. "You planned this."

Lounging on the rug, Devil raised his brows. "Of course—what else?"

He caught her hand and gently tugged; she had no choice but to sink, gracefully, onto the other half of the rug. She was careful to keep the basket between them. "You didn't even know I was going to join you."

His answer was a single raised brow and a look so outrageously patronizing she was literally lost for words.

He grinned. "Here." He reached into the basket. "Have a chicken leg."

Honoria drew in a deep breath. She looked at the portion he held out, the bone wrapped neatly in a napkin—then reached out, took it, and sank her teeth into it.

To her relief, he made no effort to converse. She shot a glance his way. He lay stretched on the rug, propped on one elbow as he worked steadily through the basket. Honoria took a long draft of champagne—and focused on distracting them both.

"Why," she asked, "did Tolly come by way of St. Ives rather than Cambridge? If he wanted to see you, why didn't he come by the faster route?"

Devil shrugged. "All of us travel via St. Ives."

"For obvious reasons?"

He grinned. "We do, of course, feel a certain link with the town." He caught Honoria's eye. "One of my ancestors built the bridge-chapel, after all."

The chapel she had entirely forgotten to demand a glimpse of. Honoria humphed. "As a penance, no doubt."

"Presumably." Devil sipped his champagne.

Honoria returned to her cogitations. "When did Charles arrive at the Place?"

"I don't know—Vane said he was there when he arrived, late that evening, just before the worst of the storm."

Honoria frowned. "If Charles followed Tolly from town, why didn't he come upon us in the lane?"

"Charles wouldn't come that way."

"I thought all Cynsters travel via St. Ives?"

"All except Charles." Sitting up, Devil started to repack the basket. He glanced at Honoria, then reached for her glass. He drained it in one gulp. "Charles, in case you hadn't noticed, is not really one of the pack."

Pack—a good word to describe them, the Cynster pack of wolves. "He does seem . . ." leaning on one arm, Honoria gestured, "in something of a different mold."

Devil shrugged. "He takes after his mother in looks *and* in disposition. Barely a Cynster trait to be discerned."

"Hmm." Honoria settled more comfortably, a warm glow spreading through her. "When did his mother die?"

"Twenty or so years ago."

"So your uncle remarried almost immediately?"

The basket repacked, Devil stretched out, crossed his arms behind his head, closed his eyes—and watched Honoria through his lashes. "Uncle Arthur's first marriage was little short of a disaster. Almira Butterworth did what no other has in the history of the family—she trapped a Cynster into marriage, much good did it do her. After twelve years of marital discord, she died of consumption—Arthur married Louise a bare year later."

"So how would Charles, not being a dyed-in-the-wool Cynster, have come to the Place? Did he drive?"

"He doesn't drive—don't ask me why. He always comes via Cambridge, hires a horse, then comes riding up the main drive. He once said something about a master always coming to the front door, rather than the back."

Charles, Honoria decided, sounded as insufferable as she'd thought him. "So it's unlikely he saw anything?"

"He said he didn't see anyone about."

Honoria tried to think, but could find no focus for further questions. It was pleasant in the sunshine. Her parasol lay furled in the grass beside her; she should open it, but could not summon the strength. A deliciously warm, relaxed sense of peace pervaded her—she was loath to break the spell.

Glancing at Devil, she noted his closed eyes, black lashes feathering his high cheekbones. Briefly, she let her gaze skim his long frame, conscious, as always, of the deep tug she'd never previously experienced, never felt for any other man. A *frisson* of pure excitement, it heightened every sense, sensitized every nerve, and set her pulse racing. Simultaneously, at some fundamental level, it drew her like a magnet, a potent attraction all too hard to deny. Every instinct she possessed screamed he was dangerous—specifically dangerous to her. Perversely, those self-same instincts insisted that with him, she was safe. Was it any wonder she felt giddy?

Yet the last was as true as the first. Not even Michael eased her mind to the same degree nor conveyed the same certainty of inviolable protection. The devil might be a tyrant, an autocrat supreme, yet he was also to be relied on, predictable in many ways, rigid in his honor.

Her eyes once more on his face, Honoria drew in a slow breath. He was dangerous indeed, but the basket sat, large and cumbersome between them. Lips gently curving, she looked away, into the soft haze of the early afternoon to the green fields of his domain.

No field came close to the pale, clear green of his eyes.

She'd reached that conclusion when the horizon abruptly fell, leaving her flat on her back, gazing up at the cloudless sky. An instant later, half the sky vanished, replaced by a black mane, hard, angular features and a pair of eyes that saw far too much. And a pair of long, mobile lips, their contours reflecting the same laughing triumph she could see in his green eyes.

The basket was no longer between them. Nothing was.

Honoria's breath caught—her gaze locked on his. Her heart thudded wildly; an uncharacteristic panic streaked through her. Could he read minds? It seemed that he could—the green gaze grew more intense, the line of his lips deepened. Then his lids lowered; slowly, deliberately, he bent his head.

Anticipation rose, an insidious temptation, stealing through her, unlocking her defenses. Honoria felt the fever rise, felt the longing grow. Each time he kissed her, it waxed stronger, more willful, harder to deny. She felt herself sinking under its influence, her lips softening. "No." The word was a whisper—all she could manage. Her heartbeat filled her; her pulse all but deafened her.

He heard her and stopped, eyes glinting from under heavy lids. "Why not?" His brows quirked—his smile grew as he searched her eyes, her face. "You like it when I kiss you, Honoria Prudence."

Her name, uttered in his deep, velvety dark voice, the 'r's gently rolled, was a sensual caress. Honoria struggled to hold back a shiver—she lost the fight when he raised one finger and traced her lower lip.

"You like my kisses—and I like kissing you. Why deny ourselves such innocent pleasure?"

Innocent? Honoria's eyes widened—she might be safe with him, but his notion of safety and hers were not the same. "Ah . . . that's not the point."

The curve of his lips deepened. "Which point is that?"

She hadn't the faintest idea. Honoria blinked blankly up at him—and saw his pirate's smile flash. His head swooped—his lips covered hers.

This time, she ought to struggle. The thought flashed into her mind—and was lost in the same instant, as anticipation exploded and wiped her mental slate clean. Further thought was beyond her; his kiss connected with some other being—a sensual, sensate being—hidden deep inside her. It was that being who reveled in the long-drawn caress, in the hard pressure of his lips on hers, that being who opened her lips, brazenly inviting him beyond, to taste, to sample, to plunder to his heart's content.

Other than through his lips, and the long fingers that framed her face, he did not touch her, yet she was surrounded by his strength, by his will, bent like a reed to his passion. Her body— skin, quivering flesh, even her bones—was achingly aware of him—of his strength, of the tense, sharply defined muscles mere inches away, of the hardness to match her melting softness.

Their lips melded, their tongues twined, sliding sensuously together. The kiss was as heady as the fine wine they'd drunk, as warm as the sunshine about them. He shifted, leaning over her as he deepened the kiss; Honoria tasted his desire. The compulsion to feed his hunger rose, flaring like a fever, an impetus steadily growing with each deep beat of her heart, a driving need to twine her arms about him, about his shoulders, his neck—to run her fingers through his thick hair. Her fingers literally itched. One hand had fallen on his upper arm, the other on his shoulder; clinging to caution, she flexed her fingers, sinking them deep in a desperate bid to deny the urge to touch, to feel, to explore.

Instead, the steely feel of him, harder than she'd imagined, something akin to warm resilient rock, seduced her; caught by her discovery, she flexed her fingers again, enthralled when his muscles shifted beneath her hands.

Immediately, his lips hardened; in a heartbeat, their kiss changed from merely hungry to ravenous. He was closer, his weight tantalizingly near yet not upon her; Honoria's senses leapt. Their lips parted; she hauled in a gasping breath. Before she could open her eyes, he took her mouth again, commanding, demanding, ravaging her senses.

His hand closed over her breast.

The shock of his touch, of the sliding caress of long, strong fingers, was muted by the cambric of her carriage dress. There was nothing to mute the shock of her reaction—like lightning it speared through her, incandescent fire arcing through her veins. Beneath his hand, her breast swelled; her nipple had tightened to a firm bud even before his fingers found it. Honoria tried to gasp, but he was still kissing her; in desperation, she took her breath from him—and discovered that she could.

His fingers stroked, gently kneaded, and her abandoned senses sang. While the warmth of his caresses spread through her, heating her, heightening the melting sensation deep inside, Honoria mastered the art of breathing through their kiss—suddenly, she was no longer so giddy.

Suddenly she could think enough to know what she felt. Enough to appreciate the quivering excitement that held her, the thrill of anticipation that invested every nerve, every square inch of her skin. Enough to recognize the desire that thrummed heavily in her veins—the compulsion to actively return his kiss, to draw his hard body to hers, to invite, incite—do whatever she could—to quench and fill the molten void within her.

The knowledge rocked her, shocked her—and gave her the strength to draw back.

Devil sensed her withdrawal. Beneath his hand, her breast was hot and swollen, the furled bud of her nipple a hard button against his palm. Yet her retreat was obvious—in their kiss, in the sudden sinking of her senses. He knew women too well, too thoroughly, to miss the battle she waged—the battle to block her own inclination, to suppress the desire that had welled within her in answer to his need.

Inwardly, he cursed; she was causing him no end of pain. He was sorely tempted to open her bodice and slide his hand in—to show her what that would do to her, what more there was yet to come. But her innocence was a cross he'd steeled himself to bear—the knowledge that he would be the one to school her in love's ways, the only man she would ever know intimately, was a powerful inducement.

She was no prude—she was attracted to him at a level so deep it excited him just to know it. She was ripe for seduction, by him; she would be his—his wife—there was no way he'd let her escape him. Raising his head, he watched as her lids fluttered, then rose, revealing misty grey eyes still silvered with passion. He trapped her gaze. "I should warn you that I've made myself four promises."

His voice, deepened by passion, gravelly with frustration, rumbled between them. Honoria blinked dazedly; Devil suppressed a feral grin. "I'm going to enjoy watching your face the first time I pleasure you." Dipping his head, he brushed her lips with his. "And the second and third time as well."

He drew back—Honoria's eyes were wide, startled. "Pleasure . . . ?"

"When I make that molten heat inside you explode."

"*Explode?*"

"In a cataclysmic starburst." Devil tightened the fingers that still lay about her breast, then let them slide in a languid caress, his thumb circling her ruched nipple. A quivering shiver raced through her. Deliberately, he caught her eye. "Trust me—I know all about it."

She searched his eyes, her own widening; suddenly, she drew a breath.

"And," Devil said, bending to taste her lips again, cutting off whatever she'd thought to say, "my fourth promise will be the culminating event."

He drew back and watched her debate her next move; eventually, she cleared her throat and asked: "What else have you promised yourself?"

Devil's face hardened. "That I'll be watching your face as I fill you, as you take me inside you, as you give yourself to me."

Honoria stilled—it took all her strength to suppress her reaction, a flaring impulse to passion and possession, a lancing desire so thrillingly vital, so compelling it literally stole her breath. The unexpected insight—into herself, into what might be—was shocking. Most shocking of all was the fact it didn't scare her. But she knew where her future lay—it couldn't be with him. Her eyes locked on his, she shook her head. "It won't happen. I'm not marrying you."

She pushed against him; he hesitated, then drew back, letting her sit up. The instant she did, his fingers closed about her chin; he turned her to face him. "Why not?"

Honoria looked into his narrowed eyes, then haughtily lifted her chin from his hold. "I have my reasons."

"Which are?"

She shot him a resigned glance. "Because you are who you are for a start."

His frown turned black. "What's that supposed to mean?"

Honoria struggled to her feet—instantly, his hand was there to help. He followed her up. She bent and picked up the rug. "You're a tyrant, an unmitigated autocrat, utterly used to your own way. But that's beside the point." The folded rug in her arms, she faced him. "I have no ambition to wed—not you, not any man."

She met his gaze and held it; he continued to frown. "Why not?" The demand, this time, was less aggressive.

Honoria swiped up her parasol and started toward the curricle. "My reason is my own and not one I need share with you." He was a duke—dukes required heirs. Reaching the curricle, she glanced back—basket in hand, he was trailing in her wake, his expression frowningly intent. When he stopped in front of her, she looked him in the eye. "Please understand, I *won't* change my mind."

He held her gaze for an instant, then he reached for the rug, tossed it into the boot, and swung the basket after it. Letting down the flap, he followed her to the side of the carriage. Honoria turned and waited; she caught her breath as his hands slid about her waist.

They firmed, but he didn't lift her. Suddenly breathless, Honoria looked up—into crystal green eyes that belonged to a conqueror.

He held her, held her gaze, for a full minute, before saying: "We have a standoff, it seems, Honoria Prudence."

Honoria attempted a look of hauteur. "Indeed?"

His lips lengthened, compressed to a line. "Indeed—for I have *no intention* of changing my mind, either."

For one finite instant, Honoria met his gaze, then she raised her brows and looked away.

Jaw clenched, Devil lifted her to the carriage seat, then followed her up. A minute later, they were back on the road; he let his horses have their heads, the whipping wind soothing his overheated brain. Possessiveness had never gripped him so hard, never sunk its talons so deep. Fate had given her to him, to have and to hold. He would have her—take her to wife—there was no alternative.

She had a reason, she said—one she wouldn't tell him. So he'd find out and eradicate it. It was that or go mad.

Chapter 9

"Yes?" Devil looked up from a ledger as Webster entered the library.

"Chatham just rode in, Your Grace—the gentleman you were expecting is waiting as directed."

"Good." Shutting the ledger, Devil stood. "Where is Miss Anstruther-Wetherby?"

"I believe she's in the rose garden, Your Grace."

"Excellent." Devil headed for the door. "I'm going riding, Webster. I'll be back in an hour with our guest."

"Very good, Your Grace."

Two grooms ran up as Devil strode into the stable yard. "Saddle up the bay and get Melton to saddle Sulieman."

"Ah—we've not sighted Melton since early, Y'r Grace."

Devil raised his eyes to the skies. "Never mind—I'll get Sulieman. You fig out the bay."

When he led Sulieman into the yard, the bay was waiting. Mounting, Devil accepted the bay's reins and rode out. Six days had passed since Honoria had dispatched her summons to her brother.

Cresting a low rise, he saw a carriage halted in the road ahead, one of his grooms chatting to the coachman. Beside the carriage, a gentleman paced impatiently. Devil's eyes narrowed, then he sent Sulieman down the road.

The gentleman glanced up at the sound of hooves. He straightened, head rising, chin tilting to an angle Devil recognized instantly. Drawing rein, he raised a brow. "Michael Anstruther-Wetherby, I presume?"

The answering nod was curt. "St. Ives."

Michael Anstruther-Wetherby was in his mid-twenties, of athletic build, with the same steady assurance, the same directness, that characterized his sister. Used to sizing men up in an instant, Devil rapidly readjusted his image of his prospective brother-in-law. Honoria's smugness had painted her brother as weaker than she, perhaps lacking the true Anstruther-Wetherby character. Yet the man eyeing him straitly, challenge and skepticism very clear in his blue eyes, had a decidedly purposeful chin. Devil smiled. "I believe we have matters to discuss. I suggest we take a ride beyond the reach of interruptions."

The blue eyes, arrested, held his, then Michael nodded. "An excellent idea." He reached for the bay's reins, then he was in the saddle. "If you can *guarantee* no interruptions, you'll have achieved a first."

Devil grinned, and set course for a nearby hillock. He halted on the crest; Michael drew up alongside. Devil glanced his way. "I've no idea what Honoria wrote, so I'll start at the beginning."

Michael nodded. "That might be wise."

Gazing over his fields, Devil outlined the events leading to Honoria's presence at the Place. "So," he concluded, "I've suggested that getting married is appropriate."

"To you?"

Devil's brows flew. "Whom else did you have in mind?"

"Just checking." Michael's grin surfaced briefly, then he sobered. "But if that's the case, why have I been summoned to escort her to Hampshire?"

"Because," Devil replied, "your sister imagines she's so long in the tooth that a reputation is neither here nor there. She plans to be the next Hester Stanhope."

"Oh, lord!" Michael cast his eyes heavenward. "She's not *still* set on Africa, is she?"

"It's her dearest wish, so I've been informed, to ride in the shadow of the Sphinx, pursued, no doubt, by a horde of Berber chieftains, then to fall victim to Barbary Coast slave traders. I understand she believes she's starved of excitement and the only way she'll get any is to brave the wilds of Africa."

Michael looked disgusted. "I'd hoped she'd grown out of that by now. Or that some gentleman would appear and give her mind a new direction."

"As to the first, I suspect she'll grow more determined with age—she is, after all, an Anstruther-Wetherby, a family renowned for its stubbornness. But as to giving her mind a new direction, I already have that in hand."

Michael looked up. "Has she agreed to marry you?"

"Not yet." Devil's expression hardened. "But she will."

There was an instant's silence, then Michael asked: "Free of any coercion?"

Devil's eyes met his; one brow lifted superciliously. "Naturally."

Michael studied Devil's eyes, then his features relaxed. He looked out over the fields; Devil waited patiently. Eventually, Michael looked his way. "I'll admit I would be glad to see Honoria safely wed, especially to a man of your standing. I won't oppose the match—I'll support it however I can. But I won't agree to pressure her into any decision."

Devil inclined his head. "Aside from anything else your sister is hardly a biddable female."

"As you say." Michael's gaze turned shrewd. "So what do you want of me?"

Devil grinned. "My brand of persuasion doesn't work well at a distance. I need Honoria to remain within reach." With a gesture, he indicated that they should ride on, and touched his heels to Sulieman's flanks.

Michael cantered alongside. "If Honoria's set on returning home, I'll need some reason to gainsay her."

Devil shot him a glance. "Is she her own mistress?"

"Until she's twenty-five, she's in my care."

"In that case," Devil said, "I have a plan."

By the time they cantered into the stable yard, Michael was entirely comfortable with his brother-in-law to be. It appeared that his sister, usually an irresistible force, had finally met a sufficiently immovable object. He matched his stride to Devil's as they headed for the house.

"Tell me," Devil said, his gaze roving the house, checking

for impending interruptions. "Has she always been frightened of storms?"

He glanced at Michael in time to see him wince.

"They still make her twitch?"

Devil frowned. "Rather more than that."

Michael sighed. "Hardly surprising, I suppose—I still get edgy myself."

"Why?"

Michael met his eyes. "She told you our parents were killed in a carriage accident?"

Devil searched his memory. "That they were killed in an accident."

"There was rather more to it than that." Michael drew a deep breath. "Neither Honoria nor I are frightened of storms— at least, we weren't. On that day, our parents took the other two for a drive."

"*Other* two?" Devil slowed his pace.

Michael looked up. "Meg and Jemmy. Our brother and sister." Devil halted, his expression blank. Michael stopped and faced him. "She didn't tell you about them?"

Devil shook his head; abruptly, he focused on Michael. "Tell me exactly what happened."

Michael looked away, across the lawns toward the house. "The pater wanted to take Mama for a drive—it started as a lovely day. Mama had been ill—she was going through one of her better patches—Papa wanted her to get some air. The little ones went with them. Honoria and I stayed home—we couldn't fit and we both had studies to attend to. Then the storm blew up—raced in out of nowhere. Honoria and I loved watching the clouds roll in. We ran up to the schoolroom to watch."

He paused, his gaze distant, fixed in the past. "The schoolroom was in the attics, overlooking the drive. We stood at the window and looked out. We never dreamed . . ." He swallowed. "We were laughing and joking, listening for the thunder, trying to spot the flashes. Then there was a massive crash overhead. In the same instant, we saw the curricle come racing up the drive. The children were frantic, clinging to Mama. The horses had panicked—Papa had his hands full managing them." He paused. "I can see them so clearly, even now. Then the lightning struck."

When he said nothing more, Devil prompted: "The carriage?"

Michael shook his head. "The bolt hit a huge elm beside the drive. It fell." Again he paused, then, drawing a deep breath, went on: "We watched it fall. The others didn't see it at first—then they did." He shuddered. "I closed my eyes, but I don't think Honoria did. She saw it all."

Devil gave him a moment, then asked: "They were killed?"

"Instantly." Michael drew a shaky breath. "I can still hear the horses screaming. We had to put them down."

Very gently, Devil said: "Go back—what happened to Honoria?"

Michael blinked. "Honoria? When I opened my eyes, she was standing, absolutely still, before the window. Then she stretched out her hands and stepped forward. I grabbed her and pulled her away. She clung to me then." He shivered. "That's the one thing I remember most vividly—how she cried. She made no sound—the tears just rolled down her cheeks, as if her sorrow was so deep she couldn't even sob." After a pause, he added: "I don't think I'll ever forget how *helpless* her crying made me feel."

Devil didn't think he'd ever forget either.

Shoulders lifting on a deep breath, Michael glanced fully at Devil. "That's the sum of it—we sorted things out and got on with our lives. Of course, the loss was worse for Honoria." He fell in beside Devil as they continued toward the house. "As Mama had been so ill, Honoria had become more mother than sister to the younger two. Losing them was like losing her own children, I think."

Devil was silent as they crossed the last of the lawn; he glanced up as they neared the portico, briefly studying the inscription on its facade. Then he glanced at Michael. "You need a drink."

He needed one, too. Then he needed to think.

Honoria was descending the main staircase, a frown puckering her brows, when the front door opened and her brother walked in.

"Michael!" Face clearing, she hurried down. "I've been expecting you for hours." Hugging him, she returned his affectionate buss. "I saw a carriage arrive and thought it must be you, but no one came in. I was wondering—" She broke off as a large shadow darkened the doorway.

Michael looked over his shoulder. "St. Ives was good enough to meet me. He's explained the situation."

"He *has*? I mean—" Her gaze trapped in crystal green, Honoria fought the urge to gnash her teeth. "How very helpful." She noted Devil's expression of guileless innocence—it sat very ill on his piratical features.

"You're looking well." Michael scanned her amethyst morning gown. "Not browbeaten at all."

Even with her gaze firmly fixed on her brother's teasing face, Honoria was aware of Devil's raised brow—and of the color that seeped into her cheeks. Tilting her chin, she linked her arm in Michael's. "Come and meet the Dowager." She steered him toward the drawing room. "Then we'll go for a walk in the grounds." So she could set the record straight.

To her chagrin, Devil strolled after them.

The Dowager looked up as they entered. With a brilliant smile, she laid aside her embroidery and held out her hand. "Mr. Anstruther-Wetherby—it is good to meet you at last. I trust your journey was without mishap?"

"Entirely, ma'am." Michael bowed over her hand. "It's indeed a pleasure to make your acquaintance."

"*Bon!*" The Dowager beamed at him. "And now we can be comfortable and talk, can we not?" Indicating the *chaise* beside her, she glanced at Devil. "Ring for tea, Sylvester. Now, Mr. Anstruther-Wetherby, you are with Carlisle, is that right? And how is the good Marguerite?"

Subsiding into an armchair, Honoria watched as her brother, who she could have sworn was impervious to all forms of flattery, fell under the Dowager's fire. Even more disturbing, time and again, she saw Michael exchange a glance with Devil; by the time Webster brought in the tea, it was clear that, somehow, Devil had succeeded in securing her brother's approval. Honoria bit into a cucumber sandwich and tried not to glower.

She dragged her brother from mother and son's seductive influence as soon as she possibly could.

"Let's go down by the lake." Tightening her hold on Michael's arm, she steered him along the terrace. "There's a seat, near the shore—it's peaceful and private there."

"It's a truly magnificent house," was Michael's only comment as they strolled down the lawn. They reached the seat, and she settled herself upon it; Michael hesitated, looking down at her, then sat beside her. "You could be very comfortable here, you know."

Honoria met his gaze levelly. "Just what has that devil told you?"

Michael grinned. "Not all that much—just the bare facts."

Honoria drew a relieved breath. "In that case, it should be clear that there's no need for any talk of marriage between myself and St. Ives."

Michael's brows rose. "Actually, that's not the impression I received."

"Oh?" Honoria made the syllable a challenge.

Michael tugged at his earlobe. "Perhaps we'd better retread events."

She was very ready to do so. While she recited her well-rehearsed version of events, Michael listened intently. "And then he left me with the Dowager," she concluded.

Michael met her eye. "That's what he told me."

Honoria had a premonition she'd just taken a wrong step.

Michael straightened, one hand clasping hers. "Honoria, you're an unmarried lady of twenty-four, of impeccable lineage and unblemished reputation. In this instance, I must agree with St. Ives—there's really no course open to you other than to accept his offer. He's behaved precisely as he should—no one could hold either of you to blame, yet the circumstances remain and require the prescribed response."

"No." Honoria made the word a statement. "You can't seriously imagine me happily married to Devil Cynster."

Michael raised his brows. "Actually, I find that easier to imagine than any other outcome."

"*Michael*! He's a tyrant! An unmitigatingly arrogant *despot*."

Michael shrugged. "You can't have everything, as Mama was wont to tell you."

Honoria narrowed her eyes; she let a pregnant moment pass

before stating, categorically: "Michael, I do not wish to marry Devil Cynster."

Letting go of her hand, Michael leaned back against the seat. "So what do you see as an alternative?"

Honoria knew relief—at least they were *discussing* alternatives. "I'd thought to return to Hampshire—it's too late to get another post this year."

"You'll never get another post, not once this gets out. And it will. St. Ives is right about that—if you marry him, the only whispers will be jealous ones; without his ring on your finger, they'll be malicious. Destructively so."

Honoria shrugged. "That's hardly a disaster. As you know, I care little for society."

"True." Michael hesitated, then added: "You might, however, have a care for our name, and our parents' memory."

Slowly, Honoria turned to face him, her eyes very narrow. "*That* was uncalled for."

His expression stern, Michael shook his head. "No—it had to be said. You cannot simply walk away from who you are and the fact that you have family connections together with the responsibility that entails."

Honoria felt chilled inside, like a general informed he'd just lost his last ally. "So," she said, haughtily tilting her chin, "you would have me marry for the sake of the family—for the sake of a name I've never claimed?"

"I would see you wed first and foremost for your *own* sake. There's no future for you in Hampshire, or anywhere else for that matter. Look about you." He gestured to the sprawling bulk of the Place, displayed like a jewel in the grounds before them. "Here you could be what you were supposed to be. You could be what Papa and Mama always *intended* you to be."

Honoria pressed her lips tightly together. "I cannot live my life according to the precepts of ghosts."

"No—but you should consider the reasons behind their precepts. They may be dead, but the reasons remain."

When she said no more but sat mulishly looking down at her clasped hands, Michael continued, his tone more gentle: "I daresay this may sound pompous, but I've seen more of our world than you—that's why I'm so sure the course I urge you to is right."

Honoria shot him an irate glance. "I am *not* a child—"

"No." Michael grinned. "If you were, this situation wouldn't exist. *But—!*" he insisted, as she opened her mouth to retort, "just hold on to your temper and listen to what I have to say before you set your mind in stone."

Honoria met his eyes. "I only have to listen?"

Michael nodded. "To the proposition St. Ives put to me—and the reasons why I think you should agree to it."

Honoria's jaw fell. "You discussed *me* with *him*?"

Michael closed his eyes for an instant, then fixed her with a distinctly male look. "Honoria, it was necessary he and I talked. We've both lived in society much longer than you—you've never done more than stick a toe in society's sea. That's a point St. Ives, thank heavens, is aware of—it's that that's behind his proposition."

Honoria glared. "*Proposition*? I thought it was a proposal."

Michael closed his eyes tight. "His proposal's on the table and will remain there until you make your decision!" He opened his eyes. "His proposition concerns how we should go on until you do."

"Oh." Faced with his exasperation, Honoria shifted, then looked across the lake. "So what is this proposition?"

Michael drew a deep breath. "Because of his cousin's death, a wedding could not be held inside three months—the Dowager will be in full mourning for six weeks, then half-mourning for another six. As you have no suitable family with whom to reside, what would normally occur is that you would remain with the Dowager and she would introduce you to the *ton* as her son's fiancée."

"But I haven't agreed to marry him."

"No—so in this case, you'll simply remain under the Dowager's wing. She intends going to London in a few weeks—you'll go with her and she'll introduce you to the *ton*. That will give you a chance to see society from a perspective you've never had—if, after that, you still wish to refuse St. Ives's offer, he and I will accept your decision and *try* to come up with some acceptable alternative."

His emphasis made it clear he did not expect to find one. Honoria frowned. "What explanation will be given for my presence with the Dowager?"

"None—Cynsters don't need to tender explanations any more than Anstruther-Wetherbys."

Honoria looked skeptical. "Surely people will wonder?"

"People will *know*, of that you may be sure. However, given the Dowager's involvement, they'll imagine an announcement is in the offing and comport themselves appropriately." Michael grimaced. "I should warn you, the Dowager is something of a force to be reckoned with."

Honoria raised a questioning brow.

Michael waved at the house. "You saw her just now. She's a consummate manipulator."

Honoria's lips twitched. "I had wondered whether you'd noticed."

"I noticed, but there's precious little point trying to resist. You called St. Ives a tyrant—I don't doubt he is, but that's probably just as well. Within the *ton*, his mother's considered a holy terror—of inestimable help if her sympathies lie with you, an enemy to be feared if they don't. No one's going to invite her ire by circulating possibly groundless rumors concerning her son and the lady who might be his duchess. There's no safer place for you than under the Dowager's wing."

Honoria could see it; slowly, she nodded, then looked frowningly at Michael. "I still think it would be much simpler for me to retire to Hampshire until all this blows over. Even if I don't get another post, as you pointed out, I *am* twenty-four. It's time I started on my travel plans."

Michael sighed, and looked away. "You can't stay in Hampshire alone—we'll have to get Aunt Hattie down."

"*Aunt Hattie?*" Honoria wrinkled her nose. "She'll drive me distracted inside of a week."

Michael pursed his lips. "Can't think of anyone else, and you can't live alone, especially once your sojourn in the woods with Devil Cynster becomes public. You'll find yourself dealing with all manner of unwanted visitors."

Honoria shot him a darkling glance, then frowned, very hard, at the lake. Michael preserved a stoic silence.

Minutes ticked past; eyes narrowed, Honoria reviewed her options. She had, indeed, regretted sending for Michael so precipitously; it was clearly going to take time to track Tolly's murderer down. Devil, initially a large hurdle to her plans, had been overcome; he now behaved as a reluctant but resigned coconspirator. The idea of them, together, unmasking Tolly's killer was attractive—quite aside from the compulsion she felt to see justice done, the situation looked set to provide the excitement she'd craved all her life. Leaving now would see all that lost.

There was also the small matter of her burgeoning desire to experience—just once—the pleasure Devil had alluded to. His words, his caresses, like Tolly's face, now haunted her. He'd made it clear physical possession and pleasure were independent events—although the thought was guaranteed to bring a blush to her cheek, she was aware of an increasing compulsion to learn what he could teach her. Of pleasure. Possession, in this case, was out of the question, beyond all possibility. Cynsters never let go anything that became theirs—she was far too wise to become his on any level.

Given she'd determined never to wed, her virtue would never be in question. It seemed wise to gain some experience of the pleasure possible between a man and a woman *before* she set off on her travels. And there was no denying the pleasure she'd thus far experienced at Devil Cynster's hands had held an excitement all its own.

With all that on offer, currently on her plate, but for Devil's matrimonial fixation, her present situation suited her admirably. She didn't *want* to go to Hampshire but with him so set on marriage, it hadn't seemed possible to stay.

Now, however, with his devilish proposition, the devil himself had cleared her path. She could remain in his household, in his mother's care, safe from him and any other gentleman, for three full months—surely, by that time, they would have laid Tolly's murderer by the heels? And she would have learned all she'd need to know of pleasure.

Which left only one quibble—was she strong enough, clever enough, to avoid any traps Devil might set for her?

Honoria straightened, and summoned a resigned grimace. "Very well." She turned and met Michael's eye. "I'll agree to remain under the Dowager's wing for three months." Michael grinned—Honoria narrowed her eyes. "After that, I'll go to Hampshire."

With a long-suffering groan, Michael rose and drew her to her feet. Arm in arm, they strolled back to the house.

Later that evening, Honoria was seated in an armchair in the drawing room, her lap full of embroidery silks, when a shadow fell across her. The Dowager was on the *chaise*, similarly occupied in sorting brilliant hanks. Michael, pleading tiredness, had retired early; Devil had retreated to the library. The tea trolley had come and gone; the evening had slipped silently into night.

Stymied in her attempt to discriminate between azure and turquoise, Honoria looked up—all the way up to Devil's face. He stood directly before her, his expression inscrutable. For a long moment, he simply held her gaze, his own shadowed, impossible to read. Then he held out his hand. "Come for a walk, Honoria Prudence."

From the corner of her eye, Honoria noted that the Dowager had been struck deaf.

Devil's lips softened fleetingly; his gaze remained intense, focused on her face. "I promise not to bite."

Honoria considered the pros and cons—she needed to talk to him, to make sure, while Michael was still here, that their bargain—his proposition—was precisely as she thought. She searched his face. "Not to the summerhouse." She might wish to learn more of pleasure, but she wanted the lessons under her control.

This time, his pirate's smile materialized fully if briefly. "Only on the terrace—I wouldn't want to distract you."

Honoria quelled an incipient shiver, elicited by the deep purring tones of his voice, and shot him a disbelieving glance.

He raised his brows resignedly. "Word of a Cynster."

And in that she could trust. Gathering her silks, Honoria set them aside, then placed her hand in his. He drew her to her feet, then settled her hand on his arm. The Dowager ignored them, apparently absorbed in lilac silks to the exclusion of all else. They strolled to where long windows stood open to the terrace, the night a curtain of black velvet beyond.

"I wished to speak to you," Honoria began the instant they gained the flags.

"And I to you." Looking down at her, Devil paused.

Regally, Honoria inclined her head, inviting his comment.

"Michael has informed me you've agreed to remain with my mother for the next three months."

Reaching the balustrade, Honoria lifted her hand from his sleeve and swung to face him. "Until the period of mourning is over."

"After which time, you'll become my duchess."

She tilted her chin. "After which time, I'll return to Hampshire."

He'd halted directly before her, no more than a foot away. With the light behind him, it was all she could do to discern his expression—arrogantly impassive; his eyes, hooded and shadowed, fixed on hers, she couldn't read at all. Honoria kept her head high, her gaze unwavering, determined to impress on him how inflexible she was.

The moment stretched—and stretched; she started to feel light-headed. Then one of his brows rose.

"We appear to have a problem, Honoria Prudence."

"Only in your mind, Your Grace."

The planes of his face shifted; his expression held a warning. "Perhaps," he said, exasperation clear beneath the polite form, "*before* we decide what will occur at the end of the three months, we should agree on the three months themselves?"

Haughtily, Honoria raised her brows. "I've agreed to remain with your mother."

"And seriously consider my proposal."

The message in his tone was unmistakable—a bargain, or no deal. Drawing in a quick breath, she nodded. "And seriously consider the prospect of becoming your wife. I should, however, inform you that I am unlikely to change my stance on that matter."

"In other words, you're bone stubborn—and I have three months to change your mind."

She did not at all like the way he said that. "I am not a vacillating female—I have no intention of changing my mind."

His teeth flashed in his pirate's smile. "You've yet to experience my powers of persuasion."

Honoria shrugged; nose in the air, she shifted her gaze beyond his shoulder. "You may persuade away—I *won't* be marrying, you or anyone."

Again, silence was his ally, slowly stretching her nerves taut.

She nearly jumped when hard fingertips slid beneath her chin, turning her face back to him.

Even in the dark she could sense the piercing quality of his gaze. feel its potency. "Women have been known, on occasion, to change their minds." He spoke slowly, softly, his tones deep and purring. "How much of a woman are you, Honoria Prudence?"

Honoria felt her eyes widen. His fingertips slid across the sensitive skin beneath her chin; sharp slivers of sensation shivered through her. Her lungs had seized; it took considerable effort to lift her chin free of his touch. Haughtily, she stated: "I'm too wise to play with fire, Your Grace."

"Indeed?" His lips curved. "I thought you wanted excitement in your life?"

"On *my* terms."

"In that case, my dear, we'll have to negotiate."

"Indeed?" Honoria tried for airy nonchalance. "Why so?"

"Because you're shortly to become my duchess—that's why."

The glance she bent on him held every ounce of exasperation she could summon, then, with a swish of her skirts, she turned and stepped out of his shadow, following the balustrade. "I've warned you—don't later say I haven't. I am *not* going to marry you at the end of three months." She paused, then, head rising; eyes widening, she swung back and waved a finger at him. "And I am *not* a challenge—don't you *dare* view me as such."

His laughter was that of a pirate—a buccaneer, a swashbuckling rogue who should have been safely on a deck in the middle of some ocean—nowhere near her. The sound, deep, rolling, and far too sure, held a threat and a promise; it enveloped her, caught her up, and held her—then he was there, before her once more.

"You are challenge personified, Honoria Prudence."

"*You* are riding for a fall, Your Grace."

"I'll be riding you before Christmas."

The deliberate reference shocked Honoria, but she wasn't about to let it show. Keeping her chin high, she narrowed her eyes. "You aren't, by any chance, imagining you're going to seduce me into marriage?"

One arrogant black brow rose. "The thought had crossed my mind."

"Well it won't work." When his second brow joined the first, Honoria smiled, supremely confident. "I cut my eyeteeth long ago—I know perfectly well you won't press me while I'm residing under your roof, in your mother's care."

For a long moment, he held her gaze. Then he asked: "How much do you know of seduction?"

It was Honoria's turn to raise her brows. Taking another step along the terrace, she shrugged lightly. "You won't be the first to try it."

"Possibly not, but I'll be the first to succeed."

Honoria sighed. "You won't, you know." Glancing up, she saw him frown. She narrowed her eyes. "*Succeed*, I mean." The frown disappeared. He paced slowly beside her as she strolled the flags. "I know you won't force me—I'll simply call your bluff."

She felt his glance; oddly, it was less intense, less disturbing than before. When he spoke, she detected faint amusement in his tone. "No force, no bluff." He met her gaze as she glanced up. "There's a lot you have to learn about seduction, Honoria Prudence, and this time, you'll be dealing with a master."

Honoria shook her head despairingly. Well, she'd warned him. He was so arrogantly confident it would do him good to be taken down a peg or two—to learn that not all things on this earth would meekly bow to his rule.

The evening reached chill fingers through her gown; she shivered.

Devil's hand on her arm halted her. "We should go in."

Honoria half turned—and found herself facing him. As she watched, his expression hardened; abruptly, he leaned closer. With a stifled shriek, she backed—into the balustrade. He set his hands on the stone parapet, one on either side of her, caging her between his arms.

Breathless, her heart racing, she blinked into his eyes, now level with hers. "You promised not to bite."

His expression was graven. "I haven't—yet." His eyes searched hers. "As you've been so ingenuously frank, the least I can do is return the favor—so that we understand each other fully." He held her gaze steadily; Honoria felt the full weight of his will. "I will not permit you to turn your back on who you are, on the destiny that was always intended to be yours. I will not let you turn yourself into a governessing drudge, nor an eccentric to titillate the *ton*.

Honoria's expression blanked.

Devil held her gaze ruthlessly. "You were born and bred to take a position at the head of the *ton*—that position now lies at your feet. You have three months to reconcile yourself to the reality. Don't imagine you can run from it."

Pale, inwardly quivering, Honoria wrenched her gaze from his. Turning, she yanked at his sleeve.

Letting go of the balustrade, Devil straightened, leaving her escape route clear. Honoria hesitated, then, her expression as stony as his, she turned and looked him straight in the eye. "You have *no right* to decree what my life is to be."

"I have *every* right." Devil's expression softened not at all; his gaze was mercilous. "You will be what you were meant to be—*mine*."

The emphasis he placed on that single word shook Honoria to her toes. Barely able to breathe, she walked quickly back to the drawing room, head high, skirts shushing furiously.

Chapter 10

～✦～

THREE DAYS LATER, Devil stood at the library windows, his gaze, abstracted, fixed on the summerhouse. Behind him, open ledgers littered his desk; a pile of letters begged for attention. He had a lot of unfinished business on his plate.

No trace had been found of Tolly's killer, and the simple task of securing his bride was proving remarkably complicated. The latter was more bothersome than the former—he was sure they'd eventually track Tolly's murderer down. He was also unshakably convinced Honoria would be his bride—he was simply no longer so sanguine about what state he'd be in by the wedding.

She was driving him demented. What power had goaded him into declaring his hand so forcefully, there, on the terrace in the moonlight? It had been sheer madness to act the tyrant as he had—yet he could feel the same emotion, the urge to conquer, to seize, to hold, flaring even now, simply at the thought of her.

Luckily, her stubbornness, her defiance, her unquenchable pride had forbidden her to flee before his heavy-handed declaration. She'd let Michael depart alone. Now, with her nose in the air, wrapped in a cloak of chill civility, she held him at a distance.

After learning of her past, common sense suggested he at least reconsider. Common sense stood not a chance against the deep-seated conviction that she was his. Where she was con-cerned he felt like one of his conquering ancestors preparing to lay siege to a much-desired prize. Given what he now suspected, her surrender, when it came, would need to be proclaimed from the battlements.

He'd wondered how she'd reached a succulently ripe twenty-four still unwed. Even hidden away as a governess, not all men were blind. Some must have seen her and appreciated her worth. A determination on her part to remain a spinster, childless, could, in this case, explain the inexplicable. Her stubbornness was a tangible thing.

In this case, her stubbornness would need to surrender.

He wasn't going to let her go. Ever.

At least she couldn't later say that *he* hadn't warned *her*.

His gaze, still on the summerhouse, sharpened; Devil straightened and reached for the handle of the French doors.

Honoria saw him coming; her hand froze in midair, then she looked down and resumed her stitching. Devil climbed the steps two at a time; she looked up and met his gaze squarely. Slowly, she raised her brows.

He held her gaze, then glanced at the seat beside her.

She hesitated, then carefully gathered up her strewn silks. "Did your man learn anything in Chatteris?"

Devil stared at her.

Honoria laid the silks in her basket. "I saw him ride in."

Swallowing his irritation, Devil sat beside her, angling his shoulders so he faced her. "Nothing—no horseman came by way of Chatteris." Perhaps he should grow screening hedges about the summerhouse? She'd adopted it as her lair; he could see a number of pertinent advantages.

Honoria frowned. "So that's all the towns 'round about—and no gentleman hired a horse anywhere."

"Except for Charles, who came by way of Cambridge."

"Is there any other place—a tavern, or some such—where horses might be hired?"

"My people checked all the hedge-taverns within reach. Short of borrowing a horse, something we can't rule out, it seems likely the murderer rode away on his own horse."

"I thought you said that was unlikely?"

"Unlikely but not impossible."

"The storm came up shortly after. Wouldn't he have had to take shelter?"

"The others checked all the inns and taverns on their way back to London. No likely gentleman took refuge anywhere. Whoever shot Tolly was either exceedingly lucky or he covered his tracks exceptionally well."

"Riding his own horse, he could have come from anywhere, not just London. He might have been a hired assassin."

Devil looked at her, silently, for a full minute. "Don't complicate things."

"Well, it's true. But I had *meant* to ask you . . ." She paused to snip a thread; in the silence that followed, Devil got her message. She'd meant to ask him *before* he'd acted the despot. Setting aside her shears, she continued: "Was it common knowledge that Tolly habitually took the lane through the wood?"

Devil grimaced. "Not *common* knowledge, but widespread enough to be easily learned."

Honoria set another stitch. "Have your cousins discovered anything in London?"

"No. But there must be something—some clue—somewhere. Young gentlemen don't get murdered on country lanes for no reason." He looked out across the lawns—and saw his mother approaching. With a sigh, he uncrossed his legs and stood.

"Is this where you are hiding, Sylvester?" The Dowager came up the steps in a froth of black lace. She held up her face for a kiss.

Devil dutifully obliged. "Hardly hiding, *Maman*."

"Indeed—you are a great deal too large for this place." The Dowager prodded him. "Sit—don't tower."

As she promptly took his place beside Honoria, Devil was reduced to perching on a windowsill. The Dowager glanced at Honoria's work—and pointed to one stitch. Honoria stared, then muttered unintelligibly, set down her needle, and reached for her shears.

Devil grabbed the opportunity. "I wanted to speak to you, *Maman*. I'll be leaving for London tomorrow."

"London?" The exclamation came from two throats; two heads jerked up, two pairs of eyes fixed on his face.

Devil shrugged. "Purely business."

Honoria looked at the Dowager; the Dowager looked at her.

When she turned back to her son, the Dowager was frowning. "I have been thinking, *chéri*, that I should also go up to London. Now that I have dear 'Onoria to keep me company, I think it would be quite *convenable*."

Devil blinked. "You're in mourning. Full mourning."

"So?" The Dowager opened her eyes wide. "I'll be in full mourning in London—so appropriate—it is always so grey there at this time of year."

"I had thought," Devil said, "that you would want to remain here, at least for another week or so."

The Dowager lifted her hands, palms upward. "For what? It is a little early for the balls, I grant you, but I am not suggesting we go to London for dissipation. No. It is appropriate, I think, that I introduce 'Onoria, even though the family is in black. She is not affected; I discussed it with your aunt 'Oratia— like me, she thinks the sooner the *ton* meets 'Onoria, the better."

Devil glanced, swiftly, at Honoria; the consternation in her eyes was a delight to behold. "An excellent idea, *Maman*." Silver glinted in Honoria's eyes; he hurriedly looked away. "But you'll have to be careful not to step on the tabbies' tails."

The Dowager waved dismissively. "Do not teach your mother to suck eggs. Your aunt and I will know just how to manage. Nothing too elaborate or such as will . . . how do you say it?—raise the wind?"

Devil hid his grin. "Raise a dust—the wind is money."

The Dowager frowned. "Such strange sayings you English have."

Devil forebore to remind her that she'd lived in England for most of her life—and that her grasp of the language always deteriorated when she was hatching some scheme. In this case, it was a scheme of which he approved.

"Everything will be *tout comme il faut*," the Dowager insisted. "You need not concern yourself—I know how conservative you are growing—we will do nothing to offend your sensibilities."

The comment left Devil speechless.

"Indeed, just this morning I was thinking that I should be in London, with your aunt Louise. I am the matriarch, no? And a matriarch's duty is to be with her family." The Dowager fixed

131

her undeniably matriarchal gaze on her silent son. "Your father would have wished it so."

That, of course, signaled the end to all argument—not that Devil intended arguing. Manufacturing an aggravated sigh, he held up his hands. "If that's what you truly wish, *Maman*, I'll give orders immediately. We can leave tomorrow at midday and be in town before nightfall."

"*Bon!*" The Dowager looked at Honoria. "We had best start our packing."

"Indeed." Honoria put her needlework in her basket, then glanced briefly, triumphantly, at Devil.

He kept his expression impassive, standing back as she and his mother exited the summerhouse. Only when they were well ahead did he descend the steps, strolling languorously in their wake, his gaze on Honoria's shapely curves, smug satisfaction in his eyes.

St. Ives House in Grosvenor Square was a great deal smaller than Somersham Place. It was still large enough to lose a battalion in, a fact emphasized by the odd individual of military mien who presided over it.

Honoria nodded at Sligo as she crossed the hall, and wondered at Devil Cynster's idiosyncracies. On arriving at dusk two days before, she'd been taken aback to find the stoop-shouldered, thin, and wiry Sligo acting as majordomo. He had a careworn face, moon-shaped and mournful; his attire was severe but did not quite fit. His speech was abrupt, as if he was still on a parade ground.

Later, she'd questioned the Dowager; Sligo, it transpired, had been Devil's batman at Waterloo. He was fanatically devoted to his erstwhile captain; on disbanding, he'd simply continued to follow him. Devil had made him his general factotum. Sligo remained at St. Ives House, acting as its caretaker when the family was not in residence. When his master *was* in residence, Honoria surmised, he reverted to his previous role.

Which, she suspected, meant that Sligo would bear watching. A footman opened the breakfast-parlor door.

"There you are, my dear." The Dowager beamed gloriously from one end of the elegant table.

Honoria bobbed a curtsy, then inclined her head toward the head of the table. "Your Grace."

The devil nodded back, his gaze roving over her. "I trust you slept well?" With a wave, he summoned Webster to hold a chair for her—the one beside his.

"Tolerably well, thank you." Perforce ignoring the nine other empty chairs about the immaculately laid table, Honoria settled her skirts, then thanked Webster as he poured her tea. The previous day had gone in unpacking and settling in. A rain squall had cut short the afternoon; she'd got no closer to the park in the Square than the drawing-room windows.

"I have been telling Sylvester that we plan to visit the modistes this morning." The Dowager waved a knife at her. "He tells me that these days the *ton* selects modistes by age."

"Age?" Honoria frowned.

Busy with toast and marmalade, the Dowager nodded. "Apparently, it is quite *convenable* that I continue with my old Franchot, but for you it must be . . ." She glanced at her son. "*Qu'est-ce que?*"

"Celestine," Devil supplied.

Honoria turned her frown on him.

He met her look with one of ineffable boredom. "It's simple enough—if you want bombazine and turbans, you go to Franchot. If frills and furbelows are your fancy, then Madame Abelard's is more likely to suit. For innocent country misses," he paused, his gaze briefly touching Honoria's fine lace fichu, "then I've heard Mademoiselle Cocotte is hard to beat. For true elegance, however, there's only one name you need know—Celestine."

"Indeed?" Honoria sipped her tea, then, setting down her cup, reached for the toast. "Is she on Bruton Street?"

Devil's brows flew. "Where else?" He looked away as Sligo approached, carrying a silver salver piled with letters. Taking them, Devil flicked through the stack. "I daresay you'll find any number of modistes that might take your fancy if you stroll the length of Bruton Street."

From the corner of her eye, Honoria watched him examine his mail. He employed a small army of agents; one had followed on their heels from the Place and spent all yesterday closeted with his master. Running estates as extensive as those of the dukedom of St. Ives would keep any man busy; thus far, from all she'd seen, business had prevented Devil from pursuing his investigations.

Reaching the bottom of the pile, he shuffled the letters together, then glanced at his mother. "If you'll excuse me, *Maman*." Briefly, his eyes touched Honoria's. "Honoria Prudence." With a graceful nod, he stood; absorbed with his letters, he left the room.

Honoria stared at his back until the door hid it from view, then took another sip of her tea.

The St. Ives town carriage had just rumbled around the corner, bearing the Dowager and Honoria to Bruton Street, when Vane Cynster strolled into Grosvenor Square. His stride long and ranging, he crossed the pavements; cane swinging, he climbed the steps to his cousin's imposing door. He was about to beat an imperious tattoo when the door swung inward. Sligo rushed out.

"Oh! Sorry, sir." Sligo flattened himself against the doorjamb. "Didn't see you there, sir."

Vane smiled. "That's quite all right, Sligo."

"Cap'n's orders. An urgent dispatch." Sligo tapped his breast—rustling parchment testified to his cause. "If you'll excuse me, sir?"

Released by Vane's bemused nod, Sligo hurried down the steps and ran to the corner. He flagged down a hackney and climbed aboard. Vane shook his head, then turned to the still-open door. Webster stood beside it.

"The master is in the library, sir. I believe he's expecting you. Do you wish to be announced?"

"No need." Surrendering his cane, hat and gloves, Vane headed for Devil's sanctum. He opened the door, instantly coming under his cousin's green gaze.

Devil sat in a leather chair behind a large desk, an open letter in one hand. "You're the first."

Vane grinned. "And you're impatient."

"You're not?"

Vane raised his brows. "Until a second ago, I didn't know you had no news." He crossed the room and dropped into a chair facing the desk.

"I take it you have no insights to offer either?"

Vane grimaced. "In a word—no."

Devil grimaced back; refolding his letter, he laid it aside. "I just hope the others have turned up something."

"What's Sligo up to?" When Devil looked up, Vane elaborated: "I bumped into him on the steps—he seemed in a tearing hurry."

Devil waved dismissively. "A small matter of forward strategy."

"Speaking of which, have you managed to convince your bride-to-be that investigating murder is not a suitable hobby for a gentlewoman?"

Devil smiled. "*Maman* can always be counted on to visit the modistes within forty-eight hours of arriving in town."

Vane raised his brows. "So you *haven't* succeeded in striking murder from Miss Anstruther-Wetherby's agenda?"

Devil's smile turned feral. "I'm directing my fire at a different target. Once that falls, her agenda will no longer apply."

Vane grinned. "Poor Honoria Prudence—does she know what she's up against?"

"She'll learn."

"Too late?"

"That's the general idea."

A brief rap on the door heralded the appearance of Richard "Scandal" Cynster; he was followed by Gabriel and Demon Harry, Vane's brother. The comfortably spacious room was suddenly very full of very large men.

"Why the delay?" Harry asked, lowering his long frame to the *chaise*. "I expected to be summoned yesterday."

"Devil had to make sure the coast was clear," Vane replied—and earned a hard look from Devil.

"Lucifer sends his regrets," Gabriel informed the room at large. "He's exhausted from his efforts to discover any news of Tolly's peccadilloes—which efforts have thus far been completely unrewarding."

"That," Harry returned, "I find exceedingly hard to believe."

"Unrewarding in terms of our investigation," Gabriel amended.

"As to that," Harry continued, "I know exactly how he feels."

Despite considerable effort in their delegated spheres, none had uncovered any evidence that Tolly had been in trouble. Devil put forward the idea that Tolly might not personally have been in trouble at all. "He may have unwittingly stumbled on something he wasn't supposed to know—he might unsuspectingly have become a threat to someone."

Gabriel was nodding. "*That* scenario sounds a lot more like Tolly."

Harry snorted. "Silly beggar would have got all fired up with innocent zeal and hared off to lay the evidence at your feet."

"Before demanding that you fix it." Richard's smile went slightly awry. "That plot rings truer than any other."

His eyes on Richard's, Devil said, "The very fact that he was coming to see me may have been what led to his death."

Vane nodded. "*That* would explain why he was killed at Somersham."

"We'll have to recanvass all Tolly's friends." Under Devil's direction, Gabriel, Harry, and Richard agreed to take on the task.

"And me?" Vane raised his brows. "What fascinating piece of detecting am I to undertake?"

"You get to wring out Old Mick."

"*Old Mick?!*" Vane groaned. "The man drinks like a fish."

"You've the hardest head of the lot of us, and someone's got to speak to him. As Tolly's man, he's our most likely lead."

Vane grumbled, but no one paid him any heed.

"We'll meet here again in two days." Devil stood; the others followed suit. Gabriel, Harry, and Richard headed for the door.

"It's occurred to me," Vane said, as he strolled after the others, "that the latest addition to the family might not be so amenable to bowing to your authority."

Devil arched a brow. "She'll learn."

"So you keep saying." At the door, Vane glanced back. "But you know what they say—beware of loose cannon."

The look Devil sent him embodied arrogance supreme; Vane chuckled and left, closing the door behind him.

*   *   *

Wringing information from a devil was not an easy task, especially when he evinced no interest in her company. Poised at the top of the stairs, Honoria debated her next move.

She'd taken Devil's advice and visited Celestine's salon. Her suspicious nature had reared its head when a note, directed in bold black script and carrying a red seal, had arrived for Celestine hard on their heels. While Honoria tried on subtly understated morning gowns, fashionable carriage dresses, and delectably exquisite evening gowns, the modiste, in constant attendance from the instant she'd read the note, had made comments enough on *monsieur le duc's* partialities to confirm her suspicions. But by then she'd seen too many of Celestine's creations to contemplate cutting off her nose to spite her face.

Instead, she'd bought an entire wardrobe, all for the express purpose of setting *monsieur le duc* back on his heels. Celestine's evening gowns, while unquestionably acceptable, were subtly scandalous—her height and age allowed her to wear them to advantage. Nightgowns, peignoirs, and chemises, all in silks and satins, were similarly stunning. Everything, naturally, was shockingly expensive—luckily, her pocket was more than deep enough to stand the nonsense.

She'd spent the ride back to Grosvenor Square imagining the look on Devil's face when he saw her in a particularly *provoking* nightgown—only as the carriage reached St. Ives House did the anomaly in her thinking strike her. When would Devil see her in her nightgown?

Never if she was wise. She'd bundled the thought from her mind.

For the past two mornings, she'd entered the breakfast-parlor wearing an encouraging smile and one of Celestine's more fetching creations; while the devil had noticed her, other than a certain glint in his green eyes, he'd shown no inclination to commit himself beyond an absentminded nod. On both mornings, in an unflatteringly short space of time, he'd excused himself and taken refuge in his study.

She could imagine that he might be busy; she was not prepared to accept that as an excuse to ignore her, particularly as he must by now have learned *something* about his cousin's death.

Drawing a determined breath, she started down the stairs.

Direct action was called for—she would beard the lion in his den. Or was that the devil in his lair? Luckily, his lair was also the library. Hand on the doorknob, she paused; no sound came from within. Mentally girding her loins, she plastered a breezily unconscious smile on her face, opened the door, and walked briskly in.

Without looking up, she closed the door and turned, taking two steps before letting her gaze reach the desk. "Oh!" Lips parting, eyes widening, she halted. "I'm sorry. I didn't realize . . ." She let her words trail away.

Her devilish host sat behind the large desk, his correspondence spread before him. By the windows, Sligo was sorting ledgers. Both men had looked up; while Sligo's expression was arrested, Devil's was unreadable.

With a longing glance at the bookshelves, Honoria conjured an apologetic smile. "I didn't mean to intrude. Pray excuse me."

Gathering her skirts, she half turned—a languid gesture halted her. "If it's distraction you seek, then by all means, seek it here."

Devil's eyes met hers; while his accompanying wave indicated the volumes and tomes, Honoria was not at all certain they were the distraction to which he referred. Lifting her chin, she inclined her head graciously. "I won't disturb you."

She already had. Devil shifted in his chair, then rearranged his letters. From the corner of his eye, he watched Honoria scan the shelves, pausing artistically here and there to raise a hand to this book or that. He wondered who she thought she was fooling.

The past two days had been difficult. Resisting the invitation in her eyes had required considerable resolution, but he'd won too many campaigns not to know the value of having her approach him. At last she'd weakened—impatience mounting, he waited for her to get to the point.

Picking up his pen, he signed a letter, blotted it, and laid it aside. Glancing up, he surprised her watching him—she quickly looked away. A sunbeam lancing through the windows burnished the gleaming chestnut knot atop her head; wispy tendrils wreathed her nape and forehead. In her cream-colored morning gown, she looked good enough to eat; for a ravenous wolf, the temptation was great. Devil watched as she put a hand to a heavy tome, one on agricultural practices; she hesitated, then pulled it out and opened it. She was vacillating.

Realizing what she was reading, she abruptly shut the book and replaced it, then drifted back to the shelves nearer the door, selecting another book at random. With an inward sigh, Devil put down his pen and stood. He didn't have all day—his cousins were due later that afternoon. Rounding the desk, he crossed the carpet; sensing his approach, Honoria looked up.

Devil lifted the book from her hands, shut it, and returned it to the shelf—then met her startled gaze. "What's it to be—a drive in the park or a stroll in the square?"

Honoria blinked. She searched his eyes, then stiffened and raised her chin. "A drive." The park might be crowded but on the box seat of his curricle she could interrogate him without restriction.

Devil's eyes didn't leave hers. "Sligo—get the bays put to."

"Aye, Capt'n Y'r Grace." Sligo darted for the door.

Intending to follow, Honoria found herself trapped, held, by Devil's green gaze. Forsaking her eyes, it slid down, lingering briefly but with a weight that sent heat rising to her cheeks.

He looked up. "Perhaps, my dear, you had better change— we wouldn't want you to catch cold."

Like she'd caught cold trying to fool him? Haughtily, Honoria raised her chin another inch. "Indeed, Your Grace. I shouldn't keep you above half an hour."

With a swish of her skirts, she escaped. Even forcibly dragging her heels, she was back in the hall in under ten minutes; to her relief, the devil forebore to comment, merely meeting her eye with a glance too arrogantly assured for her liking. His gaze swept her, neat and trim in green jaconet, then he gave her his arm; nose still high, she consented to be led down the steps.

Devil lifted her to the seat. They were bowling through the park gates, the carriages of the *ton* lining the curved avenue ahead, before she registered that a groom had swung up behind. Glancing back, she beheld Sligo.

Devil saw her surprise. "You'll no doubt be relieved that I've decided to observe the strictures wherever possible."

Honoria gestured behind. "Isn't *that* rather excessive?"

"I wouldn't let it dampen your enthusiasms, Honoria Prudence." He slanted her a glance. "Sligo's half-deaf."

A quick glance confirmed it; despite the fact Devil had not lowered his voice, Sligo's expression remained blank. Satisfied, Honoria drew a deep breath. "In that case—"

"That's the countess of Tonbridge to your right. She's a bosom-bow of *Maman's*."

Honoria smiled at the *grande dame* lounging in a brougham drawn up by the verge; a quizzing glass magnifying one protuberant eye, the countess inclined her head graciously. Honoria nodded back. "What—"

"Lady Havelock ahead. Is that a turban she's wearing?"

"A toque," Honoria replied through her smile. "But—"

"Mrs. Bingham and Lady Carstairs in the landau."

It was difficult, Honoria discovered, to smile with clenched teeth. Her breeding, however, dictated her behavior, even in such trying circumstances; calmly serene, she smiled and nodded with gracious impartiality—the truth was, she barely focused on those claiming her attention. Not even the sight of Skiffy Skeffington in his customary bilious green had the power to divert her—her attention was firmly fixed on the reprobate beside her.

She should have chosen the square. After the first three encounters, the interest directed their way registered; the glances of the ladies whose nods she returned were not idle. They were sharp, speculative—keenly acute. Her position beside Devil was clearly making some statement; Honoria had a strong suspicion it was not a statement she'd intended to make. Nodding to a beaming Lady Sefton, she asked: "How long is it since you last drove a lady in the park?"

"I don't."

"Don't?" Honoria turned and stared. "Why not? You can hardly claim you're misogynous."

Devil's lips twitched; briefly he met her eye. "If you think about it, Honoria Prudence, you'll see that appearing beside me in the park is tantamount to a declaration—a declaration no unmarried lady has previously been invited to make and one which no married lady would care to flaunt."

Lady Chetwynd was waiting to be noticed; by the time she was free again, Honoria was simmering. "And what about me?"

Devil glanced her way; this time, his expression was harder. "*You* are different. You're going to marry me."

An altercation in the park was unthinkable; Honoria

seethed, but couldn't let it show, other than in her eyes. Those, only he could see, much good did her fury do her; with an infuriatingly arrogant lift to his brows, he turned back to his horses.

Denied the interrogation she'd planned *and* the tirade he deserved, Honoria struggled, not simply to contain her wrath but to redirect it. Losing her temper was unlikely to advance her cause.

She slanted a glance at Devil; his attention was on his horses, his profile clear-cut, hard-edged. Eyes narrowing, she looked ahead, to where a line of carriages had formed, waiting to turn. Devil drew in at the end; Honoria saw her chance and took it. "Have you and your cousins learned anything of the reason behind Tolly's murder?"

One black brow quirked upward. "I had heard . . ."

Breath bated, Honoria waited.

"That Aunt Horatia intends giving a ball in a week or so." Blank green eyes turned her way. "To declare the family once more on the town, so to speak. Until then, I suspect we should curb our excursions—the park and such mild entertainments are, I believe, permissible. Later . . ."

In utter disbelief, Honoria listened to a catalogue of projected diversions—the usual *divertissements* favored by the *ton*. She didn't bother trying to interrupt. He'd accepted her help in the lane; he'd told her that his people had turned up no clues in the towns about Somersham. She'd thought he'd capitulated—understood and accepted her right to involve herself in the solving of the crime, or, at the very least, accepted her right to know what had been discovered. As the litany of pleasures in store for her continued, Honoria readjusted her thinking.

Very straight, her expression blank, she held her tongue until, the turn accomplished, he ran out of entertainments. Then, and only then, did she glance sideways and meet his eye. "You are not being fair."

His features hardened. "That's the way our world is."

"Perhaps," Honoria declared, tilting her chin, "it's time our world changed."

He made no answer; flicking the reins, he sent the horses back along the avenue.

Honoria's head was so high she nearly missed seeing the

gentleman standing by the verge; he raised his cane in greeting, then waved it.

Devil checked his team, drawing them to a stamping halt by the lawn's edge. "Good afternoon, Charles."

Charles Cynster inclined his head. "Sylvester." His gaze traveled to Honoria. "Miss Anstruther-Wetherby."

Resisting an instinctive retreat to haughtiness, Honoria returned his nod. "Sir. Might I inquire how your family is faring?" Charles wore the customary black armband, easily seen against his brown coat. Devil likewise wore the badge of mourning, virtually invisible against his black sleeve. Honoria leaned down and gave Charles her hand. "I've yet to meet your brother and sisters since coming to town."

"They are . . ." Charles hesitated. "Well, I think." He met Honoria's eyes. "Recovering from the shock. But how are you? I admit to surprise at seeing you here. I had thought your plans were otherwise?"

Honoria smiled—feelingly. "They are. *This*"—she gestured airily—"is merely a temporary arrangement. I've agreed to remain with the Dowager for three months. After that, I plan to begin my preparations for Africa. I'm considering a prolonged sojourn—there's so much to see." Her smile grew brittle. "*And do.*"

"Indeed?" Charles frowned vaguely. "I believe there's a very good exhibition at the museum. If Sylvester's too busy to escort you, pray call on me. As I assured you before, I'll always hold myself ready to assist you in any way I can."

Regally, Honoria inclined her head.

After promising to convey their regards to his family, Charles stepped back. With a flick of his wrist, Devil set his horses trotting. "Honoria Prudence, you would try the patience of a saint."

Irritation ran beneath his smooth tones. "You," Honoria declared, "are no saint."

"A point you would do well to bear in mind."

Quelling a most peculiar shiver, Honoria stared straight ahead.

They ran the gauntlet—the long line of stationary carriages holding the *grandes dames* of the *ton*—once more, then Devil turned his horses for home. By the time they reached Grosvenor

Square, Honoria had refocused on her day's objective. The objective she had yet to attain.

Devil drew up before his door. Throwing the reins to Sligo, he alighted and lifted Honoria down. By the time she caught her breath, she was on the porch; his front stoop, she decided, was no place for an argument.

The door opened; Devil followed her inside. The hall seemed crowded; as well as Webster, Lucifer was there.

"You're early."

Honoria glanced at Devil, surprised by the disapproval she detected in his tone. Lucifer's brows had quirked in surprise, but he smiled charmingly as he bowed over her hand. Straightening, he looked at Devil. "In recompense, if you will, for my previous absence."

Previous absence? Honoria looked at Devil.

His expression gave nothing away. "You'll have to excuse us, my dear. Business demands our attention."

Business her left foot. Honoria raced through her options, searching for some acceptable way to remain with them. There wasn't one. Swallowing a curse, she inclined her head regally, first to her nemesis, then to his cousin, then turned and glided up the stairs.

"I hesitate to state the obvious, but we're getting nowhere. I, for one, am finding failure a mite tedious." A general growl of agreement greeted Gabriel's pronouncement. All six cousins were present, long limbs disposed in various poses about Devil's library.

"Speaking personally," Vane drawled, "I'd prefer to have failure to report. As it is, Old Mick, longtime servitor to the second family, has departed these fair shores."

Harry frowned. "He's left England?"

"So Charles informs me." Vane flicked a speck of lint from his knee. "I went to Tolly's lodgings and found them relet. According to the landlord, who lives downstairs, Charles turned up the day after Tolly's funeral. No one had told Mick about Tolly—he was, needless to say, cut up."

Richard whistled soundlessly. "He'd been with the family forever—he was devoted to Tolly."

Vane inclined his head. "I assumed Charles would have ensured Mick was told in time to come up for the funeral—he must have been more distraught than we realized. As it transpired, there was something of a scene. According to the landlord, Mick stormed out. According to Charles, Mick was so cut up over Tolly's death that he decided to quit London and return to his family in Ireland."

Harry looked wary. "Do we know Mick's surname?"

"O'Shannessy," Richard supplied.

Devil frowned. "Do we know where his family live?"

Vane shook his head.

Harry sighed. "I'm due in Ireland within the week to look over some brood mares. I could see if I can ferret out *our* Mick O'Shannessy."

Devil nodded. "Do." His features hardened. "And when you find him, aside from our questions, make sure Charles took proper care of him. If not, make the usual arrangements and have the accounts sent to me."

Harry nodded.

"Incidentally," Vane said, "Charles's man, Holthorpe, has also left for greener fields—in his case, to America."

"America?" Lucifer exclaimed.

"Apparently Holthorpe had saved enough to visit his sister there. When Charles returned from Somersham, Holthorpe was gone. Charles's new man has rather less presence than Sligo and goes by the name of Smiggs."

Harry snorted. "Sounds like he'll suit Charles."

Lucifer sighed. "So where do we search next?"

Devil frowned. "We must be overlooking something."

Vane grinned wryly. "But not even the devil knows what it is."

Devil humphed. "Unfortunately not. But if Tolly stumbled on someone's illegal or scandalous secret, then, presumably, if we try hard enough, we can learn that same secret."

"And *whose* secret it is," Gabriel, somewhat grimly, added.

"It could be anything," Lucifer said. "Tolly could have heard it from a man on a corner or from some silly chit in a ballroom."

"Which is why we'll need to cast our net wide. Whatever it is must be out there somewhere—we'll have to trawl." Devil scanned their dissatisfied but still-determined faces. "I can't see that we have any choice other than to keep searching until we have some facts to work on."

Gabriel nodded. "You're right." He stood and met Devil's eye, a lilting smile curving his lips. "None of us are about to desert."

The others nodded; unhurriedly, they left, restrained impatience in their eyes. Devil saw them out. He turned back to the library, then hesitated. Frowning, he glanced over his shoulder. "Webster—"

"I believe Miss Anstruther-Wetherby is in the upstairs parlor, Your Grace."

Devil nodded and started up the stairs. Their lack of progress hung heavily on his mind; Honoria's wish to involve herself in the hunt was an added irritant—seducing her to his side was proving difficult enough without that complication. Gaining the top of the stairs, he smiled, grimly. There was more than one way of spiking a gun—presumably the same held true for loose cannon.

The parlor door opened noiselessly; Honoria was pacing before the hearth. She didn't hear him enter. She was muttering in distinctly forceful fashion; as Devil neared, he caught the words "fair" and "stubborn beast."

Honoria glanced up—and jumped back. Devil caught her by the elbows and yanked her to him, away from the fire.

Breathless, her heart in her mouth, Honoria pushed him away. He released her instantly; her inner shaking didn't stop. Furious, on any number of points, she put her hands on her hips and glared. "*Don't do* that!" She batted aside a distracting curl. "Hasn't anyone ever told you it's unacceptable to sneak up on people?"

"I wasn't sneaking." Devil's expression remained mild. "You didn't hear me—you were too busy rehearsing your lecture."

Honoria blinked; caution belatedly seeped into her mind.

"Now I'm here," Devil continued, "why don't you deliver it?" The invitation was the opposite of encouraging. "On the other hand," his brows quirked, "you might care to hear what my cousins had to report."

Honoria was bottling up so much spleen, she felt she might explode. There was, she understood, an "either or" buried in his words. If she poured out the tirade she'd spent the last hour preparing, she wouldn't hear what had been learned of Tolly's killer. Her head hurt. "Very well—tell me what you and your cousins have found out."

Devil gestured to the *chaise*; he waited until she sat, then settled his long frame in the opposite corner. "Unfortunately, thus far, despite considerable effort, we've turned up precisely nothing. No hint whatever of what it was that set Tolly on the road to Somersham."

"Nothing?" Honoria searched his face; there was no hint of evasion in his eyes. "Where did you look and what were you searching for?"

Devil told her; she drank in his description of the others' particular strengths and the gamut of their investigations. She was confident he wasn't lying; she did wonder if he was telling her the whole truth. She quizzed him, but his answers remained consistent. "So what now?"

In the distance, they heard the dinner gong boom. "Now," he said, rising gracefully and holding out his hand, "we keep searching." He'd explained they were looking for someone else's secret. "Until we have a scent to follow, we can do nothing more."

Honoria wasn't so certain of that. She allowed him to draw her to her feet. "Perhaps—"

One long finger slid beneath her chin; Devil tipped her face up to his. "I'll keep you informed of developments, Honoria Prudence."

His voice deepened on her name. Mesmerized, Honoria saw the color of his eyes change, a gleam silvering their depths. His gaze shifted, dropping to her lips; she felt them soften, part, felt her lids grow heavy.

"Ah . . . yes." Breathless, she lifted her chin from his finger and stepped sideways, bringing the door into view. "I'd better change."

One black brow rose, but beyond that and a quizzical glance, he made no comment, escorting her to the door and holding it while she made good her escape. It was only when, half an hour later, she sat before her mirror for her maid, Cassie, to do her hair, that understanding dawned.

He'd told her what they'd discovered—nothing. He'd promised to keep her apprised of developments—eyes narrowing,

Honoria realized he meant *after* they'd been acted upon. Even more telling, he'd prevented her from offering to assist—so that he wouldn't have to refuse and make it plain that she was still not permitted any meaningful involvement.

When she entered the drawing room, she was poised and assured, able to meet Devil's eye with calm serenity. Throughout the meal, she remained distant, listening to the conversation with but half an ear, her mind busy formulating her investigative strategy.

Nothing useful had yet been discovered, which left the field wide open. As for His Grace's antiquated notions, she was sure that, when she discovered the vital secret, he wouldn't be able to deny her. How could he?—she wouldn't tell him until after, until it was too late for him to exclude her.

Chapter 11

❧

$\mathcal{I}$NVESTIGATING TOLLY'S MURDER proved more difficult than she'd thought. While his cousins had entrée to Tolly's largely male world, Honoria did not. Likewise, they knew Tolly, his habits, his interests. On the other hand, she reasoned, she could view his last days impartially, the facts uncolored by preconceived notions. Besides, women were notoriously more observant than men.

Tolly's youngest aunt, Celia, had been elected by the conclave of Cynster wives to give the first "at home," a declaration to the *ton* that the family had emerged from deepest mourning. Even Louise was present, still in deadest black, her composure a shield against those proffering their condolences.

At St. Ives House, black crepe had wreathed the knocker ever since they had come up to town; on the Dowager's orders, it had been removed this morning. Their first week in the capital had been spent quietly, eschewing all social functions, but it was now three weeks since Tolly's death; his aunts had decreed their time in deep mourning past. They all still wore black and would for another three weeks, then they would go into half-mourning for another six weeks.

Honoria circulated amongst Celia's guests, noting those whose acuity might prove useful. Unfortunately, as it was the first time she'd ventured into society, there were many eager to claim her attention.

"Honoria." Turning, Honoria found Celia beside her, a plate of cakes in her hand, her eye on a *chaise* on the opposite side of the room. "I hate to ask, but I know you can handle it." With a smile, Celia handed her the plate. "Lady Osbaldestone—she's a veritable tartar. If I go, she'll shackle me to the *chaise*, and I'll never get free. But if one of the family doesn't appear to appease her curiosity, she'll batten on Louise. Here, let me take your cup."

Relieved of her empty teacup, Honoria was left with the cake plate. She opened her lips to point out she wasn't "family"—but Celia had disappeared into the crowd. Honoria hesitated, then, with a resigned sigh, straightened her shoulders and bore down on Lady Osbaldestone.

Her ladyship greeted her with a basilik stare. "And about time, too." A clawlike hand shot out and snaffled a petit four. "Well, miss?" She stared at Honoria. When she simply stared back, politely vacant, her ladyship snorted. "Sit down, do! You're giving me a crick. Daresay that devil St. Ives chose you for your height—I can just imagine why." This last was said with a definite leer—Honoria swallowed an urge to request clarification. Instead, she perched, precisely correct, on the edge of the *chaise*, the cake plate held where Lady Osbaldestone could reach it.

Her ladyship's black eyes studied her carefully while the petit four was consumed. "Not just in the usual way and an Anstruther-Wetherby to boot, heh? What's your grandfather say to this match, miss?"

"I have no idea," Honoria answered calmly. "But you're laboring under a misapprehension. I'm not marrying anyone."

Lady Osbaldestone blinked. "Not even St. Ives?"

"*Particularly* not St. Ives." Deciding she might as well eat, Honoria selected a small tea cake and nibbled delicately.

Her declaration had struck Lady Osbaldestone dumb. For a full minute, her black eyes, narrowed, rested on Honoria's profile, then her ladyship's face cracked in a wide smile; she cackled gleefully. "Oh, you'll do. Keep up that pose, miss, and you'll do for Devil Cynster nicely."

Haughtily, Honoria looked down her nose. "I have no interest in His Grace of St. Ives."

"Oh-*ho*!" Her ladyship poked her arm with a bony finger. "But has His Grace an interest in *you*?"

Her eyes trapped in her ladyship's black gaze, Honoria wished she could lie. Lady Osbaldestone's grin grew wider. "Take my advice, girl—make sure he never loses it. Never let him take you for granted. The best way to hold such men is to make them work for their pleasure."

Adopting a martyred expression, Honoria sighed. "I really am *not* going to marry him."

Lady Osbaldestone, suddenly terrifyingly sober, looked at Honoria through old black eyes. "Girl—you don't have a choice. *No*—!" She pointed a skeletal finger. "Don't poker up and stick that Anstruther-Wetherby chin in the air. There's no benefit in running from fate. Devil Cynster has all but declared he wants you—which means he'll have you—and if that chin is any guide, it'll be a good thing, too. And as he's too experienced to pursue where there's no reciprocating sentiment, you needn't think to deny it." Her ladyship snorted. "You'd have to be dead to be immune to his temptation—and you don't look too desiccated to me."

A blush stole into Honoria's cheeks; Lady Osbaldestone nodded. "Your mother's dead—so's your grandmother—so I'll give you the right advice in their stead. Accept fate's decree—marry the devil and *make it work*. Handsome may be as handsome is, but underneath it all he's a good man. You're a strong woman—that's the way it should be. And despite any thoughts of yours, the devil, in this case, is right. The Cynsters need you; the Anstruther-Wetherbys, strange to tell, need you as a Cynster, too. Fate has landed you precisely where you're supposed to be."

Leaning forward, she held Honoria's gaze mercilessly. "And besides, if you don't take him on, who do you imagine will? Some namby-pamby chit with more hair than wit? Do you hate him so much you'd condemn him to that—a marriage with no *passion*?"

Honoria couldn't breathe. A gust of laughter reached them; the rustle of silk heralded an approaching lady. "There you are, Josephine. Are you grilling poor Miss Anstruther-Wetherby?"

Lady Osbaldestone finally consented to release Honoria; she glanced up at the newcomer. "Good afternoon, Emily. I was merely giving Miss Anstruther-Wetherby the benefit of my experienced counsel." She waved Honoria to her feet. "Off you go—and remember what I said. And take those cakes away—they're fattening."

Shaken, her features stiff, Honoria bobbed a curtsy to Emily, Lady Cowper, then, head high, let the crowd swallow her. Unfortunately, many ladies were waiting to waylay her, to quiz her on her new relationship.

"Has St. Ives taken you to Richmond yet? The trees are quite lovely at present."

"And where are you planning to spend the festive season, my dear?"

Sidestepping such inquiries required tact and skill, difficult with her mind reeling from Lady Osbaldestone's lecture. Spying Amanda and Amelia half-hidden by a palm, Honoria sought refuge with them. Their eyes lit up when they saw the cake plate; she handed it over without comment.

"Mama said we should come and see what 'at homes' are like," Amanda said around a miniature currant bun.

"We're to be brought out next year," Amelia added.

Honoria watched them eat. "How are you?"

Both girls looked up, openly, without any trace of pain. They both screwed up their faces in thought, then Amanda offered: "All right, I think."

"We keep expecting him to come for dinner—just like he always did." Amelia looked down and picked up a last crumb.

Amanda nodded. "Laughing and joking, just like that last night."

Honoria frowned. "Last night?"

"The night before he was shot."

Honoria blinked. "Tolly came to dinner the night before he died?"

Amelia nodded. "He was in great spirits—he usually was. He played spillikins with the young ones, then after dinner, we all played Speculation. It was great fun."

"That's . . ." Honoria blinked again. "Nice—I mean, that you have such good memories of him."

"Yes." Amanda nodded. "It is nice." She appeared to dwell on the fact, then looked at Honoria. "When are you going to marry Devil?"

The question hit Honoria right in the chest. She looked into the twins' eyes, four orbs of innocent blue, and cleared her throat. "We haven't decided."

"Oh," they chorused, and smiled benignly.

Honoria beat a hasty retreat and headed for an empty alcove. Inwardly, she cursed. First Lady Osbaldestone, now Tolly's sisters. Who else was lining up to shake her resolution? The answer was unexpected.

"How are you coping with being absorbed into the clan?"

The soft question had Honoria turning, to meet Louise Cynster's still-weary eyes. Tolly's mother smiled. "It takes a little getting used to, I know."

Honoria drew a deep breath. "It's not that." She hesitated, then, encouraged by Louise's calm expression, forged on: "I haven't actually *agreed* to marry Devil—just to consider the idea." With a gesture that encompassed the room, she added: "I feel like a fraud."

To her relief, Louise didn't laugh or turn the comment lightly aside. Instead, after a moment scrutinizing her face, she put a hand on her arm. "You're not certain, are you?"

"No." Her voice was barely a whisper. After a minute, she added: "I *thought* I was." It was the truth—plain, unvarnished; the realization left her stunned. What had he—they—done to her? What had happened to Africa?

"It's normal to feel hesitant." Louise spoke reassuringly, with no hint of condescension. "Especially in such a case, where the decision is so much your own." She glanced at Honoria. "My own case was similar. Arthur was there, ready to lay his heart and all that came with it at my feet—everything hung on my whim." Her lips curved, her gaze becoming lost in reminiscence. "It's easy to make decisions when no one but yourself is involved, but when there are others to consider, it's natural to question your judgment. Particularly if the gentleman concerned is a Cynster." Her smile deepened; she glanced again at Honoria. "Doubly so if he's Devil Cynster."

"He's a tyrant," Honoria declared.

Louise laughed. "You'll get no argument from me on that score. All the Cynsters are dictatorially inclined, but Devil dictates to all the rest."

Honoria humphed. "He's inflexible—and far too used to getting his own way."

"You should ask Helena about that someday—she has stories that will curl your hair. You won't need the tongs for a week."

Honoria frowned. "I thought you were encouraging me."

Louise smiled. "I am—but that doesn't mean I can't see Devil's faults. But for all those—and you won't find a Cynster wife who's not had to cope with the same—there's a great deal to be said for a man who will unfailingly be there to shoulder the burdens, who, regardless of all else, is devoted to his family. Devil may be the leader of the pack—the president of the Bar Cynster—but give him a son or a daughter, and he'll happily sit in Cambridgeshire and play spillikins every night."

Unbidden, the image Louise's words conjured up took shape in Honoria's mind—a large, black-haired, harsh-featured male sprawled on a rug before a blazing fire with a child in petticoats clambering over him. Watching the scene, she felt a warm glow of pride, of satisfaction; she heard the child's shrill giggles over a deeper rumbling laugh—she could almost reach out and touch them. She waited—waited for the fear that had always dogged her to rise up and swallow the image whole, to banish it to the realm of unattainable dreams. She waited—and still the image glowed.

Firelight sheened on both black heads, unruly locks thick and wild. It gilded the child's upturned face—in her mind, Honoria stretched out her hand to the man's familiar shoulder, hard and stable as rock beneath her fingers. Unable to help herself, fascinated beyond recall, she reached, hesitantly, so hesitantly, for the child's face. It shrieked with laughter and ducked its head; her fingers touched hair like silky down, soft as a butterfly's wing. Emotion welled, unlike any she'd known. Dazed, she shook her head.

Then she blinked rapidly and hauled in a quick breath. She focused on Louise, idly scanning the crowd. What had she said? "The Bar Cynster?"

"Ah!" Louise sent her an arch look, then glanced about. No one was close enough to hear. "They think we don't know, but it's a standing joke among the gentlemen about town. Some wit coined the term when Richard and Harry followed Devil and Vane to London, supposedly to denote a . . . certain rite of passage. With Richard and Harry, of course, there was never any doubt that they would follow Devil and Vane into the *customary* Cynster pursuits." Her emphasis and the look in her eye left no doubt as to what those pursuits were. "Later, when Rupert and Alasdair went on the town, it was merely a matter of time before they, too, were called to the Bar Cynster."

"Like a barrister being called to Temple Bar?" Honoria kept her mind focused on the point.

"Precisely." Louise's smile faded. "Tolly would have been next."

It was Honoria's turn to lay a hand on Louise's arm and squeeze reassuringly. "I'd imagined the name derived from the heraldic term."

"The *bar sinister*?" Louise shook off her sorrow and pointedly met Honoria's gaze. "Between you, me, and the other Cynster ladies, I'm quite certain many gentlemen about town refer to our sons as 'noble bastards.' " Honoria's eyes widened; Louise grinned. "That, however, is not something anyone, gentleman or lady, would be willing to admit in our presence."

Honoria's lips twitched. "Naturally not." Then she frowned. "What about Charles?"

"Charles?" Louise waved dismissively. "Oh, he was never part of it."

Two ladies approached to take their leave; when the handclasps were over and they were private once more, Louise turned to Honoria. "If you need any support, we're always here—the others in a similar bed. Don't hesitate to call on us—it's an absolute rule that Cynster wives help each other. We are, after all, the only ones who truly understand what it's like being married to a Cynster."

Honoria glanced over the thinning crowd, noting the other family members, not just the Dowager, Horatia, and Celia, but other cousins and connections. "You really do stick together."

"We're a *family*, my dear." Louise squeezed Honoria's arm one last time. "And we hope very much that you'll join us."

"There!" Heaving a relieved sigh, Honoria propped the parchment inscribed with her brother's direction against the pigeonholes of the escritoire. Describing her doings to Michael without letting her troubled state show had proved a Herculean task. Almost as difficult as facing the fact that she might be wrong—and that Devil, the Dowager, Michael, and everyone else might be right.

She was in the sitting room adjoining her bedchamber. The windows on either side of the fireplace overlooked the courtyard below. Propping her elbow on the desk, she put her chin in her hand and stared outside.

Eight years ago she'd suffered her loss; seven years ago she'd made up her mind never to risk losing again. Until three days past, she hadn't reviewed that decision—she'd never had reason to do so. No man, no circumstance, had been strong enough to force a reevaluation.

Three days ago, everything had changed. Lady Osbaldestone's sermon had shaken her, setting the consequences of refusing Devil firmly in her mind.

Louise and the twins had compounded her uncertainty, showing her how close to the family she'd already become.

But the most startling revelation had been the image evoked by Louise, the image she'd resurrected in every spare moment since—the image of Devil and their child.

Her fear of loss was still there, very real, very deep; to lose again would be devastating—she'd known *that* for eight years. But never before had she truly *wanted* a child. Never before had she felt this driving need—a desire, a want, that made her fear seem puny, something she could, if she wished, brush aside.

The strength of that need was unnerving—not something she could readily explain. Was it simple maternal desire gaining strength because Devil would be so protective, that, because he was so wealthy, their child would have every care? Was it because, as Cynsters, both she and their child would be surrounded by a loving, supportive clan? Or was it because she knew that being the mother of Devil's child would give her a position no other could ever have?

If she gave Devil a child, he would worship at her feet.

Drawing a deep breath, she stood and walked to the window, gazing unseeing at the weeping cherry, drooping artistically in the courtyard. Was wanting Devil, wanting him in thrall, the reason she wanted his child? Or had she simply grown older, become more of a woman than she had been at seventeen? Or both? She didn't know. Her inner turmoil was all-consuming, all-confusing; she felt like an adolescent finally waking up, but compared to growing up this was worse.

A knock on the door startled her. Straightening, she turned. "Come!"

The door swung inward; Devil stood on the threshold. One black brow rose; inherently graceful, he strolled into the room. "Would you care for a drive, Honoria Prudence?"

Honoria kept her eyes on his, refusing all other distractions. "In the park?"

His eyes opened wide. "Where else?"

Honoria glanced at her letter, in which she'd carefully skirted the truth. It was too early to make any admission—she wasn't yet sure where she stood. She looked at Devil. "Perhaps you could frank my letter while I change?"

He nodded. Honoria moved past him; without a backward glance, she retreated to her bedchamber.

Ten minutes later, clad in topaz twill, she returned to find him standing before one window, hands behind his back, her letter held between his long fingers. He turned as she approached. As always, whenever he saw her anew, his gaze swept her, possessively, from head to toe.

"Your letter." He presented the folded parchment with a flourish.

Honoria took it, noting the bold black script decorating one corner. It was, she would swear, the same script that had adorned the note Celestine had, so opportunely, received.

"Come. Webster will put it in the post."

As they traveled the long corridors, Honoria inwardly frowned. Celestine had not sent in her bill. It was over a week since the last gowns had arrived.

With her letter entrusted into Webster's care, they headed for the park, Sligo, as usual, up behind. Their progress down the fashionable avenue was uneventful beyond the usual smiles and nods; her appearance in Devil's curricle no longer created any great stir.

As they left the main knot of carriages, Honoria shifted—and glanced frowningly at Devil. "*What* are they going to say when I don't marry you?" The question had been bothering her for the past three days.

The look he shot her matched her own. "You *are* going to marry me."

"But what if I *don't*?" Honoria stubbornly fixed her gaze on his equally stubborn profile. "You ought to start considering that." The *ton* could be quite vicious; until Lady Osbaldestone's sermon, she'd viewed him as an adversary comfortably impervious to the slings and arrows of society. Her ladyship had changed her perspective; she was no longer comfortable at all. "I've warned you repeatedly that I'm unlikely to change my mind."

His sigh was full of teeth-gritted impatience. "Honoria Prudence, I don't give a damn what anyone says except you. And all I want to hear from you is 'Yes.' And as for our wedding, its occurrence is far more likely than you getting within *sight* of Cairo, let alone the Great Sphinx!"

His accents left no doubt that the subject was closed. Honoria stuck her nose in the air and stared haughtily down at a group of innocent passersby.

Grim silence reined until, the turn accomplished, they headed back toward the fashionable throng. Slanting a glance at Devil's set face, Honoria heard Lady Osbaldestone's words: *make it work*. Was it possible? Fixing her gaze in the distance, she airily inquired: "Was Tolly particularly good at hiding his feelings?"

Devil stared at her—she could feel his green gaze, sharp and penetrating; stubbornly, she kept her face averted. The next instant, they were drawing in to the verge. The carriage rocked to a halt; Sligo rushed to the horses' heads.

"Hold 'em—wait here." With that terse command, Devil tied off the reins, stood, stepped past her, and jumped to the ground. Fluidly, he turned and plucked her from the seat. Ignoring her gasp, he set her on her feet, hauled her hand through his arm, and strode off across the lawn.

Honoria hung on to her hat. "Where are we going?"

Devil shot her a black glance. "Somewhere we can talk freely."

"I thought you said Sligo was half-deaf?"

"He is—others aren't." Devil scowled discouragingly at a party of young people. The fashionable throng was rapidly thinning, left behind in their wake. "Anyway, Sligo knows all about Tolly and our search."

Honoria's eyes narrowed—then flew wide. The rhododendron walk loomed ahead. "I thought you said we were to observe the strictures?"

"Wherever possible," Devil growled, and whisked her into the deserted walk. Screened by the thick bushes, he halted and swung to face her. "Now!" Eyes narrowed, he captured her gaze. "Why the devil do you want to know if Tolly was a dab hand at hiding his feelings?"

Chin up, Honoria met his gaze—and tried not to notice how very big he was. He was tall enough and broad enough to screen her completely—even if someone strolled up on them, all they would see of her was a wisp of skirt. She tipped her chin higher. "Was he—or wasn't he?"

The eyes boring into hers were crystal-clear, his gaze sharp as a surgeon's knife. She saw his jaw clench; when he spoke, his voice was a deep feral growl. "Tolly couldn't dissemble to save himself. He never learned the knack."

"Hmm." Honoria shifted her gaze to the bushes.

"Why did you want to know?"

She shrugged. "I just . . ." She glanced up—her glib reply died on her lips, slain by the look in his eye. Her heart leapt to her throat; determinedly, she swallowed it. "I just thought it was of interest that he spent the evening before he was shot playing with his brother and sisters, apparently in excellent spirits." Elevating her nose, she let her gaze drift over the glossy green leaves.

Devil stared at her. "He did?"

Honoria nodded. Silence stretched; eyes on the bushes, she waited, barely breathing. She could feel his gaze, still intense, on her face; she knew when he looked away. Then, with a deep resigned sigh that seemed to come from his boots, he set her hand back on his sleeve, and turned her along the walk. "So—tell me—what have you learned?"

It wasn't the most gracious invitation to collusion, but Honoria decided it would do. "The twins mentioned their last dinner with Tolly when I saw them on Wednesday." Strolling beside him down the secluded walk, she related the twins' description. "I had the impression Tolly and the twins were close. If he was agitated, even if he was trying to hide it, I would have thought they'd have noticed."

Devil nodded. "They would have—they're as sharp as tacks." He grimaced. "Uncle Arthur told me Tolly went there for dinner. He gave me the impression Tolly was somewhat reserved. I'd forgotten how young men react to their fathers—it was probably no more than that."

He fell silent, pacing slowly down the serpentine path; Honoria held her tongue, content to let him ponder her findings. Although he walked by her side, she felt surrounded by his strength. What had Louise said? Unfailingly protective? That was, she had to admit, a comforting trait.

Eventually the rhododendrons ended; the walk debouched onto a wide sweep of lawn. "Your information," Devil said, as they stepped clear of the walk, "narrows the field rather drastically."

"Whatever Tolly learned, whatever sent him to find you, he must have stumbled on it *after* he left the family that evening." She looked up and saw Devil grimace. "What is it?"

He glanced at her, lips thin, his gaze considering. Then he answered. "Tolly's man went home to Ireland before we could talk to him. He'll know if Tolly was in the boughs when he came in that night." Honoria opened her mouth. "And *yes*—we're tracking him down. Demon's over there now."

Honoria glanced around, noting the many nursemaids and governesses, charges in tow, dotted across the lawn. "Where are we?"

Devil stopped. "In the nursery section. The rhododendrons keep the darlings out of sight and sound of their fond mamas." He half turned to retrace their steps—an earsplitting cry rent the peace.

"Deyyyyyyyy-vil!"

All heads turned their way, most displaying disapproving expressions. Devil turned back in time to catch Simon as he flung himself against his cousin.

"Hello! Didn't 'spect to see *you* here!"

"I didn't expect to see you either," Devil returned. "Make your bow to Honoria Prudence."

Simon promptly complied. Smiling in return, Honoria noted the boy's ruddy cheeks and bright eyes, and marveled at the resilience of youth. She looked up as two women, the twins, Henrietta, and little Mary came bustling up in Simon's wake. Devil made her known to Mrs. Hawlings, the younger girls' nurse, and Miss Pritchard, the twins' governess.

"We'd thought to take advantage of the weather while we may," Mrs. Hawlings explained. "The fogs and rains will be here soon enough."

"Indeed." Honoria saw Devil draw Simon aside. She could guess the subject under discussion. Left to deal with—or was that distract?—the governess and nurse, she exchanged polite nothings with a facility born of long practice. The expectant look in the twins' bright eyes as they glanced from her to Devil and back again did not escape her. She could only be thankful they did not voice the question clearly exercising their minds.

The sun found a chink in the clouds and beamed down; the twins and Henrietta fell to weaving daisy chains. Little Mary, her fingers too plump to manage the slim stems, sat beside her sisters on the grass, big blue eyes studying first the three women chatting nearby, then Devil, still talking to Simon. After a long, wide-eyed scrutiny, she picked up her doll and, on sturdy legs, stumped up to Honoria's side.

Honoria didn't know she was there until she felt a small hand slip into hers. Startled, she glanced down. Mary looked up and smiled—confidently, openly trusting—then tightened her pudgy-fingered grip and, looking back at her sisters, leaned against Honoria's legs.

It took all Honoria's years of practice to preserve her composure, to look back at Mrs. Hawlings and Miss Pritchard and continue to converse as if nothing had happened. As if there wasn't a hot, soft hand snuggled into hers, as if there wasn't a soft weight propped against her legs, a soft cheek pressed against her thigh. Luckily, neither woman knew her well enough to know that her expression was not normally so blank.

Then Devil strolled up, one hand on Simon's shoulder. He saw Mary and glanced at Honoria. She kept her expression bland, determinedly uninformative under his sharp-eyed scrutiny; he looked down and held out a hand. Mary dropped Honoria's hand and went to him. Devil swung her up in his arms; Mary clung and snuggled her head down on his shoulder.

Honoria breathed deeply, her gaze locked on little Mary

clinging close; the emotions rolling through her, sharp need, poignant desire swamping all fear, left her giddy.

Devil declared it was time for them to go. They made their farewells; as Mrs. Hawlings turned away, Mary in her arms, the little girl wriggled about to wave a pudgy hand. Honoria smiled softly and waved back.

"Come—Sligo's probably organizing a search by now."

Honoria turned; Devil took her hand and tucked it into his elbow, leaving his fingers, warm and strong, over hers. She found his touch both comforting and disturbing as, frowning slightly, she tried to settle her emotions. They walked briskly back to the main carriageway.

The curricle was in sight when Devil spoke. "As a governess, did you ever have younger children in your care?"

Honoria shook her head. "As a *finishing* governess, my role was specifically restricted to girls a year from their come-out. If the families I worked with had younger children, they always had another, ordinary governess to take charge of them."

Devil nodded, then looked ahead.

The drive back to Grosvenor Square gave Honoria time to marshal her thoughts. Their outing had been unexpectedly productive.

She'd verified Lady Osbaldestone's theory that she was strong enough to influence Devil, even over something he had a deep antipathy to—like her involvement in the search for Tolly's murderer. She'd had it confirmed that she did, very definitely, want to have his child. Of all men, he had to be the best-qualified mate for a woman with her particular fear—and she most assuredly wanted him, arrogant tyrant that he was, worshiping at her feet.

There remained one piece of Lady Osbaldestone's vision she had yet to verify, although he had, from the first, stated that he was marrying her to get her into his bed. Did that qualify as passion? Was that what lay between them?

Ever since their interlude on the terrace at the Place, she'd given him no chance to draw her close; his *"mine"* had effectively quashed her pursuit of his *"pleasure."* Over the last three days, however, her interest in the subject had returned. Even grown.

Webster opened the door; Honoria swept over the threshold.

"If you have a moment, Your Grace, there's a matter I wish to discuss." Head high, she headed straight for the library door. A footman sprang to open it for her; she glided through—into the devil's lair.

Devil watched her go, his expression unreadable. Then he handed his driving gloves to Webster. "I suspect I won't want to be disturbed."

"Indeed, Your Grace."

Waving aside the hovering footman, Devil entered the library and shut the door.

Honoria stood before the desk, tapping her fingers on its edge. She heard the latch click; turning, she watched Devil slowly approach. "I want to discuss the *ton*'s likely reaction when it learns I'm not marrying you." That seemed a sufficiently goading topic.

Devil's brows rose. "Is that what this is about?"

"Yes." Honoria remembered to frown when he did not halt but continued his prowling advance. "It's pointless to close your eyes to the fact that such an outcome will cause a considerable stir." She turned to stroll, as slowly as he, around the edge of his desk. "You know perfectly well it will affect not just yourself but the family as well." Glancing over her shoulder, she saw him some steps behind her, following in her wake. She kept walking. "It's simply not sensible to allow the expectation to build."

"So what do you suggest?"

Rounding the desk, Honoria continued toward the fireplace. "You could hint that matters were not settled between us."

"On what grounds?"

"How should I know?" She flung a glance over her shoulder. "I'm sure you're imaginative enough to invent something."

From six feet behind, Devil's gaze remained steady. "Why?"

"Why?"

"Why should I invent something?"

"Because . . ." Gesturing vaguely, Honoria walked into the corner of the room. She stopped and stared at the volumes level with her nose. "Because it's necessary." She drew a deep breath, mentally crossed her fingers, and swung around. "Because I don't want anyone held up to ridicule because of my decision."

As she'd hoped, Devil was no longer six feet away. His eyes

held hers, mere inches distant. "*I'm* the only one risking the *ton*'s ridicule. And I'm not about to run shy."

Honoria narrowed her eyes at him, and tried not to notice she was trapped. "You are without doubt the most impossibly arrogant, conceited—" His eyes dropped from hers—Honoria caught her breath.

"Have you finished?"

The question was uttered in a conversational tone. His lids lifted and he met her gaze; Honoria managed a nod.

"Good." Again his gaze lowered; one hand rose to frame her face, then he bent his head.

Honoria's lids fell; in the instant his lips closed over hers, she gripped the bookshelves behind her tightly, fighting down her triumph. She'd got her wolf to pounce, and he hadn't even realized he'd been baited.

The thrill of success met the thrill of delight his kiss sent racing through her; she parted her lips, eager to learn of his passion, eager to experience again the pleasure she'd found in his arms. He shifted; she thought he groaned. For one instant, his weight pressed against her as his lips forced hers wider, his tongue tasting her voraciously. The sudden surge of desire surprised her; immediately, he shackled it, drawing back to a slow, steady plundering designed to reduce any resistance to dust.

That instant of raw, primitive emotion spurred Honoria on— she wanted to know it, taste it again; she needed to learn more. Her hands left the bookshelves and slid beneath his coat. His waistcoat effectively shielded his chest; the buttons, thankfully, were large. Her fingers busy, she angled her head against the pressure of his kiss. Their lips shifted, then locked; tentatively, then with greater confidence, she kissed him back.

It had been far too long since he'd kissed her.

Devil knew that was true; he was so famished, so caught up in drinking in the heady taste of her, that long minutes passed before he realized she was responding. Not passively allowing him to kiss her, not even merely offering her lips, her soft mouth. She was kissing him back. With untutored skill maybe, but also with the same determined forthrightness that characterized all she did.

The realization mentally halted him. She pressed closer, deepening the kiss of her own volition—shaking off his distraction, he took all she offered and greedily angled for more. Then he felt her hands on his chest. Palms gliding, fingers spread, she traced the heavy muscles, the fine linen of his shirt no real barrier to her touch.

She was setting him alight! Abruptly, Devil straightened, breaking off their kiss. It didn't work—Honoria's hands slid over his shoulders as she stretched upward against him; who initiated the next kiss was moot. With a groan, Devil took all she gave, his arms closing possessively about her. Did she know what she was doing?

Her eagerness, the alacrity with which she pressed herself against him, suggested she'd forgotten every maidenly precept she'd ever learned. It also suggested it was time to draw her deeper. Setting aside restraint, Devil kissed her deeply, hungrily, as ravenously as he wished, deliberately leaving her breathless. Raising his head, he drew her to the large armchair before the hearth; her hand in his, he freed the last two buttons on his waistcoat, then sat. Looking up at her, he raised one brow.

Her senses whirling, her hand clasped in his, Honoria read the question in his eyes. He'd asked it of her once before: *How much of a woman are you?* Her breasts, already heated, swelled as she drew breath. Deliberately, she stepped about his knees and sat, turning to him, sliding her hands over his chest, pushing his waistcoat wide.

Under her hands, his chest expanded; his lips found hers as he lifted her, settling her in his lap. A fleeting thought impinged on Honoria's mind—that she'd been here, like this, before. She dismissed it as nonsense—she could never have forgotten the sensation of being surrounded by him, his thighs hard beneath her, his arms a cage about her, his chest a fascinating wall of hard, shifting muscle bands over even harder bone. She pressed her hands against it, then slid them around, reaching as far as she could. His hands at her back urged her closer; her breasts brushed his chest. Then he changed the angle of their kiss and shifted her, laying her back against one arm.

Immediately, the tenor of their kiss changed; his tongue glided sensuously over hers, then alongside—she sensed his invitation. Responding, she was drawn deep into an intimate game, of thrust and parry, of artlessly evocative caresses, of steadily escalating desire. When his hand closed over her breast, she arched; his long fingers found her nipple, tantalizingly circling it before closing in a firm caress, which only left her aching for more.

Instead, his hand left her; her lips trapped beneath his, Honoria was considering pulling away to protest, when she felt her bodice give. An instant later, his hand slid beneath the twill, cupping her breast fully.

Heat seared her; as his fingers closed, then stroked, her breast grew heavy. Honoria tried to break their kiss to catch her breath; he refused to let her go, deepening the kiss instead as she felt his fingers tangle with the silk ribbons of her chemise. Giddy, her senses reeling, she felt the ribbons give, felt the silk shift and slide—then his hand, his fingers, stroked her bare skin, intimately, unhurriedly.

Sweet fever rose and spread through her; her senses sang. Every particle of awareness she possessed was fixed on where he caressed her. With each questing sweep of his fingers, he knew her more.

Devil broke their heady kiss so that he could move her back slightly and shift his attentions to her other breast. She dragged in a shuddering breath, but kept her eyes shut and didn't protest; lips curving, he gave her what she wanted. Her skin was smooth as satin, rich to the touch; his fingertips tingled as he stroked her, his palm burned when he cupped the soft weight. Her height belied her curvaceousness; each breast filled his palm, a satisfyingly sensual sensation. His only complaint was that he couldn't see what his fingers traced; her carriage dress was too stiff, the style too well cut, to brush her bodice aside.

He returned to the first breast; his fingers tightened. Honoria's eyes glinted from beneath her lashes. He caught her gaze. "I want you, sweet Honoria." Gravelly with leashed desire, his voice was very deep. "I want to watch you, naked, writhing in my arms. I want to see you, naked, spread beneath me."

Honoria couldn't stop the shiver that raced through her. Eyes trapped in his, she struggled to draw breath, struggled to steady her giddy head. The planes of his face were hard-edged; desire glowed in his eyes. His fingers shifted; a shaft of pure delight streaked through her. She shivered again.

"There's much more that I can teach you. Marry me, and

I'll show you all the pleasure I can give you—and all that you can give me."

If she'd needed any warning of how dangerous he was, how intent he was, it was there in that last phrase; Honoria heard his possessiveness ring. Any pleasure he gave her she would pay for—but would possessing her truly be such pleasure to him? And, given all she now knew, was being possessed, by him, any longer a destiny to be feared? Breathing shallowly, she raised her hand and sent it skating over his chest. Muscles shifted, then locked. Other than a hardening of his features, his face showed no reaction.

Honoria smiled knowingly; raising her hand, she boldly traced his jaw, traced the sensual line of his lips.

"No—I will go upstairs, I think."

They both froze, eyes locked on the other's. The Dowager's voice carried clearly from the hall as she issued instructions to Webster, then heels clicked as she swept past the library door.

Eyes wide, excruciatingly aware that his hand lay firm about her naked breast, Honoria swallowed. "I think I'd better go up." How long had they been here, scandalously dallying?

Devil's smile turned devilish. "In a minute."

It wasn't one, but ten. When she finally climbed the stairs, Honoria felt like she was floating. Reaching the gallery, she frowned. Devil's pleasure, she suspected, could be seriously addictive; of his possessiveness she had not a doubt. But passion?— that should be intense, uncontrollable, explosively powerful; Devil had been in control throughout. Her frown deepening, she shook her head and headed for the morning room.

Chapter 12

"*I* DON'T *BELIEVE* it!" Seated before her escritoire, Honoria stared at the single sheet of parchment in her hand. For the third time, she read the simple message, then, her jaw setting ominously, she rose and, letter in hand, headed for the library.

She didn't knock. She flung the door wide and marched in. Devil, seated in his accustomed place, raised his brows.

"I take it there's a problem."

"Indeed." Honoria's eyes glittered. "*This!*" With a flourish, she deposited her letter on the desk. "Explain *that*, if you would, Your Grace."

Devil picked up the letter and scanned it, lips firming as he realized its content. Dropping it on the blotter, he leaned back, studying Honoria still standing before the desk, arms crossed, eyes flashing—the very image of an intemperate virago. "I didn't actually think you'd ask."

"*Didn't think I'd ask?*" The look she bent on him overflowed with incredulous scorn. "When I spend a small fortune at a modiste's, I expect to receive a bill. Of *course* I asked!"

Devil glanced at the letter. "It appears you received an answer."

"Not an answer I wished to receive." Turning to pace, skirts swishing, Honoria paused long enough to inform him through clenched teeth: "It is, as you very well know, totally unacceptable for you to pay for my wardrobe."

"Why?"

Dumbfounded, she stopped and stared. "*Why?*" Then she narrowed her eyes at him. "You've been dealing with ladybirds too long, Your Grace. While it may be *de rigueur* to lavish Celestine's best on such women, it is not accepted practice for gentlemen to provide wardrobes for ladies of character."

"While I naturally hesitate to contradict you, Honoria Prudence, you're wrong on both counts." With unruffleable sangfroid, Devil picked up his pen, and his next letter. "It's perfectly acceptable for gentlemen to provide wardrobes for their wives. Ask any of *Maman's* acquaintances—I'm sure they'll verify that fact." Honoria opened her mouth—he continued before she could speak: "And as for the other, I haven't."

Honoria frowned. "Haven't what?"

Devil looked up and met her eye. "Haven't lavished Celestine's best on any of my ladybirds." Honoria's expression blanked; he lifted one brow. "That's what you meant, wasn't it?"

Honoria drew herself up. "That's irrelevant. What *is* relevant is the fact that I'm not your wife."

Devil looked down. "A minor inconsistency time will no doubt correct." With a series of bold strokes, he signed his letter.

Drawing a deep breath, Honoria clasped her hands before her and addressed the air above his head. "I am afraid, Your Grace, that I cannot acquiesce to the present situation. It is entirely inappropriate." Glancing down her nose, she watched as he reached for another letter. "Any *reasonable* being would instantly see, and acknowledge, that fact." With unimpaired calm, Devil picked up his pen and dipped it in the inkstand. Honoria set her teeth. "I must request that you inform me of the total of Celestine's bill and allow me to recompense you for the sum."

Devil signed his name, blotted it, set the pen back in its rack—and looked up. "No."

Honoria searched his eyes—his green gaze was jewel-clear, hard, and uncompromising. Her breasts swelled as she drew a portentous breath; she pressed her lips tightly together, then nodded. "Very well. I'll send everything back." She turned on her heel and headed for the door.

Devil swallowed an oath and came out of his chair. He was around the desk and striding in Honoria's wake long before she reached the middle of the room. She was reaching for the door-knob when he picked her up.

"*What*—!" Honoria batted at his hands, fastened about her waist. "Put me *down*, you arrogant oaf!"

Devil complied, but only long enough to swing her about so that she faced him. He kept his hands locked about her waist, holding her at a distance. For her own safety. The effect she had on him when in haughty mood was bad enough; haughty and angry together wound his spring far too tight. One unwary touch and he might unwind—which would certainly surprise her.

"Stop wriggling. Calm down." That advice was greeted with a furious glare. Devil sighed. "You know you can't send Celestine's things back—as I've already paid for them, she'll simply send them back here again. All you'll achieve is to inform Celestine, her staff, *and* my staff that you're throwing some incomprehensible tantrum."

"I am not throwing a tantrum," Honoria, declared. "I am behaving with exemplary reticence. If I gave vent to my feelings, I'd be *screaming*!"

Devil tightened his hold. "You are."

Honoria's glare turned baleful. "No I'm not. I can scream much louder than that."

Devil winced—and locked the muscles in his arms. He was definitely going to put that claim to the test. Later. He trapped her irate gaze in his. "Honoria, I am not going to divulge to you a figure you do not need to know, and you are not going to attempt to return Celestine's gowns."

Honoria's grey gaze turned steely. "You, my lord, are the most arrogant, overbearing, high-handed, tyrannical, dictatorial despot it has ever been my misfortune to meet."

Devil raised a brow. "You forgot autocratic."

She stared at him; he could feel the frustration mounting within her, swelling like a barely capped volcano.

"You are *impossible*!" The word came out in a hiss—like steam escaping. "*I* bought those gowns—I have a right and a duty to pay for them."

"Wrong—as your husband, that right and duty is mine."

"*Only* if I request your assistance! Which I haven't! And even if I did need help, I couldn't ask you *because*," Honoria drew a deep breath and carefully enunciated, *"we're . . . not . . . married!"*

"Yet."

Capping that terse syllable should have been impossible; Honoria resorted to a seething glare of operatic proportions and carried on regardless. "If you have some vague notion that I'm unable to pay such an amount, you're wrong. I'm perfectly willing to introduce you to Robert Child, of Child's Bank, who handles my estate. I'm sure he'll be happy to inform you that I'm no *pauper*!" She pushed again at Devil's arms; frowning, he let her go.

"I didn't pay because I thought you couldn't."

Honoria glanced at him; his eyes declared he was telling the truth. "Well," she said, somewhat mollified, "if that wasn't the reason, what was?"

Devil's jaw hardened. "I told you."

Honoria had to think back, then, her own features hardening, she shook her head. "No, no, *no! Even* if we were married, you have *no right* to pay bills that are *mine*, not unless I ask you to. In fact, I can't think why Celestine sent the bill to you at all." She tripped on the last words, and looked up, directly into his eyes. Abruptly, she narrowed hers. "It was you, wasn't it? Who sent that note to Celestine?"

Exasperated, Devil frowned at her. "It was just an introduction."

"As what? Your *wife*?" When he didn't answer, Honoria ground her teeth. "What on earth am I to *do* with you?"

Devil's features hardened. "Marry me." His voice was a frustrated growl. "The rest will follow naturally."

Honoria tilted her chin. "You are being deliberately obtuse. May I please have my account from Celestine?"

His frown deepening, darkening his eyes, Devil looked down at her. "No." The single syllable was backed by centuries of undisputed power.

Honoria held his gaze steadily—and felt her temper swell, felt indignation soar. Gazes locked, she could feel their wills, tangible entities, directly opposed, neither giving an inch. Slowly, she narrowed her eyes. "How," she inquired, her voice steely calm, "do you imagine I feel knowing that every stitch I have on was paid for by you?"

Instantly, she saw her mistake—saw it in his eyes, in the subtle shift that lightened the green, in the consideration that flashed through their depths.

He shifted closer. "I don't know." His voice had dropped to a gravelly purr; his gaze grew mesmerically intent. "Tell me."

Inwardly railing, Honoria saw any chance of getting Celestine's bill evaporate. "I do not believe we have anything further to discuss, Your Grace. If you'll excuse me?"

She heard her own words, cool and distant. His gaze hardened; his expression was as controlled as her own. He searched her eyes, then, rigidly formal, inclined his head, and stepped aside, clearing her path to the door.

Honoria's breath caught as she tried to draw it in. She bobbed a curtsy, then, regally erect, glided to the door, conscious of his gaze, shimmering heat on her back, until the door swung closed between them.

She shut the door with a definite click.

The weather, mimicking the atmosphere within St. Ives House, turned decidedly chilly. Three nights later, ensconced in one corner of the St. Ives town carriage, Honoria looked out on a dark and dreary landscape whipped by wind and incessant rain. They were on their way to Richmond, to the duchess of Richmond's ball; all the *haut ton* would be present, the Cynsters included. None of the family would dance, but appearance was mandatory.

It was not, however, the prospect of her first real ball that had knotted her nerves. The tension that held her was entirely attributable to the impressive figure, clothed in black, lounging directly opposite, his inner tension, a match for hers, radiating through the darkness. The Lord of Hell could not have had more complete command of her awareness.

Honoria's jaw tensed; her stubbornness swelled. Her gaze glued to the misery beyond the window, she conjured up an image of the Great Sphinx. Her destiny. She had started to waver, to wonder whether, perhaps . . . until his demonstration that a tyrant never changed his spots. It was, she acknowledged, deep disappointment that had left the odd emptiness inside her, as if a treat had been offered and then withdrawn.

Richmond House, ablaze with lights, shone through the

darkness. Their carriage joined the long queue leading to the portico. Innumerable stop-start jerks later, the carriage door was opened; Devil uncoiled his long length and stepped down. He assisted the Dowager up the porch steps, then returned. Avoiding his eye, Honoria placed her fingers in his and allowed him to hand her down, then escort her in the Dowager's wake.

Negotiating the stairs proved an unexpected trial; the unyielding press of bodies forced them close. So close she could feel the heat of him reach for her, feel his strength envelop her. The flimsiness of her lavender-silk gown only heightened her susceptibility; as they reached the head of the stairs, she flicked open her fan.

The duchess of Richmond was delighted to receive them. "Horatia's near the conservatory." The duchess touched a scented cheek to the Dowager's, then held out a hand to Honoria. "Hmm—yes." Surveying her critically as she rose from her curtsy, the duchess broke into a beaming smile. "A pleasure to meet you, my dear." Releasing Honoria, she glanced archly at Devil. "And you, St. Ives? How are you finding life as an almost-affianced gentleman?"

"Trying." His expression bland. Devil shook her hand.

The duchess grinned. "I wonder why?" Slanting a laughing glance at Honoria, the duchess waved them on. "I'll rely on you, St. Ives, to ensure Miss Anstruther-Wetherby is suitably entertained."

With stultifying correctness, Devil offered his arm; in precisely the same vein, Honoria rested her fingertips upon it and allowed him to steer her in the Dowager's wake. She kept her head high, scanning the crowd for familiar faces.

Many were too familiar. She wished she could take her hand from Devil's sleeve, take just one step away, enough to put some distance between them. But the *ton* had grown so used to the idea she was his duchess-in-waiting, that she was his, that any hint of a rift would immediately focus every eye on them, which would be even worse.

Her serene mask firmly in place, she had to leave her nerves to suffer his nearness.

Devil led her to a position just beyond the *chaise* where the Dowager and Horatia Cynster sat, surrounded by a coterie of older ladies. Within minutes, they were surrounded themselves, by friends, acquaintances, and the inevitable Cynsters.

The group about them swelled and ebbed, then swelled and ebbed again. Then a suavely elegant gentleman materialized from the crowd to bow gracefully before her. "Chillingworth, my dear Miss Anstruther-Wetherby." Straightening, he smiled charmingly. "We've not been introduced, but I'm acquainted with your brother."

"Michael?" Honoria gave him her hand. She'd heard of the earl of Chillingworth; by reputation, he was Devil Cynster's match. "Have you seen him recently?"

"Ah—no." Chillingworth turned to greet Lady Waltham and Miss Mott. Lord Hill and Mr. Pringle joined the group, distracting the other two ladies; Chillingworth turned back to Honoria. "Michael and I share the same club."

And very little else, Honoria suspected. "Indeed? And have you seen the play at the Theatre Royal?" Lady Waltham had waxed lyrical about the production but couldn't remember its title.

The earl's brows rose. "Quite a *tour de force*." He glanced at Devil, absorbed with Lord Malmsbury. "If St. Ives is unable to escort you, perhaps I could get up a party, one you might consent to join?"

Classically handsome, well set, tall enough to look down into her eyes, Chillingworth was a damsel's dream—and a prudent mama's nightmare. Honoria opened her eyes wide. "But you've already seen the play, my lord."

"Watching the play would not be my aim, my dear."

Honoria smiled. "But it would be *my* aim, my lord, which might disappoint you."

An appreciative gleam lit Chillingworth's eyes. "I suspect, Miss Anstruther-Wetherby, that I wouldn't find you disappointing at all."

Honoria raised a brow; simultaneously, she felt a stir at her side.

Chillingworth looked up, and nodded. "St. Ives."

"Chillingworth." Devil's deep drawl held a subtle menace. "What cast of the dice landed you here?"

The earl smiled. "Pure chance—I stopped to pay my respects to Miss Anstruther-Wetherby." His smile deepened. "But speaking of gaming, I haven't seen you at the tables recently. Other matters keeping you busy?"

"As you say." Devil's tone was noncommittal. "But I'm surprised you haven't gone north for the hunting. Lord Ormeskirk and his lady have already left, I hear."

"Indeed—but one shouldn't cram one's fences, as I'm sure you appreciate."

Devil raised a brow. "Assuming one still has fences to overcome."

Honoria resisted an urge to raise her eyes to the heavens. The following five minutes were a revelation; Devil and Chillingworth traded quips as sharp-edged as sabers, their rivalry self-evident. Then, as if they'd satisfied some prescribed routine, the conversation swung to horseflesh and thus into a more amicable vein. When that subject failed, Chillingworth turned the talk to politics, drawing her into the conversation. Honoria wondered why.

A squeaky screech was her first warning of impending difficulty. Everyone looked toward the dais at the end of the room. A whine followed by a handful of plucked notes confirmed the general supposition; a hum rose along with a bustling rush as partners were claimed for the first waltz.

Looking back at Chillingworth, Honoria saw him smile.

"Can I tempt you to the dance floor, Miss Anstruther-Wetherby?"

With that simple question, he put her on the spot. Fairly and squarely, with no room for maneuver. As she studied Chillingworth's quizzical hazel eyes, Honoria's mind raced, but she didn't need to think to know Devil's opinion. The arm under her fingers was rigid; while he appeared as languidly bored as ever, his every muscle had tensed.

She wanted to dance, had intended to dance—had looked forward to her first waltz in the capital. And she'd known that Devil, still wearing a black armband, would not take the floor. Until Celia's "at-home," she'd fully intended to waltz with others, thus making a clear statement that she would live her own life, make her own decisions, that she was her own mistress, not his. This waltz was to have been her declaration—and what better partner with which to underscore her point than Chillingworth?

He was waiting, outwardly charming but watching her like a hawk; the musicians were still tuning their strings. Devil was also watching her—he might be hedonistic, he might be unpredictable, but here, in the duchess of Richmond's ballroom, he was helpless to prevent her doing as she wished. So what did she wish?

Calmly, Honoria held out her hand. "Thank you, my lord." Satisfaction flared in Chillingworth's eyes; Honoria lifted a brow. "But I do not dance this evening."

To give him his due, the light in his eyes didn't fade although his triumphant expression certainly did. For an instant, he held Honoria's gaze, then glanced at the other ladies in their group. Looking back at Honoria, he raised a resigned brow. "How exceedingly cruel of you, my dear."

His words were too soft for anyone beyond Honoria or Devil to hear. Chillingworth raised his brows fleetingly at Devil, then, with a last nod to Honoria, he turned and, with faultless grace, solicited Miss Mott's hand.

Devil waited until the end of the dance to catch his mother's eye. She grimaced at him but when he persisted, reluctantly conceded. Setting his hand over Honoria's fingers, still resting on his sleeve, he turned her toward the *chaise*. Puzzled, she glanced up at him.

"*Maman* wishes to leave."

Collecting the Dowager, they took leave of their hostess. Taking Honoria's cloak from a footman, Devil draped it about her shoulders, fighting the urge to rest his hands, however briefly, on the smoothly rounded contours. His mother commandeered the Richmonds' butler, leaving him to lead Honoria down the steps and hand her into the carriage.

The door shut upon them, cloaking him in safe darkness; harness jingled, and they were on their way home. And he was still sane. Just.

Settled in his corner, Devil tried to relax. He'd been tense on the way to Richmond House, he'd been tense while there. He was still tense now—he didn't entirely know why.

But if Honoria had accepted Chillingworth, all hell would have broken loose. The possibility that she had refused the invitation purely to spare his feelings was almost as unacceptable as his relief that she had.

Protectiveness he understood, possessiveness he understood—both were an entrenched part of his makeup. But what the hell was this he was experiencing now—this compulsion she made him feel? He didn't know what it was but he knew he didn't like it. Vulnerability was a part of it, and no Cynster could accept that. Which begged one question—what was the alternative?

The carriage rumbled on. Devil sat in his corner, his shadowed gaze fixed on Honoria's face, and pondered the imponderable.

He'd reached no conclusion when the carriage rocked to a halt before his door. Footmen ran down the steps; his mother exited first, Honoria followed. Climbing the steps in her wake, Devil entered his hall on her heels.

"I am going straight up—I will see you tomorrow, my dears." With a regal wave, the Dowager headed up the stairs.

Cassie came running to relieve Honoria of her heavy cloak; Webster appeared at Devil's side. Devil shrugged off his evening cape.

"Master Alasdair is waiting in the library, Your Grace."

Webster delivered his message *sotto voce* but as he turned to look at his butler, Devil caught a glimpse of Honoria's face—and her arrested expression.

"Thank you, Webster." Resettling his sleeves, Devil turned to Honoria. "I bid you a good night, Honoria Prudence."

She hesitated, her eyes touching his briefly, then stiffly inclined her head. "And I bid *you* a good night, Your Grace."

With cool hauteur, she turned and climbed the stairs. Devil watched her ascend, hips swaying gently; when she passed from view, he hauled in a deep breath, slowly let it out—then headed for the library.

Wringing blood from a stone would doubtless be easier, but Honoria was not about to allow Devil to deny her the latest news. She wasn't going to marry him—she'd warned him repeatedly she would not—but she was still committed to unmasking Tolly's killer. She'd shared the information she had found; it was his turn to reciprocate.

She heard the latch of the morning-room door click; swinging to face it, she straightened. Devil entered and shut the door.

His gaze swept her, then returned to her face; with his customary languid prowl, he approached.

"I've been told you wished to see me." His tone, and the elevation of one dark brow, suggested mild boredom.

Regally, Honoria inclined her head and kept her eyes on his. All the rest of him—his distant expression, his movements so smoothly controlled, all the elements of his physical presence— were calculated to underscore his authority. Others might find the combination intimidating; she simply found it distracting. "Indeed." He halted before her. Lifting her chin she fixed him with a gaze as incisive as his was bland. "I wish to know the latest news in the search for Tolly's murderer. What did Lucifer learn?"

Devil's brows rose higher. "Nothing of any importance."

Honoria's eyes narrowed. "He waited until one in the morning to see you to report 'nothing of any importance'?"

Devil nodded. Honoria searched his eyes; her own eyes widened. "You're lying!"

Inwardly, Devil cursed. What was it that gave him away? "There was nothing Lucifer discovered that might lead us to Tolly's murderer."

Honoria stared at him. "That's not true either."

Closing his eyes, Devil swore beneath his breath. "Honoria—"

"I can't *believe* it! I helped you—it was *I* who discovered Tolly was untroubled when he left his parents' house."

Opening his eyes, Devil saw her chin tilt, her gaze shift. Before she could begin her usual peregrinations, he locked both hands on the mantelpiece, one on either side of her. Caging her. Incensed, she glared at him.

"Believe me," he said, trapping her heated gaze, "I'm grateful for your help. The others are concentrating on discovering where Tolly went after he left Mount Street. What Lucifer came to report was something else entirely." He paused, choosing his words with care. "It may be nothing, but it's not anything you can help investigate."

Honoria considered the evidence of his eyes—they remained crystal-clear. Whenever he lied, they fogged. She nodded. "Very well. I shall continue with my own investigations, in my own way."

Devil's hands clenched on the mantelpiece. "Honoria, we're discussing tracking a murderer—a cold-blooded killer—not discovering who stole the Queen of Hearts's tarts."

"I had assimilated that fact, Your Grace." Honoria tilted her chin higher. "Indeed, *before* I leave for Africa, I intended seeing the villain taken in charge."

Devil's jaw set. "You are not going to Africa, and you'll stay well clear of this villain."

Her eyes flashed; she lifted her chin one last notch. "You're very good at giving orders, Your Grace, but you've forgotten one pertinent point. *I* am not subject to your authority. And never shall be."

Those last four words were Devil's undoing; lightning-fast, he straightened, hauled her into his arms, and set his lips to hers. In his present state, it was sheer madness to try to coerce her, to attempt to enforce his will in that way.

Sheer unmitigated *madness.*

It snatched Honoria up, buffeting her senses, ripping her from reality. Only her fury and an intuitive grasp of his aim allowed her to resist. His lips were hard, demanding, searching— for a response she longed to—ached to—give. She locked her lips against him.

His arms locked about her; unyielding steel, they tightened, impressing her soft flesh with the male hardness of his. Sensation streaked through her; her skin tingled. Still she held firm, holding to her anger, using it as a shield.

He tilted his head, his lips moved on hers, a powerful, elemental call to her senses. Inwardly reeling, Honoria clung to lucidity, sure of only one thing. He was kissing her into submission. And succeeding.

Fragment by fragment, she lost her grip on her fury; familiar heat flooded her. She felt herself soften, felt her lips lose their resolution, felt all resistance melt. Desperation gripped her. Surrender was too galling to contemplate.

Which left attack her only option. Her hands were trapped against his chest; sliding them up, she found the hard planes of his face. He stilled at her touch; before he could react, she framed his jaw—and kissed him.

His lips were parted—she slid her tongue between to tangle challengingly with his. He tasted powerful—wonderfully, elementally male—a mind-whirling sensation gripped her. He hadn't moved—instinctively she deepened the caress, angling her lips against his.

Passion.

It burst upon her, upon her senses, in a hot flood tide. It rose from within him, from between them, pouring through her, cascade upon cascade of exquisite sensation, of deep, swirling emotion, of soul-stealing compulsion.

On one heartbeat, she was the leader, on the next, he resumed command, his lips hard, his body a steel cage surrounding her. A cage she no longer wished to escape. She surrendered, gladly yielding; ravenous, he stole her very breath. Breasts aching, heart thundering, Honoria stole it back.

Between them, desire smoldered, flared, then exploded, flames licking greedily, devouring all reticence. Honoria gave herself up to them, to the beckoning pleasure, to the thrill of desire, to the urge of molten need.

She pressed herself against him, flagrantly enticing, hips shifting in unconscious entreaty. Fingers sliding into his thick hair, she reveled in the raw hunger that rose, naked, elemental, between them.

Their lips parted briefly, for less than a heartbeat; who pressed the next kiss was moot. They were lost together, trapped in the vortex, neither in control, both beyond reason. Hunger welled, swelled; urgency mounted, inexorable, compelling.

An almighty crash shook them to their senses.

Devil lifted his head, arms tightening protectively as he looked toward the door. Gasping, literally reeling, Honoria clung to him; dazed, she followed his gaze.

From beyond the door came sounds of calamity—wails and recriminations exchanged between two maids—then Webster's sonorous tones cut across the commotion, bringing the plaints to an end. The sound of tinkling glass and the scrape of a whisk on the polished boards followed.

Honoria could barely make out the sounds over the thundering in her ears. Her heart thudded heavily; she had yet to catch her breath. Eyes wide, she looked into Devil's face—and saw the same driving desire, the same inchoate longing gripping her, reflected in his silvered eyes. Flames lit the crystal cores; sparks flew.

His breathing was as ragged as hers. Every muscle in his body was taut, coiled. Like a spring about to break.

"*Don't—move.*"

He bit the words out; his eyes blazed. Light-headed, barely able to drag in her next breath, Honoria didn't even think of disobeying. The planes of his face had never looked so hard, so graven. His eyes held hers steadily; she dared not blink as, rigid, he battled the force that threatened to consume them—the passion she had unleashed.

Degree by painful degree, the tension holding them decreased. His lids lowered, long lashes veiling the subsiding tempest. Gradually, his locked muscles eased; Honoria breathed again.

"The next time you do that, you'll end on your back."

There was no threat in his words; they were a statement of fact.

Hedonistic, unpredictable—she'd forgotten about the wild. A peculiar thrill shot through Honoria, immediately swamped beneath a tide of guilt. She had seen the effort her naive tactic had cost him; remnants of their passion still shimmered about them, licking at her nerves, shivering over her skin. His lids slowly rose; she met his gaze unflinchingly.

And put up a hand to touch his cheek. "I didn't know—"

Turbulence engulfed them as he brusquely drew back. "*Don't—*" His features hardened; his gaze transfixed her. "Go. *Now.*"

Honoria looked into his eyes—and obeyed. She stepped out of his arms; they fell from her but not readily. With one last, hesitant glance, she turned away; head high, shaken to her toes, she left him.

The three days that followed were the hardest Honoria had ever faced. Distracted, her nerves permanently on edge, her stomach a hard knot of reaction, she struggled to find some way out of the impasse that faced her. Hiding her state from the Dowager left her drained, yet being alone was not a desirable alternative; once free, her mind dwelled incessantly on what she had seen, what she had felt, what she had learned in the morning room.

Which only added to her distraction.

Her only consolation was that Devil seemed as distracted as she. By mutual consent, they met each other's eyes but briefly; each touch—when he took her hand or she placed it on his arm—rocked them both.

He'd told her from the first that he wanted her; she hadn't understood what he meant. Now she knew—instead of frightening her or shocking her, the physical depth of his need thrilled her. She gloried in it; at some fundamental level, her heart positively sang.

Which left her feeling exceedingly wary.

She was standing before her sitting-room window, mulling over her state, when a knock fell on the door.

Her heart skipped a beat. She straightened. "Come."

The door swung inward; Devil stood on the threshold. He raised a brow at her.

Honoria raised a brow back.

Lips thinning, he entered the room, shutting the door behind him. His expression was unreadable—not impassive so much as deliberately uninformative.

"I'm here to apologize."

Honoria met his gaze steadily, certain the word "apologize" rarely passed his lips. Her feelings took flight, only to plummet a second later. Her stomach hollow, her heart in her throat, she asked: "For what?

His quick frown was genuinely puzzled, then it evaporated; his gaze grew hard. "For appropriating Celestine's bill." His tone made it clear that if she wished for an apology for what had transpired in the morning room, she'd be waiting until hell froze.

Honoria's unruly heart sang. She fought to keep a silly—totally unnecessary—smile from her lips. "So you'll give me the bill?"

He studied her eyes, then his lips compressed. "No."

Honoria stared. "Why apologize if you won't give me the bill?"

For a long moment, he looked at her, frustration seeping into his expression. "I'm *not* apologizing for paying Celestine's account—I *am* apologizing for stepping on your independent toes—that was not my intention. But as you so rightly pointed out, the only reason such a bill would cross my desk was if you, as my wife, had referred it to me." His lips twisted. "I couldn't resist."

Honoria's jaw nearly dropped; rescuing it in time, she swallowed a gurgle of laughter. "You signed it . . . *pretending* to be my husband?" She had to struggle to keep a straight face.

The aggravation in Devil's eyes helped. "*Practicing* to be your husband."

Abruptly, Honoria sobered. "You needn't practice that particular activity on my account. *I'll* pay my bills, whether I marry you or not."

Her crisp "or not" hung between them; Devil straightened and inclined his head. "As you wish." His gaze wandered to the landscape above the fireplace.

Honoria narrowed her eyes at his profile. "We have yet to come to terms over this bill you *inadvertently* paid, Your Grace."

Both description and honorific pricked Devil on the raw. Bracing one arm along the mantelpiece, he trapped Honoria's gaze. "You can't seriously imagine I'll accept recompense—monetary recompense—from you. That, as you well know, is asking too much."

Honoria raised her brows. "I can't see why. If you'd paid a trifling sum for one of your friends, you'd allow them to repay you without fuss."

"The sum is not trifling, you are not 'one of my friends,' and in case it's escaped your notice, I'm not the sort of man to whom a woman can confess to being conscious of owing every stitch she has on, to him, and then expect to be allowed to pay him back."

Honoria's silk chemise suddenly grew hot; tightening her arms over her breasts, she tilted her chin. His conqueror's mask, all hard planes and ironclad determination, warned her she would win no concessions on that front. Searching his eyes, she felt her skin prickle. She scowled. "You . . . *devil*!"

His lips twitched.

Honoria took two paces into the room, then whirled and paced back. "The situation is beyond improper—it's outrageous!"

Pushing away from the mantelpiece, Devil raised an arrogant

brow. "Ladies who dice with me do find situations tend to end that way."

"I," Honoria declared, swinging to face him and meeting his eyes, "am far too wise to play games with you. We need some agreement over this bill."

Devil eyed her set face, and inwardly cursed. Every time he glimpsed a quick escape from the dilemma his uncharacteristically fanciful self-indulgence had landed him in, she blocked it. And demanded he negotiate. Didn't she realize *she* was the besieged and *he* the besieger? Evidently not.

From the moment he'd declared his intention to wed her, she'd flung unexpected hurdles in his path. He'd overcome each one and chased her into her castle, to which he'd immediately laid siege. He'd succeeded in harrying her to the point where she was weakening, considering opening her gates and welcoming him in—when she'd stumbled on his moment of weakness and turned it into a blunt weapon. Which she was presently wielding with Anstruther-Wetherby stubbornness. His lips thinned. "Can't you overlook it? No one knows about it other than you and me."

"And Celestine."

"She's not going to alienate a valuable customer."

"Be that as it may—"

"Might I suggest," Devil tersely interpolated, "that, considering the situation between us, you could justifiably set the matter of this bill aside, to be decided after your three months have elapsed? Once you're my duchess, you can *justifiably* forget it."

"I haven't yet agreed to marry you."

"You will."

Honoria heard the absolute decree in his words. She eyed his stony face, then raised one brow. "I can hardly accept a proposal I haven't heard."

Conquerors didn't make polite requests; his instinct was to seize what he wanted—the more he wanted, the more forceful the seizure. Devil looked into her eyes, calmly watching, calmly waiting; he read the subtle challenge in her face, the underlying stubbornness in the tilt of her chin. How much did he want this prize?

He drew a deep breath, then stepped closer and reached for her hand; his eyes on hers, he brushed his lips across her fingertips. "My dear Honoria Prudence, will you do me the honor of being my wife, my duchess—" He paused, then deliberately added: "The mother of my children?"

Her gaze flickered; she looked away. Placing one fingertip under her chin, Devil turned her face back.

After a fractional hesitation, Honoria lifted her lids and met his eyes. "I haven't yet made up my mind." He might not be able to lie—she could. But he was too potent a force to surrender to without being absolutely certain. A few more days would give her time to check her decision.

He held her gaze; between them, passion lingered, shivering in the air.

"Don't take too long."

The words, uttered softly, could have been a warning or a plea. Retrieving her fingers from his clasp, Honoria lifted her chin free of his touch. "*If* I married you, I would want to be assured no incident similar to the present *contretemps* would occur again."

"I've told you I'm not daft." Devil's eyes glinted. "And I'm certainly no advocate of self-torture."

Ruthlessly, Honoria suppressed her smile.

The planes of Devil's face shifted; he caught her hand. "Come for a drive."

"*One* more point . . ." Honoria held firm. She met the aggravation in his eyes, and tried not to feel the warmth, the seductive strength in the fingers and palm clasping hers. "Tolly's murder."

Devil's jaw firmed. "I will not let you involve yourself in the search for his killer."

Honoria met his gaze directly; again, she sensed their wills locking, this time without heat. "I wouldn't need to actively search for clues if you told me what you and your cousins discover as soon as you discover it." She'd exhausted all avenues open to her; she needed his cooperation to go on.

He frowned, then looked away; she'd started to wonder what he was thinking before he looked back. "I'll agree on one condition."

Honoria raised her brows.

"That you promise that under no circumstances whatever will you personally go searching for Tolly's killer."

Honoria promptly nodded. Her ability to come up with any male felon was severely limited by the social code; her contribution to the investigation would have to be primarily deductive. "So what did Lucifer learn?"

Devil's lips thinned. "I can't tell you."

Honoria stiffened.

"No!" He squeezed her hand. "*Don't* rip up at me—I said 'can't,' not 'won't. ' "

Honoria narrowed her eyes. "Why 'can't'?"

Devil searched her face, then looked down at their linked hands. "Because what Lucifer learned casts a far from flattering light on one of the family, probably Tolly. Unfortunately, Lucifer's information was rumor—we've yet to establish the facts." He studied her slim digits entwined with his, then tightened his grip and looked up. "However, if Tolly was involved, then it suggests a possible scenario whereby someone—someone capable of the act or of procuring the same—might have wanted him dead."

Honoria noted the fastidiousness that had crept into his expression. "It's something disreputable, isn't it?" She thought of Louise Cynster.

Slowly, Devil nodded. "Exceedingly disreputable."

Honoria drew in a long breath—then gasped as a tug set her on course for the door.

"You need some air," Devil decreed. He shot her a glance, then admitted through clenched teeth: "So do I."

Towed in his wake, Honoria grinned. Her gown was too thin, but she could don her pelisse at the front door. She had won a host of concessions; she could afford to be magnanimous. The day was fine; her heart was light. And her wolf had reached the end of his tether.

Chapter 13

❧

"*I* MAKE IT 334." Honoria restacked the lists in her lap and started counting again.

His gaze on her profile, Devil raised his brows. They were in the morning room, Honoria at one end of the *chaise* while he sprawled elegantly at the other; she was adding up the acceptances for the grand ball his aunt Horatia was to host in Berkeley Square the next night, to declare the family out of mourning. Smiling, Devil retrieved a list from the floor. "That's a goodly number for this time of year. The weather's put back the shooting, so many have stayed in town. Like Chillingworth—it appears my aunt has seen fit to invite him."

"He is an earl." Honoria glanced up, frowned, then reached over and tugged at the list. "But I gather you've known him forever."

"It certainly seems like forever. We were at Eton together."

"Rivals from your earliest years?"

"I wouldn't class Chillingworth as a rival—more like a nuisance."

Honoria looked down, hiding her grin. Devil had taken to joining her in the morning room in the post-luncheon hour during which the Dowager habitually rested. He would stay for half an hour, long limbs disposed in the opposite corner of the *chaise*, his presence filling the room, dominating her senses. They would

186

chat; if he had information from his cousins, he would tell her, simply and straightforwardly, without evasion.

From her own efforts, she'd learned nothing more. The Dowager had fulfilled her stated intention of introducing her to the *ton*; through a mind-numbing round of morning calls, "at-homes," and afternoon teas, she had met all the major hostesses and been accepted as one of their circle. But in all the gossip and scandalmongering abounding amongst the female half of the *ton*, not a single scrap had she heard regarding Tolly.

She looked up. "Have you heard anything?"

"As it happens, I have." Honoria opened her eyes wide; Devil's lips quirked wryly. "Don't get your hopes up, but Demon's back."

"Did he find Tolly's man?"

"Yes. Mick remembered that last night clearly—Tolly, to use Mick's words, was 'in a right spate' when he came in. Unfortunately, Tolly refused to tell him anything concerning the who, the why, or the what."

Honoria frowned. "Refused?"

"Mick—being Mick—asked."

"And?"

"Uncharacteristically got told, in no uncertain terms, to mind his own business."

"That was odd?"

Devil nodded. "Mick had been with Tolly since Tolly was in shortcoats. If he was troubled over something, the most likely occurrence is that Tolly would have talked it over, without reservation, with Mick."

"So." Honoria considered. "What sort of secret would Tolly refuse to discuss with Mick?"

"That, indeed, is the question." His gaze on her face, on the slight frown disturbing the sweeping arch of her brows, Devil added: "Along with the puzzle of the time."

"The time?"

"That night, Tolly got in less than an hour after he left Mount Street."

They'd assumed Tolly had been out half the night, at some function at which he'd learned the secret that led to his death. Honoria's frown deepened. "Is Mick sure?"

"Positive—he remembers particularly as he hadn't expected Tolly back so soon."

Honoria nodded. "How far is it from Mount Street to Tolly's lodgings?"

"His lodgings were in Wigmore Street—about twenty minutes from my uncle's house."

"Was there any particular house—of a friend, perhaps— where he might have stopped along the way?"

"Nothing directly in his path. And none close that we haven't checked. None of his friends saw him that night."

Honoria caught Devil's eye. "How does such a short time fit with Lucifer's discreditable rumor?"

"Not well." Devil hesitated, then added, "It doesn't rule it out, but it makes it unlikely. If Tolly had gone—" He broke off, then continued: "If what we *thought* had happened, then it most likely happened at some earlier date, which doesn't explain why Tolly only got agitated *after* he left Mount Street."

Studying his face, more revealing now that he didn't guard his expression in her presence, Honoria inwardly frowned. He remained disturbed by the discreditable rumor, even though it might now be unlinked to Tolly's death. "What is it?"

Devil looked up, then grimaced. "It's merely that, as the head of the family, I don't appreciate the idea of some skeleton not safely locked in a cupboard."

Honoria's lips softened; she looked away.

They sat silent for some minutes, Honoria puzzling over the questions Mick's recollections had raised, Devil outwardly relaxed, his gaze, gently pensive, resting on her face. Then Honoria looked at Devil. "Have you told the others?"

"They were on the doorstep with Demon. While I wrestle with our discreditable rumor, they're trying to shake information from any tree they can find. Richard and Demon have gone after the local jarveys; Gabriel, believe it or not, is hobnobbing with street sweepers. Vane and Lucifer are combing the likeliest taverns in the hope they might stumble upon some drunk who saw where Tolly went."

"That seems a very long bow to draw."

Devil sighed and leaned his head back against the *chaise*. "It is." After a moment of staring at the ceiling, he added: "I find it hard to credit but they seem as frustrated as I am." Slowly, he turned his head and looked at Honoria.

She met his gaze levelly. "Matters won't always fall into line just because you decree it."

His eyes on hers, Devil raised his brows. "So I apprehend." There was an undercurrent of subtle self-deprecation in his voice; it was followed almost immediately by a tangible ripple in the atmosphere about them. They stilled, then Devil smoothly reached out and lifted the topmost sheet from the piled lists. "I presume," he said, ostensibly scanning the list, "that every last one of the *grande dames* will be present?"

"Naturally." Equally smoothly, Honoria followed his lead, ruthlessly ignoring the breathlessness that had afflicted her. They spent the next five minutes trading inconsequential quips, while the restless hunger simmering between them subsided.

No matter how easy in each other's company they became, that flame still smoldered, ready to flare at the slightest touch, the least unwary comment. Honoria was sorely tempted to confess that she'd reached her decision, finally and firmly, incontrovertibly. She'd thought long and hard; she could see all the difficulties. She could also see the benefits, and the possibilities; she'd decided to accept the challenge.

And what better way than to start as she meant to go on? She'd determined to use Horatia's ball as the stage for her acceptance. Her speech was well rehearsed . . .

She blinked and returned to reality—and realized her voice had died in mid-sentence. Devil's gaze was on her face, too perceptive, too knowing. Heat rose in her cheeks.

He smiled—wolfishly—and fluidly rose. "I'd better see Hobden—he's come up from St. Ives with the tillage tallies." He met Honoria's eyes, then bowed elegantly. "I'll wish you a good afternoon, my dear."

"And I you, Your Grace." Honoria graciously inclined her head. As Devil strolled to the door, the black armband he still wore caught her eye. Honoria frowned. The six weeks the family had decreed as full mourning ended that night; presumably, tomorrow, he'd leave off his black armband.

Her frown deepened. He had better leave it off tomorrow night.

* * *

For Honoria, the next evening started auspiciously. Nerves wound tight, she descended the stairs, gowned for conquest. As usual, Webster materialized in the hall before she reached the last step; he crossed to the drawing-room door and placed a hand on the knob before glancing her way.

His jaw dropped—only momentarily, but the sight did wonders for Honoria's confidence. "Good evening, Webster. Is His Grace down?"

"Indeed, ma'am—I mean, miss." Webster drew in a quick breath and relocated his usual mask. "His Grace is waiting." With a deep bow, he set the door wide.

Smoothly, serenely, inwardly so tight she felt she might break, Honoria glided forward.

Standing before the fireplace, Devil swung around as she entered. As always, his gaze skimmed her, top to toe. Tonight, when he reached her silver sandals, peeking from beneath her hem, he stopped, then, excruciatingly slowly, traced his way back up her length, over the sweep of *eau de Nil* silk clinging sleekly to her long limbs. His eyes dwelled successively on each flatteringly draped curve, then rose higher, to caress her shoulders, concealed only where the simple, toga-style gown was anchored by a gold clasp on her left shoulder. The spangled silk shawl she carried over her elbows was flimsy; no real distraction. She wore no jewelry other than the gold comb in her hair, itself piled high, curl upon gleaming curl. Honoria felt the sudden intensity in his gaze.

Her breath caught.

With long, prowling stride, he crossed the room, his gaze steady on hers. As he neared, he held out one hand; without hesitation, she laid her fingers across his. Slowly, he turned her; dutifully, she twirled. She could feel the heat of his gaze as, at close quarters, it roamed her body, shielded only by gossamer silk. As she completed her revolution and faced him again, she saw his lips curve. His eyes met hers. "Celestine has my gratitude."

His voice reverberated through her; Honoria arched one brow. "Celestine?" She let her gaze linger on his. "And what, pray tell, do I receive?"

"My attention." On the words, Devil drew her closer. His

gaze lifted to her curls, then dropped to her eyes, then fell to her lips. "Unreserved."

Obedient to the pressure of his hand at her back, Honoria arched closer, lifting her lips to his. He met her halfway, yet she was sure she was floating as his lips settled, warm and firm, on hers.

It was the first kiss they'd shared since their confrontation in the morning room; beyond the fact their lips touched, this caress bore no relation to that previous embrace. This was all pleasure and warmth, delight spiced with enthralling fascination as lips melded and held, then firmed again.

Honoria's restless hands came to rest on Devil's lapels; his free hand curved possessively over one silk-clad hip. Beneath his palms, her skin burned, two layers of fine silk no real barrier to his touch. Willingly, she sank into his arms, yielding to the persuasion of his lips and her own flaring desire.

A form of magic held them fast; how many minutes they spent in that soul-stealing kiss neither could have said. The click of heels on the hall tiles brought it to an end.

Devil raised his head and looked at the door; Honoria waited, but he did not step away. His only concession as the door swung wide and his mother appeared in the doorway, was to remove his hand from her hip and, with the hand at her back, gently turn her to the door. Not by word nor, it was clear, even by deed, did he intend concealing the fact he'd been kissing her.

Honoria blinked. She was slow in following Devil's lead; when the Dowager's gaze reached them, she was still half-stretched on her toes, one hand lying on his chest. The Dowager, *grande dame* that she was, pretended not to notice. "If you are ready, my dears, I suggest we leave. There's no point waiting in *this* drawing room."

Inclining his head, Devil offered Honoria his arm; she placed her fingertips upon it. A great deal warmer than when she had entered, she left the room by his side.

The journey to Lord George Cynster's house in Berkeley Square took a bare five minutes. Another five saw Honoria, with Devil by her side, surrounded by Cynsters. The drawing room was full of them; tall, commandingly arrogant gentlemen and briskly imperious ladies, they threw the other members of the *haut ton* invited to dinner into the proverbial shade.

Her gown caused a stir—she hadn't been sure what to expect. What she received were wide smiles and nods of encouragement from the other Cynster ladies—and arrested looks from all the Cynster males. It was Lucifer who translated those looks into words. He shook his dark head at her. "You do realize, don't you, that if Devil hadn't snapped you up, you'd be facing a concerted siege?"

Honoria tried to look innocent.

Dinner had been moved forward to seven; the ball would start at nine. Across the sound of twenty conversations, Webster, borrowed for the occasion, announced that the meal was served.

Devil led his aunt into the dining room, leaving Honoria to be escorted thence by Vane. Remembering a like occasion, Tolly's funeral, Honoria glanced at Vane. "Do you always stand in for him?"

The look he sent her was startled, then his lips lifted. "It would," he murmured, with the cool hauteur that was his most notable characteristic, "be more accurate to say that we cover each other's backs. Devil's only a few months older than I am— we've known each other all our lives."

Honoria heard the devotion beneath the smooth tones and inwardly approved. Vane led her to the chair next to Devil's, taking the chair beside hers. Flanked by such partners, she looked forward to the dinner with unalloyed anticipation.

The conversation about her revolved about politics and the issues of the day; Honoria listened with an interest she hadn't previously known, registering Devil's views, reconciling them with what she knew of His Grace of St. Ives. While the second course was being served, she idly glanced around the table. And noticed the black strip about the arm of each of the Cynster cousins. Devil's left arm was by her side; she turned her head— the black band, barely noticeable against his black coat, was level with her chin.

Looking down at her plate, she swallowed a curse.

She bided her time until they were strolling the huge ballroom, ostensibly admiring the decorative wreaths. They were sufficiently private; the ball guests were only just arriving in the hall below. As they neared the ballroom's end, she slipped one finger beneath the black band and tugged. Devil looked down— and raised a brow.

"Why are you still wearing this?"

He met her gaze; she sensed his hesitation. Then he sighed and looked forward. "Because we haven't yet caught Tolly's murderer."

Given the dearth of clues, they might never catch Tolly's murderer; Honoria kept that thought to herself. "Is it really necessary?" She glanced at his stern profile. "Surely one little waltz won't addle your wits?"

His lips twisted as he glanced down, but he shook his head. "I just feel . . ." His words trailed away; frowning, he looked ahead. "I'm *sure* I've forgotten something—some key—some vital clue."

His tone made it clear he'd changed tack; Honoria followed without quibble. She could understand that he felt guilty over his inability to bring Tolly's killer to justice; she didn't need to hear him admit it. "Do you remember anything about this clue?"

"No—it's the most damnable thing. I'm sure there's something I've seen, something I've already learned, but I simply can't fasten on it. It's like a phantom at the edge of my vision—I keep turning my head to look but can never bring it into view."

Frustration rang clearly in his tone; Honoria decided to change the subject. "Tell me, is Lady Osbaldestone a Cynster connection?"

Devil glanced to where her ladyship, gimlet gaze fixed on them, sat ensconced in one corner of a nearby *chaise*. "An exceedingly distant one." He shrugged. "But that description covers half the *ton*."

They strolled, chatting with those they came upon, their perambulation slowing as the *ton* rolled up, all eager to be seen at the only Cynster ball of the season. In a short half hour, the ballroom was awash with silks and satins; perfume hung heavy on the air. The sheen of curls was fractured by the sparkle and glint of jewels; hundreds of tongues contributed to the polite hum. Being on Devil's arm guaranteed Honoria space enough to breathe; none were game to crowd her. There were, however, a definite number who, sighting her, were impelled to pay their compliments. Some, indeed, looked set to worship at her feet, even in the teeth of the very real threat of receiving a swift and well-aimed kick from her escort.

Fixed by Honoria's side, compelled to witness her effect on

other males, Devil set his jaw, and tried not to let it show. His mood was steadily turning black—not a good sign, given what he had yet to endure. He'd toyed with the idea of asking her not to dance, but she was not yet his wife. He'd transgressed once; she had, by some benign stroke of fate, consented to forgive him. He was not about to try for twice.

And she liked to dance. He knew that without asking; her attention to the music was proof enough. How he would force himself to let her waltz with some other gentleman, he did not know. He'd planned to get his cousins to stand in his place; instead, like him, they'd held to their resolution. Which left him wrestling with a rampant possessiveness he didn't at all wish to tame.

To his disgust, the musicians appeared early. Through the inevitable squeaks and plunks, Lord Ainsworth declaimed: "My dear Miss Anstruther-Wetherby, I would be most honored, indeed, overcome with gratification, should you consent to favor me with your hand and allow me to partner you in this measure." His lordship capped his period with a flourishing bow, then looked earnestly, with almost reverent devotion, at Honoria.

Devil tensed, ruthlessly denying the urge to plant his fist in Ainsworth's vacuous face. Tightening his hold on every wayward impulse, he steeled himself to hear Honoria's acceptance—and to let her go without causing a scene. Honoria held out her hand; Devil felt his control quake.

"Thank you, my lord." Her smile serene, Honoria barely touched fingers with Ainsworth. "But I won't be dancing tonight."

"My dear Miss Anstruther-Wetherby, your actions bear testimony to your exquisite sensibilities. Forgive me, dear lady, for being so gauche as to even *suggest* . . ."

Lord Ainsworth spouted on; Devil hardly heard him. When it finally dawned that the woman on his arm was in all likelihood not listening either, he cut his lordship's performance short. "Sorry, Ainsworth, but we must catch up with Lady Jersey."

As Sally Jersey had a well-developed dislike of the pompous Ainsworth, his lordship did not offer to accompany them. Crestfallen, he took his leave of them; the others in their circle smiled and dispersed, many taking to the floor as the strains of a waltz filled the room.

Devil placed his hand over Honoria's and ruthlessly drew her away. As they strolled the edge of the dance floor, their pace enough to discourage idle encounters, he searched for words, finally settling for: "There's no reason you can't dance."

His tone was dark; his delivery flat. He looked down; Honoria looked up. She studied his eyes; the smile that slowly curved her lips held understanding spiced with feminine satisfaction. "Yes, there is."

Her eyes challenged him to deny it; when he said nothing, her smile deepened and she looked ahead. "I think we should stop by Lady Osbaldestone, don't you?"

Devil didn't; the old tartar was guaranteed deliberately to bait him. On the other hand, he needed a major distraction. Dragging in a deep breath, he nodded, and set course for her ladyship's *chaise*.

"If there was ever any doubt, *that*—" with a nod, Vane indicated the group about the *chaise* on the opposite side of the ballroom, "settles it."

Standing beside Vane, one shoulder propped against the wall, Gabriel nodded. "Indubitably. Lady Osbaldestone hardly qualifies as a *desirable* interlocutor."

Vane's gaze was fixed on Devil's broad back. "I wonder what Honoria said to get him there?"

"Whatever," Gabriel said, pausing to drain his glass, "it looks like we've lost our leader."

"Have we?" Vane narrowed his eyes. "Or is he, as usual, leading the way?"

Gabriel shuddered. "What a hideous prospect." He wriggled his broad shoulders. "That felt like someone walked over my grave."

Vane laughed. "No point in running from fate—as our esteemed leader is wont to say. Which raises the intriguing subject of *his* fate. When do you think?"

Considering the tableau opposite, Gabriel pursed his lips. "Before Christmas?"

Vane's snort was eloquent. "It damn well better be before Christmas."

"*What* had better be before Christmas?"

The question had them turning; instantly, restraint entered both their expressions. "Good evening, Charles." Gabriel nodded to his cousin, then looked away.

"We were," Vane said, his tone mild, "discussing impending nuptials."

"Indeed?" Charles looked politely intrigued. "Whose?"

Gabriel stared; Vane blinked. After an instant's pause, Vane replied: "Devil's, of course."

"Sylvester's?" Brow furrowing, Charles looked across the room, then his features relaxed. "Oh—you mean that old business about him marrying Miss Anstruther-Wetherby."

"*Old* business?"

"Good heavens, yes." His expression fastidious, Charles smoothed his sleeve. Looking up, he saw his cousins' blank faces—and sighed. "If you must know, I spoke to Miss Anstruther-Wetherby at some length on the matter. She's definitely not marrying Sylvester."

Vane looked at Gabriel; Gabriel looked at Vane. Then Vane turned back to Charles. "When did you speak to Honoria Prudence?"

Charles lifted a supercilious brow. "At Somersham, after the funeral. And I spoke with her shortly after she came up to town."

"Uh-huh." Vane exchanged another look with Gabriel.

Gabriel sighed. "Charles, has anyone ever pointed out to you that ladies are prone to change their minds?"

Charles's answering glance was contemptuous. "Miss Anstruther-Wetherby is an exceedingly well-educated lady of superior sensibilities."

"Who also happens to be *exceedingly* well-structured and as such is an *exceedingly* likely target for Devil's attentions, in this case, honorable." Gabriel gestured to the distant *chaise*. "And if you won't believe us, just open your eyes."

Following his gesture, Charles frowned. Honoria, her hand on Devil's arm, leaned close to say something; Devil bent his head the better to hear her. Their stance spoke eloquently of intimacy, of closeness; Charles's frown deepened.

Vane glanced at Charles. "Our money's on Devil—unfortunately, we haven't found any takers."

"Mmm." Gabriel straightened. "A wedding before Christmas," he slanted a questioning glance at Vane, "and an heir before St. Valentine's Day?"

"Now that," Vane said, "might find us some action."

"Yes, but which way should we jump?" Gabriel headed into the crowd.

Vane followed. "Fie on you—don't you have any faith in our leader?"

"I've plenty of faith in him, but you have to admit there's rather more to producing an heir than his sire's performance. Come and talk to Demon. He'll tell you . . ."

Their words faded. Left behind, Charles continued to frown, staring fixedly at the couple before Lady Osbaldestone's *chaise*.

Chapter 14

❧❀❧

$\mathcal{A}$S THE EVENING wore on, the gaiety increased. Supper was served at one o'clock. Seated beside Devil at one of the larger tables, Honoria laughed and chatted. Smiling serenely, she studied Devil's cousins and their supper partners and knew what those ladies were feeling. The same expectation tightened her nerves, heightened her senses. Laughing at one of Gabriel's sallies, she met Devil's eye—and understood precisely why ladies of the *ton* deliberately played with fire.

The musicians summoned them back to the ballroom. The others all rose; Honoria fussed with her shawl, then untangled the ribbons of her fan. She'd intended informing Devil of her decision while sharing their first waltz; denied that opportunity, she was sure that, if she quietly suggested she had something to tell him, he would create another.

She looked up—Devil stood beside her, patient boredom in his face. She held out a hand; smoothly, he drew her to her feet. She glanced around; the supper room was empty. She turned to Devil—only to have him turn her still further, away from the ballroom. Startled, she looked up at him.

He smiled, all wolf. "Trust me."

He led her to a wall—and opened a door concealed within the paneling. The door gave onto a minor corridor, presently deserted. Devil handed her through, then followed. Blinking,

198

Honoria looked around; the corridor ran parallel to the ball-room, leading toward its end. "Where . . . ?"

"Come with me." Taking her hand, Devil strode down the corridor.

As usual, she had to hurry to keep up; before she could think of a sufficiently pointed comment, they reached a set of stairs. Somewhat to her surprise, he took the downward flight. "Where are we going?" Why she was whispering she didn't know.

"You'll see in a minute," he whispered back.

The stairs debouched into another corridor, parallel to the one above; Devil halted before a door near its end. Opening it, he looked in, then stepped back and handed her over the thresh-old.

Pausing just inside, Honoria blinked. Behind her, the lock clicked, then Devil led her down three shallow stone steps and onto a flagged floor.

Eyes wide and widening, Honoria gazed about. Huge panes of glass formed half the roof, all of one wall and half of each sidewall. Moonlight, crystal white, poured in, illuminating neatly trimmed orange trees in clay pots, set in two semicircles about the room's center. Slipping her hand from Devil's, she entered the grove. In the moonlight, the glossy leaves gleamed; she touched them—their citrus scent clung to her fingers. In the grove's center stood a wrought-iron daybed piled with silk cush-ions. Beside it on the flags sat a wickerwork basket overflowing with embroideries and lace.

Glancing back, she saw Devil, a silvered shadow prowling in her wake. "It's an orangery."

She saw his lips twitch. "One of my aunt's fancies."

The tenor of his voice made her wonder what *his* fancy was. An expectant thrill shot through her—a violin rent the peace. Startled, she looked up. "We're *under* the ballroom?"

Devil's teeth flashed as he reached for her. "My dance, I believe."

She was in his arms and whirling before she realized his intent. Not that she wished to argue, but a *soupçon* of warning might have helped, might have made the sudden impact of his nearness a little easier to absorb. As it was, with arms like iron about her and long thighs hard as oak parting hers, she imme-diately fell prey to a host of sensations, all distractingly pleasant.

He waltzed as he did most things—masterfully, his skill so assured she need do nothing but glide and twirl. They precessed down the grove, then slowly revolved about its perimeter. As they passed the entrance to the enchanted circle, he looked down, into her eyes—and deliberately drew her closer.

Honoria's breath caught; her heart stuttered, then picked up its pace. The pale silk covering her breasts shifted against his coat; she felt her nipples tingle. Their hips met as they turned, silk shushing softly, sirenlike in the night. Hardness met softness, then slid tantalizingly away, only to return, harder, more defined, a heartbeat later. The ebb and sway of the dance teased her senses; they ached—for him. Eyes wide, her gaze trapped in the clear green of his, Honoria felt the silvery touch of the moonlight and tipped up her head. Her lips, parted, were oddly dry; they throbbed to her heartbeat.

Her invitation could not have been clearer. Caught in the moment, Devil did not even think of refusing. With practised ease, he lowered his head and tasted her, confident in his mastery, only to find his head swimming as she drew him in. With an inward curse, he hauled hard on his reins and wrested back control, settling to languidly sample the riches she offered, subtly stoking her flame.

They waltzed between the orange trees; the music stopped and still they revolved. Gradually, their steps slowed; they halted by the daybed.

Honoria quelled a shiver of anticipation. Their kiss unbroken, Devil released her hand; he slid both palms over her silk-clad curves until one rested on each hip, burning through her flimsy gown. Slowly, deliberately, his hands slid further, cupping her bottom, drawing her fully against him. Honoria felt his blatant need, his desire—an answering heat blossomed within her. Her breath was his; caught in their kiss, she lifted her arms and twined them about his neck. She pressed herself against him, soothing her aching breasts against the wall of his chest. The deep shudder that passed through him thrilled her.

She'd rehearsed an acceptance speech—this was even better; actions, after all, spoke far louder than words. With a sigh of pure delight, she sank deeper into his embrace, returning his kiss with unfeigned eagerness.

Tension gripped him. He lifted her; their kiss unbroken, he

lowered her to the daybed. And followed her down; Honoria's breath fled. She knew his body was hard, but she'd never had it pressed against her, limb to limb, down her entire length. The shock was delicious; with a stifled gasp, she pushed aside his coat and eagerly spread her hands over his chest.

And felt the sudden hitch in his breathing, sensed his sudden surge of desire. From deep within, she answered it, flagrantly enticing his tongue to duel and dance with hers. She set her long legs tangling with his; her hands reached further. She would be no passive spectator; she wanted to feel, to experience, to explore.

Which was more encouragement than Devil could stand.

Abruptly, he pulled back, caught her hands and anchored them over her head. Immediately, he recaptured her lips, desire growing, escalating wildly, barely restrained. Ravenous, he deepened the kiss, searching for appeasement, fighting, simultaneously, to retain control.

Half-trapped beneath him, Honoria arched, responding to the intimacy, the steadily growing heat. Desire, a palpable entity, welled and swelled; she squirmed, silk sliding sensuously between them, then moaned and tugged against his hold. He broke their kiss only long enough to say: "No."

Twisting her head, she avoided his lips. "I only want to touch you."

"Forget it," he grated. He was dangerously overheated, driven by a desire he'd seriously underestimated; her wandering hands would be the last straw.

"Why?" Honoria tested his grip, then twisted, trying to gain greater purchase; one soft thigh pressed close, then slid downward, provocatively stroking that part of his anatomy he was desperately trying to ignore.

His breath hissed in; she pressed closer—Devil forgot why—forgot everything bar the need to assuage the driving force that filled him. Desire crystallized, hardening every muscle. Tightening every nerve. Obliterating the last remnants of caution. He caught her chin and captured her mouth in a searing kiss. He shifted, one leg trapping hers, using his weight to subdue her.

Not that she was struggling. Her lips clung to his, passionately enticing. She moaned again, this time in abandoned entreaty; her body arched, caressing his, inviting, inciting.

His hand dropped from her jaw to possessively cup one breast; he kneaded the firm mound, then rolled its tip to a tight bud.

Honoria gasped; her breast throbbed, then ached as his fingers played. She writhed, savoring his tensed muscles, shifting in response. His body was close—she ached to have him closer. Much closer. Heat flared wherever he touched her; she needed his hardness to quench the flame, to satisfy the fever that sang in her veins.

She wanted him, *needed* him—there was no longer any reason she couldn't have him. Desperately, she tugged at his grip—it firmed. His hand left her breast—before she could protest, she heard a muffled click. She stilled—the bodice of her gown peeled away. Her heart thudded, then raced. The drawstring of her chemise pulled tight, then released—the gossamer-fine fabric floated down, leaving her breasts bare.

Devil lifted his head; Honoria drew in a shuddering breath. She felt the cool touch of the moonlit air, felt the heat of his gaze. Her nipples crinkled tight. Lifting lids suddenly heavy, she looked up. His face was graven, harsh planes sharp-edged. Her breasts throbbed painfully; as if he could sense it, he bent his head.

And touched his lips to her heated skin. Honoria stiffened; her senses leapt. Devil dropped hot kisses around one aureole, then drew the soft flesh into his mouth. She tensed. He suckled—and she thought she would die. Sensation streaked through her; her toes curled. She gasped, her body tightening, lifting against him. Her fingers, still locked above her head, clenched tight.

He tortured her soft flesh until she cried out, then turned to her other breast. Only when that, too, was aching fiercely, when her body felt molten, pulsing with need, did he raise his head. From beneath her lashes, Honoria watched as he skimmed his hand down, possessively caressing the smooth curve of her hip, then tracing the long sweep of her thigh. Her lungs seized when his fingers slid beneath her hem; her heart stopped when, in one, smooth motion, he swept her skirts up to her waist.

Honoria trembled. Cool air caressed her fevered flesh; his gaze, hot as the sun, dispelled the chill, roaming comprehensively, surveying what he intended to possess. Then he turned his head and met her gaze. His hand tightened about her bare hip, then slid lower in a tantalizing caress, hard palm and long fingers stroking knowingly down, then up.

Her gaze trapped in his, Honoria shuddered. He leaned closer; she shut her eyes as his lips found hers. She gave herself up to him, up to their kiss, surrendered to the sweet wildfire that rose between them.

Devil's conqueror's soul relished the victory—he pressed on, eager for the final conquest. The long sweep of her ivory thighs was a potent attraction, her skin warm satin to his touch. Her softly rounded belly tensed beneath his hand; he slid his palm over her hip, his fingers curving about one firm buttock.

Knowingly, he traced, caressed; tangling his fingers in the soft curls at the apex of her thighs, he gently teased. Beneath him, Honoria shifted restlessly, her lips clinging to his. He drew back, fleetingly studying her face, passion-blank. At his whispered command, she parted her thighs—then gasped as he touched her, then cupped her. Only when that first flaring shock of awareness had died did he caress her, intimately stroking the delicate swollen folds, parting them to find the bud of her desire, already hard and throbbing. He circled it, and felt her passion rise—he found her slickness and gently probed, deliberately inciting the wave of desire building between them.

The higher the wave, the headier the ride, the more profound the final crash. Bringing years of experience to bear, he fed her passion until it became a raging tide.

Caught on the crest, Honoria knew nothing beyond her violent need, centered in the swollen, throbbing flesh he so knowingly stroked, so tantalizingly caressed. Then one long finger slid deeper, circled, then pressed deeper still. She caught her breath on a moan; her body lifted, helplessly seeking. He stroked—the heat within her ignited.

Again and again came that intimate invasion; eyes closed, senses raging, she wanted more. He knew her need; his lips returned to hers, his tongue claiming her mouth in the same, mesmerizingly languid rhythm with which he probed her heated body.

Her breasts swollen and heavy, Honoria arched against him, trying to ease their ache. Abruptly, he released her lips; a second later, his mouth fastened about one nipple.

A strangled shriek escaped her—lightning streaked through

her; the conflagration within her roared. The hand locked about hers disappeared. Devil shifted; using one hand to ease the ache of one breast, he caressed the other with lips and tongue. Between her thighs, his fingers slid deep, and still deeper.

Her hands free, Honoria reached for him.

Immediately, events became more heated, more urgent. She wrestled his cravat from him, then set about undoing the buttons of his shirt. Frantic, she stopped halfway and, shifting, squirming and panting, struggled with his coat. Devil struggled to hold her still. With a muttered curse, he suddenly pulled back and shrugged, then flung his coat and waistcoat aside. Honoria welcomed him back with open arms, thrilled to her toes when she finally made contact with his naked chest. His muscles tensed, shifted—greedily, she explored. Crisp hair tangled about her fingers; beneath her palms, he burned.

Devil felt her yank his shirt free of his waistband, felt her small hands slide about him, reaching to caress the broad muscles of his back. He raised his head. She tightened her hold—the twin peaks of her breasts pressed against his bare chest; the heat between her thighs scalded him. That naked embrace left him shaking, gasping, struggling to regain any glimmer of control. Every instinct he possessed urged him on, urged him to take all she offered, to sink into her slick heat and take her, claim her beyond recall. The pressure of that instinct was overwhelming; his fingers were on the buttons of his trousers, his rake's instincts running a final cursory check—when he remembered her fear.

Her reason for not marrying.

He stilled. Then blinked. He heard his ragged breathing, felt his chest swell. Raging desire pounded at his senses; passion, unleashed, fought for release. But . . . In that crazed instant, lust and will collided. The shock was almost physical. The wrenching effort required to draw his hands from Honoria, to roll away and sit up, left him giddy.

With a whimper, Honoria pulled him back. Or tried to. She couldn't get a grip on his body—clenching her hands in his loose shirt, she tugged desperately. All she did was rock herself.

Devil didn't shift. Gently, he caught her hands and disengaged her fingers. "No."

"*No?*" The question came out as a muted wail; in utter disbelief, Honoria stared at him. "You're a rake—rakes don't say 'No'!"

He had the grace to grimace. "This isn't right."

Honoria drew a deep breath; her senses were whirling, clamoring with need. "You've been bedding women for God knows how long—you must by now know what to do!"

The look Devil cast her was exceedingly sharp. "What I meant was, this isn't how I intend bedding *you*."

Honoria opened her eyes wide. "Does it matter?"

"*Yes!*" His expression grim, he shook his head. "This wasn't supposed to happen yet!"

Her hands still trapped in his, Honoria stared at him. "Why did you bring me down here, then?"

"Believe it or not, I had merely envisaged an illicit waltz—not a full-scale seduction."

"Then what are we doing on this daybed?"

Devil clenched his jaw. "I got carried away—by you!"

"I see." She narrowed her eyes. "You're allowed to seduce me, but I'm not allowed the reciprocal privilege?"

The eyes that met hers were mere green shards. "Precisely. Seduction is an art best left to the experts."

"I'm obviously a quick learner—I've had an excellent teacher." Her hands immobilized in his, she tugged, trying to topple him back down; if she could just get him back on the bed alongside her . . .

"No!" Abruptly, Devil let go of her hands and stood; grimly, he looked down at her. She hadn't seduced him—something in him had accomplished that. Whatever it was, he didn't trust it—that force that whispered within him, urging him to capitulate, to toss aside his careful plans and fall in, lustily, with hers. "When you come to me as my wife, I want you to come of your own free will. Because you've *made* the decision to become my duchess. That's not a decision you've yet made."

Staggered, Honoria stared at him. "What do you imagine *this* is all about?" Her gesture encompassed her seminaked sprawl.

Devil narrowed his eyes. "Curiosity."

"*Curi* . . . ?" Honoria's mouth fell open, then shut; lips setting ominously, she came up on one elbow.

Devil spoke before she could. "Even if it wasn't—even if

you'd made up your mind in cold blood—how the hell could I tell now, when you're so heated you're almost simmering?"

Honoria met his eyes—and wished she had an answer.

"You're all but drunk with passion—don't try to deny it."

She didn't—couldn't; just sitting up had nearly made her swoon. Her pulse thundered in her ears; she felt flushed one instant, then desperate for heat—his heat—the next. There was a curious, molten void pulsing within her; her breathing was so shallow it was difficult to think.

Devil's gaze, on her face, became more intent, then flicked down, swiftly scanning. The folds of her gown had slipped down, the hem floating on her thighs. Instantly, his eyes switched back to her face; she saw his jaw set, saw the iron shackles of his control lock.

He spoke through clenched teeth, frustration in his voice. "It's important to me to know that you've made a conscious decision—that you've decided to become my wife, the mother of my children, for your own reasons, not because I've seduced, coerced, or manipulated you into it."

"I've *made* my decision." Honoria struggled to her knees. "How can I convince you?"

"I need to hear you say it—state it—when you're fully *compos mentis*." Devil held her gaze. "I want to hear you declare that you'll be my duchess, that you *want* to bear my children."

Through the haze of her passion, Honoria glimpsed an unexpected light. She narrowed her eyes. "Just why do you need this declaration?"

Devil looked down at her—and narrowed his eyes back. "Can you deny you've avoided marrying because of your decision not to risk losing children—like you lost your brother and sister?"

Stunned, she stared at him. "How did you know?"

Devil's jaw firmed. "Michael told me about your brother and sister. The rest's obvious. You must have had a reason for not marrying—you avoid young children."

His presumption in guessing her most private fear—correctly—was infuriating; Honoria knew she should react—do something to put him in his place. Instead, their talk of children had evoked a far stronger response, a surging, primitive urge to put him in his place, in quite a different way.

206

Their discussion had done nothing to quench the desire beating steady in her veins. They were both half-naked, both breathing rapidly; passion still throbbed between them. His every muscle was sharply defined, locked against that driving need. She had no such defense.

Realization swept her—and left her quivering. "I . . ." She searched his eyes, her own widening. She spread her arms helplessly. "You can't leave me like this."

Devil looked into her eyes—and mentally cursed—himself, her—and Celestine's damned gown, gathered in sheening folds about her waist, draping her thighs in silken splendor. As he watched, a telltale shiver racked her, an almost-imperceptible quiver rippling beneath her skin.

Reaching out, she locked her fingers in his shirt and pulled. Reluctantly, he shifted closer. He'd purposely aroused her, deliberately pushed her to a state bordering on the frantic.

"Please?" The soft plea lay on her bruised lips; it glowed in her eyes.

What could a gentleman do? With one last mental curse, Devil gathered her into his arms and set his lips to hers.

She opened to him instantly, sinking against him. He gave her what she wanted, steadily fanning her flames, holding himself rigidly aloof. His demons were once more under his control—he wasn't about to let the reins slip again.

Honoria sensed his decision; the muscles that surrounded her remained locked and unyielding. She would not be his wife tonight. But she had no will left to rail against fate—her entire being was focused on the fire that raged within her. Wave upon flaming wave it seared through her, leaving her empty and yearning, weak with need. How he was going to sate her hunger she did not know; adrift, she gave herself up to his kisses, surrendered to the inferno and put herself in his hands.

When he lifted his head she was reeling, and hotter than she'd been in her life. Her whole being was one heated, aching void. Gasping, she clung to his shoulders.

"Trust me."

He whispered the words against her throat, then trailed wicked kisses down one blue vein. Honoria let her head fall back, then shuddered. The next instant, he swung her into his arms. She waited to be laid on the daybed—instead, he carried her around it; his back to it, he set her on her feet before him, facing the long mirror on the wall.

Honoria blinked. The moonlight found her skin and set it shimmering; behind her, Devil appeared a dense shadow, his hands dark against her body. Honoria licked her lips. "What are you going to do?"

He bent his head and traced one earlobe with his tongue. "Satisfy you. Release you." His eyes met hers in the mirror. "Pleasure you."

The deep purring murmur sent a sharp thrill racing through her; his hands slid around to cup both breasts—his fingers tightened and she shuddered. "All you have to do is do exactly as I say." Again he met her gaze. "Keep your eyes open and watch my hands—and concentrate on what you feel, on the sensations . . ."

His words were low, hypnotic; Honoria couldn't drag her eyes from his hands, rhythmically kneading her breasts. She watched his long fingers reach for her nipples; they swirled, then squeezed—sharp shivers lanced through her. She sucked in a short breath and leaned back—and felt his bare chest behind her, crisp hair rasping against her bare shoulders.

His hands left her breasts—she refocused on the mirror. One dark hand splayed across her midriff, holding her against him; the other gripped her gown, gathered in folds about her hips. She realized his intention and stiffened—protest welled, but never made it past her lips. He drew both gown and chemise down, over her hips, baring her, then let them slither to the floor. The costly fabrics pooled about their feet—Honoria ignored them, shocked, entranced, mesmerized by the sight of dark hands freely roaming her body.

She heard a low moan, and knew it was hers. Her head fell back against his shoulder; her spine arched. Her senses, fully alive, registered every touch, every knowing caress; from under weighted lids, she watched every erotic move. Then he shifted, his arms coming around her, surrounding her, his left hand cupping her right breast, his right hand splaying over her stomach. From behind, his knee pressed hers apart; head bent, his lips grazed the soft skin beneath her ear. "Keep watching."

Honoria did—she watched as his hand slid lower, long fingers tangling in her curls, then sliding further, pressing inward.

He touched her softness, found her molten heat and stroked. Breathless, aching, she felt the muscles in his arm shift as he reached further, felt the pressure of his hand between her thighs, felt the slow inexorable invasion as one long finger entered her.

Sensation upon sensation crashed through her; the hand at her breast fondled, fingers finding, then tightening about her budded nipple. Of their own volition, her hands found his, fastening over his broad wrists. The crisp hair of his forearms rasped the soft skin of her inner arms; beneath her fingers, hard muscle and steely sinew played.

Between her thighs, his hand shifted; as one finger slid deep, his thumb pressed, caressed.

Lightning, wildfire—pure streaks of elemental sensation lanced through her; her body tightened, arched; Honoria gasped. His caresses continued, increasingly forceful; within her, sensations swirled, then rose—a vortex of feeling.

"Keep watching."

Naked, on fire, she dragged her lids open—and saw his hand push deep between her thighs.

A starburst took her—exploded within her. Sensation crystallized, soared, then fractured, a million silver shards raining down, shooting through her, flying down overstretched nerves to melt, tingling, beneath her skin.

Release.

It swept her, washing away her tension, replacing it with a pleasure so deep she thought she'd died. She felt his lips at her temple, felt his hands soften in soothing, intimate caresses. Sweet oblivion claimed her.

When her wits reconnected with reality, Honoria discovered herself fully dressed, leaning against the daybed's back. Before her, Devil stood before the mirror, tying his cravat. She watched his fingers deftly crease and knot the wide folds, and smiled.

In the mirror, Devil's eyes met hers. Her smile widened; he raised a brow.

"I just realized," she said, leaning more heavily against the daybed, "why you don't have a valet. Being a rake necessarily means you can't rely on the services of a servant to turn you out in trim."

Settling the ends of his cravat, Devil cast her a jaundiced

glance. "Precisely." He turned. "And if you've returned to the living enough to think that through, we'd better get back to the ballroom."

He stooped to snatch his coat from the floor; Honoria opened her lips to inform him that she had, indeed, made up her mind, then thought better of it. They'd been away from the ball for too long as it was—this was no longer the time and place. Tomorrow morning would do.

She felt like she was floating, in some strange way sundered from reality. She watched Devil shrug into his coat. As he settled the lapels, something caught her eye. Turning, she peered between the orange trees.

"What is it?" Devil followed her gaze.

"I thought I saw someone, but it must have been a shifting shadow."

Devil took her hand. "Come—the gossipmongers will have enough to talk about as it is."

They walked swiftly through the orange grove; a moment later, the latch clicked and all was still. The moon continued to lay its gentle beams in wide swaths across the flagged floor.

A shadow broke the pattern.

The outline of a man was thrown across the grove, distorted to menacing proportions. Then the figure slipped away, around the corner of the orangery, and the shadow was no more.

Moonlight bathed the scene in soft white light, illuminating the orange trees, the wickerwork basket, and the daybed with its rumpled cushions.

Chapter 15

"THANK YOU, EMMY." Standing, arms folded, before her sitting-room window, Honoria watched the tweeny tidy her luncheon tray. "Has His Grace returned to the house?"

"I don't believe so, miss." Emmy straightened, hefting her burden. "I could ask Webster, if you like?"

"No—thank you, Emmy." Honoria fabricated a smile. "It was merely an idle question."

Very idle. Turning back to the window, Honoria wondered how much more idleness she could take. They'd returned from Berkeley Square well after three o'clock; sleep, deep and dreamless, had claimed her. Devil's pleasure had obviously agreed with her; on waking, she'd determined to waste no time claiming more. Gowned in one of Celestine's most fetching creations, she'd headed downstairs.

Only to discover the breakfast room empty. Devoid of wolves. Webster informed her that His Grace had broken his fast early and departed for a long drive. After breakfasting in solitary splendor—the Dowager had, the night before, declared her intention of not rising until the afternoon—she'd retreated to her sitting room. To wait. Impatiently.

How dare he demand a declaration from her and then go for a drive? She set her teeth and heard the front door slam. The sound of raised voices reached her. Frowning, she went to the door, opened it, and recognized Webster's voice raised in exclamation.

Webster shaken from his habitual imperturbability? Honoria headed for the stairs. Surely nothing short of catastrophe—

Her breath caught; eyes widening, she picked up her skirts and ran.

Reaching the gallery, she leaned over the rail. The sight that met her eyes was the opposite of reassuring. In the hall below, footmen milled about a ragged figure, supporting, exclaiming. It was Sligo, pale, shaken, one arm in a makeshift sling, cuts and abrasions all over his face.

Her heart in her mouth, Honoria started down the stairs— and heard Devil's voice, deep, strong, a forcefully coherent rumble. Relief hit her so strongly she had to lean on the balustrade to let the giddiness pass. Drawing a steadying breath, she continued down.

Devil strode out of the library; Honoria clutched the banister again. His coat was ripped in countless places, in jagged little tears. His buckskin breeches, usually immaculate, were scraped and dusty, as were his boots. Disheveled black locks framed his frowning face; an angry scatch ran along his jaw. "Get the sawbones in for Sligo—that shoulder needs setting."

"But what about *you*, m'lord?" Webster, following on his heels, raised his hands, as if tempted to seize hold of his master.

Devil swung about—and saw Honoria on the stairs. His gaze locked on hers. "There's nothing wrong with me bar a few scratches." After a moment, he glanced to his left, frowning at Webster. "Stop fussing—Cynsters are invincible, remember?" With that, he set his boot on the first stair. "Just send up some hot water—that's all I need."

"I'll bring it up directly, Your Grace." With injured dignity, Webster headed for the kitchens.

Devil climbed the stairs; Honoria waited. There were slivers of wood, some painted, caught in the tears in his coat. Her chest felt so tight it hurt. "What happened?"

Drawing abreast of her, Devil met her gaze. "The axle on my phaeton snapped."

There were small bloodstains on his shirt; he was moving briskly but without his usual fluid grace. He kept climbing; Honoria turned and followed. "Where?"

"Hampstead Heath." Without waiting for her next question, he added: "I needed some air, so I went out there and let the horses have their heads. We were flying when the axle went."

Honoria felt the blood drain from her face. "Went?"

Devil shrugged. "Snapped—there was an almighty crack. We might have hit something, but I don't think we did."

Reaching the top of the stairs, he turned and strode down the corridor; picturing the scene, and not liking what she saw, Honoria hurried in his wake. "Your horses—the bays?"

"No." Devil threw her a glance. "I had a pair of young blacks put to—to try out their paces." His features contorted. "I shot one immediately, but I only carry one pistol. Luckily, Sherringham came along—I borrowed his pistol, then he drove us back here."

"But—" Honoria frowned. "What actually happened?"

A decidedly testy glance found her. "The axle snapped under the box seat—essentially, the phaeton came apart. By hell's own luck, both Sligo and I were thrown free. I bounce better than he does."

"The carriage?"

"Is kindling."

They'd reached the end of the long corridor; opening the heavy oak door at its end, Devil strode on. He stopped in the middle of the room, in the center of a richly hued carpet. Lifting one shoulder, he started to ease off his coat—and caught his breath on an indrawn hiss.

"Here." Behind him, Honoria reached over his shoulders and gently tugged, freeing first one shoulder, then the other, then easing the sleeves off. "Great heavens!" Dropping the ruined coat, she stared.

His shirt was badly torn, the fine linen shredded down the side of his back that had taken the brunt of his fall. The abrasions had bled, as had numerous little cuts. Thankfully, his breeches and boots had provided sterner protection; there were no rips below his waist.

Before she could react, Devil pulled the shirt free of his breeches and hauled it over his head. And froze. Then his head snapped around. "What the devil are you doing here?"

It took a moment to shift her gaze from his bleeding back to his face. The look in his eyes didn't, immediately, make sense, then she looked past him—to the massive, fully canopied four-poster bed that dominated the room. In one swift glance, she took in the sumptuous hangings, all in shades of green, the ornately carved headboard and barley-sugar posts, the silk sheets and thick featherbed and the abundance of soft pillows piled high. Her expression mild, she looked back at him. "Your cuts are bleeding—they need salving."

Devil swore beneath his breath. "You shouldn't be in here." He wrestled with his shirt, trying to free his arms.

"Don't be ridiculous." Honoria caught his hands, now thoroughly tangled; deftly, she unlaced his cuffs. "The circumstances excuse the impropriety."

Devil stripped the shirt from his wrists and flung it aside. "I am not on my deathbed."

"You are, however, badly scraped." Honoria met his gaze calmly. "You can't see it."

Devil narrowed his eyes at her—then twisted, trying to look over his shoulder. "It doesn't feel that bad—I can take care of it myself."

"For goodness sake!" Honoria planted her hands on her hips and glared at him. "Stop acting like a six-year-old—I'm only going to bathe the cuts and apply some salve."

Devil's head whipped back. "That's just the point—I'm *not* a six-year-old—and I'm not dead, either."

"Naturally." Honoria nodded. "You're a Cynster—you're invincible, remember?"

Devil gritted his teeth. "Honoria, if you want to play ministering angel, you can damn well marry me first."

Honoria lost her temper—she'd been waiting to make the declaration he wanted and he turned up like this! Stepping forward, she planted her index finger in the center of his bare chest. "*If*," she declared, emphasizing the word with a definite jab. "I *do* decide to marry you." She tried another jab; when he instinctively stepped back, she closed the distance. "I would want to be *assured*." Another jab, another step. "That you will behave *reasonably*." Her finger was starting to ache. "*In—all—situations*!" Three quick jabs, three quick steps; Devil's legs hit the end of his bed. Honoria pounced. "Like now!" Glaring defiantly up at him, she prodded him one last time. "*Sit!*"

The face she looked into was uncompromisingly set; his eyes, shadowed green, smoldered darkly. They stood, gazes locked, toe-to-toe, will against will—abruptly, Devil's gaze shifted to the door.

Honoria grabbed the moment. Placing both palms on the heavy muscles of his chest, she pushed. Hard.

With a muffled expletive, Devil toppled—and sat.

"Your water, Your Grace." Webster elbowed open the door, which had swung half-shut behind them.

Turning, Honoria held out her hands. "I'll need some salve, Webster."

"Indeed, miss." Without a blink, Webster relinquished the bowl into her care. "I'll fetch some immediately."

The instant he'd gone, Honoria turned—straight into a furious glower.

"This is *not* a good idea."

She raised a brow, then bent and placed the bowl on the floor. "Stop complaining—you'll survive."

Devil watched her gown draw tight over her bottom—abruptly, he shook his head. "Maybe—but will I be sane?"

Wringing out a cloth, Honoria cast him a measuring glance. Rising, she folded the cloth, then stepped up beside him, her legs almost touching his thigh. Placing one hand on his shoulder, she drew it forward, bringing a deep cut into view. Under her fingers, his skin was warm, resilient, very much alive. "Think of something else." Carefully, she started to bathe the cut.

Closing his eyes, Devil drew a deep breath. *Think of something else.* Just as well he was sitting, or she'd know for a fact just what his "else" was. His cuts and scrapes barely rated on his scale of afflictions; his major hurt was throbbing steadily, and was only going to get worse. She was so close, leaning over, reaching around his shoulder; her perfume surrounded him, wreathing his senses, leaving him giddy with need.

Small hands touched gently, hesitantly; she started when his muscles shifted, flickering beneath her fingers. Clenching his fists, Devil anchored them to his knees; when Webster returned, salve-pot in hand, he all but sighed with relief. "How's Sligo?"

It was an effort, but he managed to keep his butler talking until, with every last scratch bathed and salved, Honoria finally stepped back.

"There." Wiping her hands on the towel Webster held for her, she slanted him a questioning glance.

Devil returned it with a blank stare. He waited while Webster gathered ruined clothes, towels, salve, and basin, then swept magisterially out. Honoria turned to watch him go—silently, Devil rose and moved up behind her. He'd lost the battle with his demons five minutes before.

"Now!" Honoria turned—straight into Devil's arms. "What—?" Her words died as she looked into his eyes. A feeling of being about to be devoured washed over her. She felt his hand at the base of her throat. It rose, framing her jaw as his head lowered.

He waited for no permission, implied or otherwise, but took her mouth rapaciously. Honoria felt her bones melt; beneath that onslaught, resistance fled. He shifted and moved her; her legs hit the bed end. Lifting her against him, he knelt on the bed, then they were toppling together. She landed on her back—he landed on top of her.

Directly on top of her.

Any thought of struggling vanished; the hunger that roared through him, the sheer muscled weight of him, tense, rigid, and ready to claim her, lit her fires instantly. Honoria wrapped her arms about his neck and feverishly kissed him back.

He pressed his hands into the down covers and slid them beneath her hips, fingers firming, then tilting her against him. More definite, more fascinating than before, she felt the rigid column of his desire ride against her. Instinctively, she writhed beneath that throbbing weight—wanting, needing.

"*God Almighty!*"

Devil's weight left her—she was plucked rudely from the bed. Trapped in his arms in a froth of petticoats, blinking wildly, Honoria saw the door approaching; juggling her, Devil swung it wide.

And deposited her on her feet in the corridor.

"*What* . . . ?" Breasts swelling, Honoria whirled to face him, the rest of her question writ large in her eyes.

Devil pointed a finger at her nose. "Your declaration." He looked wild, dark hair disheveled, black brows slashing down, lips a thin, hard line. His chest rose and fell dramatically.

Honoria drew in a deep breath.

"Not now!" Devil scowled. "When you've thought it over properly."

With that, he slammed the door.

Honoria's jaw dropped; she stared at the oak panels. Abruptly snapping her mouth shut, she reached for the doorknob.

And heard the lock fall home.

In utter disbelief, she stared at the door, her mouth open once more. Then she gritted her teeth, screwed her eyes tight and, fists clenched, gave vent to a frustrated scream.

She opened her eyes—the door remained shut.

Jaw setting ominously, Honoria swung on her heel and stalked off.

Devil escaped from his house and sought refuge at Manton's. It was late afternoon, a time when many of his peers still in town could be counted on to look in, to spend an hour or two culping wafers in convivial company.

Scanning those occupying the shooting stalls, his gaze alighted on one dark head. He strolled forward, waiting until his mark discharged his pistol before drawling: "You haven't quite corrected for the kick, brother mine."

Richard turned his head—and raised one brow. "You offering to teach me, big brother?"

Devil's teeth gleamed. "I gave up teaching you years ago— I was thinking more along the lines of a little friendly competition."

Richard grinned back. "A tenner each wafer?"

"Why not just make it a monkey the lot?"

"Done."

In perfect amity, they set to culping wafer after wafer; acquaintances strolled up, making none-too-serious suggestions, to which the brothers replied in like vein. No one, seeing them together, could doubt their relationship. Devil was the taller by an inch or so; although Richard lacked his more developed musculature, much of the difference lay in the four years between them. Their faces, seen separately, were not obviously alike, Devil's features being leaner, harder, more austere, yet when seen side by side, the same patriarchal planes, the same arrogant nose and brow line, the same aggressive chin, were readily apparent.

Standing back to let Richard take his shot, Devil smiled to himself. Other than Vane, who was as familiar as his shadow, no one was closer to him than Richard. Their similarity went deep, much deeper than the physical. Of all the Bar Cynster, Richard was the one he could predict most easily—because Richard always reacted as he did.

The retort of Richard's pistol echoed in the stall; Devil looked up, noting the hole an inch to the left of the target's center. They were using a brace plus one of Manton's specials, wicked, long-barreled specimens. While well balanced, over the distance they were shooting, the longest permitted in the gallery, there was a definite difference between the guns; using the three in rotation meant they had to constantly readjust their aim.

The assistant waiting on them had reloaded the next pistol; Devil weighed it in his hand. Richard shifted positions; Devil swung into place and raised his arm. His shot holed the wafer between the center and Richard's shot.

"Tsk, tsk! Always impulsive, Sylvester—taking a fraction more time would yield a better result."

Richard, who'd been lounging against the stall wall, stiffened, then straightened, his previously relaxed expression leaching to impassivity. He nodded briefly to Charles, then turned to supervise the reloading.

In contrast, Devil's smile broadened wickedly. "As you know, Charles, wasting time's not my style."

Charles's pale lashes flickered; a frown showed fleetingly in his eyes.

Devil noted it; unfailingly urbane, he picked up a freshly loaded pistol. "Care to show us how?" Swinging the gun about, he laid the barrel across his sleeve and presented the butt to Charles.

Charles reached for it—his hand stopped in midair. Then his jaw firmed; wrapping his fingers about the polished butt, he hefted the pistol. Stepping past Devil, Charles took up his stance. He flexed his shoulders once, then lifted his arm. He sighted, taking, as he'd said, only a moment longer than Devil, before firing.

The wafer's center disappeared.

With a sincere "Bravo," Devil clapped Charles on the shoul-

der. "You're one of the few who can do that intentionally."
Charles looked up; Devil grinned. "Care to join us?"

Charles did; despite his initial stiffness, even Richard studied
his eldest cousin's style. Shooting was one of the few gentlemanly
pursuits Charles shared with the members of the Bar Cynster;
pistol shooting was an activity at which he excelled. Charles
accepted Devil's easy compliments as his due, but after twenty
minutes recalled another engagement and took his leave.

Watching Charles's retreating back, Richard shook his head.
"If he wasn't such a prig, he might be bearable."

Devil studied the score sheets. "What's the tally?"

"I lost count when Charles appeared." Richard glanced at
the sheets, then grimaced. "You probably won—you usually
do."

"Let's declare it a draw." Devil laid the pistols aside. "For
me, it served its purpose."

"Which was?" Brows rising, Richard followed Devil from
the stall.

"Distraction." With a nod for Manton, who smiled and
bowed in return, Devil led the way from the gallery.

Richard ambled in his wake, coming up with him on the
pavement. Glancing into Devil's frowning face, Richard raised
his brows higher. "Well, you're certainly that."

Devil blinked and focused. "What?"

"Distracted."

Devil grimaced. "It's just that . . . I've forgotten something—
something about Tolly's murder."

Instantly, Richard sobered. "Something important?"

"I've an ominous feeling it might be crucial, but every time
I try to catch hold of it, it slips back into the mist."

"Stop trying so hard." Richard clapped him on the shoulder.
"Go talk to Honoria Prudence—distract yourself some more."
He grinned. "Your vital clue will probably come to mind in the
most unlikely situation."

Stifling the impulse to inform his brother that it was Honoria
Prudence he needed distracting from, Devil nodded. They parted,
Richard heading for his lodgings, Devil striding along the pave-
ments toward Grosvenor Square.

In his present condition, the walk wouldn't hurt.

*   *   *

The wind had risen by the time Devil reached his front door in the small hours of the morning. After leaving Richard, he'd returned home only to dress for the evening. Like most of his recent evenings, the past night had been devoted to what, borrowing Honoria's description, he now mentally dubbed "Lucifer's discreditable rumor." It was not something he or his cousins could investigate directly—their views were too widely known. No one would talk openly in their presence for fear of repercussions. Which meant he'd had to find a pawn to do their investigating for them—he'd finally settled on one Viscount Bromley. His lordship was bored, dissipated, a hardened gamester, always on the lookout for distraction.

A renowned cardplayer himself, Devil had found no difficulty in dangling the right lure before his lordship's nose. As of tonight, the viscount was well on the way to losing his shirt. After which, his lordship was going to prove exceedingly helpful. And after that, he'd probably never play piquet again.

Grinning grimly, Devil paused, latchkey in hand; eyes narrowing, he scanned the night sky. It was dark, but not so dark he couldn't see the thunderheads rolling in, lowering blackly over the housetops.

He quickly let himself in. He hoped Webster had remembered his instructions.

The storm broke with an almighty crash.

It flung Honoria straight into hell. Only this time, it was a different hell, with a different scene of carnage.

From above, she looked down on the wreck of a carriage, all splintered wood and crushed leather seats. The horses, tangled and torn, were screaming. Beside the carriage lay the figure of a man, sprawled, long limbs flung in impossible angles. Black locks covered his eyes; his face was pale as death.

He lay unmoving, with the absolute stillness of one gone from this world.

The black misery that welled from Honoria's heart was stronger than ever before. It caught her, effortlessly whirled her, then dragged her down into a vortex of desolation, the vale of unending tears.

He was gone—and she couldn't breathe, couldn't find voice to protest, could find no strength to call him back. With a choking sob, hands outstretched, beseeching the gods, she stepped forward.

Her fingers met solid flesh. Warm flesh.

"Hush."

The nightmare shattered; despair howled, then slid away, slinking back into the darkness, relinquishing its hold. Honoria woke.

She was not in her bed but standing before the window, her feet cold on the boards. Outside, the wind shrieked; she flinched as rain stung the pane. Her cheeks were wet with tears she couldn't recall shedding; her fine lawn nightgown was no match for the room's chill. She shivered.

Warm arms surrounded her, steadied her. Wonderingly, she looked up—for one instant, she wasn't sure which was reality and which the dream—then the heat reaching through his fine shirt registered. With a sob, she flung herself against him.

"It's all right." Devil closed his arms about her; with one hand, he stroked her hair. She was quivering; her fists, tight balls, clutched his shirt. Slipping his hand beneath the heavy fall of her hair, he stroked her nape, leaning his cheek against the top of her head. "It's all right."

She shook her head furiously. "It's *not* all right." Her voice was choked, muffled in his chest. Devil felt her tears, hot against his skin. Gripping his shirt, she tried, ineffectually, to shake him. "You were *killed*! Dead."

Devil blinked. He'd assumed her nightmare concerned her parents' and siblings' deaths. "I'm not dead." He knew that for certain; she was wearing nothing bar a single layer of fine lawn, a fact his rakish senses had immediately noted. Luckily, he'd come prepared. Reaching out, he snagged the blanket he'd left on the window seat. "Come—sit by the fire." She was tense, cold and shivering; she wouldn't sleep until she was relaxed and warm.

"There's no fire—one of the footmen put it out. There's something wrong with the chimney." Honoria imparted the information without lifting her head. She had no idea what was going on; her heart was thumping wildly, sheer panic walked her nerves.

Devil turned her to the door. "In the sitting room."

He tried to set her from him; when she wouldn't let go, he

heaved a sigh and draped the blanket about her back and shoulders, tucking it about her as best he could.

Honoria accepted his ministrations meekly—just as long as she didn't have to let go.

She felt him hesitate; he muttered something incomprehensible, then stooped and swung her into his arms. The movement broke her hold; she clutched two fresh handfuls of his shirt and pressed her cheek to his chest, relieved beyond measure when his arms tightened about her. The turbulence inside her was frightening.

As if she was a child, he carried her into the sitting room and sat in a large armchair facing the blazing fire. He settled her in his lap; she immediately curled close, pressing tightly into his hard body. Both chair and fire had changed since she'd retired, a fact she noted, but that was the most minor aspect of the confusion clouding her mind.

Her heart was still racing, high in her throat; her lips were dry. There was a metallic taste in her mouth; her skin felt coldly clammy. Her mind was awhirl, thoughts and fears, present and past, jostling for prominence, demanding responses. Reality and fearful fancy merged, then separated, then merged again, partners in a giddy dance.

She couldn't think, couldn't talk—she didn't even know what she felt.

Devil asked no questions but simply held her, stroking her hair, her back, his large palms moving slowly, hypnotically, yet without any sensual intent. His touch was pure comfort.

Honoria closed her eyes and leaned into his strength; a shuddering sigh escaped her, some of her tension drained. For countless minutes, she lay in his arms, listening to his heart, steady and sure, beating beneath her cheek. Like a rock, his strength anchored her; under its influence, the kaleidoscope of her emotions slowed, then settled—suddenly, everything was clear.

"Your phaeton." Twisting, she looked up at him. "It wasn't an accident—you were meant to die."

The flames lit his face; she could see his frown clearly. "Honoria, it was an accident. I told you—the axle broke."

"Why did it break? Do axles usually break—especially in carriages from the sort of carriagemaker you patronize?"

His lips firmed. "We might have hit something."

"You said you hadn't."

She felt his sigh. "Honoria, it was an accident—the rest is all nightmare. The fact is, I'm alive."

"But you're not *supposed* to be!" She struggled to sit up but his arms firmed, holding her still. "I don't have nightmares about deaths that didn't happen. You were *meant* to be killed. The only reason you're alive is . . ." Lost for words, she gestured.

"I'm a Cynster," he supplied. "I'm invincible, remember?"

He wasn't—he was a flesh-and-blood man, no one knew that better than she. Honoria set her lips mutinously. "If someone tampered with the axle, wouldn't it show?"

Devil looked into her eyes, unnaturally bright, and wondered if sleepwalkers got fevers. "The whole carriage, axle and all, was reduced to splinters." What could he, what should he, say to ease her mind? "Why would anyone want to kill me?"

He realized, instantly, that that wasn't a wise choice. Fighting his hold, Honoria squirmed and sat straighter. "Of course!" Eyes wide, she stared at him. "Tolly—Tolly was coming to *warn* you. Whoever's trying to kill you had to kill him before he did."

Briefly, Devil closed his eyes—in pain. Opening them, he lifted her and resettled her, clamping his arms about her. Then he met her gaze. "You are weaving this from whole cloth—and from the remnants of your nightmare. If you like, we can discuss this in the morning, when you can examine the facts in the cold light of day."

Even in her present state, he could sense the rebellion within her. Her chin firmed, then tilted. Turning her head, she settled back against his chest. "As you wish."

Too wise to take exception to her tone, he waited, patiently, for some of her haughty tension to leave her, then tightened his arms again.

Staring into the leaping flames, Honoria reexamined her newfound certainty and could not fault it. She knew what she knew, even if he refused to see it. He was a Cynster male—he believed he was invincible. She'd no intention of arguing the point, any more than she intended to change her perspective. Her "facts" might not appear all that substantial in daylight, but she wasn't about to deny them.

Her life, her purpose, was now crystal-clear. She knew, absolutely, with complete and utter conviction, precisely what she had to do. He'd challenged her to face her deepest fear; fate was now challenging her to face a deeper truth—the truth of what she felt for him.

She would give him what he asked, all he asked, and more; she would let nothing—*no one*—take him from her. She might be his, but he was hers. Nothing under heaven could change that.

Last time death had threatened those she loved, she'd been helpless, unable to save them. This time, she would not stand by; she would not let any mere mortal steal her destiny from her.

Conviction, total certainty, infused her. Her earlier confusion had passed; she felt calm, in control. Focused. Aware. She frowned. "Why are you here?"

He hesitated, then answered: "You always sleepwalk during storms."

"Always?" Then she remembered the night Tolly died. "In the cottage?"

She felt Devil nod. Safe in his arms, she considered, then shook her head. "That can't be right. It's been eight years since the accident. I haven't woken anywhere other than in my bed and I've slept in so many different houses, through so many different storms." It had only been when violent death had hovered close—at the cottage, and now, in the aftermath of his accident. Honoria mentally nodded, her conclusion confirmed. If death's presence was what evoked her nightmare, then death had stalked him that morning.

Behind her, Devil shrugged. "You walked tonight—that's all that matters. I'll stay until you sleep."

Her gaze on the flames, Honoria raised her brows. And considered that in some detail. Increasingly salacious detail. Then she grimaced. His muscles were locked, not tensed with passion but holding it at bay.

Turning her head, she looked up, into his face, all hard angles and austere planes. Raising a hand, she traced one lean cheek; at her touch, he froze. "I don't suppose you'd consider taking me to bed?"

His jaw locked; flames danced in his eyes. "No."

"Why not?"

Devil met her gaze; when he spoke, his tone was flat.

"You're upset—distraught. And you haven't made your decision yet."

Honoria sat up and twisted to face him. "I'm not upset now. And I *have* made up my mind."

Devil winced. Teeth gritted, he lifted her and set her bottom back on his thigh. "I'm not taking you to bed—to wife—purely because you're afraid of lightning!"

Honoria narrowed her eyes at him—his expression was not encouraging. "This is ridiculous." She felt soft, warm and empty inside.

"Forget it." Devil ground the words out. "*Just—sit—still.*"

Honoria stared at him, then uttered a strangled, disgusted sound and slumped back against his chest.

"Go to sleep."

She bit her tongue. In the orangery, she'd surprised him; after the accident, her tending him had simply been too much. He wouldn't again make the mistake of letting her touch him— without that, she stood no chance of getting his body to change his mind.

The warmth surrounding her had unlocked her muscles. Safe, certain—determined to prevail—she slid into untroubled slumber.

She woke the next morning neatly tucked in her bed. Blinking her eyes wide, she was almost at the point of dismissing her memories of the night as dreams when her gaze alighted on the odd blanket draped across the bed's corner. She narrowed her eyes at the inoffensive plaid; her recollections became much clearer.

With a disgusted humph, she sat up and threw back the covers. It was clearly time she had a long talk with his Obstinate Grace of St. Ives.

Gowned appropriately, she swept into the breakfast parlor primed to declare herself won—only to discover he'd left the house early, ostensibly on business. He was not expected to return until shortly before dinner, after which he would escort her to the Theater Royal.

She amended her plans—he invited some country neighbors passing through town to join them in their box. The Draycotts were charming, and utterly unshakable. At Devil's invitation,

Lord Draycott accompanied them back to Grosvenor Square, the better to discuss repairs to the Five-Mile fence.

There was no storm that night.

The next morning, Honoria rose early, determined to catch her worm. He didn't even appear, taking breakfast in his library, in the protective presence of his steward.

By evening, she'd reached the end of *her* tether. Why he was avoiding her she had no idea, but his actions left her no choice. There was one approach guaranteed to gain his complete and undivided attention—as far as she was concerned, there was no reason she couldn't employ it.

Chapter 16

*D*ONNNNNNNG.

Devil spared not a glance for the long-case clock as he passed it on the stairs. Crossing the gallery, he lifted his candle in insouciant salute to his father's portrait, then strode on, into the long corridor that led to his rooms.

His sire, he was sure, would applaud his night's work.

In his pocket lay three notes inscribed with Viscount Bromley's square script. Bromley was already deep in debt, although by how much he was probably unaware. Of course, the last hand had seen the luck change. Devil smiled. He'd have Bromley tied tight in less than a week.

Despite his success, as he drew nearer his door, he tensed; the frustration he continually held at bay exerted its power. An ache settled in his gut; muscle after muscle turned heavy, as if he was fighting himself. Grimacing, he reached for the doorknob. As long as he limited his time with Honoria to public, social venues, he could cope.

He'd told her the truth—he was more than capable of manipulating, coercing, or seducing her into marriage. Indeed, his very nature compelled him to do so, which was why he felt like a wild beast caged. He was a born conqueror—taking what he wanted came naturally. Subtleties, sensitivities, were usually of little consequence.

His expression hardening, he entered his room. Shutting the door, he crossed to the tallboy; setting the candlestick by the mirror on its top, he untied his armband, unbuttoned his waistcoat, then eased the diamond pin from his cravat. Reaching out to lay the pin in its box, his gaze slid past his reflection—white glimmered in the shadows behind him.

His head snapped around. Then, his tread utterly silent, he crossed to the chair by the fire.

Even before he touched the silk, he knew to whom it belonged. The fire, a mere glow of coals, was still warm enough to send her scent rising, wafting upward to ensorcel him. He only just stopped himself from lifting the soft silk to his face, from inhaling the beguiling fragrance. Stifling a curse, he dropped the peignoir as if it was as hot as the fire's coals. Slowly, he turned to the bed.

He couldn't believe his eyes. Even from this distance, he could see her hair, a rippling chestnut wave breaking across his pillows. She lay on her side, facing the center of the bed. The sight drew him like a lodestone. He was beside the bed, looking down on her, before he knew he'd moved.

No woman had ever slept in his bed—at least not during his tenure. His father had been of the stated opinion that a duke's bed was reserved for his duchess; he had agreed—no other woman had lain between his silken sheets. To return late at night to discover those sheets warmed by the one woman he wanted to find asleep there, breathing gently, soft, sleek limbs sunk deep into the down, left him reeling.

He couldn't think.

The realization left him shaking, battling a too-powerful urge to put aside all explanations and react—act—do what he wished with all his conqueror's soul to do.

But he needed to think—to be sure, *certain*, that he wasn't being led by the nose—no, not his nose, but another protuberant part of his anatomy—into committing a deed he would later regret. He'd taken his stance, one he knew was right. Demanding her knowing commitment, heart, mind, and soul, might not be a customary requirement, yet for him, with her, it simply had to be.

His gaze roamed her face, softly flushed, then slid lower, filling in what the sheet concealed. Swallowing a savage curse, he swung away. He fell to pacing, his footfalls cushioned by the carpet. Why the hell was she here?

He cast a glittering glance her way—it fell on her lips, slightly parted. He heard again the urgent, intensely feminine moans she'd uttered in the orangery while writhing beneath his hands. With a muted oath, he paced to the other side of the bed. From there, the view was less torturing.

Three minutes later, he still couldn't marshal a single un-lustful thought. Muttering one last, disgusted expletive, he swung back to the bed. Sitting on it was too dangerous, given her hands and her propensity to get them on him. Standing be-side the carved post at one end, he reached across and, through the covers, grasped her ankle. He shook it.

She muttered and tried to wriggle free. Devil closed his hand, locked his fingers about her slim bones and shook her again.

She opened her eyes—blinking sleepily. "You're back."

"As you see." Releasing her, Devil straightened. Folding his arms, he leaned against the bedpost. "Would you care to explain why, of all the beds in this house, you chose mine to fall asleep in?"

Honoria raised a brow. "I would have thought that was ob-vious—I was waiting for you."

Devil hesitated; his faculties remained fogged by seething lust. "To what purpose?"

"I have a few questions."

His jaw firmed. "One o'clock in the morning, in my bed, is neither a suitable nor wise choice of time and venue to ask ques-tions."

"On the contrary"—Honoria started to sit up—"it's the per-fect place."

Devil watched the covers fall, revealing her shoulders, clearly visible through translucent silk, revealing the ripe swell of her breasts—"Stop!" His jaw clenched hard. "Honoria, just—*sit—still.*"

Tartly, she hauled the covers up as she sat, then folded her arms beneath her breasts. She frowned at him. "Why have you been avoiding me?"

Devil returned the frown. "I would have thought *that* was obvious. You've a decision to make—I cannot conceive that pri-vate meetings between us, at present, would help. They certainly wouldn't help me." He'd intended giving her time—a week at least. The three days so far had been hell.

Honoria held his gaze. "About that decision—you've told me it's important to you—you haven't told me why."

For a long moment, he didn't move, didn't speak, then his folded arms lifted as he drew a deep breath. "I'm a Cynster—I've been raised to acquire, defend, and protect. My family is the core of my existence—without a family, without children, I'd have nothing to protect or defend, no reason to acquire. Given your past, I want to hear your decision declared. You're an Anstruther-Wetherby—given all I know of you, if you make a declaration, you'll stick by it. Whatever the challenge, you won't back down."

Honoria held his gaze steadily. "Given what you know of me, are you sure I'm the right wife for you?"

The answer came back, deep and sure. "You're mine."

Between them, the atmosphere rippled; ignoring the breathlessness only he could evoke, Honoria raised her brows. "Would you agree that, at present, I'm free of your seductive influence? Free of coercion or manipulation?"

He was watching her closely; he hesitated, then nodded.

"In that case—" She flung back the covers and scrambled across the bed. Devil straightened—before he could move away, Honoria grabbed the front of his shirt, and hauled herself up on her knees. "I have a declaration to make!"

Locking her eyes on his, locking both hands in his shirt, she drew a deep breath. "I *want* to marry you. I want to be your wife, your duchess, to face the world at your side. I *want* to bear your children." She invested the last with all the conviction in her soul.

He'd stilled. She tugged and he moved closer, until his legs hit the bed. He stood directly before her as she knelt, knees wide, on the bed's edge.

"Most importantly of all." She paused to draw another breath; her eyes on his, she spread her hands across his chest. "I want *you*. Now." In case he hadn't yet got her message, she added: "Tonight."

Devil felt desire soar, triumphant, compelling. Excruciatingly aware of her hands sliding as his chest swelled, he forced himself to ask: "Are you sure?" Exasperation flared in her eyes; he shook his head. "I mean about tonight." Of the rest, he had not a doubt.

Her exasperation didn't die. "*Yes!*" she said—and kissed him.

He managed not to wrap his arms about her and crush her, managed to cling grimly to his reins as she wound her arms about his neck, pressed herself to him in utter abandon and flagrantly incited his possession. He locked his hands about her waist, steadying her—then responded to her invitation. She opened to him instantly, her mouth softening, a sweet cavern to fill, to explore, to claim.

She took him in and held him, took his breath, then gave it back. Devil set his hands skimming, fingers firming, thumbs pressing inward at the tops of her thighs. Her nightgown was a mere cobweb of gossamer silk; he let his hands fall, tracing her sleek thighs before closing one hand above each knee. Slowly, he slid his fingers upward, feeling the silk slide over satiny skin, his thumbs drawing lazy circles along her inner thighs. Higher and higher, inch by inch, he raised his hands—the long muscles of her thighs tensed, then locked, then quivered.

He stopped with his thumbs just below her soft curls. Drawing back from their kiss, he watched her—and waited for her lids to rise. When they did, he trapped her gaze with his—and drew two more circles. She shivered.

"Once I take you, there'll be no turning back."

Determination flared, steely blue in her eyes. "Hallelujah."

Their lips met again; Devil loosened his reins. Desire, hot and urgent, rose between them; passion rode in its wake.

Honoria sensed the change in him, felt his muscles harden, felt his hands, still gripping her thighs, tighten. An expectant quiver ran through her tensed muscles. He released them. One hand slid around to spread across her bottom; her skin turned feverish at his touch. He caressed her in slow, sensuous circles—her senses followed, distracted by the silk shifting between hand and naked skin.

Then his hand firmed, cupping her bottom—in the same instant, she felt his other hand slide between her parted thighs.

His head angled over hers; his kiss became more demanding. He stroked her through the gossamer silk, stroked and caressed and teased until the silk clung, a second skin, muting his touch, tantalizing her senses. Honoria tensed, fingertips sinking into the muscles of his back. She felt his hand shift; one long finger slid into her, probing gently, then more deliberately.

Suddenly, she couldn't breathe. She pulled back with a gasp—he let her go, his hands leaving her. Grasping her waist, he toppled her back on the bed.

"Wait."

Devil crossed to the door to his dressing room, opened it, confirmed Sligo had not waited up, then locked it. Striding back across the room, he shrugged out of his coat and threw it on the chair. Flicking the intricate folds of his cravat undone, he tugged the yard-long strip from his neck, then stripped off his waistcoat and sent it to join his coat, before unlacing his cuffs and pulling off his shirt. The flame from the candle on the tallboy gilded the muscles of his back, then he turned and picked up the candle-stick.

Sprawled, breathless, across his bed, Honoria watched as he set flame to the two five-armed candelabra upon the mantelpiece. Concentrating on each graceful movement, on the play of the flames over his sculpted frame, she held back her thoughts, too scandalous for words. Anticipation had soared; excitement shivered over her skin. Her lungs had seized; a delicious panic had tightened every nerve.

Leaving the single candle on the mantelpiece, Devil carried one candelabra to the side of the bed, tugging the bedside table forward so that the candles' light fell across the covers. Blinking, aware that in the light she'd appear next to naked, Honoria watched as he placed the second candelabra similiarly on the bed's opposite side. She frowned. "Isn't it usually night? I mean dark?"

Devil met her gaze. "You've forgotten something."

Honoria couldn't think what and wasn't sure she cared; her gaze roamed his chest as he walked toward the bed, bathed in golden light. He stopped by her feet, then turned and sat. While he pulled off his boots, she distracted herself with his back. His cuts and scrapes had healed; she reached out a hand and traced one. His skin flickered at her touch; he muttered something beneath his breath. Honoria grinned and spread her fingers—he stood, casting one black glance back at her before stripping off his trousers. He sat to pull them free of his feet; Honoria stared at the long, broad muscles framing his spine, tailing into twin hollows below his waist. He reached, and muscles shifted; the view was almost as good as his chest.

Free of his last restriction, Devil half turned and fell back on the bed. He knew what would happen—Honoria didn't. With a valiantly smothered shriek, she rolled into him, into his arms, unable to gain any purchase on the slippery sheets. He lifted her over him, her legs tangling with his, her hair fanning over his naked chest.

He expected her to be shocked, expected her to hesitate— this had to be the first time she'd touched a naked male. The shock was certainly there—he saw it in her stunned expression; hesitation followed—it lasted a split second.

In the next, their lips met—there was no longer any distinction between him kissing her and her kissing him. He felt her hands on his chest, greedily exploring; he ravaged her mouth— and felt her fingers sink deep. He spread his hands over the firm mounds of her derriere and held her against him, easing the throbbing ache of his erection against her soft belly. She writhed, heated and eager, thin silk no barrier to his senses.

Some women were catlike, elusively seductive—she was far too bold to be a cat. She was demanding, aggressive, intent on, not just fraying his reins, but shredding them. Deliberately invoking his desire, his demons—all the possessiveness in his soul. Which, given she was a virgin, qualified as abject madness.

Breathing raggedly, he pulled back from their kiss. "For God's sake, slow down!"

Engrossed in caressing one flat nipple, Honoria didn't look up. "I'm twenty-four—I've wasted enough time."

She wriggled; Devil gritted his teeth. "You're twenty-four— you should know better. You should at least have some measure of self-preservation." Intent on impaling herself on her fate, she seemed to have no concept of how much he could hurt her, of how much his strength overshadowed hers, of how much harder than her he was.

She was intent on learning—her hands reached lower, exploring the ridges of his lower chest. Devil felt desire rise, full-blown, ravenous—too strong for her to handle. Releasing her buttocks, he grasped her upper arms.

Just as she grasped him.

The shock that lanced through him nearly shattered his control. He froze. So did Honoria.

She looked into his face—his eyes were shut, his expression graven. Carefully, she curled her fingers again, utterly fascinated by her discovery. How could something so hard, so rigid, so ridged, so blatantly, elementally male, be so silky smooth, so soft? Again, she touched the smoothly rounded head—it was akin to stroking hot steel through the finest peach silk.

Devil groaned; he reached down and closed his hand over hers—not to pull it away but to curl her fingers more tightly. Eagerly, she followed his unspoken instructions, obviously much more to her taste than slowing down.

He let her caress him until he thought his jaw would break—he had to pull her hand away. She fought him, squirming all over him, soft, hot, silk-encased flesh writhing over his by-now-painful erection.

With an oath, he caught her hands, one in each of his, and rolled, trapping her beneath him. He anchored her hands to the bed and kissed her, deeply and yet more deeply, letting his weight sink fully onto her—until she had no breath left to fight him, no strength to defy him.

They both stilled; in that instant, she was open to him, heated, her thighs spread, soft and welcoming, her hips a cradle in which he already lay. All he needed to do was reach down and rip the thin silk from between them, then sink his throbbing staff into her softness and claim her.

Simple.

Gritting his teeth, Devil let go of her hands and lifted away. He moved back. Knees spread, he sat back on his ankles in the middle of the bed. Locking his eyes on hers, he beckoned with both hands. "Come here."

Her eyes widened; they searched his, then fell—jaw locked, he suffered her scrutiny, saw the age-old question form in her eyes.

Giddy, not only from breathlessness, Honoria slowly blinked, then raised her eyes to his face. He looked like some god, seated in the candlelight, his maleness so flagrantly displayed. The soft light gilded the muscles of his arms, his chest—and the rest of him. She drew in a deep breath; her heartbeat thundered in her ears. Slowly, she rose on one elbow, then freed her legs from the folds of her nightgown and came up on her knees, facing him.

He took her hands in his and drew her closer, then closed his hands about her waist and lifted her. As he set her down astride his thighs, Honoria frowned into his eyes. "If you tell me we have to wait, I'll scream."

The planes of his face looked harder than granite. "You'll scream anyway."

She frowned harder—and saw his lips twitch.

"With pleasure."

The idea was new to her—she was still puzzling as Devil drew her closer. High on her knees as she was, her hips grazed his lower chest.

"Kiss me."

He didn't need to ask twice; willingly, she twined her arms about his neck and set her lips to his.

One hand at her back holding her upright, Devil deepened the kiss, skimming his other hand upward, over her taut abdomen, before closing it about her breast. The already heated flesh swelled and firmed; he kneaded and heard her moan. He drew back from the kiss; she let her head fall back, the exposed curve of her throat an offering he didn't refuse. He trailed hot kisses down the pulsing vein; she inched closer, pressing her breast to his palm.

Bending her back, he lowered his head. She stilled, her breathing harried. One long lick dampened the silk covering one nipple. She gasped as his lips touched the ruched peak—he suckled lightly and felt her melt.

He couldn't even remember the last time he'd bedded a virgin—even then, whoever she was, she hadn't been a gently reared, twenty-four-year-old capable of unexpected enthusiasms. He harbored no illusions over how difficult the next half hour would be; for the first time in his lengthy career, he prayed he'd be strong enough to manage—her, and the passion she unleashed in him. Head bent, he tortured one tightly budded nipple, then turned his attention to its mate.

Sinking her fingers into his upper arms, Honoria gasped and swayed. With her bones transmuted to warm honey, her weak grip, his hand at her back and the tantalizing tug of his lips were all that was keeping her upright. Hot and wet, his lips, his mouth, moved over her breasts, teasing first one aching peak, then the other until both were swollen tight. She ached to touch him, to send her hands searching, but didn't dare let go. His lips left her; a second later, his teeth grazed one crinkled nipple.

Sharp sensation lanced through her; she gave a muted cry. His lips returned, soothing her flesh, then he suckled hard—and within her heat rose. Wave upon wave, it answered his call, a primal urge building, swelling, surging ever stronger. With a long-drawn moan, she swayed forward, into his kiss.

It caught her, anchored her, as his hands roved her body, heated palms burning. Every curve she possessed, he traced; every square inch of her skin tingled, then ached for more. Her back, her sides, the curve of her stomach, the long muscles of her thighs, her arms, her bottom—none escaped his attention; her skin was flushed, dewed, when he lifted the edge of her gown.

The shiver that racked her came from deep within, a final farewell to the virgin she was but would be no more. His hands rose and he released her lips. From under weighted lids, Honoria saw the silk in his hands, already above her waist. Dragging in a huge breath that, for all her effort, was insufficient to steady her giddy head, she lifted her arms. The gown whispered from her. It screened the candles as it floated out beyond the bed; she traced its fall, feeling the air, then his hands, on her skin.

His arms closed about her.

Heat, warm skin, hard muscle surrounded her; his crisp mat of midnight black hair rasped her sensitized nipples. Hard lips found hers, demanding, commanding, ravishing her senses—no surrender requested, no quarter considered—he would take her, body and soul, and more.

For one instant, the onslaught swept her before it, then she shuddered in his arms, set her feet against desire's tide—and met his demands with her own. Passion stirred, stretched, unfolded between them; splaying her fingers, she sank the tips into his chest, and felt his muscles lock. She kissed him with a fervor to match his own, reveling in the urgency building between them, glorying in the heady rush, the growing vortex of their need.

Excitement whirled as their lips melded, each breath the other's, tongues entwined. She sank into his heat, drank it in, and felt it flood her. His hands roamed, as urgently demanding as his lips, hard palms sculpting, fingers flexing, possessing. Still on her knees, her thighs locked on either side of his, her hips pressed to his abdomen, she felt his hands curve and cup her bottom. One remained, holding her high, the other slid lower, long fingers questing. They found her heat and slid further, pressing between her thighs, probing the hot, slick folds, caressing, then pressing deep.

And deeper, igniting her fire.

The wild rush of flames seared her; she ached and burned. His only response was to deepen their kiss, holding her captive as the flames roared on. His fingers stroked slowly, deliberately—the flames grew in intensity, to a sheet, then a wall, finally erupting into an inferno, fueled by urgent need.

The inferno pulsed to her heartbeat; the same beat rang in her veins, in her ears, a tattoo of desire driving her on.

Abruptly, Devil drew back from their kiss. His fingers left her; he cupped her bottom with both hands. "Slide down."

Honoria couldn't believe the strength of the compulsion that gripped her—she needed him inside her more than she needed to breathe. Even so . . . She shook her head. "You're never going to fit."

His hands firmed about her hips. "Just slide."

She did, sinking lower, his hands guiding her. She felt the first touch of his staff, hot and hard, and stopped. He slipped his fingers between her thighs and opened her; she felt the first intimate intrusion of his body into hers. Catching her breath on a strangled gasp, she sank lower, and felt the rounded head slip inside.

He felt large, much larger than she'd expected. She sucked in a breath; under the weight of his hands, she sank still lower. Hard as forged iron, hot as unquenched steel, he pressed into her. She shook her head again. "This is not going to work."

"It will." She felt his words within her; he was, if anything, even tenser than she, rock-hard muscles flickering. "You'll stretch to take me—women's bodies are built that way."

He was the expert. Through the maelstrom of emotions besetting her—uncertainty, desire, and giddy need, laced with distant remnants of modesty, all subsumed beneath the most desperate longing she'd ever known—Honoria clung to that fact. The inferno inside her swelled; she sank down.

And stopped.

Immediately, Devil lifted her, not quite losing her clinging heat. "Sink down again." She did, until her maidenhead again impeded their progress. Under his hands, she repeated the maneuver again and again.

She was hot, slick and very tight; once she was moving freely, he brushed his lips against her temple. "Kiss me."

She lifted her head immediately, swollen lips parted, eager for more. He took her mouth voraciously, struggling to harness the wild passion that drove him, battling to remain in control long enough to avoid unnecessarily hurting her. He was going to hurt her enough as it was.

On the heels of the thought came the deed. One, powerful upward thrust, timed to meet her downward slide, enforced by the pressure of his hands on her hips, and it was done. He breached her in that single movement, forging deep into her body, filling her, stretching her.

She screamed, the sound smothered by their kiss. Her body tensed; so did his.

Focusing completely on her, waiting for her softening, the first sign of acceptance that he knew would come, Devil grimly denied the primal urge to lose himself in her heat, to plunder the scalding softness that clasped him, to assuage his driving need.

Their lips had parted; they were both breathing raggedly. From under his lashes, he watched as she moistened her lips with her tongue.

"Was that the scream you were talking about?"

"No." He touched his lips to the corner of hers. "There'll be no more pain—from now on, you'll only scream with pleasure."

No more pain. Her senses awash, overloaded with sensation, Honoria could only hope. The memory of the sharp agony that had speared her was so intense she could still feel it. Yet with every breath, with every heartbeat, the heat of him, the glow suffusing her, eased the ache. She tried to shift; his hands firmed, holding her still.

"Wait."

She had to obey. Until that moment, she hadn't appreciated how completely in his control she was. The hard, throbbing reality that had invaded her, intimately filling her, impinged fully on her mind. Vulnerability swept her, rippling through her, all the way to . . .

Her senses focused on the place where they joined. She heard Devil groan. Blinking, she looked up; his eyes were shut, his features like stone. Under her hands, the muscles of his shoulders were taut, locked in some phantom battle. Inside her, the steady throb of him radiated heat and a sense of barely reined urgency. Her pain had gone. On the thought, the last of her tension ebbed; the last vestiges of resistance fell away. Tentatively, her gaze on his face, she eased from his hold, and rose slowly on her knees.

"*Yes.*" The single word was heavy with encouragement.

He stopped her at the precise point beyond which their contact would break. She sensed his eagerness, the same compelling urgency that welled within her; she needed no direction to sink slowly down, enthralled by the feel of his steely hardness sliding, slick and hot, deep into her.

She did it again, and again, head falling back as she slid sensuously down, opening her senses completely, savoring every drawn-out second. Their guidance no longer required, his hands roved, reclaiming her breasts, the full curves of her bottom, the sensitive backs of her thighs. All awkwardness, all reticence, had vanished; lifting her head, Honoria draped her arms about his neck and sought his lips with hers. The glide of their bodies, uniting in a rhythm as old as the moon, felt exquisitely right. She gave him her mouth; as he claimed it, she tightened her arms, pressing herself to him, drawn to the promise contained within his powerful body, flagrantly demanding more.

He drew back from the kiss; under his lashes, she saw his eyes gleam.

"Are you all right?"

His hands traced mesmerizing circles over her bottom. At the peak of her rise, Honoria held his gaze—and slowly, concentrating on the rigid hardness invading her, sank down.

She felt his rippling shudder and saw his jaw firm. His eyes flashed. Greatly daring, she licked the vein pulsing at the base of his throat. "Actually, I find this quite . . ." She was so far past breathless her words shook.

"Surprising?" His voice was a rumble almost too low to be heard.

Catching a desperate breath, Honoria closed her eyes. "*Enthralling.*"

His laugh was so deep she felt it in her marrow. "Trust me." His lips traced the curve of her ear. "There's a great deal more pleasure to come."

"Ah, yes," Honoria murmured, trying desperately to cling to sanity. "I believe you claim to be a past master at this exercise." Dragging in a tight breath, she rose upon him. "Does that make me your mistress?"

"No." Devil held his breath as she sank, excruciatingly slowly, down. "That makes you my pupil." It would make her his slave, but he'd no intention of telling her that, nor that, if she applied herself diligently, the connection might just work both ways.

On her next downward slide, she pressed lower; he nudged deeper. Her breath hitched; instinctively, she tightened about him. Devil set his teeth against a groan.

Eyes wide, she looked up at him, her breathing shallow and fast. "It feels . . . very strange . . . to have you . . . inside me." Breasts rising and falling, brushing his chest, she moistened her lips. "I really didn't think . . . you'd fit."

Devil locked his jaw—along with every other muscle he possessed. After a moment of fraught silence, he managed to say: "I'll fit—eventually."

"Event . . . ?"

Her eyes grew round—he didn't wait for more. He caught her lips in a ravishing kiss and, anchoring her hips against him, tumbled her back onto the pillows.

He'd chosen their earlier position to breach her, placing a limit on how deep he could go, helpful given the force of his instincts. But the time for limits had passed; his swift rearrangement landed her on her back among the pillows, his hips between her thighs, his staff still within her.

She tensed as his weight trapped her; instantly, he lifted his chest and shoulders from her, straightening his arms, his hands sinking into the down on either side. Their kiss broken, her eyes flew open.

He trapped her gaze in his. Slowly, deliberately, he withdrew from her, then, fluidly flexing his spine, he entered her.

Inexorably, inch by inch, he claimed her; heated and slick, her body welcomed him, stretching to take him in. He watched her eyes widen, the blue-grey transmuting to silver, then fracturing as he surged deeper. He sheathed himself in her softness, sinking into her to the hilt, nudging her womb. He came to rest embedded within her; she held him in a scorching silken vice.

Gazes locked, they both held still.

Honoria couldn't breathe, he filled her so completely; she could feel the steady beat of him at the base of her throat. Staring up at his face, she saw the hard planes shift, sharp-edged with reined passion. A conqueror looked down on her, green eyes dark, ringed with silver—the conqueror she'd given herself to. A sense of possession swamped her; her heart swelled, then soared.

He was waiting—for what? Some sign of surrender? On the thought, certainty bloomed within her; a glorious confidence filled her. She smiled—slowly, fully. Her hands had come to rest on his forearms; lifting them, she reached up and drew his face to hers. She heard him groan in the instant their lips met. He came down on his elbows, his hands flicking her hair aside, then framing her face.

He deepened their kiss and her senses went spinning; his body moved on her, within her, and pleasure bloomed.

Like waves piling on the shore, they surged together. Sensations swelled like the incoming tide, rolling ever higher. She caught the rhythm and matched him, letting her body welcome him, holding him tight for a heartbeat before reluctantly releasing him. Again and again they formed that intimate embrace; each time, each devastatingly thorough thrust pushed her higher, further, onward toward some beckoning shore she could only barely perceive. Her mind and senses merged, then soared, locked in dizzying flight. Heat and light spread through her, running down each vein, irradiating each nerve. Then heat changed to fire and light to incandescent glory.

Fed by their striving bodies, by each panting breath, by each soft moan, each guttural groan, the sunburst swelled, larger, brighter, more intense.

It exploded between them—Honoria lost herself in the primal energy, all fire and light and glorious, heart-stopping sensation. Blind, she couldn't see; deaf, she couldn't hear. All she could do was feel—feel him under her hands and know he was with her, feel the warmth that filled her and know she was his, feel the emotion that held them, forged strong in the sunburst's fire—and know nothing on earth could ever change it.

The sunburst died and they drifted back to earth, to the earthly pleasures of silk sheets and soft pillows, to sleepy murmurs and sated kisses, and the comfort of each other's arms.

Devil stirred as the last candle guttered. Even before he lifted his head, he'd assimilated the fact that there was a woman, sleeping the sleep of the sated, more or less beneath him. Before he levered his shoulders away from her and looked down, he'd recalled who that woman was.

The knowledge swelled the emotion that gripped him; his gaze roved her face, gently flushed, swollen lips slightly parted. Her bare breasts rose and fell; she was deeply asleep. Triumph roared through him; smug self-satisfaction swaggered in its wake. With a grin she would probably have taken exception to, had she been in any condition to see it, he lifted from her, careful not to wake her. He'd tried to withdraw from her earlier, before he'd succumbed, but she'd clung to him fiercely and muttered an injuction he'd had insufficient strength to disobey. Despite his weight, she'd wanted to prolong their intimacy, not an aim he could argue against with any conviction.

Their intimacy had been spectacular. Superb. Sufficiently remarkable to startle even him.

He settled on his stomach, feeling her soft weight against his side. The sensation had its inevitable effect; determinedly, he ignored it. He had time and more to explore the possibilities— the rest of his life, in fact. Anticipation had replaced frustration; from the first, he'd sensed in her an underlying awareness, a sensual propensity rare in women of her kind. Now he knew it was real, he would take care to nuture it; under his tutelage, it would blossom. Then he would have time and more to reap the rewards of his control, his care, his expertise, to slake his senses in her, with her—to make her his slave.

Turning his head on the pillow, he studied her face. Lifting his hand, he brushed a stray lock from her cheek; she snuffled, then wriggled onto her side, snuggling against him, one hand searching, coming to rest on his back.

Devil stilled; the emotion that stirred within him was not one he recognized—it stole his breath and left him curiously weak. Oddly shaken. Frowning, he tried to bring it into focus, but by then it had subsided. Not left him, but sunk deep again, into the depths where such emotions dwelled.

Shaking off the sensation, he hesitated, then, very gently, slid one arm across Honoria's waist. She sighed in her sleep, and sank more heavily against him. Lips curving gently, Devil closed his eyes.

When next he awoke, he was alone in his bed. Blinking fully awake, he stared at the empty space beside him in abject disbelief. Then he closed his eyes, dropped his head back into the pillows, and groaned.

Damn the woman—didn't she know . . . ? Obviously not— it was a point of wifely etiquette on which he'd have to educate her. She wasn't supposed to leave their bed until he did—by which time she wouldn't be able to. That was the way things were. Would be. From now on.

This morning, however, he'd have to go for a long ride.

Chapter 17

SUCCESS BRED SUCCESS. Late the next night, as he let himself into his hall, Devil reflected on that maxim. He'd successes on more than one front to celebrate; only one major item on his personal agenda remained unfulfilled—and he was making slow progress even there.

Picking up the waiting candlestick, he headed for the library, crossing directly to his desk. A folded letter sat prominently displayed. He broke the plain seal. In the flickering candlelight, he scanned the single sheet, and the enclosures, then smiled. Heathcote Montague, his man of business, had, as usual, delivered the goods.

Devil drew the two notes of hand he'd extracted from Viscount Bromley that evening from his waistcoat pocket and dropped them on the blotter; selecting a key from his watch chain, he opened the middle drawer of the desk, revealing a stack of twelve other notes of hand bearing Bromley's signature. They joined the others—and the six notes discreetly bought by Montague from other gentlemen who, having observed Bromley taking a tilt at him, had been only too glad to convert the viscount's promises to hard cash.

Flicking through the stack, Devil calculated the total, then compared it with Montague's assessment of Bromley's true worth. It wasn't difficult to gauge where the viscount now stood—in the mire, well on the way to being helplessly adrift on the River Tick. Precisely where he wanted him.

With a satisfied smile, Devil placed both letter and notes back in the desk drawer, locked it, and stood. Picking up the candlestick, he left the library and headed upstairs. To celebrate one victory he'd already won.

The house lay silent about him as he strode swiftly to his room. By the time he reached his door, anticipation had dug in its spurs; he was thoroughly aroused. Opening the door, he stepped through, shutting it behind him, his eyes immediately searching the shadows of his bed.

An instant later, his fist connected with the oak panels; he swore—violently. She wasn't there.

Breathing deeply, he stood stock-still, his gaze on the undisturbed covers, struggling to free his mind of the fog of disappointment, frustration—and a nagging discomfort centerd in his chest. He needed to think. Again.

Crossing to the tallboy, he plunked the candlestick atop it; and scowled at the bed. A familiar tension took hold.

Devil swore. Closing his eyes, he uttered one, comprehensive, utterly applicable oath, then, features hardening, shrugged out of his coat. It took less than a minute to strip. Donning a robe, he glanced down at his bare feet. He hesitated, then cinched the belt of the long robe tight. Cooling his overheated blood might help. Leaving the candle wavering on his tallboy, he closed his door and strode, purposefully, down the dark corridors.

He was finished with thinking. Whatever Honoria's reasons for not being in his bed, waiting, as he'd spent the whole evening fantasizing she would be, he did not wish to know. He wasn't going to argue or even discuss it. But surely not even a well-bred, gently reared twenty-four-year-old barely ex-virgin could imagine that once was enough? That he could survive until their wedding night going on as before—not after he'd sampled her body, her passion, the challenge of her untutored wantonness?

As he marched past his ancestors, Devil cast them a narrowed-eyed look. He left the gallery, then swung left, into the corridor leading to Honoria's rooms.

And collided with a wraith in ivory satin.

She would have bounced off him but he caught her, trapping

her against him. His body knew her instantly. Desire lanced painfully through him, her satin-clad curves stroking him to throbbing life as he juggled her. Her instinctive shriek never made it past a first gasp—he stopped it, sealing her lips with his.

Instantly, she relaxed, wriggling her arms free, then twining them about his neck. She pressed closer, kissing him back, flagrantly inciting. She offered her mouth—he took it rapaciously. Swaying seductively, she caressed his chest with her breasts; one arm tightening about her, Devil closed his hand about one firm mound, finding it already swollen, the peak a hard pebble against his palm.

With a gasp, she sank against him, a melting surrender so delicious it left him reeling. Her hands slid beneath his robe, searching out the muscles of his chest, fingers tangling in the crisp hair. Each touch was driven, invested with urgency, the same urgency coursing his veins.

Swallowing a guttural groan, Devil cupped her bottom and drew her hard against him. He lifted her, tilting her hips so his aching erection rode heavily against her. Suggestively, he rocked her, his tongue mimicking the rhythm; she closed her lips and held him, warm and wet, soft and slick.

The deliberate temptation, the flagrant promise in the intimate caress, set his demons raging; the gentle tug as her fingers found the tie of his robe sounded a belated alarm.

Stunned, staggered, his control in shreds, Devil couldn't summon enough strength for even an inward groan. She was going to kill him. The door to his mother's bedroom lay across the corridor.

If she'd been more experienced, he'd have been tempted to do it anyway—to set her bottom on the top of the side table by his mother's door and bury himself between her thighs. The illicit pleasure, knowing they dared not make a sound, would have wound them both tight.

But they were already tight enough—and even if she could handle the position, she would never be able to keep quiet. She'd screamed last night, more than once, an achingly sweet sound of feminine release. He wanted to hear it again—and again. Tonight. Now. But not here.

Breaking their kiss, Devil scooped her up in his arms.

"What—?"

"Sssh," he hissed. His robe had parted; if he'd waited a second longer, she'd have touched him—and God only knew what might have happened then. Striding rapidly down the corridor, he made for her rooms.

Juggling her, he threw open the door to her sitting room and strode through. He turned to shut the door; Honoria wriggled in his hold until she was stretched against him, her arms about his neck. The door locked, Devil turned back—directly into her kiss.

He set her on her feet; relinquishing all restraint, he let his hands have their way. They already knew her—knew her intimately—and wanted to know her again. The caresses he pressed on her were blatant, expressly gauged to set her need soaring. His followed; in self-preservation he fended off her hands. Their caresses—his successful, hers less so—quickly degenerated into a panting, heated game, rapidly fueling the conflagration that already had them in its grip.

With a sound of keen frustration, Honoria drew back from their kiss. "I want—"

"Not here," Devil ground out. "The bedroom." He took her mouth again; the game resumed, neither willing to break free.

In desperation, with a sound close to a scream, Honoria wrenched away from his roving hands. Her skin was alight, on fire, her body no less so. If he didn't fill her soon, she'd swoon. Grabbing one of his hands, she hauled him to her bedchamber door. Flinging it open, she dropped his hand and entered.

Halting in the pool of moonlight streaming through the window, she faced him; tugging the bow of her translucent overrobe undone, she shrugged the sheer garment from her shoulders. As it pooled at her feet, she held out her hands—Devil had closed the door, then paused. She felt his gaze, hot as the sun, slide over her body, still shielded by soft satin.

Devil kept his hand on the cool metal of the doorknob and clung to the moment like a drowning man. He tried to remind himself about control, and that he'd taken her only once, that she might still be sore, that she would certainly still need time to adjust to his invasion. The facts registered with his conscious mind, the small remnant that still functioned. The rest was centered on her, on the throbbing ache in his loins—on his desperate need to claim her.

Her nightgown was a fascinating creation—solid satin with slits to her hips. The long line of her legs had showed briefly, tantalizingly, then she'd halted, and the skirts had fallen primly straight—an illusion of virtuous womanhood.

Her fingers flickered in entreaty—slowly, he strolled forward, letting his robe fall to the ground behind him. Naked, he ignored her hands, letting her touch him as she would. With his own, he cupped her face, then, slowly, stretching each moment until they both quivered, he bent his head and set his lips to hers.

He kissed her deeply, ravenously—forcefully—he needed to stay in control. He locked his muscles as her hands slid about his waist. They halted, gripping him as she accepted his kiss, opening herself to it without restraint. Then she slid her hands over his back; she pressed herself briefly against him, then, to his surprise, pulled away. Puzzled, Devil let her go.

Her gaze shadowed, mysterious, she took his hand and led him to the canopied bed. Halting beside it, she faced him; her eyes on his, she raised her hands and opened the shoulder clasps that anchored her gown. It slithered down, revealing the full globes of her breasts, pale ivory in the moon's faint light. The gown gathered at her waist; with a wriggle, she freed it, letting it whisper to the floor.

With no hint of reticence, of coyness or shyness—with a directness that stole his breath and much more—she stepped close. She placed her hands on his ribs, then sent them gliding upward; she stretched sensuously against him, wrapping her arms about his neck, lifting her lips for his kiss, pressing her breasts to his chest, sinking her hips against his thighs. Offering herself to him.

Something inside him shattered.

He reached for her and she was there—he wasn't certain if he'd hauled her hard against him or if she'd pressed closer. Her lips were under his, open and eager; their tongues twined, invoking all the devils of passion that ever were. Nothing else mattered.

Completion, fulfillment, was their only aim—the only thought in their fevered brains. Devil knew his horses had bolted but could summon no will to haul on their reins. She commanded his senses, his strength, every particle of his awareness;

her needs, heightening to near frenzy, were the perfect counter-
part of his own.

The desire to join flowed strongly through them, a powerful,
fiery force. It beat in their veins, found expression in their gasping breaths; it invested each touch, each bold caress, with pleasure so intense it was close to pain.

Pulling back on a gasp, Honoria lifted one knee to the bed;
Devil lifted her and placed her upon it, letting her draw him
down. He let her feel his weight, reveling in the supple softness
of the arms that slid around him, of her body undulating beneath
him. She parted her thighs; he drew away only enough to reach
down and stroke her, feeling the slickness of her need, the heat
of her arousal.

An incoherent plea left her lips; she tilted her hips in unmistakable invitation. Her hands wandered down; they reached his
ribs before Devil, settling fully upon her, his hips cradled between her thighs, caught them, one in each of his.

Her eyes, glinting from beneath weighted lids, met his. Deliberately, Devil anchored first one hand, then the other, on either side of her head. He was beyond thought, far beyond any
concept of control—the force that drove him, consumed him,
compelled him to possess her. Completely. Utterly.

The slick heat between her thighs bathed his throbbing staff;
he nudged her thighs wider—she complied, but even in that, she
managed to shake him, settling her hips deeper, perfectly positioned for his penetration, letting her thighs relax, leaving herself
open. Vulnerable. Inviting him to take her.

The emotion that rolled through him was so powerful, so
deep, Devil had to close his eyes briefly, holding back the storm.
Opening them, he drew a deep breath, his chest pressing against
her breasts, and bent his head to hers.

Their lips met, then melded; their fires ignited. With one
powerful thrust, he joined with her—and the conflagration began.

He moved on her, within her; she moved beneath him, about
him. Her body caressed him in so many ways, he lost the distinction between him and her. He stroked deeply within her and
felt her rise, felt the fiery flight start.

Honoria surrendered to it, to the elemental heat that burned
between them. It consumed them, a pure fire that burned away

all pretense, leaving only truth and emotion forged in its searing flames. She felt him within her and accepted him eagerly, taking him in, both possessed and possessing. The sunburst rose and drew rapidly nearer; their bodies strove, racing to their fate.

Then it was upon them. It caught them in its heat, in its unquenchable delight, in sensation so exquisite she screamed. She clutched him tightly and he was with her. Locked together, they soared, gasped, then fractured—into a selfless void of aching peace beyond the reach of human senses.

Devil returned to the mortal plane first. Slowly, every muscle heavy with sated lust, he lifted away, then settled the pillows about them. His gaze roamed Honoria's face, serene, softly glowing. Gently, he smoothed her hair, drawing his fingers through the silken mass, letting it slip free to lie across the crisp linen. For long moments, silent and still, he studied her face. Then his gaze drifted down, skimming her body, fair skin glowing in the silvery light.

Seconds later, he reached for the covers, drawing them up to her chin. He settled on his back beside her, one arm behind his head, a frown tangling his black brows.

He was in that pose when Honoria stirred; from under heavy lids, she studied his face, dark features etched by the moonlight. He seemed pensive. Pensive herself, she let her gaze roam the broad expanse of his chest, dark hairs shading its width, each muscle band sharply defined. The covers reached to his waist; beneath them, she could feel the hair-dusted hardness of his leg beside hers.

She smiled, a cat savoring cream. Her skin was warmly flushed, her limbs deliciously weighted. She felt at peace, fulfilled—possessed. Deeply, thoroughly, possessed. Just the thought sent a *frisson* of pleasure through her.

The day was behind her. The unsettling uncertainty which had seized her the minute she'd regained her room after scurrying like a wanton maid through the corridors in the half-light of dawn, had disappeared, eradicated by the night's fire. Her lips curved; she could still feel the inner glow. On the thought, she glanced up—Devil was watching her.

His hesitation was palpable, then he shifted, raising a hand to lift a lock of hair from her forehead. "Why weren't you in my bed?"

Honoria held his gaze, even though his eyes were too shadowed for her to see. "I didn't know whether you wanted me there."

Fleetingly, his frown deepened, then eased. But his lips did not curve as, with one finger, he lightly brushed her cheek. "I want you—and I want you there."

The deep words all but shimmered in the moonlight; Honoria smiled. "Tomorrow." She heard him sigh and saw his quick grimace.

"Unfortunately not." He lay back, his eyes still on hers. "While I'd much rather have you in my bed, until we marry, I'll have to suffer the restrictions of yours." He lifted one foot, demonstrating that even high on the pillows as he was, his feet reached the footboard.

Honoria frowned. "Why can't we sleep in your bed?"

"Propriety."

She opened her eyes wide. "*This* is propriety?" Her sweeping gesture encompassed his naked presence, which took up quite half of her bed.

"You can't be seen wandering the corridors in your peignoir every morning—the servants wouldn't approve. If they see *me* wandering about in my robe, they'll accept the sight with unimpaired aplomb—this is, after all, my house."

Honoria humphed. Wriggling about, she settled on her side, facing away from him. "I suppose you know all the correct procedures."

She felt him shift; a second later, warm limbs surrounded her. The light stubble of his jaw grazed her bare shoulder; his lips touched her ear.

"Believe it." He settled behind her. "And speaking of correct procedures, I should send a notice to *The Gazette*, stating our wedding day."

Honoria studied the shadows. "When should it be?"

He kissed her nape. "That's for you to say—but I'd hoped for December first."

Four weeks away. Honoria frowned. "I'll need a gown."

"You can command any modiste—they'll scramble for the honor."

"Celestine will do." Honoria saw no reason not to avail herself of Celestine's flair just because he'd commanded the modiste's attention.

"All the other arrangements you can leave to *Maman* and my aunts."

"I know," Honoria replied with feeling. "I spent a wretchedly awkward morning—your mother decided to visit the old housekeeper who ran the Place when your parents married. The entire conversation concerned the hows and wheres of arranging a wedding at Somersham."

Devil chuckled. "How did she know?"

"I don't know," Honoria lied. It was, she was sure, her odd, utterly inexplicable blushes that had given her away. "I'll need to write to Michael."

"I'll be writing to him tomorrow—give me your letter and I'll enclose it with mine." Devil studied the back of her head. "Incidentally, I spoke to old Magnus this morning."

Honoria swung about. "Grandfather?" Incredulous, she stared. "Why?"

Devil raised his brows. "He is the head of your family."

"You don't need his permission to marry me."

"No." His lips quirked. "However, the Anstruther-Wetherbys and Cynsters go back a long way. We've been scoring points off each other since the Ark beached."

Honoria studied his face. "How did he take the news?"

Devil grinned. "Philosophically, in the end. He knew you were living within my household, so it wasn't a total shock."

Honoria narrowed her eyes, then humphed and turned her back on him.

Devil's grin dissolved into a smile. Leaning forward, he planted a kiss behind her ear. "Go to sleep—you'll need your strength."

His words held a definite promise. Smiling, Honoria settled her cheek into her pillow, snuggled her back against his chest— and did as she was bid.

The next day, their letters to Michael were duly dispatched. The day after, a notice announcing the marriage of Honoria Prudence Anstruther-Wetherby, eldest daughter of Geoffrey Anstruther-Wetherby and his wife Heather, of Nottings Grange,

Hampshire, to Sylvester Sebastian Cynster, duke of St. Ives, appeared in *The Gazette*. The marriage would take place on December 1 at Somersham Place.

Despite the *haut ton*'s preoccupation with departing London, the news spread like wildfire. Honoria gave thanks that the only social events remaining were small, select afternoon teas and "at-homes"—farewells to friends before society adjourned to the shires for the shooting and subsequently to their estates for Christmas. The dustcovers had been placed over the chandeliers—the *ton* was in retreat from London and would not return until February.

As she and Devil had foreseen, his mother and the other Cynster ladies threw themselves into organizing the wedding with undisguised relish. The Dowager warned Honoria that it was family tradition that the bride, while making all the final decisions, was not allowed to do anything—her sole role, according to all precepts, was to appear to advantage and keep her husband in line. Honoria quickly decided there was much to be said for tradition.

Devil watched from a distance, reassured by her readiness to take on the position of his wife. She'd already impressed his aunts; with their encouragement, she took up the matriarchal reins—his mother was ecstatic.

By the end of five whirlwind days, they were ready to leave London; Devil's final chore was to reel in Viscount Bromley.

When the enormity of his losses, the perilous nature of his finances, was fully explained, Bromley, a hardened case, philosophically shrugged and agreed to Devil's terms. He was in a postion to ascertain the truth of "Lucifer's discreditable rumor," to identify the Cynster involved and learn all the facts. All this he agreed to do—by the first of February.

Satisfied, on every count, Devil laid aside his black armband and, with his wife-to-be on his arm, retired to Somersham Place.

Chapter 18

❧❧❧

THE BALLROOM AT Somersham Place was filled to overflowing. Afternoon sunlight poured through the long windows, striking glints from the curls and coifs of damsels and dowagers, rakes and roués, gentlemen and haughty matrons. Gowns of every hue vied with bright jewels and equally bright eyes. The full flower of the *ton* was present—to see, to witness, to appreciate.

"She's the last marriageable Anstruther-Wetherby female *and* as rich as bedamned—isn't it just like Devil to have such a pearl fall into his lap."

"*Such* a handsome couple—Celestine designed her gown expressly."

Surrounded by such comments, by felicitations and congratulations, Honoria circulated through the throng, smiling, graciously inclining her head, exchanging the required words with all those who'd come to see her wed.

She was now the duchess of St. Ives. The past months of consideration, the last weeks of frenetic activity, had culminated in a simple service in the chapel in the grounds. The church had been packed, the overflow surrounding it like a jeweled sea. Mr. Merryweather had pronounced them man and wife, then Devil had claimed his kiss—a kiss she'd remember all her life. The sun had broken through as the crowd surged forth, forming a long aisle. Bathed in sunshine, they'd run a gauntlet of well-wishers all the way to the ballroom.

The wedding banquet had commenced at noon; it was now close to three o'clock. The musicians were resting—only six waltzes had been scheduled, but she'd already danced more. The first had been with Devil, an *affecting* experience. She'd been starved of breath by its end, only to be claimed by Vane, then Richard, followed by Harry, Gabriel, and Lucifer in quick succession. Her head had been spinning when the music finally ceased.

Scanning the crowd, Honoria spied Devil talking to Michael and her grandfather, seated near the huge fireplace. She headed toward them.

Amelia bobbed up in her path. "You're to bring Devil to cut the cake. They're setting up the trestles in the middle of the room—Aunt Helena said Devil would toe the line more easily if you ask."

Honoria laughed. "Tell her we're on our way."

Thrilled to be involved, Amelia whisked herself off.

Devil saw her long before she reached him; Honoria felt his gaze, warm, possessively lingering, as she dealt with the continual claims on her attention. Reaching his side, she met his eyes briefly—and felt her tension tighten, felt anticipation streak through her, the spark before the flame. They'd shared a bed for four weeks, yet the thrill was still there, the sudden breathlessness, the empty ache of longing, the need to give and take. She wondered if the feeling would ever fade.

Serenely, she inclined her head, acknowledging her grandfather. At Devil's behest, they'd met briefly before leaving London; focused on her future, she'd found it unexpectedly easy to forgive the past.

"Well, Your Grace!" Leaning back, Magnus looked up at her. "Here's your brother going to stand at the next election. What d'you think about that, heh?"

Honoria looked at Michael; he answered her unvoiced question. "St. Ives suggested it." He looked at Devil.

Who shrugged. "Carlisle was ready to put your name forward, which is good enough for me. With the combined backing of the Anstruther-Wetherbys and the Cynsters, you should be assured of a sound constituency."

Magnus snorted. "He'll get a safe seat, or I'll know the reason why."

Honoria grinned; stretching up, she planted a kiss on Michael's cheek. "Congratulations," she whispered.

Michael returned her affectionate kiss. "And to you." He squeezed her hand, then released it. "You made the right decision."

Honoria raised a brow, but she was smiling. Turning, she met Magnus's eye. "I am come to steal my husband away, sir. It's time to cut the cake."

"That so? Well—lead him away." Magnus waved encouragingly. "I wouldn't want to miss witnessing this phenomenon—a Cynster in tow to an Anstruther-Wetherby."

Honoria raised her brows. "I'm no longer an Anstruther-Wetherby."

"Precisely." Devil met Magnus's gaze, a conqueror's confidence in his eyes as he raised Honoria's hand to his lips. He turned to Honoria. "Come, my dear." He gestured to the room's center. "Your merest wish is my command."

Honoria slanted him a skeptical glance. "Indeed?"

"Indubitably." With polished efficiency, Devil steered her through the throng. "In fact," he mused, his voice deepening to a purr, "I'm anticipating fulfilling a goodly number of your wishes before the night is through."

Smiling serenely, Honoria exchanged nods with the duchess of Leicester. "You're making me blush."

"Brides are supposed to blush—didn't they tell you?" Devil's words feathered her ear. "Besides, you look delightful when you blush. Did you know your blush extends all the way—"

"*There* you are, my dears!"

To Honoria's relief, the Dowager appeared beside them. "If you'll just stand behind the cake. There's a knife there waiting." She shooed them around the table; family and guests crowded around. Their wedding cake stood in pride of place, seven tiers of heavy fruitcake covered with marzipan and decorated with intricate lace. On the top stood a stag, pirouetting on the Cynster shield.

"Good God!" Devil blinked at the creation.

"It's Mrs. Hull's work," Honoria whispered. "Remember to mention it later."

"Make way! Make way!"

The unexpected commotion had all turning. Honoria saw a long thin package waved aloft. Those at the edge of the crowd laughed; comments flew. A corridor opened, allowing the messenger through. It was Lucifer, his mission to deliver the package to Vane, standing before the table opposite Devil. With exaggerated ceremony, Vane accepted the package—a sword in its scabbard—reversing it and presenting it to Devil. "Your weapon, Your Grace."

The ballroom erupted with laughter.

His smile beyond devilish, Devil reached for the hilt. The blade—his cavalry saber—came singing from its sheath. To cheers and all manner of wild suggestions, he brandished it aloft—a piratical bucanneer in the heart of the elegant *ton*.

Then his eyes met Honoria's. One swift step and he stood behind her, his arms reaching around her. "Wrap your hands about the hilt."

Bemused, Honoria did so, gripping the thick-ridged rod of the hilt with both hands. Devil wrapped his hands about hers—Honoria suddenly felt faint.

A deep, soft chuckle sounded in her right ear. "Just like last night."

Last night—when he'd spent the final night of his bachelorhood with his cousins. Sighting Webster carrying a cask of brandy to the library, Honoria had resigned herself to spending her last night as a spinster alone. She'd retired to her bed and tried to fall asleep, only to discover that she'd become too used to having a large, warm, very hard body in the bed beside her. That same large, warm, very hard body had slipped quietly into her room in the small hours of the morning—and slid beneath the covers. She'd pretended to be asleep, then decided cutting off her nose to spite her face was no fun. She'd made her wishes known.

Only to be informed in a deep, sleepy chuckle, that he was too inebriated to mount her. Fiend that he was, he'd suggested she mount him—and had proceeded to teach her how. One lesson she would never forget.

Only when, utterly exhausted, sated to her toes, she'd collapsed on top of him, only to have him take control, pushing her on, possessing her so completely she had all but lost her mind, had she realized that, in keeping with the rest of their bodies, Cynster males also had hard heads. Not thick, not dense—just hard.

The memories poured through her, leaving her weak. Turning her head slightly, she met Devil's eyes—and was immensely glad she hadn't seen his smugly triumphant smile last night; she was seeing enough of it now. It took immense effort to stiffen her spine and close her hands, beneath his, about the saber's hilt, without recalling what it reminded her of. Drawing a deep breath, she poured every ounce of warning she could into her eyes, then looked at the cake. With his help, she raised the saber high.

The blade came singing down; guiding the swing, Devil drew her back, ensuring the saber cut a neat slice in each of the seven layers. Cheers and clapping erupted on all sides; ribald comments flew.

Her knees weak, Honoria fervently prayed everyone present thought those comments were the cause of her flaming cheeks. She prayed even harder that none bar the reprobate she'd married had noticed just where the rounded knob at the end of the sabre's hilt had finally come to rest. Hemmed in by the crowd behind them, they hadn't been able to move far enough back; the knobbed end of the hilt had slipped into the hollow between her thighs.

And for once, she couldn't blame him—the stillness that gripped him, the quick indrawn breath that hissed past her ear, exonerated him; he was as shaken as she. Their eyes met—were hers as nakedly wanting as his? Carefully, he drew the sword from her slackened grasp and handed it to Vane—then swiftly bent his head and brushed her lips with his. "Later."

The whispered word was a promise; Honoria shivered and felt an answering ripple pass through him. Again their eyes met—they both blinked, both drew breath—and turned aside, putting distance between their overcharged bodies.

In a daze, Honoria did the rounds of her Anstruther-Wetherby relations—the uncles and aunts she'd never known, the cousins who now regarded her with something akin to awe. It was a relief to return to the Cynster circle, to the warm smiles, openly affectionate, to the reassuring nods and the unflagging support. She stopped beside Louise; Arthur stood beside her.

Arthur took Honoria's hand. "You make a fine duchess, my dear." Despite the lines grief had etched in his face, as he raised her hand to his lips, Honoria glimpsed the debonair, devil-may-care gentleman he must once have been. "Sylvester's a lucky man."

"I'm sure your nephew appreciates Honoria as he ought," Louise put in from between them.

Arthur smiled—a typical, slow Cynster smile. "Never heard him described as a slow-top." He looked past Honoria. "Ah—here's Charles."

Honoria turned, regally acknowledging Charles as he joined them.

"And there's Lady Perry!" Louise put her hand on Arthur's arm. "Honoria—please excuse us. We must talk to her ladyship before she leaves."

With a smile for Honoria and a cool "Charles" to his son, Arthur yielded to his wife's directions and steered her into the crowd.

Bowing correctly, Charles watched them go, then turned to Honoria. "I'm glad to have a moment to speak with you, Miss—" His features hardened. "Your Grace."

Honoria didn't trust his smile. Their subsequent meetings had not allayed her first instinctive dislike. He was the only Cynster who affected her so—all the rest she instinctively liked. "I had hoped to have the pleasure of a dance with you, sir, but I believe all the dances are done."

He raised a brow, haughty arrogance one of the few Cynster traits he possessed. "I'm afraid you forget, Your Grace—I'm still in mourning." He smoothed his black armband. "The others, of course, have forgotten Tolly, but his loss still greatly affects me."

Biting her tongue, Honoria inclined her head. Of all the Cynsters present, only Charles and his father still wore black armbands.

"But I believe congratulations are *de rigueur*."

Charles's odd phrasing had her regarding him in surprise. He nodded superciliously. "I'm sure you recall the substance of our earlier conversation—in light of the reservations I expressed to you then, I most sincerely hope you do not live to regret your new state."

Honoria stiffened.

Scanning the crowd, Charles didn't notice. "But however that may be, I do wish you well—if knowing Sylvester all his life makes me hesitant as to his constancy, I ask you to believe that that circumstance in no way lessens the sincerity of my hopes for your happiness."

"Yet, if I understand you correctly, you don't believe such happiness likely." Honoria watched as her words sank in— slowly, Charles brought his gaze back to her face. His eyes were pale, cold, oddly expressionless.

"Your actions have been most unwise. You should not have married Sylvester."

Quite what she would have replied to such an outrageous assertion Honoria never discovered—Amelia and Amanda, both still in alt, came rushing up in a froth of muslin skirts.

"Aunt Helena says you should move to the door—some of the guests are starting to leave."

Honoria nodded. From the corner of her eye, she saw Charles draw back.

"By your leave, Your Grace." With a half-bow to her and a curt nod for his half sisters, he turned on his heel and walked off.

Amanda pulled a face at his back, then linked her arm in Honoria's. "He's such a stuffy old shirt—he never enjoys anything."

"Sententious," Amelia pronounced, taking Honoria's other arm. "Now—where should you stand, do you think?"

The short December day drew swiftly to a close; when the clock on the stairs chimed five, it was full dark outside. Standing on the porch by Devil's side, waving the last of the carriages away, Honoria inwardly sighed. Meeting Devil's eyes, she smiled and turned back to the hall. He fell in beside her, capturing her hand, long fingers twining. Most of the family would remain until the next day; they'd retreated to the drawing room, leaving them to do the honors alone. Immediately before the door, Devil halted.

Honoria perforce halted, too, and looked up.

A slow smile greeted her. Raising her hand, Devil brushed a kiss across her knuckles. "Well, my dear duchess?" With his other hand, he tipped her chin up—and up; automatically she rose on her toes.

He bent his head and kissed her, gently at first, then more deeply. When he lifted his head, they were both heated once more.

Honoria blinked at him. "There's dinner yet."

His smile deepened. "They're not expecting us to show." He drew her across the threshold. "This is where we slip away."

Honoria's lips formed a silent "Oh"; the hall, empty but for Webster, busy closing the door, suggested that her husband, as usual, had the procedure right. When he raised a brow, she acquiesced with a nod; calmly serene, she climbed the stairs by his side. They'd retired together often enough in the past weeks for her to feel no qualms.

A state of affairs that lasted all the way to the top of the stairs. That was when she turned right, toward the corridor that led to her rooms.

Devil's hold on her hand brought her up short. She turned in surprise—only to see him lift one brow, his gaze very green. He shook his head. "Not anymore."

Realization hit. Honoria nodded. Head high, outwardly assured, she allowed him to lead her through the gallery, into the corridor leading to the ducal apartments. Inwardly, her nerves had come alive, fluttering in ever-decreasing spirals until they tensed into knots.

It was ridiculous, she told herself, and struggled to ignore the sensation.

She'd been to the duchess's apartments only once, to approve the new color scheme—all rich creams, soft topaz, and old gold, complementing the warm patina of polished oak. Opening her door, Devil ushered her in; Honoria blinked at the blaze that greeted her.

Lighted candelabra graced the dressing table, the mantel-shelf, a chest of drawers, an escritoire against one wall, and a tantalus set before one window. In their glare, the room appeared much as she'd last seen it, with the huge, canopied bed in pride of place between the long windows. The only new items were the urn of flowers, all yellow and white, that sat upon one chest, her brushes, gleaming silver on the polished dressing table, and her nightgown of ivory silk with its matching peignoir, laid out upon the bed.

Cassie must have put it there; Honoria certainly hadn't

thought of it. She wondered if the candelabra were Cassie's idea, too—then noticed Devil seemed unsurprised. Strolling into the room, drawing her with him, he stopped before the fireplace, and drew her smoothly into his arms.

Any doubt of his intent fled before his kiss, full of barely restrained hunger and an ardor to set her alight. She sank against him, his instantaneous response driving her to take the pleasure he offered and return it fullfold. Her head was swimming, her limbs turned to water, when he raised his head. "Come. Our children can be born in your bed—we'll beget them in mine."

He swung her into his arms; Honoria twined her arms about his neck. With impatient stride, he carried her to a paneled door, left ajar, shouldering it open, revealing the short corridor that led to his room. "What was that all about?" she asked. "The candelabra?"

Devil glanced down at her; the corridor was dim, but she saw his teeth gleam. "Diversionary tactics."

She would have asked for clarification, but all thoughts of candles went winging from her head as he carried her into his room.

His room in London was large—this room was immense. The bed that stood against the near wall was the biggest she'd ever seen. Long windows marched along both sides and filled the wall opposite the bed; this room was at the end of the wing—with the curtains open, it was flooded with moonlight, turning the pale greens of the furnishings to muted silver.

Devil carried her around the bed, setting her on her feet where the moon cast a shimmering swath across the floor. Her wedding gown, layer upon layer of wide Mechlin lace, sparkled and shivered. He straightened, his gaze drawn to where the lace rose and fell; he cupped one soft mound and felt it firm. His fingers searched, finding the tightening peak and caressing it to pebbled hardness.

Honoria's breath caught; her lids fell as she swayed toward him. Devil supported her against his chest, his hand still at her breast, gently kneading. She shifted restlessly, turning so he could reach her back. "The laces are hidden beneath the lace."

Devil grinned and set to work, one hand caressing first one breast then the other, lips trailing kisses along the side of her throat. When the last knotted lace fell free and the gown, with his help, slithered to the floor, Honoria was soft and supple in his arms, arching back against him. He loved her like this, soft and womanly, abandoned but knowingly so—later, she'd be even more abandoned, but by then she would be beyond knowing anything other than the fever singing in her veins. Reaching around her, he filled both hands with her breasts, covered by a single layer of filmy silk—a low murmur of appreciation escaped her. When he rubbed the ruched peaks between thumb and forefinger, she shifted her hips suggestively against him.

"Not yet," he murmured. "Tonight should be an experience you'll never forget."

"Oh?" The single syllable was breathless. She turned and, twining her arms about his neck, pressed herself against him. "What are you intending to do?"

He smiled, slowly. "Extend your horizons."

She tried to look haughty, but only succeeded in looking fascinated. Devil stepped back, shrugging out of his coat and waistcoat. He let them fall and reached for her. She came into his arms like the siren she was—the siren he'd spent the past weeks releasing from the shackles of convention. She was still wildly innocent in so many ways, yet whatever he taught her she mastered with a wholehearted enthusiasm that sometimes left him weak. From where he now stood, his view colored by experience, the years ahead looked rosy indeed.

He was looking forward to every one of them. Right now, he was looking forward to tonight.

Her lips were open under his, her tongue twining, inciting, enticing. She stretched against him, on her toes, her body shielded only by her fine chemise. Letting desire have its way, he molded her to him, allowing his hands to know her curves again. When he slipped his palms under the back of her chemise, her skin was dewed.

Two heated minutes later, the chemise floated to the ground to puddle, ignored, in the moonlight.

Devil deepened their kiss—Honoria met him, urging and urgent. Her hands slipped from his nape and started to roam, splaying across his chest, then searching through the folds of his shirt to knead the muscles of his back, then firming about his waist, his hips, dropping lower.

Abruptly, Devil shifted, capturing her hands, forcing them

to her back, locking them there in one of his. Their kiss unbroken, he drew her hard against him, letting her feel his strength, letting her know the seductive quality of her own vulnerability. He bent her back slightly, over the arm at her waist, her hips pressed hard to his. She moaned, the sound trapped in their kiss, and wriggled—not to win free but to get closer.

The restless shifting of her hips against him was more than he could stand. Breaking their kiss, he scooped her up and deposited her on the silk sheets. She stretched, her eyes on him, her hands questing.

Quickly he drew back, out of her reach. "If you love me, keep your hands to yourself." He'd fantasized about tonight for the past week; if he let her enthusiasm get the better of him—as it had on more than one occasion—he would have no chance of converting fantasy to reality.

Stretching luxuriously, draping her arms above her head, Honoria fixed him with a sultry gaze. "I only want to touch you." She watched as he stripped off his cravat. "You liked it last night."

"Tonight is going to be different."

His eyes left her only momentarily as he pulled off his shirt. Honoria smiled, shifting seductively under the heat of his gaze, relishing the sense of power his fascination with her naked form gave her. He'd made it very plain that he liked seeing her naked, totally nude, without any hint of modesty. Being that naked had been difficult at first, but familiarity and his abiding obsession had built her confidence so that now, being wantonly, wickedly naked with him seemed natural—how it should be—at least between them. "How?" she inquired, as he sat on the bed to remove his boots.

He flicked her a glance, his gaze sliding over her breasts, then down over her stomach and thighs. "Tonight it's going to be my pleasure to lavish pleasure upon you."

Honoria eyed him consideringly. He could make her scream—scream and moan and sob with pleasure. She was the novice—he the master. "Just what are you planning?"

He grinned and stood, unbuttoning his trousers. "You'll see—or rather," he amended, his voice deepening, "you'll feel."

The anticipation simmering in her veins abruptly heightened; Honoria's nerves flickered. That familar tension had hold of her again, a sweet vise locking tight. A second later, as naked as she, he came onto the bed in a prowling crawl. Elementally male, fully aroused, on hands and knees he straddled her, then lowered his body to hers.

Honoria's breath fled. Eyes wide, she studied his, glittering in the weak light. Then his lids fell and he lowered his head; his lips found hers.

His searching kiss reached deep—deep to where her wanton self dwelled. He called her forth and she came, eagerly seeking his pleasure. She opened to him, enticing him in, her body softening beneath his; she murmured his name and shifted beneath him, but he made no move to claim her. His hands locked about hers, one on either side of her head; as the kiss went on, her skin burned for his touch. Driven, she arched beneath him but his weight held her trapped; his legs outside hers, he held her immobile, granting her no relief from the heat building between them.

Then his lips left hers, trailing hot kisses down the column of her throat. Panting, Honoria pressed her head back into the pillows, eager for much more. He shifted and his lips traced her collarbone, then returned by way of her shoulder and upper breast. He repeated the maneuver, this time following the curve of her arm to her elbow, then on to her wrist, eventually ending with her fingertips.

Tickled by his lips, by the abrasion of his chest and chin against her smooth skin, Honoria giggled; she saw his brow quirk, but he said nothing, merely lifting her hand and draping her arm over his shoulder. He repeated the entire exercise on her other arm, until it, too, went to join its fellow. Locking her fingers at his nape, she settled back expectantly, and waited to see what came next.

His lips on her breasts was a familar sensation, sweet and full of promise. When his mouth fastened over one nipple and he suckled, she gasped; the caress continued, hot and wet, pulsing wildfire down her veins. She moaned, hips restlessly lifting, seeking. But he'd shifted lower; she could make no contact with that part of his anatomy most susceptible to persuasion. Premonition bloomed—his "tonight" would be a long-drawn affair.

He'd told her more than once that she rushed ahead too fast, that, if she let him spin out their time, the sensations would be better—more heightened, more intense. As she could barely cope with what she felt as it was, she wasn't at all sure "slower" was such a good idea. He was used to it—she was not. She wasn't even sure the exercise affected him in the same, mind-dazzling, soul-shattering, heart-twisting way in which it affected her.

His lips left her breasts; panting she waited, then felt him nuzzling beneath their fullness. His lips swept across her sensitive midriff and down to the hollow of her waist.

She was so caught by the novel sensations, by the heated tingling of her skin, that he'd flipped her onto her stomach before she had a chance to protest. He shifted, rising over her then lowering his body along the length of hers. His lips found her nape—he proceeded to cover her back with kisses, soft and warm across her shoulders, changing to soft nips as he worked his way down. Her fires had died to smouldering embers, but when he reached the full swell of her bottom, anticipation exploded into flame again. She squirmed, her breath coming in soft gasps. One heavy arm across her waist kept her still; when he pushed her knees wide apart and held them so, Honoria dragged in a shuddering breath—and waited. He was lying beside her, his weight no longer upon her. Cool air caressed her heated skin; she longed for him to cover her. Expectation welled; she willed him to shift and come between her thighs.

Instead, she felt the soft brush of his hair and the light graze of his stubble as he laid a line of warm kisses down the back of one thigh. He paid homage to the sensitive spot at the back of her knee, first one, then the other, then worked his way back up her other thigh. Honoria slowly exhaled, and waited to be allowed to roll over.

The next instant, her breath hissed in—and in. Her hands clenched on the pillow. In stunned disbelief, she felt tiny tender kisses dot their inexorable way up the inside of one thigh. Her skin shivered and flickered; as the kisses steadily neared the place where she burned, she let out a small shriek, stifled in the pillow.

She felt, rather than heard his deep chuckle. He swung over her and repeated the exercise on the inside of her other thigh. Honoria gritted her teeth, determined not to repeat her shriek; her whole body quivered with mounting need. When he reached the limit of his trail, pressing one last lingering kiss to skin that had never before felt a man's lips, she sighed—then shrieked, as his tongue swept tender, pulsing flesh—just once, but it was more than enough.

He seemed to think so, too; he drew back, rolling her onto her back, his weight pinning her again as his lips returned to hers, his kiss searing, conflagrationary—exactly as she wished it. Wrapping her arms about his neck, Honoria gave him back fire for flame, passion for desire, in a frenzy of escalating need. This time, her thighs were spread and he lay between; she could feel his throbbing staff nudging her thigh.

Abruptly, he drew back, onto his knees. Dazed, she saw him seize a fat pillow. Lifting her, he wedged it under her hips, then, leaning over her, he found her lips again. When he lifted his head she was panting in earnest, every nerve in her body alive, every vein afire. One hand was on her breast; swiftly, he lowered his head and suckled until she moaned.

"Please—now." Honoria reached for him but he shifted back.

"Soon."

He lowered his body to hers again, but too low—his head was at her breasts. He laved each burning peak until she could take no more, then trailed kisses to her navel. He circled the dimple with his tongue, then probed; the slow, repetitive thrusting brought tears of frustration to her eyes. She twisted and arched, her hips lifted high by the pillow.

"Soon." He whispered the word across the sensitive skin of her stomach, and followed it with a kiss. And another and another, slowly descending; when the first kiss fell amongst her soft curls, Honoria's eyes flew wide.

"Devil?"

The sensations streaking through her were unlike any she'd yet experienced, sharper, stronger, fiercer. More kisses followed the first and she gasped, hands reaching, fingers locking in his hair.

"*Oh God!*" The exclamation was wrung from her as his lips touched her softness. The sudden bolt of sensation was enough to melt her mind. "No." She shook her head.

"Soon," came the answer.

His lips left her swollen flesh to trail kisses along the inside of her thighs, lifting them as he slid still lower, draping a knee over each shoulder.

Well-nigh mindless, Honoria felt his breath caress her throbbing flesh. Speech was beyond her; she was going to die. From excitement—from pleasure so intense it was frightening. Gripping the sheets convulsively, she hauled in a huge breath, and shook her head violently.

Devil took no notice. Deliberately, he set his lips to her soft flesh, hot and swollen, intimately caressing each soft fold; a strangled sound, neither shriek nor scream, was his reward. He found her throbbing nubbin, already swollen and tight; he laved it gently, swirling his tongue, first this way then that, about the sensitive spot. He wasn't surprised by the subsequent silence; he could hear her ragged breathing, could feel the tension that gripped her. As usual, she was rushing—he set himself to slow her down, bringing her to that plane where she could appreciate his expertise, savor all he could give her, rather than fly headlong to her fate.

He repeated his caresses, again and again, until she grew familiar with each new sensation. Her breathing slowed, deepened; her body softened beneath his hands. She moaned softly and twisted in his hold, but she no longer fought him; she floated, senses alive to each explicit caress, receptive to the pleasures he wished her to know.

Only then, deploying every ounce of his considerable expertise, did he open the door and introduce her to all that might be. With lips and tongue, he pressed on her caresses that sent her soaring, anchoring her with an intimacy that could not be denied. Again and again, she rose to the heavens; again and again, he drew her back. Only when she could take no more, when her breathing grew frantic and every muscle in her body quivered, begging for release, did he let her fly free, filling her with his tongue, feeling her hands clench tight in his hair—then relax as ecstasy washed through her. He savored her, taking pleasure in the warm piquancy that was her, letting her essence sink to his bones. When the last of her rippling shudders had died, he slowly rose over her.

Pressing her thighs wide, he settled between—with one slow, powerful thrust he filled her, feeling her softness, slick and hot, stretch to take him, feeling her body adjust to his invasion, to being his.

She was fully relaxed, fully open; he moved within her, powerfully plundering, unsurprised when, scant moments later, she stirred and, eyes glinting beneath weighted lids, joined him in the dance. He watched her until he was sure she was with him, then, closing his eyes, letting his head fall back, he lost himself in her.

The explosion that took them from the mortal plane was stronger than any he'd felt before—just as he had known it would be.

Hours later, he awoke. Honoria lay soft and warm by his side, her hair a tangled mass on his pillow. Devil allowed himself a smile—a conqueror's smile—then carefully edged from the bed.

In her room, the candles were still burning. Warmed by recent memory, he padded, naked, to the tantalus before the window. Watered wine had been left waiting, along with suitable sustenance. He poured a glass of wine and swallowed half, then lifted the lid of the serving dish, grimaced and replaced it. He was hungry, but not for food.

On the thought, he heard a sound behind him—turning, he watched Honoria emerge, blinking, from his room. Wrapped in one of his robes, her hand shading her eyes, she squinted at him. "What are you doing?"

He held up the glass.

Lowering her hand, she came forward, holding the robe closed with one hand. "I'll have some, too."

In the garden below all was silent and still. From the distant wilderness, six pairs of startled eyes fastened on the lit window of the duchess's bedchamber, screened by lacy gauze. Six men saw Devil turn and raise his glass in salute; all six lost their breaths when Honoria joined him. The idea of what was happening in that brilliantly lit chamber exercised all six minds.

They watched, breath bated, as Honoria, cloaked in a flowing robe, her hair an aureole about her head, took the glass from Devil and sipped. She handed the glass back; Devil drained it. Setting the glass down, he lowered his head as Honoria went into his arms.

Eyes on stalks, six watched their cousin and his wife share a lengthy, amazingly thorough kiss; five shifted uncomfortably when it ended, then were struck to stillness, paralyzed anew, when Honoria raised her hands and let her robe fall. Her shadow merged again with Devil's, her arms about his neck, his head bent to hers as they resumed their kiss.

Silence filled the wilderness—not even an owl hooted. Then Devil's head rose. His arm about Honoria, their shadows still one, they moved away from the window.

"*God!*" Harry's stunned exclamation said it all.

Richard's eyes were alight. "You didn't seriously imagine Devil married purely to ensure the succession?"

"By the looks of it," Gabriel dryly observed, "the succession's in no danger. If they've got that far in five hours, then St. Valentine's Day's odds-on for our wager."

Vane's deep chuckle came out of the dark. "I hesitate to mention it, but I don't believe Devil started from scratch five hours ago."

Four heads turned his way.

"Ah-hah!" Lucifer turned to his brother. "In that case, I'll sport my blunt on St. Valentine's Day definitely. If he's got a head start, then he'll have more than three months to accomplish the deed—*more* than enough."

"True." Gabriel fell into step beside Lucifer as the party turned toward the house. Their impromptu stroll had been unexpectedly revealing. "Given Devil's reputation, it's fair to assume anyone could guess as much, so we don't need to be overly concerned about taking bets against St. Valentine's Day as the limit for conception."

"I think," Richard said, following in Gabriel's wake, "that we should be rather careful about letting any of the ladies learn about our book—they're unlikely to appreciate our interest."

"Too true," Harry replied, joining the straggling line back through the bushes. "The female half of the species has a distinctly skewed view of what's important in life."

Vane watched them go, then raised his eyes to the blazing windows in the east wing. After a moment, he shifted his gaze to the unlit windows of the large bedroom at the end of the wing. Silent and still in the dark, he considered the sight, his grin deepening to a smile. Hands in his pockets, he turned—and froze. His eyes, adjusted to the dark, picked out the square figure of a man moving slowly through the wilderness, heading toward the house.

Then the tension left his shoulders. Hands still in his pockets, he strolled forward. "What ho, Charles? Getting a breath of fresh air?"

The heavy figure came to a sudden halt, swinging to face him. Then Charles inclined his head. "As you say."

It was on the tip of Vane's tongue to ask whether Charles had caught the ducal exhibition; Charles's propensity to lecture kept the words from his lips. Falling into step as Charles gained the path back to the house, he asked instead: "You planning to stay for a few days?"

"No." Charles walked a few steps before adding: "I'll be returning to town tomorrow. Do you have any idea when Sylvester plans to return?"

Vane shook his head. "I haven't heard it mentioned, but I'd be surprised to see them up before Christmas. It's to be held here as usual."

"Really?" There was genuine surprise in Charles's voice. "So Sylvester intends to take on the role of 'head of the family' at all levels?"

Vane sent him a cool glance. "When has he not?"

Charles nodded vaguely. "True—very true."

Chapter 19

WHEN, YEARS LATER, Honoria looked back on the first months of her marriage, she wondered what benevolent fate had ordained they would marry on December 1. The season was perfect, fine-tuned to her needs—December and January, cold and snowy, kept society at bay; the week of Christmas, when the whole family descended, was a happy interlude. Those quiet winter months gave her time to find her feet, to assume the mantle of the duchess of St. Ives, to learn what she needed to go on.

Taking up the reins of the ducal household was of itself easy enough. The staff was excellent, well trained and well disposed; she faced few difficulties there. However, the decisions it fell to her to make were wide-ranging, from cows to flower beds to preserves to linens. Not just for the Place, but for the three other residences her husband maintained. The organizational logistics were absorbing. Within the family, she was expected to play the matriarch, a demanding yet satisfying role.

All this and more fell to her lot in that first December and January, yet throughout that time, the aspect of her life that commanded her deepest attention remained her interaction with Devil.

Quite what she'd expected, she couldn't have said—she had come to her marriage with no firm view of what she wanted from it beyond the very fact of laying claim to the role, of being the mother of his children. Which left, as she discovered during those long quiet weeks, a great deal to be decided. By them both.

Time and again, as their wills crossed in daily life, their eyes would meet and she would see in his an expression of arrest, of calculation, consideration—and know the same emotions were visible in her eyes.

There were adjustments in other spheres, too. Like finding time to be alone, to be easy in each other's company, to discuss the myriad matters affecting their now-mutual life, all within the framework of who they were and what they were and what they could both accept. Some adjustments came easily, without conscious effort; others required give-and-take on both sides.

And if their nights remained a constant, an arena where the lines had already been drawn, where they'd already made their decisions, even there, while their physical need of each other continued, a steady, unquenchable flame, with each night that passed, their involvement deepened, became more profound, more heavily invested with meaning.

By the time January waned and the thaws set in, they were both conscious of, not only change, but the creation of something new, some palpable entity, some subtle web within which they both now lived. They never discussed it, nor in any way alluded to it. Yet she was conscious of it every minute of the day—and knew he felt it, too.

"I'm for a ride."

Seated at a table by one window, a pile of chandler's accounts before her, Honoria looked up to see Devil strolling across the back parlor.

His gaze swept her, then returned to her face. "The going will be heavy—very slow. Do you care to chance it?"

The ice in the lanes and the general bad weather had vetoed riding for the past few weeks. But today the sun was shining—and if he was the one suggesting it, riding had to be safe once more. "I'll need to change." Forsaking her accounts without a second thought, Honoria rose.

Devil grinned. "I'll bring the horses to the side door."

They were away ten minutes later. In perfect amity, they rode across his fields, taking a roundabout route to a nearby rise. They returned by way of the village, stopping to chat with

Mr. Postlethwaite, as ever in the vicarage garden. From there, their route home was via the track through the wood.

Gaining the straight at the top of the rise, they fell silent, slowing from a canter to a walk. They passed the spot where Tolly had fallen; reaching the track to the cottage, Devil drew rein.

He glanced at Honoria—halting beside him, she held his gaze. He searched her eyes, then, without a word, turned Sulieman down the narrow track.

In winter, both cottage and clearing appeared very different. The undergrowth was still dense, impenetrable, but the trees had lost their leaves. A dense carpet of mottled brown blanketed the earth, muffling hoofbeats. The cottage was neater, tidier, the stone before the door scrubbed; a wisp of smoke curled from the chimney.

"Keenan's in residence." Devil dismounted and tied his reins to a tree, then came to Honoria's side.

As he lifted her down, she recalled how distracted she'd felt when he'd first closed his hands about her waist. Now his touch was reassuring, a warmly familiar contact. "Will he be inside?"

"Unlikely. In winter, he spends his days in the village."

He secured her reins, and together they walked to the cottage. "Is it all right to go in?"

Devil nodded. "Keenan has no real home—he simply lives in the cottages I provide and keeps my woods in trim."

Opening the door, he led the way in; Honoria followed. She watched as he crossed the small room, his ranging stride slowing as he neared the raised pallet on which Tolly had died. He came to a halt at its foot, looking down on the simple grey blanket, his face a stony mask.

It had been a long time since she'd seen his face that way—these days, he rarely hid his feelings from her. She hesitated, then walked forward, stopping by his side. That was where she belonged—sometimes he needed reminding. With that aim in mind, she slid her fingers across his palm. His hand remained slack, then closed, strongly, firmly.

When he continued to stare at the uninformative bed, Honoria leaned against him. That did the trick—he glanced at her, hesitated, then lifted his arm and drew her against him. And looked frowningly back at the pallet. "It's been six months, and we've not got him yet."

Honoria rested her head against his shoulder. "I don't imagine the Bar Cynster are the sort to accept defeat."

"*Never.*"

"Well, then." She glanced up and saw his frown deepen.

He met her gaze, the tortured frown darkening his eyes. "That something I've forgotten—it was something about *how* Tolly died. Something I noticed—something I should remember." He looked back at the pallet. "I keep hoping it'll come back to me."

The intensity in his eyes, his words, precluded any light reassurance. A minute later, Honoria felt his chest swell, felt his arm tighten briefly about her, then he released her and gestured to the door. "Come—let's go home."

They rode slowly back through the gathering dusk. Devil did not mention Tolly's killer again; they parted in the hall, he heading for the library, Honoria climbing the stairs, considering a bath before dinner.

Attuned as she now was to his moods, she knew immediately when he returned to the subject. They were in the library, he in a well-stuffed armchair, she on the *chaise*, her embroidery on her lap. The fire burned brightly, warming the room; the curtains were drawn against the night. Webster had supplied Devil with a glass of brandy, then retreated; the Dowager had gone up.

From beneath her lashes, Honoria saw Devil take a long sip of brandy, then he looked at her. "I should return to London."

She looked up, studied his face, then calmly asked: "What information do you have regarding Tolly's death that necessitates our going back now?"

His gaze locked on hers. She held it steadily, calmly, without challenge, even when the green eyes narrowed and his lips compressed. Then he grimaced and leaned back against the chair, his gaze shifting to the ceiling. Setting aside her needlework, Honoria waited.

Devil thought long and hard, then thought again, yet she *was* his duchess—and too intelligent and too stubborn to swallow any glib tale. He lowered his gaze to her face. "Viscount Bromley is currently working for me."

Honoria frowned. "Do I know him?"

"He's not the sort of gentleman you need to know."

"Ah—that sort of gentleman."

"Precisely. The Viscount is currently endeavoring to discover the truth of 'Lucifer's discreditable rumor.' He's due to report next week."

"I see." Frowning, Honoria looked at the fire, then, absent-mindedly, gathered her silks. "We have no engagements here—I'll speak to Mrs. Hull and Webster immediately." She rose, then glanced back. "I assume we'll be leaving tomorrow?"

Devil held her wide gaze for a pregnant moment, then, sighed and inclined his head. "Tomorrow. After lunch."

With a nod, Honoria turned away; Devil watched her hips sway as she walked to the door. When it closed behind her, he drained his glass—and wondered, not for the first time, just what had come over him.

"How far beyond his limit did Bromley go?"

Vane asked the question as he eased into the chair before Devil's desk. Viscount Bromley had left a bare minute before, looking decidedly green.

Locking the viscount's notes of hand back in his desk drawer, Devil named a sum; eyes widening, Vane whistled. "You really did him up in style."

Devil shrugged. "I like to be thorough."

The door opened; glancing up, Devil deduced from the distracted expression in Honoria's eyes that she'd overheard his last remark. His smile when he met her gaze was unambiguously rakish. "Good morning, my dear."

Honoria blinked, then inclined her head regally.

He watched while she exchanged greetings with Vane; she was dressed to go out in a golden merino pelisse, a velvet bonnet with a ruched rim dangling by its ribbons from her hand. The same hand, gloved in ivory kid, carried a muff of golden velvet lined with swansdown; the inner face of her pelisse's upstanding collar was trimmed with the same expensive stuff. Her hair was swept up in a sleek knot—no longer the wild tangle it had been that morning when he'd left her in their bed. The memory raised a warm glow, which he knowingly allowed to infuse his smile.

Tucking the key to the desk drawer into his waistcoat pocket, he strolled, smugly satisfied, to her side. She turned as he approached—and raised her brows. "Did the viscount have the information you expected?"

Devil halted, his eyes steady on hers. He didn't need to look to be aware of Vane's surprise. "As it happens, no. Bromley needs more time."

"And you gave it to him?"

After a fractional hesitation, Devil nodded.

Honoria raised her brows. "If his lordship's so tardy, isn't there someone else you could employ in his place?"

"It's not that simple." Forestalling the question he could see in her eyes, Devil went on: "Bromley has certain attributes that make him ideal for the job."

Honoria looked even more surprised. "I only caught a brief glimpse, but he didn't strike me as the sort to inspire any great confidence." She paused, frowning slightly, looking up at Devil's uninformative face. "Now we're here, couldn't you dispense with Bromley and investigate the matter yourself? There's quite a crowd already in residence; if you tell me what it is you need to know, I might be able to learn something myself."

Vane choked—and tried to disguise it as a cough.

Honoria stared at him; capturing Vane's gaze, Devil frowned.

Witnessing that silent exchange, Honoria narrowed her eyes. "What, precisely, is Bromley investigating?"

The question brought both men's gazes to her face; Honoria met their eyes, read their instinctive response and lifted her chin. Devil eyed the sight for a bare second, then flicked a loaded glance at Vane.

Suavely, Vane smiled at Honoria. "I'll leave you to your questions." She gave him her hand; he bowed over it, then, with a speaking look for Devil, he turned to the door.

As it closed behind him, Devil looked down, into Honoria's eyes. Her expression spoke of unshakable resolve. "You don't need to know the details of Bromley's task."

He would have shifted nearer, but her quiet dignity held him back. She searched his eyes—what she read there he couldn't tell; despite all, he was conscious of admiration of a sort he'd never thought to feel for a woman—he fervently hoped it didn't show.

Honoria straightened, her chin lifting fractionally. "I'm your wife—your duchess. If something threatens *our* family, I need to know of it."

Devil noted her emphasis; she did not look away but continued to face him with unwavering resolution.

The moment stretched, charged, thick with unspoken argument. She was challenging his authority and she knew it—but she would not back down. Her eyes said so very clearly.

Devil narrowed his eyes. "You are an exceedingly stubborn woman."

Haughtily, Honoria raised a brow. "You knew that before we wed."

He nodded curtly. "Unfortunately, that trait was an integral part of the package."

His clipped accents stung; Honoria tilted her chin. "You accepted me—for better or worse."

Devil's eyes flashed. "You did the same."

Again, their gazes locked; after a moment's fraught silence, Honoria, very slowly, lifted an imperious brow. Devil eyed the sight with undisguised irritation—then, with a low growl, gestured to the *chaise*. "The matter is hardly one fit for a lady's ears."

Hiding her triumph, Honoria obediently sat; Devil sat beside her. Briefly, concisely, he told her the essence of Lucifer's rumor—how a number of contacts had reported that a Cynster had been frequenting the "palaces."

"Palaces?" Honoria looked blank.

Devil's jaw set. "Brothels—highly exclusive ones."

Honoria looked him in the eye. "You don't believe it's one of the Bar Cynster."

A statement, not a question; grimly, Devil shook his head. "I *know* it isn't one of us. Not one of us would cross the threshold of such a place." He saw no reason to edify Honoria with details of what transpired at the "palaces"—the worst excesses of prostitution was not something his wife needed to know. "It's possible Tolly attended out of curiosity and, while there, saw or heard something that made him a threat to someone." He met Honoria's eyes. "Patrons of the 'palaces' are necessarily wealthy, most are powerful in the true sense of the word. The sort of men who have secrets to hide and the capability to silence those who learn them."

Honoria studied his face. "Why do you need Bromley?"

Devil's lips twisted. "Unfortunately, the opinions of the Bar Cynster on that particular topic are widely known. The proprietors are careful; none of us could get answers."

After a moment, Honoria asked: "Do you really think it was Tolly?"

Devil met her gaze, and shook his head. "Which leaves . . ." He frowned, then grimaced. "But I believe that even less than that it was Tolly."

They both frowned into space, then Honoria focused—and glanced at the clock. "Great heavens—I'll be late." Gathering her muff, she rose.

Devil rose, too. "Where are you going?"

"To call on Louise, then I'm due at Lady Colebourne's for lunch."

"Not a hint of any of this to Louise—or *Maman*."

The glance Honoria sent him was fondly condescending. "Of course not."

She turned to the door—Devil halted her with one finger beneath her chin, turning her back to face him, tilting her head up. He looked into her eyes, waited until he saw awareness blossom, then bent his head and touched his lips to hers.

As a kiss, it was a whisper, a tantalizing, feathering touch, too insubstantial to satisfy yet too real to ignore.

When he raised his head, Honoria blinked wildly, then she saw his smile and only just stopped her glare. She drew herself up and regally inclined her head. "I will bid you a good day, my lord."

Devil smiled, slowly. "Enjoy your day, my lady."

Throughout her afternoon, Honoria cursed her husband—and the lingering effects of his devilish kiss. Unable to explain the occasional shivers that racked her, she was forced to humor Louise's supposition and drink a glass of ratafia to drive away her chill. Seated on the *chaise* in Louise's drawing room, the twins on footstools at her feet, she grasped the opportunity to air the idea that had taken root in her mind. "I'm thinking of giving a ball." She felt it imperative to publicly stamp her claim as the new duchess of St. Ives—an impromptu ball seemed the perfect solution.

"A ball?" Amanda's eyes grew round. She swung to face her mother. "Will we be allowed to attend?"

Observing her daughters' glowing faces, Louise struggled to hide a smile. "That would depend on whether you were invited and what sort of ball it was to be."

Amanda and Amelia swung back to face Honoria; she pretended not to notice, and spoke to Louise. "I believe it should be an *impromptu* ball—just for family and friends."

Louise nodded. "Not many of the *ton* are yet in residence—it would hardly do for the duchess of St. Ives to hold her first formal ball when fully half of society is still on the hunting field."

"Indeed—tantamount to social indiscretion. A sure way of putting the *grandes dames'* noses out of joint. Too many would be offended if I held my first formal ball now—but an *impromptu* ball should raise no ire."

Louise sat back, gesturing magnanimously. "As business has necessitated your return to town, no one would question your right to a little informal entertainment. And, of course, Helena has yet to come up—you couldn't hold your first formal ball without her."

"Precisely." Honoria nodded; the Dowager had gone to visit friends and was not expected to join them until the start of the Season proper. "And if it's just for friends . . ."

"And family," Louise added.

"Then," Honoria mused, "it could be held quite soon."

Amanda and Amelia looked from one distant expression to the other. "*But will we be invited?*" they wailed.

Honoria blinked and regarded them with apparent surprise. "Good heavens! You've put up your hair!"

Louise laughed; the twins pulled faces at Honoria, then leapt up from their footstools to flank her on the *chaise*.

"We promise to be models of decorum."

"The most proper young ladies you ever did see."

"And we've plenty of cousins to dance with, so you won't need to be forever finding us partners."

Honoria studied their bright eyes, and wondered how they would view their magnificent cousins once they saw them in their true colors, their true setting, prowling a *ton* ballroom. Her hesitation earned her two abjectly imploring looks; she laughed.

"Of course you'll be invited." She glanced from one ecstatic face to the other. "But it will be up to your mama to decide if you should attend or not."

They all looked at Louise; she smiled fondly but firmly at her daughters. "I'll reserve my decision until I've spoken with your father *but*, given you're to be presented this Season, an *impromptu* family ball, particularly one at St. Ives House, would be an excellent start to your year."

Expectation took flight; the twins glowed with delight.

Leaving them in alt, already badgering Louise over their ball gowns, Honoria traveled on to Lady Colebourne's town house, to partake of luncheon amidst a host of young matrons. Any lingering reservations over the need for her ball were swiftly laid to rest. Considering gleams appeared in too many eyes at the news that her husband had returned to town, a married gentleman now, far safer, in terms of dalliance, than the unattached rake he used to be.

Smiling serenely, Honoria considered stamping her claim on him, too. Perhaps with a tattoo?—on his forehead, and another relevant part of his anatomy. The *ton*'s bored matrons could look elsewhere for entertainment. Devil was hers—she had to fight an urge to declare the point publicly.

By the time she climbed into her carriage to return to Grosvenor Square, rampant possessiveness had taken firm hold. The strength of the feeling shocked her, but she knew well enough from whence it sprang. Within the *ton*, there was more than one way to lose a husband.

Not since the night of the storm, when she'd woken to find him in her room, had she thought again of losing him. Despite her fears, despite the fact Sligo and Devil's head stableman had shared her suspicions, nothing further had occurred—it now seemed likely that Devil had been right, and the disintegration of his phaeton nothing more than freakish accident.

Staring at the streetscape, Honoria felt a totally unexpected determination well. She recognized it for what it was—it surprised her, but she did not fight it. Too many people had told her that it was her fate to be his bride.

Which meant he was hers—she intended keeping it that way.

*   *   *

Devil lunched with friends, then dropped in at White's. It was their third day back in the capital; despite the acquisition of a wife, the comfortable regime of former days was slowly settling into place. "The only difference," he explained to Vane as they strolled into the reading room, "is that I no longer need to exert myself over the matter of warming my bed."

Vane grinned. Nudging Devil's elbow, he nodded to two vacant armchairs.

They settled companionably behind newssheets. Devil gazed at his, unseeing. His mind was full of his wife and her stubbornness. Quite how he had come to marry the one woman in all the millions impervious to intimidation, he did not know. Fate, he recalled, had arranged the matter—his only option seemed to be to hope fate would also provide him with the means to manage her *without* damaging the subtle something growing between them.

That was unique, at least in his experience. He couldn't define it, could not even describe it—he only knew it was precious, too valuable to risk.

Honoria was also too valuable to risk, at any level, in any way.

He frowned at the newssheet—and wondered what she was doing.

Later that afternoon, having parted from Vane, Devil strolled home through the gathering dusk. He crossed Piccadilly and turned into Berkeley Street.

"Ho! Sylvester!"

Devil halted and turned, then waited until Charles joined him before strolling on. Charles fell into step; he had lodgings in Duke Street, just beyond Grosvenor Square.

"Back to your old haunts, I take it?"

Devil smiled. "As you say."

"I'm surprised—I thought Leicestershire would hold you rather longer. They've had excellent sport, so I've heard."

"I didn't go to the Lodge this season." Manor Lodge was the ducal hunting box. "I went out with the Somersham pack but the runs were hardly worth it."

Charles looked puzzled. "Is Aunt Helena well?"

"Perfectly." Devil shot him a sidelong glance; his lips twitched. "I've had other distractions to hand."

"Oh?"

"I married recently, remember?"

Charles's brows rose briefly. "I hadn't imagined marriage would cause any change in your habits."

Devil merely shrugged. They circumnavigated Berkeley Square, then turned down a alleyway that ran between two houses, connecting the square with Hays Mews.

"I take it Honoria remained at Somersham?"

Devil frowned. "No. She's here—with me."

"She is?" Charles blinked. After a moment, he murmured: "I must remember to pay my respects."

Devil inclined his head, unwilling to commit Honoria to any transports of delight. He knew perfectly well how his other cousins viewed Charles; for his part, he'd always tried for tolerance. They strode on, eventually halting at the corner of Grosvenor Square. Duke Street lay ahead; Devil was but yards from his door.

Abruptly, Charles swung to face him. "I hesitate to allude to such a delicate matter, but I feel I must speak."

Coolly, Devil raised his brows—and took a firm grip on his tolerance.

"Bringing Honoria to London, so early in her tenure, to require her to countenance your wider liaisons within months of your marriage, is unnecessarily cruel. She may not be experienced in *ton*nish behavior but her understanding is, I believe, superior. She will doubtless realize you're bestowing your interest elsewhere. Women are sensitive to such matters—if you had left her at Somersham, she would not be exposed to such hurt."

His expression blank, Devil looked down at Charles; he'd lost all touch with tolerance—instead, he was battling to keep the lid on his formidable temper. If Charles had not been family, he'd be choking on his teeth. It took concerted effort to keep a snarl from his face. "You mistake the matter, Charles. It was Honoria's wish that she accompany me, a wish I saw no reason to deny." His rigidly even tone had Charles stiffening; his gaze would have frozen hell. "Furthermore, you appear to be laboring under a misapprehension—at present, I have no intention of seeking any 'wider liaison'—my wife holds my interest to the exclusion of all others."

It was the truth, the literal truth, stated more clearly than he'd allowed his own mind to know it.

Charles blinked—he looked stunned.

Devil's lips twisted in chilly self-deprecation. "Indeed—there's more to marriage than even I foresaw. You should try it—I can recommend it as a challenging experience."

With a curt nod, he strode for his door, leaving Charles, blank-faced, staring after him.

Chapter 20

THE NEXT MORNING, as soon as he was free of his most urgent business, Devil climbed the stairs to the morning room.

Honoria looked up as he entered; she smiled warmly. "I thought you'd be busy for hours."

"Hobden's on his way back to the Place." Devil strolled to the *chaise* and sat on the arm beside her. Resting one arm along the *chaise*'s back, he picked up one of the lists from Honoria's lap. "Our guests?"

She peeked. "That's the connections. These are the friends."

Devil took the lists and scanned them. They'd discussed her notion of an impromptu ball the evening before. Reasoning that the exercise would keep her occupied—distracted from Bromley and his doings—he'd readily concurred. "There are a few names you might add."

Honoria picked up a pencil and dutifully scribbled as he reeled off a short list of his own. When he said "Chillingworth" she looked up in surprise. "I thought the earl was no favorite of yours?"

"On the contrary—he's a prime favorite." Devil smiled, one of his Prince of Darkness smiles. "Who would I taunt if I didn't have Chillingworth by?"

Honoria looked her reply but left the earl on the list. Chillingworth could look after himself.

"I had wondered," Devil said, studying her profile, "if you were free to come for a drive?"

Honoria looked up, her arm brushing his thigh. Her eyes touched his, then she grimaced. "I can't." She gestured to the writing materials on the table. "If the ball's to be next Friday, I need to send the invitations out today."

Devil had never written a ball invitation in his life. He was about to suggest he might learn, when Honoria continued: "Louise is bringing the twins by to help."

With a swift smile, Devil uncoiled his long legs. "In that case, I'll leave you to your endeavors."

His fingers trailed against her cheek as he stood, then he grinned and strolled to the door; Honoria watched it close behind him. She stared at the panels, her expression wistful, then she grimaced and went back to her lists.

The next morning, when the morning room door opened, Honoria looked up with an eager smile. Only to discover it was Vane who sought an audience.

"Devil said I'd find you here." Smiling charmingly, he strolled forward. "I've a request to make."

The gleam in his eye suggested just what that request might be; Honoria eyed it with matriarchal disapproval. "Who?" she asked.

"Lady Canterton. And Harry suggested Lady Pinney."

Honoria held his gaze for a pregnant moment, then reached for her pencil. "I'll send the invitations today."

"Thank you."

"With one proviso." She looked up in time to see wariness creep into his eyes.

"What proviso?"

There was a hint of steel in the question; Honoria ignored it. "You will each dance one dance with each of the twins."

"The *twins*?" Vane stared at her. "How old are they?"

"Seventeen. They'll be presented this year—Friday will be their first ball."

Vane shuddered.

Honoria raised a brow. "Well?"

He looked at her, grim resignation in his eyes. "Very well—one dance each. I'll tell Harry."

Honoria nodded. "Do."

Her next visitors followed in quick succession, all on the same errand. Gabriel succeded Vane; Lucifer followed. The last through the morning-room door was Richard. "I know," Honoria said, reaching for her much-amended list. "Lady Grey."

"Lady Grey?" Richard blinked. "Why Lady Grey?"

Honoria blinked back. She'd seen him slip away from Horatia's ball with the dark-haired, alabaster-skinned beauty. "Isn't she . . . ?" She gestured with her pencil.

"Ah, no." Richard's grin was reminiscent of Devil at his worst. "That was last year. I was going to ask for Lady Walton."

Ask for—like a treat. And, like a treat, Lady Walton would doubtless fall, a ripe plum into his lap. Honoria decided it was useless disapproving; she added Lady Walton to her list.

"And I dutifully promise to stand up with both Amanda and Amelia."

"Good." Honoria looked up in time to witness Richard's insouciant bow.

"A very good idea, this ball of yours." He paused at the door, a Cynster smile on his lips. "We were all looking for a way to get the Season rolling. Nothing could be better than an *impromptu* ball."

Honoria shot him a warning look; chuckling, he left.

She went on with her planning, trying not to listen for footsteps beyond the door, trying not to wonder whether Devil would drop by to hear of his cousins' selections, to ask her what she was doing, to offer his views.

He didn't.

When she entered the breakfast parlor the next morning, she was pleased to find Devil still present, sipping coffee and scanning *The Gazette*. Her place was now at the table's other end, an expanse of polished mahogany between them. Taking her seat, she beamed a warm smile across the silver service.

Devil returned the gesture, the expression more evident in his eyes than on his lips. Folding *The Gazette*, he laid it aside. "How are your plans progressing?"

Although he'd dined at home the previous night, he'd been preoccupied with business; he had come to bed late, conversation very far from his mind. Between sipping tea and nibbling toast, Honoria filled him in.

He listened attentively, interpolating comments, ending with: "You're setting a new fashion, you know. I've already heard of two other hostesses who are planning early, *impromptu* entertainments."

Smiling radiantly, Honoria shrugged. "Where St. Ives leads, the others will follow."

He grinned appreciatively, then his eyes locked on hers. "I've had the horses brought up from the Place. It's fine outside—I wondered if you'd care to ride?"

Honoria's heart leapt—she sorely missed their private hours. "I—"

"Your pardon, Your Grace."

Turning, Honoria watched as Mrs. Hull bobbed a curtsy to Devil, then faced her. "The caterers have arrived, ma'am. I've put them in the parlor."

"Oh—yes." Happiness deflating like a pricked balloon, Honoria smiled weakly. "I'll join them shortly." The florists were also due that morning, as were the musicians.

Mrs. Hull withdrew; Honoria turned back to meet Devil's eyes. "I'd forgotten. The supper menu needs to be decided today. I won't have time to ride this morning."

With a suave smile, Devil waved dismissively. "It's of no account."

Honoria held back a frown—that smile did not reach his eyes. But she could think of nothing appropriate to say; with an apologetic smile, she stood. "By your leave."

Devil inclined his head, his superficial smile still in place. He watched Honoria leave, then set down his cup and stood. Slowly, a frown replaced his smile. He walked into the hall; behind him, Webster gave orders for the parlor to be cleared. An instant later, he appeared at his elbow.

"Shall I send for your horse, Your Grace?"

Devil focused, and found his gaze resting on the stairs up which Honoria had gone. "No." When he rode alone, he rode early, before others were about. His features hardening, he turned to the library. "I'll be busy for the rest of the morning."

*　　*　　*

The day of the duchess of St. Ives's impromptu ball dawned crisp and clear. In the park, wispy mist wreathed beneath the trees; shrill birdcalls echoed in the stillness.

Devil rode along the deserted tan track, the heavy thud of his horse's hooves drumming in his ears. He rode with single-minded abandon, fast yet in absolute control, his body and his mount's in fluid concert as they flew through the chill morning. At the end of the track, he hauled the snorting chestnut's head about—and rode back even faster.

Nearing the end of the tan, he eased back, pulling up before a stand of oak. The deep-chested horse, built for endurance, blew hard, and dropped his head. Devil loosened the reins, chest swelling as he drew the air deep.

There was no one in sight, nothing but trees and well-tended lawns. The tang of damp grass rose as the chestnut shifted, then settled to crop. Devil filled his chest again, and felt the cold reach his brain. And, as often happened in this solitude, his unease, the nagging disquiet that had gnawed at him for days, crystallized, clarified. The insight was not encouraging.

The idea that he was irritated because his wife was so busy organizing her ball that she had no time for him did not sit well—yet denying his jealousy, the waiting, the wanting to be with her, was pointless. Even now, he could feel the black emotion roiling inside. Yet he had no justifiable cause for complaint. Duchesses were supposed to give balls. Honoria was behaving precisely as a wife should—she'd made no awkward demands, no requests for attention he didn't wish to give. She hadn't even accepted the attention he'd been only too willing to bestow.

That fact rankled. Deeply.

Frowning, Devil shook his shoulders. He was being unreasonable—he'd no right to expect his wife to be different, to comport herself by some different code—one he couldn't, even now, define. Yet that was precisely what he did want, the desire at the heart of his dissatisfaction.

Unbidden, his mind conjured up that moment when, in his woodsman's cottage, she'd leaned against him. He'd looked down, seen the warmth and understanding in her eyes, and felt her weight, soft and womanly, against him. And realized just how much he now had that Tolly would never have, never have a chance to experience.

He drew a deep breath; the crisp cold sang through his veins. He wanted Honoria—had wanted her from the first—but his want was not quite what he'd thought it. The physical want, the possessive want, the protective want, the need for her loyalty, her commitment—all these he'd fulfilled. What remained?

Something, certainly—something strong enough, powerful enough, to unsettle him, to obsess him, to undermine effortlessly his normally unassailable control. Something beyond his experience.

Brows quirking, he examined that conclusion and could not fault it. Lips firming, he took up his reins. He wasn't going to get any real peace until he fulfilled this want, too.

Both he and the chestnut had cooled. Leaning forward, he patted the horse's sleek neck and dug in his heels. The chestnut obediently stepped out, shifting fluidly into a loping canter.

The bark of the tree before which they'd stood splintered. The sound reached Devil; glancing back, he saw the fresh lesion in the trunk, level with his chest. In the same instant, a telltale "cough" reached his ears.

He didn't stop to investigate; he didn't rein in until he reached the park gate where others were now gathering for their morning ride.

Devil halted to let the chestnut settle. Guns were not permitted in the park. The keepers were exempt, but what would they shoot at—squirrels?

The chestnut had calmed; deadly calm himself, Devil headed back to Grosvenor Square.

The duchess of St. Ives's impromptu ball was an extravagant success. Held, not in the large ballroom, but in the relative intimacy of the music room, the evening overflowed with laughter, dancing, and an easy gaiety not often encountered within the rigid confines of the *ton*.

Many present, of course, were related; the rest were long-standing acquaintances. The tone was set from the first, when the duke and duchess led the company in a vigorous, breathless waltz. All hundred guests took the hint, setting themselves to enjoy the relaxed atmosphere, the champagne that flowed freely, the excellent supper and the similarly excellent company. Some five hours after the first had arrived, the last guests, weary but smiling, took their leave. Webster shut the front door, then set the bolts.

In the center of the hall, Devil looked down at Honoria, leaning on his arm. Lights still danced in her eyes. He smiled. "A signal success, my dear."

Honoria smiled back, resting her head against his arm. "It went very well, I think."

"Indeed." His hand over hers where it lay on his sleeve, Devil turned her toward the library. It had become their habit to end their evenings there, sipping brandy, exchanging comments. They halted on the threshold; footmen and maids were clearing glasses and straightening furniture. Devil glanced at Honoria. "Perhaps, tonight, we should take our drinks upstairs."

Honoria nodded. Devil accepted a lighted candelabrum from Webster; together they started up the stairs.

"Amelia and Amanda were exhausted."

"For quite the first time in their lives."

Honoria smiled fondly. "They danced every dance bar the waltzes. And they would have danced those if they could have." Glancing up, she noted the slight frown marring her husband's handsome countenance; looking forward, she inwardly grinned. The twins' presence had triggered an intriguing reaction in their male cousins—repressive looks had been *de rigueur*. She could foresee certain interesting scenes as the Season unfolded.

The thought reminded her of another interesting scene, one in which she'd participated. "Incidentally, I give you fair warning, I will not again invite Chillingworth if you behave as you did tonight."

"*Me?*" The look of innocence Devil sent her would have done credit to a cherub. "*I* wasn't the one who started it."

Honoria frowned. "I meant both of you—*he* was no better."

"I could hardly let him get away with casting a slur on my ability to satisfy you."

"He *didn't!* It was you who twisted his words that way."

"That was what he meant."

"Be that as it may, you didn't have to inform him that I—" Honoria broke off, cheeks flaming—again. She caught the gleam in Devil's green eyes. Pulling her hand from under his, she pushed him away; he didn't even stagger. "You're *incorrigible.*"

Lifting her skirts, she climbed the last stairs. "I don't know why you insisted on inviting him when all the conversation you exchanged was a litany of thinly veiled insults."

"*That's* why." Retaking her arm, Devil drew it through his as they crossed the gallery. "Chillingworth's the perfect whetstone to sharpen my wit upon—his hide's as thick as a rhinoceros's."

"Humph!" Honoria kept her chin high.

"I did let him waltz with you."

"Only because I made it impossible for you to do otherwise." She'd used the waltz to separate the two dueling reprobates—unsuccessfully as it transpired.

"Honoria, if I do not wish you to waltz with a particular gentleman, you won't."

She looked up, a protest on her lips. The undercurrent beneath his words registered, she met his eye—and decided it was safer simply to humph again.

When she looked forward, Devil grinned. He'd enjoyed the evening without reservation; even the emergence of the twins as budding Aphrodites couldn't tarnish his mellow mood. As they turned toward the ducal apartments, he slid his arm about Honoria and drew her against him.

Honoria let him, enjoying his nearness. She remained puzzled by his relationship with Chillingworth. While waltzing with Vane, she'd asked his opinion; he'd smiled. "If they weren't so busy being rivals, they'd be friends." Their rivalry, now she'd viewed it at close quarters, was not entirely facetious, yet neither was it serious. From any distance, however, they appeared deadly rivals.

"Is Charles always so subdued?" She'd noticed him watching as she waltzed with Chillingworth; his expression had been oddly blank.

"Charles? Now there's one who won't approve your innovation—unfettered gaiety was never his strong suit."

"Your other cousins reveled in 'unfettered gaiety.'" Honoria cast him a pointed glance. "*Totally* unfettered." Each one of the Bar Cynster, excepting only Devil, had disappeared from the festivities at some point, reappearing later with smug, cat-who-had-found-the-cream smiles.

Devil grinned. "Gabriel tendered his felicitations along with the firm hope that you'll make your impromptu ball a yearly event."

Honoria opened her eyes wide. "Are there really that many accommodating ladies within the *ton*?"

"You'd be surprised," Devil held his door wide.

Honoria threw him a speaking glance, then, nose high, swept over the threshold. But she was smiling as she glided deeper into the room, lit by a fire burning cheerily in the grate. The candelabra held high, dispelling the shadows, Devil crossed to the tallboy, setting the candlestick beside a silver tray holding a crystal decanter and two glasses.

Pouring brandy into one glass, he handed it to Honoria. Warming the glass between her hands, she waltzed to the armchair by the hearth and sank onto its well-stuffed arm. Raising the glass, she breathed in the fumes.

And froze. She blinked. Across the rim of her glass, she saw Devil grasp the second glass, half-full of amber liquid. He raised it.

"*No!*"

Her breathless shout made him turn. But the glass still rose— any second, he'd swallow his usual first gulp.

Honoria dropped her glass; it fell, amber liquid splashing across the jewel-hued rug. Vocal cords paralyzed, she flung herself at Devil, striking the glass from his grasp. It shattered against the tallboy.

"What—?" Devil lifted her, swinging her clear of the shards raining down. White-faced, Honoria clung to him, her gaze fixed on the liquid dripping down the tallboy.

"What's wrong?" Devil stared at her; when she didn't answer, he looked around, then, grasping her arms, set her from him and looked into her face. "What?"

She drew a shaky breath, then looked into his face. She gulped. "The brandy." Her voice was weak, quavery; she hauled in another breath. "Bitter almonds."

Devil froze—literally. The cold started at his feet and spread upward, claiming muscle after muscle until he was chilled through. His hands fell from Honoria as she pressed close, sliding her arms around him, clinging so tight he could barely breathe. Breathing, indeed, was an effort. For one instant, he stopped altogether—the instant when he realized he'd handed her a glass of poison. His gut clenched tight. He closed his eyes, resting his cheek against her curls, closing his arms about her. Her perfume reached him; he tightened his hold, feeling her body, warm and alive, against his.

Suddenly, Honoria looked up, nearly hitting his chin with her head. "You were nearly *killed!*" It was an accusation. Her expression mutinous, she clutched his waistcoat, and tried to shake him. "I told you before—I *warned* you! It's *you* they're trying to kill."

A conclusion he could hardly argue. "They didn't succeed. Thanks to you." Devil tried to draw her back into his arms. Honoria resisted.

"You were one gulp away from death—I *saw* you!"

Her eyes were fever-bright, her cheeks flushed. Devil bit back a curse—not at her, but at his would-be murderer. "I'm not dead."

"But you nearly *were!*" Her eyes flashed blue fire. "*How dare they?*"

Devil recognized shock when he heard it. "We're both alive."

His calming words fell on deaf ears; Honoria swung away and started to pace. "I can't believe it!" She threw out one hand. "This is utterly *wrong!*"

Devil followed as she paced toward the bed.

"I won't allow it—I *forbid* it! You're *mine*—they can't have you." She swung around; finding him close, she grabbed his lapels. "Do you hear?" Her eyes were silver saucers, sheened with tears. "I am *not* going to lose you, too."

"I'm here—you won't ever lose me." Devil slid his arms about her; she was so tense she was quivering. "Trust me."

She searched his eyes; tears spangled her lashes.

"Hold me," he commanded.

She hesitated, then obeyed, slowly unclenching her fists, sliding her arms about him. She rested her head against his shoulder but remained tense, taut—determined.

Framing her jaw, Devil lifted her face, looked down on pale cheeks, at eyes awash with tears, then he bent his head and kissed her set lips. "You'll never lose me," he whispered. "I'll *never* leave you."

A shudder rippled through her. Damp lashes lowered, Honoria lifted her face, offering her lips. Devil took them, then took her mouth. The caress lengthened, deepened, slowly, inexorably spiraling into passion. He needed her—she needed him—an affirmation of life to chase away death's specter.

Honoria drew back only long enough to wrap her arms about his neck. She clung to him, to the vibrant life enshrined in their kiss. His arms locked about her, his chest hard against her breasts, his heartbeat a heavy, repetitive thud reverberating through her. Her defensive tension shifted, transmuted; she pressed herself to him. She answered his kiss and desire rose, not in passionate frenzy, but as a swelling presence impossible to deny. Like rivers unleashed, it welled from them both, merging to a torrent, carrying all thought, all conscious will before it, impelling, compelling, not with need but with the need to give.

Neither questioned its rightness, neither attempted to fight it—a force more than strong enough to deny the deaths they'd faced. Surrendering, to it, to each other, they stripped, barely aware of the clothes they left strewn across the floor. The touch of skin against warm skin, of hands searching, of lips and tongues caressing, played on their senses, feeding the swelling crescendo.

Naked, aroused, they took to their bed, limbs twining, then parting, only to close intimately again. Soft murmurs rose, Devil's deep rumble beneath Honoria's breathless gasps. Time stretched; with freshly opened eyes and heightened senses, they learned each other anew. Devil revisted every soft curve, every square inch of Honoria's ivory skin, every fluttering pulse point, each and every erogenous zone. No less ensorcelled, Honoria rediscovered his hard body, his strength, his perception, his unfailing expertise. His commitment to her fulfilment—matched only by hers to his.

Time suspended as they explored, lavishing pleasure on each other, their murmurs transmuting to soft cries and half-suppressed groans. Only when there was no more left to give did Devil lie back, lifting Honoria over him. Straddling him, she arched and took him in, sinking slowly down, savoring every second, until he was buried deep.

Time fractured. A crystal moment, it hung between them, quivering, invested with sensation. Gazes locked, they both held still, then Honoria let her lids fall. Heart thundering, hearing—feeling—his heartbeat deep within her, she savored the strength that had invaded her, silently acknowledging the power that held her in its coils. Beneath her, Devil closed his eyes, his mind awash with the softness that had accepted him, that now held him so powerfully he could never break free.

Then they moved, their bodies in perfect communion, their souls committed beyond will or thought. Too experienced to rush, they savored each step down the lengthy road, until the gates of paradise opened before them. Together, they entered in.

"Under no circumstances is Her Grace to be left unattended at any time." Devil reinforced that edict with a flat look, trained impartially on the three retainers ranged before him on the library rug.

All three—Webster, poker-straight, his expression more impassive than ever, Mrs. Hull, rigidly upright, lips pinched with concern, and Sligo, his face more mournful than ever—looked uncertain.

Grudgingly, Devil amended: "Other than in our apartments."

That was where Honoria presently was and, if experience was any guide, where she'd remain for a good few hours yet. She'd been deeply asleep when he'd left her—after fully sating his senses and hers; the exercise had left him feeling more vulnerable than he'd ever felt before. But she was safe in their rooms, given the burly footman stationed within sight of the door.

"When I'm absent from the house, Webster, you'll admit no one other than one of my aunts or Vane. If any call, Her Grace is indisposed. We will not be entertaining in the immediate future—not until this matter is resolved."

"Indeed, Your Grace."

"Both you and Mrs. Hull will ensure no one has any chance to tamper with any food or provisions. Incidentally," Devil's gaze fixed on Webster's face, "did you check the rest of that brandy?"

"Yes, Your Grace. The rest of the bottle was uncontaminated." Webster straightened. "I can assure Your Grace I did not fill that decanter with poisoned spirits."

Devil met his gaze directly. "So I had assumed. I take it we've hired no new staff lately?"

Webster's stiffness eased. "No, Your Grace. As is our habit, we brought up more of our people from Somersham to assist last night, hands already familiar with our ways. There were no strangers amongst the staff, m'lord." Fixing his gaze on a point above Devil's head, Webster continued: "Last night, every member of the staff had some prescribed activity they had to perform at virtually any given time." Webster let his gaze drop to meet Devil's eyes. "The long and the short of it is that none of our staff were missing from their duties long enough to have reached your apartments and returned undetected. We must assume, I believe, that some guest aware of the location of the ducal apartments introduced the poison, my lord."

"Quite." Devil had already thought through that point, that and a great deal more; he shifted his gaze to Sligo. "You, Sligo, will accompany Her Grace wherever she goes. If she should decide to walk in public, you will be by her side—not behind her." He met Sligo's gaze levelly. "You're to guard her with your life."

Sligo nodded; he owed Devil his life several times over and saw nothing odd in the request. "I'll make sure no one gets to her. But . . ." He frowned. "If I'm to be with Her Grace, who's to be with you?"

"I've faced death before—this is no different."

"If I could suggest, Your Grace," Webster intervened. "At least a footman—"

"No." The single word cut off all protest. Devil eyed his servitors straitly. "I'm more than capable of protecting myself." His tone dared them to contradict him; naturally, none of them did. He nodded a dismissal. "You may go."

He stood as they filed to the door; Webster and Sligo left, but Mrs. Hull hung back. When, tight-lipped, she looked at him, Devil, resigned, lifted a brow.

"You're not really invincible, you know."

Devil's lips twisted wryly. "I know, Hully, I know. But for God's sake, don't tell Her Grace."

Mollified by his use of his childhood name for her, Mrs. Hull sniffed. "As if I would. You just busy yourself finding whoever was so lost to all proper feeling as to put poison in that decanter—*we'll* look after Her Grace."

Devil watched her leave, and wondered if any of the three had any idea how much he was entrusting to their care. He'd told them true—he'd faced death many times. Honoria's death he couldn't face at all.

"I'm putting my trust in you to ensure that no harm comes to His Grace." Pacing before the morning-room windows, Honoria sent a raking glance over the three servitors lined up on the rug—Webster, Mrs. Hull, and Sligo. "I assume he's already spoken to you regarding the incident last night?"

All three nodded; Webster acted as spokesman. "His Grace gave us orders to ensure no repetition of the incident, ma'am."

"I'm sure he did." Devil had left the house before she'd awoken, an occurrence delayed by him. He'd kept her awake into the small hours—she'd never known him so demanding. When he'd stirred her awake at dawn, she'd applied herself wholeheartedly to appeasing his considerable appetite, assuming, with what little wit she'd been able to command, that it was some long-overdue realization of his mortality that made him so hungry for life.

She'd expected to discuss the shocking incident of the poison with him over breakfast—instead, she'd missed breakfast altogether.

"It is not my intention to counteract any of His Grace's orders—whatever he has decreed must be done. *However*"—pausing, she glanced at the three faces before her—"am I right in assuming he gave no orders for his own protection?"

Webster grimaced. "We did make the suggestion, ma'am—unfortunately, His Grace vetoed the idea."

"Flat," Sligo corroborated, his tone making it clear what he thought of that decision.

Mrs. Hull's lips thinned to a prim line. "He always was exceedingly stubborn."

"Indeed." From the way all three were watching her, Honoria knew she had only to say the word. The context, however, was somewhat delicate—she could not, in all conscience, contradict her husband's edicts. She looked at Webster. "What was the suggestion His Grace vetoed?"

"I suggested a footman as a guard, ma'am."

Honoria raised her brows. "We have other suitable men in our employ, do we not—men who are not footmen?"

Webster blinked only once. "Indeed, ma'am. From under-butlers to scullery boys."

"And there's the grooms and stablelads, too," Sligo added.

Honoria nodded. "Very well." She met each pair of eyes. "To preserve my peace of mind, you will ensure you are always in a position to tell me where His Grace is at any time while he is absent from this house. Nothing, however, must be done against His Grace's expressed wishes. I trust that's clear?"

Webster bowed. "Indeed, ma'am. I'm sure His Grace would expect us to do all possible to keep you from fretting."

"Precisely. Now, do you have any idea where he is at present?"

Webster and Mrs. Hull shook their heads. Sligo looked at the ceiling. "I believe" he said"—he rocked slightly on his toes—"that the Cap'n's with Mister Vane." Lowering his gaze, he met Honoria's eyes. "At his lodgings in Jermyn Street, ma'am." When Honoria, along with both his peers, looked their question, Sligo opened his eyes wide. "A lad from the stables had to go that way with a message, ma'am."

"I see." For the first time since smelling bitter almonds, Honoria felt a touch of relief. She had allies. "Do you think this stablelad might still be about his business when His Grace leaves his cousin?"

Sligo nodded. "Very likely, ma'am."

Honoria nodded back, decisively, dismissively. "You have your orders, from both myself and His Grace. I'm sure you will carry them out diligently."

Sligo nodded; Mrs. Hull curtsied. Webster bowed low. "You may rely on us, Your Grace."

Chapter 21

VANE STARED AT Devil, unfeigned horror in his face. "Just how many attempts on your life have there been?"

Devil raised his brows. "If Honoria's supposition is correct, three. There's still nothing to suggest my phaeton was tampered with, but, given these other two episodes, I'm inclined to think she may be right." They were in Vane's parlor; seated at the table, Devil raised a tankard of ale and took a long sip.

Standing before the windows, Vane was still staring. "The phaeton, the poison—what was the third?"

"Someone took a shot at me in the park yesterday morning."

"You were out early?"

Devil nodded. Vane's gaze blanked; he turned to stare, unseeing, out of the window. Devil waited. After the dramatic events of the night, he felt deadly calm. In between making love to his wife, he'd spent the night thinking. Near death was a wonderful focuser—nearly losing Honoria had eradicated all pretense, exposed all the logical reasons he'd used to justify their marriage as the facade they actually were. What he felt for his wife had nothing to do with logic.

Abruptly, he shifted, and glanced at Vane—then inwardly, mockingly, shook his head. At himself. Whenever his thoughts even touched on that point—that emotion he could not, would not, define—he pulled back, edged away. That unnameable emotion left him feeling so vulnerable he found it near impossible to countenance, to even admit its existence. It opened up a gaping hole in his defenses; his instinctive response was to rebuild his walls with all speed.

But he would have to face it soon. Insecurity lay, a leaden weight in his gut; the uncertainty was driving him insane. Honoria cared for him—last night had proved that. She might even care in the way women sometimes did, at some different level from any sexual interest. On some other plane. He desperately needed to know.

Finding out without asking, without revealing his intense interest in the answer, was a challenge he intended to devote his entire attention to—just as soon as he'd dealt with his would-be murderer.

Who'd very nearly murdered his wife.

He looked up as Vane turned, fixing him with a worried look. "This is more than serious." Vane started to pace. "Why only in London?" He shot a glance at Devil. "There weren't any other suspicious happenings at the Place?"

Devil shook his head. "London because it's safer—more people about. Cambridgeshire is open country, and my fields are rather full of my workers."

"That didn't help us locate Tolly's killer."

Devil looked down, swirling the ale in his tankard.

"To sabotage your phaeton, they had to get into your stables undetected, know which carriage, and how best to make it look like an accident, which presupposes some knowledge of your driving habits. Whoever shot at you in the park must have known you make a habit of riding that early. And whoever put the poison in the decanter"—his expression grim, Vane met Devil's eye—"whoever did that had to know where the ducal appartments lie as well as your peculiar method of drinking."

Devil nodded. "If they hadn't known that, they'd have been far more circumspect in their dosage—there was enough in one mouthful to fell an ox, which was why Honoria detected it so easily."

"So," Vane said, "whoever it is knew all the above, but—" He broke off and looked at Devil.

Who grimaced. "But didn't know that Honoria shares my brandy as well as my bed."

Vane grimaced back. "Even I didn't know that, so it doesn't help us thin the ranks." He paused, then asked: "So was Tolly killed because he was coming to warn you?"

Slowly, Devil nodded. "That scenario makes sense of what he said at the cottage as well as, if not better, than any other."

Both fell silent, then Vane asked: "What will you do?"

"Do?" Devil raised his brows. "Precisely what I was planning before, only with both eyes fully open."

"*And* with me to cover your back."

Devil grinned. "If you insist."

It was a familiar sally between them; some of Vane's tension eased. He sat in the chair opposite Devil's. "So, has Bromley finally turned up trumps?"

"Not yet—but he thinks he's laid his hand on a winning card. He came by yesterday with the offer of a meeting—the madam in question wanted certain guarantees. I told him what she could have—he's gone off to negotiate time and date."

"Place?"

"The palace itself."

Vane frowned. "You'll go?"

Devil shrugged. "I can see why she'd want it that way."

"It could be a trap."

"Unlikely—she's got more to lose by siding against me rather than with me. And Bromley's too enamored of his comforts to encourage any double-dealing."

Vane didn't look convinced. "I don't like any of this."

Draining his tankard, Devil shook his head. "No—but I'd rather not miss any clue for want of looking." He glanced at Vane. "I still haven't remembered that something I've forgotten about Tolly's murder."

"You're still positive it's something vital?"

"Oh, yes." His expression grim, Devil rose. "It was something so vital I noticed it particularly, but Tolly dying wiped it from my mind."

Vane grimaced. "It'll come back."

Devil met his eyes. "But will it come back in time?"

Firm footsteps approached the morning room; Honoria left the window and sat on the *chaise*. She'd spent the day methodically analyzing the attempts on Devil's life. And had reached the only logical conclusion. While her immediate impulse was to lay her findings before Devil, further consideration had suggested he might not, in this case, accept her conclusion readily. After considerable cogitation, she'd sent a message to the one person she knew he trusted without question.

Her "Come in" coincided with a peremptory knock. The door opened; Vane strolled in. His gaze found her; closing the door, he strolled forward, his gait reminiscent of Devil's prowl. "How are you?"

Honoria grimaced. "Distracted."

He nodded and sat in the chair facing her. "How can I help?" One brown brow rose. "Your note said the matter was urgent."

Lips compressed, Honoria studied his face. "I've been thinking over all that's happened. There has to be a reason someone's trying to kill Devil."

His gaze on her face, Vane nodded. "Go on."

"There's only one compelling reason I know of connecting Devil and a person who would know enough to tamper with his phaeton and put poison in his brandy. The inheritance—which, after all, is more than considerable. That might also explain why the attacks only started after it became obvious we would wed."

Light dawned in Vane's face. "Of course. I've been concentrating on Tolly—I didn't think of that angle."

"You agree?" Honoria leaned forward. "You agree it must be Richard?"

Vane stared in blank astonishment. "Richard?"

Honoria frowned. "Devil's heir."

"Ah." Swiftly, Vane searched her face. "Honoria, your logic's impeccable—unfortunately, Devil's neglected to give you all the details necessary to arrive at the correct outcome." He hesitated, then shook his head. "I'm sorry, but it's not my place to explain—you'll have to ask Devil."

Honoria eyed him straitly. "Ask him *what*?"

Vane's eyes turned hard. "Ask him who his heir is."

"It's not Richard?"

Lips compressed, Vane rose. "I must go—but promise me you'll tell Devil your conclusions."

Honoria's eyes flashed. "I can give you an absolute assurance on that point."

"Good." Vane met her gaze. "If it makes it any easier, I'd wager he's already followed the same train of thought."

"You think he knows?" Honoria held out her hand.

"He knows, but, as he does with such matters, he won't say until he's sure—until he has proof." Vane released Honoria's hand. "By your leave, I've an idea to pursue—the sooner we get your husband the proof he requires, the sooner we'll be free of this murderer."

Unwilling to do anything to delay that outcome, Honoria nodded and let him go. Long after the door had closed behind him, she sat staring at the panels, unable to make head or tail of what was going on.

Cynsters—a law unto themselves. With a disgusted humph, she stood and headed upstairs to change.

His Grace of St. Ives dined at home that evening. Honoria waited until they retired, then stripped off her gown, donned her nightgown, scurried like an eager chambermaid into the ducal chamber, dropped her peignoir, kicked off her slippers, and scrambled beneath the covers.

From the other side of the room, engaged in untying his cravat, Devil watched her performance with interest—an interest she ignored. Propped against the pillows, she fixed her gaze on his face. "I've been thinking."

Devil's hands stilled, then he drew the white linen from about his throat. Unbuttoning his waistcoat, he approached the bed. "What about?"

"About who would want you dead."

He shrugged out of his waistcoat, then sat on the bed to pull off his boots. "Did you reach any conclusion?"

"Yes—but Vane told me my conclusion wasn't right."

Devil looked up. "Vane?"

Honoria explained. "Naturally, I thought your heir was Richard."

"Ah." Devil dropped his second boot. He stood, stripped off his shirt and trousers, then slid beneath the covers. Honoria tumbled against him; he settled her beside him. "I suppose I should have told you about that."

Honoria squinted through the shadows; she was almost sure

he was grinning. "I suspect you should have. What is it I don't know?"

Devil lay back against the pillows. "You know Richard's nickname?"

"Scandal?"

Devil nodded. "Like mine being a shortened form of 'That Devil Cynster,' Richard's is also a truncation. His full sobriquet is 'The Scandal That Never Was.' "

"*He's* a scandal?"

"Richard's my brother, but he's not my mother's son."

Honoria blinked. "Ah." Then she frowned. "But you look so alike."

"We look like my father—you've seen his portrait. Only our coloring, and in my case my eyes, come from our respective mothers—Richard's was also dark-haired."

This was scandal on a major scale—Richard was younger than Devil. Yet Honoria had detected not the slightest whiff of disapprobation in any of the *ton*'s dealings with Richard Cynster. "I don't understand." She looked up in time to see Devil's teeth gleam.

"The truth of Richard's birth has been an open secret for three decades—it's very old news. *Maman*, of course, is the key."

Honoria crossed her arms on his chest and fixed her gaze on his face. "Tell me."

Devil settled his arms about her. "When I was three, my father was asked to undertake a diplomatic mission to the Highlands. There'd been an outbreak of dissaffection and the Court boffins wanted to rattle sabers without sending troops. Sending a Cynster was considered the next best thing. *Maman* decided not to accompany him. She was told at my birth that she wouldn't be able to have more children, so she was hideously overprotective of me, much to my disgust. So m'father went north alone. The laird he was sent to . . ." He paused, searching for words.

"Intimidate?" Honoria suggested.

Devil nodded. "This laird, a redhead, had recently married—an arranged marriage with a lowlands beauty."

"She would be a beauty," Honoria muttered.

Devil glanced at her. "We Cynsters have standards, you know."

Honoria humphed and poked his chest. "What happened next."

"Strangely enough, we're not entirely sure. We do know my father's mission was a success; he was home within four weeks. Richard appeared twelve months later."

"*Twelve* months?"

"His mother died a few months after his birth. Whether she confessed or whether her husband simply assumed from his coloring that Richard was none of his, we don't know. But there was no doubt, even then, that Richard was my father's—he looked exactly like me at the same age, and there were enough about who remembered. Whatever, Richard's fate was sealed when Webster picked him up from before the front door—a carriage had driven up, the wrapped bundle deposited, and the horses whipped up immediately. No message—just Richard. Webster carried him in and Richard immediately started squalling."

"The sound was *horrendous*—I remember because I hadn't heard it before. *Maman* was brushing my hair in the nursery—we heard it all the way up there. She dropped the brush and rushed downstairs. She beat me down. I reached the last landing to see her descend on Webster and my father, who were trying to hush Richard. *Maman* plucked him out of their arms—she cooed and Richard stopped crying. She just smiled—brilliantly—you know how she can."

Her chin on his chest, Honoria nodded.

"I realized immediately that Richard was a godsend—*Maman* was so caught up with him she forgot about the knots in my hair. From that moment, Richard had my full support. My father came up—I think he was about to attempt an explanation—in retrospect I'm sorry I didn't hear it, even if I wouldn't have understood it then. But *Maman* immediately told him how immensely clever he was to have provided her with the one, truly most important thing she wanted—another son. Naturally, he kept quiet. From there on, *Maman* rolled over any objections—she'd been my father's duchess for five years and was an eminent social power. She publicly decreed Richard was her son—none were game, then or now, to contradict her." Honoria heard the smile in his voice.

"There's no doubt that having Richard to rear really did make *Maman* happy. The matter caused no one any harm; my father acknowledged him and made provision for him in his will." Devil drew a deep breath. "And that's the story of the Scandal That Never Was."

Honoria lay still; Devil's hand stroked her hair. "So now you know Richard's not my heir." His hand slid to her nape. "He's not the one trying to kill me."

Honoria listened to the steady thud of his heart. She was glad it wasn't Richard—she liked him, and knew Devil was fond of him. Without lifting her head, she murmured: "Your mother's a fascinating woman."

Devil rolled, rolling her under him; on his elbows, he brushed her hair from her face. "She certainly fascinated my father." Honoria felt his eyes on her face, then his head dipped. His lips brushed hers. "Just as my duchess fascinates me."

They were the last logical words said that night.

She needed to have a long, serious talk with her husband. Clad in a translucent ivory peignoir trimmed with feathers, Honoria paced the ducal bedchamber and waited for him to appear.

They'd met at breakfast and again at dinner, but she could hardly interrogate him in front of the servants. He was presently at White's, meeting with Viscount Bromley. That much she knew, that much he'd told her. What he hadn't told her was what he thought, who he suspected.

As Richard was illegitimate, he couldn't inherit, not with so many legitimate males in the family. After learning how Scandal had come by his name, she hadn't needed to ask who Devil's heir was. In the weeks before their marriage, she'd questioned Horatia about Devil's father—in passing, Horatia had mentioned that George, her husband, Vane's father, was a bare year younger than Devil's father. Which meant that, with Richard ineligible, George was Devil's heir, with Vane next in line.

Not in her wildest dreams could she imagine George as the villain of the piece. Devil treated him as a surrogate father, an affection George openly returned. And Vane's devotion to Devil was beyond question. So the killer wasn't Devil's heir, but as soon as she'd drawn Vane's attention to the point, he'd seen a blinding light.

With a frustrated growl, Honoria kicked her feathered hem aside. "So what *is* it about the heir that makes all obvious?"

Devil knew; Vane was sure he'd followed the same reasoning and come up with an answer. Presumably, as it wasn't the heir, some process of elimination illuminated the true killer. Who was . . .

Honoria glared at the clock. And tried not to think of the other reason she was pacing, eager to set eyes on her husband again. Someone was trying to kill him. This house was a safe haven; he was safe here. But outside . . . ?

She wanted him here, safe in her arms.

Honoria shivered; she wrapped her arms about her and, frowning, looked at the clock again. Lips setting, she made for the door. Opening it, she listened; as the clock on the mantel had correctly foretold, the clock on the stairs whirred, then chimed. Twelve deep booms resonated through the house. Midnight—and Devil was still not back.

She was closing the door when the front knocker sounded— a curt, peremptory summons. Honoria paused, her frown deepening. Who would come calling at midnight? Devil had a latchkey, so . . .

The blood drained from her face. Her heart stuttered, then started to race. She was halfway down the corridor before she realized she'd moved. Then she picked up her skirts and flew.

She raced through the gallery to the top of the stairs. Breathless, she clutched the wide banister and looked down. Webster swung the door wide, revealing a shadowy figure. The figure stepped forward; the light from the hall lamps burnished Vane's chestnut locks.

He handed his cane to Webster. "Where's Devil?"

Accepting the cane, Webster shut the door. "His Grace has not yet returned, sir."

"He hasn't?"

Even from the top of the stairs, Honoria heard Vane's surprise.

"I believe he went to White's, sir."

"Yes, I know." Vane sounded vague. "I left before him—I

had to call at a friend's, but he intended leaving on my heels. I would have thought he'd be here by now."

Her heart thumping, Honoria watched the men stare at each other—the black specter she'd held at bay all day suddenly swirled closer. She leaned over the banister. "Vane?"

He looked up, then blinked. Surprise leached from his face, leaving it curiously blank. Webster glanced up, too, but immediately lowered his gaze.

Vane cleared his throat, and tried not to focus. "Yes, Honoria?"

"Go and look for him. *Please?*" The last word was heavy with latent fear.

Vane tried an unfocused frown. "He probably fell in with some friends and was delayed."

Honoria shook her head violently; inside, a familiar panic was rising. "No—something's happened. I *know* it." Her fingers tightened on the banister; her knuckles showed white. "*Please*— go now!"

Vane was reaching for his cane before her last words had died—the emotion investing her "please" was compelling. Infected by her concern, her fear overriding the logical excuses his mind freely concocted, he turned to the door.

Webster, reacting with similar speed, opened it. Swiftly, Vane descended the steps. His stride lengthening, he mentally retraced Devil's habitual route home from his favorite club. Ten yards from the steps, Vane remembered the alleyway between Berkeley Square and Hays Mews. Cursing, he broke into a run.

Back inside St. Ives House, Honoria clutched the banister and fought down her panic.

Closing the door, Webster briefly glanced her way. "By your leave, ma'am, I'll notify Sligo."

Honoria nodded. "Please do." She remembered she'd ordered Devil watched—with relief, she grasped that branch and hung on. Sligo, protective, watchful Sligo, would have made sure his "Cap'n" was well guarded.

Beneath her, the baize door was flung open, crashing against the wall. Sligo rushed into the hall, flung open the front door and raced down the steps. As he disappeared, Honoria felt the slim branch she'd clutched ripped from her grasp—and found herself facing the black pit of her fears again.

* * *

"*Hah!*" Devil didn't waste breath putting much force into the shout—the alleyway was long and narrow; there were no windows in the tall brick walls. Swinging the thin blade of his swordstick in a wide arc, he grabbed the moment as his three attackers flinched back to reach down and tug the body slumped on the alley's cobbles within his guard.

Leaving room for his feet, he straightened immediately, sword flicking back and forth, steel tip scenting blood. In his other hand, he held the empty scabbard, the rigid rod a foil against another weapon. With a feral grin, he gestured with the scabbard. "Well, gentlemen? Who'll be first?"

His challenging glance swept the faces of the men sent to kill him. They'd waited until he was in the alley, striding along, thinking of other things. Two had followed him in, the third had closed from the other end. All three were brawny, hulking brutes—sailors from their ill-fitting garments. All three carried swords—not slim blades like the one keeping them at bay but long, straight, single-sided weapons.

His gaze steady, his expression taunting, Devil mentally searched for escape. And found none. Chance—in the form of two large barrels left in the usually empty alley, and a man who'd chased the sailors into the dimly lit passage—had kept him alive this far. With a yell, the man had thrown himself at the pair, alerting him to their presence. The man's intervention had been more heroic than wise; after momentarily grappling with him, one sailor had raised his arm and, with his sword grip, struck him down.

But by then he'd had his back against the wall, unsheathed sword and scabbard in his hands, the barrels immediately to his left restricting the front he had to defend. "Come along," he taunted, waving them forward. "No need to feel reticent about dying."

Their eyes shifted one to the other, each waiting to see who'd be first. It was his only hope—to keep them hanging back in indecision. From the corners of his eyes, he kept watch on the ends of the alley, lit by the flares in the street and square beyond. If anyone passed, their shadows would be thrown in—he'd have to hold his attackers back until that happened, and he could call for help. Unfortunately, it was past midnight in an area of fashionable residences with the Season yet to start. There were few people abroad.

Feet shifted on the cobbles; the largest of the sailors, the one directly in front, tried a slashing thrust. Devil blocked, catching the blade on his scabbard, sword hissing forward to slice the man's forearm. With a curse, the man jumped back, scowling, piggy eyes considering.

Devil prayed he wouldn't consider too hard—one on one, he could win, or hold them off forever. They were all heavier, but he was taller and had a longer, more flexible reach. If they rushed him all at once, they'd have him. Indeed, he couldn't understand why they hadn't already overwhelmed him; despite his black coat, his snowy cravat and white cuffs marked him clearly. Then he saw all three exchange another wary glance; inspiration dawned. He smiled, devilishly. "Hell's not such a bad place—take my word for it. Fiendishly hot, of course, and the pain never ends, but I can guarantee you'll all be found a place."

The three exchanged another glance, then the leader tried a less-than-successful sneer. "You may look like Satan, but you ain't him. You're just a man—your blood'll run free enough. 'Tisn't us slated to die tonight." He glanced at the others. "C'arn—let's get this done."

So saying, he raised his sword.

His warning, of course, was not wise. Devil met them, front and right; the man on his left, impeded by the barrels, predictably hung back. Sparks flew as one sword met the sweetly tempered steel of the swordstick and slid away; blocking the leader's stroke with his scabbard, Devil followed up with a swift thrust that pierced flesh.

He disengaged, simultaneously blocking the leader's second blow; the sword, wielded with force, sheered along the polished wood and struck his hand, clenched around it. The cut was not serious, he'd been pulling back at the time, but the scabbard quickly turned sticky beneath his fingers. Suppressing all reaction to the wound, Devil sent his thin blade reaching for the leader. The man jumped back as the fine point pricked his chest.

Devil cursed; the man to his left pressed closer, anxious to be in on the kill. The three assassins regrouped, all raising their weapons.

"Hi! *Hold hard!*"

311

A tall figure blocked out the light from Hays Mews. Running footsteps echoed from the walls; a second figure followed the first.

Devil grabbed the moment, striking cleanly at the leader.

The man yelped, then staggered back, clutching his right arm. His sword dropped from nerveless fingers. The clatter shocked his comrades—they looked around, then dropped their weapons. All three turned and fled.

Devil started in pursuit—and tripped over the slumped form of his would-be savior, still lying at his feet.

Vane, his own scabbard and unsheathed sword in his hands, skidded to a halt beside him. "Who the hell were they?"

Side by side, the cousins watched the three burly shadows disappear into the glare of Berkeley Square. Devil shrugged. "We didn't exchange introductions."

Vane looked down. "You got one." Bending down, he turned the man onto his back.

"No." Devil peered at his comatose good Samaritan. "He tried to help and got a clout over the ear for his pains. Strange to tell, I think he's one of my undergrooms."

Puffing, Sligo clattered up. His gaze swept Devil, then he slumped against the wall. "You all right?"

Devil raised his brows, then sheathed his swordstick, clicking the blade into place. Transferring the innocent-looking cane to his right hand, he examined his left. "Other than a cut, which doesn't seem serious."

"Thank Gawd for that." Propped against the wall, Sligo closed his eyes. "The missus would never forgive me."

Devil frowned—first at Sligo, then at Vane.

Vane was studying the three discarded swords. "Funny business." Bending, he scooped them up. "Not your usual backstreet weapon."

Devil took one of the swords and hefted it. "Odd indeed. They look like old cavalry issue." After a moment, he added: "Presumably they knew I carry a swordstick and would use it."

"They also knew they'd need three to get the job done."

"If it hadn't been for him," Devil indicated the man on the ground, "they'd have succeeded." He turned to Sligo. "Any idea what he's doing here?"

The tone of the question was mild; Sligo clung to the shadows and shook his head. "Most likely out for the evening and on his way home. Saw you and the others—you're easy enough to recognize."

Devil humphed. "You'd better get him home and make sure he's cared for. I'll see him tomorrow—such timely devotion shouldn't go unrewarded."

Making a mental note to explain to the second undergroom that he'd had the night off, Sligo hefted the man over his shoulder. Wiry and used to such loads, he started off up the alley, plodding steadily.

Devil and Vane strolled in his wake. As they left the alley, Devil glanced at Vane. "Speaking of opportune events, what brought you two here?"

Vane met his look. "Your wife."

Devil's brows rose. "I should have guessed."

"She was frantic when I left." Vane glanced at him. "She worries about you."

Devil grimaced; Vane shrugged. "She may jump to conclusions, but too often they've proved right. I decided not to argue. The alley was an obvious place for an ambush."

Devil nodded. "Very obvious."

Vane looked ahead; Sligo was making his way about Grosvenor Square. Vane slowed. "Did Honoria speak to you about your heir?"

Devil sent him a sidelong glance. "Yes."

Eyes narrowing, Vane sent the glance right back. "How long have you known?"

Devil sighed. "I still don't *know*—I suspect. I can't say exactly when I realized—I just suddenly saw the possibility."

"So?"

Devil's features set. "So I want to find out what I can from this madam—tie up that loose end, if loose end it proves. Bromley confirmed the where and when of the meeting. After that—" He grimaced. "We've precious little evidence—we may need to draw him into the open."

"A trap?"

Devil nodded.

Vane's expression hardened. "With you as bait?"

They'd reached the steps of St. Ives House. Devil looked up at his door. "With me—and Honoria Prudence—as bait."

The suggestion stunned Vane; when he refocused, Devil was climbing the steps. Webster opened the door as Sligo, lugging his burden, reached it. Setting the door wide, Webster called for assistance, then helped Sligo.

Pacing in the gallery, wringing her hands with frustrated impotence, Honoria heard the commotion. In a froth of silk and feathers, she rushed to the balustrade. The sight that met her eyes was not designed to reassure.

Webster and Sligo were carrying a body.

Honoria paled. For one instant, her heart stopped; her chest squeezed so tight, she couldn't breathe. Then she realized the body wasn't Devil's—relief hit her in a dizzying wave. The next instant, her husband strolled over his threshold, ineffably elegant as always. Vane followed.

Vane was carrying three swords and his walking cane.

Devil was carrying his silver-topped cane. The cane was streaked with blood; the back of his left hand was bright red.

Honoria forgot everything and everyone else. In a whisper of silk, feathers scattering in her wake, she flew down the stairs.

Sligo and two footmen had the unconscious groom in charge; Webster was closing the door. It was Vane who saw her first; he jogged Devil's elbow.

Devil looked up—and only just managed not to gape. His wife's peignoir was not transparent but left little to the imagination; the soft, sheer silk clung to gently rounded contours and long sleek limbs. Abruptly, his face set; biting back a curse, he strode for the stairs. He only had time to toss his cane to Webster before Honoria flung herself against him.

"Where are you hurt? What happened?" Frantic, she ran her hands across his chest, searching for wounds. Then she tried to draw back and examine him.

"I'm fine." With his right arm, Devil locked her to him. Lifting her, he continued up the stairs, his body shielding her from the hall below.

"But you're *bleeding*!" Honoria wriggled, trying to pursue her investigation of his hurts.

"It's just a scratch—you can tend it in our room." Devil gave the last three words definite emphasis. Reaching the top of the stairs, he glanced down at Vane. "I'll see you tomorrow."

Vane met his gaze. "Tomorrow."

"Is the wound on your hand or your arm?" Honoria half tipped in Devil's hold, trying to see.

Devil swallowed a curse. "On my hand. Stay still." Tightening his hold, he headed for their chamber. "If you're going to work yourself into a frenzy waiting up for me, you'll need to invest in more suitable nightwear."

The terse comment didn't even impinge on Honoria's consciousness.

Resigned, Devil set her down in their room and surrendered to the inevitable. Obediently stripping off his shirt, he sat on the end of the bed and let her bathe his cut. He answered all her questions—truthfully; she'd hear the details from her maid tomorrow anyway.

Mrs. Hull appeared with a pot of salve and bandages. She joined Honoria in clucking over him. Together, they bandaged the cut, using twice as much bandage as he deemed necessary. However, he kept his tongue between his teeth and submitted meekly; Mrs. Hull cast him a suspicious glance as she left. Honoria rattled on, her voice brittle and breathless, her gaze skittish.

"*Swords!* What sort of ruffians attack gentlemen with swords?" She gestured wildly. "It shouldn't be allowed."

Devil stood, caught her hand and towed her across the room. He stopped before the tallboy, poured two glasses of brandy, then, taking both in one hand, towed Honoria, her litany of exclamations gradually petering out, to the armchair before the fire. Dropping into the chair, he drew her down onto his lap, then handed her one glass.

Taking it, she fell silent. Then she shivered.

"Drink it." Devil guided the glass to her lips.

Cradling the glass in both hands, Honoria took a sip, then another. Then she shuddered, closed her eyes and leaned against him.

His arm about her, Devil held her close. "I'm still here." He pressed his lips to her temple. "I told you I won't leave you."

Dragging in a breath, Honoria snuggled closer, settling her head in the hollow of his shoulder.

Devil waited until she'd drained her glass, then carried her to their bed, divesting her of her *peignoir* before putting her between the sheets. Moments later, he joined her, drawing her into his arms. And set about demonstrating in the most convincing way he knew that he was still hale and whole, still very much alive.

Honoria slept late the next morning, yet when she awoke she felt far from refreshed. After tea and toast on a tray in her chamber, she headed for the morning room. Her head felt woolly, her wits still skittish. Settling on the *chaise*, she picked up her embroidery. Fifteen minutes later, she'd yet to set a stitch.

Sighing, she put the canvas aside. She felt as fragile as the delicate tracery she should have been creating. Her nerves were stretched taut; she was convinced a storm was brewing, roiling on her horizon, poised to sweep in and strike—and take Devil from her.

He meant so much to her. He was the center of her life— she couldn't imagine living without him, arrogant tyrant though he was. They were *growing* together so well, yet someone was not content to let them be.

The thought made her frown. She might think of the murderer as a black cloud, billowing ever higher, yet he was only a man.

She'd woken early to find Devil sitting beside her on the bed, stroking her hair. "Rest," he'd said. "There's no reason you need be up and about." He'd searched her face, then kissed her. "Take care. I won't approve if I find you peaked and wan." With a twisted smile, he'd stood.

"Will you be about?" she'd asked.

"I'll be back for dinner."

Which was all very well, but dinner was hours away.

Honoria stared at the door. Something was about to happen—she could feel it in her bones. A chill stole down her spine; she shivered, but didn't let go of her disturbing thoughts. Yet she could identify no action, nothing she could do to avert the impending doom. She was impotent. Helpless.

A tap on the door interrupted her dismal reverie. Sligo entered, balancing a tray. "Mrs. Hull thought as you might like her special tea. Makes it up herself, she does." He set the tray on the sidetable and deftly poured a cup.

Honoria's instant reaction was a definite veto—her stomach felt as fragile as her mental state. The soothing aroma that rose with the steam changed her mind.

"Chamomile, it is." Sligo handed her the cup.

Honoria took it and sipped, then remembered the groom. "How is Carter?"

"Better. Got a lump the size of an egg, but the Cap'n thanked him special this morning—Carter says as how he hardly feels it now."

"Good. Please convey my thanks to him as well." Honoria sipped. "Did Carter have any idea where the men who attacked His Grace hailed from?"

Sligo fiddled with the doily on the tray. "Not as such. He did say they looked like sailors."

Honoria fixed her gaze on his face. "Sligo—did Carter overhear anything?"

Sligo shifted. "He heard the two he followed agree to meet up later at the Anchor's Arms."

"The Anchor's Arms?"

"A tavern by the docks."

A demon prodded Honoria to act; she ignored it. "Has His Grace been informed of Carter's recollections?"

"No, ma'am. Carter only fully came to his wits an hour ago."

Honoria chose the course of wisdom. "Inform His Grace immediately of Carter's information."

Sligo bit his lip and shifted his weight.

Honoria studied his unprepossessing features in dawning disbelief. "Sligo—where is he?"

Sligo straightened. "The Cap'n must've fallen to our plan. When the lads set out to follow 'im this morning, he lost 'em. Neat as you please."

"*Neat!*" Honoria sat bolt upright. "There's nothing neat about it."

Here they were, with a potentially valuable avenue to explore, and her husband had taken himself off. Away from their watchful eyes. She handed Sligo her teacup, inwardly congratulating herself on not having thrown it. She wasn't so lost to all sense as to wax hysterical over someone trying to kill Devil in the middle of London during the day. She did, however, want his would-be-murderer caught without delay. Narrow-eyed, she considered Sligo. "Where does His Grace normally lunch?"

"One of his clubs, ma'am—White's, Waitier's, or Boodles."

"Send footmen to wait at all three. They are to inform His Grace immediately he arrives that I wish to speak with him as soon as may be."

"Very good, ma'am."

Chapter 22

B̶y two, Honoria had started to pace. At four, she summoned Sligo.

"Have you located His Grace?"

"No, ma'am. I've men at White's, Waitier's, and Boodles—we'll know the instant he shows."

"Would Carter recognize the ruffians he followed?"

"Aye—he'll know them again, so he says."

"How long do ships normally remain at the docks?"

"Two, three days at most."

Honoria drew a deep breath. "Have the carriage brought around—the unmarked one."

Sligo blinked. "Ma'am?"

"I presume Carter's well enough to assist us?"

"Assist us?" Sligo's expression blanked.

Honoria frowned. "To identify the men who attacked His Grace should they be at the Anchor's Arms."

"The *Anchor's Arms?*" Horror replaced Sligo's blankness. "You can't go there, ma'am."

"Why not?"

"You . . . you simply can't. It's a dockside tavern—not the sort of place you'd feel comfortable."

"At present, my comfort is not of great importance."

Sligo grew desperate. "The Cap'n wouldn't approve."

Honoria transfixed him with a look as baleful as any of his master's. "Sligo, your 'Cap'n' isn't here. He's slipped his leash and taken himself off God knows where. We are presently in receipt of information which, if acted on promptly, might identify his would-be killer. If we wait until your Cap'n deigns to return, our opportunity might have sailed with the evening tide. In His Grace's absence, we—you and I—will accompany Carter to the Anchor's Arms. I trust I've made myself clear?"

Sligo opened his mouth—then shut it.

Honoria nodded. "The carriage. I'm going to change."

Ten minutes later, attired in a deep brown carriage dress, she crossed the gallery. Mrs. Hull was standing by the stairs. "Begging your pardon, ma'am, but I heard as you were planning to visit that inn by the docks. A terrible rough area, it is. You don't think, perhaps, that it would be better to wait . . . ?"

"Mrs. Hull, you can't expect me to allow my husband's would-be murderer to continue to stalk him for want of a little courage. The Anchor's Arms may be all you fear, but I'm sure I'll survive."

Mrs. Hull grimaced. "I'd do the same meself, ma'am—but the master's not going to like it."

Honoria started down the stairs. Webster was waiting on the landing; he fell into step beside her. "I would like to suggest, ma'am, that you permit me to go in your stead. If we discover the blackguards who attacked His Grace, Sligo and I will persuade them to return here and speak with His Grace."

"There!" Mrs. Hull, following on Honoria's heels, leaned forward. "That's another way to scour the pot."

Honoria stopped on the last stair. Sligo stood waiting by the newel post. "Webster, neither you nor Sligo can offer sufficient inducement to secure such men's cooperation. Should we discover them at the Anchor's Arms, it is my intention to offer them a sizeable reward if they will swear to the name of the man who hired them. They will not fear me because I'm a female—they'll consider my proposition. When they ask for the reward, it's my intention to repair to Child's Bank. Mr. Child will assist me in any negotiations."

She paused, her gaze touching each concerned face. "While His Grace is unlikely to approve of my involvement, I do not approve of someone trying to kill him. I would rather face His

Grace's displeasure than risk His Grace's death." She stepped down from the stair. "I'm taking you into my confidence because I appreciate your concern. I am, however, determined on my course."

After an infinitesimal hesitation, Webster followed her. "Indeed, ma'am. But please—take care."

With a haughty nod, Honoria swept out of the door and down the steps. Sligo had to scurry to open the carriage door because, at that moment, there was not a single footman, or groom, left within St. Ives House.

The hitch in Honoria's plan became apparent the instant they reached the Anchor's Arms, in a mean, narrow street close by the docks. Sulfurous fog, dense and thick, wreathed the inn's low eaves. A rumble of male voices rolled out through the open door, punctuated by occasional female shrieks.

Sligo and Carter had traveled up top; descending nimbly to the cobbles, Sligo glanced around, then eased open the carriage door.

Her face lit by one of the carriage lamps, Honoria raised a brow.

"There's a problem."

"Problem?" Honoria glanced through the door at the inn beyond. The carriage's leather window flaps were down. "What problem?"

"This area's not safe." Sligo scanned the shadows. 'We should have brought more men."

"Why? I'll remain here while you and Carter go in. If the men are there, bring them out to me here."

"Who's going to watch over you while we're in the inn?"

Honoria blinked. "John Coachman's up top." Even as she said it, Sligo's unease reached her.

He shook his head. "He'll have his hands full with his team. If any wanted to grab you, all they need do is spook the horses. And I don't want to send Carter in alone. If those men are there, he might not come back."

Honoria understood, yet she had to find out if the men were there. "I'll come in with you. It's not particularly well-lit—if I cling to the shadows, no one will pay any attention to me." On the words, she left her seat.

Sligo gaped—Honoria scowled and he let down the steps. Defeated he handed her down, then beckoned Carter closer. "If we walk in front, shoulder to shoulder, you'll be less noticeable, ma'am."

Honoria nodded curtly. She followed close on Sligo's heels as he and Carter crossed the tavern's threshold.

They entered a smoke-filled, low-ceilinged room—a deathly silence fell. Every conversation was suspended, instantly cut off. Sligo and Carter halted; Honoria sensed their defensiveness. Men lounged, slumped over a long counter; others sat on crude benches about rough tables. All heads had snapped their way; eyes used to sifting shadows focused without difficulty on her. The expression on some faces was surprised; most quickly turned calculating. Some turned malevolent. Danger, palpable, cloying, hung on the smoky air. Honoria tasted it, felt it crawl across her skin.

The barman, a harrassed-looking individual, reacted first. "You've come to the wrong place." He shooed them back. "We don't have what you want."

"Now, now." A beefy arm stopped him in his tracks. A body to match the arm heaved its way off a bench. "Don't be so hasty, Willie. Who's to say wha' the fancy want?"

The leer that went with this, directed at Honoria, convinced her the barman was right.

"Tha's right. Lady walks in—must know what she's a-lookin' for." Another grinning navvy, wide as a tug, lumbered to his feet. "Any number of us 'ere might have wha' she's after."

Honoria looked him in the eye. "You're quite right." The only way out was through sheer, brazen bluff. Pushing Carter aside, she stepped forward. "You might well be able to assist me. However"—she let her gaze roam the tables—"I must warn you that my husband and his cousins—the Bar *Sinister*, as they're called—are presently on their way here. All six of them." She considered the navvy. "They're all taller than you."

She turned to the barman: "I daresay you can imagine how their group got its name. And now they've learned that three of your patrons attacked one of them last night. They're coming for revenge, but when they get here, they're not going to waste time on identification."

Barman and patrons struggled through her words; Honoria

inwardly sighed. "I think they're going to wreck this tavern—and everyone in it as well."

The navvies bristled; rebellious rumblings flew. "If it's a rough-house they're after, we'll give it 'em," one brawny salt declared.

"I'll complain to the magistrate," the barman bleated.

Honoria eyed the navvies measuringly. "Six of them—all rather large. And . . ." She looked at the barman. "Did I mention my husband's a duke?" The man's face blanked; she smiled. "His nickname's Devil. Lucifer and Demon will be with him." She peered out through the open door. "I didn't see the Watch out there."

The navvies exchanged glances. Tales of the forays mounted by the less civilized of society's males were commonplace; the poorer classes bore the brunt of such destructive routs. The crowd in the Anchor's Arms were too old to risk getting their skulls cracked unnecessarily.

The man who'd spoken first eyed her challengingly. "And just what might *you* be a-doing 'ere, then? A duchess an'all?"

Honoria looked down her nose at him. "My dear man, surely you've heard that duchesses are required to do charitable deeds? Saving the Anchor's Arms is my deed for today." She paused. "Provided, of course, that you tell me what I need to know."

The navvy glanced at his cronies—many nodded. Still suspicious, he turned back to her. "How d'we know if'n we help you, you'll be able to stop this 'ere Devil from laying waste anyway?"

"You don't." Honoria held his gaze. "You can only hope."

"What'd you want to know?" came from the back of the room.

Honoria lifted her head. "Three sailors met here recently. I need to talk to them. Carter—describe the two you saw."

Carter did; more than a few remembered them.

"In here yesterday evenin'—off the *Rising Star*."

"*Rising Star* upped anchor this mornin' for Rotterdam."

"You're sure?" Confirmation came from several points in the room.

Then silence fell. Dense, cold, it chilled the air. Even before she turned, Honoria knew Devil had arrived.

She swung to face him—and only just stopped her blink. She swallowed instead. It was him, but not the man she habitually saw. This man filled the space before the door with a menacing presence; barely restrained aggression poured from him in waves. His elegant attire did nothing to conceal his powerful frame, nor the fact that he was fully prepared to annihilate anything or anyone unwise enough to give him the slightest excuse. He fitted the image she'd created to perfection.

His eyes, cold and flat, left her, scanning the room, holding not challenge but a promise, an intent every man could feel. Vane stood at his shoulder; just the two of them made the tavern seem uncomfortably overcrowded.

As Devil's gaze fastened on the wide-eyed barman, Honoria conjured a smile and swept into the breach. "There you are, my lord. I fear the men you seek are not here—they sailed this morning."

Devil didn't blink. His gaze fastened on her face—flames replaced the chill in his eyes but they remained oddly flat. One brow rose fractionally. "Indeed?"

The single word, uttered in his deep voice, gave no hint of his thoughts. For one definable instant, the entire tavern held its breath. Then he nodded at the barman. "In that case, you must excuse us."

On the words, Devil turned, catching Honoria's arm, propelling her over the threshold, lifting her through the carriage door Sligo raced to open and into the safety beyond.

Vane swung out of the inn behind them; he loomed at Devil's shoulder as he paused, one boot on the carriage steps. "I'll take the hackney." Vane nodded to where the small carriage waited.

His expression beyond grim, Devil nodded—he followed Honoria into the carriage. Sligo slammed the door; John Coachman flicked the reins.

It took three tense, silent minutes before the coach maneuvered its way free of the narrow street. And a further, equally silent half-hour before it drew up in Grosvenor Square. Devil alighted. He waited until Sligo let down the steps, then held out his hand. Honoria placed hers in it; he helped her down and led her up the steps.

Webster opened the door, his relief so intense it showed in his face. Then he saw his master's face—immediately his expression leached to impassivity. Gliding into the hall, her fingers on an arm more like rock than human flesh, Honoria held her head high.

Devil halted in the hall. "If you'll excuse me, my dear, I must speak with Sligo." His tone was glacial, bleak, and not quite steady, the icy surface rippling with barely suppressed rage. "I'll join you shortly. Upstairs."

For the first time that evening, Honoria saw his face clearly, lit by the chandelier high above. It was paler than usual, each harsh plane starkly edged, the whole no more animated than a death mask in which his eyes burned oddly dark. She met that black gaze directly. "Sligo was acting on my orders."

Devil raised a brow, his expression cold. "Indeed?"

Honoria studied his eyes, then inclined her head. And turned for the stairs. In the mood he was in, saying anything further might be counterproductive.

Rigid, Devil watched her ascend. When she passed from sight, he switched his gaze to Sligo. "In the library."

Sligo scurried in; Devil followed more slowly. Crossing the threshold, he paused; a footman closed the door. Sligo stood at attention to one side of the desk. Devil let silence stretch before slowly closing the distance.

Normally, he would have sat at his desk; tonight, the rage consuming him would not let him rest. He halted before the long windows giving onto the dark courtyard.

Words filled his head, jostled for prominence on his tongue, a ranting rave of fury clamoring to spill free. Jaw clenched, he fought to hold it back. Never before could he recall such rage— so fraught he was chilled to the marrow, so powerful he could barely contain it.

He glanced at Sligo. "I was informed by a footman who chanced upon me in St. James that Her Grace was on her way to the Anchor's Arms. Before I could summon a hackney, three others of my household appeared, bearing like tidings. It appears that fully half my staff were scouring the streets for me, instead of *obeying my orders and looking after my wife! How the devil did she even* hear *about the Anchor's Arms?*"

Sligo flinched. "She asked—I told her."

"*What in all the saints' names did you mean by* taking *her there?*"

The door opened at the height of that roar. Devil glared balefully at Webster. "I do not wish to be disturbed."

"Indeed, Your Grace." Webster stepped around the door, held it open for Mrs. Hull, then closed it. "Mrs. Hull and I wished to make sure you were not laboring under any misapprehension."

"It is exceedingly difficult to misapprehend discovering my wife in a dockside tavern."

The words had an edge like cut glass; Webster paled but persevered. "I believe you wish to learn how that came about, my lord. Sligo did not act on his own. We were all, myself, Mrs. Hull, and Sligo, aware of Her Grace's intent. We all attempted to dissuade her, but, having heard her reasons, we couldn't legitimately stand in her way."

His fists clenched so tight they hurt, his jaw all but locked, Devil spoke through his teeth. "What reasons?"

Webster outlined Honoria's plan; Mrs. Hull elucidated her reasons. "Perfectly understandable, to my mind." She sniffed defensively. "She was worried—as were we. It seemed a perfectly sensible thing to do."

Devil swallowed the tirade that leapt to his tongue. His temper seething, roiling behind the flimsy façade of civilized behavior, he eyed them narrowly. "*Out!* All of you."

They went, carefully shutting the door. Swinging around, Devil stared into the night. Sligo didn't approve of *ton*nish women, Webster was as starchily devoted as they came, and Mrs. Hull was an arch-conservative—yet all had been suborned by his wife. And her reasons.

Ever since marrying Honoria Prudence *Anstruther-Wetherby*, he'd been knee-deep in reasons—her reasons. He had reasons, too—good, sound, solid reasons. But it wasn't his staff he need to share them with. Having reached that conclusion, Devil swung on his heel and stalked out of the library.

Striding toward the ducal apartments, he reflected that Honoria had succeeded in shielding her three co-conspirators from his anger, without even being present. Of course, if he'd been able to lose some of the red-hot fury swirling inside him by venting it on them, she wouldn't be about to face it all herself. As it was . . .

Reaching the end of the corridor, he threw open the door, then slammed it shut behind him.

Honoria didn't even jump. She stood before the fireplace, head erect, unshakable resolve in every line. The skirts of her brown velvet carriage dress were gilded by the fire behind her; the soft chestnut curls atop her head glowed. Her hands were loosely clasped before her; her face was pale but composed, her eyes wide, the soft blue-grey showing no hint of trepidation. Her neatly rounded, Anstruther-Wetherby chin was set.

Deliberately, Devil stalked toward her, watching her chin rise as she kept her eyes on his. He stopped directly before her. "You gave me your *word* you would not actively pursue Tolly's killer."

Calmly, Honoria raised a brow. "*Tolly's* killer—I gave no undertaking to sit idly by while someone tried to kill *you*."

Shadows flitted through Devil's darkened eyes. He inclined his head. "Very well—you may give me such an undertaking now."

Honoria straightened. Devil still towered over her. "I can't do that."

His eyes mere slits, more black than green, he shifted closer. "Can't—or won't?"

Honoria held her ground. "Can't." Her eyes on his, her jaw slowly firmed. "*And* won't. You can't seriously expect it of me."

For three heartbeats, Devil held her gaze. "I'm deathly serious." He braced one hand on the mantelpiece, his body settling closer, his face nearer hers. "Women—wives—are supposed to sit quietly at home and embroider, *not* actively hunt villains. They're *supposed* to be at home when their husbands get in, *not out courting danger on the docks!*" Briefly closing his eyes, he fought down the impulse to roar. Then he trapped Honoria's gaze and continued: "I want your promise that you will not again indulge in any escapade such as today's, that you will remain safely at home and that you will not further concern yourself with tracking *anyone's* killer." His eyes locked on hers, he raised one black brow. "Well?"

Honoria held his gaze steadily. "Well what?"

Devil only just managed to hold back a roar. "*Well give me your promise!*"

"When hell freezes!" Honoria's eyes flashed. "I will *not* sit tamely by while someone tries to take you from me. I'm your *duchess*—not some disinterested spectator. I will *not* sit quietly embroidering, waiting for news when that news could tell of your death. As your wife, I have a duty to help you—if in this case that means walking a dangerous path, so be it." Her chin, defiantly high, rose another notch. "I'm an Anstruther-Wetherby—I'm every bit as capable of facing danger and death as you are. If you wanted a tame, complaisant wife, you shouldn't have married *me*."

Momentarily stunned, more by her vehemence than her words, Devil stared at her. Then, his frown deepening, he shook his head. "No."

Honoria frowned back. "No what?"

"No to all the above, but most especially no, you do not have a duty to assist me in hunting a murderer. As my wife, you have no duties other than those I deem proper. In my eyes, there's nothing—no duty, no reason whatever—that could justify you placing yourself in danger."

Their faces were six inches apart; if Honoria had not sensed the throttled fury investing his large frame, radiating from it, she could not have missed the jagged edge to his words. Her eyes narrowed. "That I do not accept." She was not about to bow before his rage.

Devil's lips curved slightly; his voice, when he spoke, was mesmerically low. "*That* you *will* accept."

It was an effort not to shiver, to submissively shift her gaze from his, so penetrating, so compelling, it resembled a physical force. By sheer will, sheer stubbornness, Honoria met that intimidating gaze levelly. "You're wrong on all counts. I've lost others before, to forces I could not influence—I couldn't help them, I couldn't save them." Her jaw set; momentarily, her teeth clenched. "I *will not* sit by and let you be taken from me."

Her voice quavered; flashes of silver lit Devil's eyes. "Damn it!—do you think I'm going to *let* myself be taken?"

"Not intentionally, but it was *me* who detected the poison."

Devil waved that aside. "That was here." He studied her face, her eyes. "Within this house, you may watch over me to your heart's content, but you will *stay away from all danger*. You spoke of duty—it's *my* duty to protect you, *not* yours to protect me."

Honoria went to shake her head; Devil caught her chin on the edge of his hand and trapped her gaze with his. "Promise me you'll do as I ask."

Honoria drew as deep a breath as her tight chest would allow, then shook her head. "No—leave duty aside—we spoke also of reasons, a reason to justify my doing all and anything to safeguard your life." She spoke quickly, breathlessly; she *had* to make him understand. "My reason is one that will stand against any objection."

Devil's face hardened. His hand fell; he drew back. Her eyes locked on his, Honoria clung to the contact, refusing to let him withdraw totally behind his mask. She drew a swift breath, and let it out on the words: "I love you—more than I've ever loved anyone. I love you so profoundly it goes beyond all reason. And I could *never* let you go—let you be taken from me—that would be the same as letting life itself go, because you are life to me."

Devil stilled. For one, heart-stopping moment, he looked into Honoria's eyes; what he saw there locked his chest. He wrenched his gaze free and swung away. He paced toward the door, then stopped. Hands in fists by his sides, chest swelling, he dropped his head back, and stared at the ceiling. Then exhaling, he looked down. He spoke without turning. "Your reason's not good enough."

Honoria lifted her chin. "It is to me."

"*Damn it woman!*" Furious, Devil turned on her. "How by all that's holy do you imagine *I'm* supposed to function, knowing that, at any instant, *you* may be courting heaven knows what danger—all in the name of keeping *me* safe?" His voice rose to a bellow that literally shook the chandelier. Gesticulating violently, he paced viciously, like some trapped jungle cat. "Do you have any *idea* what I felt when I learned where you'd gone today?" Brilliant with accusation, his eyes raked her. "Can you even *conceive* what I felt when I walked in that tavern door?" He halted directly before her.

Honoria caught her breath as his eyes locked on hers.

"Do you know what might have happened in such a place?" His voice had lowered, his tones chillingly prophetic.

Honoria didn't move.

"They could have knifed Sligo and Carter—killed them

without a qualm. Then they'd have raped you—one after another. If you'd survived, they'd have slit your throat."

Devil spoke with deadpan conviction; it was the truth—a truth he'd had to face. The muscles across his shoulders rippled; he tensed, holding back his reactive rage, clinging grimly to the reality of the woman standing slim, straight, and unharmed before him. A second later he caught himself reaching for her— abruptly, he swung away, pacing again, then he stopped.

His back to Honoria, he dragged in a deep breath. "How the hell do you think I would have felt *then*?—if anything had happened to you?" He paused, then flatly stated: "I cannot countenance you putting yourself in danger over me. *You* can't ask that of *me*."

Silence fell; Devil looked back at Honoria. "Will you give me your word you will not knowingly go into danger?"

Honoria held his gaze, then, slowly, shook her head. "I can't."

He looked forward immediately, his fury clearly delineated in the rigid lines of his back, clearly expressed in a single, violent expletive.

"I simply *can't*." Honoria spread her hands. "I'm not trying to be wilful, but you must see I can't—" Her words were drowned out by a half-strangled roar; the next instant, Devil flung open the door. Honoria stiffened. "Where are you going?"

"Downstairs."

"Don't you *dare* leave." If he did, would he come back? "I haven't finished—"

His hand on the doorknob, Devil turned, his green gaze impaling her. "If I *don't* leave, you won't sit comfortably for a sennight."

Before she could react, he slammed the door shut. Honoria listened to his footsteps, uncharacteristically heavy, retreat. She stood before the fire, her gaze fixed unseeing on the panels of the door, for a very long time.

Reaching the library, Devil flung himself into an armchair. An instant later, he sprang up and fell to pacing. He never paced—the action was too indicative of lost control for his liking. If he kept on as he was, he'd wear a track in the rug.

Uttering a long-drawn groan, he halted; eyes closed, he

dropped his head back and concentrated on breathing, on letting his impotent rage settle. Into the morass of emotions that swirled inside him, all called forth by the woman he'd taken to wife.

Both jaw and fists clenched; then again he forced himself to relax. One by one, tensed muscles uncoiled; eventually, he stood easy. Eyes still closed, he looked inward, sifting through his reactions to what lay beneath.

When he saw what it was, he wasn't impressed.

Honoria was dealing with this unexpected development far better than he. Then again, she'd been through it before, albeit unhappily. He'd never experienced the like before.

He hadn't, in fact, known real fear, even on the battlefield. He was a Cynster; fate took care of Cynsters. Unfortunately, he wasn't sanguine enough to assume fate's benevolence extended to Cynster wives. Which left him battling a fear he'd no idea how to combat.

Exhaling slowly, he opened his eyes. Spreading his fingers, he studied them. They were almost steady. His muscles, tensed for so long, now felt chilled. He glanced at the decanter, then grimaced. Switching his gaze to the flames cheerily dancing in the hearth, he paused, then, deliberately, opened the door of his memory. And let Honoria's words warm him.

He stared at the flames for so long that when he heaved a long sigh and turned to the door, they still danced before his eyes.

Honoria shivered beneath the unfamiliar covers of her bed. After much mental debate, she'd returned to her apartments, undressed, and climbed between the sheets. She hadn't had any dinner—not that it mattered; she'd lost her appetite. Whether she'd find it again was moot, but if she could relive her scene with Devil, she would not change one word she'd said.

Her declaration had been necessary—she hadn't expected him to like it. She had no idea how he viewed her confession— he'd turned from her the instant he'd seen her words confirmed in her eyes.

Frowning, she stared into the dark, trying, for the umpteenth time, to make consistent sense of his reaction. On the surface, he'd appeared his usual tyrannical, domineering self, insisting without quarter that she fall in with his dictates, resorting to intimidation when she stood firm. Yet not all he'd said fitted that image—the mere thought of her being in danger had agitated him to a remarkable degree. It was almost as if . . .

The nebulous thought went round and round in her head, and followed her into sleep.

She woke to find a very large, dense shadow looming over her.

"Damn fool woman—what the devil are you doing here?"

His tone made it clear the question was rhetorical; Honoria valiantly stifled a giggle. He sounded so put upon—poor aggrieved male—not one of the most powerful men in the land. Her eyes adjusted to the dark, she saw him, hands on hips, shake his head. Then he leaned over her.

He loosened her covers, then pressed down on the soft mattress and slid his hands under her. He lifted her easily; Honoria played dead.

"*And* a bloody nightgown."

The disgust in his voice made her jaw ache.

"What the hell does she think she's about?"

He shouldered through the door into the short corridor; seconds later, very gently, she was deposited in his bed. Honoria decided a murmur and a wriggle were required for authenticity.

She heard him humph, then listened to the familiar sounds of him undressing, her mind supplying what she could not see.

The relief she felt when he slid into bed beside her, curling around her, warm, hard, reassuringly solid, made her chest ache. Carefully, he slid one arm over her waist; his hand gently pushed between her breasts, long fingers draping possessively over the lower.

She felt him heave a long, deep sigh; the last of his tension left him.

Minutes later, before she could decide whether or not to "wake up," his breathing deepened. Smiling, still wondering, Honoria closed her eyes.

Chapter 23

~◆~

THE NEXT MORNING, Honoria woke late, alone, Devil long gone, up and about his business. His unflagging energy struck her as unfair—the events of the night had left her drained. Her gaze, unfocused, fell on the swath of ivory silk adorning the richly hued carpet. Her nightgown.

They'd engaged in a midnight tussle—half-asleep, she'd been reluctant to relinquish the gown's warmth. He, however, had insisted, then compensated admirably. Even now, she felt pleasurably aglow, inside and out. Smiling, she sank deeper into the bed, luxuriating in the lingering sense of warm fulfilment.

Who'd made the first move she neither knew nor cared; they'd turned to each other and let their bodies seal their unvoiced commitment that, regardless of any differences, they remained man and wife, their alliance rock-solid, as enduring as the Place.

The door from her apartments cracked open; Cassie peeked, then bustled in. "G'morning, ma'am." She swiped up the nightgown. "It's nearly eleven."

"Eleven?" Honoria blinked her eyes wide.

"Webster asked if you wanted any breakfast kept. Having missed dinner and all."

Honoria sat up. "We ate later." An hour after her nightgown had hit the floor, Devil's mind had turned to food. She'd been sound asleep again; he'd made a trip to the kitchens, then ruthlessly harried her awake, insisting she eat morsels of chicken, ham, and cheese, all washed down with white wine.

"There's kedgeree, boiled eggs, and sausages."

Honoria wrinkled her nose. "I'll take a bath."

The bath suited her mood: lazy, disinclined to move. She stared through the steam, reviewing the previous evening—and heard in her mind, in the depths of the night, her husband's deep voice as, sated, replete, he'd slumped beside her. *"You can't fear losing me half as much as I fear losing you."* It had been a grudging admission; he'd thought her already asleep.

Why would he fear losing her even more than she feared losing him?

The minutes ticked by, the water grew cold, and still she could find only one answer. As she rose from the bath, her spirits soared—she spent the next half hour sternly lecturing herself on the unwisdom of leaping to conclusions, especially conclusions like that.

She retired to the morning room but couldn't settle, idly drifting between window and fireplace, consumed by a longing to see her husband again. To look into his face; to study his clear eyes. Mrs. Hull brought up a pot of herbal tea. Grateful, she accepted a cup, but it grew cold while she stared at the wall.

Louise and the twins provided a welcome diversion; they came to lunch, the girls eager to describe their latest gowns. Honoria toyed with a portion of steamed fish and listened with half an ear. She'd canceled all her other engagements, although the news that the new duchess of St. Ives was indisposed was certain to lead to speculation.

In this instance, speculation would be accurate. She'd hesitated to let the thought form in her mind, but it now seemed beyond question. Her dullness every morning, her fragile appetite, all testified to the fact.

She was carrying Devil's child.

The very thought made her giddy with happiness, with eager anticipation tinged only by understandable apprehension. Real fear had no chance of intruding, not with Devil and his family so constantly about her.

As if to emphasize that last, with the twins on the front steps, Louise glanced at her affectionately. "You're looking well, but if you have any questions, there's me or Horatia or Celia—we've all been there before you."

"Oh—yes." Honoria blushed—she hadn't told Devil; she could hardly tell his aunts first. "That is—" She gestured vaguely. "If . . ."

Smiling, Louise patted her arm. "Not if, my dear. *When.*" With a nod and a wave, she left, the twins falling in behind her.

Climbing the stairs, Honoria debated just how to tell Devil the news. Every time she imagined doing so, the specter of his would-be murderer intruded. They were closing in; before he'd left that morning, Devil had told her that he and Vane were searching for proof, precisely what he hadn't said. He'd promised to reveal all tonight. The last thing they needed now was a distraction—announcing the impending birth of his heir would create a major stir, focusing society's rabid interest on them.

Entering the morning room, Honoria inwardly shook her head. She would inform Devil of his impending fatherhood *after* they'd caught his would-be killer. Until then, his safety consumed her—not even his child meant more to her than he. Besides, she wanted the telling to be a happy event, a memorable moment between them, not overshadowed by a killer.

As she sank onto the *chaise*, Webster knocked and entered. "A message, ma'am." He proffered a silver salver.

Lifting the folded sheet, Honoria saw black lettering, conservative, precise, not her husband's extravagant scrawl. "Thank you, Webster." Breaking the plain seal, she returned the knife to the tray and nodded a dismissal. Webster left as she unfolded the note.

To Her Grace, the duchess of St. Ives:

Should you wish to learn more of he who intends your husband ill, come at once to No. 17 Green Street. Come alone—tell no one of your errand, else all will be lost. Most especially destroy this note that none may chance upon it and follow you, scaring away the little bird that would whisper in your ear.

A Well-wisher.

For a long moment, Honoria stared at the note, then she reread it. Then, drawing a steadying breath, she sank back against the *chaise*.

Devil wouldn't want her to go. But if she didn't?

There was clearly a potential threat to herself, but that she dismissed out of hand; far more relevant was how Devil would react. Not, of course, that such a consideration would sway her—her fear was more compelling than his.

Glancing at the note's thick black script, she grimaced. Devil's words of the night replayed in her mind; if she understood them correctly, then his fear was a mirror image of hers. There was only one emotion which gave rise to such fear. That emotion, if he felt it, demanded her consideration, her care. The same emotion impelled her to go to Green Street. How to do both?

Five minutes later, she stood and crossed to the escritoire. Fifteen minutes later, she shook sand across her letter, folded it, and sealed it with the seal Devil had given her—the Cynster stag rampant imposed on the Anstruther-Wetherby chevrons. Blowing on the wax, she rose, crossed the room, and tugged the bellpull three times.

Sligo answered her summons. "Yes, ma'am?"

Honoria glanced at the clock on the mantelpiece. Nearly three o'clock. "Where is His Grace at present?"

"At White's with Master Vane." Sligo almost smiled. "He didn't try to lose the men I set to follow him today."

"Good." Honoria held out her letter. "I want this delivered into His Grace's hands with all possible speed."

"Right away, ma'am." Accepting the letter, Sligo turned for the door.

"And have Webster call up a hackney for me."

"A hackney, ma'am?" Sligo turned back, his expression watchful. "John Coachman can have the carriage around in a trice."

"No." Honoria let authority tinge her tone. "A hackney. I'm only going a short distance—there's no need to get the carriage out." With a regal nod, she dismissed Sligo. "Tell Webster I wish to leave in ten minutes."

Sligo departed. Honoria picked up the letter from her "well-wisher." She glanced at it again, then, folding it neatly, headed upstairs.

Ten minutes later, arrayed in her golden pelisse and clutching an ivory-beaded reticule, she settled in one corner of the hackney. The footman bowed and started to close the door. It was wrenched from his grasp—Sligo bundled himself into the carriage, then shrank back in the other corner. Honoria stared at him. "Where's my letter?"

Sligo watched her like a chicken shut in with a vixen. "On its way—I sent Daley with it. He'll see it into His Grace's hands, just like you wanted."

"Indeed? And what are you doing here?"

"Ah . . ." Sligo blinked. "I thought as how it wasn't right you going about alone—you might get lost, not being used to Lunnon an' all."

Lips compressed, Honoria straightened her skirts. "I'm only going a few streets away to visit an acquaintance."

Sligo swallowed. "Be that as it may, ma'am, I'll go with you—if you don't mind."

Looking up, Honoria was about to inform him that she did mind, when suspicion dawned. "Did His Grace order you to stay with me?"

Glumly, Sligo nodded.

Honoria sighed. "Very well—but you'll have to remain in the carriage."

The hatch above opened; the jarvey peered down. "We goin' somewhere? Or did you just want to use me carriage for a chat?"

Honoria silenced him with a glare. "Green Street. Drive along it slowly—I'll tell you where to stop."

"Right you are." The jarvey dropped the hatch; an instant later, they were off.

Green Street was where her grandfather lived, at Number 13. Number 17 was closer to the park. The jarvey walked his horse along; Honoria studied the facades. Number 17 was an elegant residence, a gentleman's abode. She waited until they'd passed two more houses before saying: "Have the jarvey pull up. Wait for me here."

Sligo relayed her orders. The hackney drew up; Sligo leapt down and helped her out. Beside the hackney, screened from Number 17 on the other side of the road, Honoria fixed Sligo with a commanding look. "Wait for me here—*inside* the carriage."

Sligo blinked. "Shouldn't I walk you to the door?"

"Sligo, this is Green Street, not Billingsgate. You will stay in the carriage."

Mournfully, Sligo nodded; Honoria waited until he resumed his seat, then turned on her heel, walked back a short distance, and swiftly crossed the road. Briskly determined, she climbed the steps of Number 17. Reaching for the knocker, she froze, her hand in midair. The brass knocker was a sylph—a naked sylph. Honoria frowned, then closed her gloved hand about the indiscreet figure and beat an imperious tattoo.

She waited, clutching her reticule, trying not to think of the expletives her husband would utter when he read her letter—she hoped the committee of White's would understand. Then footsteps approached on the other side of the door. Not the measured tread of a well-trained butler but a slow, familiar, prowling gait. Even before the door opened, Honoria knew she would not be facing a butler.

When she saw who held the door wide, her jaw dropped.

The earl of Chillingworth's jaw dropped, too.

For one instant, they stood stock-still, staring at each other. Honoria mentally reeled, possibilities and conjectures whirling wildly.

Then Chillingworth scowled. "For God's sake, don't just stand there! Someone might see you."

Honoria blinked dazedly and remained rooted to his front step. Smothering a growl, Chillingworth grabbed her arm and hauled her inside. He shut the door, then faced her.

Although he was not as tall as Devil, Chillingworth was not a small man. In the narrow hall, Honoria was acutely conscious of that fact. Straightening, without a clue as to what was going on, she fixed him with an imperious look. "Where's your butler?"

Chillingworth returned her look with one she found unreadable. "My butler is out. As are the rest of my staff." Honoria's eyes widened; grimly, Chillingworth shook his head. "I can't believe you're serious." He searched her face, her eyes.

Honoria tilted her chin defiantly. "Of *course* I'm serious."

Chillingworth's expression showed a medley of disbelief and disillusionment, then hardened into a mask very like his greatest rival's. Fluidly, he shrugged. "If you insist."

Without further ado, he bent his head to Honoria's.

Uttering a strangled shriek, she jerked back and hit him.

Just before two o'clock, Devil had absentmindedly climbed the steps of White's. On the threshold, he'd literally run into Vane.

"*There* you are!" Vane had dropped back. "Where in all hell have you been? I've been looking all over."

Devil had grinned. "Surprising you didn't find me then, for that's where I've been. All over."

Frowning, Vane opened his lips—Devil waved the question aside. "Have you eaten?"

Still frowning, Vane nodded. Devil handed his cane to the doorkeeper; Vane did the same. "I'll talk while you eat."

The dining room was companionably crowded with gentlemen lingering over their brandies. Served with remarkable promptness, Devil started on the sole—and lifted an inquiring brow.

Vane grimaced at the bodies about them. "I'll tell you later."

Devil nodded and applied himself to his meal, pleased to have an excuse not to talk. Explaining why he'd spent the whole morning roaming the town, exercising the two grooms Sligo had set to tail him, was beyond him. He suspected it would always be beyond him—his affliction wasn't improving with time. And he could hardly tell Vane he was avoiding his wife because she'd said she loved him.

Said it, declared it, in unequivocal terms, with absolute conviction. Pausing, Devil quaffed half his glass of wine.

It was heady stuff, to know your wife felt that way. About you. That she would face danger without a blink, and refuse to back down, even when faced with sufficient intimidation to break a troop sergeant—all because she loved you.

There was only one snag, one fly in the ointment.

Taking another sip of wine, he returned to his sole. And the dilemma with which he'd spent all morning wrestling. If he told Honoria how he felt about her loving him, if he even acknowledged her declaration, he would simultaneously acknowledge the validity of her "justification" for going into danger. Which was something he could never do.

In times of trouble, as far as he and, he was quite sure, all his ancestors were concerned, Cynster wives were supposed to retreat to the donjon, there to remain in safety while their husbands manned the walls. Honoria's vision was apparently different—she wanted to be on the walls with him.

He understood her point—he simply couldn't accept it.

Explaining that was not going to be easy, not even after he'd made the confession he'd convinced himself he was honor-bound to make.

Feeling vulnerable was bad enough—admitting to vulnerability, out loud, in words, was infinitely worse. And, once said, the words couldn't be taken back. He would, in essence, be handing her a *carte blanche* of a kind he'd never used before. Given how she reacted to his being in danger, he wasn't at all sure that was wise.

Whether she suspected his state he did not know—he did know he couldn't count on her remaining in blissful ignorance for long. Not his Honoria Prudence. Which meant that the only way he could keep her out of danger was to remove the danger—by laying Tolly's killer by the heels.

Pushing aside his plate, he looked at Vane. "What have you learned?"

Vane grimaced. "Let's go into the smoking room."

They found a deserted nook and settled in; Vane began without preamble. "Basically, I was right. My source has checked every—"

"Excuse me, Your Grace."

They both looked up; one of the club's footmen stood at Devil's elbow, proffering a salver bearing a folded note. "This arrived a moment ago, Your Grace. The man was most insistent it be delivered to you immediately."

"Thank you." Taking the letter, Devil broke the seal, absentmindedly nodding a dismissal. Unfolding the letter, he scanned it—Vane saw his face harden. Devil's eyes flicked back up to the start of the letter; his face unreadable, he read it through again.

"Well?" Vane asked, when Devil looked up.

Devil's brows rose. "Something's come up." He didn't meet Vane's eyes. "An unexpected development." Refolding the letter, he rose. "You'll have to excuse me—I'll send for you as soon as I'm free."

With that, he turned and, putting the letter in one pocket, walked out.

Stunned, Vane stared after him. Then his face hardened. "Honoria Prudence—what the devil have you got up to now?"

"No! Wait! You can't just walk out the door."

"Why not?" Honoria swung around.

Holding a cold compress to the bridge of his nose, Chillingworth followed her up the hall. "Because there's no sense in taking unnecessary chances. Your husband's not going to appreciate this as it is—there's no sense in making things worse." Setting the compress down on the hall table, he looked her over. "Your bonnet's not straight."

Lips compressed, Honoria swung to face the mirror. Adjusting her bonnet, she studied Chillingworth's reflection. He was still very pale; she wasn't sure it was wise to leave him—his servants had not yet returned. On the other hand, she could understand his insistence that she leave without delay. "There!" She turned. "Does that meet with your approval?"

Chillingworth narrowed his eyes. "You'll pass." He met her gaze. "And don't forget—show that note to Devil as soon as you see him. *Don't* wait for him to ask."

Honoria lifted her chin.

Chillingworth eyed it with open disapproval. "Thank the heavens you're his and not mine. Wait here while I check if anyone's about. Like your grandfather or his butler."

Honoria watched as he opened the door; standing on the front step, he looked up and down the street.

"All clear." Chillingworth held the door open. "Other than your hackney, there's no one in sight."

Head high, Honoria swept out, then stopped and looked back. She frowned. "Don't forget to lie down with your feet higher than your head. And for goodness sake put that compress back, or your eye will be worse than it need be."

For the second time that day, Chillingworth's jaw dropped. Momentarily. Then he glowered. "Good God, woman—get *going!*"

Honoria blinked. "Yes, well—take care of yourself." With that, she turned and briskly descended the steps. Gaining the pavement, she saw her hackney waiting. She glanced the other way—a black carriage rolled slowly around the corner into Green Street. Behind her, Chillingworth's latch clicked. It was after four; dusk was drawing in. As Chillingworth had said, there was no one about. With an inward sigh, Honoria started along the pavement.

She didn't see the dark figure, cloaked in black, who emerged from the area stairs beside Chillingworth's steps. She had no inkling, felt no presentiment of danger, when the figure drew close, looming behind her. Harness jingled, hooves clacked as the black carriage drew abreast of her, blocking out the hackney. Honoria glanced at the carriage—a black pall dropped over her, cutting off the light, wrapping her in impenetrable folds. She gasped, and grasped the material, only to feel it wind tighter. She opened her mouth to scream; a hard hand clapped over her lips.

Honoria froze. An arm like steel wound about her waist and lifted her.

She didn't struggle but patiently waited for Devil to set her down. He eventually did—on the carriage seat. The carriage jerked and picked up speed. "Wait!" Still enveloped in what she assumed was Devil's cloak, Honoria struggled to break free. "What about Sligo?"

Silence.

Then, "Sligo?" Devil sounded as if he couldn't believe his ears.

"You ordered him to watch over me, remember?" Honoria wrestled with the cloak. The next instant, it was lifted from her—she let out an explosive breath, and discovered her husband watching her with an expression she couldn't read at all. "He's in the hackney, waiting for me."

Devil stared at her, then, frowning dazedly, shook his head. "Wait here."

He tapped on the hatch and ordered John Coachman to pull over, then leapt down. Honoria heard him stride back along the pavement. She couldn't see anything; the flaps were all down.

Two minutes later, the carriage dipped as Sligo scrambled up behind.

"Around the park until I say otherwise." Devil yanked open the door, climbed in, closed the door, then resumed his seat beside her.

The carriage lurched into motion; Devil met Honoria's wide, totally open gaze. He drew a careful breath, trying to disguise the tension that still held him. "Perhaps you'd better tell me what's going on."

He'd obviously made a horrendous mistake—he didn't want her to guess what he'd thought, how he'd felt, when he'd seen Chillingworth, stripped to his shirt, look out of his door, then seen her come waltzing out, turning back for a few last words before strolling away.

From the depths of the area, he hadn't been able to hear her words; his imagination, however, had supplied words enough, with actions to match. Her betrayal had chilled him; the thought that her declaration of love had been worthless—mere words without meaning—had struck him to the heart. Black rage had consumed him, far beyond mere temper; he could barely remember following her. He could remember the instant when he'd held her trapped before him—and thought how easy it would be to put an end to the torment before it began. The recollection left him chilled, even as relief poured through him. Guilt over his lack of trust made him inwardly ache.

Honoria was watching him, a frown forming in her eyes. Devil cleared his throat. "Sligo said you got a note?"

He threw out the question to get her talking—instead, she frowned more definitely. "I told you about the note in my letter."

Devil slowly blinked. "What letter?"

Rummaging in her reticule, Honoria dragged a sheet from the clutter. "I got this—"

Devil took it and scanned it, then glanced accusingly at her. She tilted her chin. "It said I had to come immediately, so I wrote you a letter explaining and asked Sligo to deliver it; he knew you were at White's. I didn't know you'd ordered him to stay by me—he sent Daley to deliver my letter so he could obey your orders."

Devil frowned, then looked down at the note. "I didn't get your letter—I must have left before Daley arrived." The admission was past his lips before he'd considered.

"But—" Honoria's brow was a mass of furrows. "If you didn't get my letter, why are you here?"

Devil stilled. A minute passed; slowly, he lifted his head and met Honoria's puzzled gaze. She searched his face—abruptly, he looked down. "I came because I got this." He forced himself to draw the folded note from his pocket. He didn't want to give it to her, but her straightforwardness, her honesty—her love—left him no choice. His heart a leaden weight in his chest, he handed it over.

Honoria unfolded the note, then read it. When she got to the end, she paused and drew an unsteady breath. A vise locked painfully about her chest; her heart beat heavily. Without lifting her head, she read the note again.

As she worked out what must have happened, her hands, holding the note, shook—she fought to steady them. Then, very slowly, she raised her head—and looked straight at Devil, into those eyes that usually saw too much but could also be blinded by fury. Time stretched; she stared into his eyes, her own full of pleading and disbelief. "It's not true—I would *never* do that. You *know* I wouldn't." In a painfully soft whisper, she added: "I *love* you."

Devil closed his eyes. "I *know*." His jaw clenched; savage rage swirled within him, directed at his would-be killer who had struck through the one, truly vulnerable chink in his armor— and hurt her. He dragged in a huge breath; opening his eyes, he locked them on hers. "I didn't think—I reacted. When I got that note, I *couldn't* think. Then I saw you come out of Chillingworth's—" He broke off; his jaw clenched tighter, but he forced himself to hold Honoria's gaze. Very low, he said: "*I care for you—too much*."

His words reached Honoria; what she saw in his eyes wiped away her pain. The vise about her chest eased; she drew a deep breath. "That's only fair." Shifting along the seat, she slid her arms about him and laid her head against his chest. "I love you so much it hurts, too."

If he couldn't say the words, she'd say them for him; the truth was there, shining in his eyes. His arms closed about her, then locked painfully tight; after a moment, he rested his cheek on her curls. He was so tense, his muscles flickered. Gradually, as the carriage rolled on, she felt his tension ease, felt the muscles in his arms unlock.

His warmth enveloped her; his heart beat steadily beneath

her cheek. He drew in a deep breath, then slowly exhaled; long fingers found her chin and tipped her face up.

Their eyes met, and held, then he lowered his head. Honoria's lashes fell as Devil touched his lips to hers in a gentle, inexpressibly sweet kiss.

He drew back, one brow rising. "I don't suppose you'd like to tell me just what *did* happen?"

No command or demand, just a mild request; Honoria couldn't help but grin. "Actually, Chillingworth was very insistent that I tell you all, which must be a first."

"Very likely. Start at the beginning—when you knocked on his door. Was he expecting you?"

"Not exactly." Honoria wriggled upright. "He'd received a note, too—I saw it. Written in the same hand as ours." She placed the note she still held next to the one on the seat beside Devil. "See? You can't tell if it's a man or a woman."

"Hmm—so he knew you were coming to see him?"

"No." Honoria spoke distinctly, mindful of Chillingworth's instructions—and her husband's propensities. "His note was from a mysterious unnamed lady, making an assignation for this afternoon. It was quite . . ." she gestured airily, "titillating."

Devil narrowed his eyes. "By which you mean Chillingworth was raring to go—what did he say when you arrived on his front stoop?"

Honoria shot Devil a mischievous look. "Actually, I think he was even more surprised than I was. He was almost disapproving."

Devil raised his brows skeptically. "And?"

"What followed was actually my fault—he told me I couldn't possibly be in earnest. Naturally, I assured him I was."

"*And?*"

Honoria held Devil's gaze. "He tried to kiss me—and I hit him."

Devil blinked—then blinked again. "You *hit* him?"

Honoria nodded. "Michael taught me how before he allowed me to go governessing." She frowned. "I suppose I should have used my knee, but I didn't think of it at the time."

Devil only just managed not to choke. "I think," he said, his voice not entirely steady, "that Chillingworth is probably quite grateful you hit him." Honoria was uncommonly tall, and Chillingworth was shorter than he was. Devil's lips twitched. "I must remember to inform him of his close escape."

Honoria frowned. "Yes, well—unfortunately that's not all. When I hit him, his nose started to bleed."

It was too much; Devil succumbed to gales of laughter. "Oh, God," he said, when he could speak again. "*Poor* Chillingworth."

"He seemed to think so, too. His waistcoat was ruined."

One hand pressed to his aching ribs, Devil fisted Honoria's left hand. "You must have used your left."

Honoria nodded. "How did you know?"

Devil's grin was pure devilish delight. "I caught him with a left at Eton—the same thing happened. He bled like a stuck pig."

"Precisely." Honoria sighed. "I'm afraid he's feeling rather put-upon."

"I can imagine."

Devil's tone had hardened; Honoria looked up inquiringly. He met her eyes. "He and I will have to sort this out."

Honoria straightened. "What do you mean?"

Devil's lips softened as he drew her back into his arms. "Just that we'll need to make sure we've got our stories straight in case someone noticed or starts a rumor." He hugged Honoria close. "Don't worry—I'm hardly likely to call a man out because my wife bloodied his nose."

Honoria frowned. "Yes—but is *he* likely to call *you* out because I bloodied his nose?"

Devil's chest quaked. "I really don't think that's likely." Grinning, he tilted Honoria's face up. "You're a remarkably resourceful woman, you know."

She blinked her eyes wide. "Naturally—I was raised an Anstruther-Wetherby."

Smiling, Devil lowered his head. "You were raised to be a Cynster."

He kissed her—and kept kissing her. The carriage rolled slowly through the gathering gloom, through the quiet shadows beneath the trees.

Breathless moments later, Honoria discovered that he could be remarkably resourceful, too. "*Great heavens!*" She had barely enough breath to whisper the words. "We *can't*—" Her hands closed tightly about Devil's wrists; her head fell back as she struggled for breath. "Where are we?"

"In the park." Intent on what he was doing, Devil didn't raise his head. "If you look outside, you'll see a number of carriages slowly rolling around the circuit."

"I can't *believe*—" A burst of pleasure stripped the thought from Honoria's mind; she struggled to hold back a moan. The thought that replaced the first had her blinking her eyes wide. "What about John and Sligo?" On a gasp, she met Devil's eyes. "Won't they realize?"

The grin on her husband's lips could only be described as devilish. "The trick's in the timing—trust me, they won't feel a thing."

They didn't—but she, and he, certainly did.

It seemed like hours—an infinite number of panting, gasping, *desperately* silent minutes later—when, slumped against Devil's chest, Honoria wriggled, then wriggled again. Frowning, she sat up and examined the buttons on his coat.

"Horrible things—they're sticking into me." She turned the mother-of-pearl buttons about. "They're not as big as the ones Tolly had, but they're quite bad enough."

Devil's eyes, closed in blissful peace, snapped open. "What?"

"These buttons—they're too large."

"No—what else did you say?"

Honoria frowned even more. "That they're like the ones on Tolly's coat?"

Devil stared into the distance, then he closed his eyes—and closed his arms about Honoria, drawing her close. "That's it." He spoke the words into her hair. "That's what I've been trying to remember about Tolly's death."

Honoria held him. "The button deflecting the ball? Does it help?"

His chin resting in her hair, Devil nodded. "It helps. It's the final nail in our would-be-murderer's coffin."

Honoria tried to look at Devil's face, but he held her too tightly. "You're sure who it is?"

Devil sighed. "Beyond doubt."

Three minutes later, their clothes precisely correct once more, the duke and duchess of St. Ives headed back to Grosvenor Square.

Chapter 24

❧❈❧

$\mathcal{V}$ANE WAS WAITING in the library when Honoria and Devil entered. He searched their faces, then relaxed.

"The end is nigh." Devil handed Honoria to the *chaise*, then sat beside her.

Vane sat in an armchair. "What happened?"

Devil gave him a severely edited account, proffering only the note Honoria had received. "The one I got was in the same hand." Vane studied the note, then frowned. Devil suggested: "Look at the writing itself, not the style."

Vane's face cleared. "The nib! He always uses those wide nibs so his writing looks heavier. We've got him!"

"Yes, and no. Everything we've discovered is circumstantial. Given what I've remembered today—"

"*And* my news, which I've yet to tell you," Vane cut in.

"Put it together," Devil continued, "and the murderer's identity's obvious. Obvious, however, isn't proof."

Vane grimaced; Devil's expression was bleak. Honoria glanced from one to the other. "But *who is it?*" When they looked at her blankly, she nearly ground her teeth. "You haven't told me yet."

Devil blinked. "But it was you who told me. You were the first to put it into words."

"I thought it was Richard, remember? You *both* told me I was wrong."

348

"Well, you were," Vane said. "It isn't Richard."

"You suggested the murderer was my heir." Devil waited until Honoria looked his way. "Effectively, he is."

Honoria's eyes flew wide. She glanced at Vane, then looked back at Devil. "But . . . You mean *George* . . . ?"

"George?"

"*Father?*"

Devil and Vane stared at her. "Why George?" Devil asked. "He's not my heir."

"He's *not?*" It was Honoria's turn to stare. "But Horatia told me he's a bare year younger than your father was."

"He is," Vane corroborated.

"Great heavens!" Honoria's eyes couldn't get any wider. "How many Cynster skeletons are there? Is George another Cynster like Richard?"

"You've missed a vital point—George and Arthur are twins." Devil caught Honoria's gaze. "Arthur's the elder twin—and no, it's not him either."

"*Charles?*" Honoria's expression blanked, then hardened. "How . . ." For a full minute, words failed her, then her eyes flashed. "How *cowardly*." She met Devil's eyes. "He killed his younger brother."

"Half brother," Devil corrected. "As he used to be very quick to point out. He's also now tried to kill me."

"Several times," Vane put in.

"He's also tried to kill you." Devil reached for Honoria's hand.

"And it now looks like he's killed his previous man, Holthorpe."

Devil and Honoria looked at Vane. "What did you discover?" Devil asked.

"Circumstantial evidence still, but I've had all the shipping lists checked—no Holthorpe embarked for America, or anywhere else. Holthorpe never left England."

Devil frowned. "Let's start at the beginning. Tolly left Mount Street the evening before he died. As far as we can tell, he headed home on foot. His lodgings were in Wigmore Street, so he'd walk past here. According to Sligo, he called in and learned I'd gone up to the Place. He continued on in good spirits—"

"And stopped in to see Charles," Vane said. "Around the corner in Duke Street."

"Given Holthorpe's disappearance, that seems a reasonable assumption." Devil's frown grew. "Presumably Tolly learned something, possibly overheard something—something that told him Charles was planning to kill me. Let's take that as read—what would Tolly do?"

"Tax Charles with it," Vane replied. "Tolly wouldn't have paused to think of any danger—he was too open and honest and naive to imagine others might be less so."

"We'll presume Charles didn't recant, so Tolly left."

"Probably saying enough on his way out to seal Holthorpe's fate." Vane looked grim. "The next morning, as soon as he could, Tolly left for the Place."

"But Charles took the faster route—we know he did. We didn't find anyone who could place Charles near the lane when Tolly was shot, but we did exhaustively prove no one else was in the area. No other gentleman arrived from London that day." Devil glanced at Vane.

"Right. So Charles shot Tolly—"

"That's what I'd forgotten. The button on Tolly's coat."

Vane looked puzzled. "What about it?"

Devil sighed. "The shot that killed Tolly was nothing short of perfect—the only reason he didn't die immediately with a hole through his heart was because one of his coat buttons"—Devil glanced down at the buttons on his coat—"like these, only larger, deflected the shot." He met Vane's eyes, then glanced at Honoria. "Charles's one real talent is that he's an exceptional marksman."

"Particularly with a long-barreled pistol." Vane nodded. "All right—so we have Tolly dead. Charles "arrives" at the Place then plays the grieving brother the next day."

"Very convincingly." Devil's face hardened.

"He must have got one hell of a shock when he realized Tolly had lived long enough to talk to you."

Devil nodded. "But he kept mum and saw it through, Tolly's funeral and all."

"But then came the biggest shock of all." Vane looked from Devil to Honoria. "Charles learned you were going to marry Honoria."

Honoria frowned. "Actually, no. Not then. I put him off." When Devil looked his question, she grimaced. "He came to see me in the summerhouse after the wake. He offered to marry me in your stead, assuming I was concerned over protecting my name."

"He *what?*" Devil stared at her.

Honoria shrugged. "I told him I'd no intention of marrying you or anyone."

"He believed you," Vane said. "He was taken aback later, at Mama's ball, when Gabriel and I suggested you'd changed your mind."

"Hardly surprising." Devil glanced at Honoria. "He'd stopped us in the park not long before and you as good as assured him you were off to Africa in a few weeks."

Honoria shrugged again.

"And that," Vane said, "was when the attacks on you started."

"Your phaeton accident." Honoria paled.

Devil squeezed her hand. "An impulsive first attempt. I was very busy after that, then came our wedding."

Honoria shivered. "I just remembered—Charles warned me on our wedding day that I shouldn't have married you."

Devil drew her against him. "While we remained at the Place, he didn't attempt anything."

"Too dangerous," Vane said. "Too likely he'd be spotted there."

"But as soon as we returned to town, he started plotting in earnest." Devil looked at Honoria. "First, he tried to convince me to send you back to the Place." His lips twisted. "I'm afraid I told him precisely where you stood in my affections. So, from then on, you, too, were in his sights—he wouldn't risk a posthumous heir."

Turning to Vane, Devil missed Honoria's startled expression. "The episode with the brandy came next, then the three sailors with swords who knew my route home. Both attempts were well within Charles's capabilities."

Vane held Devil's gaze. "That brandy should have done for you, you know."

Feeling Honoria shiver, Devil shot him a warning glance. "But it didn't, so he persevered. The sailors, I suspect, was an opportunity he couldn't pass up—he's walked home with me from White's often enough."

Vane frowned. "What about this business with the palaces? Where does that fit?"

Devil grimaced. "It might not—but I'll wager it'll turn out to be Charles. Whatever, I'll find out tonight."

"Tonight?" Vane blinked. "What with everything else, I'd forgotten. What's our plan?"

Devil glanced at Honoria; absorbed with her own thoughts, she eventually felt his gaze. Looking up, she blushed. "I was just recalling," she said, her eyes locking on Devil's, "something Lady Herring mentioned."

Devil's expression blanked. "Lady Herring?"

Honoria nodded. "She said Charles approached her—something about replacing her last paramour. She refused him—from the sound of it, quite contemptuously."

"Hmm." Devil looked thoughtful.

"That wouldn't have helped Charles at all." Vane shook his head. "He always resented your successes—apparently on that level, too."

The look Devil shot him was sharply reproving; Vane simply raised his brows. "It might explain why he started frequenting the palaces—the timing's right. A Cynster couldn't patronize such places for long without us hearing of it, and we heard of it soon after Tolly's funeral."

Devil nodded. "But I still want to know definitely."

"When's the meeting?"

"Midnight."

Vane looked at the clock. "I'll drive—Sligo can travel behind. Lucifer'll keep watch from the street—Scandal'll be at the corner." Devil stared; Vane raised his brows. "You didn't seriously imagine we'd let you waltz in there without pickets?"

Honoria kept her lips firmly shut on the response she knew Devil would not, in this instance, appreciate—"Thank God for the Bar Cynster" was not what he was thinking.

Devil scowled. "What *else* have you organized?"

"Nothing." Vane's expression was mild. "But there's no earthly use imagining we'll let Charles take another easy crack at you. If you die, he'll be the head of the family—there's not one of us can stomach the thought."

Devil glanced at Honoria; when she said nothing, he looked back at Vane. "All right. But I don't want the cavalry charging in before the bugle sounds—we need to let Charles run with his master plan and let him take enough rope to hang himself."

"His master plan." Vane glanced at the note in his lap. "Is that what this is?"

Devil nodded. "It fits. I'd worried that all the other attempts were too simple, too spontaneous—simply not like Charles. You know how he thinks. Any plan of his is convoluted and complicated. He's also very conservative, socially rigid. This latest effort has his character stamped all over it. Involved, heavy with intrigue, and solidly based in society's view of me, Honoria, and Chillingworth."

"Chillingworth?" Vane frowned. "Why him?"

"Because he *appears* to be the perfect goad."

"For what?"

Devil smiled—chillingly. "My temper."

Vane blinked, remembering the note Devil had received, the note he hadn't been allowed to see. His expression leached. "Oh."

"Indeed. This time, Charles has outdone himself—it's really a very good plan. It might have worked." Devil glanced at Honoria. "If things had been otherwise."

Studying his eyes, she raised a brow. "I'm not well acquainted with Charles's mental processes—could you explain his master plan to me?"

Devil's lips twisted; raising her hand, he brushed a kiss across her knuckles. "Charles needs to kill me—and now you as well—to take the title. He's tried to avoid direct action; the phaeton, the brandy, the sailors—there's no way of connecting them with him. But such chancy methods haven't succeeded. So, consider—he needs both me and you dead *with a reason*. After Tolly's death, accidental shooting of even one of us would cause a furore."

"No one would swallow that twice," Vane put in. "And he knows the rest of us wouldn't let your death under suspicious circumstances rest."

"Which is why he's focused on the one type of death for both of us that society will swallow without a qualm, and, even more importantly, the family will not only accept, but work with him to hide."

Vane's jaw firmed. "I don't like what I'm thinking, but if that's how he's set it up, he's read us very well."

Devil nodded. "He's clever. Not wise, but clever."

"I still don't understand," Honoria said. "What exactly is this death Charles has planned for us?"

Devil looked at her, his expression bleak. "Charles has known me all my life. He knows of my temper, of the scope of my rage; he has a reasonable idea of what might touch it off. With his three carefully structured notes, he arranged for me to find you coming out of Chillingworth's house."

"I'd worked that much out."

"From there on, he's relying on me—and my rage—to set the scene. He's counting on me to enact the role of jealously furious husband to the hilt, so he can kill us both and blame it on my sufficiently well-known temper."

Honoria held his gaze. "He's going to make it appear that you killed me in a jealous rage, and then killed yourself?"

Devil nodded.

Honoria's eyes narrowed, then flashed. Her chin firmed. "Charles," she declared, "is clearly not a Cynster." She looked at Devil. "How do we plan to catch him?"

"The only way we can—by letting him show his hand."

"So what's our next move?" Vane handed the note back to Devil.

"Our next move is to make our own plans, which must include all the right actions to make Charles believe *his* plan is succeeding. In any good play, the villain only reveals himself in the last scene; Charles won't appear unless we, the intended victims, play out the earlier scenes correctly." Devil glanced at Vane, leaning forward, intent, then looked at Honoria, calmly expectant by his side. He smiled, coldly. "We've already completed the opening scene in our melodrama. For the next . . ."

At six o'clock the next morning, wreathed in mist, two tall figures, pistol in hand, faced each other on Paddington Green. Their seconds stood aside; a scrap of white drifted down. Two shots rang out. One of the principals crumpled to the ground; the other, clothed in black, waited while the doctor swooped down on his patient, then handed his pistol to his second and stiffly turned away.

He and his second climbed into a black, unmarked carriage and departed the scene.

The third scene in the tragedy was played out later that morning.

Gentlefolk taking their morning stroll in Grosvenor Square— nurses and their charges, governesses and young misses, old and young alike—all witnessed the unexpected sight of the St. Ives traveling carriage rolling into the square. It drew up before St. Ives House; an army of footmen descended to strap on a mountain of luggage.

Diverted, many watched, wondering, then the door opened; His Grace of St. Ives, his face like stone, appeared, leading a heavily veiled woman. Given her height, there were few who did not recognize his duchess; her stiff manner and the way she held her head led most to speculate that there'd been some falling-out, some possibly scandalous rift in what had, until then, appeared a remarkably felicitous relationship.

Before a host of round eyes, the duke handed the duchess into the carriage and followed her in. A footman shut the door; the coachman whipped up his horses.

The word was winging, on whispers uttered with wide eyes, on hushed confidences traded behind elegantly gloved hands, long before the carriage had quit the fashionable precincts. The St. Iveses had left London unexpectedly, just before the beginning of the Season. What was the *ton* to think?

Predictably, the *ton* thought—and said—precisely what had been intended.

Four powerful blacks drew the St. Ives carriage rapidly into Cambridgeshire. Leaning against Devil's shoulder, Honoria watched the countryside flash by. "I've been thinking."

Devil opened his eyes only enough to look down at her. "Oh?"

"We'll have to give a formal ball as soon as we return to town. To dispel the mistaken impression we've been at such pains to instill."

Devil's lips twitched. "You'll have to invite Chillingworth, of course."

Honoria flicked him a warning glance. "I suppose that's unavoidable."

"Quite." Devil studied the weak sunlight playing across her features. "Incidentally, I should warn you that, despite its being midnight, it's possible someone might have seen me at the palace last night." The unknown Cynster had proved to be Charles; the madam's story had been utterly convincing.

Honoria lifted a haughty shoulder. "If any should think to mention your presence there to me, I can assure you they'll meet with a very cool reception."

Observing the imperious tilt of her chin, Devil decided it was unlikely even the most thick-skinned gabblemonger would dare—his wife was fast becoming as matriarchally intimidating as his mother.

"Do you think anyone was watching at Paddington Green this morning?" Honoria asked.

"Gabriel spotted a fellow resembling Charles's new man, Smiggs."

"So we assume Charles knows you and Chillingworth met?"

"It's a reasonable bet." Devil settled her more comfortably against him. "Try to rest." When she looked at him blankly, he added: "Tomorrow might be exhausting."

Honoria frowned vaguely. "I'm not sleepy." She looked away and so missed Devil's exasperated grimace.

After a moment, he ventured: "I just thought—"

"When do you think Charles'll appear?"

Devil inwardly sighed. "Either tonight, in which case he'll come up to the house and announce his presence, or sometime tomorrow, in which case he might not." *When* was she going to tell him? "I'll send a couple of grooms to Cambridge, to warn us the instant he arrives there."

"You think he'll use his usual route?"

"There's no reason for him to do otherwise." Studying her profile, noting her firm, not to say resolute, chin, Devil stated: "Incidentally, whatever transpires, you'll need to keep one point uppermost in your mind."

Tilting her head, Honoria blinked up at him. "What?"

"You're to obey my orders without question. And if I'm not

about, then I'll have your promise that you'll do what Vane tells you, without giving him a headache in the process."

Honoria searched his eyes, then looked forward. "Very well. I'll abide by your edicts. And Vane's in your absence."

Devil drew her back against him and touched his lips to her hair. "Thank you." Beneath his confident facade, he was deeply uneasy. The need to allow Charles to act and thus incriminate himself, to have to follow his lead and so enter the fray with no plan at all, was risky enough; having Honoria involved made it a hundred times worse. Tightening his hold on her, he settled his cheek on her hair. "We'll need to work together—rely on each other, and Vane—if we're going to spike Charles's guns."

Clasping her hands over his at her waist, Honoria humphed. "Given guns are Charles's favorite weapon, we may literally have to do so."

Devil closed his eyes and prayed it wouldn't come to that. To his relief, Honoria nodded off, lulled by the swaying of the carriage and the mild sunshine bathing the countryside. She woke as the carriage halted before the front steps of the Place.

"Ho-*hum*." Stifling a yawn, Honoria allowed Devil to lift her down.

Webster was there to greet them. "No trouble, Your Grace?"

"None." Devil glanced around. "Where's Vane?" Vane had left for Cambridgeshire the instant they'd quit Paddington Green; Webster and Mrs. Hull had left Grosvenor Square at first light.

"Trouble with the windmill at Trotter's Field." Webster directed the footmen to the luggage. "Master Vane was here when Kirby reported it—he went to take a look."

Devil met Honoria's eye. "I should go and check. It's only a few fields away—I won't be long."

Honoria waved him away. "Go and shake the fidgets from that black demon of yours. He's probably scented your return—he'll be pawing up the pasture with impatience."

Devil chuckled. Capturing her hand, he pressed a kiss to her wrist. "I'll be back within the hour."

Honoria watched him stride away, then, with a contented sigh, trod up the steps to her home. And it was home—she felt it immediately she entered. Throwing off her bonnet, she smiled at Mrs. Hull, passing with a bowl of open bulbs for the drawing room. Drawing a deep breath, she felt calm strength infuse her—the strength of generations of Cynster women.

She took tea in the back parlor, then, restless, wandered the downstairs rooms, reacquainting herself with the views. Returning to the hall, she paused. It was too early to change for dinner.

Two minutes later, she was climbing the summerhouse steps. Settling on the wickerwork settee, she studied the house, the imposing facade that had so impressed her at first sight. Recalling how Devil had hauled her along that day, she grinned. The thought of her husband increased her restlessness; he'd been gone for nearly an hour.

Rising, she left the summerhouse and headed for the stables. There was no one about when she entered the yard, but the stables were never unmanned. The stablelads would be out exercising her husband's prize cattle; the older men were probably assisting with the broken mill. Melton, however, would be hiding somewhere; he would come if she called, but otherwise tended to remain out of sight.

Honoria entered the main stable block—neither Devil nor Sulieman was there. Unperturbed, she spent the next five minutes communing with her mare. Then she heard hoofbeats. Lifting her head, she listened—a horse clattered into the yard. Smiling, she fed the mare one last dried apple, then, dusting her hands on her skirts, walked quickly back down the stable and swung through the archway into the yard.

And ran into a man.

She fell back, eyes widening, a shriek stuck in her throat.

"Your pardon, my dear. I didn't mean to startle you." With a brief, self-deprecatory smile, Charles stepped back.

"Ah . . ." One hand pressed to her palpitating heart, Honoria couldn't think what to say. Where was Devil? Or Vane? They who were supposed to tell her the plan? "I . . . er . . ."

Charles frowned. "I've truly overset you. I apologize. But I fear I bring grave news."

The blood drained from Honoria's face. "What news?"

"I'm afraid . . ." Lips pinched, Charles's gaze swept her face. "There's been an accident," he finally said. "Sylvester's hurt—he's asking for you."

Eyes wide, Honoria searched his face. Was it true—or was

this the first step in his final scene? If Devil was hurt, she didn't care—she would go to him regardless. But was Charles lying? She steadied her breathing, and tried to rein in her racing heart. "Where? Where is he?"

"At the cottage in the wood."

She blinked. "The one where Tolly died?"

"Alas, yes." Charles looked grave. "An unhappy place."

Indeed—but the broken windmill was in the opposite direction. "Oh dear." Striving for blankness, Honoria wrung her hands, something she'd never done in her life. In Devil's and Vane's absence, she'd have to script the scene herself. Delaying tactics came first. "I feel quite faint."

Charles frowned. "There's no time for that." When she tottered sideways and slumped against the stable wall, his frown deepened. "I wouldn't have thought you the sort to have the vapors."

Unfortunately, Honoria had no idea what succumbing to the vapors entailed. "What—what happened? To Devil?"

"He's been shot." Charles scowled with what was obviously supposed to be cousinly feeling. "Clearly some blackguard with a grudge against the family is using the wood as his cover."

The blackguard was facing her; Honoria struggled to hide her reaction. "How badly is he hurt?"

"Severely." Charles reached for her. "You must come quickly—God knows how long he'll last."

He grasped her elbow; Honoria fought the impulse to twist free. Then she felt the strength in his grip and was not sure she could. Half-lifting her, Charles propelled her into the stables. "We have to hurry. Which horse is yours?"

Honoria shook her head. "I can't ride."

Charles glanced at her sharply. "What do you mean?"

Pregnant women did not ride. Honoria blinked blankly. "I'm nervous of horses." As far as she could recall, Charles had never seen her ride. "And Devil's horses are impossible." She managed to wriggle her elbow free. "We'll have to take the gig."

"Gig!" Charles's scowl was quite real. "There's no time for that!"

"But—but—then I won't be able to go!" Honoria stood in middle of the stable and stared at him helplessly. Pathetically. Charles glared at her; she wrung her hands.

He ground his teeth. "Oh—*very well!*" He flung out of the stable and headed for the barn.

Honoria stopped in the yard. As soon as Charles disappeared into the barn, she searched, scanning the connecting yards, peering into the dimness of the opposite stable block. Where *was* Melton? Then she heard the rumble of wheels. "Damn!"

She scurried back across the yard. Her role was clear—she should go along with Charles's plan and let him incriminate himself. Panic feathered her nerves and tickled her spine; mentally, she stiffened it. They had to catch Charles—he was like a sword hanging over their heads, Devil's, hers, and the child she carried. But how would Devil rescue her if he didn't know where she was? Weakly, she slumped against the stable wall.

And saw Melton in the shadows of the stable directly opposite.

Honoria swallowed a whoop of joy; she hurriedly blanked her features as Charles maneuvered a light gig from the barn.

He threw her a black scowl. "Come hold the shafts while I fetch a horse."

Softening her chin, hiding any hint of resolution, Honoria limply complied. Charles entered the stable; Honoria glanced at the one opposite. Melton's cap was just visible through the open stable door; he was hugging the shadows to one side of the entrance.

Then Charles was back, leading a strong grey. "Hold the shafts steady."

Honoria dropped them once, then surreptitiously jostled the horse so he shouldered them loose again. Face set grimly, Charles worked frantically, buckling the harness, clearly conscious of time passing. Honoria fervently hoped she'd judged that commodity correctly, and that Devil would not decide to go for a longer ride.

Charles tugged on the final buckle, then stood back, scanning the rig. For one instant, his expression was unguarded—the smile that twisted his lips, oozing anticipation, Honoria could have done without. In that instant, she saw the killer behind the mask.

Melton might be old but his hearing was acute, which was how he so successfully avoided Devil. Honoria fixed Charles with her most helpless look. "Is Keenan with Devil?" She kept her expression vague, distracted. "You did say he's at Keenan's cottage, didn't you?"

"Yes, but Keenan's not there." Charles sorted the reins.

"You mean he's alone?" Honoria let her eyes grow round. "Dying in Keenan's cottage all alone?"

"*Yes!*" Charles grabbed her arm and all but forced her into the gig. "He's dying there while you're having hysterics here." He shoved the reins into her hands. "We have to hurry."

Honoria waited until he was mounted on his chestnut, turning toward the stable entrance before asking: "Are you going to ride back direct?"

Charles frowned back at her. "Direct?"

"Well . . ." She gestured weakly at the gig. "This can't go through the arch in the wall—I'll have to leave by the main gate and then find the bridle path back to the cottage."

Charles audibly ground his teeth. "I had better," he said, enunciating slowly, "stay with you. Or else you might get lost."

Dumbly, Honoria nodded. Meekly, she clicked the reins and set the gig rolling. She'd done all she could—delayed by all means she dared. The rest was up to Devil.

Chapter 25

$\mathcal{D}$EVIL KNEW SOMETHING was desperately wrong the instant he spied Melton, standing beneath the stable yard arch, wildly waving his cap. Cursing, he set his heels to Sulieman's sides; Vane's exclamation died behind him, then hooves thundered as Vane followed in his wake.

"What?" he asked, hauling Sulieman to a sliding halt.

"Master Charles." Melton clutched his cap to his chest. "Your lady went with him—he told her you were shot and a-dying in Keenan's cottage."

Devil swore. "How long since they left?"

"Five minutes, no more. But your lady's a bright one—she insisted on taking the gig."

"The gig?" Devil sat back. "Charles went with her?"

"Aye—he wanted to make sure she didn't lose her way."

Slamming a mental door on the chill fear that howled inside him, Devil flicked a glance at Vane. "Coming?"

"Nothing on earth could stop me."

They made straight for the cottage; there was no one there. Tethering their horses down the bridle path leading south, opposite the one Charles and Honoria would use, they scouted the area. Within the wood facing the cottage, they discovered a ditch, deep enough to hide them. It ringed the clearing on either side of the track from the lane. They were considering how best to use it when hoofbeats approached. Scrambling into the ditch, they watched.

Charles rode up. He dismounted by the stable, checked that Honoria was still following, then led his horse inside.

Halting the gig before the cottage, Honoria made no attempt to leave it. The instant Charles was out of sight, she looked wildly about. Both action and expression spoke of real fear.

In the ditch twenty-five yards away, Devil swore softly. "This time, I *am* going to beat you!" He didn't dare wave; he would bet his entire fortune Charles had come armed. Both he and Vane had loaded weapons in their hands, but he wanted no shooting with Honoria in the line of fire.

Dusting his hands, Charles came out of the stable. He frowned when he saw Honoria still in the gig, the reins lax in her hands. "I would have thought you'd be eager to see your husband." He waved to the cottage.

Honoria met his cold gaze. "I *am* keen to see him." She knew in her bones Devil was not in the cottage—for one fleeting instant, she'd thought he was in the wood, close, but she'd seen nothing. But he had to be coming—and she'd gone far enough with Charles. Charles slowed, his frown deepening. Drawing a deep breath, Honoria straightened her shoulders. "But he's not in the cottage."

Charles stilled; for one instant, there was no expression of any sort on his face. Then his brows rose, condescendingly superior. "You're overset." Stepping to the gig's side, he reached for her arm.

"No!" Honoria jerked back. The planes of Charles's face shifted. What she saw in his eyes had her swallowing her panic; this was no time to lose her head. "We *know*. Did you think we wouldn't realize? We know you've been trying to kill Devil—we know you killed Tolly."

Charles paused; as she watched, the veneer of civilization peeled, layer by layer from his face, revealing an expression of blank calculation, dead to any human emotion. "Knowing," Charles said, his voice unnaturally level, "isn't going to save you."

Honoria believed him—her only hope was to keep him talking until Devil arrived. "We know about your man Holthorpe—and about the sailors you set on Devil, about the poison in the brandy." What else did they know? Her recital wouldn't hold Charles for long. Fired by fear, she tilted her head and frowned. "We know everything you've done, but we don't know why you did it. You killed Tolly so he wouldn't warn Devil that you planned to kill him. But *why* are you so intent on taking the title?"

Desperate, she called up everything she'd ever felt about Charles, every intuitive hint she'd gleaned. "It isn't for money— you're rich enough as it is. You want the title, but you hold the family in contempt. Why, then, do you want to be their head?" She paused, hoping he would read true interest in her face. "What deep reason drives you?"

Charles regarded her without expression; Honoria felt her heart slow. Then he lifted one brow in typically arrogant Cynster style. "You're very perceptive, my dear." He smiled, a slight curve of his lips. "And, as you'll die shortly, I don't suppose there's any harm telling you." He looked directly into her eyes. "My name may be Cynster, but I've never been one of them— I've always felt closer to my mother's family. They're all dead now."

Bracing one hand on the gig, Charles looked into the wood, his eyes glowing. "I'm the last of the Butterworths—an infinitely superior breed, not that any Cynsters would admit that." His lips curved mockingly. "Soon, they won't have a choice. Once I take over the reins, I plan to change the family entirely—not just in the behavior associated with our name, but I'll change the name, too." He looked at Honoria. "There's nothing to stop me."

Honoria stared in openmouthed amazement. Smiling, Charles nodded. "Oh, yes—it can be done. But that was how it was meant to be—the Butterworths were destined to become the main line; my mother was to be the duchess. That's why she married Arthur."

"But—" Honoria blinked. "What about . . ."

"Sylvester's father?" Charles's expression turned petulant. "Mama didn't expect him to marry. When she married Arthur, it seemed all clear—eventually Arthur would inherit, then his son. Me." His frown grew black. "Then that slut Helena wriggled her hips and Uncle Sebastian fell for it, and Sylvester was born. But even then, my mother knew all would eventually be well—after Devil, Helena couldn't have any more brats, which left father, then me, next in line." Charles trapped Honoria's gaze. "Do you want to know why I left it so long? Why I waited until now to make away with Sylvester?"

Honoria nodded.

Charles sighed. "I was explaining that point to Mama, to her portrait, when Tolly came in that night. I didn't hear him— that cretin Holthorpe let him show himself in. Fitting enough that because of his laziness, Holthorpe had to die." His voice had turned vicious; Charles blinked, then refocused on Honoria. "As I told Mama, I needed a reason—I couldn't simply kill Sylvester and hope no one noticed. When he was young, Vane was always with him—the accidents I engineered never worked. I waited, but they never grew apart. Worse—Richard joined them, then the rest." Charles's lips curled. "The Bar Cynster." His voice strengthened, his features hardened. "They've been a thorn in my side for years. I want Sylvester dead in a way that will wean them, *and* the rest of the family, from their adulation. I want the title—I want the *power*." His eyes glowed. "Over them all."

Abruptly, his face changed, his features leaching of all expression. "I promised Mama I'd take the title, even if she wasn't here to see it. The Butterworths were always meant to triumph— I explained to her why I'd held off for so long and why I thought, perhaps, with Devil becoming so restless, the time might, at last, have come."

Again, he was with his past; Honoria sat perfectly still, content to have his attention elsewhere. The next instant, he turned on her viciously. "But then *you* came—and my time ran out *completely*!"

Honoria shrank back; the horse shifted, coat flickering. Charles's eyes blazed; for an instant, she thought he might strike her.

Instead, with a visible effort, he drew back, struggling to control his features. When he was again composed, he continued, his tone conversational: "Initially, I thought you too intelligent to fall for Devil's tricks." His gaze flicked her contemptuously. "I was wrong. I warned you marrying Sylvester was a mistake. You'll lose your life because of it, but you were too stupid to listen. I'm not going to risk being moved further from my goal. Arthur's old—he'll be no trouble. But if you and any son you bear survive Devil, I'll have all the rest of them to contend with—they'll never let Devil's son out of their sight!"

Clutching the back of the gig tightly, Honoria kept her eyes locked on Charles's, and prayed that either Devil or Vane had arrived in time to hear at least some of his ranting. He'd taken the rope she'd handed him and run, unreeling enough to hang himself twice over.

Charles drew a deep breath and looked away, into the woods. He straightened; letting go of the gig, he tugged his coat into place.

Honoria grabbed the moment to look around—she still had the feeling someone was watching. But not even a twig shifted in the wood.

She'd achieved her primary objective. Her disappearance and death would give proof enough of Charles's guilt; Melton could testify Charles had lured her away. Devil would be safe—free of Charles and his endless machinations. But she'd much rather be alive to share the celebrations, and to enjoy their child. She definitely didn't want to die.

Charles grabbed her—Honoria shrieked. Dropping the reins, she struggled, but he was far too strong. He hauled her from the gig.

They wrestled, waltzing in the leaves carpeting the clearing. Snorting, the grey backed; Charles bumped the gig. The horse bolted, the gig rattling behind it. Honoria saw it go, caught by a sense of *déjà vu*. Another grey horse bolting with another gig, this time leaving her stranded with the murderer, not his victim. *She* was to be the next victim.

Locking one arm about her throat, Charles hauled her upright.

"*Charles!*"

Devil's roar filled the clearing; Honoria nearly fainted. She looked wildly about; holding her before him, Charles swung her this way, then that, but couldn't locate Devil's position. Charles cursed; the next instant, Honoria felt the hard muzzle of a pistol pressing beneath her left breast.

"Come out, Sylvester—or do you want to see your wife shot before your eyes?"

Pushing her head back, Honoria glimpsed Charles's face, full of gloating, his eyes glittering wildly. Frantic, she tried struggling; Charles squeezed her throat. Raising his elbow, he forced her chin up; she had to stretch on her toes, losing all purchase on the ground.

"Devil?" Honoria spoke to the sky. "Don't you *dare* come out—do you hear? I'll never forgive you if you do—so don't." Panic gripped her, sinking its talons deep; black shadows danced across her eyes. "I don't want you to save me. You'll have other children, there's no need to save me."

Her voice broke; tears choked her. A dull roaring filled her ears. She didn't want to be saved if the price was his life.

In the ditch, Devil checked his pistol. Vane, brows nearly reaching his hairline, stared at him. "*Other* children?"

Devil swore through his teeth. "Fine time she picks to announce her condition."

"You *knew?*"

"One of the prime requirements of being a duke—you have to be able to count." His face grimly set, Devil stuck his pistol into the back of his waistband and resettled his coat. "Make for the other end of the ditch, beyond the track."

Honoria was babbling hysterically; he couldn't afford to listen. He pulled Tolly's hip flask from his pocket; he'd carried it since Louise had given it back to him, a reminder of his unavenged cousin. Working feverishly, he wriggled the flask into the inside left breast pocket of his coat; swearing softly, he carefully ripped the lining—finally, the flask slid in. Resettling his coat, he checked the position of the flask.

Vane stared. "I don't believe this."

"Believe it," Devil advised. He looked up; Honoria was still in full spate. Charles, his pistol at her breast, scanned the wood.

"I don't suppose there's any point trying to talk you out of it?" On his back, Vane checked his pistol. When Devil made no reply, he sighed. "I didn't think so."

"Sylvester?"

"Here, Charles."

The answer allowed Charles to face in their general direction. "Stand up. And don't bring any pistol with you."

"You do realize," Vane hissed, wriggling onto his stomach, "that this wild idea of yours has the potential to severely dint the family's vaunted invincibility?"

"How so?" Devil unbuttoned his coat, making sure the buttons hung well clear of his left side.

"When Charles kills you, I'll kill Charles, then your mother will kill me for allowing Charles to kill you. This madness of yours looks set to account for three of us in one fell swoop."

Devil snorted. "You're starting to sound like Honoria."

"A woman of sound sense."

Getting ready to stand, Devil shot a last glance at Vane. "Cover my back?"

Vane met his gaze. "Don't I always?" Then he swung about; crouched low, he started for the far end of the ditch.

Devil watched him go, drew in a long breath, then stood.

Charles saw him—he tightened his hold on Honoria.

"Let her go, Charles." Devil kept his voice even; the last thing he wanted was to panic Charles—the one he was counting on to shoot straight. "It's me you want, not her." He started forward, stepping over the scrubby undergrowth, sidestepping new canes and saplings. He didn't look at Honoria.

"Go back!" she screamed. "*Go away!*" Her voice broke on a sob. "Please . . . no." She was crying in earnest. "No . . . *No!*" Shaking her head, she gulped back sobs, her eyes pleading, her voice trailing away.

Devil walked steadily forward. He neared the edge of the clearing and Charles smiled—a smugly victorious smile. Abruptly, he flung Honoria away.

She screamed as she fell; Devil heard the scuffling of leaves as she frantically tried to free her feet from her skirts. Calmly, he stepped into the clearing. Charles raised his arm, took careful aim—and shot him through the heart.

The impact was greater than he'd expected; it rocked him back on his heels. He staggered back, hung motionless for a split second—the second in which he realized he was still alive, that Charles had clung to habit and aimed for his heart, not his head, that Tolly's hip-flask had been up to the task—then he let himself fall, slipping his right hand under the back of his coat as he went down. He landed on his left hip and shoulder; beneath him, his right hand held his pistol, already free of his waistband. Artistically, he groaned and rolled onto his back, his boots closest to Charles. All that remained was for Honoria—for once in her life—to behave as he expected.

She did; her scream all but drowned out the shot—the next instant, she flung herself full length upon him. Tears streaming down her cheeks, she framed his face; when he didn't respond, she sobbed and frantically searched—for the wound he didn't have.

Beyond thought, beyond all rational function, Honoria pushed aside Devil's coat—and found nothing but unmarked white shirt covering warm hard flesh. Gasping, her throat raw from her scream, her head pounding, she couldn't take it in. Devil was dead—she'd just seen him shot. She pulled his coat back—a wet stain was starting to spread. Her fingers touched metal.

She stilled. Then her eyes flicked up to Devil's; she saw green gleam beneath his long lashes. Beneath her hand, his chest lifted fractionally.

"*Such* a touching scene."

Honoria turned her head. Charles strolled closer, stopping ten paces away. He'd dropped the pistol he'd used to shoot Devil; in his hand was a smaller one. "A pity to put an end to it." Still smiling, Charles raised the pistol, pointing it at her breast.

"*Charles!*"

Vane's shout had Charles spinning around. Devil half rolled, coming up on his left elbow, freeing his right arm, simultaneously flinging Honoria to the ground, shielding her with his body.

Charles's head snapped back; his lips curled in a feral snarl. He raised his pistol. And paused for an infinitesimal second to correct his aim.

Neither Devil nor Vane hesitated. Two shots rang out; Charles jerked once. The look on his face was one of stunned surprise. He staggered back; his arm slowly fell. The pistol slid from his fingers; his eyes closed—slowly, he crumpled to the ground.

Devil swung around—a stinging blow landed on his ear.

"*How dare you?*" Honoria's eyes spat fire. "How *dare* you walk out to be killed like that!" Grabbing his shirt, she tried to shake him. "If you ever do that again, I'll—"

"*Me?* What about you? Happily going off with a murderer. I should tan your hide—lock you in your room—"

"It was *you* he shot—*I* nearly died!" Honoria hit his chest hard. "How the hell do you think I could live without you, you impossible man!"

Devil glared. "A damned sight better than I could without *you!*"

His voice had risen to a roar. Their gazes locked, sizzling with possessive fury. Honoria searched his eyes; he searched hers. Simultaneously, they blinked.

Honoria dragged in a breath, then flung her arms about him. Devil tried to cling to righteous fury, then sighed and wrapped his arms about her. She was hugging him so tightly he could barely breathe. He lifted her into his lap. "I'm still here." He stroked her hair. "I told you I'll never leave you." After a moment, he asked: "Are you all right? Both of you?"

Honoria looked up, blue-grey eyes swimming; she searched his face, then hiccupped. "We're all right."

"You didn't get hurt when you fell?"

She shook her head. "I don't think so. Nothing *feels* amiss."

Devil frowned. "I'll take you home." To Mrs. Hull, who knew about such things. "But first . . ." He glanced at Charles, sprawled on the leaves.

Honoria looked, then, sniffing, flicked her skirts straight and struggled up. Devil helped her up, then stood. Drawing a deep breath, he stepped forward—Honoria pressed close. Devil hesitated, then put his arm around her and felt hers slide about his waist. Together, they walked to where Vane stood, looking down on Charles.

Two bullets ripping into it from different angles had made a mess of Charles's chest. It was instantly apparent he couldn't survive. But he hadn't yet died. When Devil halted at his right hip and looked down, Charles's lids flickered.

"How?" he whispered, his voice hoarse.

Devil pulled Tolly's flask from his pocket. It would never hold liquid again; the ball had pierced one side and lodged in the other. He held it out.

Charles stared. Recognition dawned; his features twisted. "So," he gasped, each word a fight. "My little half brother won through in the end. He was so set on saving you—" A cough cut him off.

Devil quietly said: "Tolly was a far better man than you."

Charles tried to sneer.

"If I was you," Vane said, "I'd use what time you have left to make your peace with God. Heaven knows, you'll never make it with the Cynsters." So saying, he walked away.

His expression supercilious, Charles opened his mouth to comment—his features contorted, his eyes opened wide. He stiffened. Then his lids fell; his head lolled to one side.

Honoria tightened her hold on Devil, but did not take her eyes from Charles's face. "Is he dead?"

Devil nodded. "It's finished."

Hoofbeats approached, coming from the south. Vane came out of the cottage and looked at Devil. Devil shrugged. They moved to intercept the newcomers. Honoria moved with Devil; she wasn't yet ready to let him go.

Horsemen appeared on the bridle path, riding briskly. The next instant, the clearing was overflowing with Cynsters.

"What are you doing here?" Devil asked.

"We came to help," Richard replied, in the tone of one offended to be asked. Looking at the body sprawled on the ground, he humphed. "Looks like you've managed without us. He was so damned sure he had you dancing to his tune, he left London before you did."

"What next?" Gabriel, his horse tied to a tree, came to join them.

"You can't seriously consider passing this off as an accident." Lucifer followed on his heels. "Aside from anything else, I, for one, will refuse point-blank to attend Charles's funeral."

"Quite." Harry ranged himself beside Vane. "And if you can stomach burying Charles next to Tolly, *I* can't."

"So what do we do with the body, brother mine?" Richard raised his brows at Devil.

They all looked at Devil.

Honoria glanced up, but he had his mask on. He glanced down at her, then looked at the cottage. "We can't risk burying him—someone might stumble across the grave." His gaze lingered on the cottage, then swept the wood around them. "There hasn't been much rain. The wood's fairly dry."

Vane studied the cottage. "It's yours after all—no one would know except Keenan."

"I'll take care of Keenan—there's a widow in the village who's quite keen to have him as a boarder."

"Right." Richard shrugged out of his coat. "We'll have to bring the roof down and push the walls in to make sure it burns well enough."

"We'd better get started." Gabriel glanced at the sky. "We'll need to make sure the fire's out before we leave."

Honoria watched as they stripped off coats, waistcoats, and shirts, Devil and Vane included. Richard and Gabriel unearthed axes from the stable; Harry and Lucifer led the horses away, taking Charles's hired chestnut with them.

"Turn him loose in the fields closest to the Cambridge Road," Devil called after them.

Harry nodded. "I'll do it this evening."

Moments later, the sound of axes biting into seasoned timber filled the clearing. Devil and Vane each took one of Charles's hands; they dragged his body into the cottage. Honoria followed. From the threshold, she watched as they manhandled Charles onto the bare pallet on which Tolly had died.

"Most appropriate." Vane dusted his hands.

Honoria stepped back—a woodchip went flying past her face.

"*What the*—!" Richard, axe in hand, glared at her, then raised his head. "Devil!"

He didn't need to explain what the problem was. Devil materialized and frowned at Honoria. "What the devil are you doing here? Sit down." He pointed to the log across the clearing—the same log he'd made her sit on six months before. "Over there—safe out of the way."

Six months had seen a lot of changes. Honoria stood her ground. She looked past his bare chest and saw Vane, with one blow, smash a rickety stool to pieces. "What are you doing with the furniture?"

Devil sighed. "We're going to bring this place down about Charles's body—we need lots of fuel so the fire burns hot enough to act as his pyre."

"But—" Honoria stepped back and looked at the cottage, at the wide half logs of the walls, the thick beams beneath the eaves. "You've got plenty of wood—you don't need to use Keenan's furniture."

"Honoria, the furniture's mine."

"How do you know he isn't attached to it by now?" Stubbornly, she held his gaze.

Devil pressed his lips together.

Honoria's chin firmed. "It'll take two minutes to carry it out. We can use the blankets to cover it, then Keenan can take it away later."

Devil threw up his hands and turned back into the cottage. "All right, all right—but we'll have to hurry."

Vane simply stared when Devil explained. He shook his head, but didn't argue. He and Devil shifted the heavier pieces; Honoria gathered the smaller items into baskets and pails. Harry and Lucifer returned—and couldn't believe their eyes. Honoria promptly conscripted Lucifer; Harry escaped on the pretext of fetching Devil's and Vane's horses and taking them upwind of the cottage.

While Richard and Gabriel weakened the joints, the pile of Keenan's possessions grew. Finally, Harry, whom Honoria had collared and sent to clear out the stable, came back with an old oilcloth and dusty lamp. He put the lamp on the pile, then flicked the oilcloth over the whole.

"There! Done." He looked at Honoria, not in challenge, not in irritation, but in hope. "*Now* you can sit down. Out of the way."

Before she could reply, Lucifer pulled the big carved chair out from under the oilcloth, picked up the tasseled cushion, and plumped it. Coughing furiously, he dropped it back down and made her a weak but extravagant bow. "Your chair, madam. *Please* be seated."

What could she say?

Her slight hesitation was too much for Gabriel, strolling up to hand his axe to his brother. "For God's sake, Honoria, sit down—*before* you drive us all demented."

Honoria favored him with a haughty stare, then, sweeping regally about, she sat. She could almost hear their sighs.

They ignored her thereafter, as long as she stayed in the chair. When she stood and strolled a few paces, just to stretch her legs, she was immediately assailed by frowning glances—until she sat down again.

Swiftly, efficiently, they pulled the cottage down. Honoria watched from her regal perch—the acreage of tanned male chests, all gleaming with honest sweat, muscles bunching and rippling as they strove with beams and rafters, was eye-opening, to say the least. She was intrigued to discover that her susceptibility to the sight was severely restricted.

Only her husband's bare chest affected her—that particular sight still held the power to transfix her, to make her mouth go suddenly dry. One thing that hadn't changed in six months.

Between them, little else was the same. The child growing within her would take the changes one stage further—the start of their branch of the family. The first of the next generation.

Devil came over once they'd got the fire started. Honoria looked up, smiling through her tears. "Just the smoke," she said, in reply to his look.

With a sudden "swhoosh," the flames broke through the collapsed roof. Honoria stood; Devil put the carved chair back under the oilcloth, then took her hand. "Time to go home."

Honoria let him lead her away. Richard and Lucifer remained to ensure the fire burned out. Harry rode off, Charles's hired horse in charge. The rest of them made their way back through the wood, riding through the lengthening shadows. In front of Devil, Honoria leaned back against his chest, and closed her eyes.

They were safe—and they were heading home.

Hours later, chin-deep in the ducal bath, soothed by scented steam, Honoria heard sudden mouselike rustlings. Cracking open her eyes, she saw Cassie scurry out, closing the door behind her.

She would have frowned, but it was too much effort. Minutes later, the mystery was solved. Devil climbed into the bath. It was more than big enough for both of them—he'd had it specially designed.

"*Aarrghhh.*" Sinking into the water, Devil closed his eyes and leaned back against the bath's edge.

Honoria studied him—and saw the tiredness, the deep world-weariness, the last days had etched in his face. "It had to be," she murmured.

He sighed. "I know. But he was family. I'd rather the script had been otherwise."

"You did what had to be done. If Charles's deeds ever became known, Arthur's life, and Louise's, would be ruined, let alone Simon, the twins and the rest—the whispers would follow them all their lives. Society's never fair." She spoke quietly, letting the truth carry its own weight, its inherent reassurance. "This way, I presume Charles will simply disappear?"

"Inexplicably." After a moment, Devil added: "Vane will wait a few days, then sort out Smiggs—the family as a whole will be mystified. Charles's disappearance will become an unsolved mystery. His soul can find what peace it can, buried in the woods where Tolly died."

Honoria frowned. "We'll have to tell Arthur and Louise the truth."

"Hmm." Devil's eyes gleamed from beneath his lashes. "Later." Lifting his arm, he reached for the soap, then held it out to Honoria.

Opening her eyes, she blinked, then took it. Softly smiling, she came up onto her knees between his bent legs. This ranked as one of her favorite pastimes—soaping his chest, washing his magnificent body. Quickly raising a lather in the crisp mat of hair on his chest, she splayed her hands, caressing each heavy muscle band, lovingly sculpting each shoulder, each arm.

I love you, I love you. The refrain sang in her head; she let her hands say the words, give voice to the music, infusing every touch, every caress, with her love. His hands rose in answer, roaming her curves, unhurriedly possessing every one, orchestrating an accompaniment to her song.

She'd only let him use the soap on her once; the room had ended up completely flooded. To her abiding delight, his control was stronger than hers.

One large palm splayed over her gently rounded belly. Looking up, Honoria caught the gleam of green eyes beneath his lashes; she frowned. "You knew."

One brow lifted in his usual arrogant way; his lips slowly curved. "I was waiting for you to tell me."

She raised her brows haughtily. "Tomorrow's St. Valentine's Day—I'll tell you then."

He grinned—his pirate's grin. "We'll have to devise a suitable ceremony."

Honoria caught his eye—and struggled not to grin back. She

humphed and clambered over one rock-hard thigh. "Turn around."

She soaped his back, then lathered his hair and made him duck to rinse it. She'd returned to sit before him, between his thighs, her back to him, soaping one long leg, when Devil leaned forward, his arms closing around her. He nuzzled her ear. "Are you sure you're all right?"

"I'm perfectly well, and so's your son. Stop worrying."

"*Me* stop worrying?" He snorted. "That's a fine thing coming from you."

Dropping his leg, Honoria smiled and leaned back, luxuriating in the feel of the warm, hard, wet wall of his chest against her shoulders and back. "Oh, I've given up worrying about you."

Devil gave vent to an excessively skeptical sound.

"Well—just consider." Honoria gestured with the soap. "In recent times alone, you've been thrown from a disintegrating phaeton, poisoned, attacked with swords, and now shot through the heart. And you're still here." Dramatically, she spread her arms wide. "In the face of such trenchant invincibility, it's obviously wasted effort to worry about you. Fate, as I've been told often enough, quite clearly takes care of the Cynsters."

Behind her, Devil grinned. She would stop worrying about him on the same day he stopped worrying about her. Closing his hands about her waist, he lifted her, drawing her hips back against him. "I told you you were fated to be a Cynster wife— an *invincible* husband was obviously required." He underscored his emphasis by nudging the softness between her thighs, his erection sinking a tantalizing inch into that familiar haven.

Dropping the soap over the edge of the tub, Honoria arched—and drew him deeper. "I warn you, the staff are going to start wondering if we have to paint the downstairs ceiling again."

"Is that a challenge?"

She grinned. "Yes."

He chuckled, the sound so deep she felt it in her bones.

"Not a single splash," she warned him.

"Your desire is my command."

It was; he rose to her challenge—in every way—rocking her in the cradle of his hips until she thought she'd go mad. His hands roamed, fondling her swollen breasts, teasing her aching nipples. The slight ripples caused by their movement lapped at the sensitive peaks, a subtle, thoroughly excruciating sensation. Sweet fever blossomed, heating her skin, making the cooling water seem colder, impressing her with her own nakedness, sensitizing her skin to the crisp abrasion of his hair-dusted body rubbing so intimately against her.

Steadily, the fever built; Honoria shifted her knees to the outside of his. She tried to rise higher—he held her down, his hands firming about her hips. "No splashing—remember?"

She could only gasp as he pulled her lower, his hot hardness pressing deeper. Three restricted yet forceful thrusts later her fever exploded. She gasped his name as her senses soared; eyes shut, she savored the flight, hung briefly in the selfless void at the peak, then drifted gently back to earth.

He hadn't joined her; his arms came around her, holding her safe as her senses returned. Blissfully content, Honoria smiled and inwardly embraced him as possessively as he embraced her. He hadn't said he loved her, but after all that had happened, she didn't need to hear the words. He'd said enough, and, like any Cynster, his actions spoke loudest.

She was his; he was hers—she needed nothing more. What had grown between them, what was growing within her, was theirs—their life from now on. As her mental feet touched earth, she concentrated and caressed him, expertly, intimately—encouragingly.

And felt his muscles lock. Abruptly, he lifted her from him; the next instant, he stood and scooped her into his arms. As he stepped from the bath and headed for their bedroom, Honoria's eyes flew wide. "We're still wet!"

"We'll dry fast enough," replied her thoroughly aroused spouse.

They did, rolling, twisting, tangling amidst their silken sheets in a glorious affirmation of life, and the love they shared. Later, as he lay flat on his back, Honoria slumped fast asleep on his chest, Devil's lips quirked.

True Cynsters—all the male ones—died in their beds.

Stifling a chuckle, he peered down at his wife. He couldn't see her face. Gently, he shifted her to the side, settling her against him; she snuggled closer, her hand sliding across his chest. He touched his lips to her temple, and closed his arms about her.

"*To have and to hold*" was the family motto—it was also in the wedding vows. One of his ancestors had paid a horrific sum to put it there. Having married Honoria Prudence, Devil could understand why.

The having was very nice; the holding—the loving, the never letting go—was even better.

Epilogue

Somersham Place, Cambridgeshire
September 1819

THE BAR CYNSTER was in session.

They were all there, lounging about the library, languorously at ease like so many well-fed predators. Devil had pushed the chair back from his desk and propped one boot on his knee to make a makeshift cradle for his heir. Sebastian Sylvester Jeremy Bartholomew Cynster. The star attraction of the present gathering of the clan had been baptized several hours before; he was now getting his head wet in a different temple.

Vane was in the armchair by the desk; Gabriel and Harry occupied the *chaise*. Lucifer lay sprawled in one armchair by the hearth, Richard a mirror image in its mate. Each held a brandy balloon well filled with His Grace of St. Ives's best; a somnolent air of deep male satisfaction permeated the room.

The staccato click of feminine heels in the hall was the first intimation of impending fate. Then the door flew open; Honoria swept in. One look at her face, one glance at her flashing eyes, was enough to inform them that *someone* was in deep trouble.

Secure in the knowledge that, whatever was exciting her ire, *he* had to be innocent, Devil gave her a vague smile. Honoria returned it with a brief, ominously serious nod; when the others made to rise, she waved them back to their seats. Skirts swishing, she marched across the room, then whirled before Devil's desk. Crossing her arms, she faced them, her gaze impartially distributing her ire. *Only* Devil was safe.

"It has come to my notice," Honoria intoned, her words clipped and precise, "that a set of wagers—I believe the term is a book?—was run on the question of, not the date of Sebastian's birth, which would have been bad enough, but on the date of his conception." Her gaze settled on Gabriel; she raised her brows. "Is that correct?"

Gabriel eyed her warily; a tinge of color crept into his lean cheeks. He flicked a glance at Devil, who merely raised his brows back. Frowning, Gabriel looked at Honoria. "Your information is accurate."

"Indeed?" Honoria's eyes flashed pure steel. "And exactly how much did you—all of you—win?"

Gabriel blinked. To his left, Sebastian gurgled—there was no point looking to Devil for help; His Grace of St. Ives was besotted with his son as well as his wife. At the edge of his vision, Gabriel saw colors gathering in a phalanx by the door—Honoria's supporters, their mothers. Nearer to hand, he sensed Harry's tension. Vane shifted, uncrossing his legs; Richard and Lucifer both slowly sat up. Gabriel had no difficulty interpreting their silent message.

Which was all very well—they weren't the ones facing Her Grace of St. Ives's fire.

"Seven thousand, six hundred and forty-three pounds."

Honoria's brows flew. Then she smiled. "Mr. Postlethwaite *will* be pleased."

"Postlethwaite?" Richard's tone reflected their escalating unease. "What's he got to do with it?"

Honoria opened her eyes wide. "The village church needs a new roof. Mr. Postlethwaite's been at his wit's end—good lead is becoming so costly. And, of course, as we endow the chapel here, he didn't like to approach us."

Gabriel glanced at Vane; Vane looked to Richard, who was looking at Harry. Lucifer bent a look of disbelief on his brother. Jaws aching, Devil kept his head down, his gaze locked on his son's cherubic countenance.

It was Vane who stepped into the breach. "So?" The single syllable was steeped in unchallengeable superiority; with any other woman, it might have worked.

Honoria merely turned her head, looked Vane in the eye, then turned back to Gabriel. "You will donate the entire proceeds from your enterprise, with any interest accrued, to Mr. Postlethwaite, to use as he sees fit. As *you* were in charge of this infamous book, I will hold you responsible for collecting the funds and conveying them to the vicar." Her tone was that of a magistrate pronouncing sentence—it left no room for argument. "Furthermore, as a final penance, you will all attend the dedication." She paused; her gaze swept the gathering. "I trust I've made myself clear?"

Her eyes challenged them to gainsay her; each considered it—none did.

Briskly, Honoria nodded.

Sebastian cried, an eloquent warning of impending hunger. Honoria immediately lost interest in wagers, lead roofs, and indelicate speculation. Turning, she held out her arms commandingly; Devil handed his son over, an unholy smile lighting his eyes, lifting the corners of his lips.

With Sebastian at her shoulder, Honoria headed for the door, utterly ignoring the five large males she passed. She swept straight out of the room, the ladies closing ranks behind her.

Six males watched her go—one with glowing pride, the other five with uneasy trepidation.

They paid up without a whimper. Mr. Postlethwaite was delighted.

One month later, they attended the dedication; each uttered a prayer that fate wouldn't, just yet, turn her attention their way.

Unfortunately for them, fate wasn't listening.

A RAKE'S VOW

Chapter 1

October 1819
Northamptonshire

"YOU WANT TO get a move on. Looks like the Hounds of Hell are on our heels."

"What?" Jerked from uneasy contemplation, Vane Cynster lifted his gaze from his leader's ears and glanced around, bringing Duggan, his groom, into view—along with the bank of lowering thunderheads sweeping down on them from behind. "Blast!" Vane looked forward and flicked the reins. The pair of matched greys harnessed to his curricle stepped out powerfully. He glanced over his shoulder. "Think we can outrun it?"

Considering the storm clouds, Duggan shook his head. "We got three miles on it, maybe five. Not enough to turn back to Kettering, nor yet to make Northampton."

Vane swore. It wasn't the thought of a drenching that exercised his mind. Desperation dug in its spurs; his eyes on the road as the greys swept on, he searched for some option, some route of escape.

Only minutes before, he'd been thinking of Devil, Duke of St. Ives, his cousin, boyhood companion, and closest friend—and of the wife fate had handed him. Honoria, now Duchess of St. Ives. She who had ordered Vane and the other four as-yet-unmarried members of the Bar Cynster not only to pay for but attend the dedication service for the roof of the church in Somersham village, close by the ducal seat. Admittedly, the money she'd decreed they surrender had been ill-gotten gains, their winnings from a wager of which neither she nor their mothers had approved. The age-old adage that the only women Cynster males need be wary of were Cynster wives still held true for this generation as it had for those past. The reason why was not something any male Cynster liked to dwell on.

Which was why he felt such a driving need to get out of the path of the storm. Fate, in the guise of a storm, had arranged for Honoria and Devil to meet, in circumstances that had all but ensured their subsequent marriage. Vane wasn't about to take unnecessary chances.

"Bellamy Hall." He clung to the idea like a drowning man. "Minnie will give us shelter."

"That's a thought." Duggan sounded more hopeful. "The turnoff should be close."

It was around the next bend; Vane took the turn at speed, then cursed and slowed his cattle. The narrow lane was not as well surfaced as the road they'd left. Too fond of his high-stepping horses to risk injuring them, he concentrated, easing them along as fast as he dared, grimly conscious of the deepening gloom of an unnatural, too-early twilight and the rising whine of the wind.

He'd left Somersham Place, Devil's principal residence, soon after luncheon, having spent the morning at church, at the dedication service for the roof he and his cousins had paid for. Intending to visit friends near Leamington, he'd left Devil to enjoy his wife and son and headed west. He'd expected to reach Northampton and the comfort of the Blue Angel with ease. Instead, thanks to fate, he would be spending the night with Minnie and her inmates.

At least he would be safe.

Through the hedges to their left, Vane glimpsed distant water, leaden grey beneath the darkening sky. The River Nene, which meant Bellamy Hall was close; it stood on a long, sloping rise looking down on the river.

It had been years since he'd visited—he couldn't offhand remember how many, but of his welcome he had not a doubt. Araminta, Lady Bellamy, eccentric relict of a wealthy man, was his godmother. Unblessed with children, Minnie had never treated him as a child; over the years, she'd become a good friend. A sometimes too-shrewd friend uninhibited in her lectures, but a friend nonetheless.

Daughter of a viscount, Minnie had been born to a place in the *ton*. After her husband, Sir Humphrey Bellamy, died, she'd retired from socializing, preferring to remain at Bellamy Hall, presiding over a varying household of impecunious relatives and worthy charity cases.

Once, when he'd asked why she surrounded herself with such hangers-on, Minnie had replied that, at her age, human nature was her main source of entertainment. Sir Humphrey had left her wealthy enough to stand the nonsense, and Bellamy Hall, grotesquely gargantuan, was large enough to house her odd *ménage*. As a sop to sanity, she and her companion, Mrs. Timms, indulged in the occasional bolt to the capital, leaving the rest of the household in Northamptonshire. Vane always called on Minnie whenever she was in town.

Gothic turrets rose out of the trees ahead, then brick gateposts appeared, the heavy wrought-iron gates left ajar. With a grimly satisfied smile, Vane turned his horses through; they'd beaten the storm—fate had not caught him napping. He set the greys trotting down the straight drive. Huge bushes crowded close, shivering in the wind; ancient trees shrouded the gravel in shifting shadows.

Dark and somber, its multitude of windows, dull in the encroaching gloom, watching like so many flat eyes, Bellamy Hall filled the end of the tunnel-like drive. A sprawling Gothic monstrosity, with countless architectural elements added cheek by jowl, all recently embellished with Georgian lavishness, it ought to have looked hideous, yet, in the overgrown park with the circular courtyard before it, the Hall managed to escape outright ugliness.

It was, Vane thought, as he swept about the courtyard and headed for the stables, a suitably esoteric dwelling for an eccentric old woman and her odd household. As he rounded the side of the house, he saw no sign of life.

There was, however, activity in the stables, grooms hurriedly settling horses in preparation for the storm. Leaving Duggan and Minnie's stableman, Grisham, to deal with the greys, Vane strode to the house, taking the path through the shrubbery. Although overgrown, it was navigable; the path debouched onto a stretch of poorly tended lawn which continued around the corner of one wing. Around that corner, Vane knew, stood the side door, facing a wide sweep of lawn hosting a small army of huge stones, remnants of the abbey upon which the Hall was partly built. The ruins stretched for some distance; the Hall itself had grown about the guesthall of the abbey, otherwise ransacked during the Dissolution.

As he neared the corner, the blocks of weathered sandstone came into view, scattered crazily over a thick green carpet. In the middle distance, a single arch, all that remained of the abbey's nave, rose against the darkening sky. Vane smiled; all was exactly as he remembered. Nothing about Bellamy Hall had changed in twenty years.

He rounded the corner—and discovered he was wrong.

He halted, then blinked. For a full minute, he stood stock-still, gaze riveted, his mind entirely focused. Then, gaze still transfixed, his mind fully occupied by the vision before him, he strolled forward, his footsteps muffled by the thick lawn. He halted opposite a large bow window, two paces from the semi-circular flower bed before it.

Directly behind the lady, clothed in fine, wind-driven sprigged muslin, bent over, fossicking in the flowers.

"You could help." Patience Debbington blew aside the curls tangling with her eyelashes and frowned at Myst, her cat, sitting neatly in the weeds, an enigmatic expression on her inscrutable face. "It's got to be here somewhere."

Myst merely blinked her large blue eyes. With a sigh, Patience leaned as far forward as she dared and poked among the weeds and perennials. Bent over at the waist, reaching into the flower bed, gripping its soft edge with the toes of her soft-soled shoes, was hardly the most elegant, let alone stable, position.

Not that she need worry over anyone seeing her—everyone else was dressing for dinner. Which was precisely what she should be doing—would have been doing—if she hadn't noticed that the small silver vase which had adorned her windowsill had vanished. As she'd left the window open, and Myst often used that route to come and go, she'd reasoned that Myst must have toppled the vase in passing and it had rolled out, over the flat sill, and fallen into the flower bed below.

The fact that she had never known Myst unintentionally to

knock over anything she'd pushed aside; it was better believing that Myst had been clumsy than that their mysterious thief had struck again.

"It's not here," Patience concluded. "At least, I can't see it." Still bent over, she looked at Myst. "Can you?"

Myst blinked again, and looked past her. Then the sleek grey cat rose and elegantly padded out of the flower bed.

"Wait!" Patience half turned, but immediately swung back, struggling to regain her awkward balance. "There's a storm coming—this is *not* the time to go mousing."

So saying, she managed to straighten—which left her facing the house, looking directly at the blank bow windows of the downstairs parlor. With the storm darkening the skies, the windows were reflective. They reflected the image of a man standing directly behind her.

With a gasp, Patience whirled. Her gaze collided with the man's—his eyes were hard, crystalline grey, pale in the weak light. They were focused, intently, on her, their expression one she couldn't fathom. He stood no more than three feet away, large, elegant and oddly forbidding. In the instant her brain registered those facts, Patience felt her heels sink, and sink—into the soft soil of the flower bed.

The edge crumbled beneath her feet.

Her eyes flew wide—her lips formed a helpless "Oh." Arms flailing, she started to topple back—

The man reacted so swiftly his movement was a blur—he gripped her upper arms and hauled her forward.

She landed against him, breast to chest, hips to hard thighs. The breath was knocked out of her, leaving her gasping, mentally as well as physically. Hard hands held her upright, long fingers iron shackles about her arms. His chest was a wall of rock against her breasts; the rest of his body, the long thighs that held them braced, felt as resilient as tensile steel.

She was helpless. Utterly, completely, and absolutely helpless.

Patience looked up and met the stranger's hooded gaze. As she watched, his grey eyes darkened. The expression they contained—intensely concentrated—sent a most peculiar thrill through her.

She blinked; her gaze fell—to the man's lips. Long, thin yet beautifully proportioned, they'd been sculpted with a view to fascination. They certainly fascinated her; she couldn't drag her gaze away. The mesmerizing contours shifted, almost imperceptibly softening; her own lips tingled. She swallowed, and dragged in a desperately needed breath.

Her breasts rose, shifting against the stranger's coat, pressing more definitely against his chest. Sensation streaked through her, from unexpectedly tight nipples all the way to her toes. She caught another breath and tensed—but couldn't stop the quiver that raced through her.

The stranger's lips thinned; the austere planes of his face hardened. His fingers tightened about her arms. To Patience's stunned amazement, he lifted her—easily—and carefully set her down two feet away.

Then he stepped back and swept her a negligent bow.

"Vane Cynster." One brown brow arched; his eyes remained on hers. "I'm here to see Lady Bellamy."

Patience blinked. "Ah . . . yes." She hadn't known men could move like that—particularly not men like him. He was so tall, large, lean but well muscled, yet his coordination had been faultless, the smooth grace investing the languid courtesy rendering it compelling in some ill-defined way. His words, uttered in a voice so deep she could have mistaken it for the rumble of the storm, eventually impinged on her consciousness; struggling to harness her thoughts, she gestured to the door at her right. "The first gong's gone."

Vane met her wide gaze, and managed not to smile wolfishly—no need to frighten the prey. The view he now had—of delectable curves filling a gown of ivory sprigged muslin in a manner he fully approved—was every bit as enticing as the view that had first held him—the gorgeous curves of her derriere clearly delineated beneath taut fabric. When she'd shifted, so had those curves. He couldn't remember when a sight had so transfixed him, had so tantalized his rake's senses.

She was of average height, her forehead level with his throat. Her hair, rich brown, lustrously sheening, was confined in a sleek knot, bright tendrils escaping to wreathe about her ears and nape. Delicate brown brows framed large eyes of hazel brown, their expression difficult to discern in the gloom. Her nose was straight; her complexion creamy. Her pink lips simply begged to be kissed. He'd come within a whisker of kissing them, but tasting an unknown lady before the requisite introductions was simply not good form.

His silence had allowed her to steady her wits; he sensed her growing resistance, sensed the frown gathering in her eyes. Vane let his lips curve. He knew precisely what he wanted to do—to her, with her; the only questions remaining were where and when. "And you are . . . ?"

Her eyes narrowed fractionally. She drew herself up, clasping her hands before her. "Patience Debbington."

The shock hit him, heavy as a cannonball, and left him winded. Vane stared at her; a chill bloomed in his chest. It quickly spread, locking muscle after muscle in reactive denial. Then disbelief welled. He glanced at her left hand. No band of any sort decorated her third finger.

She *couldn't* be unmarried—she was in her mid-twenties; no younger woman possessed curves as mature as hers. Of that, he was sure—he'd spent half his life studying feminine curves; in that sphere he was an expert. Perhaps she was a widow—potentially even better. She was studying him covertly, her gaze sliding over him.

Vane felt the touch of her gaze, felt the hunter within him rise in response to that artless glance; his wariness returned. "*Miss* Debbington?"

Looking up, she nodded—Vane almost groaned. Last chance—a spinster, impecunious, and without connections. He could set her up as his mistress.

She must have read his mind; before he could formulate the question, she answered it. "I'm Lady Bellamy's niece."

A crack of thunder all but drowned out her words; under cover of the noise, Vane swore beneath his breath, only just resisting the impulse to direct his ire heavenward.

Fate looked at him through clear hazel eyes.

Disapproving hazel eyes.

"If you'll come this way"—with a wave, she indicated the nearby door, then haughtily led the way—"I'll have Masters inform my aunt of your arrival."

Having assimilated the style, and thus the standing, of Minnie's unexpected caller, Patience made no attempt to hide her opinion; dismissive contempt colored her tone. "Is my aunt expecting you?"

"No—but she'll be pleased to see me."

Was that subtle reproof she detected in his far-too-suave tones? Swallowing a hoity humph, Patience swept on. She felt his presence, large and intensely masculine, prowling in her wake. Her senses skittered; she clamped a firm hold on them and lifted her chin. "If you'll wait in the parlor—it's the first door on your right—Masters will fetch you when my aunt is ready to receive you. As I mentioned, the household is presently dressing for dinner."

"Indeed."

The word, uttered softly, reached her as she halted before the side door; Patience felt a cool tingle slither down her spine. And felt the touch of his grey gaze on her cheek, on the sensitive skin of her throat. She stiffened, resisting the urge to wriggle. She looked down, determined not to turn and meet his eyes. Jaw firming, she reached for the door handle; he beat her to it.

Patience froze. He'd stopped directly behind her, and reached around her to grasp the handle; she watched his long fingers slowly close about it. And stop.

She could feel him behind her, mere inches away, could sense his strength surrounding her. For one definable instant, she felt trapped.

Then the long fingers twisted; with a flick, he set the door swinging wide.

Heart racing, Patience sucked in a breath and sailed into the dim passage. Without slowing her pace, she inclined her head in regal, over-the-shoulder dismissal. "I'll speak to Masters directly—I'm sure my aunt won't keep you long." With that, she swept on, down the passage and into the dark hallway beyond.

Poised on the threshold, Vane watched her retreat through narrowed eyes. He'd sensed the awareness that had flared at his touch, the quiver of consciousness she hadn't been able to hide. For gentlemen such as he, that was proof enough of what might be.

His gaze fell on the small grey cat which had hugged Patience Debbington's skirts; it now sat on the runner, considering him. As he watched, it rose, turned, and, tail high, started up the corridor—then stopped. Turning its head, it looked back at him. "*Meeow!*"

From its imperious tone, Vane deduced it was female.

Behind him, lightning flashed. He looked back at the darkened day. Thunder rolled—a second later, the heavens opened. Rain pelted down, sheets of heavy drops obliterating the landscape.

Fate's message couldn't have been clearer: escape was impossible.

His features grim, Vane closed the door—and followed the cat.

"Nothing could be more fortuitous!" Araminta, Lady Bellamy, beamed delightedly at Vane. "Of course you must stay. But the second gong will go any minute, so cut line. How is everyone?"

Propping his shoulders against the mantelpiece, Vane smiled. Wrapped in expensive shawls, her rotund figure encased in silk and lace, a frilled widow's cap atop sprightly white curls, Minnie watched him through eyes bright with intelligence, set in a soft, lined face. She sat enthroned in her chair before the fire in her bedchamber; in its mate sat Timms, a gentlewoman of indeterminate years, Minnie's devoted companion. "Everyone," Vane knew, meant the Cynsters. "The youngsters are thriving—Simon's starring at Eton. Amelia and Amanda are cutting a swath through the *ton*, scattering hearts right and left. The elders are all well and busy in town, but Devil and Honoria are still at the Place."

"Too taken with admiring his heir, I'll wager. Daresay that wife of his will keep him in line." Minnie grinned, then sobered. "Still no word of Charles?"

Vane's face hardened. "No. His disappearance remains a mystery."

Minnie shook her head. "Poor Arthur."

"Indeed."

Minnie sighed, then slanted an assessing glance at Vane. "And what about you and those cousins of yours? Still keeping the *ton*'s ladies on their toes?"

Her tone was all innocence; head bowed over her knitting, Timms snorted. "More like on their backs."

Vane smiled, suavely charming. "We do our poor best."
Minnie's eyes twinkled. Still smiling, Vane looked down and
smoothed his sleeve. "I'd better go and change, but tell me—
who do you have staying at present?"

"A whole parcel of odds and ends," Timms offered.

Minnie chuckled and drew her hands free of her shawl.
"Let's see." She counted on her fingers. "There's Edith Swithins—she's a distant Bellamy connection. Utterly vague, but quite
harmless. Just don't express any interest in her tatting unless
you've an hour to spare. Then there's Agatha Chadwick—she
was married to that unfortunate character who insisted he could
cross the Irish Sea in a coracle. He couldn't, of course. So Agatha
and her son and daughter are with us."

"Daughter?"

Minnie's gaze lifted to Vane's face. "Angela. She's sixteen
and already a confirmed wilter. She'll swoon away in your arms
if you give her half a chance."

Vane grimaced. "Thank you for the warning."

"Henry Chadwick must be about your age," Minnie mused,
"but not at all in the same mold." Her gaze ran appreciatively
over Vane's elegant figure, long muscular legs displayed to advantage in tight buckskins and top boots, his superbly tailored
coat of Bath superfine doing justice to his broad shoulders. "Just
setting eyes on you should do him some good."

Vane merely raised his brows.

"Now, who else?" Minnie frowned at her fingers. "Edmond
Montrose is our resident poet and dramatist. Needless to say,
he fancies himself the next Byron. Then there's the General and
Edgar, who you must remember."

Vane nodded. The General, a brusque, ex–military man, had
lived at Bellamy Hall for years; his title was not a formal one,
but a nickname earned by his emphatically regimental air. Edgar
Polinbrooke, too, had been Minnie's pensioner for years—Vane
placed Edgar in his fifties, a mild tippler who fancied himself a
gamester, but who was, in reality, a simple and harmless soul.

"Don't forget Whitticombe," Timms put in.

"How could I forget Whitticombe?" Minnie sighed. "Or Alice."

Vane raised a questioning brow.

"Mr. Whitticombe Colby and his sister, Alice," Minnie supplied. "They're distant cousins of Humphrey's. Whitticombe trained as a deacon and has conceived the notion of compiling the *History of Coldchurch Abbey*." Coldchurch was the abbey on whose ruins the Hall stood.

"As for Alice—well, she's just Alice." Minnie grimaced. "She must be over forty and, though I hate to say it of one of my own sex, a colder, more intolerant, judgmental being it has never been my misfortune to meet."

Vane's brows rose high. "I suspect it would be wise if I steered clear of her."

"Do." Minnie nodded feelingly. "Get too close, and she'll probably have the vapors." She glanced at Vane. "Then again, she might just have hysterics anyway, the instant she sets eyes on you."

Vane cast her a jaundiced look.

"I think that's it. Oh, no—I forgot Patience and Gerrard." Minnie looked up. "My niece and nephew."

Studying Minnie's radiant face, Vane didn't need to ask if she was fond of her young relatives. "Patience and Gerrard?" He kept the question mild.

"My younger sister's children. They're orphans now. Gerrard's seventeen—he inherited the Grange, a nice little property in Derbyshire, from his father, Sir Reginald Debbington." Minnie frowned at Vane. "You might be too young to remember him. Reggie died eleven years ago."

Vane sifted through his memories. "Was he the one who broke his neck while out with the Cottesmore?"

Minnie nodded. "That's the one. Constance, m'sister, died two years ago. Patience has been holding the fort for Gerrard pretty much since Reggie died." Minnie smiled. "Patience is my project for the coming year."

Vane studied that smile. "Oh?"

"Thinks she's on the shelf and couldn't care less. Says she'll think about marrying after Gerrard's settled."

Timms snorted. "Too single-minded for her own good."

Minnie folded her hands in her lap. "I've decided to take Patience and Gerrard to London for the Season next year. She thinks we're going to give Gerrard a little town bronze."

Vane raised a cynical brow. "While in reality, you plan to play matchmaker."

"Precisely." Minnie beamed at him. "Patience has a tidy fortune invested in the Funds. As for the rest, you must give me your opinion once you've seen her. Tell me how high you think she can reach."

Vane inclined his head noncommittally.

A gong boomed in the distance.

"Damn!" Minnie clutched her slipping shawls. "They'll be waiting in the drawing room, wondering what on earth's going on." She waved Vane away. "Go pretty yourself up. You don't stop by that often. Now you're here, I want the full benefit of your company."

"Your wish is my command." Vane swept her an elegant bow; straightening, he slanted her an arrogantly rakish smile. "Cynsters never leave ladies unsatisfied."

Timms snorted so hard she choked.

Vane left the room to chortles, chuckles, and gleeful, anticipatory whispers.

Chapter 2

SOMETHING ODD WAS afoot. Vane knew it within minutes of entering the drawing room. The household was gathered in groups about the large room; the instant he appeared, all heads swung his way.

The expressions displayed ranged from Minnie's and Timms's benevolent welcomes, through Edgar's approving appraisal and a similar response from a young sprig, who Vane assumed was Gerrard, to wary calculation to outright chilly disapproval—this last from three—a gentleman Vane tagged as Whitticombe Colby, a pinch-faced, poker-rigid spinster, presumably Alice Colby, and, of course, Patience Debbington.

Vane understood the Colbys' reaction. He did, however, wonder what he'd done to deserve Patience Debbington's censure. Hers wasn't the response he was accustomed to eliciting from gently bred ladies. Smiling urbanely, he strolled across the wide room, simultaneously letting his gaze touch hers. She returned his look frostily, then turned and addressed some remark to her companion, a lean, dramatically dark gentleman, undoubtedly the budding poet. Vane's smile deepened; he turned it on Minnie.

"You may give me your arm," Minnie declared the instant he'd made his bow. "I'll introduce you, then we really must go in, or Cook will be in the boughs."

Before they reached even the first of Minnie's "guests," Vane's social antennae, exquisitely honed, detected the undercurrents surging between the groups.

What broth was Minnie concocting here? And what, Vane wondered, was brewing?

"It's a pleasure to meet you, Mr. Cynster." Agatha Chadwick gave him her hand. A firm-faced matron with greying blond hair half-hidden by a widow's cap, she gestured to the pretty, fair-haired girl beside her. "My daughter, Angela."

Round-eyed, Angela curtsied; Vane returned a noncommittal murmur.

"And this is my son, Henry."

"Cynster." Heavily built and plainly dressed, Henry Chadwick shook Vane's hand. "You must be glad to be able to break your journey." He nodded at the long windows through which the rain could be heard, drumming on the terrace flags.

"Indeed." Vane smiled. "A fortuitous chance." He glanced at Patience Debbington, still engrossed with the poet.

The General and Edgar were both pleased that he remembered them. Edith Swithins was vague and flustered; in her case, Vane surmised that wasn't due to him. The Colbys were as frigidly disapproving as only those of their ilk could be; Vane suspected Alice Colby's face would crack if she smiled. Indeed, it occurred to him that she might never have learned how.

Which left, last but very definitely not least, the poet, Patience Debbington, and her brother Gerrard. As Vane approached, Minnie on his arm, both men looked up, their expressions eager and open. Patience did not even register his existence.

"Gerrard Debbington." Brown eyes glowing beneath a shock of brown hair, Gerrard thrust out his hand, then colored; Vane grasped it before he could tie himself in knots.

"Vane Cynster," he murmured. "Minnie tells me you're for town next Season."

"Oh, yes. But I wanted to ask—" Gerrard's eyes were alight, fixed on Vane's face. His age showed in the length of his lanky frame, his youth in his eager exuberance. "I came past the stables just before the storm broke—there's a bang-up pair of greys stabled there. Are they yours?"

Vane grinned. "Half-Welsh. High-steppers with excellent endurance. My brother, Harry, owns a stud; he supplies all my cattle."

Gerrard glowed. "I *thought* they looked prime-uns."

"Edmond Montrose." The poet leaned across and shook Vane's hand. "Have you come up from town?"

"Via Cambridgeshire. I had to attend a special church service near the ducal seat." Vane glanced at Patience Debbington, mute and tight-lipped on the other side of Minnie. The information that he was permitted to enter a church did not melt her ice one jot.

"And this is Patience Debbington, my niece," Minnie put in, before Gerrard and Edmond could monopolize him further.

Vane bowed elegantly in response to Patience's abbreviated bob. "I know," he drawled, his gaze on her stubbornly averted eyes. "We've met."

"You have?" Minnie blinked at him, then looked at Patience, now staring, dagger-eyed, at Vane.

Patience glanced, somewhat evasively, at Minnie. "I was in the garden when Mr. Cynster arrived." The glance she flicked Vane was exceedingly careful. "With Myst."

"Ah." Minnie nodded and scanned the room. "Right then—now everyone's been introduced, Vane, you may lead me in."

He dutifully did so, the others filing in in their wake. As he conducted Minnie to the foot of the long table, Vane wondered why Patience did not want it known she'd been searching for something in the flower bed. As he settled Minnie in her chair, he noticed a place had been set directly opposite, at the table's head.

"Daresay you'd like to chat with your godson." Whitticombe Colby stopped beside Minnie's chair. He smiled unctuously. "I would be happy to surrender my place—"

"No need for that, Whitticombe," Minnie cut in. "What would I do without your erudite company?" She looked up at Vane, on her other side. "You take the chair at the head, dear boy." She held his gaze; Vane raised a brow, then bowed—Minnie tugged and he leaned closer. "I need a man I can trust sitting there."

Minnie's whisper reached only him; Vane inclined his head slightly and straightened. As he strolled down the room, he studied the seating arrangements—Patience had already claimed the chair to the left of his alloted place, with Henry Chadwick beside her. Edith was settling in opposite Patience while Edgar was making for the next seat along. Nothing in the arrangement suggested a reason for Minnie's comment; Vane couldn't imagine that Minnie, with wits like quicksilver, thought her niece, presently armored in cold steel, could possibly need protection from the likes of Colby.

Which meant Minnie's utterance had some deeper meaning; Vane inwardly sighed, and made a mental note to ferret it out. Before he escaped from Bellamy Hall.

The first course was served the instant they all sat. Minnie's cook was excellent; Vane applied himself to the meal with unfeigned appreciation.

Edgar started the conversational ball rolling. "Heard that the Whippet's odds on for the Guineas."

Vane shrugged. "There's been a lot of blunt laid on Blackamoor's Boy and Huntsman's well fancied, too."

"Is it true," Henry Chadwick asked, "that the Jockey Club's thinking of changing their rules?"

The ensuing discussion even drew a tittering comment from Edith Swithins: "Such fanciful names you gentlemen give the horses. Never anything like Goldie, or Muffins, or Blacky."

Neither Vane, Edgar, or Henry felt qualified to take that point further.

"I had heard," Vane drawled, "that the Prince Regent's battling debtors again."

"Again?" Henry shook his head. "A spendthrift through and through."

Under Vane's subtle direction, the talk turned to Prinny's latest eccentricities, on which Henry, Edgar, and Edith all entertained firm opinions.

On Vane's left, however, perfect silence reigned.

A fact which only increased his determination to do something about it, about Patience Debbington's adamant disapproval. The itch to tweak her nose, to prick her into response, waxed strong. Vane kept the lid on his temper; they were not alone—yet.

The few minutes he'd spent changing, slipping into a familiar routine, had settled his mind, cleared his vision. Just because fate had succeeded in trapping him here, under the same roof as

Patience Debbington, was no reason to consider the battle lost. He would stay the night, catch up with Minnie and Timms, deal with whatever was making Minnie uneasy, and then be on his way. The storm would probably blow itself out overnight; at the worst, he'd be held up only a day or so.

Just because fate had shown him the water, didn't mean he had to drink.

Of course, before he shook the gravel of the Bellamy Hall drive from his boots, he'd deal with Patience Debbington, too. A salutary jolt or three should do it—just enough to let her know that he knew that her icy disapproval was, to him, a transparent facade.

He was, of course, too wise to take things further.

Glancing at his prey, Vane noted her clear complexion, soft, delicate, tinged with gentle color. As he watched, she swallowed a mouthful of trifle, then sent her tongue gliding over her lower lip, leaving the soft pink sheening.

Abruptly, Vane looked down—into the big blue eyes of the small grey cat—the cat known as Myst. She came and went as she pleased, generally hugging Patience's skirts; she was presently seated beside Patience's chair, staring unblinkingly up at him.

Arrogantly, Vane lifted a brow.

With a silent mew, Myst stood, stretched, then padded forward to twine about his leg. Vane reached down and rubbed his fingers over the sleek head, then ran his nails down her spine. Myst arched, tail stiffening; the rumble of her purr reached Vane.

It also reached Patience; she glanced down. "Myst!" she hissed. "Stop bothering Mr. Cynster."

"She's not bothering me." Capturing Patience's gaze, Vane added: "I enjoy making females purr."

Patience stared at him, then blinked. Then, frowning slightly, she turned back to her plate. "Well, as long as she doesn't bother you."

It took a moment before Vane could get his lips back to straight, then he turned to Edith Swithins.

Not long after, they all rose; Minnie, with Timms beside her, led the ladies to the drawing room. Her gaze on Gerrard, Patience hesitated, her expression alternating between consterna-

tion and uncertainty. Gerrard didn't notice. Vane watched
Patience's lips set; she almost glanced his way, then realized he
was watching—waiting. She stiffened and kept her lids lowered.
Reaching out, Vane drew her chair farther back. With a brief,
excessively haughty inclination of her head, Patience turned and
followed in Minnie's wake.

Her pace wouldn't have won the Guineas.

Dropping back into his chair at the head of the table, Vane
smiled at Gerrard. With a lazy wave, he indicated the vacant
chair to his right. "Why don't you move up?"

Gerrard's grin was radiant; eagerly, he left his place for the
one between Edgar and Vane.

"Good idea. Then we can talk without shouting." Edmond
moved closer, taking Patience's chair. With a genial grunt, the
General moved up the table. Vane suspected Whitticombe would
have kept his distance, but the insult would have been too obvious. His expression coldly severe, he moved to Edgar's other
side.

Reaching for the decanter Masters had placed before him,
Vane looked up—directly at Patience, still lingering, half-in and
half-out of the door. Obviously torn. Vane's eyes touched hers;
coolly arrogant, he raised his brows.

Patience's expression blanked. She stiffened, then slipped out
of the door. A footman closed it behind her.

Vane smiled to himself; lifting the decanter, he poured himself a large glass.

By the time the decanter had circulated once, they'd settled
on the best tip for the Guineas. Edgar sighed. "We really don't
see much excitement here at the Hall." He smiled self-
consciously. "I spend most of my days in the library. Reading
biographies, y'know."

Whitticombe sniffed contemptuously. "Dilettante."

His gaze on Vane, Edgar colored but gave no other sign of
having heard the jibe. "The library's quite extensive—it includes
a number of journals and diaries of the family. Quite fascinating,
in their way." The gentle emphasis he placed on the last three
words left him looking much more the gentleman than Whitticombe.

As if sensing it, Whitticombe set his glass down and, in superior accents, addressed Vane. "As I daresay Lady Bellamy in-

formed you, I am engaged on an extensive study of Coldchurch Abbey. Once my investigations are complete, I flatter myself the abbey will once again be appreciated as the important ecclesiastical center it once was."

"Oh, yes." Edmond grinned ingenuously at Whitticombe. "But all that's the dead past. The ruins are perfectly fascinating in their own right. They stir my muse to remarkable effect."

Glancing from Edmond to Whitticombe, Vane got the impression this was an oft-trod argument. That impression deepened when Edmond turned to him, and Vane saw the twinkle in his expressive eyes.

"I'm scripting a play, inspired by the ruins and set amongst them."

"Sacrilege!" Whitticombe stiffened. "The abbey is God's house, not a playhouse."

"Ah, but it's not an abbey any longer, just a heap of old stones." Edmond grinned, unrepentant. "And it's such an *atmospheric* spot."

Whitticombe's disgusted snort was echoed by the General. "Atmospheric, indeed! It's damp and cold and unhealthful—and if you plan to drag us out to be your audience, perched on cold stone, then you can think again. My old bones won't stand for it."

"But it *is* a very beautiful place," Gerrard put in. "Some of the vistas are excellent, either framed by the ruins or with the ruins as a focal point."

Vane saw the glow in Gerrard's eyes, heard the youthful fervor in his voice.

Gerrard glanced his way, then colored. "I sketch, you see."

Vane's brows rose. He was about to express interest, polite but unfeigned, when Whitticombe snorted again.

"Sketches? Mere childish likenesses—you make too much of yourself, m'boy." Whitticombe's eyes were hard; headmasterlike, he frowned at Gerrard. "You should be out and about, exercising that weak chest of yours, rather than sitting in the damp ruins for hours on end. Yes, and you should be studying, too, not frittering away your time."

The glow vanished from Gerrard's face; beneath the youthful softness, the planes of his face set hard. "I am studying, but I've already been accepted into Trinity for the autumn term next year. Patience and Minnie want me to go to London, so I will—and I don't need to study for that."

"No indeed," Vane smoothly cut in. "This port is excellent." He helped himself to another glass, then passed the decanter to Edmond. "I suspect we should offer due thanks for the late Sir Humphrey's well-qualified palate." He settled his shoulders more comfortably; over the rim of his glass, he met Henry's eye. "But tell me, how has the gamekeeper managed with Sir Humphrey's coverts?"

Henry accepted the decanter. "The wood over Walgrave way is worth a visit."

The General grunted. "Always plenty of rabbits about by the river. Took a piece out yesterday—bagged three."

Everyone else had some contribution to make—all except Whitticombe. He held himself aloof, cloaked in chilly disapproval.

When the talk of shooting threatened to flag, Vane set down his glass. "I think it's time we rejoined the ladies."

In the drawing room, Patience waited impatiently, and tried not to stare at the door. They'd been passing the port for more than half an hour; God only knew what undesirable views Gerrard was absorbing. She'd already uttered innumerable prayers that the rain would blow over and the following morning dawn fine. Then Mr. Vane Cynster would be on his way, taking his "gentlemanly elegance" with him.

Beside her, Mrs. Chadwick was instructing Angela: "There are six of them—or were. St. Ives married last year. But there's no question on the matter—Cynsters are so well bred, so very much the epitome of what one wishes to see in a gentleman."

Angela's eyes, already round as saucers, widened even more. "Are they *all* as well set-up as this Mr. Cynster?"

Mrs. Chadwick shot Angela a reproving glance. "They are all very elegant, of course, but I've heard it said Vane Cynster is the most elegant of them all."

Patience swallowed a disgusted humph. Just her luck—if she and Gerrard had to meet a Cynster, why did it have to be the most elegant one? Fate was playing games with her. She'd accepted Minnie's invitation to join her household for the autumn and winter and then to go to London for the Season, sure that fate was smiling benevolently, intervening to smooth her path. There was no doubt she'd needed help.

She was no fool. She'd seen months ago that, although she'd been nursemaid, surrogate mother, and guardian to Gerrard all his life, she could not provide the final direction he needed to cross the last threshold into adulthood.

She couldn't be his mentor.

Nowhere in his life had there been a suitable gentleman on whose behaviour and standards Gerrard could base his own. The chances of discovering such a gentleman in deepest Derbyshire were slight. When Minnie's invitation had arrived, informing her that there were gentlemen staying at Bellamy Hall, it had seemed like fate's hand at work. She'd accepted the invitation with alacrity, organized for the Grange to run without her, and headed south with Gerrard.

She'd spent the journey formulating a description of the man she would accept as Gerrard's mentor—the one she would trust with her brother's tender youth. By the time they reached Bellamy Hall, she had her criteria firmly fixed.

By the end of their first evening, she'd concluded that none of the gentlemen present met her stringent requirements. While each possessed qualities of which she approved, none was free of traits of which she disapproved. Most especially, none commanded her respect, complete and absolute, which criterion she'd flagged as the most crucial.

Philosophically, she'd shrugged and accepted fate's decree, and set her sights on London. Potential aspirants to the position of Gerrard's mentor would clearly be more numerous there. Comfortable and secure, she and Gerrard had settled into Minnie's household.

Now comfort and security were things of the past—and would remain so until Vane Cynster left.

At that instant, the drawing-room door opened; together with Mrs. Chadwick and Angela, Patience turned to watch the gentlemen stroll in. They were led by Whitticombe Colby, looking insufferably superior as usual; he made for the *chaise* on which Minnie and Timms sat, with Alice in a chair beside them. Edgar and the General followed Whitticombe through the door; by mutual consent, they headed for the fireplace, beside which Edith Swithins, vaguely smiling, sat tatting industriously.

Her gaze glued to the door, Patience waited—and saw Edmond and Henry amble in. Beneath her breath, she swore, then coughed to disguise the indiscretion. *Damn Vane Cynster*.

On the thought, he strolled in, Gerrard by his side.

Patience's mental imprecations reached new heights. Mrs. Chadwick had not lied—Vane Cynster was the very epitome of an elegant gentleman. His hair, burnished chestnut several shades darker than her own, glowed softly in the candlelight, wave upon elegant wave sitting perfectly about his head. Even across the room, the strength of his features registered; clear-cut, hard-edged, forehead, nose, jaw, and cheeks appeared sculpted out of rock. Only his lips, long and thin with just a hint of humor to relieve their austerity, and the innate intelligence and, yes, wickedness, that lit his grey eyes, gave any hint of mere mortal personality—all else, including, Patience grudgingly acknowledged, his long, lean body, belonged to a god.

She didn't want to see how well his grey coat of Bath superfine hugged his broad shoulders, how its excellent cut emphasized his broad chest and much narrower hips. She didn't want to notice how precise, how wondrously elegant his white cravat, tied in a simple "Ballroom," appeared. And as for his legs, long muscles flexing as he moved, she definitely didn't need to notice them.

He paused just inside the door; Gerrard stopped beside him. As she watched, Vane made some smiling comment, illustrating with a gesture so graceful it set her teeth on edge. Gerrard, face alight, eyes glowing, laughed and responded eagerly.

Vane turned his head; across the room, his eyes met hers.

Patience could have sworn someone had punched her in the stomach; she simply couldn't breathe. Holding her gaze, Vane lifted one brow—challenge flashed between them, subtle yet deliberate, quite impossible to mistake.

Patience stiffened. She dragged in a desperate breath and turned. And plastered a brittle smile on her lips as Edmond and Henry reached them.

"Isn't Mr. Cynster going to join us?" Angela, oblivious of her mother's sharp frown, leaned around to stare past Henry to where Vane and Gerrard still stood talking by the door. "I'm sure he'd be much more entertained talking to us than to Gerrard."

Patience bit her lip; she did not agree with Angela, but she fervently hoped Angela would get her wish. For an instant, it seemed she might; Vane's lips curved as he made some comment to Gerrard, then he turned—and strolled to Minnie's side.

It was Gerrard who joined them.

Hiding her relief, Patience welcomed him with a serene smile—and kept her gaze well away from the *chaise*. Gerrard and Edmond immediately fell to plotting the next scene in Edmond's melodrama—a common diversion for them. Henry, one eye on Patience, made a too-obvious effort to indulgently encourage them; his attitude, and the too-warm look in his eye, irked Patience, as it always did.

Angela, of course, pouted, not an especially pretty sight. Mrs. Chadwick, inured to her daughter's witlessness, sighed and surrendered; she and Angela, now beaming with delight, crossed to join the group about the *chaise*.

Patience was content to remain where she was, even if that meant withstanding Henry's ardent gaze.

Fifteen minutes later, the tea trolley arrived. Minnie poured, chatting all the while. From the corner of her eye, Patience noted Vane Cynster discoursing amiably with Mrs. Chadwick; Angela, largely ignored, was threatening to pout again. Timms looked up and offered some comment which made everyone laugh; Patience saw her aunt's wise companion smile affectionately up at Vane. Of all the ladies about the *chaise*, only Alice Colby appeared unimpressed—not, however, unaffected. To Patience's eyes, Alice was even more tense than usual, as if holding back her disapproval by sheer force of will. The object of her ire, however, seemed to find her invisible.

Inwardly humphing, Patience tuned her ears to her brother's conversation, currently revolving about the "light" in the ruins. Undoubtedly a safer topic than whatever glib sally caused the next wave of laughter from the group about the *chaise*.

"Henry!"

Mrs. Chadwick's call had Henry turning, then he smiled and nodded to Patience. "If you'll excuse me, my dear, I'll return in a moment." He glanced at Gerrard. "Don't want to miss any of these scintillating plans."

Knowing full well Henry had no real interest in Gerrard or in Edmond's drama, Patience simply smiled back.

"I'd actually favor doing that scene with the arch in the background." Gerrard frowned, clearly picturing it. "The proportions are better."

"No, no," Edmond returned. "It *has* to be in the cloister." Looking up, he grinned—at a point past Patience. "Hello—are we summoned?"

"Indeed."

The single word, uttered in a voice so deep it literally rumbled, rang in Patience's ears like a knell. She swung around.

A teacup in each hand, Vane, his gaze on Edmond and Gerrard, nodded toward the tea trolley. "Your presence is requested."

"Right-ho!" With a cheery smile, Edmond took himself off; without hesitation, Gerrard followed.

Leaving Patience alone, stranded on an island of privacy in the corner of the drawing room with the one gentleman in the entire company she heartily wished at the devil.

"Thank you." With a stiff inclination of her head, she accepted the cup Vane offered her. With rigid calm, she sipped. And tried not to notice how easily he had isolated her—cut her out from her protective herd. She'd recognized him immediately as a wolf; apparently, he was an accomplished one. A fact she would henceforth bear in mind. Along with all the rest.

She could feel his gaze on her face; resolutely, she lifted her head and met his eyes. "Minnie mentioned you were on your way to Leamington, Mr. Cynster. I daresay you'll be eager to see the rain cease."

His fascinating lips lifted fractionally. "Eager enough, Miss Debbington."

Patience wished his voice was not so very deep; it made her nerves vibrate.

"However," he said, his gaze holding hers, his words a languid rumble, "you shouldn't sell the present company short. There are a number of distractions I've already noted which will, I'm convinced, make my unplanned stay worthwhile."

She was not going to be intimidated. Patience opened her eyes wide. "You intrigue me, sir. I wouldn't have imagined there was anything at Bellamy Hall of sufficient note to claim the attention of a gentleman of your . . . inclinations. Do, pray, enlighten me."

Vane met her challenging look, and considered doing just that. He raised his teacup and sipped, holding her gaze all the while. Then, looking down as he set his cup on its saucer, he stepped closer, to her side, so they stood shoulder to shoulder, he with his back to the room. He looked at her along his shoulder, and raised a brow. "I could be a rabid fan of amateur theatricals."

Despite her patently rigid resolve, her lips twitched. "And pigs might fly," she returned. Looking away, she sipped her tea.

Vane's brow quirked; he continued his languid prowl, slowly circling her, his gaze caressing the sweep of her throat and nape. "And then there's your brother." Instantly, she stiffened, as poker-rigid as Alice Colby; behind her, Vane raised both brows. "Tell me," he murmured, before she could bolt, "what's he done to get not only Whitticombe and the General, but Edgar and Henry, too, casting disapproving glances his way?"

The answer came, swift, decisive, and in distinctly bitter tones. "Nothing." After a second's pause, during which the defensive tension in her shoulders eased slightly, she added: "They've simply got totally inaccurate views of how youths of Gerrard's age might behave."

"Hmm." The explanation, Vane noted, shed very little light. Finishing his stroll, he halted by her side. "In that case, you owe me a vote of thanks." Surprised, she looked up; he met her eyes and smiled. "I stepped into the breach and stopped Gerrard responding to one of Whitticombe's set-downs with rather too much heat."

She searched his eyes, then looked away. "You only did so because you didn't want to listen to a deal of pointless wrangling."

Watching as she sipped, Vane haughtily raised his brows; she was, as it happened, half-right. "You also," he said, lowering his voice, "haven't yet thanked me for saving you from sitting in the flower bed."

She didn't even look up. "It was entirely your fault that I nearly did. If you hadn't sneaked up on me, I wouldn't have been in any danger of landing in the weeds." She glanced briefly at him, a touch of color in her cheeks. "A gentleman would have coughed or something."

Vane trapped her gaze, and smiled—a slow, Cynster smile.

"Ah," he murmured, his voice very low. He shifted fractionally closer. "But, you see, I'm not a gentleman. I'm a Cynster." As if letting her into some secret, he gently informed her: "We're conquerors—not gentlemen."

Patience looked into his eyes, into his face, and felt a most peculiar shiver slither down her spine. She'd just finished her tea, but her mouth felt dry. She blinked, then blinked again, and decided to ignore his last comment. She narrowed her eyes at him. "You're not, by any chance, attempting to make me feel grateful—so that I'll imagine myself in your debt?"

His brows quirked; his mesmerizing lips curved. His eyes, grey, intent, and oddly challenging, held hers. "It seemed the natural place to start to undermine your defenses."

Patience felt her nerves vibrate to the deep tenor of his voice, felt her senses quake as she registered his words. Her eyes, locked on his, widened; her lungs seized. In a mental scramble, she struggled to marshal her wits, to lay her tongue on some sharp retort with which to break his spell.

His eyes searched hers; one brow lifted arrogantly, along with the ends of his long lips. "I didn't cough because I was entirely distracted, which was entirely *your* fault." He seemed very close, totally commanding her vision, her senses. Again his eyes scanned hers, again one brow quirked. "Incidentally," he murmured, his voice velvety dark, "what were you searching for in the flower bed?"

"*There* you are!"

Breathless, Patience turned—and beheld Minnie, descending like a galleon in full sail. The entire British fleet wouldn't have been more welcome.

"You'll have to excuse an old woman, Patience dear, but I really must speak with Vane privately." Minnie beamed impartially on them both, then laid her hand on Vane's sleeve.

He immediately covered it with his. "I'm yours to command."

Despite his words, Patience sensed his irritation, his annoyance that Minnie had spiked the gun he'd turned on her. There was an instant's hiatus, then he smiled charmingly down at Minnie. "Your rooms?"

"Please—so sorry to drag you away."

"Not at all—you're the reason I'm here."

Minnie beamed at his flattery. Vane raised his head and met Patience's eyes. His smile still in place, he inclined his head. "Miss Debbington."

Patience returned his nod and quelled another shiver. He might have surrendered gracefully, but she had the distinct impression he hadn't given up.

She watched him cross the room, Minnie on his arm, chattering animatedly; he walked with head bent, his attention fixed on Minnie. Patience frowned. From the instant she'd recognized his style, she'd equated Vane Cynster with her father, another smooth-tongued, suavely elegant gentleman. All she knew about the species she'd learned from him, her restless, handsome sire. And what she'd learned she'd learned well—there was no chance she'd succumb to a well-set pair of shoulders and a devilish smile.

Her mother had loved her father—dearly, deeply, entirely too well. Unfortunately, men such as he were not the loving kind—not the kind wise women loved, for they did not value love, and would not accept it, nor return it. Worse, at least in Patience's eyes, such men had no sense of family life, no love in their soul to tie them to their hearth, their children. From all she had seen from her earliest years, elegant gentlemen avoided deep feelings. Avoided commitment, avoided love.

To them, marriage was a matter of estate, not a matter of the heart. Woe betide any woman who failed to understand that.

All that being so, Vane Cynster was high on her list of gentlemen she would definitely *not* wish Gerrard to have as his mentor. The very last thing she would allow was for Gerrard to turn out like his father. That he had that propensity none could deny, but she would fight to the last gasp to prevent him going that road.

Straightening her shoulders, Patience glanced around the room, noting the others, before the fireplace and about the *chaise*. With Vane and Minnie gone, the room seemed quieter, less colorful, less alive. As she watched, Gerrard threw a brief, watchful glance at the door.

Draining her teacup, Patience inwardly humphed. She would need to protect Gerrard from Vane Cynster's corrupting influence—nothing could be clearer.

A niggle of doubt slid into her mind, along with the image

of Vane behaving so attentively—and, yes, affectionately—toward Minnie. Patience frowned. Possibly corrupting. She shouldn't, she supposed, judge him by his wolf's clothing, yet that characteristic, in all her twenty-six years, had never proved wrong.

Then again, neither her father, nor his elegant friends, nor the others of that ilk she had met, had possessed a sense of humor. At least, not the sort of sparring, fencing humor Vane Cynster deployed. It was very hard to resist the challenge of striking back—of joining in the game.

Patience's frown deepened. Then she blinked, stiffened, and swept across the room to return her empty teacup to the trolley.

Vane Cynster was *definitely* corrupting.

Chapter 3

❧❦❧

VANE HELPED MINNIE up the stairs and down the gloomy corridors. After Sir Humphrey's death, she'd removed to a large suite at the end of one wing; Timms occupied the room next door.

Minnie paused outside her door. "A stroke of fate you should stop by just now."

I know. Vane suppressed the words. "How so?" He set the door wide.

"There's something strange going on." Leaning heavily on her cane now she was no longer "in public," Minnie crossed to the armchair by the hearth. Closing the door, Vane followed. "I'm not at all sure what it is"—Minnie settled in the chair, arranging her shawls—"but I do know I don't like it."

Vane propped his shoulder against the mantelpiece. "Tell me."

Minnie's brow furrowed. "I can't recall when it actually started, but it was sometime after Patience and Gerrard arrived." She looked up at Vane. "That's not to say I think they have anything to do with it—their arrival is merely a convenient gauge of time."

Vane inclined his head. "What did you notice?"

"The thefts started first. Little things—small items of jewelry, snuff boxes, trinkets, knickknacks. Anything small and portable—things that could fit in a pocket."

Vane's face hardened. "How many thefts have there been?"

"I don't know. None of us do. Often, things have been gone for days, even weeks, before they're noticed as missing. They're those sort of things."

Things that might fall into a flower bed. Vane frowned. "You said the thefts came first—what followed?"

"Odd happenings." Minnie's sigh overflowed with exasperation. "They're calling it 'the Spectre.' "

"A ghost?" Vane blinked. "There are no ghosts here."

"Because you and Devil would have found them if there had been?" Minnie chuckled. "Quite right." Then she sobered. "Which is why I know it's the work of someone alive. Someone in my household."

"No new servants—new helpers in the gardens?"

Minnie shook her head. "Everyone's been with me for years. Masters is as mystified as I."

"Hmm." Vane straightened. The disapproval aimed at Gerrard Debbington started to make sense. "What does this Spectre do?"

"It makes noises, for a start." Minnie's eyes flashed. "Always starts up just after I've fallen asleep." She gestured to the windows. "I'm a light sleeper, and these rooms look out over the ruins."

"What sort of noises?"

"Moans and clunks—and a grating noise, as if stones are grinding against each other."

Vane nodded. He and Devil had shifted enough stones in the ruins for him to remember the sound vividly.

"And then there's lights darting about the ruins. You know what it's like here—even in summer, we get a ground fog at night, rolling up from the river."

"Has anyone attempted to catch this Spectre?"

Chins setting, Minnie shook her head. "I refused to countenance it—I insisted they all give me their word they won't venture it. You know what the ruins are like, how dangerous it can be, even in broad daylight. Chasing a will-o'-the-wisp at night through the fog is insanity. Broken limbs, broken heads— no! I won't hear of it."

"And have they all held to their promise?"

"As far as I know." Minnie grimaced. "But you know this

house—there's doors and windows aplenty they could get in or out. And I *know* one of them is the Spectre."

"Which means if he's getting out and in without being detected, others could." Vane folded his arms. "Go through the household—who has any interest in the ruins?"

Minnie held up her fingers. "Whitticombe, of course. I told you of his studies?" Vane nodded. Minnie went on: "Then there's Edgar—he's read all the biographies of the abbots and those of the early Bellamys. He has quite an interest there. And I should include the General—the ruins have been his favorite walk for years." She progressed to her last finger. "And Edmond with his play—and Gerrard, of course. Both spend time in the ruins—Edmond communing with his muse, Gerrard sketching." She frowned at her hand, having run out of fingers. "And lastly, there's Patience, but her interest is simply abiding curiosity. She likes to poke about on her walks."

Vane could imagine. "None of the other women or Henry Chadwick has any particular interest?"

Minnie shook her head.

"That's quite a cast of characters—five men all told."

"Exactly." Minnie stared at the fire. "I don't know what worries me more, the Spectre or the thief." She heaved a sigh, then looked up at Vane. "I wanted to ask, dear boy, if you would stay and sort it out."

Vane looked down, into Minnie's face, at the soft cheeks he'd kissed innumerable times, at the bright eyes that had scolded and teased and loved him so well. For one instant, the image of another face interposed, that of Patience Debbington. Similar bone structure, similar eyes. Fate, once again, stared him in the face.

But he couldn't refuse, couldn't walk away—every particle of his Cynster character refused to consider it. Cynsters never accepted defeat, although they often courted danger. Minnie was family—to be defended to the death.

Vane refocused on Minnie's face, her own once again; he opened his lips—

A shrill scream split the stillness, rending the night.

Vane hauled open Minnie's door before the first echo faded. Less intense screeches guided him through the maze of the Hall, through the ill-lit corridors, up and down stairways joining the uneven levels. He tracked the screams to the corridor in the wing opposite Minnie's, one floor up.

The source of the screams was Mrs. Chadwick.

When he reached her she was near swooning, propped against a side table, one hand pressed to her ample breast.

"A man!" She clutched Vane's sleeve and pointed down the corridor. "In a long cloak—I saw him standing there, just in front of my door."

The door in question was shrouded in gloom. Only one sconce holding a single candle lit the corridor, casting a weak glow by the intersection behind them. Footsteps came hurrying, pounding on the polished floors. Vane put Mrs. Chadwick from him. "Wait here."

Boldly, he strode down the corridor.

There was no one lurking in the shadows. He strode to the end, to where stairs led up and down. There was no sound of retreating footsteps. Vane retraced his steps. The household was gathering about Mrs. Chadwick—Patience and Gerrard were there; so, too, was Edgar. Reaching Mrs. Chadwick's door, Vane set it wide, then entered.

There was no one in the room, either.

By the time he returned to Mrs. Chadwick, she was bathed in light cast by a candelabrum Patience held high and sipping water from a glass. Her color had improved.

"I'd just come from Angela's room." She glanced fleetingly at Vane; he could have sworn her color deepened. "We were having a little chat." She took another sip, then continued, her voice strengthening, "I was going to my room when I saw him." She pointed down the corridor. "Right there."

"Standing before your door?"

Mrs. Chadwick nodded. "With his hand on the latch."

Just going in. Considering the time it had taken him to traverse half the house, the thief—if that's who it had been—would have had ample time to disappear. Vane frowned. "You said something about a cloak."

Mrs. Chadwick nodded. "A long cloak."

Or the skirts of a woman's dress. Vane looked back down the corridor. Even with the additional light thrown by the candelabrum, it would be hard to be sure if a figure was male or female. And a thief could be either.

"Just *think*! We could be murdered in our beds!"

All heads, and it was indeed all—Minnie's household had assembled in its entirety—swung Angela's way.

Eyes huge, she stared back. "It must be some madman!"

"Why?"

Vane had opened his mouth to voice the question; Patience beat him to it. "Why on earth would someone come all the way out here," she continued, "struggle into this particular house, go to your mother's door—and then vanish as soon as she screamed? If it was a madman intent on murder, he had plenty of time to do the deed."

Both Mrs. Chadwick and Angela stared at her, stunned by her ruthless common sense.

Vane forced his lips straight. "There's no need for melodrama—whoever it was is long gone." But possibly not far away.

The same thought had occurred to Whitticombe. "Is everybody here?" He looked about, as did the others, comfirming that indeed, everyone was present, even Masters, who stood at the back of the crowd. "Well, then," Whitticombe said, scanning the faces, "where *was* everyone? Gerrard?"

Vane was quite sure it wasn't chance that had brought that name first to Whitticombe's lips.

Gerrard was standing behind Patience. "I was in the billiard room."

"Alone?" Whitticombe's insinuation was transparent.

Gerrard's jaw set. "Yes, alone."

The General grunted. "Why on earth would someone spend time in the billiard room alone?"

Color crept into Gerrard's cheeks. He flicked a glance at Vane. "I was just knocking a few balls around."

That swift glance was enough for Vane; Gerrard had been practicing shots, waiting for him to come down. The billiard room was precisely the sort of place a gentleman such as he might be expected to choose to spend an hour or so before retiring. Indeed, if events had not taken the course they had, he would have gone there himself.

Vane didn't like the accusing stares that were being aimed at Gerrard. Neither did Patience, Minnie, or Timms. He spoke before they could. "That's you accounted for. Where was everyone else?"

He made each one state their last location. Bar himself and Minnie, Angela, Mrs. Chadwick, Patience, and Timms, not one had been in sight of anyone else. Whitticombe had returned to the library; Edgar had gone in to retrieve a tome, then retreated to the back parlor. Edmond, oblivious to all once his muse had taken hold, as apparently it had, had remained in the drawing room. The General, irritated by Edmond's spontaneous spoutings, had slipped back to the dining room. From his deepened color, Vane suspected the brandy decanter had been his goal. Henry Chadwick had retired to his room.

When Vane asked for her whereabouts, Alice Colby glared at him. "I was in my room, one floor below this."

Vane merely nodded. "Very well. I suggest that now the thief is long gone, we should all retire."

In the face of that dampeningly dull suggestion, most of the party, muttering and grumbling, did so. Gerrard hung back, but when Patience noticed and gave him a push, he shot an apologetic glance at Vane and went. Predictably, Patience, Minnie, and Timms stood their ground.

Vane eyed their set faces, then sighed and waved them back. "In Minnie's room." He took Minnie's arm, concerned when he felt how heavily she leaned on him. He was tempted to carry her, but knew her pride of old. So he matched his pace to hers. By the time they reached her rooms, Timms had the fire blazing and Patience had plumped the cushions in Minnie's chair. Vane helped her to it and she sank down with a weary sigh.

"It wasn't Gerrard."

The trenchant statement came from Timms. "I can't abide how they all cast suspicion his way. They're making him a scapegoat."

Minnie nodded. Patience simply met Vane's eyes. She stood by Minnie's chair, head up, hands clasped too tightly before her, daring him to accuse her brother.

Vane's lips twisted wryly. "He was waiting for me." Strolling forward, he took up his customary position, shoulders propped against the mantelpiece. "Which, the last time I checked, wasn't a crime."

Timms sniffed. "Exactly so. That much was obvious."

"If we're agreed on that, then I suggest we forget the incident. There's no way I can see to link it to anyone."

"Masters couldn't fault any of the other alibis." Patience lifted her chin when Vane looked her way. "I asked him."

Vane regarded her for a moment, then nodded. "So tonight has revealed nothing—there's nothing more to do but head for bed."

He kept his eyes on Patience's face; after a moment, she inclined her head. "As you say." She bent down to Minnie. "If you don't need me, ma'am?"

Minnie forced a tired smile. "No, my love." She clasped Patience's hand. "Timms will take care of me."

Patience kissed Minnie's cheek. Straightening, she exchanged a conspiratorial look with Timms, then glided to the door. Vane fell in in her wake, reaching around her as she halted before the door to open it. Their positions were the same as they'd been that afternoon, when he'd deliberately discomposed her. This time it was she who hesitated, then glanced up, into his face. "You don't believe it was Gerrard."

Half question, half statement. Vane held her gaze, then shook his head. "I know it wasn't Gerrard. Your brother couldn't lie to save himself—and he didn't try."

Briefly, she searched his eyes, then inclined her head. Vane opened the door, closed it behind her, then headed back to the fire.

"Well," Minnie sighed. "Will you take on my commission?"

Vane looked down at her and let his Cynster smile show. "After that little interlude, how could I refuse?" How indeed.

"Thank heavens!" Timms declared. "Lord knows we need a little sound sense around here."

Vane stored that comment up in case of later need—he suspected Patience Debbington thought she had the sound sense market cornered. "I'll start nosing around tomorrow. Until then—" He looked at Minnie. "As I said, it would be best to forget about tonight."

Minnie smiled. "Knowing you'll be staying will be enough to ease my mind."

"Good." With a nod, Vane straightened and turned.

"Oh—ah, Vane . . . ?"

He glanced back, one brow rising, but didn't halt in his progress to the door. "I know—but don't ask me for a promise I won't keep."

Minnie frowned. "Just take care of yourself—I wouldn't want to have to face your mother if you break a leg, or, worse yet, your head."

"Rest assured—I don't intend to break either." Vane glanced back from the door, one brow arrogantly high. "As you've no doubt heard, we Cynsters are invincible."

With a rakish grin, he left; Minnie watched the door close. Reluctantly smiling, she tugged at her slipping shawls. "Invincible? Huh!"

Timms came to help. "Given all seven of the present generation returned from Waterloo, unscathed and with nary a scratch, I'd say they have some claim to the title."

Minnie made a distinctly rude sound. "I've known Vane and Devil from the cradle—and the others almost as well." She poked Timms's arm affectionately. With her help, she struggled to her feet. "They're very much mortal men, as hot-blooded and bold as they come." Her words gave her pause, then she chuckled. "They may not be invincible, but be damned if they're not the next best thing."

"Precisely." Timms smiled. "So we can leave our problems on Vane's shoulders—Lord knows, they're broad enough."

Minnie grinned. "Very true. Well, then—let's get me to bed."

Vane made sure he was early down to breakfast. When he entered the breakfast parlor, only Henry was present, working his way through a plate of sausages. Exchanging an amiable nod, Vane headed for the sideboard.

He was heaping a plate with slices of ham when Masters appeared, bearing another platter. He set it down on the sideboard. Raising a brow, Vane caught his eye. "No sign of any break-in?"

"No, sir." Masters had been Minnie's butler for twenty and more years. He knew Vane well. "I did my rounds early. The ground floor had already been secured before the . . . incident. I checked again afterward—there was no door or window left open."

Which was no more nor less than Vane had expected. He nodded noncommittally and Masters left.

Strolling to the table, Vane drew out the chair at its end.

Henry, in the next chair along, looked up as he sat. "Dashed odd business, last night. The mater's still shaken. Hate to say it, but I really do feel young Gerrard's gone far enough with this 'Spectre' nonsense."

Vane raised his brows. "Actually—"

A snort from the door cut him off; Whitticombe entered. "The young bounder should be thrashed—scaring gently bred females like that. Needs a firm hand applied to his reins—he's been left in the care of women too long."

Inwardly, Vane stiffened; outwardly, not a ripple marred his habitually urbane expression. He swallowed an impulse to defend Patience, and Minnie, too. Instead, he manufactured an expression of boredom only mildly piqued. "Why are you so sure it was Gerrard last night?"

At the sideboard, Whitticombe turned, but was beaten to speech by the General. "Stands to reason," he wheezed, stumping in. "Who else could it have been, heh?"

Again, Vane's brows rose. "Almost anyone, as far as I could see."

"Nonsense!" the General huffed, leaning his stick against the sideboard.

"Other than myself, Minnie, Timms, Miss Debbington, Angela, and Mrs. Chadwick," Vane reiterated, "any one of you could have been the culprit."

Turning, the General glared at him from under overhanging brows. "You've shaken a screw loose with too much racketing about. Why the devil would any of *us* want to put the wind up Agatha Chadwick?"

Gerrard, bright-eyed, swung through the door—and came to a dead halt. His face, initially filled with boyish anticipation, drained of expression.

Vane trapped Gerrard's gaze, then, with his eyes, indicated the sideboard. "Indeed," he drawled as Gerrard, now stiff and tense, moved to serve himself, "but, using precisely the same reasoning, why would Gerrard?"

The General scowled and shot a glance at Gerrard's back. Carrying a plate piled high with kedgeree, the General pulled out a chair farther along the table. Whitticombe, tight-lipped, censoriously silent, took a place opposite.

Frowning, Henry shifted in his seat. He, too, looked at Gerrard, busy at the sideboard, then studied his now-empty plate. "I don't know—but I suppose boys will be boys."

"As one who used that excuse to extremes, I feel compelled to point out that Gerrard is several years past the stage where that explanation applies." Vane met Gerrard's eyes as he turned from the sideboard, a full plate in his hands. Gerrard's face was lightly flushed, his gaze watchful. Vane smiled easily and waved to the chair beside his. "But perhaps he can suggest something? What say you, Gerrard—can you give us a reason why someone might want to scare Mrs. Chadwick?"

To his credit, Gerrard didn't rush into speech; he frowned as he set his plate down, then shook his head slowly as he sat. "I can't think of any reason why anyone would want to make Mrs. Chadwick screech." He grimaced at the memory. "But"— he flicked a grateful glance at Vane—"I did wonder if the fright was incidental and the person at the door was really the thief."

The suggestion made all at the table think—after a moment, Henry nodded. "Could be—indeed, why not?"

"Regardless," Whitticombe put in, "I can't conceive who this thief could be either." His tone made it clear he still suspected Gerrard.

Vane directed a mildly questioning glance at Gerrard.

Encouraged, Gerrard shrugged. "I can't see what any of us would want with all the knickknacks and fripperies that have disappeared."

The General gave one of his distinguishing snorts. "Perhaps because they're fripperies? Just the sort of things to woo a flighty maid with, heh?" His penetrating stare again fixed on Gerrard.

Ready color rose to Gerrard's cheeks.

"Not guilty! On my honor, I swear it!"

The words came in ringing tones from the doorway. They all looked around—on the threshold, Edmond stood poised in the attitude of a supplicant pleading for justice from the bench. He broke from his pose; grinning, he bowed, then straightened and loped to the sideboard. "Sorry to disappoint you, but I feel obliged to puncture that fantasy. None of the maids here would accept such tokens of esteem—the staff have all been alerted to the thefts. And as for the surrounding villages"—he paused dramatically and rolled an anguished eye at Vane—"*believe me,* there's not a likely miss within a day's ride!"

Vane hid his grin behind his coffee cup; over the rim, he met Gerrard's laughing eyes.

The sound of briskly swishing skirts drew all eyes to the door. Patience appeared in the doorway. Chairs scraped as they all made to rise. She waved them back. Pausing on the threshold, she swiftly scanned the room, her gaze fixing at the last on Gerrard. And his affectionate smile.

Vane noticed the way Patience's breasts rose and fell, noticed the light blush in her cheeks. She'd been scurrying.

She blinked, then, with a general nod, headed for the sideboard.

Vane redirected the conversation to matters less fraught.

"The Northants Hunt is the nearest," Henry replied to his question.

At the sideboard, Patience forced herself to breathe deeply while absentmindedly filling her plate. She'd intended to wake early and be here in time to protect Gerrard. Instead, she'd slept in, drained by escalating worry, followed by unsettling dreams. The other ladies generally took breakfast on trays in their chambers, a habit to which she'd never subscribed. Ears tuned to the rumble of conversation behind her, she heard Vane's lazy drawl and felt her skin prickle. She frowned.

She knew the male members of the household too well—there was no possiblity they'd omitted to mention last night's contretemps, nor that they hadn't, in one way or another, accused Gerrard of it. But he was clearly unperturbed, which could mean only one thing. For whatever reason, Vane Cynster had taken up the cudgels in her stead and deflected the household's unreasoning suspicions of Gerrard. Her frown deepened as she heard Gerrard's voice, youthful enthusiasm ringing as he described a nearby ride.

Eyes widening, Patience picked up her plate and whirled. She advanced on the table, to the chair beside Gerrard. Masters drew it out and held it while she sat.

Gerrard turned to her. "I was just telling Vane that Minnie kept the best of Sir Humphrey's hunters. And the rides hereabouts are quite reasonable."

His eyes glowed with a light Patience hadn't seen in them before. Smiling, he turned back to Vane. Her heart sinking, Patience looked to the head of the table, too. Vane sat relaxed, wide shoulders encased in a grey hacking jacket settled comfortably against the chair back, one hand resting on the chair's arm, the other stretched on the table, long fingers crooked about the handle of a coffee cup.

In daylight, his features were as hard-edged as she'd thought them, his face every bit as strong. His heavy lids hid his eyes as, with lazy interest, he listened to Gerrard extol the equestrian virtues of the locality.

To her right, the General snorted, then pushed back his chair. Whitticombe rose, too. One after the other, they left the room. Frowning, Patience applied herself to her breakfast and tried to think of another subject with which to capture the conversation.

Vane saw her frown. The devil in him stirred and stretched, then settled to contemplate this latest challenge. She would, he felt sure, avoid him. Shifting his hooded gaze, he studied Gerrard. Vane smiled. Lazily. He waited until Patience took a bite of her toast.

"Actually," he drawled, "I was thinking of filling in the morning with a ride. Anyone interested?"

Gerrard's eager response was instantaneous; Patience's response, though far less eager, was no less rapid. Vane stifled a grin at the sight of her stunned expression as, with her mouth inhibitingly full, she heard Gerrard accept his invitation with undisguised delight.

Patience looked out through the long parlor windows. The day was fine, a brisk breeze drying the puddles. She swallowed, and looked at Vane. "I thought you would be leaving."

He smiled, a slow, devilish, fascinating smile. "I've decided to stay for a few days."

Damn! Patience bit back the word and looked across the table at Edmond.

Who shook his head. "Not for me. The muse calls—I must do her bidding."

Patience inwardly cursed, and switched her gaze to Henry. He considered, then grimaced. "A good idea, but I should check on Mama first. I'll catch up if I can."

Vane inclined his head, and slanted a smiling glance at Gerrard. "Looks like it's just the two of us, then."

"No!" Patience coughed to disguise the abruptness of her answer; then took a sip of tea and looked up. "If you'll wait while I change, I'll come, too."

She met Vane's eyes, and saw the grey glint wickedly. But he smoothly, graciously, inclined his head, accepting her company, which was all she cared about. Setting down her teacup, she rose. "I'll meet you at the stables."

Rising with his customary grace, Vane watched as she left, then sank back, elegantly asprawl. He lifted his coffee cup, thus hiding his victorious smile. Gerrard, after all, wasn't blind. "Ten minutes, do you think?" He lifted a brow at Gerrard.

"Oh, at least." Gerrard grinned and reached for the coffee-pot.

Chapter 4

B Y THE TIME she gained the stable yard, Patience had the bit firmly between her teeth. Vane Cynster was not a suitable mentor for Gerrard, but, given the evidence of her eyes, Gerrard was already well on the way to an unhealthy respect, which could all too easily lead to adulation. Hero worship. Dangerous emulation.

It was all very clear in her mind.

The train of her lavender-velvet riding habit over her arm, she strode into the yard, heels ringing on the cobbles. Her reading of the situation was instantly confirmed.

Vane sat a massive grey hunter with elegant ease, effortlessly controlling the restive beast. Beside him, on a chestnut gelding, Gerrard blithely chatted. He looked happier, more relaxed, than he had since they'd arrived. Patience noted it, but, halting in the shadows of the stable arch, her attention remained riveted on Vane Cynster.

Her mother had often remarked that "true gentlemen" looked uncommonly dashing on horseback. Quelling an inward sniff—her normal reaction to that observation, which had invariably alluded to her father—Patience reluctantly conceded she could now see her mother's point: There was something about the harnessed power of the man, dominating and harnessing the power of the beast, that made her stomach tighten. The clop of hooves had drowned out her approach; she stared for a minute longer, then gave herself a mental shake, and walked forward.

Grisham had the brown mare she favored saddled and waiting; Patience ascended the mounting block, then climbed into the saddle. She settled her skirts and picked up the reins.

"Ready?"

The question came from Vane. Patience nodded.

Naturally, *he* led the way out.

The morning greeted them, crisp and clear. Pale grey clouds dotted the washed-out sky; the smell of damp greenery was all-pervasive. Their first stop was a knoll, three miles from the Hall. Vane had ridden the fidgets from his mount in a series of short gallops that Patience had tried hard not to watch. After that, the grey had cantered beside her mare. Gerrard had ridden on her other side. None of them had spoken, content to look about and let the cool air refresh them.

Reining in beside Vane on the top of the knoll, Patience looked around. Beside her, Gerrard scanned the horizon, gauging the view. Twisting in his saddle, he eyed the steep mound beyond Vane, covering one end of the knoll.

"Here." Thrusting his reins into her hands, Gerrard dismounted. "I'm going to check the view."

Patience glanced at Vane, sitting his grey with deceptive ease, hands crossed on the saddlebow. He smiled lazily at Gerrard but made no move to follow. They watched as Gerrard scrambled up the steep sloping side of the mound. Gaining the top, he waved, then looked about. After a moment, he sank down, his gaze fixed in the distance.

Patience grinned and transferred her gaze to Vane's face. "I'm afraid he might be hours. He's very much taken with landscapes at present."

To her surprise, the grey eyes watching her showed no sign of alarm at that news. Instead, Vane's long lips curved. "I know," he said. "He mentioned his current obsession, so I told him about the old burial mound."

He paused, then added, his eyes still on hers, his smile deepening, "The views are quite spectacular." His eyes glinted. "Guaranteed to hold a budding artist's attention for a considerable space of time."

Patience, her gaze locked in the grey of his, felt a tingling sensation run over her skin. She blinked, then frowned. "How kind of you." She turned to study the views herself. And again felt that odd sensation, a ripple of awareness sliding over her nerves, leaving them sensitized. It was most peculiar. She would have put it down to the touch of the breeze, but the wind wasn't that cold.

Beside her, Vane raised his brows, his predator's smile still in evidence. Her lavender habit was not new, hardly fashionable, yet it hugged her contours, emphasizing their softness, leaving him with an urgent longing to fill his arms with their warmth. The grey shifted; Vane steadied him. "Minnie mentioned you and your brother hail from Derbyshire. Do you ride much while there?"

"As much as I can." Patience glanced his way. "I enjoy the exercise, but the rides in the vicinity of the Grange are rather restricted. Are you familiar with the area around Chesterfield?"

"Not specifically." Vane grinned. "That's a bit farther north than my usual hunting grounds."

For foxes—or females? Patience stifled a humph. "From your knowledge of the locality"—she glanced at the mound beside them—"I take it you've visited here before?"

"Often as a child. My cousin and I spent a few weeks here most summers."

Patience humphed. "I'm surprised Minnie survived."

"On the contrary—she thrived on our visits. She always delighted in our exploits and adventures."

When she returned no further comment, Vane softly said, "Incidentally, Minnie mentioned the odd thefts that have occurred at the Hall." Patience looked up; he trapped her gaze. "Is that what you were looking for in the flower bed? Something that disappeared?"

Patience hesitated, searching his eyes, then nodded. "I told myself Myst must have knocked it out of the window, but I hunted high and low, in the room and in the flower bed. I couldn't find it anywhere."

"What was 'it'?"

"A small silver vase." She sketched the shape of a bud vase. "About four inches high. I've had it for years—I don't suppose it's particularly valuable, but . . ."

"You'd rather have it than not. Why were you so keen not to mention it last night?"

Her face setting, Patience met Vane's eyes. "You aren't going to tell me the *gentlemen* of the household didn't happen to mention over the breakfast table this morning that they think Gerrard is behind all these odd occurrences—the Spectre, as they call it, and the thefts as well?"

"They did, as it happens, but we—Gerrard, myself, and, surprisingly enough, Edmond—pointed out that that notion has no real foundation."

The unladylike sound Patience made was eloquent—of irritation, frustration, and overstretched tolerance.

"Indeed," Vane concurred, "so you have yet another reason to feel grateful to me." As Patience swung his way, he frowned. "And Edmond, unfortunately."

Despite herself, Patience's lips quirked. "Edmond would gainsay the elders simply for a joke—he doesn't take anything seriously, other than his muse."

"I'll take your word for it."

Instead of being distracted, Patience continued to study his face. Vane raised one brow. "I did tell you," he murmured, holding her gaze, "that I'm determined to put you in my debt. You needn't concern yourself over the gentlemen's attitude to Gerrard while I'm about." He didn't think her pride would allow her to accept an outright offer of a broad shoulder to deflect the slings and arrows of the present Hall society; presenting his aid in the guise of a rake's machinations, would, he hoped, permit her to let the matter go with a shrug and a tart comment.

What he got was a frown. "Well, I do thank you if you tried to set them straight." Patience glanced up to where Gerrard was still communing with the horizon. "But you can see why I didn't want to make a fuss over my vase—they'd only blame Gerrard."

Vane raised his brows noncommittally. "Whatever. If anything more disappears, tell me, or Minnie, or Timms."

Patience looked at him and frowned. "What—"

"Who's this?" Vane nodded at a horseman cantering toward them.

Patience looked, then sighed. "Hartley Penwick." Although her expression remained bland, her tone grimaced. "He's the son of one of Minnie's neighbors."

"Well met, my dear Miss Debbington!" Penwick, a well-set gentleman attired in tweed jacket and corduroy breeches, and astride a heavy roan, swept Patience a bow more wide than it was elegant. "I trust I find you well?"

"Indeed, sir." Patience gestured to Vane. "Allow me to make you known to Lady Bellamy's godson." Briefly, she introduced Vane, adding the information that he had stopped to take shelter from last night's storm.

"Ah." Penwick shook Vane's hand. "So your visit's in the nature of a forced halt. Daresay you'll be on your way soon. The sun's drying the roads nicely, and there's nothing in this backwater to compare with *ton*nish pursuits."

If Penwick had declared that he wanted him gone, he could not have been more explicit. Vane smiled, a gesture full of teeth. "Oh, I'm in no especial hurry."

Penwick's brows rose; his eyes, watchful from the instant he had beheld Vane, grew harder. "Ah—on a repairing lease, I take it?"

"No." Vane's gaze grew chilly, his diction more precise. "I'm merely in the way of pleasing myself."

That information did not please Penwick. Patience was about to step into the breach, to protect Penwick from likely annihilation, when Penwick, searching for the person to match the third horse, glanced up.

"Great heavens! *Get down* from there, you scallywag!"

Vane blinked and glanced up. Eyes glued to the horizon, the scallywag feigned deafness. Turning back, Vane heard Patience haughtily state: "It's perfectly all right, sir. He's looking at the views."

"Views!" Penwick snorted. "The sides of that mound are steep and slippery—what if he should fall?" He looked at Vane. "I'm surprised, Cynster, that you permitted young Debbington to embark on a mad scheme guaranteed to overturn his sister's sensiblities."

Patience, suddenly no longer sure of Gerrard's safety, looked at Vane.

His gaze on Penwick, Vane slowly raised his brows. Then he turned his head and met Patience's potentially worried gaze. "I thought Gerrard was seventeen?"

She blinked. "He is."

"Well, then." Vane sat back, shoulders relaxing. "Seventeen is more than old enough to be responsible for his own safety. If he breaks a leg on his way down, it will be entirely his own fault."

Patience stared at him—and wondered why her lips insisted on twitching upward. Vane's eyes met hers; the calm, rocklike confidence she saw in the grey steadied her—and steadied her confidence in Gerrard.

The unsuccessfully muffled laugh that drifted over their heads forced her to straighten her lips and turn to Penwick. "I'm sure Gerrard is more than capable of managing."

Penwick came close to scowling.

"Here's Edmond." Patience looked past Penwick as Edmond urged his mount up the rise. "I thought you were trapped by your muse?"

"Fought free of it," Edmond informed her with a grin. He nodded at Penwick, then turned back to Patience. "Thought you might be glad of more company."

While Edmond's expression remained ingenuous, Patience was left with little doubt as to his thinking. She fought an urge to glance at Vane, to see if he, too, had picked up the implication; she was quite sure he would have—the man was certainly not slow.

That last was borne out by the purring murmur that slid past her right ear. "We've just been admiring the views."

On the instant, before she'd even turned to him, that tingling sensation washed over her again, more intense, more wickedly evocative than before. Patience caught her breath and refused to meet his eyes. She allowed her gaze to rise only as far as his lips. They quirked, then eased into a teasing smile.

"And here's Chadwick."

Patience swallowed a groan. She turned and confirmed that Henry was, indeed, trotting up to join them. Her lips set; she'd only come on the ride because none of them had been interested in riding—and now here they all were, with even Penwick thrown in, riding to her rescue!

She didn't need rescuing! Or protecting! She wasn't in the slightest danger of succumbing to any "elegant gentleman's" rakish lures. Not, she had to concede, that Vane had thrown any her way. He might be considering it, but his subtlety left the others looking like floundering puppies, yapping in their earnest haste.

"Such a fine day—couldn't resist the thought of a brisk ride." Henry beamed engagingly at her; the image of a panting puppy, tongue lolling in a hopeful canine grin, impinged forcefully on Patience's mind.

"Now we're all gathered," Vane drawled, "perhaps we should ride on?"

"Indeed," Patience agreed. Anything to cut short this farcical gathering.

"Gerrard, come down—your horse has forgotten why it's out here." Vane's command, delivered in world-weary tones, elicited nothing more than a chuckle from Gerrard.

He stood, stretched, nodded to Patience, then disappeared around the other side of the mound. Within minutes, he reappeared at ground level, dusting his hands. He grinned at Vane, nodded to Edmond and Henry, and ignored Penwick. Accepting his reins, he flashed Patience a smile, then swung up to the saddle. "Shall we?"

A lift of one brow and a brief wave accompanied the question. Patience stiffened—she stared. She knew precisely where Gerrard had picked up both those little mannerisms.

"How were the views?" Edmond paired his horse with Gerrard's. They led the way down the rise, Gerrard responding readily, describing various vistas and expounding on the interplay of light, cloud, and haze.

Her gaze fixed on Gerrard, Patience set her horse to follow his. Consternation ensued. With Vane holding steady on her right, Penwick and Henry jostled for the position on her left. By dint of defter management, Penwick secured the prize, leaving Henry sulking in the rear. Inwardly, Patience sighed, and made a mental note to be kind to Henry later.

Within three minutes, she would gladly have strangled Penwick.

"I flatter myself, Miss Debbington, that you are clear-sighted enough to comprehend that I have your best interests at heart." That was Penwick's beginning. From there he progressed to: "I cannot but be convinced it does your sisterly sensitivities, those softer emotions with which gentlewomen are so well endowed, no good at all to be constantly abraded by the youthful but sadly inconsiderate exploits of your brother."

Patience kept her gaze on the fields and let Penwick's dissertation pass her by. She knew he wouldn't notice her abstraction. Other men always brought out the worst in Penwick—in his case, the worst was an unassailable belief in his own judgment, combined with an unshakable certainty that she not only shared his views, but was well on the way to being Mrs. Penwick. How he'd arrived at such a conclusion Patience was at a loss to understand; she'd never given him the slightest encouragement.

His portentous pronouncements flowed past her as they ambled on. Henry fidgeted, then coughed, then butted in with: "Do you think we'll get more rain?"

Patience fell on the witless question with relief and used it to distract Penwick, whose other obsession, beyond the sound of his own voice, was his fields. By dint of a few artless inquiries, she set Henry and Penwick to arguing over the effect of the recent rain on the crops.

Throughout, Vane said nothing. He didn't have to. Patience was quite sure of his thoughts—as cynical as her own. His silence was more eloquent, more powerful, more successful in impinging on her senses, than Penwick's pedantic statements or Henry's garrulous chatter.

To her right lay a sense of security, a front she did not, for the moment, need to defend. His silent presence gave her that; Patience inwardly sniffed. Yet another thing, she supposed, for which she should be grateful to him. He was proving adept at that cool, arrogant, subtle yet unrelenting maneuvering she associated with "elegant gentlemen." She was not surprised. From the first, she'd identified him as an expert practitioner.

Focusing on Gerrard, Patience heard him laugh. Over his shoulder, Edmond threw her a smiling glance, then reapplied himself to Gerrard. Then Gerrard made some comment, underscoring his point with the same indolent wave he'd used before.

Patience set her teeth. There was nothing wrong, *per se*, with the gesture, although Vane did it better. At seventeen, Gerrard's artist's hands, although well made, had yet to gain the strength and mature form Vane Cynster's hands possessed. When he performed that gesture, it reeked of a masculine power Gerrard had yet to attain.

But copying gestures was one thing—Patience worried that Gerrard's emulation would not stop there. Still, she reasoned, glancing swiftly at Vane riding quietly beside her, it was only a mannerism or two. Despite Penwick's beliefs, she was not a female overburdened with nonsensical sensivities. She was, perhaps, more acutely conscious of Vane Cynster and his propensities, more watchful than she would be with other men. But there seemed no real reason to intervene. Yet.

With a laugh, Gerrard broke away from Edmond; wheeling his horse, he brought his chestnut alongside Vane's grey. "I've been meaning to ask"—Gerrard's eyes shone with enthusiasm as he looked into Vane's face—"about those greys of yours."

A disturbance on her other side forced Patience to glance that way, so she missed Vane's answer. His voice was so deep that, when he was facing away from her, she couldn't discern his words.

The disturbance proved to be Edmond, taking advantage of Penwick's distraction with Henry to insinuate his horse between Penwick's and Patience's. "There!" Edmond blithely ignored Penwick's outraged glare. "I've been waiting to ask your opinion of my latest verse. It's for the scene where the abbot addresses the wandering brothers."

He proceeded to declaim the recent fruits of his brain.

Patience gritted her teeth; she felt literally torn. Edmond would expect her to comment intelligently on his work, which he took with all the seriousness he failed to devote to more worldly matters. On the other hand, she desperately wanted to know what Vane was saying to Gerrard. While one part of her mind followed Edmond's rhymes, she strained her ears to pick up Gerrard's words.

"So their chests are important?" he asked.

Rumble, rumble, rumble.

"Oh." Gerrard paused. "Actually, I thought weight would give a fair indication."

A long series of rumbles answered that.

"I see. So if they do have good stamina . . ."

Patience glanced to her right—Gerrard was now closer to Vane. She couldn't even hear his half of the conversation.

"So!" Edmond drew in a breath. "What do you think?"

Head snapping back, Patience met his eyes. "It didn't hold my interest—perhaps it needs more polish?"

"Oh." Edmond was deflated, but not cast down. He frowned. "Actually, I think you might be right."

Patience ignored him, edging her mare nearer Vane's grey. Vane glanced her way; both eyes and lips appeared gently amused. Patience ignored that, too, and concentrated on his words.

"Assuming they're up to the weight, the next most important criterion is their knees."

Knees? Patience blinked.

"High-steppers?" Gerrard suggested.

Patience stiffened.

"Not necessarily," Vane replied. "A good action, certainly, but there must be power behind the stride."

They were still talking about carriage horses; Patience almost sighed with relief. She continued to listen, but heard nothing more sinister. Just horses. Not even wagering or the racecourses.

Inwardly frowning, she settled back in her saddle. Her suspicions of Vane were well-founded, weren't they? Or was she overreacting?

"I'll take my leave of you here." Penwick's acid declaration cut across Patience's musing.

"Indeed, sir." She gave him her hand. "So kind of you to drop by. I'll mention to my aunt that we saw you."

Penwick blinked. "Oh, yes—that is, I trust you'll convey my regards to Lady Bellamy."

Patience smiled, coolly regal, and inclined her head. The gentlemen nodded; Vane's nod held an element of menace—how he managed it, Patience couldn't have said.

Penwick wheeled his horse and cantered off.

"Right then!" Free of Penwick's trenchantly disapproving presence, Gerrard grinned. "How about a race back to the stables?"

"You're on." Edmond gathered his reins. The lane to the stables lay on the other side of an open field. It was a straight run, with no fences or ditches to cause difficulty.

Henry chuckled indulgently and flicked Patience a smile. "I suppose I'll be in on it, too."

Gerrard looked at Vane.

Who smiled. "I'll give you a handicap—lead off."

Gerrard waited for no more. With a "Whoop!" he sprang his horse.

Edmond made to give chase, as did Henry, but, as Patience tapped her heels to her mare's sides, they moved off with her. Letting her mare have her head, Patience followed in her brother's wake; Gerrard was forging ahead, unchallenged. The three other men held their horses back, matching the mare's shorter strides.

Ridiculous! What possible benefit could any of them gain by keeping to her side over one short field? Patience fought to keep a straight face, to keep from grinning and shaking her head at the sheer silliness of men. As they neared the lane, she couldn't resist a brief glance at Vane.

Keeping station on her right, the grey held easily in check, he met her gaze—and raised one brow in weary self-deprecation.

Patience laughed—an answering gleam lit Vane's eyes. The lane drew near; he glanced forward. When he looked back, the light in his eyes had hardened, sharpened.

He edged his grey closer, crowding her mare. The mare reacted by lengthening her stride. Henry and Edmond fell behind, forced to hold back as the grey and the mare swept into the lane, only wide enough for two horses abreast.

Then they were clattering under the arch and into the yard. Pulling up, Patience dragged in a breath and looked back; Edmond and Henry were some way behind.

Gerrard, having won the race, laughed and set his chestnut prancing. Grisham and the grooms came running.

Patience looked at Vane and saw him dismount—by bringing his leg over the saddlebow and sliding to the ground, landing on his feet. She blinked, and he was by her side.

His hands closed about her waist.

She almost gasped when he lifted her from the saddle as if she weighed no more than a child. He didn't swing her down, but slowly lowered her to earth, setting her on her feet beside the mare. Less than a foot from him. He held her between his hands; she felt the long fingers flex about her, fingertips on either side of her spine, thumbs against her sensitive midriff. She felt . . . captured. Vulnerable. His face was a hard mask, his expression intent. Her eyes locked on his, Patience felt the cobbles beneath her feet, but her world continued to spin.

It *was* he—the source of those peculiar sensations. She'd thought it must be, but she'd never felt such sensations before— and those streaking through her now were far stronger than those she'd felt earlier. It was his touch that did it—the touch of his eyes, the touch of his hands. He didn't even need to contact bare skin to make every square inch she possessed react.

Patience dragged in a breath. A flicker at the edge of her vision made her shift her focus. To Gerrard. She saw him dismount, exactly as Vane had done. Grinning, brimming with prideful good humor, Gerrard crossed the cobbles toward them.

Vane turned, smoothly releasing her.

Patience dragged in another breath and fought to steady her giddy head. She plastered a bright smile on her lips for Gerrard's benefit—and continued to breathe deeply.

"A wily move, Cynster." Edmond, grinning good-naturedly, dismounted in the customary way. Patience noted it was a great deal slower than the way Vane had achieved the same end.

Henry also dismounted; Patience got the impression he hadn't liked seeing Vane lift her down. But he directed one of his hearty smiles at Gerrard. "Congratulations, my boy. You beat us fairly and squarely."

Which was laying it on a great deal too thick. Patience glanced swiftly at Gerrard, expecting some less than gracious response. Instead, her brother, standing beside Vane, merely raised one brow—and smiled cynically.

Patience gritted her teeth; her jaw set. Of one thing she was quite sure—she wasn't overreacting.

Vane Cynster was going too far, far too fast—at least with respect to Gerrard. As for the rest—his teasing of her senses— she suspected he was merely amusing himself without any serious intent. As she was not susceptible to seduction, there seemed no reason to call him to account for that.

Over Gerrard, however . . .

She mulled over the situation as the horses were led away. For a few moments, all four men stood together in the center of the yard; a little to one side, she studied them—and acknowledged she could hardly blame Gerrard for choosing Vane to emulate. He was the dominant male.

As if sensing her regard, he turned. One brow quirked, then, inherently graceful, he offered her his arm. Patience steeled herself and took it. As a group, they walked to the house; Edmond left them at the side door. They climbed the main stairs, then Gerrard and Henry turned aside, heading for their rooms. Still on Vane's arm, Patience strolled into the gallery. Her room was down the same corridor as Minnie's. Vane's was on the floor below.

There wasn't any point voicing her disapproval unless there was a real need. Patience paused in the archway leading from the gallery, from where they would go their separate ways. Drawing her hand from Vane's arm, she looked up, into his face. "Are you planning a long stay?"

He looked down at her. "That," he stated, his voice very low, "depends largely on you."

Patience looked into his grey eyes—and froze. Every muscle was paralyzed, all the way to her toes. The idea that he was amusing himself, without any real intent, died—slain by the look in his eyes.

The *intent* in his eyes.

It couldn't have been clearer had he put it into words.

Bravely, drawing on an inner reserve she hadn't known she possessed, she lifted her chin. And forced her lips to curve, just enough for a cool smile. "I think you'll find you're mistaken."

She uttered the words softly, and saw his jaw lock. A premonition of intense danger swept her; she didn't dare say anything more. With her smile still in place, she haughtily inclined her head. Sweeping about, she passed through the arch and into the safety of the corridor beyond.

Narrow-eyed, Vane watched her go, watched her hips sway as she glided along. He remained in the archway until she reached her door. He heard it shut behind her.

Slowly, very slowly, his features eased, then a Cynster smile tugged at his lips. If he couldn't escape fate, then, *ipso facto*, neither could she. Which meant she would be his. The prospect grew more alluring by the minute.

Chapter 5

❧❖❧

$\mathcal{I}$T WAS TIME to act.

Later that evening, waiting in the drawing room for the gentlemen to reappear, Patience found it increasingly difficult to live up to her name; inside, she mentally paced. Beside her, Angela and Mrs. Chadwick, occupying a settee, were discussing the best trim for Angela's new morning gown. Nodding vaguely, Patience didn't even hear them. She had weightier matters on her mind.

A dull ache throbbed behind her temples; she hadn't slept well. Worries had consumed her—worry over the increasingly pointed accusations aimed at Gerrard, worry over Vane Cynster's influence on her impressionable brother.

Added to that, she now had to cope with the distraction occasioned by her odd reaction to Vane Cynster, "elegant gentleman." He'd affected her from the first; when she'd finally succumbed to sleep, he'd even followed her into her dreams.

Patience narrowed her eyes against the ache behind them.

"I think the cerise braid would be *much* more dashing." Angela threatened a pout. "Don't you think so, Patience?"

The gown they were discussing was palest yellow. "I think," Patience said, summoning up what she could of that virtue, "that the aquamarine ribbon your mother suggested would be much more the thing."

Angela's pout materialized; Mrs. Chadwick promptly warned her daughter of the unwisdom of courting wrinkles. The pout magically vanished.

Drumming her fingers on the arm of her chair, Patience frowned at the door and returned to her preoccupation—to rehearsing her warning to Vane Cynster. It was the first time she'd had to warn any male off—she would much rather she didn't have to start now, but she couldn't let things go on as they were. Quite aside from her promise to her mother, tendered on her deathbed, that she would always keep Gerrard safe, she simply couldn't countenance Gerrard getting hurt in such a way—by being used as a pawn to win her smiles.

Of course, they all did it to some degree. Penwick treated Gerrard as a child, playing to her protectiveness. Edmond used his art as a link to Gerrard, to demonstrate his affinity with her brother. Henry pretended an avuncular interest patently lacking in real emotion. Vane, however, went one better—he actually did things. Actively protected Gerrard, actively engaged her brother's interest, actively interacted—all with the avowed intention of making her grateful, of placing her in his debt.

She didn't like it. They were all using Gerrard, but the only one from whom Gerrard stood in danger of taking any hurt was Vane. Because the only one Gerrard liked, admired, potentially worshiped, was Vane.

Patience surreptitiously massaged her left temple. If they didn't finish with the port soon, she would have a raging migraine. She would probably have one anyway—after her disturbed night, followed by the surprises of the breakfast table, capped by the revelations of their ride, she'd spent most of the afternoon thinking of Vane. Which was enough to warp the strongest mind.

He distracted her on so many levels she'd given up trying to untangle her thoughts. There was, she felt sure, only one way to deal with him. Directly and decisively.

Her eyes felt gravelly, from staring unblinking at nothing for too long. She felt like she hadn't slept in days. And she certainly wouldn't sleep until she'd taken charge of the situation, until she'd put a stop to the relationship developing between Gerrard and Vane. True, all she'd seen and heard between them thus far had been innocent enough—but no one—*no one*—could call Vane innocent.

He wasn't innocent—but Gerrard was.

Which was precisely her point.

At least, she thought it was. Patience winced as pain shafted from one temple to the other.

The door opened; Patience sat up. She scanned the gentlemen as they wandered in—Vane was the last. He strolled in, which was of itself enough to assure her that her tortuous reasoning was right. All that prowling, arrogant masculinity set her teeth on edge.

"Mr. Cynster!" Without a blush, Angela beckoned. Patience could have kissed her.

Vane heard Angela and saw her wave; his gaze flicked to Patience, then, with a smile she unhesitatingly classed as untrustworthy, he prowled in their direction.

As a group, the three of them—Mrs. Chadwick, Angela, and Patience—rose to greet him, none wishing to risk a crick in the neck.

"I wanted to ask particularly," Angela said, before anyone else could essay a word, "whether it's true that cerise is currently the most *fashionable* color for trimming for young ladies."

"It's certainly much favored," Vane replied.

"But not on pale yellow," Patience said.

Vane looked at her. "I devoutly hope not."

"Indeed." Patience took his arm. "If you'll excuse us, Angela, ma'am"—she nodded to Mrs. Chadwick—"I have something I really must ask Mr. Cynster." So saying, she steered Vane toward the far end of the room—and thanked the deity he consented to move.

She felt his gaze, slightly surprised, distinctly amused, on her face. "My dear Miss Debbington." Beneath her hand, his arm twisted—and then he was steering her. "You need only say the word."

Patience flashed him a narrow-eyed glance. The purring tones in his voice sent shivers down her spine—delicious shivers. "I'm very glad to hear you say that, for that's precisely what I intend to do."

His brows rose. He searched her face, then raised a hand and gently rubbed one fingertip between her brows.

Patience stilled, shocked, then drew her head back. "Don't do that!" A warm glow suffused the area he'd touched.

"You were frowning—you look like you have a headache."

Patience frowned harder. They'd reached the end of the room; halting, she swung to face him. And plunged into the attack. "I take it you're not leaving tomorrow?"

He looked down at her. After a moment, he replied, "I can't see myself departing in the foreseeable future. Can you?"

She had to be sure. Patience met his gaze directly. "Why are you staying?"

Vane studied her face, her eyes—and wondered what was bothering her. The feminine tension gripping her rippled about him; he translated it as "bee in her bonnet," but, from long association with strong-willed women, his mother and aunts, let alone Devil's new duchess, Honoria, he had learned the wisdom of caution. Uncertain of her tack, he temporized. "Why do you imagine?" He raised one brow. "What, after all, could possibly exercise sufficient interest to hold a gentleman like me, here?"

He knew the answer, of course. Last night, he'd seen how the land lay. There were situations where justice, blindfolded as she was, could easily be misled—the situation here was one such. The undercurrents were considerable, running unexpectedly, inexplicably, deep.

He was staying to help Minnie, to defend Gerrard—and to aid Patience, preferably without letting on he was aiding her. Pride was something he understood; he was sensitive to hers. Unlike the other gentlemen, he saw no reason to suggest that she'd failed in any way with Gerrard. As far as he could tell, she hadn't. So it could be said he was acting as her protector, too. The role felt very right.

He'd capped his question with a charming smile; to his surprise, it made Patience stiffen.

She drew herself up, clasped her hands before her, and fixed him with a censorious look. "In that case, I'm afraid I must insist that you refrain from encouraging Gerrard."

Inwardly, Vane stilled. He looked down, into her disapproving eyes. "What, exactly, do you mean by that?"

Her chin rose. "You know very well what I mean."

"Spell it out for me."

Her eyes, like clear agates, searched his, then her lips compressed. "I would rather you spent as little time as possible with Gerrard. You're only showing an interest in him to win points with me."

Vane arched one brow. "You take a lot to yourself, my dear."

Patience held his gaze. "Can you deny it?"

Vane felt his face set, his jaw lock. He couldn't refute her accusation; it was in large part true. "What I don't understand," he murmured, his eyes narrowing on hers, "is why my interaction with your brother should occasion the slightest concern. I would have thought you would be glad to have someone extend his horizons."

"I would be," Patience snapped. Her head was pounding. "But you're the very last person I would want to guide him."

"Why the devil not?"

The steel sliding beneath Vane's deep voice was a warning. Patience heard it. She was heading for thin ice, but, having come thus far, she was determined not to retreat. She set her teeth. "I don't want you guiding Gerrard, filling his head with ideas, because of the sort of gentleman you are."

"And what sort of gentleman am I—in your eyes?"

Rather than rising, his tone was becoming softer, more lethal. Patience quelled a shiver, and returned his edged glance with one equally sharp. "In this instance, your reputation is the opposite of a recommendation."

"How would you know of my reputation? You've been buried in Derbyshire all your life."

"It precedes you," Patience retorted, stung by his patronizing tone. "You only need walk into a room, and it rolls out like a red carpet before you."

Her sweeping gesture elicited a grunt. "You don't know what you're talking about."

Patience lost her temper. "What I'm talking about is your propensities with respect to wine, women, and wagering. And, believe me, they're obvious to the meanest intelligence! You may as well have a banner carried before you." With her hands, she sketched one in the air. "Gentleman rake!"

Vane shifted; he was suddenly closer. "I believe I warned you I was no gentleman."

Looking into his face, Patience swallowed, and wondered

how she could possibly have forgotten. There was nothing remotely gentlemanly in the presence before her—his face was hard, his eyes pure steel. Even his austerely elegant attire now seemed more like armor. And his voice no longer purred. At all. Clenching her fists, she drew a tight breath. "I don't want Gerrard turning out like you. I don't want you to—" Despite her best efforts, innate caution took hold—it froze her tongue.

Almost shaking with the effort of restraining his temper, Vane heard himself suggest, his tone sibilantly smooth, "Corrupt him?"

Patience stiffened. She lifted her chin, her lids veiling her eyes. "I didn't say that."

"Don't fence with me, Miss Debbington, or you're liable to get pinked." Vane spoke slowly, softly, only just managing to get the words past his teeth. "Let's be sure I have this correctly. You believe I've stayed at Bellamy Hall *purely* to dally with you, that I've befriended your brother *for no other reason* than to further my cause with you, and that my character is such that you consider me unsuitable company for a minor. Have I forgotten anything?"

Poker-straight, Patience met his eyes. "I don't think so."

Vane felt his control quake, felt his reins slither from his grasp. He clenched his jaw, and both fists. Every muscle in his body locked, every mental sinew strained with the effort of holding on to his temper.

All Cynsters had one—a temper that normally lazed like a well-fed cat but could, if pricked, change to a snarling predator. For one instant, his vision clouded, then the beast responded to the rein and drew back, hissing. As his fury subsided, he blinked dazedly.

Hauling in a deep breath, he swung halfway around and, dragging his gaze from Patience, forced himself to scan the room. Slowly, he exhaled. "If you were a man, my dear, you wouldn't still be upright."

There was an instant's pause, then she said, "Not even you would strike a lady."

Her "not even" nearly set him off again. Jaw clenched, Vane slowly turned his head, caught her wide hazel gaze—and raised his brows. His hand itched to make contact with her bottom. Positively burned. For one instant, he teetered on the brink—her widening gaze, as, frozen like prey, she read the intent in his eyes, was small comfort. But the thought of Minnie made him fight down the nearly overpowering compulsion to bring Miss Patience Debbington to an abrupt understanding of her temerity. Minnie, supportive though she was, was unlikely to prove *that* forgiving. Vane narrowed his eyes, and spoke very softly. "I have only one thing to say to you, Patience Debbington. You're *wrong*—on every count."

He turned on his heel and stalked off.

Patience watched him go, watched him stride directly across the room, looking neither left nor right. There was nothing languid in his stride, no vestige of his usual lazy grace; his every movement, the rigid set of his shoulders, shrieked of reined power, of temper, of fury barely leashed. He opened the door and, without even a nod to Minnie, left; the door clicked shut behind him.

Patience frowned. Her head throbbed remorselessly; she felt empty and—yes—cold inside. As if she'd just done something terribly wrong. As if she'd just made a big mistake. But she hadn't, had she?

She woke the next morning to a grey and dripping world. Through one eye, Patience stared at the unrelenting gloom beyond her window, then groaned and buried her head beneath the covers. She felt the dipping of the mattress as Myst jumped up, then padded closer. Settling against the curve of her stomach, Myst purred.

Patience sank her head deeper into her pillow. This was clearly a morning to avoid.

She dragged her limbs from the comfort of her bed an hour later. Shivering in the chilly air, she hurriedly dressed, then reluctantly headed downstairs. She had to eat, and cowardice was not, in her book, sufficient reason to put the staff to the unexpected trouble of making up a tray for her. She noted the time as she passed the clock on the stairs—nearly ten o'clock. Everyone else should have finished and departed; she should be safe.

She walked into the breakfast parlor—and discovered her error. *All* the gentlemen were present. As they rose to greet her most nodded benignly—Henry and Edmond even conjured smiles. Vane, at the head of the table, didn't smile at all. His grey gaze settled on her, coldly brooding. Not a muscle in his face flickered.

Gerrard, of course, beamed a welcome. Patience summoned a weak smile. Steps dragging, she headed for the sideboard.

She took her time filling her plate, then slipped into the chair beside Gerrard, wishing he was somewhat larger. Large enough to shield her from Vane's darkling gaze. Unfortunately, Gerrard had finished all but his coffee; he lay sprawled comfortably back in his chair.

Leaving her exposed. Patience bit her tongue against the impulse to tell Gerrard to sit straight; he was still too coltish to bring off that lounging pose. Unlike the gentleman he was copying, who brought it off all too well. Patience kept her eyes on her plate and her mind on eating. Other than the brooding presence at the head of the table, there was precious little other distraction.

As Masters cleared their plates, the gentlemen fell to discussing the day's possibilities. Henry looked at Patience. "Perhaps, Miss Debbington, if the skies clear, you might be interested in a short walk?"

Patience glanced very briefly at the sky beyond the windows. "Too muddy," she pronounced.

Edmond's eyes gleamed. "How about charades?"

Patience's lips thinned. "Perhaps later." She was in a waspish mood; if they weren't careful, she'd sting.

"There's a pack of cards in the library," Edgar volunteered.

The General, predictably, snorted. "Chess," he stated. "Game of kings. That's what I shall do. Any takers?"

There were no volunteers. The General subsided into vague mutterings.

Gerrard turned to Vane. "How about a round of billiards?"

One of Vane's brows rose; his gaze remained on Gerrard's face, yet, watching him from beneath her lashes, Patience knew his attention was on her. Then he looked directly at her. "A capital idea," he purred, then both voice and face hardened. "But perhaps your sister has other plans for you."

His words were soft, distinct, and clearly loaded with some greater significance. Patience ground her teeth. She was avoiding his eye; he was focusing every eye on her. Not content with that, he was making no attempt to mask the coolness between them.

It colored his words, his expression; it positively shrieked in the absence of his suavely charming smile. He sat very still, his gaze unwaveringly fixed on her. His grey eyes were coldly challenging.

It was Gerrard, the only one of the company apparently insensitive to the powerful undercurrent, who broke the increasingly awkward silence. "Oh, Patience won't want me about, under her feet." He flicked a confident grin her way, then turned back to Vane.

Vane's gaze didn't shift. "I rather think that's for your sister to say."

Setting down her teacup, Patience lifted one shoulder. "I can't see any reason you shouldn't play billiards." She made the comment to Gerrard, steadfastly ignoring Vane. Then she pushed back her chair. "And now, if you'll excuse me, I must look in on Minnie."

They all rose as she stood; Patience walked to the door, conscious of one particular gaze on her back, focused right between her shoulder blades.

There was nothing wrong with playing billiards.

Patience kept telling herself that, but didn't believe it. It wasn't the billiards that worried her. It was the chatting, the easy camaraderie that the exercise promoted—the very sort of interaction she did not wish Gerrard to engage in with *any* elegant gentleman.

Just the knowledge that he and Vane were busily potting balls and exchanging God knew what observations on life reduced her to nervous distraction.

Which was why, half an hour after she'd seen Gerrard and Vane head for the billiard room, she slipped into the adjacent conservatory. One section of the irregularly shaped garden room overlooked one end of the billiard room. Screened by an assortment of palms, Patience peered between the fringed leaves.

She could see half the table. Gerrard stood leaning on his cue beyond it. He was talking; he paused, then laughed. Patience gritted her teeth.

Then Vane came into view. His back to her, he moved around the table, studying the disposition of the balls. He'd taken off his coat; in form-fitting waistcoat and soft white shirt, he looked, if anything, even larger, more physically powerful, than before.

He halted at the corner of the table. Leaning over, he lined up his shot. Muscles shifted beneath his tight waistcoat; Patience stared, then blinked.

Her mouth was dry. Licking her lips, she refocused. Vane took his shot, then, watching the ball, slowly straightened. Patience frowned, and licked her lips again.

With a satisfied smile, Vane circled the table and stopped by Gerrard's side. He made some comment; Gerrard grinned.

Patience squirmed. She wasn't even eavesdropping, yet she felt guilty—guilty of not having faith in Gerrard. She should leave. Her gaze went again to Vane, taking in his lean, undeniably elegant form; her feet remained glued to the conservatory tiles.

Then someone else came into view, pacing about the table. Edmond. He looked back up the table and spoke to someone out of her sight.

Patience waited. Eventually, Henry came into view. Patience sighed. Then she turned and left the conservatory.

The afternoon continued damp and dreary. Grey clouds lowered, shutting them in the house. After luncheon, Patience, with Minnie and Timms, retired to the back parlor to set stitches by candlelight. Gerrard had decided to sketch settings for Edmond's drama; together with Edmond, he climbed to the old nurseries for an unrestricted view of the ruins.

Vane had disappeared, only God knew where.

Satisfied Gerrard was safe, Patience embroidered meadow grasses on a new set of cloths for the drawing room. Minnie sat dozing in an armchair by the fire; Timms, ensconced in its mate, busily plied her needle. The mantelpiece clock ticked on, marking the slow passage of the afternoon.

"Ah, me," Minnie eventually sighed. She stretched her legs, then fluffed up her shawls and glanced at the darkening sky. "I must say, it's a huge relief that Vane agreed to stay."

Patience's hand stopped in midair. After a moment, she lowered the needle to the linen. "Agreed?" Head down, she carefully set her stitch.

"Hmm—he was on his way to Wrexford's, that's why he

was passing so close when the storm struck." Minnie snorted. "I can just imagine what devilry that crew had planned, but, of course, once I asked, Vane immediately agreed to stay." She sighed fondly. "No matter what else one might say of the Cynsters, they're always reliable."

Patience frowned at her stitches. "Reliable?"

Timms exchanged a grin with Minnie. "In some ways, they're remarkably predictable—you can always rely on help if needed. Sometimes, even if you don't ask for it."

"Indeed." Minnie chuckled. "They can be quite terrifyingly protective. Naturally, as soon as I mentioned the Spectre and the thief, Vane wasn't going anywhere."

"He'll clear up this nonsense." Timms's confidence was transparent.

Patience stared at her creation—and saw a hard-edged face with grey, accusing eyes. The lump of cold iron that had settled in her stomach the previous night grew colder. Weightier.

Her head throbbed. She closed her eyes, then snapped them open as a truly sickening thought occurred. It couldn't be, wouldn't be, true—but the dreadful premonition wouldn't go away. "Ah . . ." She tugged her last stitch tight. "Who are the Cynsters, exactly?"

"The family holds the dukedom of St. Ives." Minnie settled herself comfortably. "The principal seat is Somersham Place, in Cambridgeshire. That's where Vane was coming from. Devil's the sixth duke; Vane's his first cousin. They've been close from the cradle, born a mere four months apart. But the family's quite large."

"Mrs. Chadwick mentioned six cousins," Patience prompted.

"Oh, there's more than that, but she would have been referring to the Bar Cynster."

"The Bar Cynster?" Patience looked up.

Timms grinned. "That's the nickname the *ton*'s gentlemen use to refer to the six eldest cousins. They're all male." Her grin widened. "In every way."

"Indeed." Minnie's eyes twinkled. "The six of them all together are a veritable sight to behold. Known to make weak females swoon."

Looking down at her stitching, Patience swallowed an acid

retort. Elegant gentlemen, all, it seemed. The lead weight in her stomach lightened; she felt better. "Mrs. Chadwick said that . . . Devil had recently married."

"Last year," Minnie corroborated. "His heir was christened about three weeks ago."

Frowning, Patience looked at Minnie. "Is that his real name—Devil?"

Minnie grinned. "Sylvester Sebastian—but better, and, to my mind, more accurately known as Devil."

Patience's frown grew. "Is 'Vane' Vane's real name?"

Minnie chuckled evilly. "Spencer Archibald—and if you dare call him that to his face, you'll be braver than any other in the *ton*. Only his mother can still do so with impunity. He's been known as Vane since before he went to Eton. Devil named him—said he always knew which way the wind was blowing and what was in the breeze." Minnie raised her brows. "Oddly far-sighted of Devil, actually, for there's no doubt that's true. Instinctively intuitive, Vane, when all's said and done."

Minnie fell pensive; after two minutes, Patience shook out her cloth. "I suppose the Cynsters—at least, the Bar Cynster—are . . ." Vaguely, she gestured. "Well, the usual gentlemen about town."

Timms snorted. "It would be more accurate to say that they're the pattern card for 'gentlemen about town.' "

"All within the accepted limits, of course." Minnie folded her hands across her ample stomach. "The Cynsters are one of the oldest families in the *ton*. I doubt any of them could be bad *ton*, not even if they tried—quite out of character for them. They might be outrageous, they might be the *ton*'s most reckless hedonists, they might sail within a whisker of that invisible line—but you can guarantee they'll never cross it." Again, she chuckled. "And if any of them sailed too close to the wind, they'd hear about it—from their mothers, their aunts—and the new duchess. Honoria's certainly no insipid cypher."

Timms grinned. "It's said the only one capable of taming a Cynster male is a Cynster woman—by which they mean a Cynster wife. Strange to tell, that's proved true, generation after generation. And if Honoria's any guide, then the Bar Cynster are not going to escape that fate."

Patience frowned. Her previously neat, coherent mental image of Vane as a typical, if not the archetype, "elegant gentle-man" had started to blur. A reliable protector, amenable if not positively subject to the opinions of the women in his family—none of that sounded the least like her father. Or the others—the officers from the regiments based about Chesterfield who had so tried to impress her, the London friends of neighbors who, hearing of her fortune, had called, thinking to beguile her with their practiced smiles. In many respects, Vane fitted the bill to perfection, yet the Cynster attitudes Minnie had expounded were quite contrary to her expectations.

Grimacing, Patience started on a new sheaf of grasses. "Vane said something about being in Cambridgeshire to attend a church service."

"Yes, indeed."

Detecting amusement in Minnie's tone, Patience looked up, and saw Minnie exchange a laughing glance with Timms. Then Minnie looked at her. "Vane's mother wrote to me about it. Seems the five unmarried members of the Bar Cynster got ideas above their station. They ran a wagers book on the date of con-ception of Devil's heir. Honoria heard of it at the christening—she promptly confiscated all their winnings for the new church roof and decreed they all attend the dedication service." A smile wreathing her face, Minnie nodded. "They did, too."

Patience blinked and lowered her work to her lap. "You mean," she said, "that just because the duchess said they had to, they did?"

Minnie grinned. "If you'd met Honoria, you wouldn't be so surprised."

"But . . ." Brow furrowing, Patience tried to imagine it—tried to imagine a woman ordering Vane to do something he didn't wish to do. "The duke can't be very assertive."

Timms snorted, choked, then succumbed to gales of laugh-ter; Minnie was similarly stricken. Patience watched them dou-ble up with mirth—adopting a long-suffering expression, she waited with feigned patience.

Eventually, Minnie choked her way to a stop and mopped her streaming eyes. "Oh, dear—that's the most ridiculously funny—ridiculously *wrong*—statement I've ever heard."

"Devil," Timms said, in between hiccups, "is the most out-rageously arrogant dictator you're ever likely to meet."

"If you think Vane is bad, just remember it was Devil who was born to be a duke." Minnie shook her head. "Oh, my—just the thought of a nonassertive Devil . . ." Mirth threatened to overwhelm her again.

"Well," Patience said, frowning still, "he doesn't sound particularly strong, allowing his duchess to dictate to his cousins over what is held to be a male prerogative."

"Ah, but Devil's no fool—he could hardly gainsay Honoria on such a matter. And, of course, the reason Cynster men always indulge their wives was very much to the fore."

"The reason?" Patience asked.

"Family," Timms replied. "They were all gathered for the christening."

"Very family-focused, the Cynsters." Minnie nodded. "Even the Bar Cynster—they're always so good with children. Entirely trustworthy and utterly reliable. Probably comes from being such a large brood—they always were a *prolific* lot. The older ones are used to having younger brothers and sisters to watch out for."

Cold, heavy, the weight of dismay started to coalesce in Patience's stomach.

"Actually," Minnie said, chins wobbling as she resettled her shawls, "I'm very glad Vane will be staying for a while. He'll give Gerrard a few hints on how to go on—just the thing to prepare him for London."

Minnie looked up; Patience looked down. The lump of cold iron swelled enormously; it sank straight through her stomach and settled in her gut.

In her head, she replayed her words to Vane, the thinly veiled insults she'd leveled at him in the drawing room the previous night.

Her gut clenched hard about the lump of cold iron. She felt positively ill.

Chapter 6

❦

$\mathcal{T}$HE NEXT MORNING, Patience descended the stairs, a brittlely bright smile on her face. She swept into the breakfast parlor and nodded with determined cheerfulness to the gentlemen sitting at the table. Her smile froze, just for an instant, when she saw, wonder of wonders, Angela Chadwick, chatting loquaciously, greatly animated, in the chair to Vane's left.

He sat at the table's head as usual; Patience allowed her smile to flow over him, but didn't meet his eyes. Despite Angela's outpourings, from the moment she'd appeared, Vane's attention had fixed on her. She helped herself to kedgeree and kippers, then, with a smile for Masters as he held her chair, took her place beside Gerrard.

Angela immediately appealed to her. "I was just saying to Mr. Cynster that it would be *such* a welcome diversion if we could get up a party to go to Northampton. Just *think* of all the shops!" Eyes bright, she looked earnestly at Patience. "Don't you think that's a *wonderful* idea?"

For one instant, Patience was sorely tempted to agree. Anything—even a day shopping with Angela—was preferable to facing what had to be faced. Then the idea of sending Vane shopping with Angela occurred. The vision that rose in her mind, of him in some milliner's establishment, teeth gritted as he coped with Angela's witlessness, was priceless. She couldn't stop herself glancing up the table . . . her priceless image evaporated. Vane wasn't interested in Angela's wardrobe. His grey gaze was fixed on her face; his expression was impassive, but there was a frown in his eyes. He narrowed them slightly, as if he could see through her facade.

Patience immediately looked at Angela and increased the intensity of her smile. "I think it's a little far to do much shopping in a day. Perhaps you should ask Henry to escort you and your mother down for a few days?"

Angela looked much struck; she leaned forward to consult Henry, farther down the table.

"It looks like it'll stay fine." Gerrard glanced at Patience. "I think I'll take my easel out and make a start on the scenes Edmond and I decided on yesterday."

Patience nodded.

"Actually"—Vane lowered his voice so its rumble ran beneath Angela's excited chatter—"I wondered if you'd show me the areas you've been sketching."

Patience looked up; Vane trapped her gaze.

"If"—his voice turned steely—"your sister approves?"

Patience inclined her head graciously. "I think that's an excellent idea."

A frown flashed through Vane's eyes; Patience looked down at her plate.

"But what can we do today?" Angela looked about, clearly expecting an answer.

Patience held her breath, but Vane remained silent.

"I'm going sketching," Gerrard declared, "and I won't want to be disturbed. Why don't you go for a walk?"

"Don't be silly," Angela returned scornfully. "It's far too wet to go strolling."

Patience inwardly grimaced and forked up her last mouthful of kedgeree.

"Well then," Gerrard retorted, "you'll just have to amuse yourself doing whatever it is that young ladies do."

"I will," Angela declared. "I'll read to Mama in the front parlor." So saying, she stood. As the gentlemen rose, Patience blotted her lips with her napkin and grasped the moment to make her exit, too.

She needed to hunt out her most waterproof walking shoes.

An hour later, she stood at the side door and surveyed the expanse of sodden grass between her and the ruins. Between her and the apology she had to make. A brisk breeze was blowing, carrying the scent of rain; there seemed little likelihood the grass would dry soon. Patience grimaced and glanced down at Myst, sitting neatly beside her. "I suppose it's part of my penance."

Myst looked up, enigmatic as ever, and twitched her tail.

Patience determinedly stepped out. In one hand, she twirled her furled parasol; there was just enough weak sunshine to excuse it, but she'd really picked it up simply to have something in her hands. Something to fiddle with, something defensive— something to glance at if things got truly bothersome.

Ten yards from the door, and the hem of her lilac walking dress was wet. Patience gritted her teeth and glanced around for Myst—and realized the cat wasn't there. Looking back, she saw Myst, sitting primly on the stone stoop of the side door. Patience pulled a face at her. "Fine-weather friend," she muttered, and resumed her stroll.

Her hem got wetter and wetter; gradually, water found its way through the seams of her kid boots. Patience doggedly slogged on. Wet feet might be part of her penance, but she was sure it would be the lesser part. Vane, she was certain, would provide the greater.

Abruptly, she pushed that thought aside—it was not a thought she need dwell on. What was to come would not be easy, but if she allowed herself to think too much, her courage would desert her.

Quite how she had come to be so wrong she really couldn't fathom. To have been wrong on one point would have been bad enough, but to find herself so comprehensively off target was incomprehensible.

As she detoured around the first of the fallen stones, her jaw set. It wasn't fair. He *looked* like an elegant gentleman. He *moved* like an elegant gentleman. In many ways, he *behaved* like an elegant gentleman! How could she have known that in non-physical ways he was so different?

She clung to the thought, trying it on for comfort, seeing if it would bolster her courage—then relucantly shrugged it aside. She couldn't duck the fact that she was very much at fault. She'd judged Vane entirely by his wolf's clothing. Although he was, indeed, a wolf, he was, apparently, a *caring* wolf.

There was no way out but to apologize. Her self-respect wouldn't accept anything less; she didn't think he would either.

Reaching the ruins proper, she looked about. Her eyes ached; she'd got even less sleep last night than she had the night before. "Where are they?" she muttered. If she could get this over with, and free her mind of its most vexing problem, perhaps she could nap this afternoon.

But first, she had to give the wolf his due. She was here to apologize. She wanted to do it quickly—before she lost her nerve.

"Really? I didn't know that."

Gerrard's voice led her to the old cloisters. His easel before him, he was sketching the arches along one side. Stepping into the open courtyard, Patience searched—and spotted Vane lounging in the shadows of a half-shattered cloister arch some paces behind Gerrard.

Vane had already spotted her.

Gerrard glanced up as her boots scraped on the flags. "Hello. Vane's just been telling me that sketching's considered quite the thing among the *ton* at present. Apparently, the Royal Academy holds an exhibition every year." Charcoal in hand, he turned back to his sketch.

"Oh?" Her gaze on Vane, Patience wished she could see his eyes. His expression was unreadable. Shoulders propped against the stone arch, arms folded across his chest, he watched her like a hawk. A brooding, potentially menacing hawk. Or a wolf anticipating a meal.

Giving herself a mental shake, she stepped up to Gerrard's shoulder. "Perhaps we can visit the Academy when we go up to town."

"Hmm," Gerrard said, entirely absorbed with his work.

Patience studied Gerrard's sketch.

Vane studied her. He'd seen her the instant she'd appeared, framed by a break in the old wall. He'd known she was near an instant before that, warned by some sixth sense, by a faint ripple in the atmosphere. She drew his senses like a lodestone. Which, at present, was not helpful.

Gritting his teeth, he fought to block his memories of the

previous night from crystallizing in his mind. Every time they did, his temper took flight, which, given she was near, within easy reach, was the opposite of wise. His temper was very like a sword—once unsheathed, it was all cold steel. And it took real effort to resheathe it. Something he hadn't yet accomplished.

If Miss Patience Debbington was wise, she would keep her distance until he had.

If he was wise, he'd do the same.

His gaze, dwelling, entirely without his permission, on her curves, on the play of her skirts about her legs, dropped to inspect her ankles. She was wearing kid half boots—and her skirts were distinctly wet.

Inwardly, Vane frowned. He stared at her wet hems. She *had* changed tack—he'd thought she had over breakfast, then dismissed the idea as hopeful fancy. He couldn't see why she would have changed her mind. He'd already convinced himself there was nothing he could say to refute her accusations—they all held a grain of truth, and, if he was honest, he'd set himself up with his attempts at masterful manipulation. He'd concluded there was only one way to correct her misguided notions—he would *prove* them wrong, not by word, but by deed. And then he would be able to savor her confusion, and her apologies.

Straightening, pushing away from the stone arch, Vane realized that, somehow or other, her apologies were coming early. He wasn't about to place extra hurdles in her path. Slowly, he strolled forward.

Patience was instantly aware of him. She glanced swiftly his way, then looked back at Gerrard's sketch. "Will you be much longer?"

"Hours," Gerrard replied.

"Well . . ." Patience lifted her head and boldly met Vane's eyes. "I wonder, Mr. Cynster, if I could prevail on you to lend me your arm back to the house. It's more slippery than I'd thought. Some of the stones are quite treacherous."

Vane raised one brow. "Indeed?" Smoothly, he offered her his arm. "I know a route back that has a number of advantages."

Patience shot him a suspicious look, but she placed her fingers on his sleeve and allowed him to turn her toward the old church. Gerrard absentmindedly acknowledged their good-byes, and Patience's sisterly admonition to return to the house in time for lunch.

Giving her no time to think of anything further to tell Gerrard, Vane led her into the nave. The single remaining arch soared above them; within minutes they were out of Gerrard's sight and hearing, strolling side by side down the long central aisle.

"Thank you." Patience made to lift her hand from his sleeve; Vane covered it with his.

He felt her fingers jerk, then still, sensed the ripple of awareness that streaked through her. Her head came up, chin tilting, lips firming. He caught her gaze. "Your hems are wet."

Hazel eyes flashed. "So are my feet."

"Which suggests you came on this expedition for a purpose."

She looked forward. Vane watched, with interest, as her breasts swelled, straining the bodice of her dress.

"Indeed. I came to aplogize."

The words were bitten off, uttered through clenched teeth.

"Oh? Why?"

Abruptly, she stopped and, eyes narrowing, faced him. "Because I believe I owe you an apology."

Vane smiled, directly into her eyes. He didn't try to hide his steel. "You do."

Lips compressed, Patience met his gaze, then nodded. "So I apprehend." She drew herself up, clasping her hands on the top of her parasol, tilting her chin determinedly. "I apologize."

"For what, exactly?"

One long look into his grey eyes told Patience she was not going to escape lightly. She narrowed her eyes anew. "For casting unjustified aspersions on your character."

She could see him considering, matching that against her unwise words. Rapidly, she did the same. "And your motives," she grudgingly added. Then she thought again. And frowned. "At least, some of them."

His lips twitched. "Definitely only some of them."

His voice had regained its purr; a shivery sensation slid down Patience's spine.

"Just to be clear, I take it you rescind absolutely all your *unjustified* claims?"

He was teasing her; the light in his eyes was definitely untrustworthy. "Unreservedly," Patience snapped. "There! Now what more can you want?"

"A kiss."

The answer came back so fast, so definitely, Patience's head whirled. "A kiss?"

He merely raised one arrogant brow, as if the suggestion barely rated a blink. None-too-subtle challenge lit his eyes. Patience frowned and bit her lip. They stood in the open central aisle, nothing within yards of them. Totally unscreened, totally exposed. Hardly a site that lent itself to impropriety. "Oh, very well."

Swiftly, she stretched on her toes; putting one hand on his shoulder for balance, she placed a quick peck on his cheek.

His eyes opened wide, then filled with laughter—more laughter than she could stand.

"Oh, no." He shook his head. "*Not* that sort of kiss."

She didn't need to ask what sort of kiss he wanted. Patience focused on his lips—long, lean, hard. Fascinating. They were not going to get any less fascinating. Indeed, the longer she contemplated them . . .

Hauling in a quick breath, she held it, stretched upward, shut her eyes, and fleetingly touched her lips to his. They were as hard as she'd imagined, very like sculpted marble. Sensation flared at the brief contact; her lips tingled, then throbbed.

Patience blinked her eyes wide as she lowered her heels to earth. And refocused on his lips. She saw the ends curve upward, heard his low, wickedly teasing laugh.

"Still not right. Here—let me show you."

His hands came up to frame her face, her jaw, tilting her lips up as his descended. Of their own volition, her lids fell, then his lips touched hers. Patience couldn't have quelled the shudder that passed through her had her life depended on it.

Stunned, poised to resist, she mentally paused. Strong, sure, his lips covered hers, moving slowly, langorously, as if savoring her taste, her texture. There was nothing threatening in the unhurried caress. Indeed, it was beguiling, luring her senses, focusing them on the practiced slide and glide of cool lips which seemed to instinctively know how to soothe the heat rising in hers. Hers throbbed; his pressed, caressed, as if drinking in her heat, stealing it from her.

Patience felt her lips soften; his firmed in response.

No, no, noo. . . . Some small part of her mind tried to warn her, but she was long past listening. This was new, novel—she'd never felt such sensations before. Never known such simple delight existed.

Her head was whirling, but not unpleasantly. His lips still seemed hard, cool—Patience couldn't resist the temptation to return the pressure, to see if his lips would soften to hers.

They didn't, they only became harder. The next instant, she felt a searing heat sweep over her lips. She stilled; the questing heat returned—with the tip of his tongue, he traced her lower lip. The contact lingered, an unspoken question.

Patience wanted more. She parted her lips.

His tongue slid between, slowly, with his customary assured arrogance, quite certain of his welcome, confident in his expertise.

Vane held the reins of his desire in a grip of iron and refused to let his demons loose. Deep, primal instincts urged him on; experience held him back.

She'd never yielded her mouth to any man, never shared her lips willingly. He knew that absolutely, sensed the truth in her untutored response, read it in her lack of guile. But she was rising to him, her passion, her desire, answering his call, sweet as the dew on a crisp spring morning, virginal as snow on an inaccessible peak.

He could reach her—she would be his. But there was no need for any hurry. She was untouched, unused to the demands of a man's hands, a man's lips, much less a man's body; if he pressed too fast, she'd turn skittish and balk. And he'd have to work harder to bring her to his bed.

Angling his head over hers, he kept every caress slow, every plundering stroke deliberate. Passion lay heavy, languid, almost somnolent between them; as he claimed every sweet inch of the softness she offered him, he laced the heady sensation into every caress, and let it sink into her senses.

It would lie there, dormant, until next time he touched her, until he called it forth. He would let it rise by degrees, feed it, nurture it until it became the inescapable compulsion that would, in the end, bring her to him.

He would savor her slowly, savor her slow surrender—all the more sweet because the end was never in doubt.

Distant voices reached him; inwardly, he sighed, and reluctantly brought the kiss to an end.

He raised his head. Patience's eyes slowly opened, then she blinked, and stared straight at him. For one instant, the look on her face, in her eyes, had him puzzled—then he recognized it. Curious—she wasn't shocked, stunned, or thrown into a maidenly fluster. She was curious.

Vane couldn't stop his rakish grin. Nor could he resist the temptation to brush his lips over hers one last time.

"What are you doing?" Patience whispered as his head bent to hers. Even at close quarters, she could still see his smile.

"It's called 'kiss and make up.' " The curve of his lips deepened. "It's what lovers do when they fall out."

A vise locked about Patience's heart; panic—it had to be that—streaked through her. "We aren't lovers."

"Yet."

His lips touched hers and she shivered. "We never will be." She might be giddy, but she was quite sure of that.

He stilled, but his confident smile didn't waver. "Don't wager your fortune on it." Again, his lips brushed hers.

Patience's head reeled. To her relief, he straightened and drew back, looking over her head. "Here they come."

She blinked. "They who?"

He looked down at her. "Your harem."

"My *what*?"

His brows rose in unlikely innocence. "Isn't that the correct term for a group of slaves of the opposite sex?"

Patience dragged in a deep breath—she straightened, flicked him a warning glance, then turned. To meet Penwick, Henry, and Edmond, all striding up the aisle. Beneath her breath, Patience groaned.

"My dear Miss Debbington." Penwick took the lead. "I rode over expressly to ask if you would care to essay a ride?"

Patience gave him her hand. "I thank you for your kindness, sir, but I fear I've had a surfeit of fresh air this morning." The breeze was rising, whipping stray tendrils of hair across her forehead, teasing more strands free. Penwick directed a suspicious glance at the large presence looming by her shoulder. Half-turning, Patience saw Vane return Penwick's brief nod with one a great deal more supercilious. "Actually," she stated, "I was about to return indoors."

"Capital!" Henry pressed closer. "I wondered where you'd got to. Thought you must have come out for a walk. Be a pleasure to escort you back."

"I'll come, too." Edmond beamed an understanding smile at Patience. "I came to see how Gerrard's doing, but he gave me my *congé*. So I may as well go in."

There would, Patience felt sure, have been a fight for the position on her right, to be the one whose arm she took, except that the position was already filled. "It seems we're quite a party," Vane drawled. He flicked a glance at Penwick. "Coming, Penwick? We can go by way of the stables."

Patience drew in a deep breath, placed her hand on Vane's arm—and pinched him.

He looked down at her, brows rising innocently. "I was only trying to be helpful." He turned her. The others jostled behind them as he led her up the nave.

The route he took was expressly designed to try her temper. More specifically, to have the others try her temper; Vane wisely kept quiet and let them make the running. With her wet feet now positively frozen from standing too long on cold stone, Patience discovered her stock of forebearance had dipped dangerously low.

By the time they reached the stables, and she gave Penwick her hand in farewell, it was all she could do to fabricate a smile and a polite good-bye.

Penwick squeezed her fingers. "If the rain holds off, no doubt you'll wish to ride tomorrow. I'll call by in the morning."

As if he was in charge of her rides! Patience bit her tongue on a tart rejoinder. Withdrawing her hand, she raised her brows, then haughtily turned away, refusing to fall into the trap of giving Penwick a nod—which could be construed as acceptance. One glance at Vane's face, at the expression in his eyes, was enough to confirm he'd read the exchange clearly.

Luckily, Henry and Edmond drifted off without pushing once they entered the house. As she and Vane climbed the stairs,

Patience inwardly frowned. It was almost as if both Henry and Edmond thought they had to protect her from Vane, and Penwick, too, but, once she was in the house, they considered her safe. Even from Vane.

She could imagine why they thought that—this was, after all, Vane's godmother's house. Even rakes, she understood, had lines they would not cross. But she'd already learned she couldn't predict Vane's rakishness—and she wasn't at all sure where *his* lines lay.

They reached the end of the gallery; the corridor to her room stretched ahead. Halting, she drew her hand from Vane's arm and turned to face him.

His expression mild, his eyes gently amused, he met her gaze. He read her eyes, then raised a brow, inviting her question.

"Why did you stay?"

He stilled; again, Patience felt the net draw tight, felt paralysis set in as his predator's senses focused on her. It was as if the world stopped spinning, as if some impenetrable shield closed about them, so that there was nothing but her and him— and whatever it was that held them.

She searched his eyes, but couldn't read his thoughts beyond the fact that he was considering her, considering what to tell her. Then he lifted one hand. Patience caught her breath as he slid one finger beneath her chin; the sensitive skin came alive to his touch. He tipped her face up so that her eyes locked on his.

He studied her, her eyes, her face, for one instant longer. "I stayed to help Minnie, to help Gerrard . . . and to get something I want."

He uttered the words clearly, deliberately, without any affectation. His heavy lids lifted. Patience read the truth in his eyes. The force that held them beat in on her senses. A conqueror watched her through cool grey eyes.

Giddy, she fought for enough strength to lift her chin from his finger. Breathless, she turned and walked away to her door.

Chapter 7

LATE THAT NIGHT, Patience paced before the fire in her bed-chamber. About her, the house was silent, all the occupants retired to their rest. She couldn't rest; she hadn't even bothered to undress. There wasn't any point—she wouldn't fall asleep. She was getting very tired of missing out on her sleep, but . . .

She couldn't get her mind off Vane Cynster. He commanded her attention; he filled her thoughts, to the exclusion of everything else. She'd forgotten to eat her soup. Later, she'd tried to drink tea from an empty cup.

"It's all his fault," she informed Myst, sitting, sphinxlike, on the armchair. "How am I supposed to behave sensibly when he makes declarations like that?"

Declared they would be lovers—that he wanted her in that way. Patience slowed. "Lovers, he said—not protector and mistress." She frowned at Myst. "Is there any pertinent distinction?"

Myst looked steadily back.

Patience grimaced. "Probably not." She shrugged and resumed her pacing.

After all Vane had said and done, every precept she'd ever learned stated categorically that she avoid him. Cut him dead if need be. However . . . She halted, and stared at the flames.

The truth was, she was safe. She would be the very last lady to throw her cap over the windmill for a gentleman like Vane Cynster. He might be caring in some ways, he might be so powerfully attractive she couldn't focus on anything else while he was by, but she could never forget what he was. His appearance, his movements, his attitudes, that dangerous purr in his voice—all were constant reminders. No—she was safe. He wouldn't succeed in seducing her. Her deep-seated antipathy to elegant gentlemen would protect her from him.

Which meant she could, with impunity, satisfy her curiosity. Over those odd sensations he evoked, sometimes knowingly, at other times apparently unconsciously. She'd never felt the like before.

She needed to know what they meant. She wanted to know if there was more.

Brow furrowing, she paced on, formulating her arguments. Her experience of the physical was severely limited—she herself had ensured that was so. She'd never before felt the slightest inclination to so much as kiss any gentleman. Or to allow any gentleman to kiss her. But the one, amazingly thorough, astonishingly lengthy kiss she'd shared with Vane had demonstrated beyond doubt that he was a master in that sphere. From his reputation, she'd expected nothing less. Who better to learn from?

Why shouldn't she take advantage of the situation and learn a little more—all within the bounds of the possible, of course. She might not know where his lines lay, but she knew where hers were drawn.

She was safe, she knew what she wanted, and she knew how far she could go.

With Vane Cynster.

The prospect had consumed her thoughts for most of the afternoon and all of the evening. It had been exceedingly difficult to keep her eyes from him, from his large, lean frame, those strong, long-fingered hands, and his increasingly fascinating lips.

Patience frowned and continued to pace.

She looked up as she neared the end of her well-worn route—her curtains were still undrawn. Crossing to the window, she reached a hand to each drape to twitch them shut—in the gloom below, a light gleamed.

Patience froze and stared down. The light was quite clear, a ball glowing through the fog shrouding the ruins. It bobbed, then moved. Patience didn't wait to see more. Whirling, she hauled open her wardrobe, grabbed her cloak, and ran for the door.

Her soft-soled slippers made no sound on the runners or stair carpet. A single candle left burning in the front hall threw her shadow back up to the gallery. Patience didn't pause. She flew down the dark corridor to the side door.

It was bolted. She wrestled with the heavy bolts, dragging them back, then pulled open the door. Myst shot out. Patience stepped quickly outside, and shut the door. Then she whirled and started out—into thick fog.

Five impulsive steps from the door, she stopped. Shivering, she swung her cloak over her shoulders, quickly tying the cords at the collar. She glanced back. Only by straining her eyes could she make out the wall of the house, the blank eyes of the downstairs windows, and the darker patch that was the side door.

She looked toward the ruins. There was no sign of the light, but the Spectre, whoever he was, could not have reached the house, even using the light to guide him, not before she'd reached the side door.

In all likelihood, the Spectre was still out there.

Setting her back to the house, Patience took a few cautious steps. The fog grew denser, colder.

Tugging her cloak more tightly about her, she set her teeth and forged on. She tried to imagine she was walking in bright sunshine, tried to see in her mind's eye where she was. Then the first of the tumbled stones dotting the lawn loomed out of the fog, a reassuringly familiar sight.

Dragging in a more confident breath, she continued on, carefully picking her way between the toppled stones.

The fog was densest over the lawn; as she neared the ruins, it thinned, enough for her to make out the major structures, from which she could judge her position.

Cold, damp streamers of thick fog wound their way in and out of the shattered arches. A drifting mist obscured, then revealed, then obscured again. There was no real wind, yet a fine thread of sound seemed to whisper through the ruins, like a distant keening from ages past.

As she stepped onto the lichen-covered flags of the outer ward, Patience felt the eeriness close about her. A denser drift of fog wafted about her; one hand outstretched, she felt her way along a short wall, part of the monks' dorter. It ended abruptly; beyond was a large gap giving onto the flagged corridor leading to the remains of the refectory.

She stepped toward the gap; one slipper slid on crumbling masonry. Stifling a gasp, Patience leapt forward onto the corridor flags.

And collided with a man.

She opened her mouth to scream—a hard hand clamped over her lips. An arm like steel locked about her waist, trapping her against a long, hard frame. Patience relaxed; her panic flowed out of her. There was only one body within ten miles like the one she was pressed against.

Reaching up, she pulled Vane's hand from her lips. She drew breath to speak, opened her lips—

He kissed her.

When he eventually consented to stop, he only lifted his lips a bare fraction from hers. And breathed: "Quiet—sound travels very well in fog."

Patience gathered her wits. And breathed back: "I saw the Spectre—there was a light bobbing about."

"I think it's a lantern, but it's gone or shielded now."

His lips touched hers again, then settled, not cool but warm against hers. The rest of him was warm, too, an oasis of heat in the chilly night. Her hands trapped against his chest, Patience fought an urge to snuggle closer.

When he next lifted his head, she forced herself to ask, her words still no more than a whispered breath: "Do you think he'll come back?"

"Who knows? I thought I'd wait for a while."

He followed up the tantalizing brush of his breath against her lips with a much more satisfying caress.

Patience's head spun. "Maybe I'll wait, too."

"Hmmm."

Some unknown minutes later, while taking a necessary pause for breath, Vane commented: "Did you know your cat's here?"

She hadn't known if Myst had followed her or not. "Where?" Patience looked about.

"On the stone to your left. She can probably see better than us, even in the fog. Keep an eye on her—she'll probably disappear if the Spectre returns."

Keep an eye on her. That was difficult while he was kissing her.

Patience snuggled closer to the warm wall of his chest. He adjusted his hold; his hands slid about her waist, beneath her cloak. He drew her more firmly against him, shifting so she was trapped—very comfortably—between him and the old wall. One arm and shoulder protected her from the stones; the rest of him protected her from the night. His arms tightened; Patience felt the strength of him down her length, felt the press of his chest against her breasts, the weight of his hips against her stomach, the solid columns of his thighs hard against her softer limbs.

His lips found hers again; his hands spread over her back, molding her to him. Patience felt heat rise—from her, from him, between them. They were in no danger of taking a chill.

Myst hissed.

Vane raised his head, instantly alert.

A light flashed through the ruins. The fog had grown denser, making it difficult to tell where the lantern was. Reflections bounced off the cut faces of broken stones, setting up distracting glows. It took a moment to locate the strongest source of light.

It shone from beyond the cloisters.

"Stay here." With that whispered command, Vane set her from him, leaving her in the lee of the wall. In the next instant, he disappeared, merging into the fog like a wraith.

Patience swallowed her protest. She looked around—just in time to see Myst slip away in Vane's wake.

Leaving her totally alone.

Stunned, Patience stared after them. Somewhere ahead, the Spectre's lantern still glowed.

"You have to be joking!" With that muttered statement, she hurried after Vane.

She saw him once, as he crossed the courtyard within the cloisters. The light bobbed some way before him—not near the church but on the other side of the cloister, heading toward the remnants of other abbey buildings. Patience hurried on, glimpsing Myst as she leapt over the stones of the ruined wall of the cloister. As she followed, Patience tried to remember what lay beyond that wall.

A hole, as it happened—she tumbled headlong into it.

Patience valiantly smothered her instinctive shriek, nearly choking in the process. Luckily, it wasn't stone she fell on, but a grassed incline; the impact knocked the air from her lungs and left her gasping.

Twenty yards ahead, Vane heard her muffled shriek. He stopped and looked back, scanning the fog-shrouded stones. A yard behind him, Myst came to a quivering halt atop a stone, ears pricked as she looked back. Then the sleek cat leapt down and streaked back through the fog.

Silently, Vane cursed. He looked ahead.

The light had vanished.

Drawing a deep breath, he let it out, then turned and stalked back.

He found Patience lying where she'd fallen; she was struggling to push herself upright.

"Wait." Vane jumped down by her feet. Leaning over her, he slid his hands under her arms and lifted her. He set her on her feet beside him.

With a smothered cry, Patience crumpled. Vane caught her, lifting her, supporting her against him. "What is it?"

Patience leaned into him. "My knee." She bit her lip, then weakly added, "And my ankle."

Vane cursed. "Left or right?"

"Left."

He shifted to her left, then swung her into his arms, her left leg cradled between them. "Hang on."

Patience did. Holding her against his chest, Vane climbed the short slope. Lifting her high, he set her down on the edge of the hole, then clambered out. Then he bent and lifted her into his arms again.

He carried her into the cloisters, to where a large stone offered a convenient seat. Carefully, he set her down, letting her legs down gently.

Dead grass and damp leaves clung to her bodice. Vane brushed at them. Patience immediately brushed, too, not at all certain what she was brushing away—the detritus, or his hands. Despite the sharp pain in her knee and the duller ache in her ankle, the swift sweep of his fingers across her bodice had made the tips of her breasts crinkle tight.

The sensation left her breathless.

Vane shifted, half behind her. The next instant, she felt his hands slide about her from behind, fingers firming and feeling her ribs. Before she could gather her wits, his fingers slid upward.

"*What are you doing?*" She was so short of breath she sounded hoarse.

"Checking for broken or bruised ribs."

"Nothing hurts there." This time, her voice sounded strangled—the best she could do with his fingers pressed hard beneath her breasts.

A grunt was his answer, but at least he let her go. Patience dragged in a much-needed breath, then blinked as he knelt before her.

He flicked up her skirts.

"*What*—!" Patience desperately tried to push the soft folds back down.

"Stop fussing!"

His tone—clipped and angry—made her do just that. Then she felt his hands close about her sore ankle. His fingers searched, probed gently, then, very carefully, he moved her foot about. "No sharp pain?"

Patience shook her head. His fingers firmed, gently massaging; swallowing a sigh, she closed her eyes. His touch felt so good. The heat of his hands reduced the ache; when he finally released her ankle, it felt much better.

His hands slid upward, following the swell of her calf to her knee.

Patience kept her eyes shut, and tried not to think about how sheer her evening stockings were. Luckily, she wore her garters high, so when his hands closed about her knee, he wasn't touching bare skin.

He might as well have been.

Every nerve in her legs came alive, focused on his touch. He probed, and pain flashed; Patience jerked—but welcomed the distraction. He was very careful after that. Twice more, she hissed in pain as he tested the joint. Eventually, his hands left her.

Patience opened her eyes and quickly flicked down her skirts.

She could feel her blush heating her cheeks. Luckily, in the poor light, she doubted he could see it.

Vane stood and looked down at her. "Wrenched knee, slightly sprained ankle."

Patience shot him a glance. "You're an expert?"

"Of a sort." With that, he picked her up.

Patience clung to his shoulders. "If you would give me your arm, I'm sure I could manage."

"Really?" came the less than encouraging reply. He looked down at her. In the gloom, she couldn't make out his expression. "Luckily, you won't be called upon to put that to the test." His tones remained clipped, excessively precise. The undercurrent of irritation gained in intensity as he continued, "Why the devil didn't you stay where I left you? And didn't Minnie make you promise not to chase the Spectre in the dark?"

Patience ignored his first question, for which she had no good answer. Not that her answer to his second question was particularly good either. "I forgot about my promise—I just saw the Spectre and came rushing out. But what are *you* doing here if it's too dangerous to chase the Spectre?"

"*I* have special dispensation."

Patience felt perfectly justified in humphing. "Where's Myst?"

"Ahead of us."

Patience looked but couldn't see anything. Obviously, Vane could see better than she could. His stride didn't falter as he wound his way through the tumbled blocks; her arms locked about his neck, she was inwardly very glad she didn't have to hobble up that particular stretch of lawn.

Then the side door loomed out of the murk. Myst stood waiting on the stoop. Patience waited to be put down. Instead, Vane juggled her in his arms and managed to open the door. Once across the threshold, he kicked the door shut, then leaned his shoulders back against it.

"Set the bolts."

She did as he said, reaching about him. When the last bolt slid home, he straightened and headed on.

"You can put me down now," Patience hissed as he strode into the front hall.

"I'll put you down in your room"

In the light from the hall candle, Patience saw what she hadn't been able to see before—his face. It was set. In uncompromisingly grim lines.

To her surprise, he headed for the back of the hall, and shouldered open the green baize door. "Masters!"

Masters popped out from the butler's pantry. "Yes, sir?— oh my!"

"Indeed," Vane replied. "Summon Mrs. Henderson and one of the maids. Miss Debbington went wandering in the ruins and has turned her ankle and wrenched her knee."

That, of course, did for her. Very thoroughly. Patience had to put up with Masters, Mrs. Henderson, and Minnie's old dresser, Ada, fussing nonstop about her. Vane led the bleating procession up the stairs—as he'd said, he set her down in her room, not before.

He set her, very gently, on the end of her bed. Frowning, he stood back. Hands on hips, he watched as Mrs. Henderson and Ada fussed with a mustard bath for her ankle and the makings of a poultice for her knee.

Apparently satisfied, Vane turned and trapped Patience's gaze. His eyes were hard. "For God's sake, do as you're told." With that, he strode for the door.

Utterly dumbfounded, Patience stared after him. She couldn't think of anything halfway suitable to hurl at him before he disappeared. The door clicked shut. She snapped her mouth shut, let herself fall back on the bed, and relieved her feelings with a teeth-gritted groan.

Ada fluttered over. "It'll be all right, dear." She patted Patience's hand. "We'll make it all better in a moment."

Patience set her teeth—and glared at the ceiling.

Mrs. Henderson came to wake her the next morning. Patience, lying on her back in the middle of her bed, was surprised to see the motherly housekeeper; she'd expected one of the maids.

Mrs. Henderson smiled as she drew the curtains wide. "I'll need to remove that poultice and bind up your knee."

Patience grimaced. She'd hoped to escape a bandage. She glanced idly at her clock, then stared. "It's only seven o'clock."

"Aye. We doubted you'd sleep all that well, what with the awkwardness."

"I couldn't turn over." Patience struggled to sit up.

"It won't be so bad tonight. Just a bandage should be enough from now on."

With the housekeeper's help, Patience got up. She sat patiently while Mrs. Henderson removed the poultice, clucked over her knee, then bound it up in a fresh bandage.

"I can't walk," Patience protested, the instant Mrs. Henderson helped her to her feet.

"Of course not. You must stay off your feet for a few days if that knee's to heal."

Patience closed her eyes and stifled a groan.

Mrs. Henderson helped her to wash and dress, then let her prop against the bed. "Now, would you like a tray up here, or would you rather go downstairs?"

To *think* of spending the entire day closeted in her room was bad enough; to be forced to do so would be torture. And if she was to go down the stairs, it had best be now, before anyone else was about. "Downstairs," Patience replied decisively.

"Right then."

To her amazement, Mrs. Henderson left her and headed for the door. Opening it, she put her head out, said something, then stood back, holding the door wide.

Vane walked in.

Patience stared.

"Good morning." His expression impassive, he crossed the room. Before she could formulate her thoughts, let alone the words to express them, he stooped and scooped her into his arms.

Patience swallowed her gasp. Just like last night—with one highly pertinent alteration.

Last night, she'd been wearing her cloak; its thick folds had muted his touch sufficiently to render it undisturbing. Now, clad in a morning gown of fine twill, even through her petticoats she could feel every one of his fingers, one set gripping her lower thigh, the others firm beneath her arm, close by the swell of her breast.

As he angled her through the door, then straightened and headed for the gallery, Patience tried to steady her breathing, and prayed her blush wasn't as vivid as it felt. Vane's gaze touched her face, then he looked ahead and started down the stairs.

Patience risked a glance at his face—the hard planes were still set, locked and stony, as they had been last night. His fascinating lips were a straight line.

She narrowed her eyes. "I'm not actually incapacitated, you know."

The glance he sent her was unreadable. He studied her eyes for an instant, then looked ahead once more. "Mrs. Henderson says you must keep off your feet. If I find you on them, I'll tie you to a daybed."

Patience's jaw dropped. She stared at him, but, reaching the bottom of the stairs, he didn't look her way. His boots rang on the hall tiles. Patience drew a deep breath, intending to make her views on his high-handedness plain, only to have to swallow her words; Vane swept into the breakfast parlor—Masters was there. He hurried to pull out the chair next to Vane's, angling it so it faced the head of the table. Gently, Vane deposited her in it. Masters rolled an ottoman into position; Vane set her injured ankle upon it.

"Would you like a cushion, miss?" Masters inquired.

What could she do? Patience conjured a grateful smile. "No, thank you, Masters." Her gaze shifted to Vane, standing in front of her. "You've been more than kind."

"Not at all, miss. Now, what would you like for breakfast?"

Between them, Vane and Masters saw her supplied with suitable nourishment—then watched over her as she ate. Patience bore with their male version of fussing as stocially as she could. And waited.

Vane's shoulders were coated with fine droplets of mist. His hair was darker than usual, an occasional droplet glittering amid the thick locks. He also broke his fast, working steadily through a plate piled with various meats. Patience inwardly sniffed—he was obviously a carnivore.

Eventually, Masters returned to the kitchen, to fetch chafing dishes to keep the fare warm.

As his footsteps faded, Patience pounced. "You've been out investigating."

Vane looked up, then nodded and reached for his coffee cup.

"Well?" Patience prompted, when he simply sipped.

Lips compressing, he studied her face, then grudgingly informed her: "I thought there might be a footprint or two—a track I could follow." He grimaced. "The ground was wet enough, but the ruins are all either flags, rocks, or matted grass. Nothing to hold any impression."

"Hmm." Patience frowned.

Masters returned. He set down his tray, then crossed to Vane's side. "Grisham and Duggan are waiting in the kitchen, sir."

Vane nodded and drained his coffee cup. He set it down and pushed back his chair.

Patience caught his eye and held it. She clung to the contact; her unspoken question hung in the air.

Vane's face hardened. His lips thinned.

Patience narrowed her eyes. "If you don't tell me, I'll go to the ruins myself."

Vane narrowed his eyes back. He flicked a glance at Masters, then, somewhat grimly, looked back at Patience. "We're going to check for any sign that the Spectre came from outside. Hoofprints, anything to suggest he didn't come from the Hall itself."

Her expression relaxing, Patience nodded. "It's been so wet, you should find something."

"Precisely." Vane stood. "If there's anything to find."

Masters left the parlor, on a return trip to the kitchens. From the direction of the stairs came an airy voice, "Good morning, Masters. Is anyone about yet?"

Angela. They heard Masters's low-voiced answer; Vane looked down and met Patience's wide eyes.

"That's obviously my cue to depart."

Patience grinned. "Coward," she whispered, as he passed her chair.

A heartbeat later, he'd swung about and bent over her, his breath feathering the side of her neck. His strength flowed around her, surrounded her.

"Incidentally," he murmured, in his deepest purr, "I meant what I said about the daybed." He paused. "So, if you have the slightest inkling of self-preservation, you won't move from this chair." Cool, hard lips brushed her ear, then slid lower, to lightly caress, with just the barest touch, the sensitive skin beneath her jaw. Patience lost the fight and shivered; her lids lowered.

Vane tipped her chin up; his lips touched hers in a fleeting, achingly incomplete kiss. "I'll be back before breakfast is over."

Angela's footsteps sounded in the hall.

Patience opened her eyes to see Vane striding out of the parlor. She heard Angela's delighted greeting, then Vane's answering rumble, dying away as he continued striding. A second later, Angela appeared. She was pouting.

Feeling infinitely older, infinitiely wiser, Patience smiled. "Come and have some breakfast. The eggs are particularly good."

The rest of the breakfast crowd gradually wandered in. To Patience's dismay, they, one and all, had already heard of her injury, courtesy of the household grapevine. Luckily, neither she nor Vane had seen fit to inform anyone of the reason for her nighttime excursion, so no one knew how she'd come by her hurts.

Everyone was suitably shocked by her "accident"; all were quick to proffer their sympathy.

"Distressing business," Edgar offered with one of his meek smiles.

"Twisted m'knee once, when I was in India." The General directed a curious glance up the table. "Horse threw me. Native wallahs wrapped it up in evil-smelling leaves. Knee, not the horse. Came good in no time."

Patience nodded and sipped her tea.

Gerrard, beside her, occupying the chair she usually used, asked softly, "Are you sure you're all right?"

Ignoring the ache in her knee, Patience smiled and squeezed his hand lightly. "I'm hardly a weak creature. I promise you I'm not about to swoon from the pain."

Gerrard grinned, but his expression remained watchful, concerned.

With her pleasant smile firmly in place, Patience allowed her gaze to roam. Until, across the table, she met Henry's frown.

"You know," he said, "I don't quite understand how you came to wrench your knee." His inflection made the statement a question.

Patience kept smiling. "I couldn't sleep, so I went for a stroll."

"Outside?" Edmond's surprise faded to consideration. "Well, yes, I suppose you'd have to stroll outside—strolling *inside* this mausoleum at night would give anyone nightmares." His swift grin dawned. "And presumably you wouldn't have wanted them."

Smiling over clenched teeth was not easy; Patience managed it, just. "I did go outside, as it happened." Silence would have been wiser, but they were all hanging on her words, as avidly curious as only those leading humdrum lives could be.

"But . . ." Edgar's brow folded itself into pin tucks. "The fog . . ." He looked at Patience. "It was a pea-souper last night. I looked out before I blew out my candle."

"It was rather dense." Patience looked at Edmond. "You would have appreciated the eeriness."

"I had heard," Whitticombe diffidently commented, "that Mr. Cynster carried you in."

His words, quietly spoken, hung over the breakfast table, raising questions in every mind. A sudden stillness ensued, fraught with surprise and shocked calculation. Calmly, her smile no longer in evidence, Patience turned and, her expression distant, regarded Whitticombe.

Her mind raced, considering alternatives, but there was only one answer she could give. "Yes, Mr. Cynster did help me back to the house—it was lucky he found me. We'd both seen a light in the ruins and gone to investigate."

"The Spectre!" The exclamation came from both Angela and Edmond. Their eyes glowed, their faces lit with excitement.

Patience tried to dampen their imminent transports. "I was following the light when I fell down a hole."

"I had thought," Henry said sternly, and all heads swung his way, "that we all promised Minnie we wouldn't go chasing the Spectre in the dark." The tenor of his voice and the expression on his face were quite surprising in their intensity. Patience felt a blush touch her cheeks.

"I'm afraid I forgot my promise," she admitted.

"In the chill of the moment, so to speak." Edmond leaned across the table. "Did your spine tingle?"

Patience opened her mouth, eager to grasp Edmond's distraction, but Henry spoke first.

"I think, young man, that this nonsense of yours has gone quite far enough!"

The words were wrath-filled. Startled, everyone looked at Henry—his face was set, skin slightly mottled. His eyes were fixed on Gerrard.

Who stiffened. He met Henry's gaze, then slowly put down his fork. "What do you mean?"

"I mean," Henry replied, biting off the words, "that given the pain and suffering you've caused your sister, I'm shocked to discover you such an unfeeling whelp that you can sit there, beside her, and pretend to innocence."

"Oh, come on," Edmond said. Patience nearly sighed with relief. A second later she stiffened and stared as Edmond continued, his tone the very essence of reasonableness, "How could he know Patience would break her word to Minnie and come out after him?" Edmond shrugged and turned a winning smile on both Patience and Gerrard. "Hardly his fault she did."

With supporters like that . . . Patience swallowed a groan and charged into the breach. "It wasn't Gerrard."

"Oh?" Edgar looked at her hopefully. "You saw the Spectre then?"

Patience bit her lip. "No, I didn't. But—"

"Even if you had, you would still defend your brother, wouldn't you, my dear?" Whitticombe's smooth tones floated up the table. He directed a smile of paternalistic superiority at Patience. "Quite commendable devotion, my dear, but in this case, I fear"—his gaze switched to Gerrard; his features hardened, and he shook his head—"sadly misplaced."

"It wasn't I." Pale, Gerrard made the statement evenly. Beside him, Patience sensed the battle he waged to hold his temper in check. Silently, she sent him support. Under the table, she gripped his thigh briefly.

Abruptly, he turned to her. "I'm not the Spectre."

Patience held his furious gaze levelly. "I know." She filled those two words with complete and utter conviction, and felt some of his heat leave him.

Turning, he flung a challenging stare around the table.

The General snorted. "Touching, but there's no ducking the

truth. Boy's tricks, that's what this Spectre is. And you, boy—you're the only boy about."

Patience felt the blow strike, a direct hit to the core of Gerrard's emerging adulthood. He stilled, his face deathly pale, his expression bleak. Her heart wept for him; she longed to throw her arms about him, to shield and comfort him—but knew she could not.

Slowly, Gerrard pushed back his chair and stood. He cast a burning glance around the table, excusing only Patience from its scorn. "If none of you has any more insults to hurl my way . . ." He paused, then continued, his voice threatening to break, "I'll bid you a good morning."

Brusquely, he nodded. With a swift, blank glance for Patience, he swung on his heel and left the room.

Patience would have given her entire fortune to be able to rise and, with haughty scorn, sweep out in his wake. Instead, she was trapped—condemned by her injury to have to keep her own soaring temper within bounds and deal with her aunt's witless household. Despite her threat to Vane, she could not stand, let alone hobble.

Lips compressed, she swept a glance around the table. "Gerrard is not the Spectre."

Henry smiled wearily. "My dear Miss Debbington, I'm afraid you really must face facts."

"Facts?" Patience snapped. "What facts?"

With weighty condescension, Henry proceeded to tell her.

Vane was strolling up from the stables when he saw Gerrard, jaw grimly set, striding toward him.

"What's happened?" he demanded.

Stony-faced, eyes burning, Gerrard halted before him, drew a deep breath, met his gaze briefly, then abruptly shook his head. "Don't ask." With that, he flung past, and continued to the stables.

Vane watched him go. Gerrard's clenched fists and rigid back spoke volumes. Vane hesitated, then his face hardened. Abruptly, he turned and strode for the house.

He reached the breakfast parlor in record time. One glance, and all expression left his face. Patience still sat where he'd left her, but instead of the bright sparkle he'd left in her large eyes, the light flush that had tinted her cheeks, her hazel eyes were now narrowed, flashing with temper, while flags of color flew high on her cheekbones.

Beyond that, she was pale, almost vibrating with suppressed fury. She didn't see him immediately; Henry Chadwick was the current focus of her ire.

"There you are, Cynster! Come and add your voice to ours." The General, swiveling in his chair, appealed to him. "We've been trying to tell Miss Debbington here that she has to see sense. No point bucking the truth, don't you see? That ramshackle brother of hers needs a firmer hand on his reins. A good whipping will bring him into line and stop all this Spectre tommyrot."

Vane looked at Patience. Her eyes, positively blazing, had fixed on the General. Her breasts swelled as she drew breath. If looks could kill, the General was dead. From her expression, she was ready to throttle Henry, too, with Edmond thrown in for good measure.

Smoothly, Vane strolled forward. His movement caught Patience's attention; she looked up, and blinked. Vane trapped her gaze in his. He didn't halt until he stood beside her chair. Then he held out his hand. Commandingly. Without hesitation, Patience laid her fingers in his palm.

Vane closed his hand strongly about hers; with a shudder, Patience felt warmth and strength flow into her. Her temper, almost at the breaking point, fell back from the brink. She drew in another breath and looked again at those about the table.

Vane did the same, his cool grey gaze scanning their faces. "I do hope," he mumured, his languid drawl low but clearly audible, "that, after your ordeal of last night, no one has been insensitive enough to discompose you in any way?"

The quiet words, and the cold steel behind his eyes, were enough to make everyone else at the table still.

"Naturally," he continued, in the same smooth tones, "events such as those of last night lend themselves to speculation. But, of course"—he smiled at them all—"it is just speculation."

"Ah—" Edgar broke in to ask, "You found no evidence—no clue—to the Spectre's identity?"

Vane's smile deepened fractionally. "None. So any thoughts on the identity of the Spectre are, as I said, pure fancy." He caught Edgar's eye. "Based on rather less substance than a tip for the Guineas."

Edgar smiled briefly.

"But," interrupted the General, "stands to reason it's got to be *someone*."

"Oh, indeed," Vane replied, at his languid best. "But ascribing the blame to any particular individual without reasonable *proof* seems to me to smack of . . ." He paused and met the General's eye. "Quite unnecessary slander."

"Humph!" The General sank lower in his chair.

"And, of course"—Vane's gaze swung to Henry—"there's always the thought of how foolish one will look if one's overly enthusiastic assertions prove wrong."

Henry frowned. His gaze dropped to the tablecloth.

Vane looked down at Patience. "Are you ready to go upstairs?"

Patience looked up at him and nodded. Vane bent and scooped her into his arms. Having got used to the sensation of being lifted so easily, Patience made herself comfortable, draping her arms about Vane's neck. The men at the table all came to their feet; Patience glanced across the table—and almost smiled. The look on Henry's and Edmond's faces was priceless.

Vane turned and headed for the door. Edmond and Henry came rushing around the table, almost tripping in their haste.

"Oh, I say—here, let me help." Henry rushed to hold back the already open door.

"Perhaps if we form a chair with our arms?" Edmond suggested.

Vane paused as Edmond moved to intercept them. Patience froze Edmond with an icy glare. "Mr. Cynster is more than capable of managing on his own." She allowed the chill in her voice to strike home, before adding, in precisely the same tone, "I am going to retire—I do not wish to be disturbed. Not by any further speculation, nor unwarranted slander. And least of all"—she shifted her sights to Henry—"by any overly enthusiastic assertions."

She paused, then smiled, and looked at Vane. Utterly unmoved, he raised a brow at her. "Upstairs?"

Patience nodded. "Indeed."

Without further ado, and no further hindrance, Vane carried her from the room.

Chapter 8

"Why," Vane asked, as he steadily climbed the main stairs, "are they so convinced it's Gerrard?"

"Because," Patience waspishly stated, "they can't imagine anything else. It's a *boy's* trick; ergo it must be Gerrard." As Vane gained the top of the stairs, she continued, her tone vitriolic. "Henry has no imagination; neither has the General. They're blockheads. Edmond has imagination to spare, but doesn't care enough to engage it. He's so irresponsible, he considers it all a lark. Edgar is cautious over jumping to conclusions, but his very timidity leaves him permanently astride the fence. And as for Whitticombe"—she paused, breasts swelling, eyes narrowing—"*he's* a self-righteous killjoy who positively delights in calling attention to others' supposed misdemeanors, all with a sickeningly superior air."

Vane shot her a sidelong glance. "Clearly breakfast didn't agree with you."

Patience humphed. Looking ahead, she focused on their surroundings. She didn't recognize them. "Where are you taking me?"

"Mrs. Henderson has set up one of the old parlors for you—so you won't be bothered with the others unless you choose to summon them."

"Which will be after hell freezes." After a moment, Patience

483

glanced up at Vane. In a very different tone, she asked: "You don't think it's Gerrard, do you?"

Vane looked down at her. "I *know* it isn't Gerrard."

Patience's eyes widened. "You saw who it was?"

"Yes and no. I only caught a glimpse as he went through a thinner patch of fog. He clambered over a rock, holding his light high, and I saw him outlined by the light. A grown man from his build. Height's difficult to judge at a distance, but build is harder to mistake. He was wearing a heavy coat, something like frieze, although my impression was it wasn't that cheap."

"But you're sure it wasn't Gerrard?"

Vane glanced down at Patience riding comfortably in his arms. "Gerrard's still too lightweight to be mistaken for a fully grown man. I'm quite certain it wasn't he."

"Hmm." Patience frowned. "What about Edmond—he's rather thin. Is he eliminated, too?"

"I don't think so. His shoulders are broad enough to carry a coat well, and with his height, if he was hunched, either against the cold or because he was playing the role of 'the Spectre,' then he could have been the man I saw."

"Well, whatever else," Patience said, brightening, "you can put an end to this scurrilous talk of Gerrard being the Spectre." Her brightness lasted all of ten yards, then she frowned. "Why didn't you clear Gerrard's name just now, in the breakfast parlor?"

"Because," Vane said, ignoring the sudden chill in her voice, "it's patently obvious that someone—someone about the breakfast table—is quite content to cast Gerrard as the Spectre. Someone wants Gerrard as scapegoat, to distract attention from himself. Given the mental aptitudes you so accurately described, the gentlemen are, by and large, easily led. Present the matter right, and they'll happily believe it. Unfortunately, as none of them is *un*intelligent, it's difficult to tell just who's doing the leading."

He stopped before a door; frowning, Patience absentmindedly leaned forward and opened it. Vane shouldered the door wide and carried her in.

As he had said, it was a parlor, but not one usually in use. It lay at the end of the wing housing Patience's bedchamber, one floor down. The windows were long, reaching almost to the floor. Maids had obviously been in, throwing back dust covers, dusting ferociously, and refurbishing the huge cast-iron Empire daybed that faced the long windows. Their curtains tied back, the windows looked over the shrubbery and a section of wilderness—most of the Hall's gardens were wilderness—to the golden brown canopies of the woods beyond. It was as pleasant a prospect as could be found in the present season. Farther to the right lay the ruins; in the distance, the grey ribbon of the Nene wound its way through lush meadows. Patience could recline on the daybed and contemplate the scenery. As the room was on the first floor, her privacy was assured.

Vane carried her to the daybed and carefully lowered her onto it. He plumped the pillows, arranging them supportively about her.

Patience lay back, watching as he settled a tapestry-covered cushion under her sore ankle. "Just what are your intentions over the Spectre?"

Vane met her gaze, then, raising one brow, strolled back to the door—and turned the key in the lock. Returning with the same long-strided prowl, he sat on the bed, beside her hip, bracing one hand on the daybed's iron back. "The Spectre now knows that he was followed last night—that, but for your untimely accident, he might well have been caught."

Patience had the grace to blush.

"All the household," Vane continued, his eyes locking on hers, "the Spectre included, are coming to the realization that I know the Hall well, possibly better than they do. I'm a real threat to the Spectre—I think he'll lie low and wait for me to depart before making another appearance."

Patience made an effort to live up to her name; she pressed her lips tightly together.

Vane smiled understandingly. "Consequently, if we're to lure the Spectre to reveal himself, I suspect it would be wise to let it appear that I'm still willing to entertain the notion that Gerrard—the obvious candidate—is to blame."

Patience frowned. She studied the cool grey of his eyes, then opened her lips.

"I would suggest," Vane said, before she could speak, "that it's not going to hurt Gerrard to let the household think what they like, at least for the immediate future."

Patience's frown deepened. "You didn't hear what they said." She crossed her arms beneath her breasts. "The General called him a boy."

Vane's brows rose. "Highly insensitive, I agree—but I think you're underestimating Gerrard. Once he knows all the people he cares about *know* he's innocent, he won't worry over what the others think. I suspect he'll view it as an exciting game—a conspiracy to catch the Spectre."

Patience narrowed her eyes. "You mean that's how you'll present it to him."

Vane grinned. "I'll suggest he responds to any aspersions cast his way with scornful boredom." He raised his brows. "Perhaps he can cultivate a superior sneer?"

Patience tried to eye him with disapproval. She was sure that, as Gerrard's guardian, she shouldn't approve of such plans. Yet she did; she could see Vane's plan was the fastest way to resuscitate Gerrard's confidence, and that, above all, was her primary concern. "You're rather good at this, aren't you?" And she didn't just mean his reading of Gerrard.

Vane's grin converted to a rakish smile. "I'm rather good at lots of things."

His voice had lowered to a rumbling purr. He leaned closer.

Patience tried, very hard, to ignore the vise slowly closing about her chest. She kept her eyes on his, drawing ever nearer, determined that she wouldn't—absolutely would not—allow her gaze to drop to his lips. As her heartbeat deepened, she raised one brow challengingly. "Such as?"

Kissing—he was very, very good at kissing.

By the time Patience reached that conclusion, she was utterly breathless—and utterly enthralled by the heady feelings slowly spiraling through her. Vane's confident possession of her lips, her mouth, left her giddy—pleasurably so. His hard lips moved on hers, and she softened, not just her lips, but every muscle, every limb. Slow heat washed through her, a tide of simple delight that seemed to have no greater meaning, no deeper import. It was all pleasure, simple pleasure.

With a mental sigh, she lifted her arms and draped them over his shoulders. He shifted closer. Patience thrilled to the slow surge of his tongue against hers. Boldly, she returned the caress; the muscles beneath her hands tensed. Emboldened, she let her lips firm against his, and reveled in his immediate response. Hard transmuted to harder; lips, muscles, all became more definite, more sharply defined.

It was fascinating—she became softer—he became harder.

And behind his hardness came heat—a heat they both shared. It rose like a fever, turning the swirling pleasure hot. Beyond the caress of his lips, he hadn't touched her, yet every nerve in her body was heating, simmering with sensation. The warm tide spread, swelled; the temperature increased.

And she was flushed, restless—wanting.

The slide of hard fingers over her breasts made her gasp— not in panic but pure shock. Shock at the shaft of sheer delight that speared through her, the sharp tingling that spread over her skin. The fingers firmed, possessively cupping her soft, oddly swollen flesh—which immediately swelled more. His hand closed, fingers kneading; her heated flesh firmed, tingling and tight.

The hot tangling of their tongues and the heat of his hand proved utterly distracting. When he stroked the peak of her breast, Patience gasped again. With something akin to amazement, her senses acutely focused on his fingertips, she marveled at her response to his touch, at the flaring heat that seared her, at the tight ruching of her nipples.

She'd never imagined such sensations existed; she could barely believe they were real. Yet the caresses continued, thrilling her, heating her—she had to wonder what else she didn't know.

What else she had yet to experience.

With every ounce of expertise at his command, Vane deliberately drew her deeper. Her total lack of resistance would have made him wonder, if he hadn't earlier seen the curiosity, the calm calculated intention in her eyes. She was willing, even eager—the knowledge stirred his passions powerfully. He held them in check, aware that she was no wanton, that she'd never been down this road before—and that, despite her guileless confidence, her openness—her implicit trust was a fragile thing which could all too easily be shattered by overly aggressive loving.

She was naive, innocent—she needed to be loved tenderly, coaxed to passion gently, savored slowly.

As he was savoring her now, the softness of her mouth his

to enjoy, her breast firm under his fondling hand. Her innocence was refreshing—heady, addictive, entrancing.

Angling his head, Vane deepened the kiss for an instant, then drew back, releasing her lips. But not her breast.

He waited, fingers stroking the swollen mounds, first one, then the other, waiting . . . until he saw her eyes glint beneath her lashes. He caught her gaze, then slowly, deliberately, lifted his fingers to the top button of her bodice.

Patience's eyes widened under her heavy lids; her breasts swelled as she drew in a shocked breath. The sudden release of the top button was almost a relief. Her senses reeled as his fingers moved down—to the next button; she felt every slow beat of her heart, pulsing under her skin, as, one after another, the tiny pearl rounds slipped their moorings.

And her bodice slowly opened.

For one fraught instant, she wasn't sure what she wanted—whether she even wanted to know what came next. The hesitation lasted only a second—the second it took for Vane to slowly brush aside the soft fabric of her bodice, for his fingers to slide knowingly in.

One gentle tug, and her chemise slid down. Then came the first tantalizing touch of his fingertips on her skin; Patience's senses whirled. Aghast, agape, utterly enthralled, her every nerve tingled to his touch, to the caress of his palm, to those long, hard fingers as they closed about her breast.

Vane watched her reaction from under heavy lids, watched flaring passion light her eyes. Sparks of pure gold flashed in the hazel depths as he gently kneaded, then sent his fingers gliding over her silken skin. He knew he should kiss her, distract her, from what came next—but the compulsion to witness, to know her reaction as she learned what he would do, as he filled his senses with her, waxed strong.

Deliberately, he shifted his hand; his fingers closed confidently about one tightly budded nipple.

Patience gasped—the sweet sound filled the room. Instinctively, she arched, pressing her breast more firmly into the hard palm surrounding it, seeking relief from the sharp sensation that speared her—again and again as his fingers firmed.

Vane bent his head and his lips found hers.

Patience clung to his kiss, held to it like an anchor in her suddenly whirling world. Pure streams of heat arced through her, waves of hot pleasure sank to her bones, pooled in her loins. She clutched Vane's shoulders, and kissed him back, suddenly desperate to know, to feel, to appease the desire throbbing in her veins.

Abruptly, he broke their kiss. He shifted, and his lips touched her throat. No longer cool, they seared like a brand as he traced the long sweep of her throat. Patience pressed her head back into the pillows and fought to catch her breath.

Only to lose it entirely a bare second later.

His lips closed about one tightly furled nipple—Patience thought she would die. Gasping desperately, she clenched her hands on his shoulders, fingers sinking deep. His lips firmed, he suckled gently—Patience felt the earth quake. The heat of his mouth shocked her—the wet sweep of his tongue scalded her. She gave a strangled cry.

That sound, keenly feminine, acutely evocative, caught and focused Vane's attention. Focused every hunter's instinct. Desire heightened, need escalated. His demons turned frenzied—her siren's song lured them on. Urged him on. Compulsion swelled—tense, turbulent, powerful. Desire seethed hotly. He drew a ragged breath—

And remembered—all he'd nearly forgotten, all her wild responses had driven from his mind. This was one seduction he had to, needed to, manage perfectly—this time, there was meaning beyond the act. Seducing Patience Debbington was too important to rush—conquering her senses, her body, was only the first step. He didn't want her just once—he wanted her for a lifetime.

Dragging in a shuddering breath, Vane caught hold of his reins and hauled his impulses up short. Something in him wailed with frustration. He shut his mind to the relentless pounding of his arousal.

And set himself to soothe hers.

He knew how. There were planes of warm desire on which women could float, neither driven, nor quiescent, but simply buoyed on a sea of pleasure. With hands and lips, mouth and tongue, he soothed her fevered flesh, took the sting from her aches, the edge from her passion, and eased her into that pleasured sea.

Patience was beyond understanding—all she knew was the peace, the calm, the profound pleasure that welled and washed through her. Content, she flowed with the tide, letting her senses stretch. The whirling that had disorientated her slowed; her mind steadied.

Full consciousness, when it came, was no shock; the continuing touch of Vane's hands, the artful caress of his lips, his tongue, were familiar—no threat.

Then she remembered where they were.

She tried to open her eyes, but her lids were too heavy. Finding breath enough to whisper was just possible. "What if someone comes in?"

Her words ended on a sigh as Vane lifted his head, lifted his lips from her breast. His voice rumbled softly through her. "The door's locked—remember?"

Remember? With his lips brushing hers, with his fingers caressing her breast, Patience was hard-pressed to remember her own name. The peace holding her stretched, her senses slowly sank. Every muscle gradually relaxed.

Vane had noticed the dark rings under her large eyes. He wasn't surprised to find her drifting close to sleep. Gradually, he slowed his caresses, then stopped. Carefully, he drew back, and smiled—at the soft smile that curved her kiss-bruised lips, the soft glow that lit her face.

He left her sleeping.

Patience wasn't sure when she realized he was gone—she sleepily cracked open her lids—and saw the windows rather than him. The warm peace that pervaded her was too deep to leave; she smiled and closed her eyes again.

When she finally awoke, the morning had gone. Blinking her eyes wide, she wriggled higher on the pillows. And frowned.

Someone had left her embroidery on the table beside the daybed; dredging through her foggy memories, she vaguely recalled Timms dropping by, remembered a hand gently stroking her hair.

Remembered a hand gently stroking her breasts. Patience blinked. Other memories, other sensations, crowded into her mind. Her eyes widened. "No—that *must* have been a dream." Frowning, she shook her head—but couldn't dull the sharpness of the sensual images, rising one after another in her mind. To dispell the nagging uncertainty, she glanced down—uncertainty crystallized to fact.

Her bodice was undone.

Horrified, Patience muttered an imprecation, and rapidly did it up. "Rakes!" Frowning direfully, she glanced about. Her gaze collided with Myst's. The small grey cat was settled comfortably on a side table, sitting on her brisket, front paws neatly tucked in.

"Have you been there all this time?"

Myst blinked her wide blue eyes—and stared steadily back.

Patience felt color rise in her cheeks—and wondered if it was possible to feel shy of a cat. Because of what a cat might have seen.

Before she could make up her mind, the door opened—Vane strolled in. The smile on his face, curving those fascinating lips, was more than enough to make Patience inwardly swear that she would not, not for anything, give him the pleasure of knowing how flustered she felt. "What's the time?" Nonchalance laced her tones.

"Lunchtime," replied the wolf.

Feeling very like Red Riding Hood, Patience smothered a feigned yawn, then held up her arms and waved him closer. "You may carry me down then."

Vane's smile deepened. With elegant ease, he lifted her into his arms.

Their entry into the dining room was noted by all. The rest of the household was already assembled about the table, with one notable exception. Gerrard's chair was empty.

Minnie and Timms both smiled benignly as Vane settled Patience into her chair. Mrs. Chadwick inquired after her injury with matronly politeness. Patience responded to the ladies with smiles and gentle words—and totally ignored all the men.

Except Vane—she couldn't ignore him. Even if her senses would have allowed it, he didn't—he insisted on instituting a general conversation on mild and unprovocative topics. When, encouraged by the prevailing sense of calm, Henry, under the pretext of helping her to more ham, tried to engage her with a smile and a gentle query about her knee, Patience froze him with a reply couched in sheet ice, and felt, beneath the table, Vane's knee jog hers. She turned and fixed him with an innocent look—he met her gaze, his eyes a flat grey, then ruthlessly drew her into the conversation.

When he lifted her into his arms at the end of the meal, Patience was in no very good mood. Not only had the undercurrents at the table abraded her nerves, but Gerrard had not appeared.

Vane carried her up to her private parlor and settled her back on the daybed.

"Thank you." Patience wriggled and prodded at her pillows, then sank back and reached for her embroidery. She threw Vane a quick, somewhat darkling glance, then shook out the linen cloth.

Stepping back, Vane watched her pull colored silks from her bag, then turned and strolled to the window. The day had started clear, but now clouds were rolling in, greying the sky.

Glancing back, he studied Patience. She sat amid the pillows and cushions, her work in her hands, bright silks strewn about her. But her hands were still; an absentminded frown had settled on her face.

Vane hesitated, then his lips firmed. He swung to face her. "If you like, I'll go and look for him."

He made the offer nonchalantly, leaving her the option of declining without embarrassment.

She looked up, her expression difficult to read. Then color seeped into her cheeks—and Vane knew she was recalling all she'd accused him of only two days before. But she did not look down, did not shift her gaze from his. After a further moment of consideration, she nodded. "If you would, I would be . . ."

Patience stopped, and blinked—but couldn't stop the word that rose to her lips. "Grateful." Her lips quirked; she looked down.

The next instant, Vane was beside her. Fingers sliding beneath her chin, he tipped her face up. He looked down at her for a long moment, his expression unreadable, then he stooped and touched his lips to hers. "Don't worry—I'll find him."

Instinctively, she returned the kiss. Gripping his wrist, she held him back, searching his face, then squeezed and let him go.

When the door closed behind him, Patience drew a deep, very deep breath.

She'd just placed her trust in an elegant gentleman. More than that, she'd trusted him with the one thing on earth she held most dear. Had he addled her wits? Or had she simply lost them?

For a full minute, she gazed unseeing at the window, then frowned, shook her head, shook her shoulders, and picked up her embroidery. There was no point wrestling with facts. She knew Gerrard was safe with Vane—safer than with any other gentleman within Bellamy Hall, safer than with any other gentleman she'd ever met.

And, she thought, pulling her needle free, while she was on the subject of startling admissions, she might as well admit that she felt relieved as well—relieved that Vane was there, that she wasn't, any longer, Gerrard's sole protector.

As startling admissions went, *that* took the prize.

"Here, you must be hungry by now." Vane dropped the sack he'd brought onto the grass beside Gerrard, who jumped like a scalded cat.

Gerrard looked around, then stared as Vane lowered himself to the grassy top of the old burial mound. "How did you know I'd be here?"

His gaze on the horizon, Vane shrugged. "Just a guess." A lilting smile touched his lips. "You hid your horse well enough, but you left tracks aplenty."

Gerrard humphed. His gaze fell on the sack. He pulled it closer and opened it.

While Gerrard munched on cold chicken and bread, Vane idly studied the views. After a while, he felt Gerrard's gaze on his face.

"I'm not the Spectre, you know."

Vane raised his brows arrogantly. "I do, as it happens."

"You do?"

"Hmm. I saw him last night—not well enough to recognize but enough to know it definitely wasn't you."

"Oh." After a moment, Gerrard went on, "All that talk of me being the Spectre—well, it always was just so much rot. I mean, as if I'd be silly enough to do such a thing anywhere near Patience." He snorted derisively. "Of *course* she'd go to look.

493

Why—she's worse than I am." A second later, he asked, "She is all right, isn't she? I mean, her knee?"

Vane's expression hardened. "Her knee's as well as can be expected—she has to stay off it for at least a few days, which, as you can imagine, is not improving her temper. At the moment, however, she's worrying—about you."

Gerrard colored. Looking down, he swallowed. "I lost my temper. I suppose I'd better go back." He started to pack up the sack.

Vane halted him. "Yes, we'd better get back and put a stop to her worrying, but you haven't asked about our plan."

Gerrard looked up. "Plan?"

Vane filled him in. "So, you see, we need you to continue to behave"—he gestured widely—"exactly as you have been—like a sapskull with his nose put out of joint."

Gerrard chuckled. "All right, but I am allowed to sneer dismissively, aren't I?"

"As much as you like, just don't forget your role."

"Minnie knows? And Timms?"

Vane nodded and got to his feet. "And Masters and Mrs. Henderson. I told Minnie and Timms this morning. As the staff are all reliable, there seemed little point keeping them in the dark, and we can use all the eyes we can get."

"So," Gerrard said, untangling his legs and rising, "we let it appear that I'm still chief suspect, all but convicted, and wait for the Spectre—"

"*Or* the thief—don't forget you're prime suspect there, too."

Gerrard nodded. "So we wait and we watch for their next move."

"Right." Vane started down the mound. "That, at the moment, is all we can do."

Chapter 9

~❖~

*T*WO DAYS LATER, Patience sat in her private parlor and applied herself to her embroidery. The cloths for the drawing room were almost finished; she'd be glad to see the last of them. She was still confined to the daybed, her knee still bound, her foot propped on a cushion. Her suggestion, made earlier that morning, that she could probably hobble perfectly well using a stick, had made Mrs. Henderson purse her lips, shake her head, and pronounce that four days' complete rest would be wiser. *Four days!* Before she could voice her utter antipathy to the idea, Vane, in whose arms she'd been at the time, had weighed in, backing Mrs. Henderson.

When, after breakfast, Vane had carried her here and laid her on the daybed, he'd reminded her of his earlier threat to tie her to it should he discover her on her feet. The reminder had been couched in sufficiently intimidating terms to keep her reclining, attending to the household linens with apparent equanimity.

Minnie and Timms had come to bear her company; Timms was busy knotting a fringe while Minnie watched, lending a finger whenever an extra was needed. They were all used to spending hours in quiet endeavors; none saw any reason to fill the peace with chatter.

Which was just as well; Patience's mind was fully occupied

elsewhere—mulling over what had ensued the first time Vane had carried her to this room. What with hiding her reaction, and her worries over Gerrard and the accusations hurled his way, it had been that night before she'd had time to fully examine the event.

Ever since, she had, at one level or another, thought of little else.

She should, of course, feel scandalized, or at the very least, shocked. Yet whenever she allowed herself to recall all that had happened, sweet pleasure washed through her, leaving her skin tingling and her breasts deliciously warm. Her "shock" was exciting, thrilling, an enticing reaction, not one of revulsion. She should feel guilty, yet whatever guilt she possessed was swamped beneath a compulsion to know, to experience, and an intense recollection of how much she'd enjoyed that particular experience.

Lips firming, she set a stitch. Curiosity—it was her curse, her bane, the cross she had to bear. She knew it. Unfortunately, knowing didn't quell the impulse. This time, curiosity was prompting her to waltz with a wolf—a dangerous enterprise. For the last two days, she'd watched him, waiting for the pounce she'd convinced herself would come, but he'd behaved like a lamb—a ridiculously strong, impossibly arrogant, not to say masterful lamb, but with a guileless newborn innocence, as if a halo had settled over his burnished locks.

Squinting at her work, Patience swallowed a disbelieving humph. He was playing some deep game. Unfortunately, due to lack of experience, she had no idea what.

"Actually"—Minnie settled back in her chair as Timms shook out the shawl they'd been working on—"this thief is worrying me. Vane might have scared the Spectre off, but the thief seems made of sterner stuff."

Patience glanced at Timms. "Your bracelet's still missing?"

Timms grimaced. "Ada turned my room upside down, and Minnie's, too. Masters and the maids have hunted high and low." She sighed. "It's gone."

"You said it was silver?"

Timms nodded. "But I wouldn't have thought it of any great value. It was engraved with vine leaves—you know the sort of thing." She sighed again. "It was my mother's and I'm really quite . . ."—she looked down, fiddling with the fringe she'd just knotted—"*bothered* that I've lost it."

Patience frowned absentmindedly and set another stitch.

Minnie sighed gustily. "And now here's Agatha similarly afflicted."

Patience looked up; so did Timms. "Oh?"

"She came to me this morning." Minnie frowned worriedly. "She was quite upset. Poor woman—what with all she's had to cope with, I wouldn't have had this happen for the world."

"What?" Patience prompted.

"Her earrings." Her expression as grim as it ever got, Minnie shook her head. "The last small piece she had left, poor dear. Oval drop garnets surrounded by white sapphires. You must have seen her wearing them."

"When last did she see them?" Patience remembered the earrings well. While handsome enough, they couldn't have been overly valuable.

"She wore them to dinner two nights ago," Timms put in.

"Indeed," Minnie nodded. "That was the last she saw of them—when she took them out that night and placed them in her box on her dressing table. When she went to get them last night, they were gone."

Patience frowned. "I thought she seemed a bit distracted last night."

"Agitated." Timms nodded grimly.

"She searched everywhere later," Minnie said, "but she's now quite sure they've vanished."

"Not vanished," Patience corrected. "They're with the thief. We'll find them when we catch him."

The door opened at that moment; Vane, followed by Gerrard, strolled in.

"Good morning, ladies." Vane nodded to Minnie and Timms, then turned his smile on Patience. His eyes, teasing grey, met hers; the quality of his smile, the expression at the back of his eyes, altered. Patience felt the warmth of his gaze as it slid lazily over her, over her cheeks, her throat, the swell of her upper breasts revealed by the scooped neckline of her morning gown. Her skin tingled; her nipples tightened.

She suppressed a warning scowl. "Did you enjoy your ride?" Her tone was as guilelessly innocent as his; both yesterday and today had been gloriously fine—while she'd been stuck inside, metaphorically tied to the daybed, he and Gerrard had enjoyed themselves on horseback, cantering about the county.

"Actually," Vane drawled, gracefully settling in a chair facing the daybed, "I've been introducing Gerrard to all the hedge-taverns within reach."

Patience's head jerked up; aghast, she stared at him.

"We've been checking if any of the others have been there," Gerrard eagerly explained. "Perhaps selling small things to tinkers or travelers."

From beneath her lashes, Patience threw Vane a darkling glance. He smiled, far too sweetly. His halo continued to glow. Patience sniffed and looked down at her work.

"And?" Minnie prompted.

"Nothing," Vane replied. "No one from the Hall—not even one of the grooms—has visited any of the local dives recently. No one's heard any whispers of anyone selling small items to tinkers and the like. So we still have no clue as to why the thief is stealing things, nor what he's doing with his ill-gotten gains."

"Speaking of which." Briefly, Minnie described the loss of Timms's bracelet and Mrs. Chadwick's earrings.

"So," Vane said, his expression hardening, "whoever it is has not been dissuaded by our pursuit of the Spectre."

"So what now?" Timms asked.

"We'll need to check Kettering and Northampton. It's possible the thief has a connection there."

The mantel clock chimed the half hour—twelve-thirty. Minnie gathered her shawls. "I'm due to see Mrs. Henderson about the menus."

"I'll leave the rest of this 'til later." Timms folded the shawl they'd been fringing.

Vane rose and offered Minnie his arm, but she waved him away. "No, I'm all right. You stay and keep Patience company." Minnie grinned at Patience. "Such a trying thing—to be tied to a daybed."

Suppressing her reaction to those innocent words, Patience smiled graciously, accepting Minnie's "gift"; once Minnie had passed on her way to the door, Patience lifted her embroidery, fixed her gaze upon it, and grasped the needle firmly.

Gerrard held the door open for Minnie and Timms. They

passed through; he looked back at Vane. And grinned engagingly. "Duggan mentioned he'd be exercising your greys about now. I might just nip down and see if I can catch him."

Patience whipped her head around, just in time to catch Gerrard's brotherly wave as he went out of the door. It shut behind him. In disbelief, she stared at the polished panels.

What were they all thinking of—leaving her alone with a wolf? She might be twenty-six—but she was an inexperienced twenty-six. Worse, she had a strong notion Vane viewed her age, let alone her inexperience, more as a positive than a negative.

Looking back at her work, she recalled his earlier jibe. Her temper rose, a helpful shield. Lifting her head, she studied him, standing before the daybed some four feet away. Her gaze was coolly measuring. "I do hope you don't intend to drag Gerrard into every inn—every '*dive*'—in Kettering and Northampton."

His gaze, already fixed on her, didn't waver; a slow, untrustworthy smile curved his lips. "No inns or taverns—not even dives." His smile deepened. "In the towns, we'll need to visit the jewelers, and the moneylenders. They often advance cash against goods." He paused, then grimaced. "My one problem is that I can't see what anyone at the Hall would want with extra cash. There's nowhere about to wager or game."

Lowering her embroidery to her lap, Patience frowned. "Perhaps they need the money for something else."

"I can't see the General or Edgar—much less Whitticombe— paying upkeep for some village maid and her brat."

Patience shook her head. "Henry would be shocked at the notion—he's stolidly conservative."

"Indeed—and, somehow, the notion doesn't ring true for Edmond." Vane paused. Patience looked up—he trapped her gaze. "As far as I can see," he said, his voice lowering to a purr, "Edmond seems more inclined to planning, rather than performance."

The implication, so strong Patience couldn't doubt she'd read it aright, was that *he* placed more emphasis on the latter. Ignoring the vise slowly choking off her breathing, she raised a haughty brow. "Indeed? I would have thought planning was always to be recommended." Greatly daring, she added, "In any enterprise."

Vane's slow smile curved his lips. Two prowling strides

brought him to the daybed's side. "You misunderstand me—good planning's essential to any successful campaign." Trapping Patience's gaze, he reached for the embroidery lying forgotten in her lap.

Patience blinked free of his hold as the linen slipped from her lax grasp. "I daresay." She frowned—just what were they talking about? She followed the embroidery as Vane lifted it—and met his eyes over the top of the hoop.

He smiled—all wolf—and tossed her work—linen, hoop and needle—into the basket beside the daybed. Leaving her without protection.

Patience felt her eyes grow round. Vane's smile deepened—a dangerous glint gleamed in his grey eyes. Languidly, he lifted a hand and, long fingers sliding beneath her chin, gripped it gently. Deliberately, he brushed his thumb—gently—over her lips.

They throbbed; Patience wished she had the strength to pull free of his light hold, to wrench free of his gaze.

"What I meant," he said, his voice very deep, "was that planning without the subsequent performance is worthless."

He meant she should have hung on to her embroidery. Too late, Patience caught his drift. He'd seen through her plan to use her work as a shield. Breath bated, she waited for her temper to come to her aid, to rise in response to being read so effortlessly, to being affected so readily.

Nothing happened. No searing fury erupted.

The only thought in her head as she studied his grey eyes was what *he* was planning to do next.

Because she was watching, was so deep in the grey, she caught the change, the subtle shift, the flash of what looked suspiciously like satisfaction that glowed, briefly, in his eyes. His hand fell; lids lowering, he turned away.

"Tell me what you know of the Chadwicks."

Patience stared at him—at his back as he returned to his chair. By the time he sat and faced her, she'd managed to school her features, although they felt curiously blank.

"Well"—she moistened her lips—"Mr. Chadwick died about two years ago—missing at sea."

With the help of Vane's prompts, she recounted, stiltedly,

all she knew of the Chadwicks. As she reached the end of her knowledge, the gong sounded.

His rake's smile returning, Vane stood and strolled toward her. "Speaking of performance, would you like me to carry you to lunch?"

She wouldn't—narrowing her eyes at him, Patience would have given half her fortune to avoid the sensation of being scooped so easily into his arms, and carried away so effortlessly. His touch was unnerving, distracting; it made her think of things she really should not. And as for the sensation of being helpless in his arms, trapped, at his mercy, a pawn to his whim—that was even worse.

Unfortunately, she had no choice. Coolly, inwardly girding her loins, she inclined her head. "If you would."

He grinned—and did.

The next day—the fourth and, Patience vowed, the very last day of her incarceration—she once more found herself committed to the daybed in her quiet parlor. After their usual early breakfast, Vane had carried her upstairs—he and Gerrard were to spend the day checking Northampton for any sign of items stolen from the Hall. The day was fine. The idea of a long drive, the wind whipping her hair as she sat on his box seat, behind the greys she'd already heard far too much about, had seemed like heaven. She'd been sorely tempted to ask that they put off the excursion—just for a day or so—until her knee improved sufficiently to allow her to sit in a carriage for a few hours, but, in the end, she'd held her tongue. They needed to discover who the thief was as soon as possible, and the weather, while fine today, could not be guaranteed.

Minnie and Timms had sat with her through the morning; as she couldn't go downstairs, they'd taken lunch on trays. Then Minnie had retired for her nap. Timms had helped Minnie to her room, but hadn't returned.

She'd finished the cloths for the drawing room. Idly examining designs, Patience wondered what project she should attempt next. Perhaps a delicate tray-piece for Minnie's dresser?

A knock on the door had her looking up in surprise. Neither Minnie nor Timms usually knocked.

"Come in."

The door opened tentatively; Henry's head appeared around its edge. "Am I disturbing you?"

Patience inwardly sighed, and waved to a chair. "By all means." She was, after all, bored.

Henry's puppy grin split his face. Straightening his shoulders, he entered, one hand held rather obviously behind his back. He advanced on the daybed, then halted—and, like a magician, produced his gift—a collection of late roses and autumn border blooms, greenery provided by Queen Anne's lace.

Primed, Patience widened her eyes in feigned surprise and delight. The delight waned as she focused on the ragged stems and the dangling remnants of roots. He'd ripped the flowers from the bushes and borders, not caring of the damage he did. "How—" She forced a smile to her lips. "How lovely." She took the poor flowers from him. "Why don't you ring for a maid so I can ask for a vase?"

Smiling proudly, Henry crossed to the bellpull and yanked it vigorously. Then, clasping his hands behind his back, he rocked on his toes. "Wonderful day outside."

"Is it?" Patience tried not to sound wistful.

The maid arrived and returned quickly with a vase and a pair of garden shears. While Henry prattled on about the weather, Patience tended the flowers, loping off the ragged ends and roots and setting them in the vase. Finished, she set the shears aside and turned the small side table she'd worked on toward Henry. "There." With a gracious wave, she sat back. "I do thank you for your kindness."

Henry beamed. He opened his lips—a knock cut off his words.

Brows rising, Patience turned to the door. "Come in."

As she'd half expected, it was Edmond. He'd brought his latest stanza. He beamed an ingenuous grin at both Patience and Henry. "Tell me what you think."

It wasn't just one stanza—to Patience, trying to follow the intricacies of his phrasing, it seemed more like half a canto.

Henry shifted and shuffled, his earlier brightness fading into petulance. Patience fought to stifle a yawn. Edmond prosed on.

And on.

When the next knock sounded, Patience turned eagerly, hoping for Masters or even a maid.

It was Penwick.

Patience gritted her teeth—and forced her lips to curve over them. Resigned, she held out her hand. "Good morning, sir. I trust you are well?"

"Indeed, my dear." Penwick bowed low—too low, he nearly hit his head on the side of the daybed. Pulling back just in time, he frowned—then banished the expression to smile, far too intently, into Patience's eyes. "I've been waiting to fill you in on the latest developments—the figures on production after we instituted the new rotation scheme. I know," he said, smiling fondly down at her, "how interested you are in 'our little patch.' "

"Ah—yes." What could she say? She'd always used agriculture, and having run the Grange for so long she had a more than passing knowledge of the subject, to distract Penwick. "Perhaps—?" She glanced hopefully at Henry. Tight-lipped, his gaze was fixed, not amiably, on Penwick. "Henry was just telling me how fine the weather's been these last few days."

Henry obligingly followed her lead. "Should stay fine for the foreseeable future. I was talking to Grisham only this morning—"

Unfortunately, despite considerable effort, Patience could not get Henry to switch to the effect of the weather on the crops, nor could she get Penwick to, as he usually did, distract Henry and himself with such matters.

To crown all, Edmond kept taking snippets from both Henry's and Penwick's words and fashioning them into verse, then, across whoever was speaking, trying to engage her in a discussion of how such verses might fit with the development of his drama.

Within five minutes, the conversation descended into a three-way tug-of-war for her attention—Patience was ready to throttle whichever foolish servant it was who'd divulged her up-until-then-secret location.

At the end of ten minutes, she was ready to throttle Henry, Edmond and Penwick as well. Henry held his position and pontificated on the elements; Edmond, nothing loath, was now talking of including mythological gods as commentators on his main characters' actions. Penwick, losing out to the chorus, puffed out his chest and portentously asked: "Where's Debbington? Surprised he isn't here, bearing you company."

"Oh, he tagged along with Cynster," Henry offhandedly informed him. "They escorted Angela and Mama to Northampton."

Finding Patience's gaze riveted on his face, Henry beamed at her. "Deal of sunshine, today—shouldn't wonder if Angela doesn't claim a turn in Cynster's curricle."

Patience's brows rose. "Indeed?"

There was a note in her voice which successfully halted all conversation; the three gentlemen, suddenly wary, glanced sidelong at each other.

"I think," Patience declared, "that I have rested long enough." Tossing aside the rug that had lain across her lap, she pushed herself to the edge of the daybed, and carefully let down her good leg, then the damaged one. "If you would be so good as to give me your arm . . . ?"

They all rushed to help. In the end, it wasn't as easy as she'd thought—her knee was still tender, and very stiff. Taking her full weight on that leg was out of the question.

Which made the stairs impossible. Edmond and Henry made a chair of their arms; Patience sat and held their shoulders for balance. Puffed with importance, Penwick led the way down, talking all the while. Henry and Edmond couldn't talk—they were concentrating too much on balancing her weight down the steep stairs.

They made it to the front hall without mishap, and set her carefully on her feet on the tiles. By then Patience was having second thoughts—or rather, she *would* have entertained second thoughts, if she hadn't been so exercised by the news that Vane had taken Angela to Northampton.

That Angela had enjoyed the drive—would even now be enjoying the drive—she herself had fantasized over, but had, for the greater good, not sought to claim.

She was not in a very good mood.

"The back parlor," she declared. Leaning on both Henry's and Edmond's arms, she hobbled along between them, trying not to wince. Penwick rattled on, recounting the number of bushels "their little patch" had produced, his matrimonial assumptions waving like flags in his words. Patience gritted her teeth. Once they gained the back parlor, she would dismiss them all—and then, very carefully, massage her knee.

No one would look for her in the back parlor.

"You're not supposed to be on your feet."

The statement, uttered in a flat tone, filled the sudden gap where Penwick's babble had been.

Patience looked up, then had to tip her chin higher—Vane was standing directly in front of her. He was wearing his caped greatcoat; the wind had ruffled his hair. Behind him, the side door stood open. Light streamed into the dim corridor, but didn't reach her. He blocked it—a very large, very male figure, made even larger by the capes of his greatcoat, spread wide by his broad shoulders. She couldn't see the expression on his face, in his eyes—she didn't need to. She knew his face was hard, his eyes steel grey, his lips thin.

Irritation poured from him in waves; in the confines of the corridor, it was a tangible force. "I did warn you," he said, his tones clipped, "what would happen."

Patience opened her lips; all she uttered was a gasp.

She was no longer on her feet, she was in his arms.

"Just a minute!"

"I say—!"

"Wait—!"

The ineffectual exclamations died behind them. Vane's swift strides had them back in the front hall before Penwick, Edmond, and Henry could do more than collectively blink.

Catching her breath, Patience glared. "Put me down!"

Vane glanced, very briefly, into her face. "No." He started up the stairs.

Patience drew in a breath—two maids were coming down the stairs. She smiled as they passed. And then they were in the gallery. It had taken the others ten full minutes to get her downstairs; Vane had accomplished the reverse in under a minute. "The other *gentlemen*," she acidly informed him, "were helping me to the back parlor."

"Sapskulls."

Patience's breasts swelled. "I *wanted* to be in the back parlor!"

"Why?"

Why? Because then, if he came looking for her after his fine

505

day out at Northampton with Angela, he wouldn't have known where she was and might have been worried? "Because," Patience tartly replied, folding her arms defensively across her breasts, "I've grown sick of the upstairs parlor." The parlor he'd arranged for her. "I'm bored there."

Vane glanced at her as he juggled her to open the door. "Bored?"

Patience looked into his eyes and wished she'd used some other word. Bored was, apparently, a red rag to a rake. "It's not long to dinner, perhaps you should just take me to my room."

The door swung wide. Vane stepped through, then kicked it shut behind them. And smiled. "There's more than an hour before you need change. I'll carry you to your room—later."

His eyes had narrowed, silvery with intent. His voice had changed to his dangerous purr. Patience wondered if any of the other three would have the courage to follow—she couldn't believe they would. Ever since Vane had so coldly annihilated their senseless accusations of Gerrard, both Edmond and Henry treated him with respect—the sort of respect accorded dangerous carnivores. And Penwick knew Vane disliked him—intensely.

Vane advanced on the daybed. Patience eyed it with increasing misgiving. "What do you think you're doing?"

"Tying you to the daybed."

She tried to humph, tried to ignore the premonition tickling her spine. "Don't be silly—you just said that as a threat." Would it be wise to wind her arms about his neck?

He reached the back of the bed, and stopped. "I never issue threats." His words floated down to her as she stared at the cushions. "Only warnings."

With that, he swung her over the wrought-iron back and set her down with her spine against it. Patience immediately squirmed, trying to twist around. One large palm, splayed across her midriff, kept her firmly in place.

"And then," Vane continued, in the same, dangerous tone, "we'll have to see what we can do to . . . distract you."

"Distract me?" Patience stopped her futile wriggling.

"Hmm." His words feathered her ear. "To alleviate your boredom."

There was enough sensual weight in the words to temporarily freeze her wits—capture them and hold them in fascinated speculation—just long enough for him to grab a scarf from the pile of mending left in the basket by the daybed, thread it through the holes in the swirls of the ornate back and cinch it tight about her waist.

"What . . . ?" Patience looked down as his hand disappeared and the scarf drew tight. Then she glared. "This is ridiculous." She tugged at the scarf and tried to shift forward, but he'd already secured the knot. The silk gave just so far, then held. Vane strolled around to face her; Patience shot him a dagger glance—she didn't want to know about the smile on his lips. Compressing her own, she lifted her arms and reached over the back of the bed. The ornately worked railing reached halfway up her back—while she could lift her arms over it, she couldn't reach very far down. She couldn't touch his knot, let alone untie it.

Eyes narrowed, Patience looked up; Vane was watching her, a cool smile of ineffable male superiority etched on his too-fascinating lips. She narrowed her eyes to slits. "You will never live this down."

The curve of his lips deepened. "You're not uncomfortable. Just sit still for the next hour." His gaze sharpened. "It'll do your knee good."

Patience gritted her teeth. "I'm not some infant who needs to be restrained!"

"On the contrary it's clear you need someone to exercise some control over you. You heard Mrs. Henderson—four full days. Your four days is up tomorrow."

Astounded, Patience stared at him. "And just who appointed you my keeper?"

She caught his gaze, held the contact defiantly—and waited. His eyes narrowed. "I feel guilty. I should have sent you back to the house as soon as I found you in the ruins."

All expression drained from Patience's face. "You wish you'd sent me back to the house?"

Vane frowned. "I feel guilty because you were following me when you got hurt."

Patience humphed and crossed her arms beneath her breasts. "You told me it was *my* fault for not staying where you'd told me to stay. Anyway, if Gerrard at seventeen is old enough to be responsible for his own actions, why would it be otherwise with me?"

Vane looked down at her; Patience felt sure she'd won her point. Then he raised an arrogant brow. "*You're* the one with the wrenched knee. *And* the twisted ankle."

Patience refused to surrender. "My ankle's fine." She put her nose in the air. "And my knee's just a bit stiff. If I could test it—"

"You can test it tomorrow. Who knows?" Vane's expression hardened. "You might need an extra day or two's rest after today's excitement."

Patience narrowed her eyes. "Don't," she advised, "even suggest it."

Vane raised both brows, then, turning away, prowled to the window. Patience watched him, and tried to locate the anger she felt sure she should feel. It simply wasn't to be found. Stifling a disaffected humph, she settled more comfortably. "So what did you discover in Northampton?"

He glanced back, then fell to prowling back and forth between the windows. "Gerrard and I made the acquaintance of a very helpful individual—the Northampton Guildmaster, so to speak."

Patience frowned. "Of which guild?"

"The guild of moneylenders, thieves, and rogues—assuming there is one. He was intrigued with our investigations and amused enough to be helpful. His contacts are extensive. After two hours of consuming the best French brandy—at my expense, of course—he assured us no one had recently attempted to sell any items of the sort we're seeking."

"Do you think he's reliable?"

Vane nodded. "There was no reason for him to lie. The items, as he so succinctly put it, are of insufficient quality to attract his personal interest. He's also well-known as 'the man to contact.' "

Patience grimaced. "You'll check Kettering?"

Still pacing, Vane nodded.

Watching him, Patience conjured her most innocent expression. "And what did Mrs. Chadwick and Angela do while you and Gerrard met with this Guildmaster?"

Vane stopped pacing. He looked at Patience—studied her.

His expression was unreadable. Eventually, he said, "I haven't the faintest idea."

His voice had altered, a subtle undercurrent of awakened interest sliding beneath the suave tones. Patience opened her eyes wide. "You mean Angela didn't tell you every last detail on the drive back?"

With long, languid strides, Vane came toward her. "She traveled—both ways—in the carriage."

Vane reached the edge of the daybed. His eyes gleamed with a predator's satisfaction. He leaned nearer—

"Patience? Are you awake?"

A peremptory knock was followed immediately by the sound of the latch lifting.

Patience swung around—as far as she could. Vane straightened; as the door opened, he reached the back of the daybed. Before he could tug the knotted scarf loose, Angela breezed in.

"Oh!" Angela stopped, eyes widening with delight. "Mr. Cynster! *Perfect*! You must give us your opinion of my purchases."

Eyeing the bandbox dangling from Angela's fingers with distinct disapprobation, Vane nodded a noncommittal greeting. As Angela eagerly made for the chairs facing the daybed, he stooped slightly, fingers reaching for the knot in the scarf, screened from view by his legs—only to have to straighten quickly as the door swung wider and Mrs. Chadwick entered.

Angela, settling in a chair, looked up. "See here, Mama— Mr. Cynster can tell us if the ribbons that I bought aren't just the right shade."

With a calm nod for Vane and a smile for Patience, Mrs. Chadwick headed for the second chair. "Now, Angela, I'm sure Mr. Cynster has other engagements . . ."

"No, how can he have? There's no one else here. Besides," —Angela threw Vane a sweet, truly ingenuous smile—"that's how *ton*nish gentlemen pass their time—commenting on ladies' fashions."

The sigh of relief Patience had heard behind her was abruptly cut off. For one fractured instant, she was sorely tempted to twist about, look up—and inquire if Angela's foppish notion of his character found greater favor with him than her earlier, overly rakish one. Then again, both notions were partly right. Vane, she felt sure, when he commented on ladies' fashions, would do so while divesting the subject of his interest of them.

Mrs. Chadwick heaved a motherly sigh. "Actually, my dear, that's not quite right." She sent Vane an apologetic glance. "Not all gentlemen . . ." For Angela's edification, Mrs. Chadwick embarked on a careful explanation of the distinctions prevailing amongst *ton*nish males.

Leaning forward, ostensibly to straighten the wrap over Patience's legs, Vane murmured, "That's my cue to retreat."

Patience's gaze remained glued to Mrs. Chadwick. "I'm still tied," she murmured back. "You can't leave me like this."

Fleetingly, her eyes met Vane's. He hesitated, then his face hardened. "I'll release you on condition that you wait here until I return to carry you to your room."

Reaching farther over her, he flicked out the edge of the wrap. Patience glared at his profile. "This is all your fault," she informed him in a whisper. "If I'd made it to the back parlor, I'd have been safe.

Straightening, Vane met her gaze. "Safe from what? There's a daybed there, too."

Her gaze trapped in his, Patience tried hard not to let the likely outcomes take shape in her mind. Determinedly, she blotted out all thought of what might have transpired had Angela not arrived as she had. If she thought too much of that, she'd very likely throttle Angela, too. The ranks of her potential victims were growing by the hour.

"Anyway . . ."—Vane's gaze flicked to Angela and Mrs. Chadwick. He stooped slightly; Patience felt the tug as he worked the knotted scarf free—"you said you were bored." The knot gave, and he straightened. Patience looked up and back— and met his eyes. His lips curved, too knowingly. One brown brow arched, subtly wicked. "Isn't this what usually distracts ladies?"

He knew very well what ladies found most distracting—the look in his eyes, the sensual curve of his lips said as much, screamed as much. Patience narrowed her eyes at him, then, folding her arms, looked back at Mrs. Chadwick. "Coward," she taunted, just loudly enough for him to hear.

"When it comes to gushing schoolgirls, I freely admit it."

The words fell softly, then he stepped away from the daybed's back. The movement caught both Angela's and Mrs. Chadwick's attention. Vane smiled, smoothly suave. "I'm afraid, ladies, that I'll have to leave you. I need to check on my horses." With a nod to Mrs. Chadwick, a vague smile for Angela, and a last, faintly challenging glance for Patience, he sketched an elegant bow and made his escape.

The door closed behind him. Angela's bright face darkened into a sulky pout. Patience inwardly groaned, and swore she'd extract suitable revenge. Meanwhile . . . Plastering an interested smile on her lips, she looked at the items spilling from Angela's bandox. "Is that a comb?"

Angela blinked, then brightened. "Yes, it is. Quite inexpensive, but so pretty." She held up a tortoiseshell comb dotted with paste "diamonds." "Don't you think it's just the thing for my hair?"

Patience resigned herself to perjury. Angela had bought cerise ribbon, too—by the yard. Patience silently added that to Vane's bill, and continued to smile sweetly.

Chapter 10

❦

*D*ANGER.

It should have been his middle name.

It should have been tatooed on his forehead.

"A warning would at least make it fairer." Patience waited for Myst to react; eventually, the cat blinked. "Humph!" Patience cut another branch of autumn color. Narrow-eyed, she bent and stuffed the branch into the pannier at her feet.

Three days had passed since she'd escaped the daybed; this morning, she'd eschewed Sir Humphrey's cane. Her first excursion had been a ramble about the old walled garden. In company with Vane.

That, in retrospect, had been a most peculiar outing—it had certainly left her in a most peculiar state. They'd been alone. Anticipation had soared, only to be frustrated—by Vane. By their location. Unfortunately, there had been no other private moments in the intervening days.

Which had left her in no very good mood—as if her emotions, raised by that one, intense, unfulfilled moment in the walled garden, were still swirling hotly, as yet unappeased. Her knee was weak, but no longer painful. She could walk freely, but could not yet go far.

She'd gone as far as the shrubbery, to collect a sheaf of bright leaves for the music room.

512

Picking up the full pannier, Patience balanced it against her hip. Waving Myst ahead, she started along the grassy path leading back to the house.

Life at the Hall, temporarily disrupted by Vane's arrival and her accident, was settling back into its usual routine. The only hitch in the smooth flow of mild household events was Vane's continuing presence. He was about somewhere—she had no idea where.

Emerging from the shrubbery, Patience scanned the lawns rolling away into the ruins. The General was striding up from the river, walking briskly and swinging his cane. In the ruins themselves, Gerrard sat on a stone, his easel before him. Patience studied the stones and archways nearby, then swept the ruins and lawns again.

Then realized what she was doing.

She headed for the side door. Edgar and Whitticombe would be buried in the library—not even sunshine would lure them out. Edmond's muse had turned demanding: He barely attended meals, and even then, was sunk in abstraction. Henry, of course, was as idle as ever. He had, however, developed a penchant for billiards and was frequently to be found practicing shots.

Opening the side door, Patience waited for Myst to trip daintily in, then followed and shut the door. Myst led the way up the corridor. Resettling her pannier, Patience heard voices in the back parlor. Angela's whine, followed by Mrs. Chadwick's patient reply. Grimacing, Patience walked on. Angela was town-bred, not used to the country, with its mild pursuits and slow seasons. Vane's arrival had transformed her into a typical, bright-eyed miss. Unfortunately, she'd now tired of that image and reverted to her usual, die-away airs.

Of the rest of the household, Edith continued with her tatting. And Alice had been so silent of late one could be forgiven for forgetting her existence.

From the front hall, Patience turned into a narrow corridor, and thus reached the garden hall. Setting the pannier on a side table, she selected a heavy vase. As she arranged her branches, she considered Minnie and Timms. Timms was happier, more relaxed now that Vane was here. The same and more could be said of Minnie. She was clearly sleeping better—her eyes were back to their sparkling best and her cheeks no longer sagged with worry.

Patience frowned, and concentrated on her twigs.

Gerrard was also more relaxed. The accusations and insinuations surrounding him had died, sunk without trace, dispersed like so much river mist. Just like the Spectre.

That was also Vane's doing—another benefit his presence had brought them. The Spectre hadn't been sighted again.

The thief, however, continued to strike: His latest trophy was nothing short of bizarre. Edith Swithin's pincushion—a beaded, pink-satin cushion four inches square, embroidered with a likeness of His Majesty George III, could hardly be considered valuable. That last disappearance had perplexed them all. Vane had shaken his head and given it as his opinion that they had a resident magpie roosting within the Hall.

"Resident raven more like." Patience looked at Myst. "Have you seen one?"

Settled on her brisket, Myst met her gaze, then yawned. Not delicately. Her fangs were quite impressive. "No raven either," Patience concluded.

Despite checking all inns and "dives" within reach, Vane, happily assisted by Gerrard, had not found any clue to suggest the thief was selling the stolen goods. It all remained an ongoing mystery.

Patience put away the pannier, then picked up the vase. Myst jumped from the table and, tail high, led the way. As she headed for the music room, Patience reflected that, with the exception of Vane's presence and the thief's eccentricities, the household had indeed sunk back into its previously untrammeled existence.

Before Vane's arrival, the music room had been her retreat—none of the others was musically inclined. She'd always played, every day for most of her life. Spending an hour with a pianoforte, or, as here, a harpsichord, always soothed her, eased the load that had always been hers.

Carrying the vase into the music room, she placed it on the central table. Returning to close the door, she surveyed her domain. And nodded. "Back to normal."

Myst was making herself comfortable on a chair. Patience headed for the harpsichord.

These days, she never decided what to play, but simply let

her fingers roam. She knew so many pieces, she just let her mind choose without conscious direction.

Five minutes of restless, disjointed playing—of drifting from one piece to another in search of her mood—was enough to bring home the truth. *Not* everything was back to normal.

Putting her hands in her lap, Patience frowned direfully at the keys. Things were back the way they were, the same as before Vane's arrival. The only changes were for the good; no need for her to fret. Less need to fret than before. Everything was proceeding smoothly. She had her usual round of small chores, lending order to her days—she'd found it satisfying before.

But far from sinking back into reassuring routine, she was . . . fretful. Dissatisfied.

Patience put her hands back on the keys. But no music came. Instead, her mind, entirely against her will, conjured up the source of her dissatisfaction. One elegant gentleman. Patience looked down at her fingers resting on the ivory keys. She was trying to fool herself and not doing a particularly good job of it.

Her mood was unsettled, her temper more so. As for her emotions, they'd taken up residence on a carousel. She didn't know what she wanted, she didn't know what she felt. For someone used to being in charge of her life, of directing that life, the situation was beyond irritating.

Patience narrowed her eyes. Her situation, in fact, was insupportable. Which meant it was past time she did something about it. The source of her condition was obvious— Vane. Just him—no one else was even peripherally involved. It was her interaction with him that was causing all her problems.

She could avoid him.

Patience considered that long and hard—and rejected it on the grounds that she couldn't do that without embarrassing herself and insulting Minnie. And Vane might not deign to be avoided.

And she might not be strong enough to avoid him.

Frowning, she shook her head. "Not a good idea." Her thoughts returned to their last moment alone, in the walled garden three days before. Her frown deepened. What was he about? His "not here" she'd later understood—the walled garden was overlooked by the house. But what had he meant by "not yet"?

"That," she informed Myst, "suggests a 'later.' A 'some-time.' " Patience set her teeth. "What I want to know is *when*?"

A scandalous, inadmissible want perhaps, but . . . "I'm twenty-six." Patience eyed Myst as if she'd argued. "I'm entitled to the knowledge." When Myst responded with an unblinking stare, Patience continued: "It's not as if I intend throwing my cap over the windmill. I'm not likely to forget who I am, let alone who and what he is. And neither is he. It should all be perfectly safe."

Myst tucked her nose into her paws.

Patience went back to frowning at the keyboard. "He won't seduce me under Minnie's roof." Of that, she was certain. Which raised a most pertinent question. What did he want—what did *he* expect to gain? What was his purpose in all this—did he even have one?

All questions for which she lacked answers. While, over the last days, Vane had not engineered any moment alone with her, she was always conscious of his gaze, always conscious of him, of his watchful presence.

"Perhaps this is dalliance? Or some part thereof?"

Yet more questions without answers.

Patience gritted her teeth, then forced herself to relax. She drew in a deep breath, exhaled and drew in another, then determinedly laid her fingers on the keys. She didn't understand Vane—the elegant gentleman with unpredictable reservations—indeed, he confused her at every turn. Worse, if this was dalliance, then it apparently proceeded at his whim, under his control, entirely outside hers—and, of that, she thoroughly disapproved.

She wasn't going to think about him anymore.

Patience closed her eyes, and let her fingers flow over the keys.

Delicate, hauntingly uncertain music floated out of the house. Vane heard it as he walked up from the stables. The lilting strains reached him, then wrapped about him, about his mind, sinking into his senses. They were a siren's song—and he knew precisely who was singing.

Halting on the graveled drive before the stable arch, he listened to the moody air. It drew him—he could feel the tug as if it was physical. The music spoke—of need, of restless frustration, of underlying rebellion.

The scrunch of gravel under his boots brought him to his senses. Frowning, he stopped again. The music room was on the ground floor, facing away from the ruins; its windows gave onto the terrace. At least one window had to be open, or he wouldn't hear the music so clearly.

For a long moment, he stared, unseeing, at the house. The music grew more eloquent, seeking to ensorcel him, insistently drawing him on. For one more minute, he resisted, then shook aside his hesitation. His face set, he strode for the terrace.

When the final notes died, Patience sighed and lifted her fingers from the keys. A measure of calm had returned to her, the music had released some of her restlessness, had soothed her soul. A catharsis.

She stood, more serene, more confident than when she'd sat. Pushing back the stool, she stepped about it and turned.

Toward the windows. Toward the man who stood beside the open French door. His expression was set, unreadable.

"I had thought," she said, her words deliberate, her eyes steady on his, "that you might be thinking of leaving."

Her challenge could not have been clearer.

"No." Vane answered without thinking; no thought was required. "Aside from unmasking the Spectre and discovering the thief, I haven't yet got that something I want."

Contained, commanding, Patience's chin rose another notch. Vane studied her, his words echoing in his head. When he'd first coined the phrase, he hadn't appreciated exactly what it was that he wanted. Now he knew. His goal, this time, was different from the prizes he habitually lusted after. This time, he wanted a great deal more.

He wanted her—all of her. Not just the physical her, but her devotion, her love, her heart—all the essential her, the tangible intangible of her being, her self. He wanted it all—and he wasn't going to be satisfied with anything less.

He knew why he wanted her, too. Why she was different. But he wasn't going to think about that.

She was his. He'd known it the instant he'd held her in his arms, that first evening with the storm lowering about them.

She'd fitted—and he'd known, instinctively, immediately, at some level deeper than his bones. He hadn't come by his name by accident: he had a gift for recognizing what scent was on the breeze. An instinctive hunter, he responded to shifts in the mood, the atmosphere, taking advantage of whatever current was flowing without conscious thought.

He'd known from the first just what was in the wind—known from the instant he'd held Patience Debbington in his arms.

Now she stood before him, challenge lighting gold sparks in her eyes. That she was tired of their present hiatus was clear; what she envisioned replacing it was not so obvious. The only virtuous, willful women he'd interacted with were related to him; he'd never dallied with such ladies. He had no clue what Patience was thinking, how much she'd accepted. Taking a death grip on the reins of his own clamorous needs, he deliberately took the first steps to find out.

With slow, prowling strides, he approached her.

She didn't say a word. Instead, her eyes steady on his, she lifted one hand, one finger, and, slowly, giving him ample time to react, to stop her if he would, reached to touch his lips.

Vane didn't move.

The first tentative touch inwardly rocked him; he tightened his hold on his passions. She sensed the momentary turbulence. Her eyes widened, her breath caught. Then he stilled and she relaxed, and continued her tracing.

She seemed fascinated by his lips. Her gaze dropped to them; as her finger passed over his lower lip and returned to one corner, Vane moved his head just enough to brush a kiss across her fingertip.

Her eyes lifted again to his. Emboldened, she quested further, lifting her fingers higher to trace his cheek.

Vane returned the caress, slowly raising one hand to run the back of his fingers along the smooth curve of her jaw, then sliding them back until his palm cupped her chin. His fingers firmed; moving to the slow, steady drumbeat only he and she could hear, he tilted her face up.

Their gazes locked. Then he let his lids fall, knowing she did the same. In time with the slow beat, he lowered his lips to hers.

She hesitated for one instant, then kissed him back. He

waited one beat more before demanding her mouth; she yielded it instantly. Sliding his fingers further, beneath the silken coil of hair at her nape, he raised his other hand and framed her jaw.

He held her face steady—and slowly, systematically, moving to the compelling rhythm that held them, drove them, plundered her mouth.

That kiss was a revelation—Patience had never imagined a simple kiss could be so bold, so heavily invested with meaning. His lips were hard; they moved over hers, parting them further, confidently managing her, ruthlessly teaching her all she was so eager to learn.

His tongue invaded her mouth with the arrogance of a conqueror claiming victory's spoils. Unhurriedly, he visited every corner of his domain, claiming each inch, branding it as his—knowing it. After a lengthy, devastatingly thorough inspection, he settled to sample her in a different way. The slow, languid thrusting seduced her willing senses.

She'd yielded, yet her passive surrender satisfied neither of them. Patience found herself drawn into the game—the slide of lips against lips, the sensual glide of hot tongue against tongue. She was more than willing. The promise in the heat rising, steadily building between them, and even more the tension—excitement and something more—that surged like a slow tide behind the warm glow, drew her on. The kiss stretched and time slowed—the drugging effect of shared breaths sent her wits into a slow spin.

He drew back, breaking the kiss, letting her catch her breath. But he didn't straighten; his lips, relentlessly hard, remained mere inches from hers.

Aware only of compulsion, of the steady driving beat in her blood, she stretched upward and touched her lips to his.

He took her lips, her mouth, briefly, then again broke the contact.

Patience snatched a breath and, stretching up, followed his lips with hers. She needn't have worried—he wasn't going anywhere. His fingers firmed about her jaw; his lips returned, harder, more demanding as he angled his head over hers.

The kiss deepened. Patience hadn't dreamed there could be more, yet there was. Heat and hunger poured through her. She felt each caress, each bold, knowing stroke—she reveled in the hot pleasure, drank it in, and gave it back—and wanted more.

When next their lips parted, they were both breathing rapidly. Patience opened her eyes and met his watchful gaze. Subtle invitation, and even subtler challenge, melded in the grey; she considered the sight—and considered how much more he could teach her.

She paused. Then she stepped closer, sliding one hand, then the other, up over his broad shoulders. Her bodice touched his jacket; she moved closer still. Boldly holding his gaze, she pressed her hips to his thighs.

The locking of his control was palpable, like the sudden clenching of a fist. The reaction reassured her, allowed her to continue to meet his grey gaze. To meet the challenge in his eyes.

His hands had softened about her face; now they drifted away, resting briefly on her shoulders before, his gaze steady on hers, he swept them down, down her back, over her hips, drawing her fully against him.

Patience's breath caught. Her lids fell. Wordlessly, she lifted her face, offering her lips.

He took them, took her—as their lips fused, Patience felt his hands slide lower, deliberately tracing the ripe hemispheres of her bottom. He filled his hands, then kneaded—heat spread, prickling over her skin, leaving it fevered. Cupping her firm flesh, he molded her to him, easing her deeper into the V of his braced thighs.

She felt the evidence of his desire, felt the hard, heavy, throbbing reality pressed against her soft belly. He held her there, senses fully awake, fully aware, for one achingly intense instant, then his tongue slowly surged, thrusting deep into the softness of her mouth.

Patience would have gasped, but she couldn't. The evocative caress, his unhurried possession of her mouth, sent heat rolling through her. It pooled, hot and heavy, in her loins. As the kiss drew her in, drew her deeper, a heady langor spread, weighting her limbs, slowing her senses.

But not muting them.

She was achingly aware. Aware of the hardness that surrounded her, of the steely flex of hard muscle about her. Of her tightly furled nipples pressed hard to the wall of his chest; of the softness of her thighs held intimately against him. Of the relentless, driving passion he ruthlessly held back.

That last was a temptation, but one so potently, preeminently dangerous not even she dared prod it.

Not yet. There were other things she'd yet to learn.

Like the feel of his hand on her breast—different now he was kissing her so deeply, now she was so much in contact with him. Her breast swelled, warm and tight as his fingers closed about it; the nipple was already a ruched bud, excruciatingly sensitive to his knowing squeeze.

And their kiss went on, anchoring her to her own heartbeat, to the repetitive ebb and surge of a rhythm that played at the very edge of her consciousness. The pattern swirled and deepened, but still the beat was there, a crescendo of slow-burning desire, conducted, orchestrated, so that she never lost touch, was never overwhelmed by sensation.

He was teaching her.

Quite when that became clear, Patience couldn't have said, but she'd accepted it as truth when the gong for lunch sounded. Distantly.

She ignored it; so did Vane. At first. Then, with obvious reluctance, he drew back from their kiss.

"They'll notice if we miss lunch." He murmured the words against her lips—then resumed kissing them.

"Hmm," was all Patience cared to say.

Three minutes later, he lifted his head. And looked down at her.

Patience studied his eyes, his face. Not the smallest hint of apology, of triumph, even of satisfaction, showed in the grey, in the hard, angular planes. Hunger was the dominant emotion—in him and in her. She could feel it deep within her, a primal craving stirred to life by their kiss but as yet unappeased. His hunger showed in the tension holding him, the control he'd never once eased.

His lips twisted wryly. "We'll have to go." Reluctantly, he released her.

Equally reluctant, Patience drew back, instantly regretting

the loss of his heat and the sense of intimacy that, for the last uncounted moments, they'd shared.

There was, she discovered, nothing she wished to say. Vane offered his arm and she took it, and allowed him to lead her to the door.

Chapter 11

‍‍

FTER HIS AFTERNOON gallop with Gerrard, Vane strode determinedly back to the house.

He couldn't get Patience out of his mind. The taste of her,
the feel of her, the evocatively heady scent of her wreathed his
senses and preyed on his attention. He hadn't been this obsessed
since he'd first lifted a woman's skirts, yet he recognized the
symptoms. He wasn't going to be able to concentrate on anything else until he'd succeeded in putting Patience Debbington
in her rightful place—on her back beneath him.

And he couldn't do *that* until he'd said the words, asked the
question he'd known had been inevitable since she'd first landed
in his arms.

In the front hall, he encountered Masters. Purposefully, Vane
stripped off his gloves. "Where's Miss Debbington, Masters?"

"In the mistress's parlor, sir. She usually sits with the mistress and Mrs. Timms most afternoons."

One boot on the lowest stair, Vane considered the various
excuses he could use to extract Patience from under Minnie's
wing. Not one was sufficient to escape attracting Minnie's instant attention. Let alone Timms's. "Hmm." Lips setting, he
swung about. "I'll be in the billiard room."

"Indeed, sir."

*　　*　　*

Contrary to Masters's belief, Patience wasn't in Minnie's parlor. Excusing herself from their usual sewing session, she'd taken refuge in the parlor on the floor below, where the daybed, now no longer needed, sat swathed in Holland covers.

So she could pace unrestricted, frowning, muttering distractedly, while she attempted to understand, to accurately comprehend, to justify and reconcile all that had happened in the music room that morning.

Her world had tilted. Abruptly. Without warning.

"That much," she waspishly informed an imperturbable Myst, curled comfortably on a chair, "is impossible to deny." That heated yet masterfully controlled kiss she and Vane had shared had been a revelation on more than one front.

Swinging about, Patience halted before the window. Folding her arms, she stared out, unseeing. The physical revelations, while unnerving enough, had been no real shock—they were, indeed, no more than her curiosity demanded. She wanted to know—he'd consented to teach her. That kiss had been her first lesson; that much was clear.

As for the rest—therein lay her problem.

"There was something else there." An emotion she'd never thought to feel, never expected to feel. "At least"—grimacing, she resumed her restless pacing—"I *think* there was."

The acute sense of loss she'd felt when they'd moved apart had not been simply a physical reaction—the separation had affected her on some other plane. And the compulsion to intimacy—to satisfy the hunger she sensed in him—*that* did not stem from curiosity.

"This is getting complicated." Rubbing a finger across her forehead in a vain attempt to erase her frown, Patience struggled to come to grips with her emotions, to clarify what she truly felt. If her feelings for Vane went beyond the physical, did that mean what she thought it meant?

"How on earth can I tell?" Spreading her hands, she appealed to Myst. "I've never felt this way before."

The thought suggested another possibility. Halting, Patience lifted her head, then, with returning confidence, drew herself up and glanced hopefully at Myst. "Perhaps I'm just imagining it?"

Myst stared, unblinking, through big blue eyes, then yawned, stretched, jumped down, and led the way to the door.

Patience sighed. And followed.

The telltale tension between them—there from the first—had intensified. Vane felt it as he held Patience's chair while she settled her skirts at the dinner table that evening. Consciousness slid under his guard, like the brush of raw silk across his body, raising hairs, leaving every pore tingling.

Inwardly cursing, he took his seat—and forced his attention to Edith Swithins. Beside him, Patience chatted easily with Henry Chadwick, with no detectable sign of confusion. As the courses came and went, Vane struggled not to resent that fact. She appeared breezily unconscious of any change in the temperature between them, while he was fighting to keep the lid on a boiling pot.

Dessert was finally over, and the ladies withdrew. Vane kept the conversation over the port to a minimum, then led the gentlemen back to the drawing room. As usual, Patience was standing with Angela and Mrs. Chadwick halfway down the long room.

She saw him coming; the fleeting flare of awareness in her eyes as he drew near was a momentary sop to his male pride. Very momentary—the instant he stopped by her side, her perfume reached him, the warmth of her soft curves tugged at his senses. Decidedly stiff, Vane inclined his head fractionally to all three ladies.

"I was just telling Patience," Angela blurted out, pouting sulkily, "that it's beyond anything paltry. The thief has stolen my new comb!"

"Your comb?" Vane flicked a glance at Patience.

"The one I bought in Northampton," Anglea wailed. "I didn't even get to wear it!"

"It may still turn up." Mrs. Chadwick tried to sound encouraging, but with her own, much more serious loss clearly in mind, she failed to soothe her daughter.

"It's *unfair*!" Flags of color flew in Angela's cheeks. She stamped her foot. "I want the thief caught!"

"Indeed." The single word, uttered in Vane's coolest, most bored drawl, succeeded in dousing Angela's imminent hysterics. "We would all, I fancy, like to lay our hands on this elusive, light-fingered felon."

"Light-fingered felon?" Edmond strolled up. "Has the thief struck again?"

Instantly, Angela reverted to her histrionic best; she poured out her tale to the rather more appreciative audience of Edmond, Gerrard, and Henry, all of whom joined the circle. Under cover of their exclamations, Vane glanced at Patience; she felt his gaze and looked up, meeting his eyes, a question forming in hers. Vane opened his lips, the details of an assignation on his tongue—he swallowed them as, to everyone's surprise, Whitticombe joined the group.

The garrulous recitation of the thief's latest exploit was instantly muted, but Whitticombe paid little heed. After a general nod to all, he leaned closer and murmured to Mrs. Chadwick. She immediately raised her head, looking across the room. "Thank you." Reaching out, she took Angela's arm. "Come, my dear."

Angela's face fell. "Oh, but . . ."

For once entirely deaf to her daughter's remonstrances, Mrs. Chadwick towed Angela to the *chaise* where Minnie sat.

Both Vane and Patience followed Mrs. Chadwick's progress, as did the others. Whitticombe's quiet question had them turning back to him.

"Am I to understand that something else has gone missing?"

Entirely by chance, he was now facing the others, all arrayed in a semicircle, as if joined in league against him. It was not a felicitous social grouping, yet none of them—Vane, Patience, Gerrard, Edmond, or Henry—made any move to shift position, to include Whitticombe more definitely in their circle.

"Angela's new comb." Henry briefly recited Angela's description.

"Diamonds?" Whitticombe's brows rose.

"Paste," Patience corrected. "It was a . . . *showy* piece."

"Hmm." Whitticombe frowned. "It really brings us back to our earlier question—what on earth would anyone want with a garish pincushion and a cheap, somewhat tawdry, comb?"

Henry's jaw locked; Edmond shifted. Gerrard stared pugnaciously—directly at Whitticombe, who'd fixed his cold, transparently assessing gaze on him.

Beside Vane, Patience stiffened.

"Actually," Whitticombe drawled, the instant before at least three others spoke, "I was wondering if it isn't time we instituted a search?" He lifted a brow at Vane. "What do you think, Cynster?"

"I think," Vane said, and paused, his chilly gaze fixed on Whitticombe's face, until there wasn't one of the company who did not know precisely what he truly thought, "that a search will prove fruitless. Aside from the fact that the thief will certainly hear of the search before it begins, and have time aplenty to secrete or remove his cache, there's the not inconsiderable problem of our present location. The house is nothing short of a magpie's paradise, let alone the grounds. Things hidden in the ruins might never be found."

Whitticombe's gaze momentarily blanked, then he blinked. "Ah . . . yes." He nodded. "I daresay you're right. Things might never be found. Quite true. Of course, a search would never do. If you'll excuse me?" With a fleeting smile, he bowed and headed back across the room.

Puzzled to varying degrees, they all watched him go. And saw the small crowd gathered about the *chaise*. Timms waved. "Patience!"

"Excuse me." With a fleeting touch on Vane's arm, Patience crossed to the *chaise*, to join Mrs. Chadwick and Timms, gathered about Minnie. Then Mrs. Chadwick stood back; Patience stepped closer and helped Timms assist Minnie to her feet.

Vane watched as, her arm about Minnie, Patience helped her to the door.

Intending to follow, Mrs. Chadwick shooed Angela ahead of her, then detoured to inform the deserted group of males: "Minnie's not well—Patience and Timms will put her to bed. I'll go, too, in case they need help."

So saying, she herded a reluctant Angela out of the room and closed the door behind them.

Vane stared at the closed door—and inwardly cursed. Fluently.

"Well." Henry shrugged. "Left to our own devices, what?" He glanced at Vane. "Fancy a return match in the billiard room, Cynster?"

Edmond looked up; so did Gerrard. The suggestion obviously met with their approval. His gaze on the closed door beyond them, Vane slowly raised his brows. "Why not?" Lips firming to an uncompromising line, his eyes unusually dark, he waved to the door. "There seems little else to do tonight."

The next morning, his expression tending grim, Vane descended the main stairs.

Henry Chadwick had beaten him at billiards.

If he'd needed any confirmation of how seriously the current impasse with Patience was affecting him, *that* had supplied it. Henry could barely sink a ball. Yet he'd been so distracted, he'd been even less able to sink anything, his mind totally engrossed with the where, the when, and the how—and the likely sensations—of sinking into Patience.

Striding across the front hall, his boots ringing on the tiles, he headed for the breakfast room. It was past time he and Patience talked.

And after that . . .

The table was half-full; the General, Whitticombe, and Edgar were all there, as was Henry, blithely gay with a wide grin on his face. Vane met it without expression. He helped himself to a large and varied breakfast, then took his seat to wait for Patience.

To his relief, Angela did not appear; Henry informed him that Gerrard and Edmond had already broken their fast and gone out to the ruins.

Vane nodded, and continued to eat—and wait.

Patience didn't appear.

When Masters and his minions appeared to clear the table, Vane rose. Every muscle felt locked, every sinew taut and tight. "Masters—where is Miss Debbington?"

His accents, while even, held more than a hint of cold steel.

Masters blinked. "Her Ladyship's unwell, sir—Miss Debbington is presently with Mrs. Henderson sorting menus and going over the household accounts, it being the day for those."

"I see." Vane stared unseeing at the empty doorway. "And just how long do menus and household accounts take?"

"I'm sure I couldn't say, sir—but they've only just begun, and Her Ladyship usually takes all morning."

Vane drew a deep breath—and held it. "Thank you, Masters."

Slowly, he moved out from behind the table and headed for the door.

He was past cursing. He paused in the hall, then, his face setting like stone, he turned on his heel and strode for the stables. In lieu of talking with Patience, and the likely aftermath, he'd have to settle for a long, hard ride—on a horse.

He caught her in the stillroom.

Pausing with his hand on the latch of the half-open door, Vane grinned, grimly satisfied. It was early afternoon; many of the household would be safely napping—the rest would at least be somnolent. Within the stillroom, he could hear Patience humming softly—other than the rustling of her gown, he could hear no other sound. He'd finally found her alone and in the perfect location. The stillroom, tucked away on the ground floor of one wing, was private, and contained no daybed, *chaise*, or similar piece of furniture.

In his present state, that was just as well. A gentleman should not, after all, go too far with the lady he intended making his wife before informing her of that fact. The absence of any of the customary aids to seduction should make coming to the point easy, after which they could retire to some place of greater comfort, so he could be comfortable again.

The thought—of how he would ease the discomfort that had dogged him for the past days—wound his spring a notch tighter. Jaw set, he drew a deep breath. Setting the door wide, he stepped over the threshold.

Patience whirled. Her face lit up. "Hello. Not riding?"

Scanning the dimly lit stillroom, Vane slowly closed the door. And slowly shook his head. "I went out this morning." The last time he'd been in here, he'd been nine years old—the room had appeared much more spacious. Now . . . Ducking a dangling sheaf of leaves, he edged around the table running down the center of the narrow room. "How's Minnie?"

Patience smiled, gloriously welcoming, and dusted her hands. "Just a sniffle—she'll be better soon, but we want to keep an eye on her. Timms is sitting with her at present."

"Ah." Dodging more branches of drying herbs, carefully avoiding a rack of large bottles, Vane eased down the aisle between the central table and the side counter at which Patience was working. He only just fitted. The fact registered, but dimly; his senses had focused on Patience. His eyes locked on hers as he closed the distance between them. "I've been chasing you for days."

Desire roughened his voice; he saw the same emotion flare in her eyes. He reached for her—in precisely the same moment she stepped toward him. She ended in his arms, her hands sliding up to frame his face, her face lifting to his.

Vane was kissing her before he knew what he—they—were about. It was the first time in his extensive career he'd misstepped, lost the thread of his predetermined plot. He'd intended *speaking* first, making the declaration he knew he should make; as Patience's lips parted invitingly under his, as her tongue boldly tangled with his, all thought of speech fled from his head. Her hands left his face to slide and lock over his shoulders, bringing her breasts against his chest, her thighs against his, the soft fullness of her belly caressing the aching ridge distorting the front of his breeches.

Need burst upon him—his, and, to his utter amazement, hers. His own lust he was used to controlling; hers was something else again. Vibrant, gloriously naive, eager in its innocence, it held a power far stronger than he'd expected. And it drew something from him—something deeper, stronger, a compulsion driven by something much more powerful than mere lust.

Heat rose between them; in desperation, Vane tried to lift his head. He only succeeded in altering the angle of their kiss. Deepening it. The failure—so totally unprecedented—jerked him to attention. Their reins had well and truly slipped from his grasp—Patience now held them—and she was driving far too fast.

He forced himself to draw back from their kiss. "Patience—"

She covered his lips with hers.

Vane closed his hands about her shoulders; he felt the wrench deep in his soul as he again pulled away. "Dammit woman—I want to *talk* to you!"

"Later." Eyes glinting from beneath heavy lids, Patience drew his head back to hers.

Vane fought to hold back. "Will you just—"

"Shut up." Stretching upward, pressing herself even more

flagrantly against him, Patience brushed her lips against his. "I don't want to talk. Just kiss me—*show* me what comes next."

Which wasn't the wisest invitation to issue to a painfully aroused rake. Vane groaned as her tongue slid deep into his mouth, as he instinctively met it. The duel that followed was too heated for him to think; a haze of hot passion clouded his senses. The counter at his back made escape impossible, even if he could have summoned the strength.

She held him trapped in a net of desire—and with every kiss the strands grew stronger.

Patience gloried in their kiss, in the sudden revelation that she'd been waiting for just this—to experience again the heady thrill of desire sliding through her veins, to sense again the seductive lure of that elusive something—that emotion she had not yet named, as it wound about her—about them—and drew her deeper.

Deeper into his arms, deeper into passion. To where the desire to fulfill the craving she sensed beneath his expertise became a compulsion, a poignantly sweet urge swelling deep within her.

She could taste it on her tongue, in their kiss; she could feel it—a slow throb—gradually building in her blood.

This was excitement. This was experience. *This* was precisely what her curious soul craved.

Above all, she needed to know.

Vane's hands on her hips urged her closer; hard, demanding, they slid down, grasping her firmly, fingers sinking deep as he lifted her against him. His rigid staff rode against her, impressing her softness with the hard evidence of his need. His evocative rocking motion sent heat pulsing through her; his staff was a brand—a brand with which he would claim her.

Their lips parted briefly, so they could haul in gasping breaths before need fused their lips again. An aching, spiraling urgency flowed through them, gaining in strength, flooding their senses. She sensed it in him—and knew it in her.

And together they strove, feeding the swelling compulsion, both driven by it. The wave rose and reared over them—then it broke. And they were caught in the rush, in the furious swirling urgency, tossed and tousled until they gasped and clung. Waves—of desire, passion, and need—beat upon them, forcing awareness of the emptiness within, of the burning need to fill it, to achieve completeness on the mortal plane.

"Miss?"

The tap on the door had them flying apart. The door opened; a maid looked in. She spied Patience, turning toward her in the dim light; to all appearances, Patience had been facing the counter, her hands in a pile of herbs. The maid held up a pannier full of lavender spikes. "What should I do with these now?"

Her pulse thundering in her ears, Patience struggled to focus on the question. She gave mute thanks for the lack of lighting—the maid hadn't yet seen Vane, leaning negligently on the counter four feet away. "Ah—" She coughed, then had to moisten her lips before she could speak. "You'll need to strip the leaves and snip off the heads. We'll use the leaves and heads for the scented bags, and the stalks we'll use to freshen rooms."

The maid nodded eagerly and moved to the central table.

Patience turned back to the counter. Her head was still whirling; her breasts rose and fell. She knew her lips were swollen—when she licked them again, they felt hot. Her pounding heartbeat suffused her entire body; she could feel it in her fingertips. She'd sent the maid to gather lavender; it needed to be processed immediately. A point on which she'd lectured the maid.

If she sent the maid away . . .

She glanced at Vane, silent and still in the shadows. Only she, close as she was, could see the way his chest rose and fell, could see the light that glowed like hot embers in his eyes. One burnished lock of hair had fallen across his forehead; as she watched, he straightened and brushed it back. And inclined his head. "I'll catch up with you later, my dear."

The maid started and looked up. Vane viewed her blandly. Reassured, the maid smiled and returned to the lavender.

From the corner of her eye, Patience watched Vane retreat, watched the door close slowly behind him. As the latch clicked shut, she closed her eyes. And fought, unsuccessfully, to quell the shudder that racked her—of anticipation. And need.

The tension between them had turned raw. Taut as a wire, heightened to excruciating sensitivity.

Vane felt it the instant Patience appeared in the drawing

room that evening; the glance she threw him made it clear she felt it, too. But they had to play their parts, fill their expected roles, hiding the passion that shimmered, white-hot, between them.

And pray that no one else noticed.

Touching in any way, however innocuous, was out of the question; they artfully avoided it—until, in accepting a platter from Vane, Patience's fingers brushed his.

She nearly dropped the platter; Vane only just stifled his curse.

Jaw locked, he endured, as did she.

At last they were back in the drawing room. Tea had been drunk and Minnie, wreathed in shawls, was about to retire. Vane's mind was a blank; he had not a single clue as to what topics had been discussed over the past two hours. He did, however, recognize opportunity when he saw it.

Strolling to the *chaise*, he raised a brow at Minnie. "I'll carry you up."

"An excellent idea!" Timms declared.

"Humph!" Minnie sniffed, but, worn down by her cold, reluctantly acquiesced. "Very well." As Vane gathered her, shawls and all, into his arms, she grudgingly admitted: "Tonight, I *feel* old."

Vane chuckled and set himself to tease her into her usual, ebullient frame of mind. By the time they reached her room, he'd succeeded well enough to have her commenting on his arrogance.

"Far too sure of yourselves, you Cynsters."

Grinning, Vane lowered her into her usual chair by the hearth. Timms bustled up—she'd followed close on his heels.

So had Patience.

As Vane stood back, Minnie waved dismissively. "I don't need anyone but Timms—you two can go back to the drawing room."

Patience exchanged a fleeting glance with Vane, then looked at Minnie. "If you're sure . . . ?"

"I'm sure. Off you go."

They went—but not back to the drawing room. It was already late—neither felt any desire for aimless chat.

They did, however, feel desire. It flowed restlessly about

them, between them, fell, an ensorcelling web, over them. As he strolled by Patience's side, by unspoken agreement escorting her to her chamber, Vane accepted that dealing with that desire, with what now shimmered between them, would fall to him, would be his responsiblity.

Patience, despite her propensity to grab the reins, was an innocent.

He reminded himself of that fact as they halted outside her door. She looked up at him—inwardly Vane sternly reiterated the conclusion he'd reached after the debacle of the stillroom. Until he'd said the words society dictated he should say, he and she should not meet alone except in the most formal of settings.

Outside her bedchamber door in the cool beginning of the night did not qualify; *inside* her bedchamber—where his baser self wished to be—was even less suitable.

Jaw setting, he reminded himself of that.

She searched his eyes, his face. Then, slowly but not hesitantly, she lifted a hand to his cheek, lightly tracing downward to his chin. Her gaze dropped to his lips.

Beyond his volition, Vane's gaze lowered to her lips, to the soft rose-tinted curves he now knew so well. Their shape was etched in his mind, their taste imprinted on his senses.

Patience's lids fluttered down. She stretched upward on her toes.

Vane couldn't have drawn back from the kiss—couldn't have avoided it—had his life depended on it.

Their lips touched, without the heat, without the driving compulsion that remained surging in their souls. Both held it back, denying it, content for one timeless moment simply to touch and be touched. To let the beauty of the fragile moment stretch, to let the magic of their heightened awareness wash over them.

It left them quivering. Yearning. Curiously breathless, as if they'd been running for hours, curiously weak, as if they'd been battling for too long and nearly lost.

It was an effort to lift his heavy lids. Having done so, Vane watched as Patience, even more slowly, opened her eyes.

Their gazes met; words were superfluous. Their eyes said all they needed to say; reading the message in hers, Vane forced himself to straighten from the doorframe which at some point he'd leaned against. Ruthlessly relocating his impassive mask, he raised one brow. "Tomorrow?" He needed to see her in a suitably formal setting.

Patience lightly grimaced. "That will depend on Minnie."

Vane's lips twisted, but he nodded. And forced himself to step away. "I'll see you at breakfast."

He swung on his heel and walked back up the corridor.

Patience stood at her door and watched him leave.

Fifteen minutes later, a woolen shawl wrapped about her shoulders, Patience curled up in the old wing chair by her hearth and stared moodily into the flames. After a moment, she tucked her feet higher, beneath the hem of her nightgown, and, propping one elbow on the chair's arm, sank her chin into her palm.

Myst appeared, and, after surveying the possibilities, jumped up and took possession of her lap. Absentmindedly, Patience stroked her, gaze locked on the flames as her fingers slid over the pert grey ears and down the curving spine.

For long minutes, the only sounds in the room were the soft crackling of the flames and Myst's contented purr. Neither distracted Patience from her thoughts, from the realization she could not escape.

She was twenty-six. She might have lived in Derbyshire, but that wasn't quite the same as a nunnery. She'd met gentlemen aplenty, many of them of similar ilk to Vane Cynster. Many of those gentlemen had had some thoughts of her. She, however, had never had thoughts of them. Never before had she spent hours—not even minutes—thinking about any particular gentleman. One and all, they'd failed to fix her interest.

Vane commanded her attention at all times. When they were in the same room, he commanded her awareness, effortlessly held her senses. Even when apart, he remained the focus of some part of her mind. His face was easy to conjure; he appeared regularly in her dreams.

Patience sighed, and stared at the flames.

She wasn't imagining it—imagining that her reaction to him was different, special, that he engaged her emotions at some deeper level. That wasn't imagination, it was fact.

And there was no point whatever in refusing to face facts—that trait was alien to her character. No point in pretense, in avoiding the thought of what would have occurred if he had not been so honorable and had asked, by word or deed, to enter this room tonight.

She would have welcomed him in, without fluster or hesitation. Her nerves might have turned skittish, but that would have been due to excitement, to anticipation, not uncertainty.

Country-bred, she was fully cognizant of the mechanism of mating; she was not ignorant on that front. But what caught her, held her—commanded her curiosity—was the emotions that, in this case, with Vane, had, in her mind, become entangled with the act. Or was it the act that had become entangled with the emotions?

Whatever, she'd been seduced—entirely and utterly, beyond recall—not by him, but by her *desire* for him. It was, she knew in her heart, in the depths of her soul, a most pertinent distinction.

This desire had to be what her mother had felt, what had driven her to accept Reginald Debbington in marriage and trapped her in a loveless union for all her days. She had every reason to distrust the emotion—to avoid it, reject it.

She couldn't. Patience knew that for fact, the emotion ran too strong, too compulsively within her, for her to ever be free of it.

But it, of itself, brought no pain, no sadness. Indeed, if she'd been given the choice, even now she would admit that she'd rather have the experience, the excitement, the knowledge, than live the rest of her life in ignorance.

There was, invested within that rogue emotion, power and joy and boundless excitement—all things she craved. She was already addicted; she wouldn't let it go. There was, after all, no need.

She had never truly thought of marriage; she could now face the fact that she had, indeed, been avoiding it. Finding excuse after excuse to put off even considering it. It was marriage—the trap—that had brought her mother undone. Simply loving, even if that love was unrequited, would be sweet—bittersweet maybe, but the experience was not one she would turn down.

Vane wanted her—he had not at any time tried to hide the effect she had on him, tried to screen the potent desire that glowed like hot coals in his eyes. The knowledge that she aroused him was like a grapple about her heart—a facet from some deep, heretofore unacknowledged dream.

He'd asked for tomorrow—that was in the lap of the gods, but when the time came, she would not, she knew, draw back.

She'd meet him—meet his passion, his desire, his need—and in fulfilling and satisfying him, fulfill and satisfy herself. That, she now knew, was the way it could be. It was the way she wanted it to be.

Their liaison would last for however long it might; while she would be sad when it ended, she wouldn't be caught, trapped in never-ending misery like her mother.

Smiling, wistfully wry, Patience looked down and stroked Myst's head. "He might want me, but he's still an elegant gentleman." She might wish that were not so, but it was. "Love is not something he has to give—and I'll never—hear me well—*never*—marry without that."

That was the crux of it—that was her true fate.

She had no intention of fighting it.

Chapter 12

$\mathcal{V}$ANE ARRIVED EARLY in the breakfast parlor the next morning. He served himself, then took his seat and waited for Patience to appear. The rest of the males wandered in, exchanging their usual greetings. Vane pushed back his plate and waved for Masters to pour him more coffee.

Coiled tension had him in its grip; how much longer would it be before he could release it? That, to his mind, was a point to which Patience should give her most urgent attention, yet he could hardly begrudge Minnie her aid.

When Patience failed to appear by the time they'd finished their meals, Vane inwardly sighed and fixed Gerrard with a severe glance. "I need a ride." He did, in more ways than one, but at least he could release some of his pent-up energy in a good gallop. "Interested?"

Gerrard squinted out of the window. "I was going to sketch, but the light looks flat. I'll come riding instead."

Vane raised a brow at Henry. "You game, Chadwick?"

"Actually"—Henry sat back in his chair—"I'd thought to practice my angle shots. Wouldn't do to get rusty."

Gerrard chuckled. "It was pure luck you beat Vane last time. Anyone could tell he was a trifle out of sorts."

A trifle out of sorts? Vane wondered if he should educate Patience's brother on precisely how "out of sorts" he was. A blue powder wouldn't cure his particular ache.

"Ah—but I did win." Henry clung to his moment of victory. "I've no intention of letting my advantage slip."

Vane merely smiled sardonically, inwardly grateful Henry would not be accompanying them. Gerrard rarely spoke when riding, which suited his mood far better than Henry's locquaciousness. "Edmond?"

They all looked down the table to where Edmond sat gazing at his empty plate, mumbling beneath his breath. His hair stuck out at odd angles where he'd clutched it.

Vane raised a brow at Gerrard, who shook his head. Edmond was clearly in the grip of his muse and deaf to all else. Vane and Gerrard pushed back their chairs and rose.

Patience hurried in. She paused just inside the room, and blinked at Vane, half-risen.

He immediately subsided into his chair. Gerrard turned, and saw him reseated; he also resumed his seat.

Reassured, Patience headed for the sideboard, picked up a plate, and went straight to the table. She was late; in the circumstances, she'd settle for tea and toast. "Minnie's better," she announced as she took her seat. Looking up the table, she met Vane's gaze. "She spent a sound night and has assured me she doesn't need me today."

She swept a brief smile over Henry and Edmond, thus rendering the information general.

Gerrard grinned at her. "I suppose you'll be off to the music room as usual. Vane and I are going for a ride."

Patience looked at Gerrard, then stared up the table at Vane. Who stared back. Patience blinked, then reached for the teapot. "Actually, if you'll wait a few minutes, I'll come with you. After being cooped up these last days, I could do with some air."

Gerrard looked at Vane, who was gazing at Patience, an unfathomable expression on his face. "We'll wait" was all he said.

By agreement, they met in the stable yard.

After scurrying into her habit, then rushing out of the house like a hoyden, Patience was mildly irritated to find Gerrard not yet there. Vane was already atop the grey hunter. Both rider and horse were restless.

Climbing into her sidesaddle, Patience took up her reins and glanced back toward the house. "Where is he?"

Lips compressed, Vane shrugged.

Three minutes later, just as she was about to dismount to go and search, Gerrard appeared. With his easel.

"I say, I'm sorry, but I've changed my mind." He grinned up at them. "There's clouds coming up and the light's turned grey—it's just the look I've been waiting to capture. I need to get it down before it changes again." He shifted his burden and continued to grin. "So go on without me—at least you've got each other for company."

Gerrard's disingenuity was transparently genuine; Vane swallowed a curse. He glanced swiftly at Patience; she met his gaze, questions in her eyes.

Vane understood the questions—but Gerrard was standing there, large as life, waiting to wave them away. Jaw firming, he gestured to the stable arch. "Shall we?"

After a fractional hesitation, Patience nodded and flicked her reins. With a perfunctory wave to Gerrard, she led the way out. Vane followed. As they thundered along the track past the ruins, he glanced back. So did Patience. Gerrard, slogging in their wake, waved gaily.

Vane cursed. Patience looked forward.

By unspoken accord, they put distance between themselves and the Hall, eventually drawing rein on the banks of the Nene. The river flowed steadily, a reflective grey ribbon smoothly rippling between thickly grassed banks. A well-beaten track followed the river; slowing the grey to a walk, Vane turned along it.

Patience brought her mare up beside him; Vane let his gaze roam her face, her figure.

Fingers tightening on the reins, he looked away. Over the lush riverbanks, insufficiently formal for the discussion he needed to have with her. The grassy banks would do nicely as a couch. Far too tempting. He wasn't sure he could trust himself in such a setting, and, after the stillroom, he knew he couldn't trust her. She, however, was an innocent; *he* had no excuse. Besides which, the area was too open, and Penwick often rode this way. Stopping by the river was untenable. And Patience deserved better than a few casual words and a question on horseback.

Thanks to Gerrard, it seemed he'd have to endure yet another morning without progress. Meanwhile, he, and his demons, were champing at the bit.

Beside him, Patience, too, found the idea of wasting another morning less than appealing. Unlike Vane, she saw no reason not to use the time. Having surreptitiously filled her mind anew with the image of him on his hunter, she voiced the thought uppermost in her mind. "You mentioned having a brother—does he look like you?"

Vane glanced her way, brows rising. "Harry?" He considered. "Harry has curly blond-brown hair and blue eyes— but otherwise"—a slow smile transformed Vane's face—"yes, I suppose he does look a lot like me." He slanted Patience a rakish glance. "But then, all six of us are said to look similar—the stamp of our common ancestors, no doubt."

Patience ignored the subtle tenor of that comment. "All six? Which six?"

"The six eldest Cynster cousins—Devil, myself, Richard— he's Devil's brother—Harry, who's my only sibling, and Gabriel and Lucifer. We were all born within five or so years of each other."

Patience stared. The idea of six Vanes was . . . And two were called Gabriel and Lucifer? "Aren't there any females in the family?"

"In our generation, the females came later. The eldest are the twins—Amanda and Amelia. They're seventeen and have just weathered their first Season."

"And you all live in London?"

"For some part of the year. My parents' house is in Berkeley Square. My father, of course, grew up at Somersham Place, the ducal seat. To him, that's home. While he and my mother, indeed, the whole family, are always welcome there, my parents decided to make their primary home in London."

"So that's home to you."

Looking over the green meadows, Vane shook his head. "Not any more. I moved into lodgings years ago, and recently bought a town house. When Harry and I came of age, my father settled sizable sums on both of us and advised us to invest in

property." His smile deepened. "Cynsters always accumulate
land. Land, after all, is power. Devil has the Place and all the
ducal estates, which underpin the wealth of the family. While he
looks after those, we're each expanding our own assests."

"You mentioned that your brother owns a stud."

"Close by Newmarket. That's Harry's enterprise of choice—
he's a master when it comes to horses."

"And you?" Patience tilted her head, her eyes on his face.
"What's your enterprise of choice?"

Vane grinned. "Hops."

Patience blinked. "Hops?"

"A vital ingredient used to flavor and clarify beers. I own
Pembury Manor, an estate near Tunbridge in Kent."

"And you grow hops?"

Vane's smile teased. "As well as apples, pears, cherries, and
cob nuts."

Drawing back in her saddle, Patience stared at him. "You're
a farmer!"

One brown brow rose. "Among other things."

Recognizing the glint in his eyes, she swallowed a humph.
"Describe this place—Pembury Manor."

Vane did, quite content to follow that tack. After a brief
outline, bringing to life the orchards and fields spread over the
Kentish Weald, he turned to the house itself—the house he
would take her to. "Two stories in grey stone, with six bed-
rooms, five reception rooms, and the usual amenities. I haven't
spent much time there—it needs redecorating."

He made the comment offhandedly, and was pleased to see
a distant, considering expression on her face.

"Hmm" was all Patience said. "How far—"

She broke off and looked up; a second raindrop splattered
her nose. As one, she and Vane looked up and behind them.
With one voice, they cursed. Thunderheads had blown up, dark
grey and menacing, swelling in the sky behind them. A leaden
curtain of drenching rain steadily advanced, mere minutes away.

Looking about, they searched for shelter. It was Vane who
spotted the slate roof of the old barn.

"There." He pointed. "Along the riverbank." He glanced
behind again. "We might just make it."

Patience had already sprung her mare. Vane followed, holding the grey back, clear of the mare's heels. They thundered along the track. In the skies above, more thunder rumbled. The leading edge of the rain curtain reached them, flinging heavy drops on their backs. Doors closed, the barn nestled in a shallow depression set back from the track. Patience wrestled the now skittish mare to a halt before the doors. Vane hauled the grey to a slithering stop and flung himself from the saddle. Reins in one hand, he dragged open the barn door. Patience trotted the mare in and Vane followed, leading the grey.

Once in, he dropped the reins and strode back to the door. As he pulled it shut, thunder cracked, and the heavens opened. Rain came down in sheets. Standing catching his breath, Vane looked up at the rafters. Still perched on her mare, Patience did the same. The sound of the rain on the old roof was a steady, relentless roar.

Shaking his shoulders, Vane peered into the dimness. "This looks to be in use. The roof seems sound." His eyes growing accustomed to the gloom, he strolled forward. "There are stalls along that wall." He lifted Patience down. "We'd better settle the horses."

Eyes wide in the gloom, Patience nodded. They led the horses to the stalls; while Vane unsaddled them, Patience investigated further. She discovered a ladder leading up to the loft. She glanced back at Vane; he was still busy with the horses. Gathering her skirts, she climbed up, carefully checking each rung. But the ladder was sound. All in all, the barn was in good repair.

From the top of the ladder, Patience surveyed the loft. A wide chamber built over most of the barn, it housed a quantity of hay, some baled, some loose. The floor was sound timber. Stepping up, she dropped her skirts, brushed them down, then crossed to where the hay doors were fastened against the weather.

Lifting the latch, she peeked out. The hay doors faced south, away from the squall. Satisfied no rain would drive in, she opened the doors, admitting soft grey light into the loft. Despite the rain, perhaps because of the heavy clouds, the air was warm. The view revealed, of the river, whipped by wind, pocked with rain, and the gently sloping meadows, all seen through a grey screen, was soothing.

Glancing around, Patience lifted a brow. Her next lesson from Vane was long overdue; while the music room would have been preferable, the loft would do. With hay aplenty, there was no reason they couldn't be comfortable.

In the barn below, Vane took as long as he could tending the horses, but the rain showed no sign of abating. Not that he'd expected it to; having seen the extent of the clouds, he knew they'd be trapped for hours. When there was nothing left to do, he wiped his hands in clean straw and dusted them. Then, closing a mental fist firmly about his own reins, he set off after Patience. He'd caught a glimpse of her disappearing into the loft. His head cleared the loft floor; he looked about—and inwardly cursed.

He knew trouble when he saw it.

She turned her head and smiled, eliminating any possiblity of craven retreat. Washed by the soft light falling through the open hay doors, she sat in the midst of a huge pile of hay, her expression welcoming, her body radiating a sensual tug to which he was already too susceptible.

Drawing in a deep breath, Vane climbed the last rungs and stepped onto the loft floor. With every evidence of his customary cool command, he strolled toward Patience.

She shattered his calm—by smiling more deeply and holding out her hand. Instinctively, he took it, fingers closing firmly. Then he caught himself.

His expression rigidly impassive, he looked down at her face, into her eyes, all hazel-gold, warm and alluring, and struggled to find some way to tell her this was madness. That, after all that had passed between them, to sit together in the hay and look out at the rain was too dangerous. That he could no longer guarantee his behavior, his usual coolness under fire, his customary command. No words sprang to mind—he was not capable of making such an admission of weakness. Even though it was true.

Patience gave him no time to wrestle with his conscience— she tugged. With no excuse forthcoming, Vane inwardly sighed— sealed an iron fist about his demons' reins—and sank down to the straw beside her.

He had a trick or two up his sleeve. Before she could turn to him, he wrapped his arms about her and drew her back, settling the curve of her back against his side, so they could study the scenery together.

Theoretically a wise move. Patience relaxed against him, warm and trusting—only to impinge on his senses in a thousand different ways. Her very softness tensed his muscles; her curves, fitting against him, within his arms, invoked his demons. He drew a steadying breath—and her perfume washed through him, subtly evoking, enticing.

Her hands slid over his arms, wrapped about her waist, and came to rest on his hands, her warm palms curved over the backs of his. Outside, the rain continued; inside, heat rose. Jaw clenched, Vane fought to endure.

He might have succeeded if she hadn't, without warning, turned to him. Her head turned first—and her lips were mere inches from his. Her body followed, sliding sensuously around in his arms; he tightened his grip, sank his fingers into soft flesh, but it was already too late.

Her gaze had fixed on his lips.

Desperation could reduce even the strongest to pleading. Even him. "Patience—"

She cut him off, sealing his lips with hers.

Vane fought to hold her back, but there was no strength in his arms—not for that maneuver. Instead, his muscles strained to crush her to him. He managed to stop himself from doing that, only to feel the pair of them sinking back into the hay, the pile originally behind him increasingly beneath him as it compressed under their combined weights. Within seconds, they were close to horizontal, with her stretched against him, half-atop him. Vane inwardly groaned.

His lips had parted, and she was kissing him—and he was kissing her. Jettisoning his crusade against what had proved the inevitable, Vane focused on the kiss. Gradually, he wrested back control, distantly aware that she relinquished the reins too readily. But the small victory encouraged him; he reminded himself that he was stronger than she, infinitely more experienced than she—and that he'd successfully managed women far more knowledgeable than she in this arena for years.

He was in control.

The litany sang in his head as he rolled and pressed her into the hay. She accepted the change readily, clinging to their kiss.

Vane deepened it, plundering her mouth, hoping thus to assuage the clamoring need swelling within him. He framed her face and drank deep; she met him, sliding her hands under his loose jacket, spreading them, sending them questing over his chest, around his sides and back.

His shirt was fine lawn. Through it, her hands burned.

The final battle was so short, Vane had lost it before he'd realized—and after that, he wasn't capable of realizing anything beyond the woman beneath him and the raging tide of his need.

Her hands, her lips, her body, arching lightly beneath him, urged him on. When he opened her velvet riding jacket and closed one hand about her blouse-covered breast, she only sighed and kissed him more urgently.

Under his hand, her breast swelled; between his fingers, her nipple was a tight bud. She gasped when he squeezed, arched when he stroked. And moaned when he kneaded.

The tiny buttons of her blouse slipped their moorings readily; the ribbons of her chemise needed no more than a tug to free them. And then her softness filled his hand, filled his senses. Skin like soft silk teased him; the heated weight of her inflamed him. And her.

When he broke their kiss to raise his head and survey the bounty he'd captured, she watched, eyes glinting goldly from under heavy lids. Watched as his head descended and he took her into his mouth. He suckled, and her eyes closed.

The next fractured gasp that filled the loft was the first note of a symphony, a symphony he orchestrated. She wanted more, and he gave it, pushing aside the soft blouse, drawing down her silk chemise, to bare her breasts fully to the soft grey light, the gentle coolness of the air, and his heated attentions.

Beneath them, she burned, as in his dreams he'd imagined her doing, until she was hot and aching—and frantic for more. Her small hands were everywhere, desperately searching, opening his shirt and greedily reaching, caressing, imploring.

That was when he finally realized that control was far beyond him. He didn't have a shred left—she'd stolen it from him and thrown it away. She certainly had none. That was abundantly clear as, panting, her lips gloriously swollen, she drew his face to hers and kissed him voraciously.

Half-beneath him, she lifted, her body caressing his in flagrant entreaty—the oldest method of beckoning known to woman. She wanted him—and heaven help him, he wanted her. Now.

His body was rigid with need, tense and heavy with it; he needed to claim her, to slide into her body and find release. The buttons fastening her velvet skirts were at her back; his fingers were already on them. He'd waited too long to speak, to formally offer for her hand. He couldn't focus enough to form a garbled sentence—but he had to try.

With a groan, Vane pulled back from their kiss. On his elbows above her, he waited for her to open her eyes. When her lashes flickered, he drew a huge breath—and lost it as her nipples brushed his expanding chest. He shuddered—she shivered, quivers rippling through her stomach to her thighs. His mind immediately focused—on the soft haven between her long limbs, experience supplying in gratifying detail just what her responses were achieving.

Vane shut his eyes—he tried to shut his mind and simply speak.

Instead, her voice reached him, clear, soft, sirenlike, a whisper of pure magic in the heavily laden air.

"Show me."

Entreaty silvered the words. In the same instant, Vane felt her fingers slide, glide, then gently close about him. Her tentative touch had him locking his jaw, locking every muscle against a raging impulse to ravish her. She seemed unaware of it; her gliding caress continued, cindering the last of his will.

"Teach me," she whispered, her breath feathering his cheek. And then she breathed against his lips, "All."

That last small word vanquished the last of his resistance, the last remnant of caution, of cool command. Gone was any gentleman, any vestige of his facade—only the conqueror remained.

He wanted her—with every ounce of his body, every ounce of his blood. And she wanted him. Words were superfluous.

The only thing that still mattered was the manner of their joining. With ultimate victory assured, his demons—those spirits that moved him, drove him—were more than ready to lend their talents to achieving glory in the most satisfying way. Not control, but focused frenzy.

Patience felt it. And gloried in it—in the hardness of the hands that possessed her breasts, in the hardness of his lips as they returned to hers. She clung tight, hands clutching, then kneading the broad muscles of his back, a moment later sliding around to hungrily explore his chest.

She wanted to know—know it all—*now*. She couldn't bear to wait, to drag out the frustration. A yearning—for that knowledge—the fundamental experience all women craved—had bloomed, spread, and now consumed her. Drove her as she arched lightly, responding to the demand in his hands, in his lips, in the steady plundering of his tongue.

He was all heat and shockingly hot hardness. She wanted to draw him into her, to take his heat in and quench it, to release the fevered tension driving him—the same tension slowly suffusing her. She wanted to give herself to him—she wanted to take him into her body.

She knew it, and was long past denial. She knew who she was—she knew what was possible. She'd satisfied herself that she understood how things would be.

So there was nothing to cloud her enjoyment—of the moment, of him. She gave herself up to it gladly—to the shiver of excitement as he drew her velvet skirts down, then rolled her to spread them, a soft blanket, beneath her. Her full petticoats went the same route, becoming a wide sheet beneath her shoulders. She knew no shame as, his lips on hers, he drew her chemise from her, tossing it aside before gathering her to him.

Sharp delight was what she knew as his hands, hard and knowing, possessed her, tracing every curve, every soft mound. One hand slid beneath her waist, then slid lower to cup her bottom. Strong fingers kneaded, caressed, and sweet fever spread, pooling in her belly, dewing her skin. The hand slid lower, tracing the long curve of the back of her thigh all the way to her knee, then slid to the front, reversing direction. To her hip, to that sensitive join where thigh met torso. One finger gently, insistently, stroked downward along the crease—she shuddered, suddenly desperate for breath.

And then he was parting her thighs, gently but firmly spreading them to lavish soothing caresses along the sensitive inner faces. His lips had gentled on hers, allowing her to focus on each touch, each searing response. On the excitement, the frantic, barely reined passion that had both of them in its grip.

Then his hand reached the end of his last caress and drifted higher, to stroke flesh that had never before been stroked, never before felt a man's touch.

The shudder that racked her was pure excitement—distilled sensual anticipation. Sinking into the soft hay, Patience gasped and spread her thighs wider—and felt the caresses grow firmer, more deliberate. More intimate, more evocative.

The soft folds seemed slick; he parted them. Knowing fingers found a point, a nub of flesh, and bolts of delight lanced through her. Fiery delight, hot and urgent, it struck deep inside her, caught hold and grew. Pressing her head back, she broke from their kiss. He let her go. He continued to play in the softness between her thighs; Patience hauled in a too-shallow breath and fought to lift her lids.

And saw him, his face a mask of concentration etched with passion, watching his fingers as they stroked and twirled. Then one probed.

The sound that escaped her was more gasp than moan, more scream than groan. He glanced at her face; his eyes locked on hers. She felt his hand press between her thighs—and felt the intrusion of his finger, gently but insistently penetrating.

She gasped again, and closed her eyes. He pressed farther, deeper.

Then he stroked her—inside—deep within, where she was all slick and hot and so full of desire. So full of molten passion. A passion he stirred, deliberately inciting, stoking that inner furnace.

On a shuddering moan, Patience felt herself melt, felt her senses soar.

Vane heard her, felt her surrender—and inwardly smiled, a touch grimly. She was trying his demons to the utmost; by now, most women new to the game would have gone over the edge, or, more likely, been so overcome by need that they would be begging him to take them. Not Patience. She'd let him bare her completely, without any maidenly confusion—she seemed to enjoy writhing naked beneath him as much as he enjoyed having her do so. And now, when even accomplished ladies might be expected to break, she was floating—taking all he lavished on her and waiting for more.

He gave her more, learning her intimately, filling his male senses with her feminine secrets. Slowly, he drove her upward, turning the wheel of the rack of sensual excitement with practiced ease.

Still, she didn't break. She gasped, moaned, and arched—and her eager body begged for yet more. Her needs were not those of the ladies he was accustomed to; as he took her further still, that was brought home beyond doubt. Patience was older, more mature, more sure of her own self. She was not, he realized, the innocent he had labeled her—strictly speaking, she didn't, in fact, have very much of that commodity. She knew enough to know what they were doing, and to have made her decision.

And it was that that was different. Her character and its consequences. She was straightforward, assured, used to taking what experiences life had to offer. To picking and choosing among the fruits of life's tree. And she'd chosen. Deliberately. This—and him.

That was what was different.

Vane looked at her—at her face lightly flushed with desire, at her eyes, glinting gold from beneath heavy lids. And couldn't breathe.

From sheer lust—from sheer need. The need to be inside her. The need to claim her as his.

With a soft oath, he drew his hands from her and shrugged free of his jacket and shirt. His boots took an impatient minute, then he stood to strip off his breeches. He could feel her gaze on him, trailing down his back. He flung his breeches aside and glanced over his shoulder. She lay naked, asprawl in the hay, calmly waiting. Simmering.

Her breasts rose and fell rapidly; her skin was gently flushed. Naked, fully aroused, he turned to her.

Not a single hint of shock showed in her face—the face of a Fragonard wanton. Her gaze slid down, over him, then slowly rose to his face.

She lifted her arms. To him.

Vane went to her—covered her—took her lips in a searing kiss and eased himself into her. She was hot and tight; she tensed as he tested her maidenhead. And cried out as, with one well-judged thrust, he breached it. He held still, for one long, achingly tense moment, then she eased about him. Instinct claimed him—he thrust powerfully, deep into her body—and claimed her.

His reins broke—his demons took charge. Driving him, driving her, in a frenzied mating.

Far beyond thought, beyond reason, beyond anything except feeling, Patience held tight and let their passion take her. Every sensation was new, battering in on her mind, her overloaded senses, yet she clung to each thrill, each new intimacy, determined to miss nothing, determined to feel all.

To know the sheer delight of his hard body heavy on hers, his chest hard, hair-roughened, rasping against her sensitive nipples and the soft swells of her breasts. To glory in the hardness that filled her, the steely velvet that pressed deep into her, stretching her, claiming her. To experience, with every gasp, with every desperate pant, the power with which he repeatedly drove into her, the flexing of his spine, the rhythmic fusing of their bodies. To sense her vulnerability, in her nakedness, in the weight that anchored her hips, in the blind wanting that drove her. To revel in the excitement, shamelessly hot, unquenchably erotic, that swelled, grew, built, then flooded them, a raging tide avidly seizing them.

And to feel, deep within her, the unfurling of an anchoring force, more powerful than desire, more deep, more enduring, than anything on earth. That force, all emotion, golden and silver, swelled and caught her. She gave herself up to it and bravely, eagerly, knowingly claimed it for her own.

Ecstasy filled her—eagerly, she shared it, through her lips and their hungry kisses, through the worship of her hands, her limbs, her body.

He did the same; she tasted it on his tongue, felt its heat in his body.

Whatever he needed she gave, whatever she craved, he delivered. Mouth to mouth, breasts to chest, urgent softness gripping his hardness.

On a groan, Vane straightened his arms, and managed to find support enough in the hay to lift from her. He drove himself into her, savoring every hot inch that closed about him, pausing for an instant to feel her throb about him, before withdrawing, only to thrust deeply again. And again.

Sating himself—and her.

She writhed, heated and urgent beneath him. He'd never seen anything so beautiful as her, locked in passion's snare. She lifted and twisted, her head turning blindly from side to side as, inside, she sought release. He sank deep and pushed her higher, but still held her back from the edge—she could go higher yet. So could he.

And he wanted to watch her—so splendidly wanton, so gloriously abandoned—as she took him in and held him, as she gave herself to him for the first time. The sight stole his breath—and more. He would have her again, many times, but none would be the same as this, as vested with emotion as this moment was.

He knew when the end was upon her, felt the keen edge of tension ready to explode—and felt the hot flowering within her. He drove into it, and let go—let his body do what came naturally and sent them both over the edge. And, at the last, he watched as the explosion took her, as desire coalesced and turned her womb molten, a hot, fertile pocket for his seed.

Gritting his teeth, he hung on for the last second, and saw her ease. Saw the lines of her face, drawn tight with passion, soften; felt, deep inside her, the strong ripples of her release. On a silent sigh, her body softened beneath him. The expression that washed over her face was that of an angel in the presence of the divine.

Vane felt the shudders rack him. Closing his eyes, he let them—let her—take him.

It had been more—much more—than he'd expected.

Lying on his back in the hay, Patience curled into his side, her skirts and petticoats flipped over her to keep her warm as she slept, Vane tried to come to grips with that reality. He couldn't begin to explain it, all he knew was that no other had ever been like this.

It therefore came as no surprise to discover, as his sated senses cleared, that he was once more possessed of an urgent desire.

Not the same urgent desire that had driven him for the past

days, and which she'd so recently and so remarkably thoroughly sated, but a related desire—the compulsive need to secure her as his own.

As his wife.

The four-letter word had always made him flinch. In a reflexive manner, it still did. But he was not about to run counter to his fate—to what he knew, in his bones, was right.

She was the only one for him. If he was ever to marry, it had to be to her. And he wanted children—heirs. The thought of her, his son in her arms, had an instant effect on him. Uunder his breath, he swore.

He glanced sideways, at Patience's topmost curls, and willed her to wake. Gaining her formal agreement to their marriage had just become his top priority. His most urgent priority. In accepting him as her lover, she'd already agreed *in*formally. Once he'd made his offer and she'd said yes, they could indulge their senses as they willed. As often as they willed.

The thought intensified his growing discomfort. Gritting his teeth, he tried to think of something else.

Sometime later, Patience drifted back to consciousness. She came awake as she never had before, her body floating on a sea of golden pleasure, her mind hazed with a deep sense of golden peace. Her limbs were heavy, weighted with warm langor; her body felt buoyed, sated, replete. At peace. For long moments, no thought could pierce the glow, then, gradually, her surroundings impinged.

She was lying on her side, cocooned in warmth. Beside her, Vane lay stretched on his back, his body a hard rock to which she clung. Outside, the rain had ceased, but drips still fell from the eaves. Inside, the glow they'd created lingered, enclosing them within a heavenly world.

He had given her this—shown her the way to this state of grace. The delicious pleasure still lapped about her. Patience smiled. One hand rested on his chest; under her palm, beneath the curly brown hair, she could feel his heart beating, steady and sure. Her own heart swelled.

The emotion that poured through her was stronger than before, glowing golden and silver, so beautiful it made her heart ache, so piercingly sweet it brought tears to her eyes.

Patience closed her eyes tight. She'd been right—right to

press for the knowledge, right to take this road. No matter what happened, she would treasure this moment—and all that had brought her here. No regrets. Not ever.

The intense emotion faded, sinking from her conscious mind. Lips gently curving, she shifted, and planted a warm kiss on Vane's chest.

He looked down. Looking up, Patience smiled more deeply and, eyes closing, sank against him. "Hmm—nice."

Nice? Looking down at her face, at the smile on her lips, Vane felt something in his chest shift. Then lock. The feeling, and the emotions that coursed, tumbled and jumbled, in its wake, were not nice at all. They shook him, and left him feeling vulnerable. Lifting one hand, he brushed back Patience's honey gold hair; the tangled mass caught in his fingers. He started releasing the strands, gathering her pins as he went. "Once we're married, you can feel nice every morning. And every night."

Concentrating on her hair, he didn't see the shock flare in Patience's eyes as, stunned, she looked up at him. Didn't see the shock fade into blankness. When he glanced down, she was staring at him, her expression closed, unreadable.

Vane frowned. "What is it?"

Patience drew a shuddering breath, and desperately tried to find her mental feet. She licked her lips, then focused on Vane's face. "Marriage." She had to pause before she could go on. "I don't recall discussing that." Her voice was flat, expressionless.

Vane's frown deepened. "We're discussing it now. I'd meant to speak earlier, but, as you well know, our attempts at rational discussion haven't met with any great success." He drew the last of her hair free and, raking it back with his fingers, laid it across the hay. "So." Finding her eyes once more, he raised a cool brow. "When's it to be?"

Patience simply stared. She was lying here, naked in his arms, her body so sated she couldn't move, and he, suddenly, entirely without warning, wanted to discuss marriage? No, not even discuss it, but simply decide when it was to be.

The golden glow had vanished, replaced with an arctic chill. A chill colder than the grey misery outside the hay doors, colder than the breeze that had sprung up. Icy panic sent gooseflesh rippling over her limbs, then sank to her marrow. She felt the touch of cold steel—the jaws of the trap that was slowly, steadily, closing on her.

"No." Summoning every ounce of her strength, she pressed against Vane's chest; closing her eyes to its bare state, she struggled to sit up. She would never have made it except that he deigned to help her.

He stared—as if he couldn't credit his hearing. "No?" He searched her face, then the shutters came down over his grey eyes. His expression leached. "No what?"

His steely accents made Patience shiver. Turning away from him, keeping her skirts over her lap, she reached for her chemise. She pulled it over her head. "I have never intended to marry. Not at all."

A white lie, perhaps, but a position more easily defended than the unvarnished truth. Marriage had never been high on her agenda—marriage to an elegant gentleman had never figured in her plans. Marriage to Vane was simply impossible—even more so after the last hour.

His voice, coolly precise, came from behind her. "Be that as it may, I would have thought the activities of the last hour would suggest that a rearrangement of your intentions was in order."

Tying the ribbons of her chemise, Patience pressed her lips together and shook her head. "I don't want to marry."

The sound he made as he sat up was derisive. "*All* young ladies want to marry."

"Not me. And I'm not that young." Patience finished pulling on her stockings. Swinging about, she grabbed her petticoats.

She heard Vane sigh. "Patience—"

"We'd better hurry—we've been out all morning." Standing, she hiked up her petticoats and cinched them at her waist. Behind her, she heard the hay rustle as he rose. "They'll worry if we don't return for lunch." Under cover of swiping up her skirt, she turned. Not daring to look directly at him—he was, after all, still naked—she could nevertheless see him from the corner of her eye, and prevent him from touching her. From catching hold of her.

If he did, her shaky, somewhat confused resolution might disintegrate—and the trap might slam shut on her. She could still feel his hands on her skin, sense the imprint of his body on hers. Feel the heat of him inside her.

She yanked her skirts up. "We can't afford to dally." In a state bordering on the frenzied, she scanned the floor for her jacket. It was lying beside his breeches. She hurried over.

Aware that he was standing, naked, hands on hips, frowning at her, she picked up her jacket, and flung his breeches at his head.

He caught them before they hit. His eyes narrowed even further.

"*Do* come on," she implored. "I'll get the horses." With that, she rushed to the ladder.

"*Patience!*"

That particular tone had been known to snap unruly, half-drunk soldiers to immediate attention; to Vane's disgust, it had no discernible affect on Patience. She disappeared down the ladder as if he hadn't spoken.

Leaving him disgusted—thoroughly and absolutely—with himself.

He'd muffed it. Completely and utterly. She was annoyed with him—piqued to her toes—and she had every right to feel so. His offer—well, he hadn't even made it; he'd tried instead to slide around it, to arrogantly push her into agreeing without having to ask.

He'd failed. And now she was in a royal snit.

Not for an instant did he believe that she didn't want to marry, that was merely the first excuse that had sprung to her mind—a weak excuse at that.

Swearing roundly—the only viable way he could relieve his temper—he hauled on his breeches, then reached for his shirt. He'd tried to avoid making the declaration he knew he had to make—and now it was going to be ten times worse.

Gritting his teeth, he stomped into his boots, swiped up his jacket, and stalked to the ladder.

Now he was going to have to beg.

Chapter 13

❧◆❧

BEGGING DID NOT come naturally.

That evening, Vane led the gentlemen back to the drawing room, feeling as if he was marching to his execution. He told himself proposing wouldn't really be that bad.

Keeping the lid on his temper all the way back to the Hall, and then through the long afternoon, had tried him sorely. But having accepted the inevitable—Patience's right to a formal, precisely correct proposal—he'd swallowed his ire and forced his conqueror's instincts, which she'd very effectively raised to his surface, into line.

How long they'd toe that line was a moot point, but he was determined it would be long enough for him to propose and for her to accept him.

Strolling through the drawing-room doors, he scanned the occupants, and inwardly smiled. Patience was not present. He'd grasped the moment as the ladies were rising from the table, when they'd been close as he'd drawn back her chair, to say, *sotto voce*: "We need to meet privately."

Her eyes, wide and golden, had flown to his.

"When and where?" he'd asked, struggling to keep all command from his tone.

She'd studied his eyes, his face, then looked down. She'd waited until the last minute, when she was about to turn and walk from him, to whisper, "The conservatory. I'll retire early."

Suppressing his impatience, he forced himself to stroll to the *chaise*, where Minnie, as usual, sat in shawled splendor. She looked up as he neared. He raised a languid brow. "I take it you are, indeed, improved?"

"Pish!" Minnie waved dismissively. "It was no more than a cold—there's been far too much bother made over a mere sniffle."

She glanced pointedly at Timms, who humphed. "At least Patience had the sense to go up early, to make sure she took no lasting harm from getting so damp. I suppose you should go up early, too."

"I didn't get that wet." Affectionately brushing his fingers over Minnie's hand, Vane nodded to both women. "If you need help getting upstairs, call me."

He knew they wouldn't; only when she was truly ill would Minnie accept being carried. Turning from them, he strolled to where Gerrard and Edmond were teasing Henry.

Henry pounced the instant he joined them. "Just the one we need! These two have been bending my ear with their melodrama while I'd much rather take them on at billiards. What say you to that return match?"

"Not tonight, I fear." Vane stifled a fictitious yawn. "After spending half the day riding, I'm for bed as soon as possible." He made the comment unblushingly, but his body reacted to the veiled reference to his morning's activities, and his hopes for the night.

The others, of course, thought he was exhausted.

"Oh, come on. You can't be that tired." Edmond chided. "Must be used to being up to all hours in London."

"Indeed," Vane laconically agreed. "But being up is usually followed by a suitably long time prone." Not, of course, necessarily asleep; the conversation was doing nothing for his comfort.

"One game wouldn't take that long," Gerrard pleaded. "Just an hour or so."

Vane had no difficulty squashing a craven impulse to agree—to put off saying the inevitable words yet again. If he didn't get it right this time, present Patience with the speech he'd spent all afternoon rehearsing, God only knew what hideous punishment fate would concoct for him. Like having to go down on bended knee. "No." His determination made the answer definite. "You'll have to make do without me tonight."

The tea trolley saved him from further remonstrance. Once the cups were replaced and Minnie, steadfastly refusing his aid, had gone upstairs, Vane found himself forced to follow, to take refuge in his room until the others reached the billiard room and settled to their game. The conservatory lay beyond the billiard room, and could be reached only by passing the billiard-room door.

Fifteen minutes of pacing his bedchamber did nothing to improve his temper, but he had it well in hand when, having strolled silently past the billiard room, he opened the conservatory door. It opened and closed noiselessly, failing to alert Patience. Vane saw her instantly, peering out of one of the side windows through a bank of palms.

Puzzled, he drew closer. Only when he stood directly behind her did he see what she was so intently watching—the billiard game currently in progress.

Henry was leaning far over the table, his back to them, lining up one of his favorite shots. As they watched, he made his play, his elbow wobbling, the cue jerking.

Vane snorted. "How the devil did he beat me?"

With a gasp, Patience whirled. Eyes wider than wide, one hand pressed to her breast, she struggled to draw breath.

"Get *back*!" she hissed. She prodded him, then flapped her hands at him. "You're taller than the palms—they might see you!"

Vane obligingly backed, but stopped the instant they were beyond the line of the billiard room. And let Patience, fussing and fuming, run into him.

The impact, mild though it was, knocked what breath she'd managed to catch out of Patience. Mentally cursing, she fell back, flashing Vane a furious look as she fought to regain her composure. To calm her wretchedly leaping heart, to quell the impulse to step forward and let his arms steady her, to lift her face and let his kiss claim her.

He'd always affected her physically. Now that she'd lain naked in his arms, the effect was ten times worse.

Inwardly gritting her teeth, she infused impassivity into her features and drew herself up. Defensively. Clasping her hands before her, she lifted her head, and tried to find the right level. Not challenge, but assurance.

Her nerves had been frazzled before he'd appeared—the jolt he'd just given her had scrambled them further. And worse was yet to come. She had to hear him out. There was no alternative. If he wished to offer for her, then it was only right she allow him to do so, so she could formally and definitively decline.

He stood directly before her, a large, lean, somewhat menacing figure. She'd held him silent with her eyes. Drawing a deep breath, she raised one brow. "You wished to speak with me?"

Vane's instincts had been screaming that all was not as he'd thought; the tone of her question confirmed it. He studied her eyes, shadowed in the dimness. The conservatory was lit only by moonlight pouring through the glassed roof; he wished, now, that he'd insisted on some more illuminated meeting place. His eyes narrowed. "I think you know what it is I wish to say to you." He waited for no acknowledgment, but went on, "I wish to ask for your hand in marriage. We're well suited, in all ways. I can offer you a home, a future, a station in keeping with your expectations. As my wife, you would have an assured place in the *ton*, should you wish to claim it. For my part, I would be content to live mostly in the country, but that would be as you wish."

He paused, increasingly tense. Not a glimmer of response had lit Patience's eyes or softened her features. Stepping closer, he took her hand, and found it cool. Raising it, he brushed a kiss across her cold fingers. Of its own accord, his voice lowered. "Should you agree to be my wife, I swear that your happiness and comfort would be my primary, and my most passionate, concern."

Her chin lifted slightly, but she made no answer.

Vane felt his face harden. "Will you marry me, Patience?" The question was soft, yet steely. "Will you be my wife?"

Patience drew a deep breath, and forced herself to hold his gaze. "I thank you for your offer. It does me more honor than I deserve. Please accept my heartfelt regrets." Despite her conviction, a last, small, desperate hope had clung to life in her heart, but his words had slain it. He'd said all the right things, the accepted things, but not the one important thing. He hadn't said he loved her; he'd made no promise to love her for all time.

She drew a difficult breath and looked down, at his fingers lightly holding hers. "I do not wish to marry."

Silence—absolute and compelling—held them, then his fingers, very slowly, slid from hers.

Vane drew a not entirely steady breath, and forced himself to step back. The conqueror within him roared—and fought to reach for her, to haul her into his arms and take her, storm her castle and force her to acknowledge that she was his—only his. Fists tightly clenched, he forced himself to take a different tack. Slowly, as he had once before, he circled her.

"Why?" He asked the question from directly behind her. She stiffened; her head rose. Eyes narrowed, he watched one golden curl quiver by her ear. "I think, in the circumstances, I'm entitled to know that much."

His voice was low, sibilantly soft, lethally restrained; Patience shivered. "I've decided against marriage."

"When did you make this decision?" When she didn't immediately respond, he suggested, "After we met?"

Patience wished she could lie. Instead, she lifted her head. "Yes, but my decision was not solely an outcome of that. Meeting you simply clarified the matter for me."

Tense silence again descended. He eventually broke it. "Now how, precisely, am I to take that?"

Patience sucked in a desperate breath. She tensed, and would have whirled to face him, but his fingers on her nape, just the lightest touch, froze her.

"No. Just answer me."

She could feel the heat of his body less than a foot away, sense the turbulence he held leashed. He could let the reins fall at any minute. Her wits whirled—giddiness threatened. It was so difficult to think.

Which, of course, was what he wanted—he wanted her to blurt out the truth.

Swallowing, she kept her head high. "I have never been particularly interested in marriage. I've grown used to my independence, to my freedom, to being my own mistress. There's nothing marriage can offer me that I value as highly that would compensate me for giving up all that."

"Not even what we shared in the barn this morning?"

She should, of course, have expected that, but she'd hoped

to avoid it. Avoid facing it. Avoid discussing it. Avoid tarnishing the silver and the gold. She kept her chin high, and quietly, evenly, stated, "Not even that."

That, thank heaven, was true. Despite all she'd felt, all that he'd made her feel, all that her body now yearned for, having felt the power of that gold and silver emotion—love, what else could it be?—she was even more sure, even more certain, that her course was right.

She was in love with him, as her mother had loved her father. No other power was as great, no other power so fateful. If she made the mistake of marrying him, took the easy road and gave in, she would suffer the same fate her mother had, suffer the same lonely days and the same endless, aching, soul-destroying, lonely nights. "I do not, under any circumstances, wish to marry."

His fury escaped him; it vibrated around her. For one instant, she thought he would seize her. She only just stopped herself from whirling and stepping away.

"This is *insane*!" His anger scorched her. "You gave yourself to me this morning—or did I imagine it? Did I imagine you naked and panting beneath me? Tell me, did I imagine you writhing wantonly as I sank into you?"

Patience swallowed, and pressed her lips tightly together. She didn't want to discuss this morning—not any of it—but she listened. Listened as he used the golden moments to flay her, used the silvery delight like a lance to prick her to say yes.

But to agree would be stupid—after having been warned, having seen what would happen, to knowingly accept misery—she'd never been that witless.

And it would be misery.

That was borne out as she listened, listened carefully, as he reminded her, in graphic detail, of all that had passed between them in the barn. He was relentless, ruthless. He knew women too well not to know where to aim his barbs.

"Do you remember how you felt when I first slid inside you?"

He went on, and desire rose, flickering about her, within her. She recognized it for what it was; she heard it in his voice. Heard the passion rise, felt it, a tangible force as he appeared again beside her, looking down into her face, his features craved granite, his eyes burning darkly. When next he spoke, his voice was so deep, so low, it grated on her skin.

"You're a gentlewoman, born and bred—the position, the requirements, are in your blood. This morning you spread yourself for me—you wanted me, and I wanted you. You gave yourself to me. You took me in—and I took you. I took your maidenhead, I took your virginity—what innocence you had, I took that, too. But that was only the penultimate act in a script carved in stone. The final act is a wedding. *Ours.*"

Patience met his gaze steadily, although it took all her will. Not once had he spoken of any softer emotion—not once had he alluded to even the existence of love, let alone suggested it might live in him. He was hard, ruthless—his nature was not soft. It was demanding, commanding, as unyielding as his body. Desire and passion were his forte; that he felt both for her was beyond doubt.

That was not enough. Not for her.

She wanted, needed, love.

She had long ago promised herself she would never marry without it. She'd spent the hour before dinner staring at a cameo portrait of her mother, remembering. The images she'd recalled were still vivid in her mind—of her mother alone, weeping, lonely, bereft of love, dying for want of it.

She lifted her chin, her eyes steady on his. "I do not wish to marry."

His eyes narrowed to grey shards. A long minute passed; he studied her face, her eyes. Then his chest swelled; he nodded once. "If you can tell me this morning meant nothing to you, I'll accept your dismissal."

Not for an instant did his eyes leave hers; Patience was forced to hold his gaze while inside, her heart ached. He'd left her no choice. Lifting her chin, she struggled to draw breath—and forced herself to shrug as she looked away. "This morning was very pleasant, quite eye-opening, but . . ." Shrugging again, she swung aside and stepped away. "Not enough to commit me to marriage."

"*Look at me, dammit!*" The command was issued through clenched teeth.

Swinging back to face him, Patience saw his fists clench—and sensed the battle he waged not to touch her. She immediately lifted her chin. "You're making too much of it—you, of all men, should know ladies do not marry all the men with whom they share their bodies." Her heart twisted; she forced her voice to lighten, forced her lips to curve lightly. "I have to admit this morning was very enjoyable, and I sincerely thank you for the experience. I'm quite looking forward to the next time—to the next gentleman who takes my fancy."

For one instant, she feared she'd gone too far. There was something—a flash in his eyes, an expression that flitted over his face—that locked her breath in her throat. But then he relaxed, not completely, but much of his frightening tension—battle-ready tension—seemed to flow out of him.

She saw his chest rise as he drew breath, then he was coming toward her, moving with his usual predatory grace. She wasn't sure which she found more unnerving—the warrior, or the predator.

"So you liked it?" His fingers, cool and steady, slid under her chin and tipped her face up to his. He smiled—but the gesture didn't reach his eyes. "Perhaps you should consider the fact that if you married me, you would have the pleasure you experienced this morning every day of your life?" His eyes locked on hers. "I'm perfectly prepared to swear that you'll never want for that particular pleasure if you become my wife."

Only desperation allowed her to keep her features still, to stop them from crumpling. Inside, she was weeping—for him, and for her. But she had to turn him from her. There were no words on earth to explain to him—proud descendant of a prideful warrior clan—that it was not in his power to give her the one thing she needed to become his wife.

The effort to lift one brow archly nearly felled her. "I suppose," she said, forcing herself to look into his eyes, to infuse consideration into her expression, "that it might be quite nice to try it again, but I can't see any need to marry you for that." His eyes blanked. She was at the end of her strength and she knew it. She put her last ounce into brightening her smile, her eyes, her expression. "I daresay it would be quite exciting to be your inamorata for a few weeks."

Nothing she could have said, nothing she could have done, would have hurt him, or shocked him, so much. Or been more certain to drive him from her. For a man like him, with his background, his honor, to refuse to be his wife but consent to be his mistress was the ultimate low blow. To his pride, to his ego, to his self-worth as a man.

Her fists clenched in her skirts so tightly, her nails cut into her palms. Patience forced herself to look inquiringly at him. Forced herself not to quail when she saw the disgust flare in his eyes the instant before the steel shutters came down. Forced herself to stand firm, head still high, when his lip curled.

"I ask you to be my wife . . . and you offer to be my whore."

The words were low, laced with contempt, bitter with an emotion she couldn't place.

He looked at her for one long minute, then, as if nothing of any great moment had transpired, swept her an elegant bow.

"Pray accept my apologies for any inconvenience my unwelcome proposition may have caused you." Only the ice in his tone hinted at his feelings. "As there's nothing more to be said, I'll bid you a good night."

With one of his usual graceful nods, he headed for the door. He opened it, and, without glancing back, left, pulling the door gently closed behind him.

Patience held her position; for a long while, she simply stood there, staring at the door, not daring to let herself think. Then the cold reached through her gown, and she shivered. Wrapping her arms about her, she forced herself to walk, to take a calming turn around the conservatory. She held the tears back. Why on earth was she crying? She'd done what had to be done. She reminded herself sternly that it was all for the best. That the numbness enveloping her would eventually pass.

That it didn't matter that she would never feel that golden and silver glow—or the joy of giving her love—again.

Vane was halfway across the neighboring county before he came to his senses. His greys were pacing steadily down the moonlit road, their easy action eating the last miles to Bedford, when, like Saint Paul, he was struck by a blinding revelation.

Miss Patience Debbington might not have lied, but she hadn't told the whole truth.

Cursing fluently, Vane slowed the greys. Eyes narrowing, he tried to think. Not an exercise he'd indulged in since leaving the conservatory.

On leaving Patience, he'd gone to the shrubbery, to pace and curse in private. Much good had it done him. Never in his life had he had to cope with such damage—he'd hurt in tender places he hadn't known he possessed. And she hadn't even touched him. Unable to quell the cauldron of emotions that, by then, had been seething inside him, he'd fastened on strategic retreat as his only viable option.

He'd gone to see Minnie. Knowing she slept lightly, he'd scratched on her door, and heard her bid him enter. The room had been in darkness, relieved only by a patch of moonlight. He'd stopped her lighting her candle; he hadn't wanted her, with her sharp old eyes, to see his face, read the turmoil and pain he was sure must be etched into his features. Let alone his eyes. She'd heard him out—he'd told her he'd remembered an urgent engagement in London. He would be back, he'd assured her, to deal with the Spectre and the thief in a few days. After he'd discovered how to deal with her niece, who wouldn't marry him—he'd managed to keep that confession from his lips.

Minnie, bless her huge heart, had bidden him go, of course. And he'd gone, immediately, rousing only Masters to lock the house after him, and, of course, Duggan, presently perched behind him.

Now, however, with the moon wrapping him in her cool beams, with the night so dark about him, with his horses' hooves the only sound breaking the echoing stillness—now, sanity had deigned to return to him.

Things didn't add up. He was a firm believer in two and two making four. In Patience's case, as far as he could see, two and two made fifty-three.

How, he wondered, did a woman—a gently bred lady—who had, on first sight of him, deemed him likely to corrupt her brother simply by association, come to indulge in a far from quick roll in the hay with him?

Just what had impelled her to that?

For some women, witlessness might have been the answer, but this was a woman who'd had the courage, the unfaltering determination, to warn him off in an effort to protect her brother.

And had then had the courage to apologize.

This was also a woman who'd never before lain with a man,

never before so much as shared a passionate kiss. Never given herself in any way—until she'd given herself to him.

At the age of twenty-six.

And she expected him to believe . . .

With a vitriolic curse, Vane hauled on the reins. He brought the greys to a halt, then proceeded to turn the curricle. He steeled himself for the inevitable comment from Duggan. His hench-man's long-suffering silence was even more eloquent.

Muttering another curse—at his own temper and the woman who had, for some ungodly reason, provoked it—Vane set the greys pacing back to Bellamy Hall.

As the miles slid by, he went over everything Patience had said, in the conservatory and before. He still couldn't make head or tail of it. Replaying once again their words in the conserva-tory, he was conscious of a towering urge to lay hands on her, put her over his knee and beat her, then shake her, and then make violent love to her. How *dared* she paint herself in such a light?

Jaw clenched, he vowed to get to the bottom of it. That there was something behind her stance he had not a doubt. Patience was sensible, even logical for a woman; she wasn't the sort to play missish games. There'd be a reason, some point she saw as vitally important that he, as yet, couldn't see at all.

He'd have to convince her to tell him.

Considering the possibilities, he conceded, given her first nonsensical view of him, that she might have taken some odd, not to say fanciful, notion into her head. There was, however, from whichever angle one viewed the proposition, no reason whatever that they shouldn't wed—that she shouldn't become his wife. From his point of view, and from that of anyone with her best interests at heart, from the viewpoint of his family, and hers, and the *ton*'s, she was perfect for the position in every way.

All he had to do was convince her of that fact. Find out what hurdle was preventing her from marrying him and over-come it. Regardless of whether in order to do so he had to act in the teeth of her trenchant opposition.

As the roofs of Northampton rose before them, Vane smiled grimly. He'd always thrived on challenges.

*   *   *

Two hours later, as he stood on the lawn of Bellamy Hall and looked up at the dark window of Patience's bedchamber, he reminded himself of that fact.

It was after one o'clock; the house lay in darkness. Duggan had decided to sleep in the stables; Vane was damned if he'd do the same. But he'd personally checked all the locks throughout the Hall; there was no way inside other than by plying the front knocker—guaranteed to wake not only Masters, but the entire household.

Grimly, Vane studied Patience's third-floor window and the ancient ivy that grew past it. It was, after all, her fault that he was out here.

By the time he was halfway up, he'd run out of curses. He was too old for this. Thankfully, the thick central stem of the ivy passed close by Patience's window. As he neared the stone ledge, he suddenly realized he didn't know if she was a sound or a light sleeper. How hard could he knock on the pane while clinging to the ivy? And how much noise could he make without alerting Minnie or Timms, whose rooms lay farther along the wing?

To his relief, he didn't need to find out. He was almost up to the sill when he saw a grey shape behind the glass. The next instant, the shape shifted and stretched—Myst, he realized, reaching for the latch. He heard a scrape, then the window obligingly popped open.

Myst nudged it further with her head, and peered down. "*Meew!*"

Uttering a heartfelt prayer to the god of cats, Vane climbed up. Pushing the window wide, he hooked an arm over the top of it and managed to get one leg over the sill. The rest was easy.

Safe on solid timber, he bent down and ran his fingers along Myst's spine, then rubbed between her ears. She purred furiously, then, tail held high, the tip twitching, stalked off toward the fire. Vane straightened, and heard rustling from the direction of the huge four-poster bed. He was dusting leaves and twigs from his shoulders and the skirts of his greatcoat when Patience appeared out of the shadows. Her hair lay, a rippling bronze veil, over her shoulders; she clutched a shawl around her, over her fine lawn nightgown.

Her eyes were bigger than saucers. "What are you doing here?"

Vane raised his brows, and considered the way her night-gown clung to the long limbs beneath. Slowly, he let his gaze travel upward, until his eyes reached her face. "I've come to take you up on your offer."

If he'd had any doubt over his reading of her, the utter blankness that swamped her expression would have dispelled it.

"Ah—" Eyes still wide, she blinked at him. "Which offer is that?"

Vane decided it was wiser not to answer. He shrugged off his greatcoat and dropped it on the window seat. His coat followed. Patience watched with increasing agitation; Vane pretended not to notice. He crossed to the hearth and crouched to tend the fire.

Hovering behind him, Patience literally wrung her hands—something she'd never done in her life before—and frantically wondered which tack to take now. Then she realized Vane was building up the fire. She frowned. "I don't need a roaring blaze now."

"You'll be glad of it soon enough."

She would? Patience stared at Vane's broad back, and tried not to notice the play of his muscles beneath the fine linen. Tried not to think of what he might mean, what he might be planning. Then she remembered his greatcoat. Frowning, she drifted back to the window seat, stepping lightly, her feet cold on the bare boards. She ran a hand over the capes of the greatcoat—they were damp. She looked out of the window; the river mist was rolling in.

"Where have you been?" Had he been searching for the Spectre?

"To Bedford and back."

"Bedford?" Patience noticed the open window. She swung around to face him. "How did you get in here?" When she'd woken and seen him, he'd been standing in the moonlight looking down at Myst.

Vane glanced back at her. "Through the window."

He turned back to the fire; Patience turned back to the window. "Through the . . . ?" She looked out—and down. "Good Lord—you might have been killed!"

"I wasn't."

"How did you get in? I'm sure I locked this window."

"Myst opened it."

Patience turned to stare at her cat, curled in her favorite position atop a small table to one side of the fire. Myst was observing Vane with feline approval—he was, after all, creating a nice blaze.

He was also creating utter confusion.

"What's going on?" Patience arrived back before the hearth just as Vane rose. He turned to her, and reached for her, helping her the last step into his arms.

Muted by nothing more than fine lawn, his touch seared her. Patience gasped. She looked up. "What—"

Vane sealed her lips with his, and drew her fully against him. Her lips parted instantly; inwardly Patience cursed. His tongue, his lips, his hands, all started to weave their magic. She made a wild mental grab—for shock, surprise, anger, even witless distraction—anything that would give her the strength to distance herself from . . . this.

From the drugging wonder of his kiss, the immediate yearning that swelled within her. She knew precisely what was happening, knew precisely where he was leading her. And was powerless to prevent it. Not while all of her body—and all of her heart—was madly in alt at the prospect.

When not even hauteur would come to her aid, she gave up all resistance and kissed him back. Hungrily. Had it only been this morning she'd had her last taste of him? If so, she was addicted. Beyond recall.

Her hands slid up, over his shoulders; her fingers found their way into his thick hair. Breasts swelling, nipples sensitive against the hard wall of his chest, Patience abruptly drew back, desperate for air.

She gasped as his lips slid down her throat, then fastened hotly over the spot where her pulse thundered. She shuddered and closed her eyes. "Why are you here?"

Her words were a thread of silver in the moonlight. His answer was deep as the deepest shadows.

"You offered to be my inamorata, remember?"

It was as she'd thought; he wasn't going to let her go yet. He hadn't finished with her, had not yet had his fill of her. Eyes closed tight, Patience knew she should fight. Instead, her willful heart sang. "Why did you go to Bedford?" Had he gone in search of information, or because . . .

"Because I lost my senses. I found them and came back."

Patience was very glad he, busy branding her throat with his lips, couldn't see the smile that curved hers—soft, gentle—utterly besotted. His words confirmed her reading of his character, his reactions; he had indeed been hurt and angry—furious enough to leave her. She would have thought a great deal less of him if, after all she'd said in the conservatory, he hadn't felt that way. As for the need that had brought him back to her— the desire and passion she sensed flowing so hotly in his veins— that, she could only be grateful for.

He raised his head, his lips returned to hers. One hand caressing his lean cheek, Patience welcomed him back. The kiss deepened; desire and passion blended and swelled. When next he lifted his head, they were both heated through—both very aware of what it was that shimmered hotly about them.

Their gazes locked. They were both breathing rapidly, both totally focused.

Feeling the touch of cooler air below her throat, Patience looked down. And saw Vane's fingers quickly, deliberately, slipping free the tiny buttons down the front of her nightgown. She studied the sight for an instant, aware of the throbbing in her blood, of the beat that seemed to vibrate about them. As his fingers passed the point between her breasts, and moved lower, she drew in a shuddering breath.

And closed her eyes. "I won't be your whore."

Vane heard the tremor in her voice. He regretted the word, but . . . He glanced at her face, then looked down, watching the small white buttons slide between his fingers, watching the halves of her nightgown slowly open, revealing her soft, sumptuous body.

"I asked you to be my wife, you offered to be my lover. I still want you as my wife." Her eyes flew open. He met her gaze, his face set, etched with passion, hard with determination. "But if I can't have you as my wife, then I'll have you as my lover." Forever, if need be.

Her gown was open to her waist. He slid one hand inside, palm sliding possessively around her hip, fingers sinking into soft flesh as he drew her to him. He took her lips, her mouth—a second later, he felt the shudder that passed through her, her achingly sweet surrender.

He felt her fingers at his nape; they slid into his hair. Her lips were soft, pliant, eager to appease—he feasted, on them, on her mouth, on the warmth she so freely offered. She pressed herself to him. Inside her gown, he slid his hand down her back, to stroke, then cup the smooth swell of her bottom. The lower half of her gown was still fastened, restricting his reach; withdrawing his hand, Vane drew back from their kiss.

Patience blinked dazedly. He caught her hand and towed her the few steps to the chair. He sat, then caught her other hand, too, and drew her to stand between his knees. She watched, her breathing ragged, as he quickly unfastened the rest of her gown.

Then the two halves fell free. Slowly, almost reverently, Vane reached up and parted the gown fully, pushing it back to bare her rounded shoulders. To bare her entirely to his gaze. Chest tightening, groin aching, he looked his fill. Her body glowed ivory in the moonlight, her breasts proud mounds tipped with rose pink buds, her waist narrow, indented, the swell of her hips smooth as silk. Her belly was gently rounded, tapering to the fine thatch of bronzy curls at the apex of her thighs. Long, sleek thighs that had already clasped him once.

Vane drew a shuddering breath and reached for her.

His burning palms sliding over her back, urging her forward, broke the spell that had held Patience. On a gasp, she let him draw her near; she had to grasp his shoulders to steady herself. He looked up, the invitation in his eyes very clear. Patience bent her head and kissed him, longingly, openly, giving all she had to give.

She was his—she knew it. There was no reason she couldn't indulge him, and herself, in this way. No reason she couldn't let her body say what she would never say in words.

After a long, lengthy, satisfying kiss, his lips slid from hers to trace the curve of her throat, to heat the blood pulsing just under her skin. Patience tipped her head back to give him better access; her fingers sank into his shoulders, his tightened about her waist as he took full advantage. He held her steady as his lips drifted lower, over the ripening swells of her breasts. She drew a deep breath, murmuring appreciatively when the movement pressed her flesh more firmly to his lips.

Her murmur ended on a gasp as his teeth grazed one tightly furled nipple, then he took it into his mouth, and she felt her bones melt. One of her hands slid from shoulder to nape, then her fingers slid higher, to convulsively clutch his head as he laved her breasts, teasing the now aching peaks, soothing one moment, then tantalizing the next, easing her back one minute, then whipping her to an excruciating peak of feeling.

Her breathing was desperate long before his mouth moved on, lower, to explore the tender hollows of her waist, to feast on the sensitive cusp of her belly. His hands, palms hot and hard, fastened about her hips, supporting her. Then his tongue, hot and slick, probed her navel—the ragged hiss of her breathing fractured.

As his tongue delved, the rhythm evocatively familiar, she swayed and gasped his name. He didn't answer. Instead, he trailed lingering hot kisses down her quivering belly. And into the soft curls at its base.

"Vane!"

Her shocked protest carried little conviction; by the time it passed her lips, she was already arching, straining up on her toes, knees parting, limbs pliant, hips tilting as she instinctively offered herself for the next heated caress.

It came—a kiss so intimate she could barely cope with the shattering sensation. He followed it with more, not ruthless but relentless, not forceful but insistent. Then his tongue slid between his lips, and between hers.

For one, crystal moment, Patience was sure he'd pushed her too far and she would die—die of the glory sizzling down her nerves, of the distilled excitement searing every vein. It was too much—at the very least, she'd lose her wits.

His tongue slid lazily across her throbbing flesh—and high became higher, tight became tighter. Hot as a brand, it flicked and swirled, dipped and delved—and her limbs liquefied. Heat soared and roared through her.

She didn't die, and she didn't crumple to the ground in a witless heap. Instead, she clutched him to her, and lost any hope of pretending the truth was not real—that she wouldn't be his, be anything he wished.

He filled his palms with her, cupped her and supported her, held her steady as he tasted her. Explored her with his tongue, teased and tantalized her until she was sobbing.

Sobbing with urgency, moaning with need.

He was hungry—she let him feast; he was thirsty—she urged him to drink. Whatever he asked, she gave, even if he used no words, and she had only instinct to guide her. He took all she offered, and confidently opened further doors, walking in and claiming all as his unquestionable right. He kept her there, his, undeniably his, in a dizzying world of bright sensation, of nerve-tingling realization, of soul-stealing intimacy.

Fingers clenched in his hair, eyes closed, glory exploding, a golden haze on the inside of her lids, Patience shuddered and surrendered—to the welling heat, to the beckoning culmination.

With one last, lingering lick, savoring the tart taste of her, the indescribably erotic tang of her sinking to his bones, Vane drew back. One hand beneath the full swell of her bottom, and her convulsive grasp on his hair kept Patience upright. His gaze roaming her flushed face, he flicked the two buttons that closed his trousers undone.

She was already high, floating, pleasured to her toes; he had every intention of pleasuring her more.

It was the work of an experienced minute to ready himself, then he clasped her thighs and urged her knees onto the chair, sliding along on either side of his hips. The chair was an old one, low, deep and comfortable—made for just this.

Dazed, she followed his unspoken instructions, clearly unsure but eager to learn. He knew her body was ready—achingly empty, yearning for him to fill her. As her thighs slid past his hips, he grasped hers and drew her to him, then drew her down.

He sank into her—and saw her eyes close, lids falling as her breath expelled in a soft, long-drawn sigh. Her body stretched, her softness accommodating his hardness. Then she shifted, pressing deeper, to take more of him, to impale herself more completely.

For one fractured instant, he thought he'd lose his mind.

Certainly all control. He didn't, but it was a grim fight he waged with his demons, slavering to have her, to ravish her utterly. He beat them back, held them back—and set himself to giving her . . . everything he could.

He lifted her, then lowered her; she quickly caught the rhythm, quickly realized she could move herself. He eased his hold on her hips, let her have the illusion of setting the pace; in reality, he never let go, but counted every stroke, gauged the depth of every easy penetration.

It was a magical ride, timeless, without restraint. Using every ounce of his expertise, he created a sensual landscape for her, conjuring it out of her needs, her senses, so that all she felt, all she experienced was part of the staggering whole. His own needs he held back, his demons' cravings, allowing them only the sensations he felt as, rigid, engorged, giddy with passion, drunk on the lingering taste of her, he sank into her cloying heat, and felt her welcoming embrace.

He gave her that—unalloyed sensual joy, pleasured delight beyond description; under his subtle guidance, she gasped, swayed and panted as he filled her, thrilled her, pleasured her to oblivion. He gave her all, and more—he gave her himself.

Only when she started up the last stair, the last flight to heaven, did he loosen his reins and follow in her wake. He'd done everything he could to bind her to him with passion. At the end, as they gasped and clung and the beauty swept over them, through them, and between them, he let go and savored, in his marrow, in the deepest recesses of his heart, in the farthest corners of his being, the glory he intended to capture for all time.

Chapter 14

A DEEP, REGULAR vibration woke Vane in the eerie hour before dawn. Blinking his eyes wide, struggling to make out shapes in the dim light, it was a full minute before he realized the vibration was emanating from the warm weight in the center of his chest.

Myst lay curled in the hollow just below his breastbone, looking at his face through unblinking blue eyes.

And purring fit to wake the dead.

Another source of warmth, the soft female body curled against his side, registered. Vane glanced sideways. Patience was clearly accustomed to Myst's roar of a purr—she remained dead to the world.

He couldn't stop the grin that curved his lips. Just as well she was asleep. Despite the ups and downs of yesterday, especially the downs, the ups, particularly the last up, dominated his mind.

Coming straight back and making passionate love to her had been the right tack to take. Masterful, yet not forceful. If he pushed too hard, she would dig in her heels and resist—and he'd never learn what it was that was holding her back from marriage.

This way, he could indulge his senses, slake his demons' urges, and wrap her in a sensual web that, regardless of what she might imagine, was quite as strong as the web she'd already woven, albeit unwittingly, about him. And in between tying knot after knot in the net that would bind her to him, he would, gently, carefully, win her confidence, her trust, and she would, in the end, confide in him.

Then it would simply be a matter of slaying her particular dragon, and carrying her off. Simple.

Vane's grin turned wry. He struggled to subdue his cynical laugh. Myst did not appreciate his quaking chest; she dug in her claws, which abruptly cut off his laughter. He frowned at her, but, given her sterling assistance in the night, did not push her from her comfortable perch.

Aside from anything else, *he* was feeling decidedly comfortable—sunk in a warm bed with the lady he wanted as his wife softly sleeping beside him. At this precise moment, he couldn't think of anything else he wanted in the world; this haven was complete. Last night he'd confirmed, beyond all shadow of doubt, that Patience loved him. She might not know it—or she might, but be unwilling to admit it, even to herself. He didn't know which, but he knew the truth.

A lady like her could not give herself to him, take him into her body and love him as she had, if she didn't, truly, in her heart care for him. It needed more than curiosity, more than lust, or even trust, for a woman to give herself completely, utterly, as Patience did every time she gave herself to him.

That degree of selfless giving sprang from love and nothing else.

He'd had too many women not to know the difference, not to sense it and value it as a gift beyond price. How much Patience understood of it he didn't know, but the longer their association persisted, the more accustomed to it she would become.

Which seemed eminently desirable to him.

Vane smiled, devilishly, at Myst.

Who yawned and flexed her claws.

Vane hissed. Myst stood, stretched, then regally stepped off him and padded to the end of the bed. Pausing, she turned and stared back at him.

Frowning, Vane stared back—but the cat's action raised the question of "what next?" in his mind.

His body replied instantly, with an entirely predictable suggestion; he considered it, but rejected it. Henceforth, as far as he was concerned, Patience was his—his to care for, his to protect. At this juncture, protecting her meant preserving appearances. It would never do for some maid to stumble in and discover them, limbs entwined.

Grimacing, Vane edged to his side. Patience lay sunk in down, deeply asleep. He stared at her face, drank in her beauty, breathed in her warmth; he raised a hand to brush aside a curl—and stopped. If he touched her, she might wake—and he might not be able to leave. He stifled a sigh.

Silently, he slipped from her bed.

Before going down to breakfast, Vane detoured by Minnie's rooms. Her surprise at seeing him was written all over her face. Speculation filled her eyes. Before she could start in on him, he nonchalantly stated: "Halfway down, I realized that my London appointment was of far less moment than my obligations here. So I came back."

Minnie opened her old eyes wide. "*Indeed?*"

"Indeed." Vane saw Minnie exchange a laden glance with Timms—who'd clearly been informed of his departure. Knowing from experience the tortures they could put him to, he nodded curtly to them both. "So I'll leave you to your breakfasts, and go and find mine."

He got himself out of Minnie's room before they could recover and start to tease him.

He entered the breakfast parlor to the usual nods and greetings. The gentlemen of the household were all present; Patience was not. Suppressing a smug grin, Vane helped himself from the sideboard, then took his seat.

The glow that had suffused him since the early hours had yet to leave him; he responded to Edmond's variation on his latest scene with an easy smile and a few perfectly serious suggestions, which caused Edmond to depart in a rush, revived and eager to serve his demanding muse.

Vane turned to Gerrard. Who grinned.

"I'm determined to start a new sketch today. There's a particular view of the ruins, taking in the remains of the abbot's lodge, that I've always wanted to draw. The light's rarely good in that quarter, but it will be this morning." He drained his coffee cup. "I should get the essentials down by lunchtime. How about a ride this afternoon?"

"By all means." Vane returned Gerrard's grin. "You shouldn't spend all your days squinting at rocks."

"What I've always told him," humphed the General as he stumped out.

Gerrard pushed back his chair and followed the General. Which left Vane gazing at Edgar's mild profile.

"Which Bellamy are you currently researching?" Vane inquired.

Whitticombe's contemptuous sniff was clearly audible. He pushed aside his plate and rose. Vane's smile deepened. He raised his brows encouragingly at Edgar.

Edgar slid a careful glance at Whitticombe. Only when his archrival had passed through the door did he turn back to Vane. "Actually," Edgar confessed, "I've started on the last bishop. He was one of the family, you know."

"Indeed?"

Henry looked up. "I say—was this place—the abbey, I mean—as important as Colby makes out?"

"Well . . ." Edgar proceeded to give them a neat picture of Coldchurch Abbey in the years immediately preceding the Dissolution. His dissertation was refreshingly short and succinct; both Vane and Henry were sincerely impressed.

"And now I'd better get back to it." With a smile, Edgar left the table.

Leaving Vane and Henry. By the time Patience arrived, in a frantic froth of skirts, Vane's mellow mood had stretched to granting Henry his long-sought return match over the billiard table. Happy as a lark, Henry stood, and smiled at Patience. "Best go look in on Mama." With a nod to Vane, he ambled off.

Thoroughly enamored—softened by his mood and this unexpected consequence—Vane subsided into his chair, angling it so he could gaze unimpeded at Patience as she helped herself from the sideboard, then came to the table. She took her usual seat, separated from his by Gerrard's vacant place. With a brief smile and a warning look, she applied herself to her breakfast. To the large mound she'd heaped on her plate.

Vane eyed it, straightfaced, then lifted his gaze to her face. "Something must have agreed with you—your appetite's certainly improved."

Patience's fork froze in midair; she glanced down at her plate. Then she shrugged, ate the portion on her fork, then calmly looked at him. "I vaguely remember being excessively hot." She raised her brows, then looked back at her plate. "Quite feverish, in fact. I do hope it isn't catching." She forked up another mouthful, then slanted him a glance. "Did you pass a quiet night?"

Masters and his minions were hovering—well within earshot—waiting to clear the table.

"Actually, no." Vane met Patience's gaze. Memory had him shifting in his chair. "Whatever had you in its grip must have disturbed me, too—I suspect the malady might last for some time."

"How . . . distracting," Patience managed.

"Indeed," Vane returned, warming to his theme. "There were moments when I felt enclosed in damp hotness."

A blush spread over Patience's cheeks; Vane knew it extended to the tips of her breasts.

"How odd," she countered. She picked up her teacup and sipped. "To me, it felt like heat exploding inside."

Vane stiffened—further; he fought to avoid a telltale shuffle in his seat.

Setting down her cup, Patience pushed aside her plate. "Luckily, the affliction had vanished by morning."

They stood. Patience strolled to the door; Vane sauntered beside her. "Perhaps," he murmured as they passed into the front hall, his voice low, for her ears alone. "But I suspect you'll find your affliction will return tonight." She cast a half-wary, half-scandalized glance at his face; he smiled, all teeth. "Who knows? You might find yourself even more heated."

For one instant, she looked . . . intrigued. Then haughty dignity came to her aid. Coolly, she inclined her head. "If you'll excuse me, I think I'll go and practice my scales."

Pausing at the foot of the stairs, Vane watched as she glided across the hall—watched her hips sway with their usual unrestrained license; he couldn't quite stifle his wolfish grin. He was contemplating following—and trying his hand at disrupting her scales—when a footman came hurrying down the stairs.

"Mr. Cynster, sir. Her Ladyship's asking after you. Urgent, she says—quite in a tizz. She's in her parlor."

Vane shed his wolf's fur in the blink of an eye. With a curt nod for the footman, he started up the stairs. He took the second flight two at a time. Frowning, he strode rapidly for Minnie's rooms.

The instant he opened the door, he saw the footman hadn't lied; Minnie was huddled in her chair, shawls fluffed, looking like nothing so much as an ill owl—except for the tears streaming down her lined cheeks. Closing the door, Vane swiftly crossed the room and went down on one knee beside the chair. He clasped one of her frail hands in his. "What's happened?"

Minnie's eyes were swimming in tears. "My pearls," she whispered, her voice quavering. "They're gone."

Vane glanced at Timms, hovering protectively. Grim-faced, she nodded. "She wore them last night, as usual. I put them on the dresser myself, after we—Ada and I—helped Min to bed." She reached back, lifting a small brocade box from the side table behind her. "They were always kept in this, not locked away. Min wore them every night, so there never seemed much point. And with the thief delighting in tawdry glitter, there didn't seem much threat to the pearls."

Two long, matched strands, with matching drop earrings. Vane had seen them on Minnie for as long as he could remember.

"They were my bride gift from Humphrey." Minnie sniffed tearfully. "They were the one thing—the one piece of all he gave me—that was the most personal."

Vane swallowed the oath that sprang to this lips, swallowed the wave of anger that one of Minnie's charity cases should repay her in this way. He squeezed her hand, imparting sympathy and strength. "If they were here last night, when did they disappear?"

"It had to be this morning, when we went for our constitutional. Otherwise, there wasn't any time someone wasn't in the room." Timms looked angry enough to swear. "We're in the habit of going for a short amble around the walled garden whenever the weather permits. These mornings, we usually go as soon as the fog lifts. Ada tidies in here while we're away, but she's always gone before we return."

"Today"—Minnie had to gulp before continuing—"as soon as we got through the door, I saw the box wasn't in its usual place. Ada always leaves everything just so, but the box was askew."

"It was empty." Timms's jaw locked. "This time, the thief has gone well and truly too far."

"Indeed." Grim-faced, Vane stood. He squeezed Minnie's hand, then released it. "We'll get back your pearls—I swear on my honor. Until then, try not to worry." He glanced at Timms. "Why not go down to the music room? You can tell Patience while I set a few matters in train."

Timms nodded. "An excellent idea."

Minnie frowned. "But it's Patience's practice time—I wouldn't want to intrude."

"I think you'll find," Vane said, helping Minnie to her feet, "that Patience won't forgive you if you *don't* intrude on her practice." Over Minnie's head, he exchanged a glance with Timms. "She won't want to be left out."

After seeing Minnie and Timms to the music room, and leaving his godmother in Patience's capable hands, Vane met with Masters, Mrs. Henderson, Ada, and Grisham, Minnie's senior servants.

Their shock, and their instant anger against whoever had dared hurt their generous mistress, was palpable. After assuring them that none of them was suspected, and receiving assurances that all the current staff was utterly reliable, Vane did what he could to bolt the stable door.

"The theft has only just occurred." He looked at Grisham. "Has anyone requested a horse or the gig?"

"No, sir." Grisham shook his head. "They're not much for getting out an' about, this lot."

"That should make our task easier. If anyone asks for transportation—or even for a groom to deliver something—put them off and get word to me immediately."

"Aye, sir." Grisham's face was grim. "I'll do that, right enough."

"As for indoors . . ." Vane swung to face Masters, Mrs.

Henderson, and Ada. "I can't see any reason the staff can't be informed—the outdoor staff, too. We need everyone to keep their eyes peeled. I want to hear of anything that strikes anyone as odd, no matter how inconsequential."

Mrs. Henderson fleetingly grimaced. Vane raised his brows. "Has anything odd been reported recently?"

"Odd enough." Mrs. Henderson shrugged. "But I can't see as it could mean anything—not to do with the thief or the pearls."

"Nevertheless . . ." Vane gestured for her to speak.

"The maids have reported it again and again—it's making terrible scratches on the floor."

Vane frowned. "What's making terrible scratches?"

"Sand!" Mrs. Henderson heaved a put-upon sigh. "We can't make out where she gets it from, but we're constantly sweeping it up—just a trickle, every day—in Miss Colby's room. Scattered on and around the hearth rug, mostly." She wrinkled her nose. "She has this garish tin elephant—heathenish thing—she told one of the maids it was a memento left her by her father. He was a missionary in India, seemingly. The sand's usually not far from the elephant, but that doesn't seem to be the source. The maids have had a good go dusting it, but it seems perfectly clean. Yet still the sand is there—every day."

Vane's brows rose high, visions of Alice Colby sneaking out in the dead of night to bury pilfered items floating through his mind. "Perhaps she tracks the sand in from outside?"

Mrs. Henderson shook her head; her double chins wobbled vehemently. "Sea sand. I should have said—it's that that makes the whole so strange. Nice and silver-white, the grains are. And where, near here, could you find sand like that?"

Vane frowned, and let his fanciful images fade. He met Mrs. Henderson's eye. "I agree the matter's odd, but, like you, I can't see that it could mean anything. But that's precisely the sort of odd occurrence I want reported, whether it's obviously connected with the thief or not."

"Indeed, sir." Masters drew himself up. "We'll speak to the staff immediately. You may rely on us."

Who else could he rely on?

That question revolved in Vane's brain as, leaving Mrs. Henderson's parlor, he wandered into the front hall. In his estimation, Patience, Minnie, and Timms—and Gerrard—had always been beyond suspicion. There was an element of openness, of candor, in both Patience and Gerrard that reminded Vane of Minnie herself; he knew, soul-deep, that neither they, nor Timms, were involved.

That left a host of others—others he felt far less sure of.

His first stop was the library. The door opened noiselessly, revealing a long room, paneled with floor-to-ceiling bookshelves down its entire length. Long windows punctuated the bookcases along one side, giving access to the terrace; one window was presently ajar, letting a light breeze, warmed by autumn sunshine, waft in.

Two desks faced each other down the length of the room. The larger, more imposing example, closer to the door, was weighed down with tomes, the remaining surface blanketed by papers covered in a cramped fist. The well-padded chair behind the desk was empty. In contrast, the desk at the far end of the room was almost bare. It played host to one book only, a heavy leather-covered volume with gilt-edged pages, presently open and supported by Edgar, who sat behind the desk. His head bent, his brow furrowed, he gave no indication he had heard Vane enter.

Vane advanced down the carpeted floor. He was abreast of the wing chair flanking the hearth, its back to the door, before he realized it was occupied. He halted.

Happily ensconced in the deep chair, Edith Swithins busily tatted. Her gaze fixed on the threads she was twining, she, too, gave no sign of noticing him. Vane suspected she was partially deaf, but hid it by reading people's lips.

Stepping more heavily, he approached her. She sensed his presence only when he was close. Starting, she glanced up.

Vane summoned a reassuring smile. "I apologize for interrupting. Do you often spend your mornings here?"

Recognizing him, Edith smiled easily. "I'm here most mornings—I come down immediately after my breakfast and take my seat before the gentlemen get in. It's quiet and"—with her head she indicated the fire—"warm."

Edgar lifted his head at the sound of voices; after one myopic glance, he retreated to his reading. Vane smiled at Edith. "Do you know where Colby is?"

Edith blinked. "Whitticombe?" She peered around the edge of the wing chair. "Good heavens—fancy that! I thought he was there all the time." She smiled confidingly at Vane. "I sit here so I don't have to look at him. He's a very . . ."—she pursed her lips—"*cold* sort of man, don't you think?" She shook her head, then shook out her tatting. "Not at all the sort of gentleman one needs dwell on."

Vane's fleeting smile was genuine. Edith returned to her tatting. He resumed his progress down the room.

Edgar looked up as he neared and smiled ingenuously. "I don't know where Whitticombe is either."

There was nothing wrong with Edgar's hearing. Vane halted by the desk.

Removing his pince-nez, Edgar polished them, staring up the long room at his archrival's desk. "I must confess I don't pay all that much attention to Whitticombe at the best of times. Like Edith, I thought he was there—behind his desk." Replacing the pince-nez, Edgar looked up at Vane through the thick lenses. "But then, I can't see that far, not with these on."

Vane raised his brows. "You and Edith have worked out how to keep Whitticombe neatly at a distance."

Edgar grinned. "Were you after something from the library? I'm sure I could help."

"No, no." Vane deployed his rakish smile—the one designed to allay all suspicions. "I was just aimlessly wandering. I'll let you get back to your work."

So saying, he retraced his steps. From the door of the library, he looked back. Edgar had retreated to his tome. Edith Swithins was not visible at all. Peace reigned in the library. Letting himself out, Vane frowned.

Without, he was the first to admit, any logical basis, he had an instinctive feeling the thief was female. Edith Swithins's capacious tatting bag, which went everywhere with her, exerted an almost overpowering fascination. But to separate it from her long enough to search it was, he suspected, beyond his present powers. Besides, if she'd been in the library since before Whitticombe had left the breakfast parlor, it seemed unlikely she could have rifled Minnie's room during the short time it had been empty.

Unlikely—but not impossible.

As he headed for the side door, Vane wrestled with another, even more complicating possiblity. Minnie's thief—the one who'd stolen the pearls—may not be the same person who'd perpetrated the earlier thefts. Someone might have seen the opportunity to use the "magpie" thief as scapegoat for a more serious crime.

Nearing the side door, Vane grimaced—and hoped that scenario, while not beyond him, was at least beyond the majority of the occupants of Bellamy Hall. Minnie's household affairs were tangled enough as it was.

He'd intended to stroll to the ruins, to see if he could locate Edmond, Gerrard, Henry, and the General—according to Masters, they were all still outside. The voices emanating from the back parlor halted him.

"I can't see *why* we can't drive into Northampton again." Angela's whine was pronounced. "There's nothing to do *here*."

"My dear, you really should cultivate some thankfulness." Mrs. Chadwick sounded weary. "Minnie's been more than kind in taking us in."

"Oh, of course, I'm *grateful*." Angela's tone made it sound like a disease. "But it's just so *boring*, being stuck out here with nothing to look at but old stones."

Holding silent in the corridor, Vane could easily envisage Angela's pout.

"Mind you," she went on, "I did think that when Mr. Cynster came it would be different. You said he was a rake, after all."

"*Angela!* You're sixteen. Mr. Cynster is entirely out of your league!"

"Well, I know *that*—he's so old, for a start! And he's far too serious. I did think Edmond might be my friend, but these days he's forever mumbling verses. Most times, they don't even make sense! And as for Gerrard—"

Comforted by the fact he wouldn't have to fend off any more of Angela's juvenile advances, Vane backtracked a few steps, and took a secondary stair upward.

From all he'd gleaned, Mrs. Chadwick kept Angela close,

undoubtedly a wise decision. As Angela no longer attended the breakfast table, he suspected that meant she and Mrs. Chadwick had spent the whole morning together. Neither, to his mind, were good candidates for the role of thief, either of Minnie's pearls, or more generally.

Which left only one female member of the household as yet unaccounted for. Strolling down one of the Hall's endless corridors, Vane reflected that he had no idea how Alice Colby spent her days.

On the night he'd arrived, Alice had told him her room was on the floor below Agatha Chadwick's. Vane started at one end of the wing, and knocked on every door. If no answer came, he opened the door and looked in. Most rooms were empty, the furniture swathed in covers.

Halfway down the wing, however, just as he was about to push yet another door wide, the handle was hauled from his light grip—and he discovered himself the focus of Alice's black-eyed stare.

Malevolent black-eyed stare.

"Just what do you think you're doing, sir? Disturbing God-fearing people at their prayers! It's outrageous! Bad enough this mausoleum of a house doesn't have a chapel—not even a decent sanctuary—but I have to put up with interruptions from such as *you*."

Letting the tirade drift past him, Vane scanned the room, conscious of a curiosity to rival Patience's. The curtains were drawn tight. There was no fire in the hearth, not even embers. There was a palpable coldness, as if the room was never warmed, never aired. What furniture he could see was plain and utilitarian, with none of the items of beauty generally found scattered throughout the Hall. As if Alice Colby had taken possession of the room and stamped her character on it.

The last items he noted were a prie-dieu with a well-worn cushion, a tattered Bible open on the shelf, and the elephant of Mrs. Henderson's tale. This last stood beside the fireplace, its gaudy metal flanks glinting in the light lancing through the open door.

"What do you have to say for yourself, that's what I'd like to know. What excuse do you have for interrupting my prayers?" Alice folded her arms across her scrawny chest and stared black daggers at him.

Vane brought his gaze back to her face. His expression hardened. "I apologize for disrupting your devotions, but it was necessary. Minnie's pearls have been stolen. I wanted to know if you'd heard anything or seen anyone strange about."

Alice blinked. Her expression changed not at all. "No, you stupid man. How could I see anyone? I was *praying*!"

With that, she stepped back and shut the door.

Vane stared at the panels—and fought down the urge to break them in. His temper—a true Cynster temper—was never a wise thing to prod. Right now, it was already prowling, a hungry beast seeking blood. Someone had harmed Minnie; to some, not exactly small, part of his mind, that equated to an act of aggression against him. He—the warrior concealed beneath the veneer of an elegant gentleman—reacted. Responded. Appropriately.

Drawing a deep breath, Vane forced himself to turn from Alice's door. There was no evidence to suggest she was involved, any more than anyone else.

He headed back to the side door. He might not stumble instantly over the culprit by checking people's whereabouts, but, at present, it was all he could do. Having located all the women, he went in search of the other males.

Warring with his instinctive conviction that the "magpie" thief was a woman had been a half-fledged hope the whole affair might prove a simple misdemeanor—like Edgar, Henry, or Edmond being strapped for cash and being foolish enough, and weak enough, to be tempted to the unthinkable. As he strode over the lawn, Vane let that idea die. Minnie's pearls were worth a small fortune.

Their simple thief, assuming it was one and the same, had just made the step up to grand larceny.

The ruins appeared deserted. From the wall of the cloisters, Vane saw Gerrard's easel, set up on the other side of the ruins, facing the abbot's lodge, a section of woods at Gerrard's back. The paper pinned to the easel riffled in the breeze. Gerrard's pencil box sat beneath the easel; his painter's stool sat behind it.

All that, Vane could see. Gerrard he couldn't see at all. Assuming he'd taken a moment to stretch his legs and wander,

Vane turned away. No point asking Gerrard if he'd seen any-thing—he'd left the breakfast table with one goal in mind and had doubtless been blind to all else.

Turning back into the cloisters, Vane heard, faint on the breeze, an intense mumbling. He discovered Edmond in the nave, sitting by the ruined font, creating out aloud.

When the situation had been explained to him, Edmond blinked. "Didn't see anyone. But then, I wasn't looking. Whole troop of cavalry might have charged past, and I wouldn't have noticed." He frowned and looked down; Vane waited, hoping for some help, however slight.

Edmond looked up, his brows still knit. "I really can't decide whether this scene should be acted in the nave or the cloisters. What do you think?"

With remarkable restraint, Vane didn't tell him. After a pregnant pause, he shook his head, and headed back to the house.

He was skirting the tumbled stones when he heard his name called. Turning, he saw Henry and the General striding up from the woods. As they neared, he asked: "You went for a stroll together, I take it?"

"No, no," Henry assured him. "I stumbled across the Gen-eral in the woods. I went for a ramble to the main road—there's a track that leads back through the woods."

Vane knew it. He nodded and looked at the General, huffing slightly as he leaned on his cane.

"Always go out by way of the ruins—a good, rousing walk over uneven terrain. Good for the heart, y'know." The General's eyes fastened on Vane's face. "But why'd you want to know, heh? Not into rambles yourself, I know."

"Minnie's pearls have disappeared. I was going to ask if you'd seen anyone acting strangely on your walks?"

"Good God—Minnie's pearls!" Henry looked shocked. "She must be terribly upset."

Vane nodded; the General snorted. "Didn't see anyone until I ran into Henry here."

Which, Vane noted, did not actually answer his question. He fell into step beside the General. Henry, on his other side, re-verted to his garrulous best, filling the distance to the house with futile exclamations.

Shutting his ears to Henry's chatter, Vane mentally reviewed the household. He'd located everyone, excepting only Whitticombe, who was doubtless back in the library poring over his precious volumes. Vane supposed he'd better check, just to be sure.

He was saved the need by the gong for luncheon—Masters struck it as they reached the front hall. The General and Henry headed for the dining room. Vane hung back. In less than a minute, the library door opened. Whitticombe led the way, nose in the air, his aura of ineffable superiority billowing like a cloak about him. In his wake, Edgar helped Edith Swithins and her tatting bag from the library.

His expression impassive, Vane waited for Edgar and Edith to pass him, then followed in their wake.

Chapter 15

~≈≋≈~

MINNIE DID NOT appear at the luncheon table; Patience and Timms were also absent. Gerrard did not show either, but, remembering Patience's comments on his ability to forget all while in pursuit of a particular view, Vane didn't fret about Gerrard.

Minnie was a different story.

Grim-faced, Vane ate the bare minimum, then climbed the stairs. He hated coping with feminine tears. They always left him feeling helpless—not an emotion his warrior self appreciated.

He reached Minnie's room; Timms let him in, her expression absentminded. They'd pulled Minnie's chair to the window. A lunch tray was balanced across the broad arms. Seated on the window seat before Minnie, Patience was coaxing her to eat.

Patience glanced up as Vane neared; their eyes touched briefly. Vane stopped beside Minnie's chair.

Minnie looked up, a heart-breakingly hopeful expression in her eyes.

Exuding impassivity, Vane hunkered down. His face level with Minnie's, he outlined what he'd done, what he'd learned—and a little of what he thought.

Timms nodded. Minnie tried to smile confidently. Vane put his arm around her and hugged her. "We'll find them, never fear."

Patience's gaze locked on his face. "Gerrard?"

Vane heard her full question in her tone. "He's been out sketching since breakfast—apparently there's a difficult view rarely amenable to drawing." He held her gaze. "Everyone saw him go—he hasn't returned yet."

Relief flashed through her eyes; her swift smile was just for him. She immediately returned to her task of feeding Minnie. "Come—you must keep up your strength." Deftly, she got Minnie to accept a morsel of chicken.

"Indeed," Timms put in from along the window seat. "You heard your godson. We'll find your pearls. No sense fading to a cypher in the meantime."

"I suppose not." Picking at the fringe of her outermost shawl, Minnie glanced, woe-stricken and frighteningly fragile, at Vane. "I'd willed my pearls to Patience—I'd always intended them for her."

"And I'll have them someday, to remind me of all this, and of how stubborn you can be about eating." Determinedly, Patience presented a piece of parsnip. "You're worse than Gerrard ever was, and heaven knows, he was quite bad enough."

Manufacturing a chuckle, Vane bent and kissed Minnie's paper-thin cheek. "Stop worrying and do as you're told. We'll find the pearls—surely you don't doubt me? If so, I must be slipping."

That last gained him a weak smile. Relieved to see even that, Vane bestowed a rakishly confident smile on them all and left.

He went in search of Duggan.

His henchman was out exercising the greys; Vane passed the time in the stables, chatting to Grisham and the grooms. Once Duggan returned and the greys had been stabled, Vane strolled out to take a look at a young colt in a nearby field—and took Duggan with him.

Duggan had been a young groom in his father's employ before being promoted to the position of personal groom to the eldest son of the house. He was an experienced and reliable servant. Vane trusted his abilities, and his opinions of other servants, implicitly. Duggan had visited Bellamy Hall many times over the years, both in his parents' entourage as well as with him.

And he knew Duggan well.

"Who is it this time?" Vane asked once they were clear of the stables.

Duggan tried an innocent expression. When Vane showed no sign of believing it, he grinned roguishly. "Pretty little parlormaid. Ellen."

"Parlormaid? That might be useful." Vane stopped by the fence of the colt's field and leaned on the top rail. "You've heard of the latest theft?"

Duggan nodded. "Masters told us all before lunch—even called in the gamekeeper and his lads."

"What's your reading of the servants. Any likely prospects there?"

Duggan considered, then slowly, definitely, shook his head. "A good bunch they are—none light-fingered, none hard-pressed. Her ladyship's generous and kind—none would want to hurt her."

Vane nodded, unsurprised to have Masters's confidence echoed. "Masters, Mrs. Henderson, and Ada will watch doings in the house; Grisham will handle the stables. I want you to spend as much time as you can keeping an eye on the grounds—from the perimeter of the house to as far as a man might walk."

Duggan's eyes narrowed. "You think someone might try to pass the pearls on?"

"That, or bury them. If you see any disturbance of the ground, investigate. The gardener's old—he won't be planting anywhere at this time of year."

"True enough."

"And I want you to listen to your parlormaid—encourage her to talk as much as she likes."

"Gawd." Duggan grimaced. "You don't know what you're asking."

"Nevertheless," Vane insisted. "While Masters and Mrs. Henderson will report anything odd, young maids, not wanting to appear silly, or to draw attention to something they've come across while doing something they shouldn't, might not mention an odd incident in the first place."

"Aye, well." Duggan tugged at his earlobe. "I suppose— seeing as it's the old lady and she's always been a good'un—I can make the sacrifice."

"Indeed," Vane replied dryly. "And if you hear anything, come straight to me."

Leaving Duggan musing on how to organize his searches, Vane strode back to the house. The sun was long past its zenith. Entering the front hall, he encountered Masters on his way to the dining room with the silverware. "Is Mr. Debbington about?"

"I haven't seen him since breakfast, sir. But he might have come in and be somewhere about."

Vane frowned. "He hasn't been into the kitchen after food?"

"No, sir."

Vane's frown deepened. "Where's his room?"

"Third floor, west wing—one but the last."

Vane took the stairs two at a time, then swung through the gallery and into the west wing. As he climbed the stairs to the third floor, he heard footsteps descending. He looked up, half-expecting to see Gerrard. Instead, he saw Whitticombe.

Whitticombe didn't see him until he swung onto the same flight; he hesitated fractionally, then continued his purposeful descent. He inclined his head. "Cynster."

Vane returned his nod. "Have you seen Gerrard?"

Whitticombe's brows rose superciliously. "Debbington's room is at the end of the wing, mine is by the stairhead. I didn't see him up there."

With another curt nod, Whitticombe passed on down the stairs. Frowning, Vane continued his climb.

He knew he had the right room the instant he opened the door; the combined smell of paper, ink, charcoal, and paint was confirmation enough. The room was surprisingly neat; Vane cynically suspected Patience's influence. A large wooden table had been pushed up to the wide windows; its surface, the only cluttered area in the room, was covered with piles of loose sketches, sketchbooks, and an array of pens, nibs, and pencils, nestling amidst a straw of pencil shavings.

Idly, Vane strolled to the desk and looked down.

The light streaming low through the window glanced off the surface of the table. Vane saw that the pencil shavings had recently been disturbed, then regathered. There were scraps of shavings between the edges of the loose sketches, and between the pages of the sketchbooks.

As if someone had leafed through the lot, then noticed the disturbed shavings and tidied them again.

Vane frowned, then he shook aside the idea. Probably just a curious—or smitten—maid.

He looked out of the windows. The west wing was on the opposite side of the house from the ruins. But the sun was steadily descending; Gerrard's rare morning light was long gone.

A tingle, an unnerving touch of premonition, slithered down Vane's spine. Vividly recalling the sight of Gerrard's easel and stool, but no Gerrard, Vane swore.

He descended the stairs much more rapidly than he'd climbed them.

His expression bleak, he strode through the hall, down the corridor, and out through the side door. And halted.

He was an instant too late in wiping the grim expression from his face. Patience, strolling in company with her harem, had instantly focused on him; alarm had already flared in her eyes. Inwardly, Vane cursed. Belatedly assuming his customary facade, he strolled to meet her.

And her harem.

Penwick was there. Vane gritted his teeth and returned Penwick's nod with distant arrogance.

"Minnie's resting," Patience informed him. Her eyes searched his. "I thought I'd get some air."

"A sound notion," Penwick pronounced. "Nothing like a turn about the gardens to blow away the megrims."

Everyone ignored him and looked at Vane.

"Thought you were going riding with young Gerrard," Henry said.

Vane resisted the urge to kick him. "I was," he replied. "I'm just going to haul him in."

Edmond frowned. "That's odd." He looked back at the ruins. "I can imagine he might miss lunch, but it's not that easy to put off the pangs this long. And the light's almost gone. He can't still be sketching."

"Perhaps we'd better mount a search," Henry suggested. "He must have moved on from where he was this morning."

"He could be anywhere," Edmond put in.

Vane gritted his teeth. "I know where he was—I'll fetch him."

"I'll go with you." Patience's words were a statement. One look at her face told Vane arguing would be wasted effort. He nodded curtly.

"Allow me, my dear Miss Debbington." Unctuously, Penwick offered his arm. "Naturally, we'll all come, to make sure your mind is set at rest. I'll have a word or two to say to Debbington, never fear. We can't allow him to so heedlessly overset you."

The look Patience sent him was scathing. "You'll do no such thing. I have had quite enough of your attempted interference, sir!"

"Indeed." Seizing opportunity, Vane seized Patience's hand. Stepping forward, brushing Penwick aside, he drew her around. And set off for the ruins at a clipping pace.

Patience hurried beside him. Eyes scanning the ruins, she made no protest at having to half run to keep up.

Vane glanced down at her. "He was set up on the farside, beyond the cloister, facing the abbot's lodge."

Patience nodded. "He might have forgotten lunch, but he wouldn't have forgotten an engagement to ride with you."

Glancing back, Vane saw Edmond and Henry, throwing themselves into the excitement of a search, turn aside, Edmond heading for the old church, Henry for the opposite side of the cloisters. They, at least, were being helpful; Penwick, on the other hand, followed doggedly in their wake.

"Regardless," Vane said, as they reached the first crumbling wall, "he should have been back by now—the light's gone, and the angles would have changed by lunchtime."

He helped Patience over a patch of uneven stones, then they hurried along the west side of the cloister. Henry had just gained the east side. In the nave, they could hear Edmond, his poet's voice ringing, calling for Gerrard. No answer came.

Reaching the far wall, Vane helped Patience up onto the line of toppled stones from which she'd fallen so many nights before. Then he turned and looked toward the abbot's lodge.

The scene he beheld was as he'd seen it earlier. Precisely as he'd seen it earlier.

Vane swore. He didn't bother apologizing. Jumping down, he lifted Patience down to the old flags. Her hand tight in his, he headed for Gerrard's easel.

It took them ten minutes of scrambling—essentially crossing the entire abbey compound—to reach the grassed expanse on which Gerrard had stationed himself. The lawn rose gently as it led away from the abbot's lodge, then dipped into the scrubby edges of the wood. Gerrard had set up below the highest point of the rise, well in front of the dip, a few feet before a crumbling arched gateway, all that was left of the wall that had enclosed the abbot's garden.

Clasping Patience's hand, feeling her fingers clutch his, Vane strode straight to the easel. The page fluttering on it was blank.

Patience blanched. "He never started."

Vane's jaw set. "He started all right." He flicked the tattered remnants of paper caught under the pins. "It's been ripped away." Tightening his hold on Patience's hand, he looked toward the trees.

"Gerrard!"

His roar faded into silence.

A scuffling of boots heralded Henry's appearance. He clambered over a ruined wall, then, straightening, stared at the untended easel. Then he looked at Patience and Vane. "No sign of him the way I came."

Edmond appeared around the far edge of the ruins. Like Henry, he stared at the easel, then gestured behind him. "He's not anywhere around the church."

Stony-faced, Vane waved them to the trees. "You start from that end." They nodded and went. Vane looked down at Patience. "Would you rather wait here?"

She shook her head. "No, I'll come with you."

He'd expected nothing less. Her hand locked in his, they backtracked off the lawn and circled into the wood.

Penwick, huffing and puffing, caught up with them deep in the trees. Calling Gerrard's name, they were quartering the area; after pausing to catch his breath, Penwick tut-tutted censoriously. "If you'd allowed me to talk to Debbington earlier—bring him to a proper sense of his responsibilities—none of this nonsense, I flatter myself, would have occurred."

Pushing back a lock of hair from her forehead, Patience stared at him. "What nonsense?"

"It's obvious." Penwick had regained his breath and his customary attitude. "The boy's got an assignation with some flighty maid. Says he's busy drawing and slips away into the wood."

Patience's jaw dropped.

"Is that what you did at his age?" Vane inquired, forging ahead without pause.

"Well . . ." Penwick tugged his waistcoat into place, then he caught Patience's eye. "No! Of course not. Anyway, it's not me but young Debbington we're talking about here. Loose screw in the making, I've not the slightest doubt. Brought up by women. Pampered. Allowed to run wild without proper male guidance. What else can you expect?"

Patience stiffened.

"Penwick." Vane caught Penwick's eye. "Either go home or shut up. Or I'll take great delight in knocking your teeth down your throat."

The inflexible steel in his voice made it clear he was speaking the truth.

Penwick paled, then flushed and drew himself up. "If my assistance isn't welcome, naturally, I'll take myself off."

Vane nodded. "Do."

Penwick looked at Patience; she stared stonily back. With the air of a rejected martyr, Penwick sniffed and turned on his heel.

When the crump of his retreating footsteps died, Patience sighed. "Thank you."

"It was entirely my pleasure," Vane growled. He flexed his shoulders. "Actually, I was hoping he'd stay and keep talking."

Patience's giggle tangled in her throat.

After a further ten minutes of fruitless searching, they saw Edmond and Henry through the trees. Patience halted and heaved a troubled sigh. "You don't think," she said, turning to Vane as he stopped beside her, "that Gerrard actually might be off with some maid?"

Vane shook his head. "Trust me." He looked around—the belt of woodland was narrow; they hadn't missed any area. He looked down at Patience. "Gerrard's not that interested in females yet."

Henry and Edmond came up. Hands on hips, Vane glanced around one last time. "Let's get back to the ruins."

They stood on the lawn before Gerrard's easel and surveyed

the gigantic pile of toppled stones and crumbling rock. The sun was painting the sky red; they would have only an hour before fading light made searching dangerous.

Henry put their thoughts into words. "It's really relatively open. It's not as if there's all *that* many places someone might lie concealed."

"There are holes, though," Patience said. "I fell into one, remember?"

Vane looked at her, then he looked back at the easel—at the rise of the lawn behind it. Swinging about, he strode to the lip, and looked down.

His jaw locked. "He's here."

Patience rushed to Vane's side; clutching his arm, teetering on the lip's edge, she looked down.

Gerrard lay sprawled on his back, arms flung out, his eyes closed. The dip, which appeared gentle enough from any other vantage point, was quite steep, dropping six feet vertically into a narrow cleft, concealed by the sloping banks on either side.

The blood drained from Patience's face. "Oh, no!"

Vane jumped down, landing by Gerrard's feet. Patience immediately sank onto the edge, gathering her skirts about her legs. Vane heard the rustling. He looked around. His eyes lit with warning; Patience tilted her chin stubbornly and wriggled closer to the edge.

Cursing softly, Vane swung back, gripped her waist, and lifted her down, setting her on her feet beside Gerrard.

Immediately Vane released her, Patience flung herself on her knees beside her brother. "Gerrard?" A cold fist clutched her heart. He was dreadfully pale, his lashes dark crescents against chalk white cheeks. With a shaking hand, she brushed back a lock of hair, then framed his face in her hands.

"Gently," Vane warned. "Don't try to shift him yet." He checked Gerrard's pulse. "His heartbeat's strong. He's probably not badly injured, but we should check for broken bones before we shift him."

Relieved on one score, she sat back and watched Vane check Gerrard's torso, arms, and legs. Reaching Gerrard's feet, he frowned. "Nothing seems broken."

Patience frowned back, then reached for Gerrard's head, spreading her hands, sliding her fingers through the thick hair to check his skull. Her searching fingers found a roughness, a deep abrasion, then her palm turned sticky. Patience froze—and looked up at Vane. She drew a shaky breath, then, gently laying Gerrard's head back down, she retrieved her hand and peered at the palm. At the red streaks upon it. Her expression blanking, she held up her hand for the others to see. "He's been . . ."

Her voice died.

Vane's expression turned granite-hard. "Hit."

Gerrard came to his senses with a painful groan.

Patience immediately flew to his side. Sitting on the edge of his bed, she squeezed out a cloth in a basin perched on the bedside table. Shoulders propped against the wall beyond the bed, Vane watched as she bathed Gerrard's forehead and face.

Gerrard groaned again, but surrendered to her ministrations. Grimly impassive, Vane waited. Once they'd established Gerrard had been knocked unconscious, he'd carried him back to the house. Edmond and Henry had packed up Gerrard's gear and followed. Patience, distraught and struggling to master it, had kept by his side.

She'd come into her own once they'd got Gerrard upstairs. She'd known just what to do, and had gone about doing it in her usual competent way. While she'd remained pale and drawn, she hadn't panicked. With silent approval, he'd left her issuing orders left and right, and gone to break the news to Minnie.

Crossing the gallery, he'd seen, in the hall below, Edmond and Henry holding court, informing the other household members of Gerrard's "accident." Before leaving the ruins, they'd found the rock that had hit him—part of the old gateway arch. To Edmond and Henry, that meant Gerrard had been standing beneath the arch at the wrong moment, been struck by the falling masonry, then stumbled back and fallen into the cleft. Vane's view was not so sanguine. Concealed in the shadows of the gallery, he'd studied each face, listened to each exclamation of horror. All had rung true—true to form, true to character; none gave any indication of prior knowledge, or of guilt. Grimacing, he'd continued to Minnie's rooms.

After informing Minnie and Timms, he'd returned to assist Patience in evicting all those who'd gathered—all of Minnie's odd household—from Gerrard's room. While he'd succeeded in that, he hadn't been able to evict Minnie and Timms.

Vane glanced to where Minnie sat huddled in the old chair by the fireplace, wherein a fire now roared. Timms stood beside her, one hand gripping Minnie's shoulder, imparting wordless comfort. Their attention was focused on the bed. Vane studied Minnie's face, and chalked up another entry in the Spectre's—or was it the thief's?—account. They'd pay—for every deepening line in Minnie's face, for the worry and fretful concern in her old eyes.

"*Oh!* My head!" Gerrard tried to sit up. Patience pushed him back down.

"You have a gash at the back, just lie quietly on your side."

Still dazed, Gerrard obeyed, blinking owlishly across the now dim room. His gaze fixed on the window. The sun had set; last banners of vermilion streaked the sky. "It's evening?"

" 'Fraid so." Pushing away from the wall, Vane strolled forward to where Gerrard could see him. He smiled reassuringly. "You've missed the day."

Gerrard frowned. Patience rose to remove her basin; Gerrard raised a hand and gingerly felt the back of his head. His features contorted as he touched his wound. Lowering his hand, he looked at Vane. "What happened?"

Relieved, both by the clarity and directness of Gerrard's gaze, and his eminently sensible question, Vane grimaced. "I was hoping *you'd* be able to tell *us* that. You went out to sketch this morning, remember?"

Gerrard's frown returned. "The abbot's lodge from the west. I remember setting up."

He paused; Patience returned to sit beside him. She took one of his hands in hers. "Did you start sketching?"

"Yes." Gerrard went to nod, and winced. "I *did* sketch. I got the general lines down, then I got up and went to study the detail." He frowned in his effort to recall. "I went back to my stool, and kept sketching. Then. . . ." He grimaced, and glanced at Vane. "Nothing."

"You were hit on the back of the head with a rock," Vane informed him. "One that originally came from the gateway arch behind you. Try to think back—had you stood up, and stepped back? Or did you never leave your seat?"

Gerrard's frown deepened. "I didn't stand up," he eventually said. "I was sitting, sketching." He looked at Patience, then at Vane. "That's the last I remember."

"Did you see anything, sense anything? What's the very last thing you recall?"

Gerrard screwed up his face, then he shook his head—very slightly. "I didn't see or sense anything. I had my pencil in my hand and I was sketching—I'd started filling in the details around what's left of the abbot's front door." He looked at Patience. "You know what I'm like—I don't see anything, hear anything." He shifted his gaze to Vane. "I was well away."

Vane nodded. "How long were you sketching?"

Gerrard raised his brows in a facial shrug. "One hour? Two?" He lifted a shoulder. "Who knows. It could have been three, but I doubt it was that long. Give me a look at my sketch, and I'll have a better idea."

He looked up expectantly; Vane exchanged a glance with Patience, then looked back at Gerrard. "The sketch you were working on was torn from your easel."

"*What*?"

Gerrard's incredulous exclamation was echoed by Timms. Gerrard carefully shook his head. "That's ridiculous. My sketches aren't worth anything—why would the thief steal one? It wasn't even finished."

Vane exchanged a long glance with Patience, then transferred his gaze back to Gerrard's face. "It's possible that's why you were rendered unconscious—so you never did finish your latest view."

"But why?" The bewildered question came from Minnie.

Vane turned to face her. "If we knew that, we'd know a great deal more."

Later that night, by unanimous accord, they held a conference in Minnie's room. Minnie and Timms, Patience and Vane, gathered before Minnie's fire. Sinking onto the footstool beside Minnie's chair, one of Minnie's frail hands clasped in hers, Patience scanned the others' faces, lit by the flickering firelight.

Minnie was worried, but beneath her fragility ran a streak of pure stubbornness, and a determination to learn the truth. Timms seemed to consider the malefactors in their midst as a personal affront, if not to her dignity, then certainly to Minnie's. She was doggedly fixated on unmasking the villains.

As for Vane . . . Patience let her gaze roam his features, more austere than ever in the shifting golden light. All hard angles and planes, his face was set. He looked like . . . a warrior sworn. The fanciful notion popped into her head, but she didn't smile. The epithet fitted all too well—he looked set on eradicating, annihilating, whoever had dared disturb Minnie's peace.

And hers.

She knew that last was true—the knowledge had come to her borne by the touch of his hands on her shoulders as he'd helped her with Gerrard, in the way his eyes had searched her face, watching for worry, for signs of distress.

The sensation of being within his protective circle was sweetly comforting. Even though she told herself it was only for now—for the present and not for the future—she couldn't stop herself drinking it in.

"How's Gerrard?" Timms asked, settling her skirts in the second chair.

"Safely sleeping," Patience replied. He'd turned fretful as the evening wore on, until she'd insisted on dosing him with laudanum. "He's snug in his bed, and Ada's watching over him."

Minnie looked down at her. "Is he truly all right?"

Vane, leaning against the mantelpiece, shifted. "There was no sign of concussion that I could see. I suspect that, other than a sore head, he'll be his usual self in the morning."

Timms snorted. "But who hit him? And why?"

"Are we sure he was hit?" Minnie looked at Vane.

Grimly, he nodded. "His recollections are clear and lucid, not hazy. If he was seated as he said, there's no way a falling stone could have struck him at that angle, with that sort of force."

"Which brings us back to my questions," Timms said. "Who? And why?"

"As to the who, it must be the Spectre or the thief." Patience glanced at Vane. "Presuming they're not one and the same."

Vane frowned. "There seems little reason to imagine they're the same person. The Spectre has lain low since I chased him, while the thief has continued his activities without pause. There's also been no hint that the thief has any interest in the ruins, while they've always been the Spectre's special haunt." He didn't mention his conviction that the thief was a female, and thus unlikely to have had the strength, or intestinal fortitude, to cosh Gerrard. "We can't rule out the thief as today's culprit, but the Spectre seems the more likely villain." Vane shifted his gaze to Timms's face. "As for the why, I suspect Gerrard saw something—something he may not even realize he's seen."

"Or the villain *thought* he saw something," Timms replied.

"He's really very good with noting detail," Patience said.

"A fact the whole household knew. Anyone who's ever seen any of his sketches would be aware of the detail he includes." Vane stirred. "I think, given the disappearance of his last sketch, that we can safely conclude that he did indeed see something someone didn't want him to see."

Patience grimaced. "He doesn't remember anything special about what he'd sketched."

Vane met her gaze. "There's no reason whatever it is would appear out of the ordinary to him."

They fell silent, then Minnie asked, "Do you think he's in any danger?"

Patience's gaze flew to Vane's face. He shook his head decisively. "Whoever it is knows Gerrard knows nothing to the point, and poses no real threat to Gerrard now." Reading a lack of conviction in all their eyes, he reluctantly elaborated, "He was lying out there for hours, unconscious. If he was a real threat to the villain, said villain had ample time to remove him permanently."

Patience shuddered, but nodded. Both Minnie's and Timm's faces grew bleak. "I want this villain caught," Minnie declared. "We can't go on like this."

"Indeed." Vane straightened. "Which is why I suggest we remove to London."

"London?"

"Why London?"

Resettling his shoulders against the mantelpiece, Vane looked at the three faces turned up to him. "We have two problems—the thief and the Spectre. If we consider the thief, then, while the thefts don't follow any rhyme or reason, the chances of the perpetrator being one of the household is high. Given the number of items stolen, there must be a cache somewhere—

we've virtually eliminated any possiblity that the stolen goods have been sold. If we remove the entire household to London, then, as soon as we leave here, the staff, all of whom are above suspicion, can start a thorough search. Simultaneously, when we arrive in London, I'll arrange for all the luggage to be searched as well. In a house in London, further thefts and the hiding of items taken will be much more difficult."

Minnie nodded. "I can see that. But what about the Spectre?"

"The Spectre," Vane said, his expression growing grimmer, "is the most likely candidate for our villain of today. There's no evidence that the Spectre comes from outside—he's most likely one of the household. All that went before—the sounds and lights—could have been someone searching the ruins by night, when no one else was about. Today's events presumably arose because Gerrard unknowingly got too close to something the Spectre doesn't want seen. All that's happened suggests that the Spectre wants to hunt in the ruins without anyone else about. By removing to London, we give the Spectre precisely the situation he wants—the ruins, deserted."

Timms frowned. "But if he's one of the household, and the household's in London . . ." Her words faded as understanding lit her face. "He'll want to come back."

Vane grinned humorlessly. "Precisely. We'll just need to wait and see who makes the first move to return."

"But will he, do you think?" Minnie grimaced. "Will he persist, even after today? He must realize he needs to be more careful now—he must fear being caught."

"As for fearing being caught, I can't say. But"—Vane's jaw firmed—"I'm quite sure, if it's the empty ruins he wants, he won't be able to resist the opportunity of having them all to himself." He caught Minnie's eye. "Whoever the Spectre is, he's obsessed—whatever it is he's after, he's not going to give up."

And so it was decided: The whole household would remove to London as soon as Gerrard was fit enough to travel. As he did a final round of the silent, sleeping house, Vane made a mental list of preparations to be put in train tomorrow. The last leg of his watchman's round took him along the third floor of the west wing.

The door of Gerrard's room stood open; soft light spilled across the corridor floor.

Silently, Vane approached. He paused in the shadows of the doorway and studied Patience as, seated on a straight-backed chair set back from the bed, her hands clasped in her lap, she watched Gerrard sleep. Old Ada dozed, sunk in the armchair by the fireplace.

For long, uncounted moments, Vane simply looked—let his eyes drink their fill—of Patience's soft curves, of the sheening gloss of her hair, of her intrinsically feminine expression. The simple devotion in her pose, in her face, stirred him—thus would he want his children watched, cared for, protected. Not the sort of protection he provided, but protection, and support, of a different, equally important, sort. He would provide one, she would provide the other—two sides of the same, caring coin.

He felt the surge of emotion that gripped him; he was long past breaking free. The words he'd used to describe the Spectre rang in his head. The description applied equally well to him. He was obsessed, and was not going to give up.

Patience sensed his presence as he neared. She looked up and smiled fleetingly, then looked back at Gerrard. Vane curved his hands about her shoulders, then grasped and, gently but firmly, drew her to her feet. She frowned, but let him draw her into the circle of his arms.

Head bent, he spoke softly. "Come away. He's in no danger now."

She grimaced. "But—"

"He won't be happy if he wakes and finds you slumped asleep in that chair, watching over him as if he were six years old."

The look Patience bent on him stated very clearly that she knew precisely which string he was pulling. Vane met it with an arrogantly lifted brow. He tightened his arm about her. "No one's going to harm him, and Ada's here if he calls." He steered her to the door. "You'll be of more use to him tomorrow if you've had some sleep tonight."

Patience glanced over her shoulder. Gerrard remained sound asleep. "I suppose . . ."

"Precisely. I'm not about to leave you here, sitting through the night for no reason." Drawing her over the threshold, Vane pulled the door shut behind them.

Patience blinked her eyes wide; all she could see was darkness.

"Here."

Vane's arm slid around her waist, and tightened, locking her to his side. He turned her toward the main stairs, strolling slowly. Despite the lowering gloom, Patience found it easy to relax into his warmth, to sink into the comfort of his strength.

They walked in silence through the darkened house, and on into the opposite wing.

"You're sure Gerrard will be all right?" She asked the question as they reached the corridor leading to her room.

"Trust me." Vane's lips brushed her temple. "He'll be fine."

There was a note in his deep voice, rumbling softly through her, that reassured far more than mere words. The last of her edgy, perhaps irrational, sisterly trepidation slid away. Trust him?

Safely screened by the dark, Patience let her lips curve in a knowing, very womanly, smile.

Her door loomed before them. Vane set it wide and handed her through. A gentleman would have left at that point—he'd always known he wasn't a gentleman. He followed her in and shut the door behind him.

She needed to sleep; he wouldn't be able to rest until she was dreaming. Preferably curled in his arms.

Patience heard the latch fall home and knew he was in the room with her. She didn't look back but walked slowly to stand before the fire. It was blazing, stoked by some thoughtful servant. She stared into the flames.

And tried to clarify what she wanted. Now. This minute. From him.

He'd spoken truly—Gerrard was no longer six years old. Her time for watching over him was past. To cling would only be to hold him back. But he'd been the focus of her life for so long, she needed something to replace him. Someone to replace him.

At least for tonight.

She needed someone to take from her all she had to give. Giving was her outlet, her release—she needed to give in much the same way as she needed to breathe. She needed to be wanted—needed someone to take her as she was, for what she was. For what she could give them.

Her senses reached for Vane as he drew nearer. Drawing a deep breath, she turned.

And found him beside her.

She looked into his face, the angular planes burnished by the fire's glow. His eyes, cloudy grey, searched hers. Setting aside all thoughts of right and wrong, she raised her hands to his chest.

He stilled.

Sliding her arms upward, she stepped closer; locking her hands at his nape, she pressed herself to him and lifted her lips to his.

Their lips met. And fused. Hungrily. She felt his hands lock about her waist, then he shifted, and his arms closed, viselike, about her.

Her invitation, her acceptance, shook Vane to his soul; he only just managed not to crush her to him. His demons howled in triumph; he swiftly shackled them, leashed them, then turned his attention to her. Of her own volition, she pressed closer. Letting his hands glide down the delicate planes of her back, he molded her to him, urging her hips nearer, then, sliding his hands further, he cupped the firm curves of her derriere and drew her forcefully into the V of his braced thighs.

She gasped and offered him her mouth anew; rapaciously he claimed her. In the back of his mind rang a litany of warning, reminding him of his reined demons, of the concepts of civilized behavior, of sophisticated expertise—all the hallmarks of his rakish experience. Said experience, without conscious instruction, came up with a plan of action. It was warm before the fire—they could disrobe before it, then repair to the civilized comfort of her bed.

Having formulated a plan, he focused on its implementation. He kissed her deeply, searchingly, evocatively—and felt her flaring response. Her tongue boldly tangled with his; distracted, keen to experience the sweet response again, he tempted her, taunted her, to repeat the caress. She did, but slowly, so slowly his senses followed every flick, every sliding contact, with giddy intensity.

Not until he finally summoned his wits and eased back from

their kiss did he feel her hands on his chest. Through his shirt, her palms branded him, her fingers kneading. She swept her hands up to his shoulders; his coat impeded the movement. She tried to push the coat off. Breaking their kiss, Vane released her and shrugged. Coat and waistcoat hit the floor.

She fell on his cravat, as eager as his demons. Brushing her hands aside, Vane rapidly flicked the knotted folds undone, then dragged the long strip free. Patience had already transferred her attentions to his shirt buttons; within seconds she had them undone. Hauling the tails free of his waistband, she flung the sides wide and greedily set her hands searching, fingers tangling in the crisp hair.

Looking into her face, Vane savored the look of sensual wonder in her features, the glow of anticipation in her eyes.

He reached for her laces.

Patience was enthralled. He'd explored her, but she hadn't, yet, had a chance to explore him. She spread her fingers, and her senses, drinking in the warm resilience of taut muscle stretched over hard bone. She investigated the hollows and broad planes of his chest, the wide ridges of his ribs. Crisp brown hair curled and caught at her slim digits; the flat discs of his nipples hardened at her touch.

It was all perfectly fascinating. Eager to extend her horizons, she seized the sides of his shirt.

Just as he seized the sleeves of her gown.

What followed had her giggling—foolishly, heatedly. Hands locked on each other, they rocked and swayed. Simultaneously, they both adjusted their grips. While she fought to wrestle his shirt from him, he—far more expertly—divested her of her gown.

He hauled her into his arms and ravished her mouth, plundering deeply, one arm locking her to him while his other hand dealt with the drawstring of her petticoat.

Patience answered the challenge and returned the kiss avidly—while her busy fingers fought with the buttons of his breeches. Their lips met and melded, parting only to fuse heatedly again.

Her petticoats fell to the floor in the same instant she pushed his breeches over his hips. He broke from their kiss. Their eyes met, heated gazes colliding. With a soft curse, he stepped back and stripped off both boots and breeches.

Eyes wide, Patience drank in the sight of him, the brutally hard, sculpted planes of his body bathed in the fire's golden light.

He looked up and caught her watching. He straightened, but before he could reach for her, she grasped the lower edge of her chemise and, in one smooth movement, drew it up and over her head.

Her eyes locked on his, she let the soft silk fall, forgotten, from her fingers. Hands, arms, reaching for him, she deliberately stepped into his embrace.

The golden instant of meeting, the first touch of bare skin to bare skin, sent exquisite delight lancing through her. She sucked in a quick breath. Lids lowered, she draped her arms over his broad shoulders and pressed closer, settling her breasts against his chest, her thighs meeting his much harder ones, her soft belly a cradle for the rampant hardness of his staff.

Their bodies slid and shifted, then locked tight. His arms closed, a steel vise, about her.

And she felt the coiled tension that held him. The leashed tension he held back.

The power, the force, she sensed in his locked muscles, in the taut sinews that surrounded her, compelled her. Fascinated her. Emboldened and encouraged her. She wanted to know it— feel it, touch it, revel in it. Tightening her arms about his neck, she pressed even closer. Lifting her head, she brushed her lips across his. And whispered, "Let go."

Vane ignored her—she didn't know, couldn't know, what she was asking. Lowering his head, he captured her lips in a long, lengthy kiss designed to intensify the glorious sensation of her naked body sinking against his. She felt like cool silk, vibrant, delicate, and sensual; the slide of her against him was a potent caress, leaving him achingly aroused, achingly urgent.

He needed to get her to the bed. Soon.

She broke from their kiss to place hot, openmouthed kisses across his collarbone, across the sensitive skin just below his throat.

And to reach for him.

She touched him. Vane stilled. Delicately tentative, she

curled her fingers about his rigid length. He stiffened—and hauled in a desperate breath.

Her bed. His demons roared.

Guided by unerring instinct, her fingers closing more confidently about him, she licked one flat nipple, her tongue scalding hot, and murmured, "Let the reins go."

Vane's head reeled.

Releasing him, she raised her head. Twining her arms about his neck, she stretched upward against him, and, bending one knee, lifted one firm, ivory thigh to his hip. "Take me."

She was out of her mind—but he was already out of his.

All thoughts of beds, and civilized sophistry, vanished from his head. Without conscious direction, his hands closed about the firm globes of her bottom and he lifted her. Instantly, she wrapped her long legs about his hips and drew herself tight against him.

It was she who made the necessary adjustment to capture the throbbing head of his staff in the slick flesh between her thighs, leaving him poised, aching and desperate, at her entrance.

And it was she who made the first move to sink down, to take him into her body, to impale herself on his rigid hardness.

Every muscle locked, Vane struggled to breathe, struggled to deny the impulse to ravish her. Sinking lower, she found his lips with hers, brushing them tantalizingly. "Let go."

He didn't, couldn't—to relinquish control completely was beyond him. But he loosened the reins, slackened them as much as he dared. Muscles bunching, flexing, he lifted her—and thrust upward as she sank down.

She learned quickly. The next time he lifted her, she relaxed, then tightened as he filled her, slowing her downward slide, extending it to take even more of him than before.

Vane set his teeth. His head whirled as, again and again, she closed, scalding hot, about him. When it was that the truth dawned and he realized she was loving him, knowingly pleasuring him, lavishing the most intimate of caresses upon him, he never knew. But it was suddenly crystal-clear.

He'd never been loved like this—had a woman set herself to lavish pleasure so determinedly upon him—to ravish him.

The slick caresses continued; he was sure he'd lose his mind.

Fire rose, flame upon flame within him. He was burning, and she was the source of the heat.

He buried himself in the wet furnace she offered him, and felt her boldly embrace him. With a half-smothered groan, he sank to his knees on the rug before the hearth.

She adjusted instantly, eagerly using her new purchase on the floor to ride him more hungrily.

He couldn't take much more. Vane locked his hands about her hips and held her to him, trying to catch his breath, desperate to prolong the glorious congress. Patience squirmed, fighting to regain control. Vane set his teeth on an agonized hiss. Sliding both hands up, along her back, he tipped her back and away, arching her so her breasts, swollen and ripe, were his to feast on.

He feasted.

Patience heard her own gasp as his mouth fastened hungrily over one engorged nipple. A sobbing moan followed moments later. Hot and ravenous, he laved her breasts, then suckled the hypersensitized peaks until she was sure she would die. Within her, his heavy hardness filled her, completed her; pressed deeply into her, he rocked deeper still, claiming her—body, mind, and senses.

Trapped in his hold, she gasped and writhed; unable to rise on him, but refusing to be gainsaid, she changed direction, and rolled her hips against him.

It was Vane's turn to gasp. He felt the coiled tension inside him tighten, then tighten again, invested with a force he had no hope of controlling. Of holding back.

Reaching between them, he slid his fingers through her damp curls, and found her. Just a touch was all it took, and she shattered, fragmented, her senses exploding in a fractured cry as she tumbled over that invisible precipice and into sated oblivion.

He followed a heartbeat later.

The fire had burned to embers before they stirred. Their bodies, locked together, felt too deeply enmeshed to part. Both roused, but neither shifted, both too content with their closeness, their intimacy.

Time stretched, and still they clung, their heartbeats slowing, their bodies cooling, their souls still locked in flight.

Eventually, Vane bent his head and brushed his lips across Patience's temple. She glanced up. He studied her eyes, then kissed her gently, lingeringly. As their lips parted, he asked, "Have you changed your mind yet?"

He sensed her confusion, then she understood. She didn't pull away, but shook her head. "No."

Vane didn't argue. He held her, and felt her warmth surround him, felt her heart beating in time with his. Uncounted minutes later, he lifted her from him and carried her to her bed.

Chapter 16

~❖~

WHY WOULDN'T SHE marry him?

What did she have against marriage?

Those questions revolved in Vane's brain as he headed his horses down the London road. It was the second morning after Gerrard's accident. Pronounced fit to travel, Gerrard sat on the box seat beside him, idly studying the scenery.

Vane didn't even see his leader's ears. He was too engrossed with thoughts of Patience, and the situation he now found himself in. The lady herself, with Minnie and Timms, was traveling in the carriage following his curricle; behind that, a pageant of hired coaches bore the rest of the Bellamy Hall household away from Bellamy Hall.

Sudden pressure on his left ankle made Vane glance down; he watched as Myst recurled herself against his left boot. Instead of joining Patience in the closed carriage, Myst had surprised her mistress and elected to ride with him. While he had nothing against cats, or youthful sprigs, Vane would readily have traded both his companions for Patience.

So he could interrogate her over her inexplicable stance.

She loved him, but refused to marry him. Given her circumstances, and his, that decision more than qualified as inexplicable. His jaw setting, Vane looked ahead, staring fixedly between his leader's ears.

His original plan—to break down Patience's barriers with passion, to so addict her to his loving that she would come to view marrying him as very much in her best interests, and so admit to him what was worrying her—had developed a major hitch. He hadn't reckoned with becoming addicted himself, possessed by a desire more powerful than any he'd known. Addicted to the extent that that desire—and his demons—were no longer subject to his will.

His demons—and that mindless need—had broken free that first time in the barn. He'd excused that as understandable, given the circumstances and his pent-up frustrations. On the night he'd invaded her bedchamber, he'd had all the reins firmly in his grasp; he'd coolly and successfully retained control, even under the full force of her fire. That success had left him complacent, confidently assured.

Their third interlude, two nights ago, had shattered his complacency.

He'd come within a whisker of losing control again.

Worse—she knew it. A golden-eyed siren, she'd deliberately tempted him—and very nearly lured him to the rocks.

That a woman could reduce his vaunted self-control to the merest vestige of its usual despotic strength was not a fact he liked to contemplate. He'd slept alone last night—not well. He'd spent half the night thinking, warily wondering. The truth was he was more deeply entangled than he'd thought. The truth was, he yearned to let go—to lose himself utterly—in loving her. Just formulating that thought was enough to unnerve him—he'd always equated losing control, especially in that arena, as a form of surrender.

To knowingly surrender—knowingly let go as she'd asked—was . . . too unnerving to imagine.

Their interaction had developed dangerous undercurrents—currents he'd failed to forsee when he'd set sail on this particular tack. What would happen if she held firm to her inexplicable refusal? Would he ever be able to give her up? Let her go? Marry some other woman?

Vane shifted on the hard seat and resettled the reins in his hands. He didn't even want to consider those questions. Indeed, he refused point-blank to consider them. If she could take a stance, so could he.

She was going to marry him—she was going to be his wife. He just had to convince her there was no sane alternative.

The first step was to discover the basis for her inexplicable stance, the reason she would not agree to marriage. As the curricle rolled on, the pace slow so the carriages could keep up, he wrestled with schemes to uncover Patience's problem, which had now become his.

They stopped briefly for lunch at Harpenden. Both Patience and Timms spent their time cosseting Minnie, still under the weather. Other than a low-voiced query as to Gerrard's strength, Patience had no time to spend with him. Laying her sisterly qualms to rest, he let her return to Minnie's side, squelching all thought of taking her up in his curricle. Minnie's need was greater than his.

Their cavalcade got under way again. Gerrard settled back, surveying all with a keen and curious eye. "I've never been this far south."

"Oh?" Vane kept his gaze on his horses. "Where, exactly, is your home?"

Gerrard told him, describing the valley outside Chesterfield using words like brushstrokes; Vane had no difficulty seeing it in his mind's eye. "We've always lived there," Gerrard concluded. "For the most part, Patience runs things, but she's been teaching me the ropes for the last year."

"It must have been hard when your father died so unexpectedly—difficult for your mother and Patience to take up the reins."

Gerrard shrugged. "Not really. They'd been managing the estate for years even then—first Mama, then Patience."

"But . . ." Vane frowned. He glanced at Gerrard. "Surely your father managed the estate?"

Gerrard shook his head. "He was never interested. Well, he was never there. He died when I was six, and I couldn't remember him even then. I can't recall him ever staying for more than a few nights. Mama said he preferred London and his London friends—he didn't come home very often. It used to make her sad."

His gaze grew distant as memory took hold. "She was always trying to describe him to us, how handsome and gentlemanly he was, how he rode so well to hounds, how he carried the cloak of a gentleman so elegantly. Whenever he appeared, even if for only one day, she was always eager for us to see how impressive he was." He grimaced. "But I can't recall what he looked like at all."

A chill struck Vane's soul. For Gerrard, with his vivid visual memory, to have no recollection of his father spoke volumes. Yet for well-heeled gentlemen to behave toward their families as Reginald Debbington had was not unheard of and no crime. Vane knew it. But he'd never before been close to the children of such men, never before had cause to feel sorrow and anger on their behalf—sorrow and anger they themselves, the deprived, did not know they should feel—for what their father had not given them. All the things his own family, the Cynsters, held dear—all they stood for—family, home, and hearth. *To have and to hold* was the Cynster motto. The first necessitated the second—that was something all male Cynsters understood from their earliest years. You desired, you seized—then you accepted responsibility. Actively. When it came to family, Cynsters were nothing if not active.

As the curricle bowled along, Vane struggled to grasp the reality Gerrard had described—he could see Gerrard's home, but couldn't conceive of its atmosphere, how it had functioned. The entire concept—a family without its natural leader, its most stalwart defender—was alien to him.

He could, however, imagine how Patience—his determined, independent, practical wife-to-be—would have viewed her father's behavior. Vane frowned. "Your father—was Patience very attached to him?"

Gerrard's puzzled look was answer enough. "Attached to him?" His brows rose. "I don't think so. When he died, I remember her saying something about duty, and what was expected." After a moment, he added, "It's difficult to become attached to someone who's not there."

Someone who didn't value your attachment. Vane heard the words in his head—and wondered.

The shadows were lengthening when their cavalcade pulled up in Aldford Street, just west of South Audley Street. Vane threw the reins to Duggan and jumped down. Minnie's traveling carriage rocked to a stop behind his curricle, directly before the steps of Number 22. A discreet, gentleman's residence, Number

22 had been hired at short notice by a certain Mr. Montague, man of business to many of the Cynsters.

Opening the door of Minnie's carriage, Vane handed Patience to the pavement. Timms followed, then Minnie. Vane knew better than to attempt to carry her. Instead, with Patience lending support on her other side, he helped Minnie climb the steep steps. The rest of Minnie's household began debouching from their carriages, attracting the attention of late strollers. An army of footmen swarmed out of the house to assist with the luggage.

At the top of the steps, the front door stood open. Patience, carefully guiding Minnie, looked up as they gained the narrow porch—and discovered a strange personage standing in the front hall, holding the door wide. Stoop-shouldered, wiry, with an expression that would have done credit to a drenched cat, he was the oddest butler she'd ever encountered.

Vane, however, appeared to find nothing odd about the man; he nodded briefly as he helped Minnie over the threshold. "Sligo."

Sligo bowed. "Sir."

Minnie looked up and beamed. "Why, Sligo, what a pleasant surprise."

Following in Minnie's wake, Patience could have sworn Sligo blushed. Looking uncomfortable, he bowed again. "Ma'am."

In the melee that followed, as Minnie and Timms, then all the others, were received and shown to their rooms, Patience had ample time to observe Sligo, and the absolute rule he wielded over the junior servants. Both Masters and Mrs. Henderson, who had traveled up with their mistress, clearly recognized Sligo and treated him as a respected equal.

To Patience's relief, Vane distracted Henry, Edmond, and Gerrard, keeping them out from under everyone's feet while the other members of the household were settled. When those three at last took themselves off to explore their new accommodation in the hour left before dinner, Patience heaved a weary sigh and sank onto a *chaise* in the drawing room.

And looked up at Vane, standing in his usual pose, one shoulder propped against the mantelpiece. "Who," Patience asked, "is Sligo?"

Vane's lips curved slightly. "Devil's ex-batman."

Patience frowned. "Devil—the Duke of St. Ives?"

"One and the same. Sligo acts as Devil's caretaker when he's out of town. As it happens, Devil and his duchess, Honoria, returned to the fray yesterday, so I borrowed Sligo."

"Why?"

"Because we need someone trustworthy who knows a trick or two, here in the house. Sligo's presently coordinating the searches of all the arriving luggage. He's absolutely trustworthy and utterly reliable. If you want anything done—anything at all—ask him and he'll arrange it."

"But . . ." Patience's frown deepened. "You'll be here. Won't you?"

Vane met her gaze directly. "No." Dismay—or was it simply disappointment?—flitted through her golden eyes. Vane frowned. "I'm not deserting, but an instant's thought ought to show that Mr. Vane Cynster, known to have recently purchased a comfortable house just a stone's throw away in Curzon Street, cannot possibly have any acceptable need to reside under his godmother's roof."

Patience grimaced. "I hadn't thought of that. I suppose, now we're in London, we'll have to bow to society's dictates."

To whit, he couldn't spend the night in her bed. "Precisely." Vane suppressed his reaction. There were other options, but she didn't need to know about them yet. Once he'd manuevered their interaction onto a more manageable footing, he'd let her into the secret. Until then . . .

Straightening, he pushed away from the mantelpiece. "I'd better be on my way. I'll call tomorrow, to see how you've settled in."

Patience held his gaze, then coolly held out her hand. He grasped it, then bent and brushed his lips over her knuckles. And felt the tiny jolt that went through her.

Satisfied for the moment, he left her.

"It's all *soooo* exciting!"

Hearing Angela's paean for the tenth time that morning, Patience ignored it. Ensconced in a corner of one of the two drawing-room *chaises*, she continued stitching yet another tray-cloth. The activity had palled, but she had to do something with her mind—her hands—while she waited for Vane to appear.

Presuming he would. It was already after eleven.

Beside her, Timms sat darning; Minnie, having survived the rigors of the journey surprisingly well, was sunk in the comfort of a large armchair before the hearth. The other *chaise* played host to Mrs. Chadwick and Edith Swithins. Angela—she of the senseless pronouncements—was standing beside the window, peeking through the lace curtains at the passersby.

"I can't wait to see it all—the theaters, the modistes, the milliners." Hands clasped to her breast, Angela whirled and twirled. "It'll be so *wondrously* exciting!" Ceasing her twirling, she looked at her mother. "Are you sure we can't go before luncheon?"

Mrs. Chadwick sighed. "As agreed, we'll go for a short excursion this afternoon to decide which modistes might be suitable."

"It will have to be one in Bruton Street," Angela declared. "But the best shops, Edmond says, are on Bond Street."

"Bond Street is just beyond Bruton Street." Patience had spent the journey down reading a guidebook. "Once we stroll the length of one, we'll have reached the other."

"Oh. Good." Her afternoon's prospects assured, Angela subsided back into her daydreams.

Patience resisted an urge to glance at the mantelpiece clock. She could hear its steady tick, counting away the minutes; it seemed like she'd been listening for hours.

She already knew town life would never suit her. Used to country hours, the routine of breakfasting at ten, of taking luncheon at two and dining at eight or later, would never find favor with her. Bad enough that she'd woken at her usual hour, and, finding the breakfast parlor empty, had had to make do with tea and toast in the back parlor. Bad enough that there was no piano with which she could distract herself. Much worse was the fact that it was, apparently, unacceptable for her to walk out unescorted. Worst of all was the fact that Number 22 Aldford Street was a great deal smaller than Bellamy Hall, which meant they were all thrown together, under each other's feet— each other's noses—all the time.

To have to bear with the others at such close quarters looked set to drive her demented.

And Vane had not yet arrived.

When he did, she would inform him in no uncertain terms what she thought of his idea of removing to London. They had better flush out the thief and the Spectre. Soon.

The clock ticked on. Patience gritted her teeth and persevered with her needle.

A knock on the street door had her looking up. Along with everyone else but Edith Swithins—she happily tatted on. The next instant, a deep rumbling voice reached all their straining ears. Patience inwardly sighed—with a relief she had no intention of examining too closely. Minnie's face lit up as familiar prowling footsteps neared. Timms grinned.

The door opened. Vane strolled in, to be greeted with a panoply of smiles. His gaze flicked to Patience. She met it coolly. She studied him as he nodded to them all, then greeted Minnie elegantly and affectionately, inquiring after her health and how she'd spent the night.

"I very likely got more sleep than you," Minnie replied, a roguish twinkle in her eye.

Vane smiled lazily down at her and made no move to deny it. "Are you ready to brave the park?"

Minnie grimaced. "Perhaps tomorrow I might let you persuade me to a stroll. For today, I'm content to sit quietly, gathering my failing strength."

Her color, better than it had been for days, showed she was in no danger of fading away. Reassured, Vane glanced at Patience, watching with a reserved coolness he didn't appreciate. "Perhaps," he said, looking back at Minnie, "if you're settled today, I might take Miss Debbington up in your stead."

"By all means." Minnie beamed at Patience and made shooing motions. "So trying for Patience to be cooped up inside."

Vane slanted a rakish glance at Patience. "Well, Miss Debbington? Are you game for a turn about the park?"

Her gaze locked with his, Patience hesitated.

Angela opened her mouth and stepped forward; Mrs. Chadwick motioned her back, mouthing a definite "No!" Angela subsided, sulking.

Unable to read anything in Vane's eyes to explain the challenge in his words, Patience raised a brow. "Indeed, sir. I would be glad of the chance of some fresh air."

Vane inwardly frowned at her temperate acceptance. He waited while she set aside her work and stood, then, with a nod to Minnie and the rest, offered Patience his arm from the room.

He halted in the hall.

Patience lifted her hand from his sleeve and turned to the stairs. "I won't keep you above a minute."

Vane reached out, grasped her elbow, and drew her back to him. All the way back until he looked down into her now wide eyes. After a moment, he softly asked, "The others. Where are they?"

Patience struggled to think. "Whitticombe has taken over the library—it's well stocked but unfortunately quite small. Edgar and the General had nowhere else to go, so they've braved the chill, but I don't know how long they'll remain there. Edgar said something about looking in at Tattersalls."

"Hmm." Vane frowned. "I'll make sure Sligo knows." He refocused on Patience. "The others?"

"Henry, Edmond, and Gerrard made straight for the billiard room." Vane's grip on her elbow slackened; twisting free, Patience straightened—and shot him a severe glance. "I won't tell you what I think of a house that has a billiard room but no music room."

Vane's lips twitched. "It is a *gentleman's* residence."

Patience humphed. "Regardless, I don't believe the allure of billiards will keep that trio satisfied. They were planning all manner of excursions." She gestured widely. "To Exeter Exchange, the Haymarket, Pall Mall. I even heard them mention some place called the Peerless Pool."

Vane blinked. "That's closed."

"Is it?" Patience raised her brows. "I'll tell them."

"Never mind. I'll tell them myself." Vane glanced at her again. "I'll have a chat with them while you fetch your pelisse and bonnet."

With a haughty nod, Patience acquiesced. Vane watched as she ascended the stairs, then, frowning more definitely, strode for the billiard room—to lay down a few ground rules.

He returned to the front hall as Patience regained the tiles. Minutes later, he handed her into his curricle and climbed up beside her. The park was close; as he headed his horses toward the trees, Vane checked over the list of Minnie's household. And frowned. "Alice Colby." He glanced at Patience. "Where's she?"

"She didn't come down to breakfast." Patience's brows rose. "I suppose she must be in her room. I haven't seen her about at all, now you mention it."

"She's probably praying. She seems to spend a good part of her time thus employed."

Patience shrugged and looked ahead. Vane glanced at her, letting his gaze slide appreciatively over her. Head high, face to the breeze, she scanned the avenue ahead. Beneath the poke of her bonnet, wispy tendrils of burnished brown fluttered against her cheeks. Her pelisse was the same powder blue as the simple morning gown she wore beneath it. His brain registered the fact that neither was new, much less in the latest style, but, to his eyes, the picture she presented as she sat on the box seat of his curricle was perfect. Even if her chin was tilted a touch too high, and her expression was a touch too reserved.

Inwardly, he frowned, and looked to his horses. "We'll need to ensure that none of Minnie's menagerie has a chance to get loose on their own. I think we can assume there's no conspiracy or partnership, at least between unrelated individuals. But we must ensure none of them has a chance to pass on any stolen valuables, like the pearls, to an accomplice. Which means we— you, me, Gerrard, Minnie, and Timms, with Sligo's help—will have to accompany them whenever they leave the house."

"Angela and Mrs. Chadwick plan to visit Bruton and Bond Streets this afternoon." Patience wrinkled her nose. "I suppose I could go with them."

Vane suppressed his grin. "Do." Most ladies of his acquaintance would hie off to Bruton and Bond Streets at the drop of a hat. Patience's lukewarm enthusiasms augered well for a peaceful life in Kent. "I've agreed, suitably reluctantly, to act as guide for Henry, Edmond, and Gerrard this afternoon, and I tipped Sligo the wink to keep his eye on Edgar and the General."

Patience frowned. "There are rather many to watch if they should decide to go out on their own."

"We'll have to curb their taste for town delights." Vane noted the carriages drawn up to the verge ahead. "Speaking of which . . . behold, the *grandes dames* of the *ton*."

Even without the warning, Patience would have recognized them. They sat delicately draped over velvet or leather seats, elegant turbans nodding, sharp eyes bright, gloved hands artfully waving as they dissected and discussed every snippet of potential gossip. From youthful but elegant matrons to eagle-eyed dowagers, they were assured, secure in their social positions. Their carriages lined the fashionable route as they exchanged information and invitations.

Many heads turned their way as they bowled steadily along. Turbans were graciously inclined; Vane returned the nods easily but did not stop. Patience noted that many of the eyes beneath the turbans came to rest on her. The expressions she detected were either arrested, haughtily disapproving, or both. Chin rising, she ignored them. She knew her pelisse and bonnet were unfashionable. Dowdy. Possibly even frumpish.

But she would only be in London for a few weeks—to catch a thief—so her wardrobe hardly mattered.

At least, not to her.

She glanced sidelong at Vane, but could detect no glimmer of consciousness in his expression. She couldn't read anything in it at all. He gave no sign of registering, let along responding, to the more artful of the looks directed his way. Patience cleared her throat. "There seem to be a lot of ladies present—I didn't think so many would have returned to town."

Vane shrugged. "Not everyone does, but Parliament's back in session, so the political hostesses are in residence, exerting their influence with the usual balls and dinners. That's what draws many of the *ton* back. The few weeks of social whirl nicely fill the time between the summer and the start of the shooting season."

"I see." Scanning the carriages ahead, Patience noted one lady who, rather than reclining languidly and watching them go by, had sat bolt upright. A second later, she waved—imperiously.

Patience glanced at Vane; from the direction of his gaze and his set lips, he'd already seen the lady. His hesitation was palpable, then, gathering tension as if girding his loins, he slowed his horses. The curricle rocked to a stop beside the elegant brougham.

Occupied by the lady, of similar age to Patience, with bright chesnut hair and a pair of exceedingly shrewd, blue-grey eyes. Said eyes instantly locked on Patience's face. Their owner smiled delightedly.

Grimly, Vane nodded. "Honoria."

The lady switched her bright smile to him. It deepened fractionally. "Vane. And who is this?"

"Allow me to present Miss Patience Debbington. Minnie's niece."

"Indeed?" Without waiting for more, the lady held out her hand to Patience. "Honoria, my dear Miss Debbington."

"Duchess of St. Ives," Vane grimly announced.

Honoria ignored him. "It's a pleasure to meet you, my dear. Is Minnie well?"

"She's much better than she was." Patience forgot about her shabby clothes and responded easily to the duchess's openness. "She took a chill a few weeks back, but she survived the journey down surprisingly well."

Honoria nodded. "How long does she plan to stay in town?"

Until they caught their thief—unmasked their Spectre. Patience held the duchess's clear gaze. "Ah . . ."

"We're not certain," Vane drawled. "It's just one of Minnie's usual bolts to town, but this time she's brought her entire menagerie with her." He raised his brows in patent boredom. "Presumably for distraction."

Honoria's gaze remained steady on his face long enough to make Patience wonder how much of Vane's glib explanation she believed. Then Honoria switched her gaze to her—and smiled warmly, welcomingly—far more personally than Patience had expected. "I'm sure we'll meet again shortly, Miss Debbington." Honoria pressed Patience's fingers. "I'll let you get on—you doubtless have a busy morning ahead of you. Indeed"—she shifted her gaze to Vane—"I've some calls to make, too."

Vane, tight-lipped, nodded curtly—and gave his horses the office.

As they bowled down the avenue, Patience glanced at his set face. "The duchess seems very nice."

"She is. Very nice." Also very nosy, and definitely too perceptive. Vane inwardly gritted his teeth. He'd known the family would find out sometime, but he hadn't expected it to be quite so soon. "Honoria's effectively the matriarch of the family." He struggled to find words to explain precisely what that meant—but gave up. Acknowledging the power Honoria—or any of the Cynster women—wielded within the family was something he, and all his male relatives, always found exceedingly difficult.

Vane narrowed his eyes and headed his team toward the park gates. "I'll call for you tomorrow, at much the same time. A drive or a walk seems the best way for us to exchange information on what the others have done, and where they're intending to go."

Patience stiffened. He'd taken her for this drive so they could coordinate their plans—he viewed the outing as a campaign meeting. "Indeed," she replied, somewhat tartly. An instant later, she said, "Perhaps we should get Sligo to accompany us?" When Vane, frowning, glanced her way, she added, "So we can get his views firsthand."

Vane frowned harder—his horses distracted him.

As they negotiated the park gates and turned into the crowded thoroughfare, Patience sat, stiffly erect; inside, her emotions churned. As the horses' hooves struck the cobbles of Aldford Street, she lifted her chin. "I realize that you feel committed to identifying the thief and the Spectre, but, now you've returned to London, I daresay you have other engagements—other distractions—on which you'd much rather spend your time." She drew a tight breath; a cold vise had fastened about her chest. She felt Vane's quick glance. Head high, eyes forward, she continued, "I'm sure, now Sligo has joined us, we could find some way to get the relevant information to you without having to waste your time on unnecessary walks or drives."

She would not cling. Now they were in town, and he could see that she didn't fit within his elegant world, couldn't hold a candle to the exquisitely arrayed beauties he was accustomed to consorting with, she would not try to hold on to him. Like her mother had clung to her father. Theirs was a temporary relationship; in her mind, she could already see its end. By taking the first step and acknowledging the inevitable, she might, just possibly, prepare her heart for the blow.

"I have no intention of not seeing you at least once a day."

The words were bitten off, infused with a steely rage Patience could not possibly mistake. Taken aback, she glanced at

Vane. The carriage rocked to a halt, he tied off the reins and jumped down.

Then swung around. He grasped her waist and lifted her bodily from the seat—and placed her, with quiveringly rigid control, on the pavement before him.

Steel shards, his eyes held hers. Breathless, Patience blinked up at him. His face was hard, a warrior's mask. Waves of anger and aggression lapped about her.

"When it comes to distraction," he informed her through clenched teeth, "nothing in this world could top you."

His words were invested with meaning—a meaning she didn't understand. Mentally at sea, Patience struggled to catch her breath. Before she succeeded, Vane had marched her up the steps and deposited her in the front hall.

Narrow-eyed, he looked down at her. "Don't expect to see the last of me anytime soon."

With that, he swung on his heel and stalked out.

Chapter 17

TWO DAYS LATER, Vane stalked up the steps of Number 22 Aldford Street, on his way to see Patience. If she wasn't ready to drive out with him this morning, there'd be trouble.

He was not in a good mood.

He hadn't been for the past two days.

After last leaving Patience in Aldford Street, his temper gnashing at the bit, he'd gone off to seek refuge at White's to calm down and think. He'd assumed, given their closeness, how much of himself he'd already revealed to her, that she wouldn't—couldn't possibly—confuse him with her father. He'd obviously assumed wrong. Her attitude, her comments, made it plain she was judging him against Reginald Debbington's standard—and was failing to perceive any significant difference.

His initial reaction had been a violent hurt he had not, even now, entirely suppressed. After her earlier efforts that had sent him fleeing from Bellamy Hall, he'd thought he'd surmounted "hurt." He'd been wrong on that score, too.

Sunk in a quiet corner of White's, he'd spent fruitless hours composing terse, pithy speeches designed to elucidate precisely how and in what manner he differed from her sire—a man to whom family had meant little. His periods had grown increasingly forceful; in the end, he'd jettisoned phrases in favor of action. That, as all Cynsters well knew, spoke far louder than words.

Judging that, by that time, the damage within the family had already been done, he'd swallowed his pride and gone to call on Honoria—to ask, innocently, if she might consider giving one of her impromptu balls. Just for family and friends. Such a ball would be a useful tool in his avowed endeavor—to convince Patience that, to him as for all the Cynsters, the word "family" meant a great deal.

Honoria's wide eyes, and thoughtful consideration, had set his teeth on edge. But her agreement that an impromptu ball might, perhaps, be a good idea had gone some way to easing his temper. Leaving Devil's duchess to her plans, he'd retired to formulate his own. And to brood, darkly.

By the time yesterday morning had dawned, and he'd again set his horses' heads for Aldford Street, he'd come to the conclusion that there had to be more—more than just a simple misconception holding Patience back from marriage. He was absolutely certain what style of woman he'd chosen; he knew, soul-deep, that his reading of her was not wrong. Only a powerful reason would force a woman such as she, with so much affection and devotion to give, to view marriage as an unacceptable risk.

There was something more—something he had not yet learned about her parents' marriage.

He'd climbed the steps of Number 22 determined to learn what that something was—only to be informed Miss Debbington was not available to go driving with him. She had, it seemed, been seduced by the Bruton Street modistes. His temper had taken a downhill turn.

Luckily for Patience, Minnie had been watching for him. Unexpectedly spry, she'd claimed his escort for her promised stroll along the graveled walks of Green Park. On the way, she'd gaily informed him that, by some stroke of benign fate, Honoria had happened on Patience in Bruton Street the afternoon before, and had insisted on introducing her to her favored modiste, Celestine, the result being the fitting Patience was then attending for a series of gowns including, Minnie had taken great delight in assuring him, a positively *dashing* golden evening gown.

Arguing with benign fate was impossible. Even if, by virtue of Edith Swithins who had joined them for the stroll, said fate had ensured he had no chance to question Minnie about Patience's father, and the depths of his ignominy.

An hour later, reassured that Minnie's constitution was fully restored, he'd returned her to Number 22, only to discover Patience still absent. Leaving a tersely worded message with Minnie, he'd departed to find distraction elsewhere.

Today, he wanted Patience. If he had his way, he'd have Patience, but that was unlikely. Privacy of that sort, in the present circumstances, was unlikely to be on offer—and he had a wary premonition he'd be unwise to embark on any further seductive manuevers until he had their relationship on a steady, even keel.

With *his* hand firmly on the tiller.

Sligo opened the door to his peremptory knock. With a curt nod, Vane strode in. And stopped dead.

Patience was in the hall, waiting—the sight literally stole his breath. As his gaze, helplessly, slid over her, over the soft green merino pelisse, severely cut and snugly fitted, its upstanding collar framing her face, over the tan gloves and half boots, over the pale green skirts peeking beneath the pelisse's hem, Vane felt something inside him tighten, click, and lock.

Breathing was suddenly more difficult than if someone had buried a fist in his gut.

Her hair, glinting in the light streaming in through the door, was coiffed differently, to more artfully draw attention to her wide golden eyes, to the creaminess of her forehead and cheeks, and the delicate yet determined line of her jaw. And the soft vulnerability of her lips.

In some far corner of his thoroughly distracted brain, Vane uttered a thank-you to Honoria, then followed it with a curse. Before had been bad enough. How the hell was he supposed to cope with this?

Chest swelling, he forced his mind to draw back. He focused on Patience's face—and read her expression. It was calm, untinged by any emotion. She was dutifully waiting—as required by their plans—there was nothing more, so her expression declared, behind her drive with him.

It was her "dutiful" stance that did it—pricked his temper anew. Fighting to keep a scowl from his face, he nodded curtly and held out his arm. "Ready?"

Something flickered in her large eyes, but the hall was too dim for him to identify the emotion. Lightly, she inclined her head and glided forward to take his arm.

Patience sat, stiffly erect, on the box seat of Vane's curricle, and struggled to breathe through the iron cage locked about her chest. At least he couldn't disapprove of her appearance; she'd been assured, both by Celestine and Honoria, that her new pelisse and bonnet were all the crack. And her new gown, beneath it, was a definite improvement over her old one. Yet from his reaction, it seemed her appearance was of little consequence. She hadn't, she reminded herself sternly, really expected it would be. She'd bought the gowns because she hadn't refurbished her wardrobe for years and now seemed the perfect opportunity. After they caught the thief—and the Spectre—and Gerrard had acquired sufficient town bronze, she and he would retire once more to Derbyshire. She would probably never come to London again.

She'd bought a new wardrobe because it was the sensible thing to do, and because it wasn't reasonable to force Vane Cynster, elegant gentleman, to appear in public with a dowd.

Not that he seemed to care either way. Patience suppressed a sniff and tilted her chin. "As I told you, Mrs. Chadwick and Angela visited Bruton Street on our first afternoon. Angela dragged us into every modiste's establishment, even those designing for the dowagers. And asked the price of everything in sight. It was really most embarrassing. Luckily, the answers she received eventually took their toll. She seems to have accepted that it might be more practical to have a seamstress in to make up some gowns for her."

Eyes on his horses, Vane humphed. "Where were Angela and Mrs. Chadwick while you were in Celestine's?"

Patience colored. "Honoria came upon us in Bruton Street. She insisted on introducing me to Celestine—and things"—she gestured—"went on from there."

"*Things* have a habit of going that way once Honoria's involved."

"She was very kind," Patience retorted. "She even engaged Mrs. Chadwick and Angela in conversation all the while I was with Celestine."

Vane wondered how much Honoria was going to make him pay for that. And in what coin.

"Luckily, being able to haunt Celestine's salon and talk to a duchess quite buoyed Angela's spirits. We went on to Bond Street without further dramas. Neither Mrs. Chadwick nor Angela showed any hint of wanting to speak to any of the jewelers whose establishments we passed, nor in meeting anyone else along the way."

Vane grimaced. "I really don't think it's either of them. Mrs. Chadwick's bone-honest, and Angela's too witless."

"Indeed." Patience's tone turned ascerbic. "So witless nothing would do but she must cap the afternoon with a visit to Gunter's. Nothing would dissuade her. It was full to bursting with young sprigs, too many of whom spent the time ogling her. She wanted to go again yesterday afternoon—Mrs. Chadwick and I took her to Hatchards instead."

Vane's lips twitched. "She must have enjoyed that."

"She moaned the whole time." Patience shot him a glance. "That's all I have to report. What have the gentlemen been up to?"

"Sight-seeing." Vane uttered the word with loathing. "Henry and Edmond have been possessed by some demon which compels them to set eyes on every monument within the metropolis. Luckily, Gerrard is happy enough to go along and keep a watchful eye on them. So far, he's had nothing to report. The General and Edgar have settled on Tattersalls as the focus of their daily interest. Sligo or one of his minions follows and keeps watch, so far to no avail. I've been arranging their afternoons and evenings. The only ones who've not yet stirred from the house are the Colbys." Vane glanced at Patience. "Has Alice emerged from her room?"

"Not for long." Patience frowned. "She may actually have been the same at Bellamy Hall. I'd imagined her in the gardens, or in one of the parlors, but she might have stayed in her room the whole time. It's really rather unhealthy."

Vane shrugged.

Patience glanced sideways, studying his face. He'd headed his horses down a less-frequented drive, away from the fashionable avenue. While there were carriages about, they didn't need to exchange greetings. "I haven't had a chance to speak to Sligo, but I presume he found nothing?"

Vane's expression turned grim. "Not a thing. There was no clue in the luggage. Sligo's surreptitiously searching all the rooms in case the stolen items were somehow smuggled in."

"Smuggled? How?"

"Edith Swithins's tatting bag springs to mind."

Patience stared. "You don't think *she* . . . ?"

"No. But it's possible someone else has noticed how deep that bag is, and is using it for the pearls, if nothing else. How often do you think Edith empties the bag out?"

Patience grimaced. "Probably never."

Vane came to an intersection and turned smartly to the right. "Where is Edith now?"

"In the drawing room—tatting, of course."

"Does her chair face the door?"

"Yes." Patience frowned. "Why?"

Vane shot her a glance. "Because she's deaf."

Patience continued to frown, then understanding dawned. "Ah."

"Precisely. So . . ."

"Hmm." Patience's expression turned considering. "I suppose . . ."

Half an hour later, the drawing-room door at Number 22 opened; Patience looked in. Edith Swithins sat on the *chaise* facing the door, tatting furiously. Her large knitted bag sat on the rug beside the *chaise*. There was no one else present.

Smiling brightly, Patience entered, and set the door to, ensuring the latch did not fall home. Just *how* deaf Edith was they didn't know. With determined cheerfulness, she swept down on Edith.

Who looked up—and returned her smile.

"I'm so glad I caught you," Patience began. "I've always wanted to learn how to tat. I wonder if you could show me the basics?"

Edith positively beamed. "Why of course, dear. It's really quite simple." She held up her work.

Patience squinted. "Actually"—she looked around—"perhaps we should move over by the window. The light's much better there."

Edith chuckled. "I must confess I really don't need to *see* the stitches, I've been doing it for so long." She eased off the *chaise*. "I'll just get my bag . . ."

"I'll get it." Patience reached for the bag—and inwardly conceded Vane was right. It was deep, full, and surprisingly heavy. It definitely needed to be searched. Hefting the bag, she whirled. "I'll pull that chair into place for you."

By the time Edith, cradling her work in progress, had crossed the room, Patience had a deep armchair positioned facing the window, its back to the door. Placing the tatting bag beside it, hidden from the occupant by the overhang of the arm, she helped Edith into the chair. "Now if I sit here, on the window seat, there'll be plenty of light for us both to see."

Obligingly, Edith settled back. "Now." She held up her work. "The first thing to note . . ."

Patience gazed at the fine threads. At the edge of her vision, the door slowly opened. Vane entered, and carefully shut the door. On silent feet, he drew closer. A board creaked under his weight. He froze. Patience tensed. Edith blithely chatted on.

Patience breathed again. Vane glided forward, then sank out of sight behind Edith's chair. From the corner of her eye, Patience saw Edith's tatting bag slide away.

She forced herself to listen to Edith's lecture, forced herself to follow enough to ask sensible questions. Beaming with pride, Edith imparted her knowledge; Patience encouraged and admired, and hoped the Almighty would forgive her her perjury, given it was committed in the pursuit of justice.

Hunkered down behind the chair, Vane poked about in the bag, then, realizing the futility of that, gingerly upended it on the rug. The contents, a welter of odds and ends, many unidentifiable, at least, to him, rolled out on the soft pile. He spread them, frowning, trying to recall the list of items pilfered over the past months. Whatever, Minnie's pearls were not in the tatting bag.

"And now," Edith said, "we just need a crochet hook . . ." She looked to where her tatting bag had been placed.

"I'll get it." Patience crouched, eyes down, hands reaching as if the bag was actually there. "A crochet hook," she repeated.

"A fine one," Edith added.

Crochet hook. A fine one. Behind the chair, Vane stared at the array of unnameable implements. What the hell was a crochet hook? What did it look like—fine or otherwise? Frantically examining and discarding various items in tortoiseshell, his fingers finally closed about a thin wand sprouting a fine steel prong, hooked at the end—a miniature fisherman's net hook.

"I know it's there somewhere." Edith's voice, slightly querulous, jolted Vane to action. Reaching around the chair back, he slid the implement into Patience's outstretched palm.

She clutched it. "Here it is!"

"Oh, good. Now, we just put it in here, like this . . ."

While Edith continued her lesson, and Patience dutifully learned, Vane stuffed the contents of the tatting bag back into the gaping maw. Giving the bag a shake to settle it, he eased it back into position beside the chair. Moving with intense care, he stood and crept to the door.

Hand on the knob, he glanced back; Patience did not look up. Only when he'd regained the front hall, with the drawing room door securely closed, did he breathe freely again.

Patience joined him in the billiard room half an hour later.

Blowing aside the fine errant curls tangling with her lashes, she met his gaze. "I now know more about tatting than I could possibly need to know, even should I live to be a hundred."

Vane grinned. And leaned over the table.

Patience grimaced. "I take it there was nothing there?"

"Nothing." Vane lined up his next shot. "No one's using Edith's tatting bag as a store, presumably because, once something goes in, it might never be found again."

Patience stifled a giggle. She watched as Vane shifted, lining up the ball. As at Bellamy Hall, when she'd watched from the conservatory, he'd taken off his coat. Under his tight waistcoat, muscles rippled, then tensed. He clipped the ball neatly, sending it rolling into the pocket opposite.

Vane straightened. He looked at Patience, and noted her fixed gaze. Lifting his cue from the table, he sauntered closer. And stopped directly in front of her.

She blinked, then drew in a quick breath and dragged her gaze up to his face.

Vane captured her gaze. After a moment, he murmured, "I foresee certain complications."

"Oh?" Patience's gaze had already drifted from his, fastening instead on his lips.

Leaning more heavily on the cue, Vane let his gaze roam her face. "Henry and Edmond." The curves of her lips caught and held his attention. "They're getting restless."

"Ah." The tip of Patience's tongue appeared between her lips, then delicately traced them.

Vane hauled in a desperate breath. And leaned closer. "I can hold their reins during the day, but the evenings . . ." He angled his head. "Could be a problem."

His words died away as Patience stretched upward.

Their lips touched, brushed, then locked. Both stopped breathing. Vane's hands closed tight about the billiard cue; Patience shivered. And sank into the kiss.

"He must be in the billard room."

Vane's head jerked up; he swore and shifted, screening Patience from the door. She scooted farther into the shadows beyond the table, where her blush would be less visible. Along with the heat in her eyes. The door swung open and Vane was potting a ball with nonchalant ease.

"There you are!" Henry ambled into the room.

Followed by Gerrard and Edmond.

"Seen enough sights for one day." Henry rubbed his hands together. "Perfect time for a quick game."

"Not for me, I fear." Coolly, Vane handed his cue to Gerrard, and resisted the urge to throttle them all. He reached for his coat. "I only dallied to tell you I'll come by at three. I'm expected elsewhere for lunch."

"Oh. All right." Henry cocked a brow at Edmond. "You game?"

Edmond, having exchanged a smile with Patience, shrugged. "Why not?"

Gerrard, with a nod for his sister, joined them. Her pulse thundering, still breathless, Patience preceded Vane as he left the room.

She heard the door shut behind them, but didn't stop. She didn't dare. She led the way into the front hall; only then did she turn and, with what calm she could muster, face Vane.

He looked down at her. His lips twisted wryly. "I meant what I said about Henry and Edmond. I've agreed to take Gerrard, Edgar, and the General to White's this evening. Henry and Edmond don't want to go, and we couldn't keep them in sight if they did. Any chance you could call them to heel?"

The look Patience cast him spoke volumes. "I'll see what I can do."

"If you can keep them on their leashes, I'll be forever grateful."

Patience studied the glint in his grey eyes and wondered how to best use such indebtedness. Just what she might have him do. Then she realized her gaze had refastened on his lips. She blinked and nodded curtly. "I'll try."

"Do." Capturing her gaze, Vane raised one finger and traced the line of her cheek. Then lightly tapped. "Later." With a nod, he strode for the door.

For Patience, Lady Hendricks's musicale that evening proved to be an eminently forgettable experience. As well as herself, Minnie and Timms, all three Chadwicks, and Edmond, attended.

Inducing Henry and Edmond to join the party had been simplicity itself; over luncheon, she'd blithely asked Gerrard to escort their otherwise all-female party that evening. Put on the spot, Gerrard had blushed and stumbled into an apology; from the corner of her eye, Patience had seen Henry and Edmond glance surreptitiously at each other. Before Gerrard got to the end of his explanation, Henry interrupted to offer his services. Edmond, recalling the connection between music and drama, declared he would come, too.

As they crossed the threshold of Lady Hendricks's music room, Patience congratulated herself on her masterful success.

They made their bows to their hostess, then passed on, into the already crowded room. In Minnie's wake, Patience walked on Edmond's arm. Henry's had been claimed by his mother. Minnie and Timms were well-known; those greeting them nodded and smiled at Patience, too. Garbed in a new gown, she returned the greetings serenely, inwardly amazed at the confidence imparted by a sheath of moss green silk.

Timms steered Minnie to a half-vacant *chaise*. They took possession of the free space, striking up a conversation with the lady already ensconced in the other corner. Leaving the rest of the party milling aimlessly.

With an inward sigh, Patience took charge. "There's a chair over there, Henry. Perhaps you might fetch it for your mama."

"Oh. Right." Henry strode to where a chair remained unclaimed by the wall. At the exhortation of their hostess, all the guests were settling; seating was suddenly in short supply.

They sat Mrs. Chadwick beside Minnie's *chaise.*

"What about me?" Angela, gowned in a white dress overendowed with pink rosettes and cerise ribbon, stood twisting her fingers in said ribbon.

"There're some chairs over there." Edmond indicated a few empty seats in the ranks of straight-backed chairs lined up before the pianoforte and harp.

Patience nodded. "We'll sit there."

They headed for the chairs. They'd almost gained their objective when Angela balked. "I think the other side might be better."

Patience was not deceived. The few youthful sprigs forced by their mamas to attend had clumped in a petulant group on the other side of the room. "Your mama would expect you to sit with your brother." Deftly twining arms, she anchored Angela to her side. "Young ladies who venture about on their own rapidly gain a reputation for being fast."

Angela pouted. And cast longing looks across the room. "It's only a few yards away."

"A few yards too many." Reaching the vacant chairs, Patience sat, dragging Angela down beside her. Edmond slid into the chair on Patience's left; rather than sit beside his sister, Henry opted to sit behind Patience. As the performers appeared to polite applause, Henry shuffled his chair forward, hissing *sotto voce* to Angela to move aside.

Disapproving glances were cast their way. Patience turned her head and glared. Henry desisted.

With an inward sigh of relief, Patience settled in her chair and prepared to give her attention to the music.

Henry leaned forward and hissed in her ear: "Quite a smart gathering, isn't it? Daresay this is how *ton*nish ladies spend most of their evenings."

Before Patience could react, the pianist laid her fingers on the keys and commenced a prelude, one of Patience's favorites. Inwardly sighing, she prepared to sink into the comfort of the familiar strains.

"Bach." Edmond leaned closer, head nodding with the beat. "A neat little piece. Designed to convey the joys of spring. Odd choice for this time of year."

Patience closed her eyes and clamped her lips shut. And heard Henry shift behind her shoulder.

"The harp sounds like spring rains, don't you think?"

Patience gritted her teeth.

Edmond's voice reached her. "My dear Miss Debbington, are you feeling quite the thing? You look rather pale."

Her hands tightly clasped in her lap against the urge to box a few ears, Patience opened her eyes. "I fear," she murmured, "that I might be developing a headache."

"Oh."

"Ah."

Blessed silence reigned—for all of half a minute.

"Perhaps if . . ."

Hands clenched tight, Patience closed her eyes, closed her lips, and wished she could close her ears. The next second, she felt a definite pang behind her temples.

Denied the music, denied all natural justice, she fell back on imagining the reward she would claim in recompense for the destruction of her evening. When next she saw Vane. Later. Whenever that proved to be.

At least Edith Swithins and the Colbys had had the good sense to stay home.

At precisely that moment, in the hallowed half gloom of the cardroom of White's, Vane, his gaze on the General and Edgar, both seated at a table playing whist, took a slow sip of the club's excellent claret and reflected that Patience's evening would not be—could not be—more boring than his.

Hanging back in the shadows, cloaked in the quiet, restrained ambience, redolent with the masculine scents of fine leather, cigar smoke, and sandalwood, he'd been forced to decline numerous invitations, forced to explain, with a languidly raised brow, that he was bear-leading his godmother's nephew. That, in itself, had raised no eyebrows. The fact that he apparently believed bear-leading precluded sitting down to a game of cards had.

He could hardly explain his real aim.

Stifling a yawn, he scanned the room, easily picking out Gerrard, watching the play at the hazard table. The interest Gerrard showed was academic—he seemed to harbor no deep wish to join in the play.

Making a mental note to inform Patience that her brother showed little susceptibility to the lure that brought too many men low, Vane straightened, eased his shoulders, then returned to propping the wall.

Five totally uneventful minutes later, Gerrard joined him.

"Any action yet?" Gerrard nodded to the table at which Edgar and the General sat.

"Not unless you count the General getting clubs confused with spades."

Gerrard grinned, and glanced over the room. "This doesn't seem a likely place for someone to pass on stolen goods."

"It is, however, a very good venue in which to unexpectedly bump into an old friend. Neither of our two pigeons, however, is showing any signs of wanting to curtail their scintillating activity."

Gerrard's grin broadened. "At least it makes watching them easy enough." He glanced at Vane. "I can manage here if you'd like to join your friends. I'll fetch you if they move."

Vane shook his head. "I'm not in the mood." He gestured to the tables. "Seeing we're here, you may as well widen your horizons. Just don't accept any challenges."

Gerrard laughed. "Not my style." He moved off again to stroll between the tables, many surrounded by gentlemen vicariously enjoying the play.

Vane sank back into the shadows. He hadn't been tempted, even vaguely, to take Gerrard up on his offer. At present, he was in no good mood to join in the usual camaraderie over a pack of cards. At present, his mind was entirely consumed by one unanswered question, by one conundrum, by one glaring anomaly.

By Patience.

He desperately needed to talk to Minnie, alone. Patience's home life, her father, held the key—the key to his future.

This evening had been wasted: no headway had been made. On any level.

Tomorrow would be different. He'd see to it.

The next morning dawned bright and clear. Vane strode up the steps of Number 22 as early as he dared. In the far distance, a bell tolled—eleven deep bongs. Face set, Vane grasped the knocker. Today, he was determined to see progress.

Two minutes later, he strode back down the steps. Leaping into his curricle, he flicked the reins free, barely waiting for Duggan to scramble up behind before setting the greys clattering toward the park.

Minnie had hired a brougham.

He knew the instant he spotted them that something momentous had occurred. They were—there was no other word for it—aflutter. They were all there, packed into the brougham— Patience, Minnie, Timms, Agatha Chadwick, Angela, Edith Swithins and, amazing though it seemed, Alice Colby. She was dressed in something so dark and drab it might have been widow's weeds; the others looked much more inviting. Patience, gowned in a stylish walking dress of fresh green, looked good enough to eat.

Drawing his curricle up behind the brougham, Vane reined in his appetites along with his horses, and languidly descended to the verge.

"You've just missed Honoria," Minnie informed him before he'd even reached the carriage. "She's holding one of her impromptu balls and has invited us all."

"Indeed?" Vane summoned his most innocent look.

"A real ball!" Angela jigged up and down on the seat. "It'll be simply *wonderful*! I'll have to get a new ball gown."

Agatha Chadwick nodded in greeting. "It was very kind of your cousin to invite us all."

"I haven't been to a ball since I don't know when." Edith Swithins beamed at Vane. "It'll almost be an *adventure*."

Vane couldn't help returning her smile. "When's it to be?"

"Hasn't Honoria told you?" Minnie frowned. "I thought she said you knew—it's next Tuesday."

"Tuesday." Vane nodded, as if committing the fact to memory. He looked at Patience.

"Giddy nonsense, balls." Alice Colby very nearly sniffed. "But as the lady's a duchess, I daresay Whitticombe will say we must go. At least it's sure to be a suitably refined and dignified affair." Alice made the comment to the world at large. Concluding, she shut her pinched lips and stared straight ahead.

Vane stared, po-faced, at her. So did Minnie and Timms. All of them had attended impromptu balls Honoria had given. With all the Cynsters gathered in one room, refined and dignified tended to be overwhelmed by robust and vigorous. Deciding it was time Alice learned how the other half lived, Vane merely raised a brow and returned his attention to Patience.

At precisely the same moment she looked at him. Their gazes met and held; inwardly, Vane cursed. He needed to talk to Minnie; he wanted to talk to Patience. With her sitting there, waiting for him to invite her for a stroll, he couldn't ask Minnie instead. Not without adding to his problems, without leaving Patience feeling that he had, after all, started to ease back in his affections.

His affections, which were currently ravenous. Starved. Slavering for attention. And her.

He raised a languid brow. "Would you care for a stroll, Miss Debbington?"

Patience saw the hunger in his eyes, briefly, fleetingly, but quite clearly enough to recognize. The vise already locked about her chest tightened. Inclining her head graciously, she held out one gloved hand—and struggled to suppress the thrill that raced through her when his fingers closed strongly about hers.

He opened the door and handed her down. She turned to the carriage. Mrs. Chadwick smiled; Angela pouted. Edith Swithins positively grinned. Minnie, however, fluffed up her shawls and exchanged a quick glance with Timms.

"Actually," Timms said, "I rather think we should be getting back. The breeze is a mite chilly."

It was an Indian summer's day. The sun shone brightly, the breeze was almost balmy.

"Humph! Perhaps you're right," Minnie grumbled gruffly. She shot a glance at Patience. "No reason you can't go for your stroll—Vane can bring you home in his curricle. I know how much you miss your rambles."

"Indeed. We'll see you back at the house later." Timms

poked the coachman with the tip of her parasol. "Home, Cedric!"

Left on the verge staring bemusedly after the carriage, Patience shook her head. Vane's arm appeared beside her. Placing her fingers on his sleeve, she glanced up into his face. "What was all that about?"

His eyes met hers. His brows rose. "Minnie and Timms are inveterate matchmakers. Didn't you know?"

Patience shook her head again. "They've never behaved like that with me before."

They'd never had him in their sights before either. Vane kept that thought to himself and guided Patience across the lawn. There were many couples strolling close to the carriageway. As they nodded and smiled, returning greetings as they headed for less-crowded terrain, Vane let his senses revel in the experience of having Patience once more by his side. He'd drawn her as close as propriety allowed; her green skirts swished against his boots. She was all woman, soft and curvaceous, mere inches away; he grew harder simply at the thought. The breeze, wafting past, lifted her perfume to his face—honeysuckle, roses, and that indefinable scent that evoked every hunter's instinct he possessed.

Abruptly, he cleared his throat. "Nothing happened last evening?" It was an effort to lift his voice from the gravelly depths to which it had sunk.

"Nothing." Patience slanted him a sharp, slightly curious glance. "Distressingly, Edmond and Henry have reverted to their competitive worst. Stolen items, or the disposal of same, seemed exceedingly far from their minds. If either of them are the thief or the Spectre, I'll eat my new bonnet."

Vane grimaced. "I don't think your new bonnet's in any danger." He studied the stylish creation perched atop her curls. "Is this it?"

"Yes," Patience returned, somewhat waspishly. He could at least have noticed.

"I thought it looked different." Vane flicked the cockade perched over her eyebrow—and met her gaze with a far-too-innocent look.

Patience humphed. "I take it the General and Edgar made no suspicious moves last night?"

"Suspicious moves aplenty, but more along the line of being suspiciously foxed. More to the point, however, Masters has heard from the Hall."

Patience's eyes widened. "And?"

Vane grimaced. "Nothing." Looking forward, he shook his head. "I can't understand it. We know the items haven't been sold. We haven't found them in the luggage brought up to town. But they aren't at the Hall. Grisham and the staff have been very thorough—they even checked the wainscot for hidden panels. There are a few. I didn't tell Grisham where they were, but he found them all. Empty, of course—I'd checked before we left. They searched every room, every nook and cranny. They checked under loose floorboards. They also searched the grounds and the ruins. Thoroughly. Incidentally, they did find some disturbance just beyond the door of the abbot's lodge."

"Oh?"

"Someone had cleared off a section of the flags. There's an iron ring set in a stone—an old hatch. But the hatch *hasn't* been opened recently." Vane caught Patience's gaze. "Devil and I lifted it years ago—the cellar beneath was filled in. There's nothing beneath that stone, not even a hole in which something might be hidden. So it doesn't explain anything, least of all why Gerrard was struck down."

"Hmm." Patience frowned. "I'll ask him if he's remembered anything more about what he saw before he was hit."

Vane nodded absently. "Unfortunately, none of that sheds any light on our mystery. The puzzle of where the stolen goods, including Minnie's pearls, have gone darkens with every passing day."

Patience grimaced and briefly tightened her hold on his arm—simply because it seemed the right thing to do, to comfort and sympathize. "We'll just have to remain vigilant. On our guard. Something will happen." She looked up and met Vane's eyes. "It has to."

There was no arguing with that. Vane slid his free hand over her fingers, anchoring her hand on his sleeve.

They walked for some minutes in silence, then Vane glanced at Patience's face. "Are you excited by the prospect of Honoria's ball?"

"Indeed." Patience glanced fleetingly up at him. "I understand it's an honor to be invited. As you saw, Mrs. Chadwick and Angela are in alt. I can only hope awe is sufficient to overcome Henry. Edmond, however, will remain unimpressed. I'm sure he'll come, but I doubt even a ducal ball has sufficient weight to puncture his self-assurance."

Vane made a mental note to mention that to Honoria.

Patience glanced up at him, a frown in her eyes. "Will you be there?"

Vane raised his brows. "When Honoria issues a summons, we all fall in."

"You do?"

"She's Devil's duchess." When Patience's puzzled frown persisted; Vane elaborated: "He's the head of the family."

Looking ahead, Patience mouthed an "Oh." She was clearly still puzzled.

Vane's lips twisted wryly.

"There were two other ladies in the carriage with Honoria when she stopped to invite us." Patience looked at Vane. "I think they were Cynsters, too."

Vane kept his expression impassive. "What did they look like?"

"They were older. One was dark and spoke with a French accent. She was introduced as the Dowager."

"Helena, Dowager Duchess of St. Ives—Devil's mother." His other godmother.

Patience nodded. "The other was brown-haired, tall, and stately—a Lady Horatia Cynster."

Vane's expression turned grim. "My mother."

"Oh." Patience glanced his way. "Both your mother and the Dowager were . . . very kind." She looked ahead. "I didn't realize. All three—Honoria and the other two ladies—seemed very close."

"They are." Resignation rang in Vane's tone. "Very close. The whole family's very close."

Mouthing another "Oh," Patience looked ahead again.

Glancing sidelong, Vane studied her profile, and wondered what she'd made of his mother—and what his mother had made of her. Not that he anticipated any resistance on that front. His mother would welcome his chosen bride with open arms. And a great deal of otherwise classified information and far-too-insightful advice. Within the Cynster clan, that was the way things were done.

A deep requirement, a need, for commitment to family, formed, he was now sure, part of Patience's bulwark, one part of the hurdle that stood between her and marriage. That was one element of her problem he barely needed to take aim at—all he needed to do was introduce her to *his* family to blow that part of her problem away.

Despite the sacrifices it demanded of him, St. Ives House next Tuesday night was definitely the right address to send her to. After she saw the Cynsters all together, in their natural setting, she would rest easy on that score.

She would see, and believe, that he cared about family. And then . . .

Unconsciously, his fingers tightened about hers; Patience looked up inquiringly.

Vane smiled—wolfishly. "Just dreaming."

Chapter 18

For Patience, the next three days passed in a whirl of brief meetings, of whispered conferences, of desperate endeavors to locate Minnie's pearls, punctuated by last-minute fittings for her new ball gown, all squeezed between the social excursions necessary to keep all Minnie's household under observation. Beneath the frenetic rush ran a sense of gathering excitement, a swelling thrill of anticipation.

Highlighted whenever she met Vane, whenever they exchanged glances, whenever she sensed the weight of his personal, highly passionate, regard.

There was no hiding it, no sidestepping it; the desire between them grew stronger, more charged, with every passing day. She didn't know whether to blame him, or herself.

By the time she climbed the imposing steps of St. Ives House and passed into the brilliantly lit hall, her nerves had wound taut, coiled tight in her stomach. She told herself it was nonsense to allow the moment to so affect her, to imagine anything great would come of the evening. This was merely a private family ball, an impromptu affair, as Honoria had been at great pains to assure her.

There was no reason—no sense—to her reaction.

"There you are!" Honoria, magnificently gowned in mulberry silk, informally greeting her guests by the door, all but pounced on Patience as she crossed the music room's threshold. Nodding to Minnie, Timms, and the rest of their entourage, Honoria graciously waved them on, but kept hold of Patience. "I must introduce you to Devil."

Deftly linking arms with Patience, she swept up to where a tall, dramatically dark gentleman clothed in black stood talking to two matrons. Honoria jabbed his arm. "Devil—my husband. Duke of St. Ives."

The man turned, took in Patience, then slanted Honoria a mildly inquiring glance.

"Patience Debbington," his spouse supplied. "Minnie's niece."

Devil smiled, first at his wife, then at Patience. "It's a pleasure to meet you, Miss Debbington." He bowed gracefully. "You've just come up from Bellamy Hall, I hear. Vane seems to have found his stay there unexpectedly distracting."

The smooth tones of his deep voice, distinctly familiar, rolled over, and through, Patience. She resisted the urge to blink. Vane and Devil could have been brothers—the resemblance, the autocratic cast of their features, the aggressive line of nose and jaw, was impossible to mistake. The primary difference lay in their coloring—while Vane's hair was burnished brown, his eyes cool grey, Devil's hair was midnight black, his large eyes a pale green. There were other differences, too, but the similarities outweighed them. From their build, their distinctive height, and, most striking of all, the wicked glint in their eyes and the totally untrustworthy lilt to their lips, they were clearly as one beneath the skin. Wolves in human form.

Very masculine, distinctly distracting form.

"How do you do, Your Grace." Patience held out her hand, and would have sunk into the regulation deep curtsy, but Devil grasped her fingers and prevented it.

"*Not* 'Your Grace.' " He smiled, and Patience felt the mesmerizing power of his gaze as he raised her gloved fingers to his lips. "Call me Devil—everyone does."

For good reason, Patience decided. Despite that, she couldn't help but return his smile.

"There's Louise—I must speak with her." Honoria glanced at Patience. "I'll catch up with you later." Skirts swishing imperiously, she headed back to the door.

Devil grinned. He turned back to Patience—his gaze slid past her.

"Minnie's asking after you." Vane nodded to Patience as he halted beside her, then he returned his gaze to Devil. "She wants to relive some of our more embarrassing exploits—rather you than me."

Devil sighed feelingly. He raised his head, looking over the swelling throng to where Minnie was holding court, enthroned on a *chaise* by the wall. "Perhaps I could impress her with the weight of my ducal demeanor?" He raised his brows at Vane, who grinned.

"You could try."

Devil smiled. With a nod to Patience, he left them.

Patience met Vane's gaze; instantly, she was aware of the tension that held him. A peculiar shyness gripped her. "Good evening."

Something hot flashed through his eyes; his face hardened. He reached for her hand. She yielded it readily. He raised it, but instead of touching his lips to the backs of her gloved fingers, he reversed her hand. His eyes steady on hers, he pressed his lips to her inner wrist. Her pulse leapt beneath his caress.

"There's someone you should meet." His voice was low, gravelly. Placing her hand on his sleeve, he turned her.

"Hello, coz. Who's this?"

The gentleman who blocked their way was obviously another Cynster—one with light brown hair and blue eyes. Vane sighed, and made the introductions—and kept making them as more of them appeared. They were all similar—similarly dangerous—all large, all suavely assured—all elegant. The first went by the name of Gabriel; he was followed by Lucifer, Demon, and Scandal. Patience found it impossible not to soften under their practiced smiles. She grasped the moment to regain her breath, regain her poise. The pack—she instantly labeled them as such—chatted and sparred with effortless facility. She responded easily, but remained alert. How could one claim not to have been forewarned with names like that? She kept her hand firmly anchored to Vane's sleeve.

For his part, Vane showed no inclination to drift from her side. She told herself not to read too much into that fact. There simply might not be many ladies of the type to attract his interest in a crowd composed of family and friends.

A squeaky screech, followed by a plunk, heralded the start of the dancing. Four of the large men surrounding her hesitated; Vane did not. "Would you care to dance, my dear?"

Patience smiled her acceptance. With a gracious nod to the others, she consented to be led to the floor.

Stepping into the space rapidly clearing at the room's center, Vane confidently drew her into his arms. When her eyes widened, he raised a brow. "You do waltz in the wilds of Derbyshire, don't you?"

Patience lifted her chin. "Of course. I quite enjoy a good waltz."

"*Quite enjoy?*" The first strains of a waltz swelled. Vane's lips lifted wickedly. "Ah—but you've yet to waltz with a Cynster."

With that, he drew her closer, and whirled her into the dance.

Patience had parted her lips to haughtily ask just why Cynsters were thought such exponents of the art—by the time they'd revolved thrice, she had her answer. It took her three more revolutions before she managed to suck in a breath and close her mouth. She felt like she was airborne—swooping, sweeping. Effortlessly twirling, all in strict time.

Her startled gaze fell on the mulberry gown of the lady in the couple ahead of them, who was revolving every bit as vigorously as she. Honoria—their hostess. In the arms of her husband.

A quick glance revealed that all the Cynsters who'd been politely conversing with her earlier, had claimed ladies and taken to the floor. It was easy to pick them out among the crowd; they didn't revolve any faster than anyone else, but with greater enthusiasm, immensely greater power. Harnessed, controlled, power.

Feet flying, her skirts aswirl, compelled by the steely arms that held her, the powerful body that so effortlessly steered her, checked her, reversed her and turned her, Patience clung tight— to her wits, and to Vane.

Not that she felt in any danger of being released.

The thought brought his nearness, his strength, into sharper focus. They neared the end of the room; his hand burning like a brand through the fine silk of her gown, he drew her closer, deeper into his protective embrace. They swung into the turn; Patience dragged in a desperate breath—and felt her bodice, her breasts, shift against his coat. Her nipples constricted, excruciatingly tight.

On a muted gasp, she looked up, and her gaze collided with his, silvery grey, mesmerically intent. She couldn't look away, could barely breathe, as the room revolved about them. Her senses narrowed, until the world she knew was encompassed within the circle of his arms.

Time stopped. All that was left was the sway of their bodies, caught in the compelling, powerful rhythm only they could hear. The violins played a minor theme; the music that played between them came from a different source.

It swelled and grew. Hips and thighs met, caressed, and parted as they shifted through the turns. The rhythm called, their bodies answered, flowing effortlessly with the dance, pulsing with the beat, heating slowly. Touching tantalizingly. Teasing and promising. When the violins ceased and their feet slowed, their music still played on.

Vane hauled in a deep breath; the moment shivered about them. He forced his arms from about Patience, caught her hand, and placed it on his sleeve, unable, even though he knew too many were watching avidly, to forgo placing his free hand over her fingers.

He felt her slight shudder, took her weight as, for an instant, she leaned more heavily on him, blinking rapidly as she struggled to pull free of the magic.

She lifted her eyes and studied his face. Coolly, a great deal more coolly than he felt, he raised a brow.

Patience straightened. Looking ahead, she put her nose in the air. "You waltz quite creditably."

Vane chuckled through his teeth. His jaw was set against the urge to whisk her away, through one of the doors that led from the music room. He knew this house like the back of his hand. While she might not know their options, he did. But too many were watching them, and Honoria, for one, would never forgive him. Not so early in the evening, when sudden absences were too obvious.

Later. He'd already given up all thought that he could weather tonight without sating his demons. Not while she was wearing that dress.

Dashing, Minnie had termed it.

Dashed impossible, from his point of view.

He'd had every intention of toeing the line, at least until she'd accepted his offer. Now . . . There was such a thing as tempting a wolf too far.

He glanced down. Patience strolled serenely on his arm. The bronze-silk gown fitted snugly about her breasts, with only the tiniest wisps of sleeves, set off her shoulders, to distract from the glorious expanse of creamy skin, the ripe swells of her upper breasts, the delicate molding of her shoulders. The long straight skirts draped gently over her curvy hips, sleekly concealing her derriere; they fluttered elegantly about her legs, the hems ruffled to tantalizingly reveal her ankles as she walked.

While the neckline was low, there was nothing specifically outrageous about the gown. It was the combination of the woman wearing it and Celestine's faultlessly draped fabric that was causing his problems.

Only from his vantage point was it possible to see how deeply Patience's breasts rose and fell.

A second later, he forced himself to lift his head and look ahead.

Later.

He drew a deep breath, and held it.

"Evening, Cynster." An elegant gentleman stepped forward from the crowd, his gaze on Patience. "Miss . . . ?" Smoothly, he looked at Vane.

Who sighed. Audibly. And nodded. "Chillingworth." Vane glanced at Patience. "Allow me to present the earl of Chillingworth." He looked at Chillingworth. "Miss Debbington, Lady Bellamy's niece."

Patience curtsied. Chillingworth smiled charmingly, and bowed, as gracefully as any Cynster.

"I take it you've come up to town with Lady Bellamy, Miss Debbington. Are you finding the capital to your liking?"

"Actually, no." Patience saw no reason to prevaricate. "I fear I'm addicted to early mornings, my lord, a time the *ton* seems to eschew."

Chillingworth blinked. He glanced swiftly at Vane, then his gaze dropped fleetingly to where Vane's hand covered Patience's fingers, resting on his sleeve. He raised his brows and smiled suavely at Patience. "I'm almost tempted to explain, my dear, that our apparent dismissal of the morning hours is, in fact, a natural consequence of our activities in the *later* hours. Then again . . ." He slanted a glance at Vane. "Perhaps I had better leave such explanations to Cynster, here."

"Perhaps you had." There was no mistaking the steel in Vane's tone.

Fleetingly, Chillingworth grinned, but when he looked back at Patience, he was calmly serious once more. "You know, it's really quite odd." He smiled. "While I rarely find myself in agreement with Cynsters, one has to admit their taste in one respect resonates remarkably with mine."

"Indeed?" Patience acknowledged the veiled compliment with an assured smile. Having dealt with Vane for three weeks, the earl, charming and undeniably handsome though he was, had no chance of ruffling her feathers.

"Indeed." Chillingworth turned to quiz Vane. "Don't you find that remarkable, Cynster?"

"Not at all," Vane replied. "Some things are so blatantly obvious even you should appreciate them." Chillingworth's eyes sparked. Vane smoothly continued, "However, given your admittedly similar tastes, you might reflect on where following such tastes might land you." He nodded across the room.

Both Chillingworth and Patience followed his direction, and saw Devil and Honoria by the side of the ballroom, clearly engaged in some pointed discussion. As they watched, Honoria clasped her hands about Devil's arm and pushed to turn him down the room. The look Devil cast the ceiling, the long-suffering look he cast his wife as he acquiesced, made it clear who had won the round.

Chillingworth shook his head sadly. "Ah, how the mighty have fallen."

"You'd best be on your guard," Vane advised, "given that your tastes so parallel the Cynsters', that you don't find yourself in a situation you're constitutionally unprepared to handle."

Chillingworth grinned. "Ah, but I don't suffer from the Achilles' heel with which fate has hobbled the Cynsters." Still grinning, he bowed to Patience. "Your servant, Miss Debbington. Cynster." With a last nod, he went on his way, ignoring Vane's narrow-eyed glare.

Patience looked up into Vane's face. "What Achilles' heel?"

Vane stirred. "Nothing. It's just his notion of a joke."

If it was a joke, it had had an odd effect. "Who is he?" Patience asked. "Is he a Cynster connection of sorts?"

"He's not related—at least not by blood." After a moment, Vane added, "I suppose, these days, he's an honorary Cynster." He glanced at Patience. "We elected him for services rendered to the dukedom."

"Oh?" Patience let her eyes ask her question.

"He and Devil have a history. Ask Honoria about it sometime."

The musicians started up again. Before Patience could blink, Lucifer was bowing before her. Vane let her go, somewhat reluctantly, she thought. But as she whirled down the floor, she saw him whirling, too, a striking brunnette in his arms.

Abruptly, Patience looked away, and gave her attention to the dance, and to dealing with Lucifer's glib tongue. And ignoring her sinking heart.

The end of the measure saw them well down the room. Lucifer introduced her to a group of ladies and gentlemen, all chatting easily. Patience tried to concentrate, tried to follow the conversation.

She literally jumped when hard fingers closed about hers, lifted her hand from Lucifer's sleeve and placed it, firmly, on a familiar arm.

"Upstart," Vane growled. And deftly insinuated himself between Lucifer and Patience.

Lucifer grinned engagingly. "You need to work for it, coz. You know none of us appreciates that which comes too readily."

Vane slayed him with a look, then turned to Patience. "Come, let's stroll. Before he puts misguided notions into your head."

Intrigued, Patience allowed herself to be escorted on an amble up the room. "What misguided notions?"

"Never mind. *Good God*—there's Lady Osbaldestone! She's hated me ever since I stuck a marble up the end of her cane. She couldn't understand why it kept sliding away from her. Let's go the other way."

They tacked back and forth through the crowd, chatting here, exchanging introductions there. Yet when the music resumed, another Cynster appeared before her like magic.

Demon Harry, Vane's brother, stole her away; Vane stole her back the instant the music ceased. The voluptuous blonde he'd whirled around the room was nowhere in sight.

The next waltz brought Devil to bow, ineffably elegant before her. As he swung her into the first turn, he read the question in her eyes and grinned. "We always share."

His grin deepened as her eyes, beyond her control, widened. Only the wicked laughter in his eyes assured Patience he was teasing.

And so it went on, through waltz after waltz. After every one, Vane reappeared by her side. Patience tried to tell herself it meant nothing, that it could simply be that he'd found nothing more scintillating, no lady more enticing, with whom to spend his time.

She shouldn't make too much of it—yet her heart leapt one notch, one giddy rung higher on the ladder of irrational hope, every time he reclaimed her hand, and his position by her side.

"These balls of Honoria's are such a good idea." Louise Cynster, one of Vane's aunts, leaned on her husband, Lord Arthur Cynster's arm, and smiled at Patience. "Despite the fact we all move in the same circles, the family's so large, we can often go for weeks without meeting each other, at least not long enough to exchange our news."

"What my dearest wife means," Lord Arthur smoothly said, "is that, although the ladies of the family meet often, they miss the opportunity of seeing how the other half of the family's comporting itself, and these little gatherings of Honoria's guarantee we'll all turn out on parade." His eyes twinkled. "To be inspected, as it were."

"Bosh!" Louise tapped him smartly on the arm with her fan. "As if you men ever need any excuse to turn out on parade. And as for being inspected! There's not a lady in the *ton* who won't tell you that Cynsters are past masters at 'inspecting' themselves."

The comment brought chuckles and grins all around. The

group dissolved as the music resumed. Gabriel materialized to bow before Patience. "My turn, I believe?"

Patience wondered if Cynsters had a monopoly on wolfish smiles. They also all had quick and ready tongues: During every dance, she'd found her attention firmly held by the brisk repartee that seemed their hallmark.

A minor ruckus ensued as they started to whirl. Passing close by its epicenter, Patience discovered Honoria grappling with Devil.

"We've already danced once. You should dance with one of our guests."

"But I want to dance with *you*."

The look that went with that was uncompromising. Despite her status, Honoria was clearly not immune. "Oh, very well." The next instant, she was whirling, masterfully captured, then Devil bent his head to hers.

As she and Gabriel swirled past, Patience heard Honoria's ripple of laughter, saw the glow in her face as she looked up at her husband, then closed her eyes and let him whirl her away.

The sight caught at Patience's heart.

This time, when the music finally slowed and died, she'd lost sight of Vane. Assuming he'd soon reappear, she chatted easily with Gabriel. Demon joined them, as did a Mr. Aubrey-Wells, a dapper, very precise gentleman. His interest was the theater. Not having seen any of the current productions, Patience listened attentively.

Then, through a gap in the crowd, she saw Vane, talking to a young beauty. The girl was exquisite, with a wealth of blond hair. Her understated gown of pale blue silk positively screamed "outrageously expensive."

"I think you'll find the production at the Theatre Royal worth a visit," Mr. Aubrey-Wells intoned.

Patience, her gaze locked on the tableau on the other side of the room, nodded absently.

The beauty glanced about, then put her hand on Vane's arm. He looked behind them, then took her hand in his. Swiftly, he conducted her to a double door in the wall. Opening it, he handed her through and followed her in.

And shut the door.

Patience stiffened; the blood drained from her face.

Abruptly, she looked back at Mr. Aubrey-Wells. "The Theatre Royal?"

Mr. Aubrey-Wells nodded—and continued his lecture.

"Hmm." Beside Patience, Gabriel nodded to Demon, then inclined his head toward the fateful door. "Looks serious."

Patience's heart plummeted.

Demon shrugged. "Daresay we'll hear later."

With that, they both turned attentively to Patience. Who kept her gaze fixed on Mr. Aubrey-Wells, parroting his remarks as if the theater filled her mind. In reality, her mind was full of the Cynsters, several and singular.

Elegant gentlemen, one and all. All and one.

She should never have forgotten it, should never have let her senses shut her eyes to the reality.

But she hadn't lost anything, given anything she hadn't wanted to give. She'd expected this from the first. With an effort, she suppressed a racking shiver. She'd felt surrounded by warmth and laughter; now bleak disappointment pierced her bones and froze her marrow. As for her heart, that was so cold she was sure that, at any moment, it would fracture. Shatter into frozen shards.

Her face felt the same way.

She let Mr. Aubrey-Wells's discourse flow past her, and wondered what she should do. As if in answer, Gerrard's face swam into her restricted vision.

He smiled at her, then, more tentatively, at her escort.

Metaphorically, Patience grabbed him. "Mr. Cynster, Mr. Cynster and Mr. Aubrey-Wells—my brother, Gerrard Debbington."

She gave the men the minimum of time to exchange greetings, then, smiling too brightly, beamed at them all. "I really should check on Minnie." Mr. Aubrey-Wells looked confused; she beamed even more brightly. "My aunt, Lady Bellamy." Taking Gerrard's arm, she flung them another brilliant smile. "If you'll excuse us?"

They all bowed with ready grace, Gabriel and Demon easily outperforming Mr. Aubrey-Wells. Inwardly gritting her teeth, Patience steered Gerrard away. "Don't you ever dare bow like that."

Gerrard sent her a startled look. "Whyever not?"

"Never mind."

They had to tack through the crowd. The throng was at its height. Supper had yet to be served. All had arrived but few had yet departed.

In order to get to Minnie's *chaise*, they had perforce to pass by the double doors through which Vane and the beauty had disappeared. Patience had intended to sweep past, nose in the air. Instead, as they neared the innocent-looking panels, she slowed.

When she halted a few steps from the doors, Gerrard threw her an inquiring look. Patience saw it; she took a moment before she met it.

"You go on." Drawing a deep breath, she straightened. Lips setting, she lifted her hand from his sleeve. "I want to check on something. Can you see Minnie into supper?"

Gerrard shrugged. "Of course." Smiling, he ambled on.

Patience watched him go—then turned on her heel and marched straight to the double doors. She knew perfectly well what she was doing—even if she couldn't formulate a single coherent thought through the haze of fury clouding her brain. How *dare* Vane treat her like this? He hadn't even said good-bye. He might be an elegant gentleman to his toes, but he was going to have to learn some manners!

Besides, the beauty was too young for him, she could barely be more than seventeen. A chit out of the schoolroom—it was scandalous.

Her hand on the doorknob, Patience paused—and tried to think of an opening line—one suitable for the scene she might very likely stumble in upon. Nothing leapt to her tongue. Grimly, she shook aside her hesitation. If, in the heat of the moment, nothing occurred to her, she could always scream.

Eyes narrow, she grasped the handle and turned.

The door flew inward, pulled open from within. Yanked off her feet, Patience tripped on the raised threshold and fetched up against Vane's chest.

The impact knocked the air from her lungs; Vane's arm, locking about her, kept her breathless. Wide-eyed and gasping, Patience looked up into his face.

His eyes met hers. "Hel-*lo*."

His intent expression made Patience stiffen, only to realize the arm around her, steadying her, was also trapping her.

Hard against him.

Dazed, she glanced around; the dark shapes of huge leaves reared above the denser dark of heavy pots, grouped upon a tiled floor. Moonlight streamed through walls of long windows and panes in the ceiling, silvering paths wending between stands of palms and exotic blooms. The rich scents of earth and the warm humidity of growing things hung on the heavy air.

She and Vane stood within the shadows, just beyond the shaft of light lancing through the open door. A yard away, enveloped in soft gloom, stood the beauty, regarding her with open curiosity.

The beauty smiled and bobbed a curtsy. "How do you do? Miss Debbington, isn't it?"

"Ah—yes." Patience looked, but could see no signs of disarray—the girl appeared neat as a pin.

Into her total bewilderment Vane's voice fell, like a bell tolling. "Allow me to present Miss Amanda Cynster."

Stunned, Patience looked up; he captured her gaze and smiled. "My cousin."

Patience mouthed an innocent, "Oh."

"First cousin," he added.

Amanda cleared her throat. "If you'll excuse me?" With a quick nod, she slipped past, out of the door.

Abruptly, Vane raised his head. "Remember what I said."

"Of *course* I will." Amanda threw him a disgusted frown. "I'm going to tie him in knots, and then hoist him from his . . ." She gestured, then, with a swish of her skirts, stalked into the crowd.

Patience reflected that Amanda Cynster sounded like a beauty who would never need rescuing.

She, however, might.

Vane returned his attention to her. "What are you doing here?"

She blinked, and glanced around again—then hauled in a breath, difficult with her breasts pressed to his chest. She gestured to the room. "Someone mentioned it was a conservatory. I've been thinking of suggesting that Gerrard install one at the

Grange. I thought I'd look in." She peered into the leafy gloom. "Study the amenities."

"Indeed?" Vane smiled, the merest lifting of his long lips, and released her. "By all means." With one hand, he pushed the door shut; with the other, he gestured to the room. "I'll be only too pleased to demonstrate some of the benefits of a conservatory."

Patience cast him a swift glance and quickly stepped forward, out of his reach. She gazed at the arches forming the ceiling. "Was this room always part of the house, or was it added on?"

Behind her, Vane slid the bolt on the doors; it engaged noiselessly. "It was, I believe, originally a loggia." Strolling unhurriedly, he followed Patience down the main pathway, into the palm-shrouded depths.

"Hmm, interesting." Patience eyed a palm towering above the path, handlike leaves poised as if to seize the unwary. "Where does Honoria get such plants?" Passing beneath the palm, she trailed her fingers through delicate fern fronds surrounding the palm's base—and threw a quick glance behind her. "Do the gardeners propagate them?"

Pacing steadily in her wake, Vane caught her gaze. His brows rose fractionally. "I've no idea."

Patience looked ahead—and quickened her pace. "I wonder what other plants do well in such a setting. Palms like these might be a bit hard to come by in Derbyshire."

"Indeed."

"Ivies, I daresay, would do well. And cacti, of course."

"Of course."

Flitting along the path, absentmindedly touching this plant or that, Patience stared ahead—and tried to spot the way out. The path wound randomly about; she was no longer entirely sure of her bearings. "Perhaps, for the Grange, an orangery might be more sensible."

"My mother has one."

The words came from just behind her. "She has?" A swift glance behind revealed Vane almost at her shoulder. Gulping in a quick breath, Patience mentally acknowledged the skittering excitement that had cinched tight about her lungs, that had started, very effectively, to draw her nerves taut. Expectation, anticipation, shivered in the moonlit dark. Breathless, wide-eyed, she lengthened her stride. "I must remember to ask Lady Horatia—oh!"

She broke off. For one moment, she stood stock-still, drinking in the simple beauty of the marble fountain, the base of its pedestal wreathed in delicate fronds, that stood, glowing lambently in the soft white light, in the center of a small, secluded, fern-shrouded clearing. Water poured steadily from the pitcher of the partially clad maiden frozen forever in her task of filling the wide, scroll-lipped basin.

The area had clearly been designed to provide the lady of the house with a private, refreshing, calming retreat in which to embroider, or simply rest and gather her thoughts. In the moonlit night, surrounded by mysterious shadow and steeped in a silence rendered only more intense by the distant sighing of music and the silvery tinkle of the water, it was a hauntingly magical place.

For three heartbeats, the magic held Patience immobile.

Then, through the fine silk of her gown, she felt the heat of Vane's body. He did not touch her, but that heat, and the flaring awareness that raced through her, had her quickly stepping forward. Hauling in a desperate breath, she gestured to the fountain. "It's lovely."

"Hmm," came from close behind.

Too close behind. Patience found herself heading for a stone bench, shaded by a canopy of palms. Stifling a gasp, she veered away, toward the fountain.

The fountain's pedestal was set on a stone disc; she stepped onto the single, foot-wide step. Beneath her soles, she felt the change from tiles to marble. One hand on the rim of the basin, she glanced down, then, nerves flickering wildly, forced herself to bend and study the plants nestling at the pedestal's base. "These look rather exotic."

Behind her, Vane studied the way her gown had pulled tight over the curves of her bottom—and didn't argue. Lips lifting in anticipation, he moved in—to spring his trap.

Her heart racing, tripping in double time, Patience straightened, and went to slide around the fountain, to place it between herself and the wolf she was trapped in the conservatory with. Instead, she ran into an arm.

She blinked at it. One faultless grey sleeve enclosing solid bone well covered with steely muscle, large fist locked over the scrolled rim of the basin, it stated very clearly that she wasn't going anywhere.

Patience whirled—and found her retreat similarly blocked. Swinging farther, she met Vane's gaze; standing on the tiled floor, one step below her, arms braced on the rim, his eyes were nearly level with hers. She studied them, read his intent in the silvered grey, in the hardening lines of his face, the brutally sensual line of those uncompromising lips.

She couldn't believe her eyes.

"*Here*?" The word, weak though it was, accurately reflected her disbelief.

"Right here. Right now."

Her heart thudded wildly. Prickling awareness raced over her skin. The certainty in his voice, in the deepening tones, riveted her. The thought of what he was suggesting made her mind seize.

She swallowed, and moistened her lips, not daring to take her eyes from his. "But . . . someone might come in."

His gaze dropped from hers, his lids veiling his eyes. "I locked the door."

"You did?" Wildly, Patience glanced back toward the door; a tug at her bodice hauled her back, refocused her scattered wits. On the top button of her bodice, now undone. She stared at the gold-and-tortoiseshell whorl. "I thought they were just for show."

"So did I." Vane popped the second of the big buttons free. His fingers moved to the third and final button, below her breasts. "I must remember to commend Celestine on her farsighted design."

The final button slid free—his long fingers slid beneath the silk. Patience sucked in a desperate breath; he had very quick fingers—with locks, and other things. On the thought, she felt the ribbons of her chemise give; the fine silk slid down.

His hand, hot and hard, closed over her breast.

Patience gasped. She swayed—and grabbed his shoulders to keep herself upright. The next second, his lips were on hers; they shifted, then settled, hard and demanding. For one instant, she stood firm, savoring the heady taste of his desire—his need of her—then she yielded, opening to him, inviting him in, brazenly delighting in his conquest.

The kiss deepened, not by degrees, but in leaps and bounds, in a blind, breathless downhill rush, a giddy pursuit of sensual delights, carnal pleasures.

Parched for air, Patience drew back on a gasp. Head back, she breathed deeply. Her breasts rose dramatically; Vane bent his head to pay homage.

She felt his hand at her waist, burning through her thin gown as he held her steady before him; she felt his lips, hot as brands, tease and tug at her nipples. Then he took the engorged flesh into the wet heat of his mouth. She tensed. He suckled—her strangled cry shivered in the moonlight.

"Ah." His eyes glinted wickedly as he lifted his head and transferred his attention to her other breast. "You'll have to remember. This time, no screaming."

No screaming? Patience clung to him, clung desperately to her wits as he feasted. His mouth, his touch, drew and fragmented her attention, stoked and fed the desire already flaring hotly within her.

But it was impossible—it had to be.

There was the bench—but it was cold and narrow and surely too hard. Then she remembered how he'd once lifted her and loved her.

"My dress—it'll crush horribly. Everyone will guess."

His only response was to tuck the sides of her bodice back, completely baring her breasts.

Through her next gasp, Patience managed, "I meant my skirts. We'll never be able to . . ."

The rumbling chuckle that rolled through him left her shuddering.

"Not a single crease." His lips brushed the crests of her breasts, now tight and aching; his teeth grazed the furled tips, and daggers pierced her flesh. "Trust me."

His voice was deep, dark, heavy with passion. He lifted his head. His hands closed about her waist. Deliberately, he drew her to him, so her tingling breasts pressed against his coat. She gasped, and he bent his head and kissed her, kissed her until she had softened through and through, until her weakening limbs could barely support her.

"Where there's a will there's a way." He breathed the words against her lips. "And I *will* have you."

For one fractured instant, their gazes met—no pretense, no amount of guile could conceal the emotions driving them. Simple, uncomplicated. Urgent.

He turned her; Patience blinked at the fountain, pearly white in the moonlight, blinked at the barely robed maiden steadily filling the bowl. She felt Vane behind her, hot, solid—aroused. He bent his head; his lips grazed the side of her throat. Patience sank back against him, angling her head back, encouraging his caresses. She let her hands drop to her sides, to his thighs, hard as oak behind her. Spreading her fingers, she gripped the long, tensed muscles—and felt them harden even more.

He reached around her; she waited to feel his hands close about her breasts, to feel him fill his hands with her bounty.

Instead, with just the very tips of his fingers, he traced the swollen curves, circled the aching peaks. Patience shuddered—and sank deeper against him. His hands left her; she felt him reach out. She forced her eyes open. From under weighted lids, she watched as, with one hand, he traced the bare breast of the maiden, lovingly caressing the cool stone.

Leaving the maiden, his fingers trailed lightly in the clear water in the marble bowl. Then he raised the same fingers to her heated flesh—and touched her as he'd touched the maiden—delicately, evocatively. Enticingly.

Patience closed her eyes—and shivered. His fingers, cool, wet, trailed and traced—exquisite sensation lanced through her. Pressing her head back against his shoulder, she bit her lip against a moan, and flexed her fingers on his thighs.

And managed to gasp: "This is . . ."

"Meant to be."

After a moment, she licked her parched lips. "How?"

She sensed the change in him, the surge of passion he immediately leashed. Her flaring response, the urgent need to have him take her, completely and utterly, and give himself in the same way, stole her breath.

"Trust me." He reached around her again, moving closer; his strength flowed around her, surrounded her. His hands closed about her breasts, no longer delicately teasing but hungry.

He filled his hands and kneaded; Patience felt the flames rise—in him, in her.

"Just do what I tell you. And don't think."

Patience mentally groaned. How? What . . . ? "Just remember my dress."

"I'm an expert, remember? Grasp the rim of the bowl with both hands."

Bemused, Patience did. Vane shifted behind her; the next instant, her skirts, then her petticoats, were flipped up, over her waist. Cool air washed over the backs of her thighs, over her bottom, exposed to the moonlight.

She blushed hotly—and opened her mouth on a protest.

The next second, she forgot about protest, forgot about everything, as long, knowing fingers slid between her thighs.

Unerringly, he found her, already slick and swollen. He traced, and tantalized, teased and caressed, then evocatively probed her.

Eyes closed, Patience bit her lip against a moan. He reached deep, stroking into her softness; she gasped, and gripped the marble bowl more tightly.

Then he reached around her, one large palm sliding under her dress and petticoats, gliding over her hip to splay possessively over her naked stomach. The hand shifted, fingers searching boldly through her curls. Until one found and settled against her most sensitive spot.

She couldn't find enough breath to gasp—let alone moan or scream. Patience desperately drew air into her lungs, and felt him behind her. Felt the hot hard length of him press between her thighs. Felt the wide head nudge into her softness and find her entrance.

Slowly, he sank into her, easing her hips back, then holding her steady, bracing her as he slid fully home. And filled her.

Slowly, deliberately, he withdrew—and returned, pressing so deeply she rose on her toes.

Her gasp hung like shimmering silver in the moonlight, eloquent testimony to her state.

Again and again, with the same relentlessly restrained force, he filled her. Thrilled her. Loved her.

The hand at her belly didn't shift, but simply held her steady so she could receive him, could feel, again and again, his possession, the slow repetitive penetration impinging on her mind as well as her body, on her emotions as well as her senses.

She was his and she knew it. She gave herself gladly, received him joyfully, obediently struggled to hold back her moans as he shifted and sank deeper.

Tucking her bottom firmly against his hips, he moved more forcefully within her, thrusting more deeply, more powerfully.

The tension—within him, within her, holding them so tightly—grew, swelled, coiled. Patience swallowed a gasp—and clung to sanity. And prayed for release while dazedly wondering if this time she really would lose her mind.

Again and again he filled her. The golden glimmer she now knew and desired glowed on her horizon. She tried to reach for it—to draw it nearer—tried to tighten about him and urge him on.

And suddenly realized that, in this position, her options were limited.

She was at his mercy and could do nothing to change it.

With a gasp, she lowered her head, her fingers tightening on the bowl's rim. Pleasure, relentless, passionate, rolled through her in waves, rearing every time he sank into her and stretched her. Completed her.

Patience felt a scream building—and bit her lip—hard.

Vane sank into her again and felt her quiver. He remained sunk in her heat for a fraction longer, then smoothly withdrew. And sank into her again.

He was in no hurry. Savoring the slick, scalding softness that welcomed him, the velvet glove that fitted him so well, glorying in all the heady signs of her body's acceptance of him—the natural, abandoned way the hemispheres of her bottom, glowing ivory in the moonlight, met his body, the slick wetness that made his staff gleam, the total absence of all restraint, the completeness of her surrender—he took time to appreciate it all.

Before him, she tightened, and tensed, and helplessly squirmed.

He held her steady. And slowly filled her again. She was close to frantic. He withdrew from her, nudged her legs wider, and filled her even more deeply.

A muted squeal escaped her.

Vane narrowed his eyes, and took firm hold of his reins. "What brought you here? To the conservatory?"

After a fractured minute, Patience gasped, "I told you—the amenities."

"Not because you saw me come in here with a lovely young lady?"

"No!" The answer came back too quickly. "Well," Patience breathlessly temporized, "she was your cousin."

With his free hand, Vane reached around her, filling his palm with the swollen fullness of her breast. He searched and found the tight bud of her nipple—and rolled it gently between thumb and finger, before squeezing firmly. "You didn't know that until I told you."

Patience valiantly swallowed her scream. "The music's stopped—they must all be at supper." She was so breathless, she could barely speak. "We'll miss it all if you don't hurry."

She'd die if he didn't hurry.

Hard lips caressed her nape. "The lobster patties can wait. I'd rather have you."

To Patience's relief, he tightened his grip on her, held her even more rigidly, as he stroked more powerfully. The flames within her roared, then fused and coalesced; the bright sun of release drew steadily nearer. Grew steadily brighter. Then he paused.

"You seem to be missing something here."

Patience knew what she was missing. The bright sun stopped, three heartbeats away. She gritted her teeth—a scream welled in her throat—

"I told you—you're mine. I want you—and you alone."

The words, uttered softly, with rocklike conviction, drove all other thoughts from Patience's head. Opening her eyes, she stared unseeing at the marble maiden, shimmering softly in the moonlight.

"There's no other woman I want to be inside—no other woman I crave." She felt his body tense, gather—then he thrust deep. "Only you."

The sun crashed down on her.

Hot pleasure washed through her like a tidal wave, sweeping all before it. Her vision clouded; she was unaware that she screamed.

Shifting his hand to her lips, Vane muffled the worst of her ecstatic cry—the sound still shredded his control. His chest swelled; grimly, he struggled to contain the desire raging through him, pounding his senses, liquid fire in his loins.

He succeeded—until the ripples of her release caressed him. He felt the power gather, felt it swell, grow and build within him. And in that final moment, as the cosmos crashed about him, he surrendered.

And did as she'd once asked, let go—and poured himself into her.

The instant Minnie's carriage door closed, cloaking her in the safe dark, Patience slumped against the squabs. And prayed she'd be able to master her limbs sufficiently to leave the carriage and walk to her bed when they arrived in Aldford Street.

Her body no longer felt like hers. Vane had taken possession and left her limp. Wrung out. The half hour between their return to the ballroom and Minnie's departure had been a near-run thing. Only his surreptitious support, his careful maneuvering, had concealed her state. Her deeply sated state.

At least she'd been able to speak. Reasonably coherently. And think. In some ways, that had made things worse. Because all she could think about was what he'd said, whispered against her temple, when she'd finally stirred in his arms.

"Have you changed your mind yet?"

She'd had to search for the strength to say "No."

"Stubborn woman," in the tone of a soft curse, had been his reply.

He hadn't pressed her further, but he hadn't given up.

His question replayed in her mind. His tone—one of understated but unswerving determination—bothered her. His strength ran deep, not just a physical characteristic; overcoming it—convincing him she wouldn't acquiesce and be his wife—was proving a far harder battle than she'd foreseen. The unwelcome possibility that, unintentionally, she'd pricked his pride, taunted his conqueror's soul, and would now have to contend with the full force of that side of his character, too, wasn't a cheering thought.

Worst of all was the fact that she'd hesitated before saying "No."

Temptation, unheralded, had slunk in and slipped under her guard. After all she'd seen, all she'd observed, of the Cynsters, their wives, and their firmly stated and rigidly applied attitudes on the subject of family, it was impossible to escape the fact that Vane's offer was the best she'd ever get. Family—the one thing that was most important to her—was critically important to him.

Given all his other attributes—his wealth, his status, his handsomeness—what more could she possibly want?

The problem was, she knew the answer to that question.

That was why she had said "No." Why she would keep saying "No."

The Cynster attitude to family was possessive and protective. They were a warrior clan—the open commitment she'd initially found so surprising was, viewed in that light, perfectly under-standable. Warriors defended what was theirs. Cynsters, it seemed, regarded their family as a possession, to be defended at all costs and in all arenas. Their feelings sprang from their con-querors' instincts—the instinct to hold on to whatever they'd won.

Perfectly understandable.

But it wasn't enough.

Not for her.

Her answer still remained—had to remain—"No."

Chapter 19

◆━◆━◆

$\mathcal{S}$LIGO OPENED THE front door of Number 22 at nine the next morning.

Vane nodded curtly and strode in. "Where's Her Ladyship?" He cast a quick glance about the hall; it was mercifully untenanted. Bar Sligo, who was gaping.

Vane frowned.

Sligo blinked."Should think Her Ladyship would still be abed, sir. Should I send up—"

"No." Vane looked up the stairs. "Which room is hers?"

"Last on the right."

Vane started up. "You haven't seen me. I'm not here."

"Aye, sir." Sligo watched Vane ascend, then shook his head. And headed back to his porridge.

Locating what he fervently prayed was Minnie's door, Vane rapped lightly on the panels. An instant later, Minnie bade him enter. He did—quickly—silently shutting the door behind him.

Propped against her pillows, a steaming cup of cocoa in her hands, Minnie stared at him. "Great heavens! It's been years since I've seen you up at cockcrow."

Vane advanced on the bed. "I need some sage advice, and you're the only one who can help me."

Minnie beamed. "Well then—what's afoot?"

"Nothing." Incapable of sitting, Vane paced beside the bed.

"That's the problem. What should be afoot is a wedding." He glanced sharply at Minnie. "Mine."

"Ah-hah!" Triumph glowed in Minnie's eyes. "Sits the wind in that quarter, heh?"

"As you well know," Vane stated, his accents clipped, "the wind's been in that quarter since I first set eyes on your niece."

"Perfectly proper—as it should be. So what's the rub?"

"She won't have me."

Minnie blinked. Her smug expression faded. "*Won't have you?*"

Total bewilderment rang in her tone; Vane struggled not to gnash his teeth. "Precisely. For some ungodly reason, I'm not suitable."

Minnie said nothing; her expression said it all.

Vane grimaced. "It's not me, specifically, but men, or marriage in general, she's set her mind against." He sent a saber-edged glance Minnie's way. "You know what that means. She's inherited your stubborness with interest."

Minnie sniffed, and set aside her cocoa. "A very clear-headed girl, Patience. But if she harbors reservations about marriage, I would have thought *you*, of all men, would have been up to the challenge of changing her mind."

"Don't think I haven't tried." Exasperation rang in Vane's words.

"You must have made a muddle of it. When did you offer for her? In the conservatory last night?"

Vane tried not to remember the conservatory last night. Vivid memories had kept him awake until dawn. "I first offered for her—twice—at Bellamy Hall. And I've repeated the offer several times since." He swung on his heel and stalked down the rug. "With increasing persuasiveness."

"Hmm." Minnie frowned. "This sounds serious."

"I think—" Vane halted; hands on hips, he looked up at the ceiling. "No—I *know* she initially confused me with her father. Expected me to behave as he had." He swung about and stalked back. "She first expected me to have no interest in marriage, and when I proved to think otherwise, she assumed I had no real interest in family. She thought I was offering for purely superficial reasons—because she might suit, in effect."

"A Cynster not caring about *family?*" Minnie humphed. "Now she's met so many of you, she can't still be blind."

"No, she can't. Which is precisely my point." Vane stopped beside the bed. "Even after the family's attitudes were paraded before her, she *still* wouldn't change her mind. Which means there's something more—something deeper. I felt there was from the first. Some fundamental reason she'd set her mind against marriage." He met Minnie's eyes. "And I think it derives from her parents' marriage, which is why I'm here, asking you."

Minnie held his gaze, then her expression grew distant. Slowly, she nodded. "You could be right." She refocused on Vane. "You want to know about Constance and Reggie?"

Vane nodded. Minnie sighed. "It was not a happy story."

"Meaning?"

"Constance loved Reggie. By that, I do *not* mean the usual affection found in many marriages, nor yet some warmer degree of affection. I mean love—selfless, complete and unswerving. For Constance, the world revolved about Reggie. Oh, she loved her children, but they were Reggie's and so within her purlieu. To give Reggie his due, he tried to cope, but, of course, from his point of view, the discovery that his wife loved him to distraction was more an embarrassment than a joy." Minnie snorted. "He was a true gentleman of his time. He hadn't married for any notion as outrageous as love. It was considered a good match on all sides—not his fault, really, that matters developed in such an unlooked-for direction."

Minnie shook her head. "He tried to let Constance down lightly, but her feelings were cast in stone, never to be rewritten. In the end, Reggie did the gentlemanly thing and kept away. He lost all touch with his children. He couldn't visit them without seeing Constance, which led to situations he couldn't countenance."

His frown deepening, Vane resumed his pacing. "What, for want of a better word, *lesson*, would Patience have drawn from that?"

Minnie watched him pace, then her gaze sharpened. "You say it's this deep reason that's keeping her from accepting your offer—I presume you're therefore *certain* she would otherwise agree to your suit?"

Vane shot her a glance. "*Perfectly* certain."

"Humph!" Minnie narrowed her eyes at his back. "If that's the case," she declared, her tone tending censorious, "then, as far as I can see, the matter's perfectly obvious."

"*Obvious?*" Vane bit the word off as he rounded on the bed. "Would you care to share your insight with me?"

"Well"—Minnie gestured—"it stands to reason. If Patience is willing to accept you at *that* level, then the odds are that she's in love with you."

Vane didn't blink. "So?"

"So she watched her mother endure a life of misery through marrying a man she loved but who didn't love her, a man who cared nothing for her love."

Vane frowned and looked down. He continued to pace.

Eyes widening, Minnie raised her brows. "If you want to change Patience's mind, you'll have to convince her her love is safe with you—that you value it, rather than see it as a millstone 'round your neck." She caught Vane's eye. "You'll have to convince her to trust you with her love."

Vane scowled. "There's no reason she can't trust me with her love. I wouldn't behave like her father."

"I know that and you know that. But how does Patience know that?"

Vane's scowl turned black. He paced more aggressively.

After a moment, Minnie shrugged and folded her hands. "Funny thing, trust. People with reasons not to trust can be very defensive. The best way to encourage them to give their trust is if the same trust—the *complementary* trust—is freely given to them."

Vane shot her a far from complimentary glance; Minnie raised her brows back. "If you trust her, then she'll trust you. That's what it comes down to."

Vane glowered—mutinously.

Minnie nodded. Decisively. "You'll have to trust her as you want her to trust you, if you're going to win her to wife." She eyed him measuringly. "Think you're up to it?"

He honestly didn't know.

While he struggled with the answer to Minnie's question, Vane hadn't forgotten his other obligations. Half an hour after leaving Minnie, he was shown into the snug parlor of the house in Ryder Street shared by his uncle Martin's sons. Gabriel, so Vane had been informed, was still abed. Lucifer, seated at the table, engaged in devouring a plate of roast beef, looked up as he entered.

"Well!" Lucifer looked impressed. He glanced at the mantelpiece clock. "To what do we owe this unlooked-for—nothing less than startling—visit?" He waggled his brows. "News of an impending fixture?"

"Contain your transports." With an acid glance, Vane dropped into a chair and reached for the coffeepot. "The answer to your question is Minnie's pearls."

Like shedding a skin, Lucifer dropped his inanity. "Minnie's pearls?" His gaze grew distant. "Double strand, thirty inches if not more, exceptionally well-matched." His frown deepened. "Drop earrings, too, weren't there?"

"There were." Vane met his arrested gaze. "They're all gone."

Lucifer blinked. "Gone—as in stolen?"

"So we believe."

"When? And how?"

Briefly, Vane explained. Lucifer listened intently. Each member of the Bar Cynster had some special area of interest; Lucifer's specialty was gems and jewelry. "I came to ask," Vane concluded, "if you could sound out the cognescenti. If the pearls have slipped through our net and been passed on, I assume they'll pass through London?"

Lucifer nodded. "I'd say so. Any fence worth his salt would try to interest the denizens of Hatton Garden."

"All of whom you know."

Lucifer smiled; the gesture was not humorous. "As you say. Leave it with me. I'll report back as soon as I hear anything to the point."

Vane drained his coffee mug, then pushed back his chair. "Let me know the instant you hear."

An hour later, Vane was back in Aldford Street. Collecting a still sleepy Patience, he installed her in his curricle and made straight for the park.

"Any developments?" he asked as he headed his greys down one of the quieter avenues.

Yawning, Patience shook her head. "The only change, if change it be, is that Alice has turned even more prudishly odd." She glanced at Vane. "Alice declined Honoria's invitation. When Minnie asked why, Alice glared, and declared you were all devils."

Vane's lips twitched. "Strange to tell, she isn't the first to have labeled us that."

Patience grinned. "But to answer your *next* question, I spoke with Sligo—despite being left all alone, Alice did nothing more exciting than repair early to her chamber, where she remained for the whole evening."

"Praying for deliverance from devils, no doubt. Did Whitticombe attend the ball?"

"Indeed, yes. Whitticombe's not affected by any puritanical streak. While not jovial, he was at least willing to be entertained. According to Gerrard, Whitticombe spent most of his time chatting with various senior Cynsters. Gerrard thought he was sounding out possible patrons, although for what project remained unclear. Of course, Gerrard's not the most unbiased observer, not when it comes to Whitticombe."

"I wouldn't sell young Gerrard short. His artist's eye is remarkably keen." Vane slanted a glance at Patience. "And he still has the ears of a child."

Patience grinned. "He does love to listen." Then she sobered. "Unfortunately, he heard nothing to the point." She caught Vane's eye. "Minnie's starting to fret again."

"I've set Lucifer on the trail of the pearls. If they've made their way to London's jewelers, he'll hear of it."

"He will?"

Vane explained. Patience frowned. "I really don't understand how they can have so thoroughly disappeared."

"Along with everything else. Just consider—" Vane checked, then wheeled his team for the turn. "If there's only one thief, and, given none of the other stolen items have been found either, that seems a reasonable bet, then all the items are probably hidden in one place. But where?"

"Where indeed? We've hunted all over, yet they must be somewhere." Patience glanced at Vane. "Is there anything more I can do?"

The question hung in the air between them; Vane kept his

gaze on his horses until he could keep the words "*Agree to marry me*" from his lips. Now was not the time—pressing her was the wrong tack to take. He knew it, but swallowing the words took real effort.

"Check Minnie's inmates one more time." At a spanking pace, he set the curricle for the park gates. "Don't look for anything specific, anything suspicious. Don't prejudge what you see—just study each one." He breathed deeply, and flicked Patience a hard glance. "You're the one closest and yet most detached—look again, and tell me what you see. I'll call for you tomorrow."

Patience nodded. "Same time?"

Curtly, Vane acquiesced. And wondered how much longer he could refrain from doing something—saying something—rash.

"Miss Patience!"

Hurrying along the gallery on her way to join Vane, impatiently waiting downstairs, Patience paused, and waited for Mrs. Henderson, deserting her post supervising the maids down one corridor, to join her.

With a conspiratorial look, Mrs. Henderson came close and lowered her voice. "If you'd be so good, miss, as to tell Mr. Cynster that the sand's back."

"Sand?"

One hand to her ample bosom, Mrs. Henderson nodded. "He'll know. Same as before, just a trickle here and there about that heathenish elephant. I can see it sparkling between the floorboards. Not that it comes from the gaudy beast—I took a cloth to it myself, but it was perfectly clean. Other than that, even with these London maids—and Sligo's hired ones with the sharpest eyes in Christendom—we've not spotted anything awry."

Patience would have requested an explanation, if the expression on Vane's face when he'd called and found her in the drawing room, rather than ready, waiting for their drive, had not been indelibly imprinted on her mind.

He was impatient, champing at some invisible bit.

She smiled at Mrs. Henderson. "I'll tell him."

With that, she whirled, and, clutching her muff, hurried down the stairs.

"Sand?" Her gaze fixed on Vane's face, Patience waited for clarification. They were in the park, taking their usual route far from the fashionable throng. She'd delivered Mrs. Henderson's message; it had been received with a frown.

"Where the devil is she getting it from?"

"Who?"

"Alice Colby." Grim-faced, Vane told her of the earlier report of sand in Alice's room. He shook his head. "Heaven only knows what it means." He glanced at Patience. "Did you check out the others?"

Patience nodded. "There was nothing remotely odd about any of them, or their activities. The only thing I learned that I didn't know before was that Whitticombe brought books up from the Hall. I imagined, when he took such immediate possession of the library, that he'd found some tomes there and had settled to a new interest."

"And he hasn't?"

"Far from it. He lugged at least six huge volumes along as luggage; no wonder their coach was straggling behind."

Vane frowned. "What's he studying at the moment—still Coldchurch Abbey?"

"Yes. He goes for a constitutional every afternoon—I slipped into the library and checked. All six books focus on the Dissolution—either just before or just after. The only exception was a ledger, dated nearly a century before."

"Hmm."

When Vane said nothing more, Patience jogged his elbow. "Hmm what?"

He flicked her a glance, then looked back at his leader. "Just that Whitticombe seems obsessed with the abbey. One would have thought he'd know everything there was to know of it by now—at least enough to write his thesis." After a moment, he asked, "Nothing suspicious to report about any of the others?"

Patience shook her head. "Did Lucifer learn anything?"

"In a way, yes." Vane threw her a frustrated glance. "The pearls have *not* been cleared through London. In fact, Lucifer's sources, which are second to none, are very sure the pearls have not, in their idiom, 'become available.' "

"Available?"

"Meaning that whoever stole them still has them. No one's attempted to sell them."

Patience grimaced. "We seem to meet blank walls at every turn." After a moment, she added, "I calculated how big a space would be needed to store everything that's been stolen." She caught Vane's eye. "Edith Swithin's tatting bag, emptied of everything else, would barely hold it all."

Vane's frown turned grim. "It's all *got* to be somewhere. I had Sligo search everyone's room again, but he turned up empty-handed."

"But it *is* somewhere."

"Indeed. But where?"

Vane was back in Aldford Street at one o'clock the next morning, assisting a weak-kneed Edmond up the front steps. Gerrard was steering Henry, chortling at his own loquaciousness. Edgar, a wide, distinctly silly grin on his face, brought up the rear.

The General, thank heavens, had stayed home.

Sligo opened the door to them, and instantly took charge. Nevertheless, it took another half hour and the concerted efforts of the sober members of the group, to install Edmond, Henry, and Edgar in their respective beds.

Heaving a sigh of relief, Gerrard slumped against the corridor wall. "If we don't find the pearls soon, and get this lot back to the Hall, they'll run amok—and run us into the ground."

The comment accurately reflected Vane's thoughts. He grunted and resettled his coat.

Gerrard yawned, and nodded sleepily. "I'm off to bed. I'll see you tomorrow."

Vane nodded. "Good night."

Gerrard headed down the corridor. His expression sober, Vane crossed the gallery to the stairs. At their head, he paused, looking down into the darkened front hall. About him, the house lay slumberous, the cloak of night, temporarily disturbed, settling back, a muffling shroud.

Vane felt the night drag at him, draining his strength. He was tired.

Tired of getting nowhere. Frustrated at every turn.

Tired of not winning, not succeeding.

Too tired to fight the compulsion that drove him. The compulsion to seek succor, support, surcease from his endeavors, in his love's arms.

He drew in a deep breath and felt his chest swell. He kept his gaze locked on the stairs, denying the impulse to look right, down the corridor that led to Patience's room.

It was time to go home, time to walk down the stairs, out through the front door, stroll the few blocks to his own house in Curzon Street, let himself into the silence of an empty house, walk up the elegant stairs and into the master bedroom. To sleep alone in his bed, between silken sheets, cold, unwarmed, unwelcoming.

A whisper of sound, and Sligo materialized beside him. Vane glanced sideways. "I'll let myself out."

If Sligo was surprised, he didn't show it. With a nod, he descended the stairs. Vane waited, watched as Sligo moved through the hall, checking the front door. He heard the bolt slide home, then the bobbing candle crossed the hall and disappeared through the green-baize door.

Leaving him in the silent darkness.

Still as a statue, Vane stood at the top of the stairs. In the present circumstances, inviting himself into Patience's bed was unacceptable, even reprehensible.

It was also inevitable.

His eyes fully adjusted to the dark, he turned right. Silently, he walked down the corridor, to the room at its end. Facing the door, he raised his hand—and hesitated. Then the planes of his face shifted, and set.

He knocked. Softly.

A silent minute passed, then he heard the soft patter of bare feet on the boards. A heartbeat later, the door opened.

Flushed with sleep, her hair a tousled crown, Patience blinked at him. Her long white gown clung to her figure, outlined by the glow from the hearth. Lips parted, her breasts rising and falling, she radiated warmth and the promise of paradise.

Her eyes found his; for a long minute, she simply looked, then she stepped back and gestured him in.

Vane crossed the threshold and knew it to be his Rubicon. Patience shut the door behind him, then turned—into his arms.

He drew her close and kissed her; he needed no words for what he wanted to say. She opened to him instantly, offering all he wanted, all he needed. She sank against him, all soft womanly curves enticing, encouraging.

Vane caught his breath, caught the reins of his demons, and knew, this time, he wouldn't hold them for long. She set his blood afire too easily; she was the very essence of need to him.

The sole and dominant object of his desire.

Lifting his lids, he glanced at her bed. Reassuringly large, it was shrouded in shadow. The only light in the room came from the embers glowing in the hearth.

He wanted her in his bed, but tonight, he'd make do with hers. He also wanted to see her, to let his eyes, all his senses feast. His demons needed feeding. He also had to find a way to tell her the truth, to tell her what was in his heart. To utter the words he knew he had to say.

Minnie, damn her ancient shrewdness, had pointed unerringly to the truth. And, as much as one part of him wished to, he was powerless to duck, powerless to escape.

He had to do it.

Lifting his head, he drew in a breath so huge, his chest strained against his coat. "Come to the fire."

Sliding one arm around her, registering the glide of fine lawn over bare skin, he guided her toward the hearth. Pressing close, her head in the hollow of his shoulder, her hip against his, she acquiesced readily.

As one, they stopped before the hearth. With a naturalness he found enthralling, she turned into his arms. Sliding her hands over his shoulders, she lifted her face, her lips. He was kissing her before he thought of it.

With an inward sigh, Vane caught hold of his impulses, locked a mental fist about them, then, easing his arms from her, he closed his hands about her waist. And tried not to register the warmth beneath his palms, the softness under his fingers.

He lifted his head, breaking their kiss. "Patience—"

"Sssh." She stretched up on her toes and set her lips to his.

Hers clung, softly teased; his firmed. Instinctively, he took charge again, effortlessly sliding into the next kiss.

Inwardly, Vane cursed. His reins were steadily fraying. His demons were grinning. In devilish anticipation. He tried again, this time whispering the words against her lips. "I need to t—"

She silenced him again, just as effectively.

Even more effectively, she reached for him, slim fingers closing possessively about his already rigid length.

Vane caught his breath—and gave up. There was no point battling on—he'd forgotten what it was he had to say. He slid his hands down and around; cupping her bottom, he drew her hips hard against his thighs. Her lips parted, her tongue flicked temptingly; he accepted her invitation and plundered. Ravenously.

Patience sighed with satisfaction and sank into his hard embrace. She wasn't interested in words. She was prepared to listen to pants, moans, even groans—but no words.

She didn't need to hear him explain why he was here; she didn't need to hear any excuses for why he needed her—his reasons had been there, shining silver in his eyes, when he'd stood in the dark on her threshold, his gaze locked, so hungrily, on her. The strength of that silvery force was etched in the driven planes of his face, there for her to see. She didn't want to hear him explain—and risk tarnishing the silver with mere words. Words could never do it justice—they'd only detract from the glory.

The glory of being needed. Needed like that. It had never happened to her before; it would likely never happen again.

Only with him. His was a need she could fill; she knew, to her bones, she was made for the task. The unalloyed pleasure she received from giving to him—giving herself to him and assuaging his need—was beyond all words, beyond all earthly measures.

This was what it meant to be a woman. A wife. A lover. This, of all things, was what her soul craved.

She wanted no words to get in her way.

Patience opened her singing heart and welcomed him in. She kissed him as ravenously as he kissed her, hands greedily searching through his clothes.

With a hissed curse, he drew back. "Wait."

Dragging the long pin from his cravat, he laid it on the mantelpiece; swiftly, he unknotted and unwound the long folds. Patience smiled and reached for him; his expression granite hard, he stepped aside and around—linen folds blocked her sight.

"What . . . ?" Patience raised her hands to her face.

"Trust me." Now behind her, Vane brushed her hands aside and deftly wound the linen twice about her head, then knotted it tight at the back. Then, closing his hands about her shoulders, he bent his head and trailed his lips, feather-light, up the curve of her throat. "It'll be better this way."

Better for him—he might retain some degree of control. He felt the responsiblity of being her love keenly; taking without giving was not in his nature. He needed to tell her what was in his heart. If he couldn't manage the words, at least he could demonstrate his feelings. For now, with desire rampant, pounding through his veins, that was the best he could do.

He knew very well what being "blind" would do to her. Without sight, her remaining senses would heighten—her sexual sensitivity, physical and emotional, would reach new peaks.

Slowly, he turned her to face him, and lifted his hands from her.

Senses flickering wildly, Patience waited. Her breathing was shallow, tight with anticipation; her skin prickled. Hands lax at her sides, she listened to her heartbeat, listened to desire thrum in her veins.

The first tug was so gentle she wasn't sure it was real, then another button on her nightgown slid free. Her senses told her Vane was near, close, but precisely where she couldn't tell. Tentatively, she reached out—

"No. Just stand still."

Obedient to his deep voice, to its compelling tone, she let her arms fall.

Her gown was buttoned down the front, all the way to the floor. Only the waft of air on her skin and the slightest of tugs told her when the last button fell free. Before she could imagine what might come next, quick tugs at her wrists had the lacings undone.

Blind, helpless, she shivered.

And felt her gown part and lift away, then it was sliding

down her arms, down her back, slithering free of her hands to fall to the floor behind her.

She sucked in a tight breath—and felt Vane's gaze upon her. He stood before her; his gaze roved—her nipples puckered; heat spread beneath her skin. A warm flush followed his gaze, over her breasts, her belly, her thighs. She felt herself soften, felt anticipation surge.

He shifted—to the side. Tilting her head slightly, she strained to track his movements. Then he stepped closer. He stood to her left, bare inches away; she could sense him with every pore of her skin.

A hard fingertip slid beneath her chin and tipped her face up. Her lips throbbed; he covered them with his.

The kiss was long and deep, ardent, brutally candid. He surged deep and claimed her softness, then tasted her, languidly but thoroughly, a demonstration of what was to come. Then he drew back—and the fingertip slid away.

Naked, unable to see, with nothing beyond the soft glow from the fire and the heat of desire to warm her, Patience simmered. And waited.

One fingertip touched her right shoulder, then lazily meandered down, over the swell of her breast to circle her nipple. At the last, it flicked the achingly tight bud, then disappeared.

His second caress mirrored the first, teasing her left nipple, sending a long quivering shiver through her. She sucked in a fractured breath.

He leaned closer, reaching behind her to trace the long muscles framing her spine, one, then the other, stopping where they trailed into the hollow below her waist.

Again his touch was withdrawn; again Patience waited. Then his palm, hard, hot, slightly rough on her smooth skin, settled low on her back, in the curve below her waist, then boldly traced down. And around. Proprietorially claiming the full curves, knowingly, appreciatively assessing. Patience felt desire flare, hot and urgent inside her, felt its dew dampen her skin.

She gasped softly; the sound echoed in the stillness. Vane bent his head; she sensed it and lifted her lips. They met his in a kiss so full of aching wanting she swayed. She lifted a hand to grasp his shoulder—

"No. Stand still." He breathed the words against her lips,

then kissed her again. Then his lips trailed to her temple. "Don't move. Just feel. Don't do anything. Just let me love you."

Patience shivered—and mutely acquiesced.

The hand fondling her bottom remained, distractingly intimate. It dropped to briefly trace the backs of her thighs, then, long fingers trailing up the line between, returned to caressing her tensed curves.

Then a rogue fingertip found the hollow at the base of her throat. Involuntarily, Patience straightened. The finger slowly tracked down, sliding smoothly over her skin. It passed between her swollen breasts, continued down her sensitive midriff, over the line of her waist, to her navel. There, it circled, slowly, then trailed diagonally, to one hip, then down the midline of her thigh, stopping and disappearing just above her knee.

The fingertip returned to her throat. The long journey was followed again, this time diverting to her other hip and ending above her other knee.

Patience was not deceived. When the fingertip again came to rest below her throat, she dragged in a desperate breath. And held it.

The fingertip slid down, with the same lazy, langorous touch. Again, it circled her navel, then, deliberately, it slid into the small hollow. And probed. Gently. Evocatively. Repetitively.

Patience's breath escaped in a rush. The shiver that racked her was more like a shudder; breathing became even more difficult. She licked her parched lips, and the finger eased back.

And drifted lower.

She tensed.

The finger continued its leisurely descent, over the gentle swell of her belly, on, into the soft curls at its base.

She would have moved, but the hand behind her gripped and held her steady. With unhurried deliberation, the finger parted her curls, then parted her, and slid further.

Into the hot slickness between her thighs.

Every nerve in her body clenched tight; every square inch of her skin glowed hot. Every last fragment of her awareness was centered on the touch of that lazily questing fingertip.

It swirled, and she gasped; she thought her knees would buckle. For all she knew, they did, but the hand at her bottom supported her. Held her there, so she could feel every movement of that bold finger. It swirled again, and again, until her bones melted.

Within her, fire raged; Vane certainly knew it. But he was in no hurry—his finger pressed deeper, reached farther, and circled her, much as it had circled her above.

Breath bated, Patience waited. Waited. Knowing the moment would come when he would probe, when his finger would slide deep into her empty heat. Her breathing was so shallow she could hear the soft hiss; her lips were dry, parched, yet throbbing. Again and again, he hesitated at her entrance, only to slide away, to caress her swollen flesh, slick and throbbing with her heartbeat.

Finally, the moment came. He circled her one last time, then paused, his finger centered on her entrance. Patience shuddered and let her head fall back.

And he speared her, so slowly she thought she'd lose her mind. She gasped, then cried out as he reached deep.

His answer was to close his lips about one aching nipple.

Patience heard her responsive cry as if from a distance. Raising her hands, she clutched—and found his shoulders.

Vane shifted so she was fully before him, so he could lave first one breast, then the other, while he sank one, then two long fingers into her scalding heat. With his other hand, he gripped the firm mounds of her bottom, knowing he'd leave bruises. If he didn't, she'd be on the floor—and so would he. Which would result in even more bruises.

He'd already depleted his stock of control; it had run out when he'd touched the wet heat between her thighs. He'd reckoned correctly on blind nakedness arousing her deeply—he hadn't foreseen her blind nakedness so arousing him. But he was determined to lavish every attention on her—every ounce he was capable of giving.

Mentally gritting his teeth, mentally girding his loins—in cast iron—he hung on. And lavished more loving on her.

All he had to give, given as only he could.

Patience hadn't known her body could feel so much, so intensely. Fire seared her veins; awareness invested her skin. She was sensitive to each shifting current of air, each and every bold touch, every nuance of every caress.

Every knowing stroke of Vane's hard fingers drove pleasure

into her and through her; every tug of his lips, every wet sweep of his tongue caught the pleasure and drove it to shattering heights.

The pleasure grew, welled, swept and beat through her, then flared and coalesced into a familiar inner sun. Eyes closed beneath her blindfold, she gasped and waited for the sunburst to break over her, then fade. Instead, it swelled brighter, wider—and engulfed her.

And she was part of the sun, part of the pleasure, felt it wash through her and about her, buoy her up and lift her. She drifted, afloat on a sea of sensual bliss, pleasured to her very toes.

The sea stretched on and on; waves lapped at her senses, fed them, sated them. But still left them hungry.

Dimly, she was aware of Vane's hands shifting, aware of losing his intimate touch. Then he lifted her, cradling her against his chest, and carried her. To her bed. Gently, with soothing kisses that eased her parched lips, he laid her on top of her sheets. Patience waited for the blindfold to disappear. It didn't. Instead, she felt the cool slide of her satin coverlet over her sensitized skin.

She listened—ears straining, she heard a soft thud—one boot hitting the floor. In the dark, she smiled. Sinking into the feathers beneath her, she relaxed. And waited.

She expected him to join her beneath the coverlet; instead, a few minutes later, the coverlet was whisked away. He came onto the bed, and stopped. It took her a moment to realize where he was.

On his knees, straddling her thighs.

Anticipation struck her like lightning; in an instant, her body heated anew. Tensed, tightened—quivering with expectation.

Above her, she heard a hoarse chuckle. His hands clamped about her hips. The next instant, she felt his lips.

On her navel.

From there, things only got more heated.

When, endless panting, gasping, shatteringly intimate minutes later, he finally joined with her, she was hoarse, too. Hoarse from her muted cries, from her desperate attempts to breathe. He'd driven her into a state of endless delight, her body awash with exquisite sensation, sensitive to every touch, every unerringly intimate caress.

Now he drove into her, and drove her still further, into the heart of the sun, into the realm of glory. Patience blindly urged him on, let her body speak for her, caress him and hold him and love him as he was loving her.

Wholeheartedly. Unreservedly. Unrestrainedly.

The truth broke on her in the instant their sun imploded and shattered into a million shards. Glory rained about her—about them. Locked together, she felt his ecstasy as deeply as she felt hers.

Together they rose, buoyed on the final rapturous wave; together they fell, into deeply sated release. Wrapped in each other's arms, they floated in the realm reserved for lovers, where no mind was allowed to go.

"Hmm-hmm." Patience burrowed deeper into her warm bed and ignored the hand shaking her shoulder. She was in heaven, a heaven she couldn't remember being in before, and she wasn't interested in cutting short her stay. Even for him—he who had brought her here. There was a time for everything, especially for talking, and this was definitely not it. A warm glow lapped about her. Gratefully, she sank into it.

Vane tried again. Fully dressed, he leaned over, and shook Patience as hard as he dared. "Patience."

A disgruntled noise that sounded like "glumph" was all he got out of her. Exasperated, Vane sat back, and stared at the golden brown curls showing above the coverlet, all he could see of his wife-to-be.

As soon as he'd woken, and realized he'd have to leave, he'd tried to wake her—to tell her, simply and clearly, what he'd failed to tell her earlier. Before her passions had run away with them.

Unfortunately, he'd come to her late, and had stretched the time out as far as he'd been able. The result was that, only two hours later, she was still deeply sunk in bliss and highly resistant to being roused.

Vane sighed. He knew from experience that insisting on rousing her would result in an atmosphere totally inimical to the declaration he wanted to make. Which meant waking her was useless—worse than useless.

He'd have to wait. Until . . .

Muttering a curse, he stood, and headed for the door. He had to leave now or he'd trip over the maids. He would call and see Patience later—he'd have to do what he'd sworn he never would. Never expected he ever would.

Lay his heart on a platter—and calmly hand it to a woman.

Whether he was up to it no longer mattered. Securing Patience as his wife was the only thing that did.

Chapter 20

❧❧❧❧

*W*AS SHE IMAGINING it?

Seated at the breakfast table the next morning, Patience carefully buttered a slice of toast. About her, the household chattered and clattered. Since breakfast was served later, in keeping with town hours, all the household attended, even Minnie and Timms. Even Edith. Even Alice.

Patience glanced about—and ignored the conversations wafting up and down the board. She was too distracted by her inner musings to waste time on less-urgent affairs.

She picked up her knife and reached for the butter.

And started to spread butter. On butter. She focused on the toast—then, very precisely, laid the knife aside and picked up her teacup. And sipped.

Langorous lassitude dragged at her limbs. Sweetly salacious thoughts dragged at her mind. Pleasured exhaustion had her in its grip; it was difficult to concentrate, but, again and again, she drew her mind back to the unexpected revelation of the night before. It required supreme effort to focus on the undercurrents that had run beneath their lovemaking, rather than on the lovemaking itself, but she was certain she wasn't inventing, that the underlying intensity she'd sensed had been real. The intensity of Vane's need, the intensity he'd brought to the act of loving her.

Loving her.

He'd used the words in the physical sense. For herself, she thought first in terms of the emotion, with the act the physical outpouring. Until last night, she'd assumed Vane's meaning was strictly physical—after last night, she wasn't so sure.

Last night, the physical had reached new heights, intensified by some force too powerful to be confined within limbs and flesh. She'd felt it, tasted it, gloried in it—she'd come to know it in herself. Last night, she'd recognized it in him.

Drawing a slow breath, she stared at the cruet set.

She was certain of what she'd sensed but—and here was the rub—he was such an accomplished lover, could he conjure that, too, without it being real? Was what she'd sensed simply a facade created by his undoubted expertise?

Setting down her teacup, she straightened. It was tempting to imagine that she might, perhaps, have misjudged, and his "love" was deeper than she'd supposed. She distrusted that conclusion. It was too neat—too self-serving. One part of her mind was trying to talk the rest into it. Into entertaining the notion that he might love her in the same way she loved him.

As distractions went, that won the crown.

Lips tightening, she picked up her well-buttered toast and crunched. After arriving on her threshold unheralded, he'd taken himself off the same way—before she'd had time to wake up, let alone think. But if what she thought was even half-true, she wanted to know. Now.

She glanced at the clock; it would be hours before he called.

"I say, can you pass the butter?"

Setting aside her impatience, Patience handed Edmond the butter dish. Beside him, Angela smiled brightly. Idly scanning the faces opposite, Patience encountered Alice Colby's black-eyed stare. Intensely cold, black-eyed stare.

Alice kept staring. Patience wondered if her topknot was askew. She was about to turn to Gerrard to ask—

Alice's features contorted. "*Scandalous!*" Uttered in a voice hoarse with righteous fury, the exclamation cut across the conversations. All heads turned; all eyes, startled, fixed on Alice. Who clapped her knife down on the table. "I don't know *how* you can, miss! Sitting there like a lady, taking breakfast with decent folk." Face mottling, Alice pushed back her chair. "I, for one, do not intend to put up with it a moment longer."

"Alice?" From the bottom of the table, Minnie stared. "What is this nonsense?"

"Nonsense? *Hah*!" Alice nodded at Patience. "Your niece is a fallen woman—do you call that nonsense?"

Stunned silence gripped the table.

"Fallen woman?" Whitticombe leaned forward to follow Alice's gaze.

The others looked, too. Patience kept her gaze steady on Alice's; her face had frozen, luckily in a relaxed expression. She was leaning on her elbows, her hands, steady, gripping her teacup. Outwardly, she consciously exuded calm; inside, her wits whirled. How to respond? Coolly, she raised one brow, faintly incredulous.

"*Really*, Alice!" Minnie frowned disapprovingly. "The things you do imagine!"

"*Imagine*?" Alice sat bolt upright. "I didn't imagine a large gentleman in the corridor in the middle of the night!"

Gerrard shifted. "That was Vane." He glanced at Henry and Edmond, then looked at Minnie. "He came upstairs with us when we got in."

"Yes. Indeed." Distinctly pale, Edmond cleared his throat. "He . . . ah . . . ." He glanced at Minnie.

Who nodded, and looked at Alice. "See, there's a perfectly logical explanation."

Alice glowered. "That doesn't explain why he walked down the corridor to your niece's room."

Timms sighed. Dramatically. "Alice, Minnie doesn't have to explain all she does to everyone. After the disappearance of her pearls, naturally, Vane has been keeping an eye on the house. When he returned to the house late, he simply did a last watchman's round."

"Naturally." Minnie nodded, chins in unison. "Just the sort of thing he would do." She glanced, challengingly, at Alice. "He's very considerate in such ways. As for these aspersions you're casting on both Patience's and Vane's characters, you should really be careful of making outrageous accusations without foundation."

Flags flew in Alice cheeks. "I *know* what I saw—"

"Alice! That's enough." Whitticombe rose; his gaze locked

with his sister's. "You mustn't distress people with your fantasies."

There was an emphasis in his words Patience didn't understand. Alice gaped. Then her color surged. Hands clenched, she glared at her brother. "I am *not*—"

"Enough!" Leaving his seat, Whitticombe quickly rounded the table. "I'm sure everyone will excuse us. You're clearly overwrought."

He manhandled Alice, incoherent with rage, from her chair and locked an arm about her scrawny shoulders. With a strained smile for the rest of the company, he turned her and marched her, stiff-legged, from the room.

Slightly dazed, Patience watched them go. And wondered how she'd weathered potential calamity without uttering a single word.

The answer was obvious, but she didn't understand it.

Somewhat subdued, the rest of the household dispersed. All made a point of smiling at Patience, to show they hadn't believed Alice's slander.

Retreating to her room, Patience paced. Then she heard the tap of Minnie's cane in the corridor. An instant later, Minnie's door opened, then shut.

An instant after that, Patience tapped on the panels, then entered. Minnie was easing into an armchair by the windows. She beamed at Patience.

"Well! That was a bit of unexpected excitement."

Patience fought not to narrow her eyes. Indeed, she fought to retain a proper degree of calm in the face of Minnie's twinkling eyes. Timms's smug smile.

They knew. And *that* was even more scandalous, to her thinking, than the fact Vane had spent the night—a number of nights—in her bed.

Lips thinning, Patience swept to the windows, and fell to pacing alongside Minnie. "I need to explain—"

"No." Minnie held up a commanding hand. "Actually, you need to keep your lips shut and concentrate on not saying anything I don't wish to hear."

Patience stared at her; Minnie grinned.

"You don't understand—"

"On the contrary, I understand very well." Minnie's impish smile surfaced. "Better than you, I'll warrant."

"It's obvious," Timms chimed in. "But these things take time to sort themselves out."

They thought she and Vane would marry. Patience opened her mouth to set them right. Minnie caught her eye. Reading the stubbornness behind Minnie's faded blue gaze, Patience snapped her lips shut. And muttered through them, "It's not that simple."

"Simple? Bah!" Minnie fluffed up her shawls. "You should be relieved. Simple and easy is never worthwhile."

Pacing again, Patience recalled similar words—after a moment, she placed them as Lucifer's—to Vane. Arms folded, pacing slowly, she wrestled with her thoughts, her feelings. She should, she supposed, feel some measure of guilt, of shame. She felt neither. She was twenty-six; she'd made a rational decision to take what life offered her—she'd embarked on an affair with an elegant gentleman with her eyes fully open. And she'd found happiness—perhaps not forever, but happiness nonetheless. Bright moments of glory infused with heady joy.

She felt no guilt, and not the slightest regret. Not even for Minnie would she deny the fulfillment she'd found in Vane's arms.

But honesty insisted she set the record straight—she couldn't leave Minnie imagining wedding bells on the breeze. Drawing a deep breath, she halted by Minnie's chair. "I haven't accepted Vane's proposal."

"Very wise." Timms bent over her stitching. "The last thing you want is a Cynster taking you for granted."

"What I'm *trying* to say—"

"Is that you're far too wise to accept without being convinced. Without gaining a few meaningful assurances." Minnie looked up at her. "My dear, you're going about this in precisely the right way. Cynsters never give ground easily—their version of the matter is that, once seized, things, even wives, become theirs. The fact that in the instance of a wife, they might need to negotiate a trifle won't at first enter their heads. And even when it does, they'll try to ignore the issue as far as you'll allow them. I'm really very proud of you, standing firm like this. Until you gain sufficient promises, sufficient concessions, you most certainly shouldn't agree."

Patience stood, stock-still, for a full minute, staring into Minnie's face. Then she blinked. "You *do* understand."

Minnie raised her brows. "Of course."

Timms snorted. "Just make sure he gets it right."

Minnie grinned. Reaching out, she squeezed Patience's hand. "It's up to you to judge what will finally tip the scales. However, I have a few sage words, if you'll accept advice from an old woman who knows both you and Vane better than either of you seem to realize?"

Patience blushed. She waited, suitably penitent.

Minnie's grin turned wry. "There are three things you should remember. One, Vane is not your father. Two, you are not your mother. And, three, don't imagine—not for a moment—that you won't be marrying Vane Cynster."

Patience looked long into Minnie's wise eyes, then turned aside and sank onto the window seat.

Minnie, of course, was right. She'd hit all three proverbial nails soundly on the head.

She had from the first visited her father's character on Vane. Now, holding one up against the other, that was patently a false image, a superficial glamor. Vane was an "elegant gentleman" in appearance only, not in character. Not in any of the ways that were important to her.

As for her not being her mother, that was unquestionably true. Her mother had possessed a quite different nature—if her mother had sighted her father going into a conservatory with a youthful beauty, she would have put on her most brittle smile and clung to the pretense of not knowing. Not for her such meekness.

She knew what would have transpired if the beauty Vane had retired with had not been so innocent—so related. It would not have been a pleasant scene. While her mother had accepted infidelity as her lot, she would accept no such thing.

If she married Vane . . . The thought drew her into a day-dream—of ifs, buts, and possibilities. Of how they'd interact, adjust to each other, if she took the risk, grabbed fate by the throat, and accepted him. It was a full five minutes before her mind moved on and the implication of Minnie's third statement dawned.

Minnie had known Vane from childhood. She also understood her own dilemma, that she would insist on love as her talisman for the future. That she would not accept Vane without his love declared. And Minnie was sure, convinced beyond all possibility, that she and Vane would marry.

Patience blinked. Abruptly, she looked at Minnie and discovered her aunt waiting, watching, a deep smile in her old eyes.

"Oh." Lips lifting, her heart leaping, Patience could think of nothing more to say.

Minnie nodded. "Precisely."

The incident at breakfast cast a long shadow. When the household sat down to lunch, the conversation was subdued. Patience noted it, but, her heart light, paid it little heed. She was waiting, as patiently as she could, to see Vane. To look deep into his eyes, to search for what Minnie was so certain must be there, concealed behind his elegant gentleman's mask.

He hadn't appeared for their usual midmorning drive. As she settled her skirts, Patience wryly reflected that, even a few days ago, she would have interpreted his absence as evidence of waning desire. Now, buoyed by an inner confidence, she was convinced that only some urgent matter to do with Minnie's pearls would have kept him from her side. The inner glow that went with that confidence was very pleasant indeed.

Alice did not join the table. As if in apology for her morning's outburst, Whitticombe set himself to be more pleasant than usual. Edith Swithins, beside him, was the main beneficiary of his careful erudition. At the end of one particularly tedious explanation, she beamed.

"How fascinating." Her gaze alighted on Edgar, sitting opposite. "But dear Edgar has studied that period, too. As I recall, his conclusions were different?" Her tone made the words a question. Everyone at the table held their breath.

Except Edgar, who launched into his own perspective.

To everyone's amazement, even, Patience suspected, Edith's and Edgar's, Whitticombe listened. His attitude had about it the air of gritted teeth, but he heard Edgar out, then nodded curtly. "Quite possibly."

Patience caught Gerrard's eye and fought to suppress a giggle.

Edmond, still pale and limply disheveled, chased a pea

around his plate. "Actually, I was wondering when we might be heading back to the Hall."

Patience stiffened. Beside her, Gerrard straightened. They both looked at Minnie.

So did Edmond. "I really should get on with my drama, and there's precious little inspiration, and a great deal of distraction, here in town."

Minnie smiled. "Bear with the foibles of an old lady, my dear. I've no immediate plans to return to the Hall. Besides, there's only a skeleton staff left—we gave the maids leave, and Cook has gone to visit her mother."

"Oh." Edmond blinked. "No cook. Ah." He subsided into silence.

Surreptitiously, Patience grimaced at Gerrard. He shook his head, then turned to speak to Henry.

Patience glanced—for the fiftieth time—at the clock.

The door opened; Masters entered, his expression stiff. Approaching Minnie's chair, he bent and spoke quietly. Minnie blanched. Her face grew instantly old.

From the end of the table, Patience looked her concern and her question. Minnie saw; sinking back in her chair, she gestured to Masters to speak.

He cleared his throat, gathering all attention. "Some . . . gentlemen from Bow Street have arrived. It seems a report was lodged. They've come with a warrant to search the house."

An instant of stunned silence ensued, then cacophony erupted. Exclamations of shock and surprise came from all sides. Henry and Edmond competed for prominence.

Patience stared helplessly up the table at Minnie. Timms was patting Minnie's hand. The cacophony continued unabated. Lips setting, Patience grasped a soup ladle and wielded it against a dish cover.

The clangs cut through the din—and silenced the din makers. Patience raked the offenders with an irate glance. "Who? Who notified Bow Street?"

"I did." Pushing back his chair, the General stood. "Had to be done, don't y'know."

"Why?" Timms asked. "If Minnie'd wanted those dreadful Runners in her house, she'd have requested it."

The General flushed a choleric red. "Seemed that was the

problem. Women—ladies. Too softhearted for your own good."
He slid a glance Gerrard's way. "Had to be done—no sense in
ducking it any longer. Not with the pearls missing, too." Regi-
mentally stiff, the General drew himself upright. "I took it upon
myself to notify the authorities. Acting on information received,
don't y'know. Plain as a pikestaff it's young Debbington at fault.
Search his room, and it'll all come to light."

Premonition seized Patience; she shook it off as irrational.
She opened her mouth to defend Gerrard—he kicked her ankle.
Hard. Sucking in a breath, she turned—and met a very straight
stare.

"Let be," Gerrard whispered. "There's nothing there—let
them play out their hand. Vane warned me something like this
might happen. He said best to shrug and grin cynically and see
what transpires."

To Patience's utter amazement, he proceeded to do just that,
managing to convey an impression of patent boredom.

"By all means—search all you like." He grinned cynically
again.

Pushing back from the table, Patience bustled to Minnie's
side. Minnie clasped her hand tightly, then nodded to Masters.
"Show the gentlemen in."

There were three of them, subtly unsavory to a man. Standing at Minnie's shoulder, firmly clasping her hand, Patience
watched as, sharp eyes darting about the room, the Runners
edged in and formed up in a row. Sligo slipped through the door
after them.

The tallest Runner, in the center, bobbed a bow at Minnie.
"Ma'am. As I hope yer man told you, we've a-come to search
the premises. Seems there's some valuable pearls gone missing
and a villain about."

"Indeed." Minnie studied them, then nodded. "Very well.
You have my permission to search the house."

"We'll start with the bedchambers, if you don't mind,
ma'am."

"If you must. Masters will accompany you." Minnie nodded
a dismissal. Sligo held the door open, and Masters ushered the
men out.

"I think," Minnie said, "that we should all remain here until
the search is concluded."

Gerrard slouched, relaxed, in his chair. The others shifted and looked uncomfortable.

Patience turned on Sligo.

"I know, I know." He held up a placating hand as he reached for the door. "I'll find him and get him here." He slipped out. The door closed softly behind him.

Patience sighed and turned back to Minnie.

Half an hour had passed, and Patience was certain the face of the ormolu clock on the mantel was indelibly imprinted on her mind, before the door opened again.

Everyone straightened. Breaths caught.

Vane strode in.

Patience knew an instant of giddy relief. His gaze touched her, then passed on to Minnie. He went straight to her, pulling up a vacant chair.

"Tell me."

Minnie did, her voice lowered so the others, now gathered in groups about the room, could not hear. Aside from Minnie with Timms beside her, and Patience hovering, only Gerrard remained at the table, alone at the other end. As Minnie whispered her news, Vane's face hardened. He exchanged a charged glance with Gerrard.

Glancing up, Vane met Patience's eyes, then he looked back at Minnie. "It's all right—a good sign, in fact." He, too, spoke softly; his words reached no further than Patience. "We know there's nothing in Gerrard's room. Sligo searched only yesterday. And Sligo's very thorough. But this means something, at long last, is afoot."

Minnie's look was tremulous.

Somewhat grimly, Vane smiled. "Trust me." Minnie drew in a breath, then smiled, weakly. He squeezed her hands, then stood.

He turned to Patience. Something shifted in his face, in his eyes.

Patience lost her breath.

"I apologize for not arriving this morning, but something came up."

He took her hand, raised it to his lips, then changed his grip and grasped firmly; Patience felt warm strength flow into her, around her. "Anything helpful?" she asked.

Vane grimaced. "Another blank wall. Gabriel heard of our problem—he has some surprising contacts. While we learned nothing about where the pearls are, we did learn where they haven't been. To wit, pawned." Patience opened her eyes wide. Vane nodded. "It was another possibility, but we've exhausted that avenue, too. For my money, the pearls have never left Minnie's household."

Patience nodded. She opened her mouth—

The door swung open and the Runners returned.

One glance at their triumphant expression, and Patience's premonition returned with a vengeance. Her heart stopped, chilled, then sank. Vane's grip on her fingers tightened; she curled her fingers and clung.

Carrying a small sack, the senior Runner advanced portentously on Minnie—then spilled the contents of the sack onto the table before her. "Can you identify these baubles, ma'am?"

The baubles included Minnie's pearls. They also included everything else that had gone missing.

"My comb!" Gleefully, Angela swooped down and plucked the gaudy trinket free.

"Dear me—there's my pincushion." Edith Swithins poked it aside.

The items were nudged apart—Timms's bracelet, the pearls and their matching earrings, Patience's bud vase. Everything was there—except—

"Only one." Agatha Chadwick looked down at the garnet drop earring she'd separated from the pile.

Everyone looked again. The Runner upended the sack, then peered into it. He shook his head. "Nothing here. And there wasn't any goods left lying in the drawer."

"Which drawer?" Patience asked.

The Runner glanced over his shoulder—to where his comrades had taken up position one on either side of Gerrard's chair. "The drawer of the bureau in what I 'ave been told is Mister Gerrard Debbington's bedchamber. Which bedchamber he has on his own, not sharing with anyone else."

The Runner made that last sound like a crime in itself. Her

heart constricted, sunk to her slippers, Patience looked at Gerrard. And she saw he was struggling not to laugh.

Patience stiffened; Vane pinched her fingers.

"You'll a-have to come along of us, young gent." The Runner advanced on Gerrard. "There's some serious questions the magistrate'll have for you. You come along nice and quiet, and we won't have no fuss."

"Oh, indeed. No fuss."

Patience heard the suppressed laughter in Gerrard's voice as he obligingly stood—how *could* he be so flippant? She wanted to shake him.

Vane shook her—her hand, at any rate. She glanced at him; he frowned at her and shook his head fractionally.

"Trust me."

The words reached her on a whisper, a mere thread of sound.

Patience looked into his eyes, calmly grey—then she looked at Gerrard, her young brother, light of her life. Drawing in a steadying breath, she glanced back at Vane and almost imperceptibly nodded. If Gerrard could trust Vane, and play out his alloted role, how much more reason had she to place her trust in him.

"What's the charge?" Vane asked, as the Runners formed up around Gerrard.

"No charge as yet," the senior Runner replied. "That's up to the magistrate, that is. We just lay the evidence before him and see what he thinks."

Vane nodded. Patience saw the glance he exchanged with Gerrard.

"Right then." Gerrard grinned. "Which round house is it to be? Or do we go directly to Bow Street?"

Bow Street it was. Patience had to bite her lip to stop herself from intervening, or begging to go, too. Sligo, she noticed, at a nod from Vane, slid out in the Runners' wake. All the rest of the household remained in the dining room until the front door clanged shut behind the Runners and their charge.

For one instant, the tension held, then a sigh ran through the room.

Patience stiffened. Vane turned to her.

"I said it again and again, but you would pay no heed, Miss

Debbington." Righteously patronizing, Whitticombe shook his head. "And now it's come to this. Perhaps, in future, you will take more note of those with more years in their cup than yourself."

"Hear, hear," came from the General. "Said it from the first. Boys' tricks." He frowned at Patience.

Emboldened, Whitticombe gestured at Minnie. "And just think of the sore distress you and your brother have so heedlessly caused our dear hostess."

Color high, Minnie thumped her cane. "I'll thank you not to get your causes muddled. I'm certainly distressed, but my distress, as far as I can see, has been occasioned by whoever called the Runners down on our heads." She glared at Whitticombe, then at the General.

Whitticombe sighed. "My dear cousin, you really must see the light."

"Actually." Vane's drawl, laced with an undercurrent of sharpened steel, sliced through Whitticombe's sugary tones. "Minnie *needs* do nothing. A charge is not a conviction—indeed, a charge has yet to be made." Vane held Whitticombe's gaze. "I rather think that, in this case, time will reveal who is at fault, and who needs adjust their thinking. It seems somewhat premature to make sweeping conclusions just yet."

Whitticombe tried to look down his nose contemptuously; as Vane was a half head taller, he didn't succeed. Which irritated him even more. Face setting, he eyed Vane, then, deliberately, let his gaze slide to Patience. "I rather think you're in no position to act as defender of the righteous, Cynster."

Vane tensed; Patience locked her hand about his.

"Oh?"

At Vane's quiet prompt, Whitticombe's lips curled. Patience inwardly groaned and shifted her hold to Vane's arm. Everyone else in the room stilled, holding their collective breaths.

"Indeed," Whitticombe smiled spitefully. "My sister had some very interesting—quite riveting—insights to offer this morning. On you and Miss Debbington."

"Is that so?"

Deaf to anything but his own voice, Whitticombe failed to hear the warning in Vane's lethally flat tone. "Bad blood," he pronounced. "Must run in the family. One a bald-faced thief, the other—"

Belatedly, Whitticombe focused on Vane's face—and froze.

Patience felt the aggression lance through Vane; under her hands, the muscles of his arm locked, rock-hard. She clung, literally, and hissed a furious, "No!"

For one instant, she thought he might shake free and then Whitticome might just be dead. But she'd set her sights on living in Kent, not in exile on the Continent.

"Colby, I suggest you retire—now." Vane's tone promised instant retribution should he decline.

Stiffly, not daring to take his gaze from Vane's face, Whitticombe nodded to Minnie. "I'll be in the library." He backed to the door, then paused. "The righteous will be rewarded."

"Indeed," Vane replied. "I'm counting on it."

With a contemptuous glance, Whitticombe left. The tension gripping the room drained. Edmond slumped into a chair. "Gad, if I could only capture that on stage."

The comment sent a ripple of uneasy laughter through the others. Timms waved to Patience. "After that excitement, Minnie should rest."

"Indeed." Patience helped Timms gather Minnie's myriad shawls.

"Shall I carry you?" Vane asked.

"No!" Minnie waved him away. "You've other things on your plate just now—more urgent things. Why are you still here?"

"There's time."

Despite Minnie's shooing, Vane insisted on helping her up the stairs and seeing her installed in her room. Only then did he consent to leave. Patience followed him into the corridor, pulling the door shut behind her.

Vane pulled her to him and kissed her—hard and quick.

"Don't worry," he said the instant he raised his head. "We had a plan in case something like this happened. I'll go and make sure all's fallen into place."

"Do." Patience met his eyes, searched them briefly, then nodded and stepped back. "We'll hold the line here."

Swiftly, Vane raised her hands and kissed them, then stepped back. "I'll keep Gerrard safe."

"I know." Patience clutched his hand. "Come to me later."

The invitation was deliberate; she acknowledged it with her eyes.

Vane's chest swelled; his face was a conqueror's mask, hard and unyielding. His eyes held hers, then he nodded. "Later."

With that, he left her.

Chapter 21

C̓OME TO ME *later*, she'd said.

Vane returned to Aldford Street just after ten o'clock.

The house was quiet when Masters let him in. His expression implacable, Vane handed Masters his cane, hat, and gloves. "I'll go up to Her Ladyship and Miss Debbington. You needn't wait up—I'll show myself out."

"As you wish, sir."

As he climbed the stairs, Vane recalled Chillingworth's words: *How the mighty have fallen.* The steely determination that had taken possession of him wound a notch tighter. He wasn't sure how deep the changes within him had gone, but as of this afternoon, he'd sworn off all attempts to hide his connection with Patience Debbington. The lady who would be his wife.

There was no doubt of that fact, no possibility of error, no room for maneuver—and absolutely none for negotiation. He was finished with excuses, with playing the game according to society's rules. Conquerors wrote their own rules. That was something Patience would have to come to terms with—he intended shortly to inform her of the fact.

But first, he'd set Minnie's heart at rest.

He found her propped on her pillows, eyes expectantly wide. Timms was present; Patience was not. Quickly, concisely, he explained and reassured. Then he left Timms to tuck Minnie, at ease once again, up for the night.

He knew they were grinning behind his back, but was not about to acknowledge it. Shutting Minnie's door with a definite click, he turned and strode down the corridor.

With a token, peremptory tap, he opened Patience's door and walked in, then shut it behind him. Rising from the chair by the hearth, she blinked, then resettled the shawl she'd draped over her shoulders, and calmly waited.

Beneath the soft shawl, she was wearing a fine silk night-gown, cinched with a drawstring under her breasts. And nothing else.

The blaze in the hearth roared.

One hand on the doorknob, Vane drank in the sight, luscious curves and sleek limbs outlined by the flames. The embers inside him ignited; a rush of fiery lust seared his veins. He straightened and slowly stalked toward her.

"Gerrard's with Devil and Honoria at St. Ives House." The words fell from his lips slowly, as, starting at her nightgown's hem, he let his gaze rise, noting the fascinating way the silk clung to each curve, to her long, sleek thighs, rounded hips, the soft swell of her belly, how it cradled the warm globes of her breasts. Her nipples peaked as his gaze feasted.

She tightened her hold on her shawl. "Was that part of your plan?"

Halting before her, Vane lifted his gaze to her face. "Yes. I hadn't imagined Bow Street, but something along those lines was in the cards. Someone had, from the first, tried to cast Gerrard as the thief."

"What happened?" Patience's words were breathless; her lungs had seized. She held Vane's gaze and tried not to shiver. Not with fear, but anticipation. The stark planes of his face, the silvery flames in his eyes, all screamed of reined passion.

He studied her eyes, then raised one brow. "By the time I reached Bow Street, Devil had descended and whisked Gerrard away. I followed them to St. Ives House. According to Gerrard, he didn't even have time to look around Bow Street before Devil arrived, courtesy of Sligo. He must have run all the way to Grosvenor Square."

Her eyes locked on his, Patience licked her lips. "He's really been a big help over this business."

"Indeed. As he could swear that the stolen goods were not in Gerrard's room yesterday, and nor was the sack in which they were found, the magistrate was understandably diffident over laying any charge." Vane's lips lifted. "Particularly with Devil leaning on the charge desk."

Bracing one hand on the mantelpiece, he leaned closer. Decidedly giddy, Patience tilted her chin. "I suspect your cousin enjoys intimidating people."

Vane's lips quirked. His gaze lowered to her lips. "Let's just say Devil's rarely backward in exercising his authority, especially in support of one of the family."

"I . . . see." Her gaze fixed on his long lips, Patience decided to let his description of Gerrard as "family" pass unchallenged. The tension investing his large frame, so close beside her, was fascinating—and deliciously unnerving.

"The magistrate decided something odd was going on. The report hadn't come from Minnie, and, of course, there was the matter of Sligo, Devil's servant, masquerading as Minnie's hired help. He couldn't understand it, so he elected to make no finding at present. He released Gerrard into Devil's care, pending any further developments."

"And Gerrard?"

"I left him happily ensconced with Devil and Honoria. Honoria told me to tell you they were grateful for the excuse to stay home. While they keep up appearances, they only came to town to catch up with the family. They'll be returning to Somersham any day."

Patience licked her lips again; under his gaze, they'd started to throb. "Will that—them leaving town—create problems if Gerrard's still in Devil's care?"

"No." Vane lifted his gaze to her eyes. "I'll assume the charge."

Patience mouthed a silent "Oh."

"But tell me." Vane pushed away from the mantelpiece and straightened. "Has anything happened here?" He started to unbutton his coat.

"No." Patience managed to find enough breath for a sigh.

"Alice hasn't been sighted since this morning." She glanced at Vane. "She saw you in the corridor last night."

Vane frowned, and shrugged out of his coat. "What the devil was she doing up at that hour?"

Patience shrugged, and watched him toss his coat on the chair. "Whatever, she didn't come down for dinner. Everyone else did, but all were understandably subdued."

"Even Henry?"

"Even Henry. Whitticombe preserved a censorious silence. The General spent the entire time grumbling, and snapping at anyone who loomed in his path. Edgar and Edith kept their heads down, together for the most part, whispering. About what I know not." Vane's fingers closed about the buttons of his waistcoat. Patience drew a tight breath. "Edmond's succumbed to his muse again. Angela is quietly happy because she got her comb back. Henry, however, was idling about because he couldn't find anyone with whom to play billiards."

Patience shifted, giving Vane space to strip off his waistcoat. "Oh—there was one point of interest—Mrs. Chadwick quietly asked Minnie and me if she could search Gerrard's bureau for her missing earring. Poor dear, it seemed the least we could do. I went with her—we searched high and low, and through all the other drawers, too. There was no sign of it anywhere."

She turned to Vane—just as he freed his cravat and drew the long strip from his neck. His gaze on her, he held it between his hands. "So," he murmured, his tone deep, "nothing of any moment happened here."

Her gaze transfixed by the long strip of linen, Patience tried to speak and couldn't—she shook her head.

"Good." The word was a feral purr. With a negligent flick, Vane sent the cravat to join his coat. "So there's nothing to distract you."

Patience dragged her gaze up to his face. "Distract me?"

"From the subject we need to discuss."

"You want to discuss something?" She hauled in a breath and tried to steady her giddy head.

Vane trapped her gaze. "You. Me." His face hardened. "Us."

With a supreme effort, Patience raised her brows. "What about 'us'?"

A muscle in his jaw flickered. From the corner of her eye, she saw his fist clench. "I," he declared, "have reached the end of my tether."

He stepped toward her; she took a sliding step back.

"I do not approve of any situation that leaves you a target for the likes of such as the Colbys—regardless of whether said situation arises from my actions or otherwise." His lips a thin line, he stepped forward; Patience instinctively edged back. "I cannot, and will not, condone any scenario whereby your reputation is in any way sullied—even by me with the best of intentions."

He continued to stalk her; she continued to retreat. Patience longed to whirl around and scurry out of his reach, but she didn't dare take her eyes from his. "What are you doing here then?"

She was trapped, mesmerized—she knew he'd soon pounce. As if to confirm that, his eyes narrowed, and he tugged his shirt from his waistband. Without taking his eyes from her, he started undoing the buttons, still advancing, still forcing her to retreat. Toward the bed.

"I'm here"—he bit the words off—"because I can't see any sense in being anywhere else. You're *mine*—henceforth, you sleep with me. As you're sleeping here at the moment, *ergo*, so do I. If my bed is not yet yours, then yours will have to be mine."

"You just said you didn't want my reputation sullied."

His shirt fell fully open. He continued to advance. Patience didn't know where to look. Where she most wanted to look.

"Precisely. So you'll have to marry me. Soon. Which is what we need to discuss." With that, he looked down, and unlaced his cuffs.

Poised to seize the moment to dash to safety, Patience froze. "I don't *have* to marry you."

He looked up, and stripped off his shirt. "Not in that sense, no. But for you, marriage to me is inevitable. All we need to determine—what we are *going* to determine—tonight—is what it's going to take to make you agree."

His shirt hit the floor—he stepped forward.

Belatedly, Patience scurried three steps back—and fetched up against the bedpost. Before she could whisk around it, Vane was there, reaching around her, hands locking about the post behind her. Trapping her within the circle of his arms, facing him, and his bare chest.

Dragging in a desperate breath, Patience locked her eyes on his. "I told you—I will *not* simply marry you."

"I think I can guarantee there'll be nothing simple about our marriage."

Patience opened her lips on an acid retort—he sealed them, with a kiss so potent by the time he raised his head, she was clinging for dear life to the bedpost.

"Just listen." He said the words against her lips, as if they were forced from him.

Patience stilled. Her heart thumping wildly, she waited. He didn't straighten, or draw away. Lids lowered, her gaze fixed on his lips, she watched the words form as he spoke.

"I'm renowned within the *ton* as being cool under fire—around you, I'm never cool. I'm heated—I seethe—I burn with desire. If I'm in the same room, all I can think about is heat—your heat—and how you'll feel around me."

Patience felt the heat rise, a real force between them.

"I've gained the reputation of being the soul of discretion—now look at me. I've seduced my godmother's niece—and been seduced by her. I share her bed openly, even under my god-mother's roof." His lips twisted wryly. "So much for discretion."

He drew a deep breath; his chest brushed her breasts.

"And as for my vaunted, up-until-you *legendary* control—the instant I'm inside you that evaporates like water on hot steel."

What prompted her Patience never knew. His lips were so close—with her teeth, she nipped the lower. "I told you to let go—I won't break."

The tension, pouring off him in waves, eased, just a little. He sighed, and rested his forehead on hers. "It's not that." After a moment, he went on, "I don't like losing control—it's like losing myself—in you."

She felt him gather himself, felt the tension swell and co-alesce about them.

"It's giving myself to you—so that I'm in your keeping."

The words, low and gravelly, rolled through her; closing her eyes, she drew in a shallow breath. "And you don't like doing that."

"I don't like it—but I crave it. I don't approve of it, yet I yearn for it." His words feathered her cheek, then his lips touched hers. "Do you understand? I haven't any choice."

Patience felt his chest swell as he drew a deep breath.

"I love you."

She shivered, eyes shut tight, and felt the world shift about her.

"Losing myself in you—giving my heart and soul into your keeping—is part of that."

His lips brushed hers in an inexpressibly tender caress.

"Trusting you is part of that. Telling you I love you is part of that."

His lips touched hers again; Patience didn't wait for more. She kissed him. Letting go of the post, she slid her hands up, framing his face, so she could let him know—let him feel—her response to all he'd said.

He felt it, sensed it—and reacted; his arms locked tight about her. She couldn't breathe, but she didn't care. All she cared about was the emotion that held them, that flowed so effortlessly between them.

Silver and gold, it wound about them, investing each touch with its magic. Silver and gold, it shimmered about them, and quivered in their fractured breaths. It was immediate compulsion and future promise, heavenly delight and earthly pleasure. It was here and now—and forever.

With a soft oath, Vane drew back and stripped off his trousers. Released, Patience lowered her arms and let her shawl fall, then tugged the tie of her nightgown free. A quick shift and a shrug sent the silk sliding to the floor.

Vane straightened—she stepped into his arms, setting her naked limbs to his.

He sucked in a breath, then let it out in a groan as she stretched sinuously against him. He wrapped her in his arms and bent his head to hers; their lips met, and desire ran free.

He lifted her and laid her on the sheets, and followed her down. She welcomed him to her, took him into her body with joyous abandon.

And this time, there was no holding back, no reticence, no control, no vestige of rational thought. Passion and desire bloomed, then ran riot. They were one—in mind, in thought, in deed. Pleasure for one was the other's delight. They gave themselves, again and again, and still found more to give.

And over and between ran the shimmering glory, stronger than steel and more precious than pearls.

When they crested the final wave, and clung to each other as the maelstrom took them, it intensified and filled them. Until all existence became that wondrous glow; as they drifted, deeply sated, into dreamless sleep, it settled over them.

A blessing—the most desired of benedictions.

What followed was entirely Myst's fault.

Vane woke, as he had once before, to discover the small cat once again curled on his chest, purring furiously. Sleepily sated, he scratched one grey ear while waiting for his senses to refocus. His limbs were heavy with deep satiation—a drugging glow still filled him. He glanced toward the window. The sky had started to lighten.

He and Patience needed to talk.

Vane lifted his hand from Myst's ear.

The cat promptly flexed her claws.

Vane hissed—and glared. "Your claws are more lethal than your mistress's."

"Hmm?" Heavy-eyed, Patience emerged from beneath the sheets.

Vane waved at Myst. "I was about to ask if you'd consider removing your resident predator."

Patience stared at him, then blinked, and looked down. "Oh. Myst." Fighting free of the tangled sheets, she leaned over and scooped Myst up. "Off, Myst. Come on." Wriggling, Patience slid fully across Vane—her hips slid over his—as Vane sucked in an agonized breath.

Patience grinned, and dropped Myst over the side of the bed. "Off you go." She watched the cat stalk off, offended, then, entirely deliberately, wriggled back across Vane.

And stopped halfway.

"Hmm." Finding her lips level with one flat nipple, she stuck out her tongue and licked. The jolt that shook him made her smile. "Interesting."

She uttered the word as she wriggled some more, so her torso was more or less atop him, her legs sliding over his.

Vane frowned. "Patience . . ."

Warm flesh encased in smooth satin slithered over his hips, over the rigid length of his erection. Vane blinked, several times, and tried to recall what he'd been about to say.

"Hmm?"

Patience's tone suggested she had other things on her mind: She was busily trailing warm, openmouthed kisses down his increasingly tense torso.

Jaw setting, Vane gathered his resolve—and reached for her. "Patience, we need to—" A groan cut off his words—he was almost surprised to recognize it as his. Muscle after muscle tensed and locked. Lust roared through him—in response to her artless, inquisitive touch, to the husky chuckle she gave. Soft fingers trailed up his rigid length, then slid about him and tentatively closed. She traced and caressed, then explored further, squirming downward as she did—clearly delighted by his helpless reaction.

Rigid to his toes, Vane jerked as she circled his sensitive, swollen head. "*Good God, woman!* What . . . ?" His voice suspended as she reached further still, and closed her hand. Vane groaned, and closed his eyes. The inside of his lids burned with raging lust.

He dragged in a desperate breath, and reached down, fighting through the tangled sheets to try to capture her hand. She chuckled again and eluded him easily; he slumped back, breathing too fast. His limbs had turned heavy, weighted with lust, burning with desire.

"Don't you like it?" The teasing question, clearly rhetorical, floated up from under the sheets. Then she squirmed again. "Perhaps you'd like this better."

Vane did, but he wasn't about to say so. Gritting his teeth, he suffered the hot, wet sweep of her tongue, the gentle caress of her lips. She didn't have the faintest idea what she was doing—thank God. What she was doing was bad enough. If expertise was added to the equation, he'd be dead.

He tried to remind himself that the experience was hardly new to him—the rationalization didn't work. He couldn't distance himself from Patience's touch, couldn't imagine she was some faceless lady with whom he was sharing a bed. No logic seemed strong enough to quench or control the fire she was igniting.

He heard himself gasp. He licked lips suddenly dry. "Where the devil did you get the idea . . . ?"

"I heard some maids talking."

Inwardly cursing all wanton maids, he summoned the last of his strength. She'd gone far enough. Jaw clenched so hard his teeth ached, he reached for her. Beneath the soft sheets, he found her head; he threaded his fingers through her hair, searching downward for her shoulders.

Beneath his hands, she shifted.

Hot wetness closed about him.

His fingers spasmed and clutched. The rest of his body reacted equally predictably. For one instant, Vane thought he'd die. Of heart failure. Then she released him. He groaned—and she took him into her mouth again. Eyes closed, he fell back on the pillows, and surrendered.

She had him at her mercy.

She knew it—she set about enjoying her newfound mastery. To the hilt. Extrapolating wantonly. Inventing with gay abandon.

Until, with a desperate groan, he was driven to expend his last ounce of strength and capture her, wrestle free, and find her waist and lift her. Over him. He lowered her, expertly nudging into the slick flesh between her thighs. Then he pulled her down, impaling her on the achingly urgent phallus she'd spent the last ten minutes inciting.

She gasped, then sank farther, her hands fastening tight about his forearms as she deliberately took him all. She rose on her knees immediately, pushing his hands from her, refusing to allow him to set the pace.

He acquiesced, filling his hands with her breasts instead, drawing the tight peaks to his mouth. She rode him with reckless abandon; he filled her and feasted, until, in a glorious, giddy rush, they fell over the edge of the world and, locked together, plunged into the selfless void.

They had no time to talk, no time to speak, no time to discuss anything at all. When, with the house waking about them, Vane, mildly irritated, left her, Patience was incapable of conscious thought.

* * *

Some four hours later, Patience sat at the breakfast table. Smiling. Glowingly. She'd seen the sight in her mirror, but hadn't been able to find any expression capable of disguising her joy.

She'd woken to find the tweeny quietly cleaning her grate, and Vane nowhere in sight. Which was undoubtedly just as well. The last sight she'd had of him would have driven the tweeny into hysterics. Lolling in her bed, which had looked like a whirlwind had struck it, she'd considered going and telling Minnie her news. But she'd decided against saying anything yet, not until she and Vane had discussed the details. From what she'd seen of the Cynsters, and what she knew of Minnie, once they made an announcement, *things* would simply happen.

So she'd lolled some more, replaying Vane's declaration, committing every word, every nuance, to memory. No doubt of the veracity, or the strength of his feelings, could ever assail her—not with memories like that. She had, indeed, started to wonder if her desire to hear that particular assurance stated, in words, might, in the end, be too much to ask, an unrealistic expectation from a man like him. Men like the Cynsters did not set their tongue to that four-letter word lightly. "Love" was not something they gave readily, and, as Minnie had warned her, even once given, they did not easily acknowledge it.

Vane had.

In simple words so laden with feeling she could not doubt, could not question. She'd wanted that, needed it, so he'd given it. No matter the cost.

Was it any wonder her heart was light, singing joyfully?

In contrast, the rest of the household remained subdued; Gerrard's empty place cast a pall over the conversation. Only Minnie and Timms, at the other end of the table, were unaffected; Patience beamed a happy smile up the board, and knew in her heart that Minnie understood.

But Minnie waggled her head at her and frowned. Recalling that she was supposed to be the anguished sister of a young sprig hauled off to face justice, Patience dutifully tried to mask her glow.

"Have you heard anything?" Henry's nod to Gerrard's empty chair clarified his question.

Patience hid her face behind her teacup. "I haven't heard of any charges."

"I fancy we'll hear by this afternoon." Whitticombe, his expression coldly severe, reached for the coffeepot. "I daresay the magistrate was not available yesterday. Theft, I fear, is a common enough crime."

Edgar shifted uneasily. Agatha Chadwick looked shocked. But no one said anything.

Henry cleared his throat, and looked at Edmond. "Where shall we go today, do you think?"

Edmond humphed. "Not really in the mood for more sights today. Think I'll dust off my script."

Henry nodded glumly.

Silence fell, then Whitticombe eased back his chair. He turned to Minnie. "By your leave, cousin, I believe Alice and I should return to Bellamy Hall." Patting his thin lips with his napkin, he laid it aside. "We are, as you know, somewhat rigid in our beliefs. Old-fashioned, some might call it. But neither my dear sister nor I can countenance close association with those we believe transgress acceptable moral codes." He paused long enough for his meaning to sink in, then smiled, unctuously patronizing, at Minnie. "Of course, we appreciate your position, even applaud your devotion, misguided though it sadly seems to be. However, Alice and I seek your permission to repair to the Hall, there to await your return."

He concluded with an obsequious nod.

Everyone looked at Minnie. There was, however, nothing to be read in her unusually closed expression. She studied Whitticombe for a full minute, then solemnly nodded. "If that is what you wish, then certainly, you may return to the Hall. However, I warn you I do not have any immediate plans to return there myself."

Whitticombe raised his hand in a gracious gesture. "You need not concern yourself with us, cousin. Alice and I can entertain ourselves well enough." He glanced at Alice, all in black. At no time since she'd entered the room had she looked anywhere but at her plate. "With your permission," Whitticombe continued, "we'll leave immediately. The weather looks like turning, and we have no reason to dally." He glanced at Minnie, then looked up at Masters, standing behind her chair. "Our boxes could be sent on."

Minnie nodded. Tight-lipped, she glanced up at Masters, who bowed. "I'll arrange it, ma'am."

Bestowing a last unctuous, ingratiating smile on Minnie, Whitticombe rose. "Come, Alice. You'll need to pack."

Without a word, without a glance, Alice rose and preceded Whitticombe from the room.

The instant the door closed behind them, Patience looked at Minnie. Who waved her to silence. To some semblance of discretion.

Patience bit her lip, and munched her toast, and waited.

A few minutes later, Minnie heaved a sigh and pushed back her chair. "Ah, me. I'm going to rest for the morning. All these unexpected happenings." Shaking her head, she rose and looked down the table. "Patience?"

She didn't need to be summoned twice. Dropping her napkin on her plate, Patience hurried to assist Timms help Minnie from the room. They went straight to Minnie's bedchamber, summoning Sligo on the way.

He arrived as Minnie sank into her chair.

"Whitticombe's making a dash for the Hall." Minnie pointed her cane at Sligo. "Go fetch that godson of mine—fast!" She shot a glance at Patience. "I don't care if you have to drag him from his bed, just tell him our hare has finally bolted."

"Indeed, ma'am. Right away, ma'am." Sligo headed for the door. "Even in his nightshirt."

Minnie grinned grimly. "Right!" She thumped the floor with her cane. "And not before time." She looked up at Patience. "If it does turn out to be that worm, Whitticombe, behind it all, I'll disown him utterly."

Patience gripped the hand Minnie held out to her. "Let's wait and see what Vane thinks."

There was one problem with that—Vane couldn't be found.

Sligo returned to Aldford Street an hour later, with the news Vane was not at any of his habitual haunts. Minnie sent Sligo back out with a flea in his ear and a dire warning not to return without Vane.

"Where could he be?" Minnie looked at Patience.

Mystified, Patience shook her head. "I'd assumed he'd gone home—to Curzon Street."

She frowned. He couldn't possibly be walking the streets with a creased, reused cravat. Not Vane Cynster.

"He gave you no hint as to any lead he might be following?" Timms asked.

Patience grimaced. "I was under the impression he'd run out of possiblities."

Minnie humphed. "So was I. So *where* is he?"

No one answered. And Sligo didn't return.

Not until late afternoon, by which time Minnie, Timms, and Patience had reached the end of their collective tether. Whitticombe and Alice had departed at noon in a hired carriage. Their boxes were piled in the front hall, awaiting the carter. Lunch had come and gone, the household marginally more relaxed. Edmond and Henry were playing billiards. The General and Edgar had taken their usual constitutional to Tattersalls. Edith was tatting with Mrs. Chadwick and Angela for company in the drawing room.

In Minnie's room, Patience and Timms took turns by the window; it was Patience who saw Vane's curricle bowl up and stop before the door. "He's here!"

"Well you can't run downstairs," Minnie admonished her. "Just contain your transports until he gets here. *I* want to hear where he's *been*."

Minutes later, Vane strolled in, smoothly elegant as ever. His eyes went straight to Patience, then he bent and kissed Minnie's cheek.

"Where, by all that's holy, have you *been*?" she demanded.

Vane raised his brows. "Out. Sligo told me Whitticombe's left. What did you want to see me for?"

Minnie stared at him, then swiped at his leg with one hand. "To find out what comes *next*, of course!" She glared at him. "Don't try your high-handed Cynster ways with me."

Vane's brows rose higher. "I wouldn't dream of it. But there's no need for any panic. Whitticombe and Alice have gone—I'll follow, and see what they get up to. Simple."

"I'm coming, too," Minnie declared. "If Humphrey's nephew's a bad egg, I owe it to Humphrey to see the proof with my own eyes. After all, it's me who'll have to decide what to do."

"Of course, I'll go with Minnie," Timms added.

Patience caught Vane's eye. "If you think I'm staying behind, think again. Gerrard's my brother—if Whitticombe's the one who knocked him on the head . . ." She didn't finish her sentence—her expression said it all.

Vane sighed. "There's really no need—"

"Cynster! Have to show you—"

With a clatter of boots, the General, followed by Edgar, burst into the room. Seeing Minnie, the General flushed, and ducked his head. "Apologies, Minnie, and all that, but thought you'd all be interested. Best see this."

Crossing the room, he bent and awkwardly slid a small object from his large palm onto Minnie's lap.

"Great *heavens*!" Minnie picked the object up, and held it to the light. "Agatha's earring." She looked at the General. "The other one?"

"Must be," Edgar put in. He glanced at Vane. "We found it in the elephant sitting in the front hall."

"The *elephant*?" Vane looked from Edgar to the General.

"Indian contraption. Recognized it instantly. Seen ones like it in India, don't y'know." The General nodded. "Couldn't resist opening it—showed it to Edgar here. One of the tusks is the catch. Twist it, and the beast's back opens up. Indian wallahs used the things to store treasure."

"It's full of sand," Edgar said. "Fine, white stuff."

"Used for weight," the General explained. "The sand stabilizes the beast, then the treasure's settled in the sand. I grabbed up a handful to show Edgar—sharp eyes, he has—spotted the gleam of that trinket in the pile."

"I'm afraid we made rather a mess unearthing it." Edgar looked at the earring in Minnie's fingers. "But it is Agatha's, isn't it?"

"Isn't what?"

They all looked up; Mrs. Chadwick entered, followed by Angela, with Edith Swithins trailing vaguely behind. Agatha Chadwick grimaced apologetically at Minnie. "We heard the commotion . . ."

"Just as well." Minnie held up the earring. "This is yours, I believe."

Agatha took it. The smile that broke across her face was all the answer anyone needed. "Where was it?" She looked at Minnie—who looked up at Vane.

Who shook his head in amazement. "In Alice Colby's room, in the elephant she kept by her hearth." He glanced at Patience—

"There's sand all over the front hall!" Mrs. Henderson swept in, a galleon in full sail; Henry, supported by Edmond and Masters, hobbled in in her wake. Mrs. Henderson gestured at him. "Mister Chadwick slipped and nearly broke his head." She looked at Vane. "It's from *inside* that evil elephant!"

"I say." Edmond had focused on the earring in Agatha Chadwick's hand. "What's going on?"

The question drew a spate of garbled answers. Recognizing opportunity, Vane edged to the door.

"Stop right there!" Minnie's order brought an abrupt end to the cacophony. She waved her cane at Vane. "Don't you *dare* try to leave us behind."

Patience swung about—and glared daggers at Vane.

"What's afoot?" Edmond demanded.

Minnie folded her arms and snorted, then glared at Vane. Everyone turned and looked at Vane.

He sighed. "It's like this." His explanation—that whoever attempted to return to the Hall without the rest of the household was odds on to be the Spectre, and said Spectre was almost certainly the villain who'd coshed Gerrard in the ruins—even stripped to the bare bones, still raised everyone's hackles.

"Colby! *Well*!" Henry straightened, and eased his full weight onto his wrenched ankle. "First, he coshes young Gerrard, then he makes out Gerrard's the thief, and *then* he gloats so . . . so . . . *superiorly*." He tugged his coat straight. "You may count me in—I certainly want to see Whitticombe get his just desserts."

"Blissful thought!" Edmond grinned. "I'll come, too."

"And me." The General glowered. "Colby must have known his sister was the thief—or perhaps it was him, and he used his sister's room as a store. Whatever, the bounder talked me into sending for the Runners—wouldn't have entered my head but for him. He should be strung up!"

Vane drew a deep breath. "There's really no need—"

"I'm coming, too." Agatha Chadwick lifted her head high. "Whoever was the thief, whoever has so grievously wronged Gerrard, I want to see justice done!"

"Indeed!" Edith Swithins nodded determinedly. "I even had my tatting bag searched, all because of this thief. I'll certainly want to hear his—or her—explanation."

It was at that point Vane gave up arguing. By the time he'd crossed the room to Minnie's side, the whole household, bar only Masters and Mrs. Henderson, had resolved to follow Whitticombe and Alice back to the Hall.

Bending over Minnie, Vane spoke through his teeth. "I'm taking Patience—I'll pick Gerrard up on the way. As far as I'm concerned, the rest of you would do well to remain in London. If you want to hie across the counties with the weather closing in, you'll have to organize it yourselves. *However*!"—he let his exasperation show—"whatever you do, *for God's sake remember* to come up the back track, *not* the main drive, and *don't* come closer to the house than the second barn."

He glared at Minnie, who glared belligerently back. Then tipped her nose in the air. "We'll wait for you there."

Swallowing a curse, Vane grabbed Patience's hand and strode for the door. In the corridor, he glanced at Patience's gown. "You'll need your pelisse. There's snow on the way."

Patience nodded. "I'll meet you outside."

She hurried down the steps minutes later, rugged up against the deepening chill. Vane handed her into the curricle, then climbed up beside her. And sprang his horses for Grosvenor Square.

"Well, the drought's broken." Looking up as Vane walked through his library door, Devil grinned. "Who is it?"

"Colby." Vane nodded to Gerrard, perched on the arm of a chair beside Devil, who was sprawled on the rug before the hearth.

Following Vane in, Patience noted that last with surprise, until, moving closer, she saw the small being rolling on the soft rug, fists and feet waving madly, protected from any chance of a flying cinder by Devil's large body.

Following the direction of her gaze, Devil grinned. "Allow me to present Sebastian, Marquess of Earith." He looked down. "My heir."

The last words were infused with such deep and abiding love, Patience found herself smiling mistily. Devil scratched the baby's tummy; Sebastian cooed and gurgled and batted clumsily at his father's finger. Blinking rapidly, Patience glanced at Vane. He was smiling easily—he clearly found nothing odd in the sight of his powerful, domineering cousin playing nursemaid.

She looked at Gerrard; he laughed as Sebastian latched on to Devil's finger and wrestled.

"Vane?" All turned as Honoria swept into the room. "Ah—Patience." As if they were already related, Honoria enveloped Patience in a scented embrace and touched cheeks. "What's happened?"

Vane brought them up-to-date. Honoria sank onto the *chaise* beside Devil. Patience noted that, after a quick glance to check, Honoria left Sebastian in Devil's care. Until, recognizing her voice as she questioned Vane, Sebastian lost interest in Devil's finger and, with a cry, waved his arms for his mother. Devil passed his heir over, then glanced at Vane.

"Is Colby likely to prove dangerous?"

Vane shook his head. "Not in our terms."

Patience didn't need to ask what their terms were. Devil got to his feet, and the room shrank. It was clear that, if Vane had said there'd be danger, Devil would have accompanied them. Instead, he grinned at Vane. "We're going back to the Place tomorrow. Head our way once you've finished tidying up for Minnie."

"Indeed." Honoria seconded her husband's edict. "We'll need to discuss the arrangements."

Patience stared at her. Honoria smiled, openly affectionate. Both Devil and Vane shot Honoria, then Patience, identical, unreadable, masculine looks, then exchanged a long-suffering glance.

"I'll see you out." Devil gestured to the hall.

Honoria came, too, Sebastian at her shoulder. While they stood chatting, waiting for Gerrard to fetch his coat, the baby, bored, fell to tugging Honoria's earring. Noticing his wife's difficulty, without pausing in his discussion with Vane, Devil reached out, scooped his heir out of Honoria's arms, and settled Sebastian against his chest, so the diamond pin anchoring his cravat was level with the baby's eyes.

Sebastian cooed, and happily grasped the winking pin in a chubby fist—and proceeded to destroy what had been a perfectly tied *Trone d'Amour*. Patience blinked, but neither Devil, Vane, nor Honoria seemed to find anything remarkable in the sight.

An hour later, as London fell behind and Vane whipped up his horses, Patience was still mulling over Devil, his wife, and his son. And the atmosphere that hung, a warm, welcoming glow, throughout their elegant house. Family—family feeling, family affection—of the sort the Cynsters took for granted, was something she'd never known.

Having a family like that was her dearest, deepest, wildest dream.

She glanced at Vane, beside her, his eyes fixed on the road, his face a mask of concentration as he drove his horses into the lowering night. Patience smiled softly. With him, her dream would come true; she'd made her decision—she knew it was right. To see him with their son, lounging by the fire like Devil, caring without even stopping to think—that was her new aim.

It was his aim, too—she knew without asking. He was a Cynster—that was their code. Family. The most important thing in their lives.

Vane glanced down. "Are you warm enough?"

Wedged between him and Gerrard, with, at his insistence, two rugs tucked firmly around her, she was in no danger of taking a chill. "I'm fine." She smiled, and snuggled closer. "Just drive."

He grunted, and did.

About them, an eerie twilight fell; thick, swirling clouds, pale grey, hung low. The air was bitter, the wind laced with ice.

Vane's powerful greys drew the curricle on, wheels rolling smoothly over the macadam. They raced through the evening, into the night.

On toward Bellamy Hall, to the last act in the long drama,

to the final curtain call for the Spectre and their mysterious thief. So they could bring the curtain down, send the players on their way—and then get on with living their lives.

Creating their dream.

Chapter 22

Ⓘt was full dark when Vane eased his horses off the road onto the back track leading to the Bellamy Hall stables. The night had turned icy, crisply chill; the horses's breaths steamed in the still air.

"The fog will be heavy tonight," Vane whispered.

Beside him, pressed close, Patience nodded.

The back barn, second of two, loomed ahead; Vane uttered a silent prayer. It went unanswered. As he rolled the curricle to a halt just inside the barn, he saw Minnie's menagerie milling at the other entrance, peering toward the main barn, the stables, and the house beyond. They were all there, even, he noted, glimpsing a grey shadow darting about, Myst. He jumped to the ground, then lifted Patience down. The others came hurrying up, Myst in the lead.

Leaving Patience to deal with Minnie and the rest, Vane helped Duggan and Gerrard stable the greys. Then, grim-faced, he returned to the whispering group thronging the barn's center.

Minnie immediately stated, "If you're entertaining the notion of ordering us to wait in this drafty barn, you may save your breath."

Her belligerence was reflected in her stance and was echoed by the usually practical Timms, who nodded direfully. Every member of Minnie's ill-assorted ménage was likewise imbued with decisive determination.

The General summed up their mood. "Blighter's kinged it over us all—need to see him exposed, don't y'know."

Vane scanned their faces, his features set. "Very well." He spoke through clenched teeth. "But if any of you makes the *slightest* sound, or are so witless as to alert Colby or Alice to our presence *before* we've gained sufficient details to prove beyond doubt who the Spectre and the thief are . . ."—he let the moment stretch as he scanned their faces—"they'll answer to me. Is that understood?"

A flurry of nodding heads replied.

"You'll need to do exactly as I say." He looked pointedly at Edmond and Henry. "No bright ideas, no sudden elaborations to the plan."

Edmond nodded. "Right."

"Indubitably," Henry swore.

Vane glanced around again. They all looked back, meek and earnest. He gritted his teeth and grabbed Patience's hand. "Come on, then. And *no* talking."

He strode for the main barn. Halfway there, shielded from the house by the bulk of the stables, he halted, and, rigidly impatient, waited for the others to catch up.

"Don't walk on the gravel or on the paths," he instructed. "Keep to the grass. It's foggy; sound travels well in fog. We can't assume they're snug in the parlor—they might be in the kitchen, or even outside."

He turned and strode on, blocking out all thoughts of how Minnie was coping. She wouldn't thank him, and, at the moment, he needed to concentrate on other things.

Like where Grisham was.

Leading Patience, with Gerrard close behind, he reached the stables. Grisham's quarters gave off it. "Wait here," Vane whispered, his lips close by Patience's ear. "Stop the others here. I'll return in a moment."

With that, he slid into the shadows. The last thing he wanted was Grisham imagining they were intruders and sounding the alarm.

But Grisham's room was empty; Vane rejoined his ill-assorted hunting party at the rear of the dark stables. Duggan had checked the grooms' rooms. He shook his head and mouthed, "No one here." Vane nodded. Minnie had mentioned she'd given most of the staff leave.

"We'll try the side door." They could force the window of the back parlor—that wing was farthest from the library, Whittcombe's favorite bolt-hole. "Follow me, not too close together. And remember—*no sound*."

They all nodded mutely.

Swallowing a futile curse, Vane made for the shrubbery. The high hedges and grassed paths eased his mind of one worry, but as he and Patience, Duggan and Gerrard at their backs, neared the place where the hedges gave way to open lawn, a light flashed across their path.

They froze. The light disappeared.

"Wait here." On the whisper, Vane edged forward until he could look across the lawn. Beyond lay the house, the side door closed. But a light was bobbing up from the ruins—the Spectre was walking tonight.

The light rose again briefly; in its beam, Vane saw a large, dark figure lumbering along the side of the lawn, heading their way.

"Back!" he hissed, pushing Patience, who'd edged up to his shoulder, into the hedge behind him. In the lee of the hedge, he waited, counting the seconds, then the lumbering figure swung into the path—and was upon them.

Vane grabbed him in a headlock; Duggan clung to one muscled arm. The figure tensed to fight.

"Cynster!" Vane hissed, and the figure went limp.

"Thank Gawd!" Grisham blinked at them. Vane released him. Looking down the path, Vane was mollified to see that the rest of the party had frozen, strung out in the shadows. Now, however, they clustered closer.

"I didn't know what to do." Grisham rubbed his neck.

Vane checked; the carrier of the bobbing light was still some distance away, negotiating the tumbled stones. He turned back to Grisham. "What happened?"

"The Colbys arrived late afternoon. I figured it was the sign we was watching for. I told 'em straight off there was only me and two maids in the house—if anything, Colby seemed well pleased. He had me make up the fire in the library, then called for dinner early. After that, he told us we could retire, as if he was doing us a favor an'all." Grisham snorted softly. "I kept a close eye on 'em, of course. They waited a while, then took one of the library lamps and headed for the ruins."

Grisham glanced back. Vane checked, then nodded for him to continue. They still had a few minutes before whispers became too dangerous.

"They went all the way across to the abbot's lodge." Grisham grinned. "I stayed close. Miss Colby grumbled all the way, but I wasn't near enough to make out what she said. Colby went straight for that stone I told you about." Grisham nodded at Vane. "Checked it over real careful-like, making sure no one had lifted it. He was right pleased with himself after that. They started back then—I came on ahead, so's I'd be here to see what's next."

Vane raised his brows. "What indeed?"

The light flashed again, much closer now—everyone froze. Vane clung to the edge of the hedge, aware of Patience pressed to his side. The others edged closer, wedged together so they could all see the section of lawn before the side door.

"It's not *fair*! I don't see *why* you had to give back my treasure." Alice Colby's disgruntled whine floated on the frosty air. "You're going to get *your* treasure, but *I* won't have anything!"

"I told you those things weren't yours!" Whitticombe's tone turned from aggravated to scathing. "I would have thought you'd have learned after last time. I won't have you caught with things that *aren't yours*. The very idea of being branded the brother of a thief!"

"Your treasure isn't yours *either*!"

"That's different." Whitticombe stumped into view before the side door; he looked around at Alice, trailing after him. And sniffed contemptuously. "At least, this time, I could put your little foible to some use. It was just what I needed to deflect Cynster's attention. While he's getting young Debbington cleared, I'll have the time I need to complete my work."

"*Work*?" Alice's contempt matched Whitticombe's. "You're obsessed with this foolish treasure hunt. Is it here, or is it there?" she parroted in a singsong voice.

Whitticombe threw open the door. "Just go inside."

Still singing her little ditty, Alice walked in.

Vane looked at Grisham. "Run like the devil—through the

kitchen, into the old parlor behind the library. We'll come to the windows."

Grisham nodded and set off at a run.

Vane turned to the others; they all looked at him in mute expectation. He set his teeth. "We're going to backtrack, quickly and quietly, around the house to the terrace. On the terrace, we'll have to be especially quiet—Whitticombe will probably make for the library. We need to know more about this treasure of his, and whether he was, indeed, the one who struck Gerrard."

As one, they all nodded. Resisting a strong urge to groan, Vane, Patience's hand locked in his, led the way back through the shrubbery.

They picked their way along the verge bordering the carriage drive, then gingerly climbed to the terrace flags. Myst, a swift shadow, ran ahead; Vane silently cursed—and prayed the fiendish animal would behave.

Grisham was waiting, a wraith at the long parlor windows. He eased back the catch—Vane stepped in, then helped Patience over the raised sill.

"They're arguing in the hall," Grisham whispered, "over who owns some elephant or other."

Vane nodded. He looked back and saw Timms and Edmond help Minnie in. Turning, he strode to the wall—and opened a door concealed in the paneling—revealing the back of another door, set into the paneling of the next room, the library. His hand on the latch of the second door, Vane glanced, frowning, over his shoulder.

The assembled company obediently held their breaths.

Vane eased opened the door.

The library was empty, lit only by the flames dancing in the hearth.

Scanning the room, Vane saw two large, four-paneled screens, used during summer to protect the old tomes from sunlight. The screens hadn't been folded away; they stood open, parallel to the fireplace, effectively screening the area before the hearth from the terrace windows.

Stepping back, Vane drew Patience to him. Nodding to the screens, he gently pushed her through the door. Quickly, her gaze on the library door, she scooted across the floor, blessedly covered in a long Turkish rug, and took refuge behind the farthest screen.

Before Vane could blink, Gerrard followed his sister.

Vane glanced back, nodded the others toward the room, then followed his brother-in-law-to-be.

When footsteps fell outside the library door, the entire company, barring only Grisham, who'd elected to remain in the parlor, were all crammed behind the two screens, eyes glued to the fine slits between the panels.

Vane prayed no one would sneeze.

The door handle turned; Whitticombe led the way in, his expression disdainful. "It matters not who *owned* the elephant. The fact is, the goods *inside it* weren't *yours*!"

"But *I* wanted them!" Face mottled, Alice clenched her fists. "The others lost them, and they became mine—but you took them away! You always take my things away!"

"That's because they're not yours to begin with!" Grinding his teeth, Whitticombe pushed Alice into the chair by the fire. "Just sit there and keep quiet!"

"I will *not* keep quiet!" Alice's eyes blazed. "You always tell me I can't have things I want—that it's wrong to take them— but you're going to take the abbey treasure. And *that* doesn't belong to *you*!"

"*It's not the same!*" Whitticombe thundered. He fixed Alice with a baleful eye. "I know the distinction is hard for you to grasp, but retrieving—resurrecting—lost church plate—restoring the magnificence of Coldchurch Abbey—is not the same as *stealing*!"

"But you want it all for *yourself*!"

"*No!*" Whitticombe forced himself to draw a calming breath, and lowered his voice. "*I* want to be the one to *find* it. I fully intend to hand it over to the proper authorities, *but . . .*" He lifted his head and straightened. "The *fame* of finding it, the glory of being the one who, through his tireless scholarship, traced and restored the lost plate of Coldchurch Abbey—*that*," he declared, "will be *mine*."

Behind the screen, Patience caught Vane's eye. He smiled grimly.

"All very well," Alice grumped. "But you needn't make out

you're such a saint. Nothing saintly about hitting that fool boy with a rock."

Whitticombe stilled. He stared down at Alice.

Who smirked. "Didn't think I knew, did you. But I was in dear Patience's room at the time and chanced to look out over the ruins." She smiled maliciously. "I saw you do it—saw you pick up the rock, then creep up close. Saw you strike him down."

She sat back, her gaze fixed on Whitticombe's face. "Oh, no, dear brother, *you're* no saint."

Whitticombe sniffed, and waved dismissively. "Just a concussion—I didn't hit him that hard. Just enough to make sure he never finished that sketch." He started to pace. "When I think of the shock I got when I saw him poking about the abbot's cellar door! It's a wonder I didn't hit him too hard. If he'd been more curious, and mentioned it to one of those other dunderheads—Chadwick, Edmond, or, heaven forbid, Edgar—Lord knows what might have happened. The fools might have stolen my discovery!"

"*Your* discovery?"

"*Mine*! The glory will be *mine*!" Whitticombe paced on. "As it is, everything's worked out perfectly. That tap on the head was enough to scare the old woman into taking her precious nephew off to London—mercifully, she took all the others as well. So now—tomorrow—I can hire some itinerants to help me lift that stone, and then—!"

Triumphant, Whitticombe whirled—and froze.

All those peeking through the screens saw him, hand upraised as if to exhort adulation, staring, goggle-eyed, into the shadows at the side of the room. Everyone tensed. No one could see, or imagine, what he was staring at.

His mouth started to work first, opening and closing to no effect. Then: "*Aaarrrrgh!!!*" His face a mask of abject horror, Whitticombe pointed. "*What's that cat doing here?*"

Alice looked, then frowned at him. "That's Myst. Patience's cat."

"I *know*." Whitticombe's voice shook; his gaze didn't shift.

Risking a glance around the screen, Vane sighted Myst, sitting neatly erect, her ancient, all-seeing blue gaze fixed, unwinking, on Whitticombe's face.

"But it was in *London*!" Whitticombe gasped. "How did it get here?"

Alice shrugged. "It didn't come down with us."

"*I know that*!"

Someone choked on a laugh; the second screen wobbled, then teetered. A hand appeared at the top and righted it, then disappeared.

Vane sighed, and stepped out, around the other screen. Whitticombe's eyes, which Vane would have sworn could not get any wider, did.

"Evening, Colby." Vane waved Minnie forward; the others followed.

As the company assembled in full sight, Alice chortled. "So much for your secrets, dear brother." She sank back in her chair, grinning maliciously, clearly unconcerned by her own misdemeanors.

Whitticombe threw her a swift glance and drew himself up. "I don't know how much you heard—"

"All of it," Vane replied.

Whitticombe blanched—and glanced at Minnie.

Who stared at him, disgust and disaffection clear in her face. "Why?" she demanded. "You had a roof over your head and a comfortable living. Was fame so important you would commit crimes—and for what? A foolish dream?"

Whitticombe stiffened. "It's *not* a foolish dream. The church plate and the abbey's treasure were buried before the Dissolution. There's clear reference made in the abbey records—but after the Dissolution there's no mention of it at all. It took me forever to track down where they'd hidden it—the crypt was the obvious place, but there's nothing but rubble there. And the records clearly state a cellar, but the old cellars were excavated long ago—and nothing was found." He drew himself up, inflated with self-importance. "Only *I* traced the abbot's cellar. It's there—I found the trapdoor." He looked at Minnie, avaricious hope lighting his eyes. "You'll see—tomorrow. Then you'll understand." Confidence renewed, he nodded.

Bleakly, Minnie shook her head. "I'll never understand, Whitticombe."

Edgar cleared his throat. "And I'm afraid you won't find anything, either. There's nothing to be found."

Whitticombe's lip curled. "Dilettante," he scoffed. "What would you know of research?"

Edgar shrugged. "I don't know about research, but I do know about the Bellamys. The last abbot was one—not in name—but he became the grandfather of the next generation. And he told his grandsons of the buried treasure—the tale was passed on until, at the Restoration, a Bellamy asked for and was granted the old abbey's lands."

Edgar smiled vaguely at Minnie. "The treasure is all around us." He gestured to the walls, the ceiling. "That first Bellamy of Bellamy Hall dug up the plate and treasure as soon as he set foot on his new lands—he sold them, and used the proceeds to build the Hall, and to provide the foundation for the future wealth of the family."

Meeting Whitticombe's stunned stare, Edgar smiled. "The treasure's been here, in plain sight, all along."

"No," Whitticombe said, but there was no strength in his denial.

"Oh, yes," Vane replied, his gaze hard. "If you'd asked, I—or Grisham—could have told you the abbot's cellar was filled in more than a hundred years ago. All you'll find under that trapdoor is solid earth."

Whitticombe continued to stare, then his eyes glazed.

"I rather think, Colby, that it's time for some apologies, what?" The General glared at Whitticombe.

Whitticombe blinked, then stiffened, and lifted his head arrogantly. "I don't see that I've done anything particularly reprehensible—not by the standards of *this* company." Features contorting, he scanned the others. And gestured disdainfully. "There's Mrs. Agatha Chadwick, struggling to bury a nincompoop of a husband and settle a daughter with not two wits to her name and a son not much better. And Edmond Montrose—a poet and dramatist with so much flair he never accomplishes anything. And we mustn't forget you, must we?" Whitticombe glared vituperatively at the General. "A General with no troops, who was nothing but a sergeant major in a dusty barracks, if truth be known. And we shouldn't forget Miss Edith Swithins, so sweet, so mild—oh, no. Don't forget her, and the fact she's consorting with Edgar, the rambling historian, and thinking no one knows. At her age!"

Whitticombe poured out his scorn. "And last but not least," he pronounced with relish, "we have Miss Patience Debbington, our esteemed hostess's niece—"

Crunnnch! Whitticombe sailed backward and landed on the floor, some yards away.

Patience, who'd been standing beside Vane, quickly stepped forward—to come up with Vane, who'd stepped forward as he delivered the blow that had lifted Whitticombe from his feet.

Clutching Vane's arm, Patience looked down—and prayed Whitticombe had the sense to stay down. She could feel the steel in the muscles beneath her fingers. If Whitticombe was foolish enough to fight back, Vane would demolish him.

Stunned, Whitticombe blinked back to full consciousness. As the others gathered about, he raised one hand to his jaw. And winced. "Assault!" he croaked.

"The battery might yet follow." The warning—entirely un-neccessary from Patience's perspective—came from Vane. One look at his face, as hard as granite and equally unyielding, would have informed any sane person of that fact.

Whitticombe stared—then he scanned the circle about him. "He hit me!"

"Did he?" Edmond opened his eyes wide. "Didn't see it myself." He looked at Vane. "Would you care to do it again?"

"No!" Whitticombe looked shocked.

"Why not?" the General inquired. "A sound thrashing—do you good. Might even knock some sense into you. Here—we'll all come and watch. Ensure fair play and all that. No blows below the belt, what?"

The horrified look on Whitticombe's face as he gazed around the circle of faces—and found not one showing the slightest glimmer of sympathy—would have been comic if any had been in the mood to be amused. When his gaze returned to Vane, he sucked in a breath, and sniveled: "Don't hit me."

Narrow-eyed, Vane looked down at him, and shook his head. His battle-ready tension eased; he stepped back. "A coward—through and through."

The verdict was greeted with nods and humphs of agreement. Duggan pushed forward and grasped Whitticombe by the collar. He hauled the miserable figure upright. Duggan looked at Vane. "I'll lock him in the cellar, shall I?"

Vane looked at Minnie. Tight-lipped, she nodded.

Alice, who had watched it all, face alight with vindictive glee, laughed and waved at Whitticombe. "Off you go, brother! You wanted to look at a cellar all these months—enjoy it while you can." Cackling, she slumped back in her chair.

Agatha Chadwick laid a hand on Minnie's arm. "Allow me." With considerable dignity, she descended on Alice. "Angela."

For once, Angela did not drag her heels. Joining her mother, her face a mask of determination, she grasped Alice's other arm; together, they hoisted Alice to her feet.

"Come along, now." Mrs. Chadwick turned to the door.

Alice glanced from one to the other. "Did you bring my elephant? It *is* mine, you know."

"It's on its way from London." Agatha Chadwick glanced at Minnie. "We'll lock her in her room."

Minnie nodded.

All watched the trio pass through the door. The instant it closed behind them, the iron that had kept Minnie's spine straight for the past hours dissolved. She slumped against Timms. Vane softly cursed—without requesting permission, he scooped Minnie up in his arms and gently eased her into the chair Alice had vacated.

Minnie smiled tremulously up at him. "I'm all right—just a bit rattled." She grinned. "But I enjoyed seeing Whitticombe fly through the air."

Relieved to see that grin, Vane stepped back, letting Patience get closer. Edith Swithins, likewise at the end of her resources, was being solicitously helped into the second armchair by Edgar.

As she sank down, she, too, smiled at Vane. "I've never seen any fisticuffs before—it was quite exciting." Rummaging in her bag, she retrieved two bottles of smelling salts. She handed Minnie one. "I thought I'd lost this one years ago, but lo and behold, it turned up at the top of my bag last week."

Edith sniffed from her bottle, eyes twinkling at Vane.

Who discovered he could still blush. He glanced around; the General and Gerrard had been conferring—the General looked up. "Just discussing the dispositions, what? No staff here—and we haven't dined yet."

The observation got them all moving, lighting fires, making up beds, and preparing and serving a hot, sustaining dinner.

Grisham, Duggan, and the two maids assisted, but everyone, bar only Alice and Whitticombe, readily contributed their share.

As no fire had been lit in the drawing room, the ladies remained at the table while the port did the rounds. The glow of common experience, of camaraderie, was evident as they shared thoughts of the past weeks.

At the end, as yawns started to interrupt their reminiscences, Timms turned to Minnie. "What will you do with them?"

Everyone quieted. Minnie grimaced. "They really are pitiful. I'll speak to them tomorrow, but, in all Christian charity, I can't throw them out. At least not at the moment, not into the snow."

"Snow?" Edmond raised his head, then rose and pulled back one of the drapes. Fine flakes swirled across the beam of light shining out. "Well, fancy that."

Vane did not fancy that. He had plans—a heavy fall of snow was not part of them. He glanced at Patience, seated beside him. Then he smiled, and quaffed the last of his port.

Fate couldn't be that cruel.

He was the last to climb the stairs, after walking a last round about the huge house. All was silent, all was still. It seemed the only other life in the old house was Myst, darting up the stairs before him. The small cat had elected to follow him on his round, weaving about his boots, then dashing into the shadows. He'd walked out of the side door to study the sky. Myst had disappeared into the dark, only to return a few minutes later, sneezing snowflakes off her pink nose, shaking them disdainfully from her fur.

His thoughts in the future, Vane followed Myst up the stairs, through the gallery, down one flight, and along the corridor. He reached his room and opened the door; Myst darted through.

Vane grinned and followed—then remembered he'd meant to go to Patience's room. He looked around, to call Myst back— and saw Patience, dozing in the chair by the fire.

Lips curving, Vane closed the door. Myst woke Patience before he reached her—she looked up, then smiled, rose—and walked straight into his arms. He closed them about her.

Eyes shining, she looked into his. "I love you."

Vane's lips lifted as he bent to kiss her. "I know."

Patience returned the gentle caress. "Was I that obvious?"

"Yes." Vane kissed her again. "That part of the equation

was never in doubt." Briefly, his lips brushed hers. "Nor was the rest of it. Not from the moment I first held you in my arms."

The rest of it—his part of the equation—his feelings for her.

Patience drew back so she could study his face. She lifted a hand to his cheek. "I needed to know."

The planes of his face shifted; desire flared in his eyes. "Now you do." He lowered his head and kissed her again. "Incidentally, don't ever forget it."

Already breathless, Patience chuckled. "You'll have to make sure you remind me."

"Oh, I will. Every morning and every night."

The words were a vow—a promise. Patience found his lips with hers and kissed him until she was witless. Chuckling, Vane lifted his head. Wrapping one arm around her, he steered her to the bed. "Theoretically, you shouldn't be here."

"Why? What's the difference—your bed or mine?"

"Quite a lot, by servants' standards. They'll accept the sight of gentlemen wandering the house in the early hours, but for some reason, the sight of ladies flitting through the dawn in their nightgowns incites rampant speculation."

"Ah," Patience said, as they halted by the bed. "But I'll be fully clothed." She gestured to her gown. "There'll be no reason for speculation."

Vane met her gaze. "What about your hair?"

"My hair?" Patience blinked. "You'll just have to help me put it up again. I assume 'elegant gentlemen,' such as you, learn such useful skills very early in life."

"Actually, no." Straight-faced, Vane reached for her pins. "Us rakes-of-the-first-order . . ." Dropping pins left and right, he set her hair cascading down. With a satisfied smile, he caught her about the waist and drew her hard against him. "We," he said, looking into her eyes, "spend our time concentrating on rather different skills—like letting ladies' hair down. And getting them out of their clothes. Getting them into bed. And other things."

He demonstrated—very effectively.

As he spread her thighs and sank deeply into her, Patience's breath fractured on a gasp.

He moved within her, claiming her, pressing deep, only to withdraw and fill her again. Arms braced, he reared above her, and loved her; beneath him, Patience writhed. When he bent his head and found her lips, she clung to the caress, clung to the moment. Clung to him.

Their lips parted, and she sighed. And felt his words against her lips as he moved deeply within her.

"With my body, I thee worship. With my heart, I thee adore. I love you. And if you want me to say it a thousand times, I will. Just as long as you'll be my wife."

"I will." Patience heard the words in her head, tasted them on her lips—she felt them resonate in her heart.

The next hour passed, and not a single coherent phrase passed their lips. The warm stillness within the room was broken only by the rustling of sheets, and soft, urgent murmurs. Then the silence gave way to soft moans, groans, breathless pants, desperate gasps. Culminating in a soft, piercingly sweet scream, dying, sobbing, into a deep guttural groan.

Outside, the moon rose; inside, the fire died.

Wrapped in each other's arms, limbs and hearts entwined, they slept.

"Bye!" Gerrard stood on the front steps and, smiling hugely, waved them away.

With a cheery wave, Patience faced forward, settling herself under the thick rug. The rug Vane had insisted she needed in order to go driving with him. She glanced at him. "You aren't going to fuss over me, are you?"

"Who? Me?" He threw her an uncomprehending glance. "Perish the thought."

"Good." Patience tipped her head back and looked at the sky, still threatening snow. "There's really no need—I'm perfectly accustomed to looking after myself."

Vane kept his eyes on his horses's ears.

Patience slanted him another glance. "Incidentally, I meant to mention . . ." When he merely raised an inquiring brow, and kept his gaze forward, she put her nose in the air and baldly stated, "If you dare, ever, to go into a conservatory with a beautiful woman, even if she's related—even a first cousin—I will not be held accountable for the outcome."

That got her a glance, a mildly curious one.

"Outcome?"

"The fracas that will inevitably ensue."

"Ah." Vane looked forward again, easing his horses down the lane to the main road. "What about you?" he eventually asked. Meekly mild, he raised his brows at her. "Don't you like conservatories?"

"You may take me to see any conservatory you please," Patience snapped. "My liking for pot plants is not, as you well know, the subject of this discussion."

Vane's lips quirked, then lifted—lightly. "Indeed. But you may put that particular subject from your head." The look in his eyes told Patience he was deadly serious. Then he smiled, his wolfish, Cynster smile. "What would I want with other beautiful women, if I can show you conservatories instead?"

Patience blushed, and humphed, and looked ahead.

A fine sprinkling of snow covered the landscape and sparkled in the weak sunshine. The breeze was chilly, the clouds leaden grey, but the day remained fine—fine enough for their drive. They reached the main road, and Vane turned north. He flicked the reins, and his greys stepped out. Lifting her face to the breeze, Patience thrilled to the steady rolling rhythm, to the sense of traveling quickly along a new road. In a new direction.

The roofs of Kettering lay ahead. Drawing a deep breath, she said, "I suppose we should start making plans."

"Probably," Vane conceded. He slowed the greys as they entered the town. "I'd imagined we'd spend most of our time in Kent." He glanced at Patience. "The house in Curzon Street is big enough for a family, but other than the obligatory appearances during the height of the Season, I can't imagine we'll be there all that much. Unless you've discovered a liking for town life?"

"No—of course not." Patience blinked. "Kent sounds wonderful."

"Good—did I mention there's a deal of redecorating to do?" Vane grinned at her. "Infinitely better you than me. Most of the house needs attention—especially the nurseries."

Patience mouthed an "Oh."

"Of course," Vane continued, deftly steering his cattle through the main street, "*before* we get to the nurseries, I suppose we should consider the main bedchamber." His expression impossibly innocent, he caught Patience's eye. "I daresay you'll need to make changes there, too."

Patience narrowed her eyes at him. "*Before* we get to the main bedchamber, don't you think we should get to a church?"

Vane's lips twitched; he looked ahead. "Ah, well. Now that poses some problems."

"Problems?"

"Hmm—like which church."

Patience frowned. "Is there some tradition in your family?"

"Not really. Nothing we need concern ourselves with. It really comes down to personal preference." With the town behind then, Vane set the greys pacing. And turned his attention to Patience. "Do you want a big wedding?"

She frowned. "I hadn't given it much thought."

"Well, do. And you might like to ponder the fact that there are approximately three hundred friends and connections who will have to be invited from the Cynster side alone, should you elect to go that route."

"Three *hundred*?"

"That's just the close ones."

It didn't take Patience long to shake her head. "I really don't think a big wedding is called for. It sounds like it'll take forever to organize."

"Very likely."

"So—what's the alternative?"

"There are a few," Vane admitted. "But the fastest method would be to marry by special license. That can be done at virtually anytime, and would take next to no time to organize."

"Beyond obtaining the license."

"Hmm." Vane looked ahead. "So, the question is, when would you like to marry?"

Patience considered. She looked at Vane, at his profile, puzzled when he kept his eyes forward and refused to meet her gaze. "I don't know," she said. "You pick a date."

He looked at her then. "You're sure? You won't mind what I decide?"

Patience shrugged. "Why should I? The sooner the better, if we're to go on as we are."

Vane let out a breath, and whipped up his horses. "This afternoon."

"This after . . ." Patience swiveled on the seat to stare at him. Then she snapped her mouth shut. "You've already got a license."

"In my pocket." Vane grinned—wolfishly. "That was where I was yesterday, while Sligo was hunting high and low."

Patience slumped back against the seat. Then their pace, Gerrard's wide grin, and the distance they'd already traveled, registered. "Where are we going?"

"To get married. In Somersham." Vane smiled. "There's a church in the village by the ducal estate, which you could say I've a connection with. Of all the churches in this land, I'd like to be married there. And the vicar, Mr. Postlethwaite, will fall over himself to do the honors."

Feeling slightly dizzy, Patience drew in a deep breath—then let it out. "Well, then—let's be married in Somersham village."

Vane glanced her way. "You're sure?"

Meeting his eyes, reading the uncertainty, the question, in the grey, Patience smiled, and slid closer. "I'm overwhelmed." She let her smile deepen, let her joy show. "But I'm sure."

Tucking one hand in Vane's arm, she gestured grandly. "Drive on!"

Vane grinned, and complied. Patience clung close, and listened to the wheels' steady clatter. Their journey together had already begun. Their dream was waiting—just beyond the next bend.

Epilogue

*T*HEIR WEDDING WAS small, select, intensely personal; their wedding breakfast, held one month after the initiating event, was enormous.

Honoria and the other Cynster ladies organized it. It was held at Somersham Place.

"You took your time!" Lady Osbaldestone poked Vane with a skeletal finger, then wagged the same finger at Patience. "Make sure you keep him in line—there've been too many Cynsters loose for too long."

She stumped off to speak to Minnie. Vane breathed again—Patience caught his eye. "She's a terror," he said defensively. "Ask anyone."

Patience laughed. Gowned in silk the color of old gold, she tightened her hold on Vane's arm. "Come do the pretty."

Vane smiled, and let her lead him into the throng, to chat with the guests gathered to wish them well. She was all he could ask for, all he needed. And she was his.

He was perfectly willing to listen to congratulations on that fact until the sky fell.

Circulating through the guests, they eventually came up with Honoria and Devil, doing the same.

Patience hugged Honoria. "You've done us proud."

A pleased and proud matriarch, Honoria glowed. "I think

the cake was the highlight—Mrs. Hull surpassed herself." The many-tiered marzipan-covered fruit cake had been topped by a weather vane, delicately executed in spun sugar.

"Very inventive," Vane commented dryly.

Honoria humphed. "You men never appreciate such things as you ought." She glanced at Patience. "At least there'll be no wagers for you to contend with."

"Wagers?" A great many cheers, and ribald and raucous suggestions, had flown when they'd cut the cake. But wagers? Then she remembered. Oh.

Honoria smiled tightly, and flicked Vane a darkling glance. "Hardly surprising your husband has a fondness for the church in Somersham. He, after all, helped pay for its roof."

Patience glanced at Vane—his expression all innocence, he looked at Devil.

"Where's Richard?"

"Gone north." Deftly snagging Honoria in one arm, Devil anchored her to his side, preventing her from embroiling them in further social conversations. "He got a letter from some Scottish clerk regarding an inheritance from his mother. For some reason, he had to be present in the flesh to collect."

Vane frowned. "But she's been dead for—how long? Nearly thirty years?"

"Almost." Devil looked down as Honoria tugged. "It was a ghostly whisper from the past—a past he'd thought long buried. He went, of course—out of curiosity if nothing else." Looking up, Devil shot Vane a pointed glance. "Town life, I fear, has begun to pall for our Scandal."

Vane met Devil's gaze. "Did you warn him?"

Devil grinned. "Of what? To beware storms and unattached ladies?"

Vane grinned. "Put like that, it does sound a mite far-fetched."

"No doubt Scandal will return, hale and whole, safe and sound, with nothing more than a few battle scars and several new notches on his—"

"That's the duchess of Leicester to your right!" Honoria hissed. She glared at Devil. "Behave!"

The soul of injured innocence, he put his hand to his heart. "I thought I was."

Honoria made a distinctly rude sound. Winning free of his hold, she whirled and pushed him toward the duchess. She nodded over her shoulder at Patience. "Take him"—her nod indicated Vane—"the other way, or you'll never meet everyone."

Patience grinned, and obeyed. Vane went quietly. His gaze dwelling on Patience's face, on her figure, he found it no chore to play the proud and besotted groom.

From the other side of the ballroom, Vane's mother, Lady Horatia Cynster, watched him, and Patience, and sighed. "If only they hadn't married in such a rush. There was obviously no need for it."

Her second son, Harry, better known as Demon, to whom this was addressed, shot her a glance. "I suspect your notion of 'need' and Vane's differ in certain pertinent respects."

Horatia humphed. "Whatever." Deserting the sight of her firstborn, so well and appropriately settled, she turned her sights on Harry. "Just as long as you never try the same thing."

"Who? Me?" Harry was honestly shocked.

"Yes—*you*." Horatia jabbed his chest. "I hereby give you fair warning, Harry Cynster, that if you *dare* marry by special license, I'll never, *ever*, forgive you."

Harry promptly held up his hand. "I swear by all that's holy that I will never marry by special license."

"Humph!" Horatia nodded. "Good."

Harry smiled—and completed his vow in silence. *Or any other way.*

He was determined to be the first Cynster in history to escape fate's decree. The notion of tying himself up to some chit— of restricting himself to one woman—was ludicrous. *He* wasn't getting married—ever.

"Think I'll go see how Gabriel's doing." With a sweeping, ineffably elegant bow, he escaped his mother's orbit, and went in search of less scarifying company. People who weren't fixated on weddings.

The afternoon passed; the shadows slowly lengthened. Guests started to take their leave, then the bulk left in a rush. The long day drew to a close with Vane and Patience on the front porch of the Place, waving the last of the guests away. Even the family had departed. Only Devil and Honoria remained at the Place—and they'd retired to their apartments to play with Sebastian, who'd spent much of the afternoon with his nurse.

As the last carriage rumbled away down the drive, Vane glanced at Patience, close by his side.

His wife.

The four-letter word no longer shook him, at least, not in the same way. Now, in his head, it rang with possessiveness, a possessiveness that satisfied, that sat well with his conqueror's soul. He'd found her, he'd seized her—now he could enjoy her.

He studied her face, then raised one brow. And turned her back into the house.

"Did I tell you this place has an extremely interesting conservatory?"